THE LEPER BISHO

EL OBISPO LEPROSO

ARIS & PHILLIPS HISPANIC CLASSICS

THE LEPER BISHOP

EL OBISPO LEPROSO

by

GABRIEL MIRÓ

Translated by

Walter Borenstein

Aris & Phillips Hispanic Classics
are published by
Oxbow Books, Oxford

ISBN   978-0-85668-797-6 cloth
ISBN   978-0-85668-792-1

A CIP record for this book is available from the British Library

*Cover illustration: Gonder, Ethiopia, Miracles of Mary (Te'amire
Maryam), Late 17th century, reign of Yohannes (1667–82) or Iyyasu I
(1682–1706), Parchment, ink, tempera, wood, leather, cotton, and string,
36.8 × 31.8 × 9.5 cm. (14 1/2 × 12 1/2 × 3 3/4 in.), Ada Turnbull Hertle
and Marian and Samuel Klasstorner endowments, G18800, Illustration,
Miracle 23, The story of the leper Bishop Mercurious (111 verso, 112
recto). The Art Institute of Chicago.
Photography © The Art Institute of Chicago.*

Printed and bound by
The University Press, Cambridge

CONTENTS

ACKNOWLEDGMENTS

I dedicate this book to the memory of Professor Edmund L. King, who died on December 25, 2005 at the age of 91. He had dedicated a good part of his scholarly life to the work of Gabriel Miró, and, more than anyone else, made the name of the Spanish novelist more widely known in the English-speaking world. It was he who considered the two Olezan novels, *Nuestro Padre San Daniel* and *El obispo leproso* as Miró's highest achievement as a novelist.

Professor King considered these novels as virtually untranslatable. He wrote: "All knowledge, including knowledge in the form of literary art, is the recollection of experience." He added: "For Miró, the very act of naming the objects of his experience completes their existence, and it is this act, not informative, not utilitarian, but celebrative, that we participate in when we read him." He felt that "to eliminate the peculiarly regional from his artistic concern because it might be of too limited interest would have been for Miró to deny the basic premise of his art: fidelity to his own experience and vision." He argued that even when we read "in partial lexical darkness, we sense the constant aesthetic experience behind the word."

As a translator, I thought that many of the difficulties I encountered in trying to find appropriate meanings in English for so many of the words deliberately selected by Miró, for the "things" that were so vital a part of his experience, were equally perplexing to readers in his own language, as they strove to grasp his intended meaning within the "lexical darkness" to which King refers. A goodly part of the language of many great writers may often prove to be as great a problem for readers in the original as for those reading it in translation. No translator can ever assume to have found the proper word in his own language to recreate the experience and the feeling in the words meticulously chosen by an author to describe them.

When Charlotte Remfrey-Kidd chose to translate Miró's novel as *Our Father San Daniel* in 1930, she recreated the scene in what Arthur Machen in his introduction to the work, called a kind of English Barchester, the imaginary town described by Anthony Trollope in his Barset novels. It is not that the English language was not adequate to capture the meaning of the words chosen by Miró. It is that the writer was in love with these words, especially the sounds he heard in his mind, and the emotions they evoked by

their very use. A translator can't be expected to capture this. My translation, at best, can only offer a reader a limited vision of all that Miró intended to project, and such a reader is really not more limited than a young reader in Spanish today struggling with archaic and often irrelevant words.

I completed this translation in 1993 and made only a few attempts to find a publisher. In December of 2005, Doctor Jonathan Thacker of Merton College, Oxford, wrote to me saying he had been informed that I had this translation of Miró and, as Series Editor for the Hispanic Classics series, he would very much like to see it. Less than two years later, the work will become a part of that series. I can't adequately express my appreciation for his efforts to make this and many other translations available to the English-reading public.

I would also like to offer my very sincere thanks to Clare Litt and Tara Evans of Oxbow books for their patient, kind and understanding support for the project.

Throughout the more than half a century that I have been engaged in translating a dozen literary works, my sole encouragement, my faithful advisor, inspiration and source of consolation in moments of adversity and rejection, has been my wife Audrey, a widely published author in many genres in her own right. When I sought interpretation or correct English usage, when difficult choices had to be made, when help in transfer to a computer was required, she was ever present to move the project along. I can never fully express my gratitude to her for her contribution to my work.

Finally, as only a translator of another writer's genius can say, in some mystical and wonderful way, I owe a genuine debt to Gabriel Miró who was always present in my mind's eye, encouraging me to forge ahead in moments when the dauntless task seemed all but impossible.

INTRODUCTION

Miró and the Generation of 1898

The Generation of 1898 in Spain was undoubtedly the most influential and widely discussed literary, artistic and cultural movement of the twentieth century. It was not surprising, therefore, that there was passionate and even bitter controversy as to who were the most genuine members of that select and respected group, and critics spent an inordinate amount of time scrutinizing the credentials of potential candidates, some of whom had no inclination whatsoever to be associated with them. Azorín, who along with Miguel de Unamuno, Pío Baroja and Antonio Machado, was considered one of the most bona fide and widely accepted members of this generation of *noventayochistas*, was primarily responsible for popularizing the name of the movement in 1910 and 1913.[1] In his proposal for a definition of the Generation of 1898 in his definitive book on the subject, Donald L. Shaw writes that "the test of membership of the Generation is therefore, in my view, bound up with three considerations: participation in a personal quest for renewed ideals and beliefs; interpretation of the problems of Spain in related terms, i.e., as a problem of mentality, rather than as political or economic and social; and acceptance of the role of creative writing primarily as an instrument for the examination of these problems."[2] Shaw mentions Gabriel Miró only once in his book, referring to the "polished elegance of his style."

In the introduction to his edition of *Nuestro Padre San Daniel*, Manuel Ruiz-Funes takes up the issue of Miró and the Generation in a lengthy section discussing the author in the literature of his time. He qualifies his remarks saying: "Perhaps, by assigning a writer to trends or movements, we may fall into a kind of schematism and reduce his creative richness into something entirely too simple."[3] He further explains his fear of reductionism in the thirty years of Miró's creative work. In spite of such fears, he devotes nine pages to a detailed discussion of the author's place in the Generation. He cites numerous outstanding critics who have dealt with this question. Pedro Laín Entralgo, for example, adds Juan Ramón Jiménez and Miró as tangential *noventayochistas*. He quotes extensively from Margarita de Mayo, Emma Napolitano de Sanz and especially from Paciencia Ontañon de Lope, who

compares Miró's *El obispo leproso* to Pío Baroja's *Camino de perfección*. Some critics have considered Miró as not only a member of the Generation, but as a prominent *modernista*, referring to the importance of style in his work. Other critics cited include Marcus Parr, Vicente Ramos, Mariano Baquero Goyanes, Ramón María Tenreiro, Guillermo Díaz-Plaja, A.W. Becker, Raymond Vidal and Ricardo Gullón. One of the few to disagree was Edmund L. King, perhaps the most important of the Mironian critics, who found that Miró and the members of the Generation "remained separated in a friendly relationship." He saw him as living isolated because "he was a man who didn't live amidst the literary dinners of his time, nor did he even want to mingle with them."[4] In a letter to a close friend in 1929, Miró wrote that he shunned literary gatherings and preferred to live withdrawn from the social literary scene and from newspaper editorial offices. "Socially," he wrote, "I do not function as a writer."[5]

Pío Baroja, one of the most accepted members of the Generation, was also the most iconoclastic and individualistic, and always questioned the very existence of the movement. Although he may have been taking an extreme position and teasing those who seemed so proud of their membership in so prestigious a movement, he wrote an article entitled "La influencia del 98," in which he proclaimed that such a generation never really existed. He wrote: "A generation that has no common points of view, or similar aspirations, or spiritual solidarity, or even the nexus of a movement, is not a generation."[6] He attacked all the criteria critics used to create the air of a group that used a form of classification to enhance its existence, meaning and influence, and concluded: "Spain has never been a country of literary schools."[7] Baroja elaborated on all the political and social differences of its members, their varied literary tastes and styles and their contradictory ideas, out of which no system could be drawn. He was most critical of their possible influence, including the rise of the republic in 1931, and sarcastically pointed out that writers would like to believe their work may have some impact, but are most often mistaken.

Gabriel Miró has much in common with many of the accepted and purported members of the Generation of 1898. He was born at the right time and was influenced by many of the same ideas. However, he never sought to attach himself to any literary movements and kept his distance from their activities all of his life. His close relationship with Azorín and his occasional contact with Unamuno were at a very personal level. Edmund L. King concludes that writers like Miró may be *in* , but not *of* a generation. He

argues: "A writer belonging chronologically to the Generation, but in whom the preoccupations of the noisy and commanding figures are absent, may be relegated to secondary status if not overlooked entirely." He concludes: "Gabriel Miró must be detached from the label that doesn't fit him and be seen for what he is, an anomaly and an artistic figure of superior stature.[8]

Gabriel Miró: His Life

Gabriel Francisco Miró Ferrer was born on July 28, 1879 in Alicante on the Costa Blanca some eighty miles south of Valencia. His father, Don Juan Miró Moltó was a chief highway engineer in the Spanish civil service. He came from a family of bankers and industrialists and had briefly studied for the priesthood. On July 4, 1876, he married Doña Encarnación Ferrer Ons, a native of Orihuela and thirteen years younger than her husband. They had two sons, Juan, the older, born on June 21, 1877, and Gabriel. His father was dedicated to the upbringing of his sons and made every effort to instill proper values in them. His mother was quite devout and fond of speaking her mind.

His early education was in Alicante. Although many of the country people around the city spoke a dialect of Valencian, the city still maintained Castilian as its official and cultural language. As a child, Gabriel would play at the home of Antonino Maignon, the French consul in the city, and it was here that he met Eufrasio Coloma, who was to be his lifelong friend, and the consul's daughter Clemencia, who was later to become his wife. He very likely developed an interest in the French language and culture here. Miró wasn't recognized as a writer in the city and never had a warm feeling for it, though he did have an attachment to the physical environment and ordinary people.

In 1885 he began to frequent the art studio of Lorenzo Casanova, a painter who was married to his aunt, and he would continue visiting him in Alicante till he died in 1900. He would later look back at the influence of painting in his life and wonder whether he should have followed that path instead of literature. Edmund King believes that it was his uncle's interest in literature that played an even greater role in his decision to turn in that direction. Although Miró later claimed that he had never written a line of poetry in his life, some critics, including the noted Jorge Guillén, have called him a true poet. King writes: "If he was to be a poet, an artist, and not just a writer, he must be utterly faithful to the experience of his own clearest vision."[9]

In 1887, at the age of eight, Gabriel's parents sent him away to a boarding school in nearby Orihuela, the Jesuit Colegio de Santo Domingo that would become the "Jesús" in his novel *The Leper Bishop*. Ruiz-Funes tells us that the five years the boy spent here "were not only bitter and sad, but also left a deep scar upon him, in every way, for the rest of his days."[10] Edmund King takes a more generous view and, though he recognizes the contrast between Gabriel's happy life at home with doting friends and family as well as the pervasive influence of his freethinking uncle Lorenzo, and the strict, military-like life at the school, finds compensations that would serve him well as a writer in later life. If Miró brought upon himself the lasting hatred of most Jesuits and many of the conservative traditionalists of his time for his ironic depiction of their impact on education at the school in four of his novels, he did acquire a deeper understanding of himself through the self-examination the Jesuits imposed on schoolboys in their Spiritual Exercises. King tells us "the constant injunction throughout the Exercises is to employ the five senses imaginatively in calling to mind the divine realities, the penitent's frailties and sins, and his possible punishment or salvation." He adds that the "ultimate as well as the most immediate realities must be contemplated sensorially as seen, tasted, smelled, heard, touched." He concludes that the "literary sensualism that has its dual origin in the doctrines of Lorenzo Casanova and of Ignatius Loyola is not limited to those Biblical evocations. It is the foundation of Miró's art."[11] The boy remained at the school in Orihuela until 1892, when he returned to Alicante at the age of thirteen to complete his studies at the Institute there, graduating with his *bachillerato* in 1896. He continued his visits to his uncle's studio during all this time. The family was compelled to move to Ciudad Real in Castile for a brief time when his father was sent there by the government, but they returned in time for the boy to complete his studies and receive his degree. Ruiz-Funes feels that even this brief sojourn in the heart of Castile left its imprint on the sensitive soul of the budding writer.

He began his university studies in September of 1896 and completed the program in law in October of 1900. Most critics agree that he showed little if any interest in the study of law. He attended the University of Valencia as a student in residence for only the first year, turned out to be a mediocre student, and transferred to the University of Granada because he felt it might be less demanding there. When his expectations failed to materialize, he returned to study in Valencia, living at home as an external student, studying the prescribed courses of the curriculum on his own and only taking his examinations at the school, a common practice at the time.

Edmund King points out that a major factor in this decision was his apparent hypochondria, a condition found among many young men of his social class at the time. He was overly aware of his physical symptoms and could be considered "hyperaesthetic." He would interrupt his studies over a supposed "heart condition," temporarily interrupting his required reading and devoting himself to more eclectic books on ancient and modern literature and inspiring conversations with friends on literary and cultural questions.

A good part of his reading was done aloud for a friend he had made at the university, Francisco Figueras Pacheco, who had gone blind at the age of eighteen. King offers a fascinating interpretation of the importance of this practice and its impact on his feeling for words in his writing.

> One wonders at once which writers in the history of literature have been readers to the blind. Is it too much to suppose that the experience returns the spoken word to the reader with interest? In the society of the word that is written and silently read, the passage of meaning from writer to reader may possibly become so smooth that the peculiarities of the meaning, the peculiar edges and wrinkles in the word, may scarcely be perceived. Any word within a certain range of synonymity will do. Can we not see in this phase of Miró's development as an artist a kind of unsought training? First, he strengthens his power to grasp sensorial values by compensating for another person's blindness and then he necessarily refines his awareness of language, the means of expressing these values. When we consider certain qualities of Miró's art – the importance of sensation, the importance of words, and the *tempo lento* in which Miró seems to form and savor every word separately – we have no reason to think that we will find the sources of its special grace and effectiveness, but it is reasonable to look for experiences that might have furthered the growth of such qualities...[12]

Miró read aloud not only to his blind friend but also to many of his acquaintances who appreciated his fine elocution.

When he received his *licenciatura* in law from the University of Valencia on October 13, 1900, it was with the lowest possible passing grades. His biographer, Vicente Ramos, refers to his indifference to legal studies, implying that the young man was only fulfilling his obligations to his family and that what he had learned would serve no purpose whatsoever in his life.[13]

After his graduation, he traveled about his native province, acquiring

experiences that he would use in his later writing. On November 16, 1901, when he was twenty-two years old, he married his childhood friend, Clemencia Maignon. In early 1901, his first short work, De mi barrio, appeared, a character sketch of a friend. His first novel, La mujer de Ojeda, was published in Alicante in March of 1901. According to the critic Ricardo Landeira, this work was later repudiated by the author along with a second novel, Hilván de escenas (1903), and was not included in his Obras completas.[14] At about this time he was having essays and stories published in Alicante in El Ibero, which was directed by his blind friend Figueras Pacheco.

His first daughter Olympia was born on October 5, 1903, the same year that his first major work, Del vivir, was completed, and it was published the following year. His second daughter, Clemencia, was born on December 30, 1905. Miró was not sure that he could support a wife and family by pursuing a literary career, and soon realized he would have to seek some gainful employment and find the spare time to continue with his writing. He took civil service examinations twice, once in 1905 and again in 1907, and wasn't appointed to the posts he sought. This struggle to earn sufficient money for himself and his family while finding the time to pursue his true interests would plague him for the rest of his life. In 1906, he finally acquired a secretarial position in the provincial government of Alicante.

He continued to write stories for publication and entered a competition at a newspaper in Madrid, but his work was rejected. In January of 1908, his short novel Nómada won a prize granted by the magazine El cuento semanal. It is interesting to note that the judges for this competition were Ramón del Valle-Inclán, Pío Baroja and Felipe Trigo. On March 6 of this same year, Miró's father died.

He remained in Alicante until 1914, devoting his spare time to writing, study and some travel, always dedicated to his family, which was the centerpiece of his life. He was named the official chronicler for the province of Alicante in 1908, and two years later, he was appointed assistant to the representative of the government for port authority of Alicante, spending several months in Alcoy, a city several miles north of his home.

In 1911, he traveled to Barcelona with the intention of expanding his literary sphere. Here he met writers associated with the Ven de Catalunya – Joan Maragall, Eugenio d'Ors, Josep Carner, Joaquím Riura, August Pi Sunyer and many others. With their support, he began to publish pieces in the newspaper Diario de Barcelona. It was at this time that he began the

study of the antiquity of the Middle East and its relationship to the Bible. After publishing several articles in La Vanguardia of Barcelona in 1913, he and his family moved here the following year, and he accepted a position in the accounting department of the Casa de Caridad.

The family lived on the Calle de la Diputación in Barcelona, and he spent his mornings at his job, the remainder of the day given to his literary preoccupations and his evenings with his family or with newly acquired friends. One of them recalled an evening in June when the noted composer Enrique Granados invited a number of people to his studio and played the piano for them; Miró read some pages from his ongoing work "El abuelo del rey." Years afterward, he explained his reactions to his move from the small city where he had lived so many years to this invigorating life of a major metropolis, powerful, noisy and filled with so many people he did not know. At the time, he seemed to have lost some of his desire for the intimacy of his former provincial life. However, in his two Olezan novels, he did not reflect this loss of feeling as he returned for the scene of his novels to the more sheltered life of Orihuela.

At this point in his life, he was offered an opportunity he could not refuse, when in August of 1914 he was offered the editorship of a projected Catholic encyclopedia to be funded by the publishing house of Vecchi y Ramos in Barcelona. For almost a year he was completely dedicated to this undertaking, and he was devastated when the company declared bankruptcy in April of 1915, and the work was never resumed. The failure of a project that could have supported his needs and fulfilled his ambitions only intensified his sense of futility, but many critics point out that the year of dedicated research offered him "an accumulation of knowledge that would serve him well intellectually and be useful for the rest of his life."[15] The influence of this year of such assiduous study can clearly be discerned in a number of his works, especially his Figures of the Passion and The Leper Bishop.

By the time his close friend Enrique Granados died in March of 1916, Miró had begun to lose the feeling he had earlier had for his life in Barcelona. He continued to publish his books, and the first volume of his most famous work Figures of the Passion of the Lord appeared early in 1917. It was nominated for the Fastenrath Prize offered by the Royal Spanish Academy, but was rejected. The second volume appeared shortly thereafter, published by the Editorial Doménech. On April 6, 1917, Valdés Prida, the editor of El Noroeste in Gijón, published one chapter of this work and was later jailed for bringing out so sacrilegious a work on Good Friday. The author's

troubles with certain elements of the Catholic hierarchy in Spain and the traditionalist forces allied with it can be traced to this period of his career.
As early as 1917, Miró began to consider moving to Madrid, seeking a position in Barcelona that would allow him to be transferred to Madrid. He finally accepted a post in November of 1918 as cronista in the Municipal government of Barcelona. During this same year, chapters from one of his most important works, El humo dormido, were published as separate articles in La Publicidad in Barcelona (Feb. 28, 1918–Jan. 31, 1919). In July of 1920, he and his family finally moved to Madrid, where they were to remain until his untimely death ten years later. Almost immediately, he was beset by a family tragedy when two of his brother's children died and their mother lost her mind. To add to his difficulties, a position that had been promised to him in the Ministry of Public Instruction by Antonio Maura, who was a leader of the Conservative party, failed to materialize. He was appointed to a temporary post in the General Technical Secretariat of the Ministry of Labor. Maura, a devout Catholic and a great admirer of Miró's work, had been a Prime Minister, a director of the Spanish Academy, and had attempted to help Miró advance in his career.

The family took a summer home in the village of Polop de la Marina near Alicante, and the writer took the opportunity to go on a number of excursions that were later to fill the pages of his books. He was able to serve as a contributor of material for the newspaper *El Sol* in Madrid and *La Nación* in Buenos Aires. In 1922 he was appointed Secretary of National Competitions, a position created especially for him in the division of Fine Arts of the Ministry of Public Education. This post was the result of the efforts of his friend Antonio Maura, and he held it until his death eight years later.

On April 5, 1924, one chapter, "Señorita y sor," from his novel *The Leper Bishop*, was published in *El Cuento Semanal*. He also received the Mariano de Cavia prize from the newspaper *ABC* for his article "Huerto de cruces" on March 25, 1925. He traveled to Gijón to give a lecture on "Lo viejo y lo santo en manos de ahora" to show his support for the editor, Valdés Prida, who had been jailed earlier for publishing his work. On November 1, 1925, he became a grandfather for the first time. He signed a contract with Biblioteca Nueva to publish his *Obras completas*, for which he could choose the works to be included. His novel, *The Leper Bishop*, was published in December of 1926 by Biblioteca Nueva in Madrid. He had begun writing it as early as 1916.

On February 24, 1927, Miró was nominated for membership in the Spanish Royal Academy by Azorín, Palacio Valdés and Ricardo León. In April of that same year, he was rejected for this prestigious honor, much to the chagrin of his good friend Azorín and many of his loyal supporters. A year earlier, he was turned down for the Fastenrath Prize for the second time.

Miró felt a sense of rejection even more and began to withdraw from much of public life. He was disturbed by the attacks on his work and the slanderous remarks that were made by his enemies. He lived even more in the intimacy of his home and his family and the few intimate friends who were a consolation for him. Out of his isolation came the book *Años y leguas*, published in May of 1928. He suffered even greater anguish when he felt compelled to defend himself against criticism of his novel *The Leper Bishop* by the eminent philosopher José Ortega y Gasset.

One evening, he attended a gathering in homage to an old friend Miguel de Unamuno. When he returned home, he felt ill and was hospitalized for an acute attack of appendicitis. Following the surgery, he died of peritonitis at his home at the Paseo del Prado, number 20, on May 27, 1930. He was buried in the Cementerio de la Almudena in Madrid, where his remains lie in a tomb alongside those of his wife, who died in 1953, and his younger daughter Clemencia, who died the same year. It is interesting to note that the great Spanish Realistic novelist Benito Pérez Galdós was buried in this same cemetery ten years earlier. Few writers could be so different as these two Spanish novelists. While more than thirty thousand of his many admirers filed past his coffin and followed Galdós's funeral cortège to take him to his final resting place, only a small number of family members and friends bade farewell to Gabriel Miró. The public figure versus the private figure. Each had followed his chosen and destined path in life.

Gabriel Miró: His Works

The most decisive blow to Miró's self esteem occurred in January of 1927, three years before he died, when a review by José Ortega y Gasset of the novel the author and many critics believed to be his culminating work, appeared in the newspaper *El Sol* in Madrid.[16] He was clearly shaken by this unforeseen attack on him as a novelist and never really recovered from its impact. Ortega, with endless apologies and reservations as to his remarks, asked the public whether Miró was truly a novelist, and if he was, was he a

good one. He praised him as a writer for his perfection of style, but called his work static and paralytic. He based his criticism upon extraneous elements in the description of some characters, and the inverisimilitude between the intellectual capacity of a number of individuals, like the priest Don Magín and María Fulgencia, and their words and thoughts.

Most critics since that time have come to Miró's defense and taken Ortega to task for the narrow view he held of the novel and also because of the extent to which our critical vision of the novel in general has grown since the time of writers like James Joyce. Others, however, like Eugenio G. de Nora and Gonzalo Torrente Ballester, supported Ortega's contention and emphasized the difficulty encountered in reading Miró, and even accused the novelist of failing to avail himself of the best qualities of an excellent and objective writer. Although this criticism of his novels did not possess the vitriolic antagonism he had encountered some ten years earlier when his *Figures of the Passion* was published, one can not help but think that many of the forces hostile to his earlier work were, for similar reasons, still unwilling to forgive him, and others were simply finding new reasons to find fault with his writing. All this took place only four years before the coming of the republic, and Spain, divided in so many ways, was preparing for a conflict that would bring two visions of the direction of a nation into open conflict.

Among the many who came to Miró's defense was the eminent poet Jorge Guillén, who found the genre of the novel ideally suited for Miró, because he felt that everything fitted in the novel.[17] Andrés Amorós found all the discussion of what was truly a novel to be tedious and pointless. He felt that many of the newer forms of the novel could be accused of the same deficiencies as Miró's.[18] Miguel de Unamuno, among others, had already affirmed that even philosophy is, strictly speaking, a novel. The critic, Mariano Baquero Goyanes defended Miró's novel, expounding on Ortega's three criteria for the genre and finding the novel as fitting a more inventive definition of its nature.[19] Eminent writers in many places, like Baroja and Henry James had long struggled with the elusive interpretation of what was a novel, and the many innovations of the second half of the twentieth century only served to make the definition include virtually everything. Baroja had defined his sense of the novel in precisely these terms. The critic Ricardo Gullón, considering the works of this epoch, declared that "the most outstanding characteristics of these works are...the internalizing, the breaking with temporal linearity, narrative simultaneity, the use of stream

of consciousness and internal monologues..."[20] So it is that Miró confronted literary traditionalists and religious reactionaries at the same time, and it was they who deplored the more liberal directions he espoused in religion and literature.

Richard Chandler and Kessel Schwartz, in a brief analysis of Miró's work, say that he "excelled all in the beauty of his language, in his harmonies and rhythms and in his virtuosity." They compare him to the "spirit of the artistic endeavors of the Generation of 98," and they conclude "in addition to their lyrical note, they contain a psychological analysis which at times reminds one of Proust or Joyce. Miró is pure sensation and has a sensual attitude toward life, overshadowed at times by a kind of simple mysticism and at others by spiritual anguish."[21] G.G. Brown, in his history of Spanish literature in the twentieth century, devotes eight pages to Gabriel Miró out of 161 pages in the book.[22] He is among the few to remark on the author's desire to repudiate his earliest writing up to 1904. Brown notes Miró's rejection of his earliest novels and he sees *Las cerezas del cementerio* in 1910 as a turning point in his career as a writer. He speaks of the fact that "the exultant intensity and luxuriousness of his communication of beauty as perceived by all the senses, but particularly those of sight, smell and taste, had been remarked by all his commentators." He takes note of "his prodigious linguistic artistry, his enormously rich vocabulary, and his Valencian regionalism. What is less observed is that Miró's quest for beauty and happiness is accompanied by a preoccupation with ugliness and cruelty – usually expressed in gratuitously sadistic acts practiced by humans on small and helpless animals."[23] He considers *The Leper Bishop* to be the author's last and greatest novel.

As I have pointed out, Miró has been compared to Azorín more than to any other writer of his time. Salvador de Madariaga gives an entire chapter of his book *The Genius of Spain* to discuss these two writers from the same region of Spain and find the similarities and differences between them. He quotes Miró as saying: "From the moment we are born, our eyes are filled with the blueness of the waters."[24] He says of Miró that "he has the powers of minute observation which go with the plastic attitude, those powers which seem to consist in a mere capacity for stating what is there, before everybody's eyes, and yet are ever so much deeper rooted to the recesses of sensibility." Madariaga points out in Miró "the impression that the material which he shapes is more rebellious to the hand than the light and air with which Azorín paints his little pictures." He concludes: "As a rule, however, it is the creation of a bright, penetrating, and sensitive imagination, sustained by

a poetic feeling of such simplicity and truth that it can elevate the statement of commonplaces to heights of limpid beauty..."[25]

What some critics refer to as Miró's mature period of writing began in 1910 with the publication of *Las cerezas del cementerio*. Until then, he had written two early novels in 1901 and 1903, both of which he considered inferior and excluded from his *Obras completas*. In addition, he had written *Del vivir* in 1904, a work in which he first introduced the character Sigüenza, who would reappear in *Libro de Sigüenza* in 1917 and *Años y leguas* in 1928. Most critics consider this character to be the author's alter ego, who goes about seeking beauty and joy, but most often fails to find it and only sees other things that appeal to him. He wrote a short novel *Nómada* in 1908 that earned him a first prize for fiction, and also another short novel, *La novela de mi amigo*, that same year. The novel he published in 1909, *Amores de Antón Hernando*, would later become the better-known *Niño y grande*.

G.G. Brown believes that the period beginning in 1910 produced only three novels, *El abuelo del rey* (1915), *Nuestro Padre San Daniel* (1921) and *El obispo leproso* (1926).[26] He points out that "a large part of Miró's output does not consist of novels, but of the kind of short pieces," that form the books about Sigüenza, the *estampas* of his controversial *Figures of the Passion* (1916–17) and *El ángel, el molino, el caracol del faro* (1921). He probably wrote more than 250 short pieces and fragments of longer works in many Spanish periodicals and newspapers. He began to contribute them after 1902 to *El Ibero* of Alicante, the *Revista Latina* of Madrid, *Los Lunes de el Imparcial* of Madrid, the *Diario de Alicante*, the *Heraldo de Madrid*, the *Diario de Barcelona*, *La Vanguardia* of the same city, *La Publicidad* of Barcelona, *La Nación* of Buenos Aires and *El Sol* of Madrid.

Much of what has been written about the author's work in Spanish has not been about his novels, and an even larger part of the criticism in English has been about his *Figuras de la Pasión*. Edmund King, in the introduction to his edition of *El humo dormido*, takes up the question of genre that has caused critics such difficulty in assigning a proper category to his works.[27] He says that the author preferred to call many of his varied works *estampas* or *tablas*, *viñetas* and *glosas*. The fact is that he may be the kind of writer for whom we can have no label, and the eminent poet Jorge Guillén, when he dedicated a copy of his *Cántico*, his best known volume of verse, to Gabriel Miró, referred to him as the only poet who refused to be one. In a certain way, then, he can be compared to his compatriot Azorín, where choice of genre would always prove difficult and whose much praised book

Confessions of a Little Philosopher, which he called a novel, always baffled admiring readers.

It should therefore be apparent that in order to discuss Miró as a novelist, one must inevitably speak primarily of his two novels of Oleza, *Our Father San Daniel* and *The Leper Bishop*. Manuel Ruiz-Funes, who edited and annotated editions of both these novels, takes up the question of the general theme and structure of the Olezan novels in a lengthy introduction to the first novel.[28] In this work, the author presents us "a small Levantine city, wrapped in a fertile and rich natural background, almost Eden-like; but – in contrast – it is a closed, asphyxiating, Levitical city. The subtitle of this first novel – 'a novel of priests and devotees' – is enough to confirm this vision."[29] Not everyone sees this world from the same perspective. Arthur Machen, in his introduction to the English translation of the first novel says that the book presents "the sense of Spain, that sacred Spain of *Don Quixote*; of the hot white road, the fruitful vineyards and olive garths, the sunlight burning on the fields, the scented shade of orchards and gardens, the bells jangling from the church towers, the cloaked priests pacing the narrow ways, the cloud of incense about the altars, and the harsh criers from the street breaking in on the chanting choir..."[30] He tends to emphasize the author's ability to offer the reader this extraordinary and endearing picture of a small Spanish city in order to counteract his awareness of many of the less palatable aspects and the narrowness of the scene. He sees more of a balance between the positive and the negative.

Miró reinforces the sense of conservative values dominant here by calling the place a "brazier and archive of regional Carlism." Ruiz- Funes finds many double themes throughout the novel, revealing the inevitable lack of happiness of the people brought about by the struggle of the two points of view. María Fulgencia, the principal female character of the second novel, envisions Oleza as a place where nobody really loves. The divisions in Oleza are geographical, spiritual and political. The river divides the two contrasting districts, one, impoverished, the other more affluent. There are two factions at war: the traditionalist, conservative one, living in the past, with no desire for renovation, opposing the construction of a railroad that might bring the enlightenment of the outside world into their midst; and the more liberal, sensitive, open individuals who have a great need for freedom and progress.

Many critics see the two novels as really one, in which symbolic descriptions and narrative techniques are the same for both. The author

announces the coming of the second novel at the end of the first. F. Márquez Villanueva conceives of one vast novel, constituting "a great mural of the whole life of a small city in the second half of the XIXth century."[31]

The first part of *Our Father San Daniel* is dominated by the figure of San Daniel, who becomes the patron saint of Oleza. Its four chapters present us with the background necessary to understand what will follow. The reader is introduced to the story of San Daniel and all the many details surrounding his cult. We see the effigy carved in his likeness, the temple dedicated to him and the parish church related to his worship. The second part has six chapters and makes us aware of the secular characters of the community and the priests and other churchmen who relate to them. The first group includes Don Daniel Egea, his daughter Paulina, their housekeeper, the outspoken Jimena, Don Amancio Espuch, Doña Corazón and the many other townspeople who will appear throughout this first as well as the second novel. The principal priests are Don Magín, Padre Bellod, Don Jeromillo and Don Cruz. The two high-ranking prelates are the first Bishop who dies early in the novel, and the new Bishop who comes to Oleza at the end of the second part and becomes a major figure of the second novel.

The third part of the first novel introduces a new character, who will soon dominate the conservative faction, who arrives in the city as a total stranger. He will eventually marry Paulina. Don Álvaro is the father of Pablo, the young boy who is perhaps the major figure of the second novel. In this third part of the work, which contains seven chapters, we will meet many other characters, including the homeopath Monera and his wife, as well as Elvira, Don Álvaro's austere and forbidding sister, and "Cara-rajada," among the most interesting and atypical of the author's creations. C.A. Longhurst, who has written the most comprehensive analysis of both novels in English,[32] sees the two almost simultaneous arrivals, that of the new Bishop and that of Don Álvaro, as representing the "two rather different approaches to religion," evoking "rather different responses among the *olecenses*."[33] Miró does not limit himself to introducing Don Álvaro and portraying him in an almost charismatic role in the more reactionary community. He continues to develop the many other characters already present in his novel.

The fourth and final part, which contains ten chapters, takes the reader from Don Álvaro and Paulina's wedding to the birth of their son Pablo less than one year later. Three new characters are introduced here, the Count and Countess of Lóriz and their son Máximo; he becomes a close friend of Pablo, and plays a major role in the second novel. Miró develops the theme

of the growing friendship between the new Bishop and Don Magín, and offers a melodramatic event in the shooting of the latter during a public riot. An even more critical, gripping and momentous occurrence is the extensive flooding that brings the novel to a conclusion. Whereas the first novel has a limited time space of a year and a half, the second covers nine or ten years. Pablo is eight years old when it begins and he is finishing his studies at "Jesús" at the end, when he is fifteen or sixteen. It should be noted that some seven years in between are not included in the novels.

The struggle for the control of the minds of the Olezans is one of the principal themes of the second novel in which the major character can be said to be the city of Oleza. The added elements of the Jesuit school to which Pablo is sent by his father and the powerful influence of Elvira, Pablo's aunt, as a countervailing force to the presence of his mother and the company of Don Magín and the Bishop, make the conflict ever clearer. The fanaticism and closed mindedness of the faction led by Don Álvaro, dominated by extremist Carlist sympathies and a brand of the Catholic faith that would brook no opposition and traced its heritage to the time of the Inquisition, seem to be repudiated by Miró as something belonging to the past. Longhurst concludes his insightful analysis of both novels, saying that the conclusion is "to reject the apocalyptic God of punishment and death and follow instead the God of love and life."[34]

The second novel ends with the death of the Bishop, followed by Doña Purita's departure from Oleza for good, as Don Magín bids her farewell. G.G. Brown sees the Bishop's martyrdom caused by leprosy, Elvira's shameful and hurried departure from Oleza and the return of Pablo and his family to the home of his grandfather, Don Daniel, as implying "for Oleza wisdom rather than victory." The struggle between innocence and evil is tempered now by understanding. "Paulina and Pablo go off, silent, reflective, on the road to happiness... They have learnt that following their natural impulses does not necessarily produce happiness." They still have a long way to go. The Bishop "loved life with a pure and spontaneous joyfulness; life responded by inflicting on him a loathsome, disfiguring disease. Yet the disease never reached his soul, and by enduring it steadily, he was able to play his part in bringing to Oleza and its inhabitants a civilized maturity which they had formerly lacked."[35]

Ruiz-Funes brings up an interesting point in his edition of *El obispo leproso*.[36] He points out that Miró had been thinking of a work of fiction about a leprous Bishop since perhaps 1914. By 1924, he was able to publish

the short piece *Señorita y sor*. This lengthy period of gestation gave the author the opportunity to give considerable thought to his intentions. Even more interesting is the evidence that the author was forced to eliminate many pages of his manuscript, for a variety of reasons, in order to see it published. His daughter Clemencia claimed that she had seen him burn chapters of the completed work, including the death and burial of the bishop, not long before the novel was published. And Ruiz-Funes poses the fascinating conjecture that the earlier novel, *Our Father San Daniel*, may actually have been inspired by the second one, rather than the reverse.

In Conclusion

In the introduction to several critical comments on Miró's works, Edmund L. King, one of the leading Miró scholars, is cited as explaining why so few of the author's works have been translated into English. "He is of Spain's most untranslatable writers. As a result of this limited exposure in the English-speaking world, Miró is usually perceived as a writer of slow-paced religious works," and, while praising his careful descriptions and craftsmanship, "few have come to appreciate his underlying humanitarian concerns and his technical innovations, such as the manipulation of narrative chronology, which give his stories an aura of timeliness."[37] In a dissertation written in 1958, Marcus Parr translated Miró's work *Años y leguas*, and pointed out in detail the many difficulties he encountered in trying to complete the work.[38] Ruiz-Funes's annotated editions of the two Olezan novels contain forty-two pages of a glossary of Spanish words used by the author that require definition.

The noted Spanish poet Jorge Guillén, in a book on language and poetry, points out how Miró used language in ways uncommon to most writers of prose.[39] He sees him as an artist, "cheerful, sorrowful, passionate, with a vehemence shot through with the most exquisite sensibility; and sensitive, sensitive, sensitive to everything, and expressive, as much so as anyone, more so than anyone else."[40]

Although Miró always chose to maintain a distance between himself and the activist members of the Generation of 1898, he was often on the mind of Azorín, who dedicated his book of stories *Blanco en azul*, written in 1929, to his close friend Gabriel Miró, "a marvelous painter...of one of the finest regions of Spain: that of Alicante; a place of soft, diffuse, tenuous grays; bluish grays, greenish grays, purplish grays, golden grays..."[41] He referred to

him as "his friend, his admirer, his compatriot." Azorín wrote two chapters of his *Libro de Levante* about Miró, and it was he, along with two other noted writers, who nominated Miró for membership in the Spanish Royal Academy.

In one of the chapters of his dedication "In Memoriam" to Miró, written one year before the latter's untimely death, Azorín wrote of "the entire landscape of Alicante – the beautiful landscape of Alicante – touched by Gabriel Miró. And made eternal, always present. In other artists one has the sensation of the past; time is always past; the present minute and second isn't present, it is already past." And he ends saying: "In Miró, everything eternal is in the present second; in the second in which his hands keep caressing and retaining things. Retaining them so that they ... may not be dragged off terribly and tragically toward the fathomless pit of the past."[42]

THE TEXT AND ITS VARIANTS

I have used the edition of Manuel Ruiz-Funez of *El obispo leproso* (1989) for the Spanish text and the English translation. It is generally considered the most authoritative version of the novel. He chose the text of the *Obras Completas*, volume XI (1947) as the basis for his text, and explains his choice by saying that the original was revised and annotated by Pedro Carabia, who compared all the previous editions. I collated his text with the later editions of the novel of 1957 and 1969.

SELECTED BIBLIOGRAPHY

Works of Miró in English translation

Años y leguas Parr, Marcus, "Gabriel Miró: The Years and the Leagues." Introduction and translation. Dissertation. University of Utah, 1958.

Figuras de la pasión del Señor: Figures of the Passion of the Lord. Tr. C.J. Hogarth. London: Chapman, 1924. New York: Knopf, 1925.

"Las hermanas" ("The Sisters"). Tr. Grant Kohler Smith. In *International Short Stories*, V.W.F. Church, ed. Dallas, Chicago: Lyons and Carnahan, 1934.

"Herod Antipas." (Excerpt). In *The Ways of God and Man: Great Stories from the Bible in World Literature*, Ruth Selden, ed. New York: Daye, 1950.

El humo dormido (Sleeping Smoke). "The Man in Mourning and the Sprig of Parsley." (Excerpt). In *The European Caravan.* Samuel Putnam, ed. New York: Warren and Putnam, 1934.

El libro de Sigüenza, Libro de Sigüenza: Corpus. (Fragments). Tr. W. Wilson. New York: W. Norton, 1935.

Niño y grande (Niño y grande). Tr. Winifred L. Saunt. London: n.p. 1928.

Nuestro padre San Daniel: Novela de capellanes y devotos: Our Father San Daniel: Scenes of Clerical Life. Tr. Charlotte Remfrey-Kidd. London: E. Benn, Ltd., 1930.

"Pasión de Nuestra Señora" (uncertain title) (*Passion of Our Lady*). In *The Greatest Bible Stories: A Catholic Anthology from World Literature*, Anne Jackson Freemantle, ed. Garden City, N.Y.: Image Books, 1957.

"Señor Cuenca and His successor." (Excerpt). Tr. Anon. *Alhambra*, I, (1929) 66– .

"Señor Cuenca and His Successor." (Excerpt). Tr. Angel Flores. In *Best of Modern European Literature*, Klaus Mann and Hermann Kesten, eds. Philadelphia: Blakiston, 1945.

"Señor Cuenca and His successor." (Excerpt). Tr. Angel Flores. In *Great Spanish Short Stories*, Angel Flores, ed. New York: Dell, 1962. Pp.202–207.

"El señor maestro," (From *Corpus, y otros cuentos*) ("The Schoolmaster"). Tr. Warre Wells. In *Great Spanish Short Stories Representing the Work of the Leading Writers of the Day*, Warre G. Wells, ed. Boston: Houghton Mifflin, 1932. Pp.137–149. Also in *The Spanish Omnibus*. London: Eyre and Spottiswoode, 1932.

"Woman of Samaria." (Excerpt). in *World of Great Stories*, H.Haydn and J. Cournos, eds. New York: Crown, 1947.

Books and articles in English on Miró

Adams, Nicholson B., "Two Stylists: Azorín and Gabriel Miró. In *Contemporary Spanish Literature in English Translation.* Chapel Hill, N.C.: University of North Carolina Press, 1929: 27–29.

Barbará, Frederic, *Gabriel Miró and Catalan Culture: The Forging of the Literary Language in the Context of His Poetics.* New Orleans: The University Press of the South, 2004.

Bentley, Mercedes Clarasó and Douglas Gifford, eds, "Caminos y lugares: Gabriel Miró's *El obispo leproso,"* *Modern Language Review,* 77 (3); 1982 July: 606–617.

Bentley, Mercedes Clarasó and Douglas Gifford, eds, *Gabriel Miró: His Private Library and His Literary Background.* London: Tamesis Books, 1975.

Bentley, Mercedes Clarasó and Douglas Gifford, eds, "Why Is Miró's Bishop a Leper?", *Anales de la Literatura Española Contemporánea,* 7 (1982): 59–77.

Brown, Gerald G., "The Biblical Allusions in Gabriel Miró's Oleza Novels." *Modern Language Review;* 1975 Oct; 70 (4): 786–94.

Brown, Gerald G., "Gabriel (Francisco Victor) Miró (Ferrer)." In *Twentieth Century Literary Criticism,* Sharon K. Hall, ed. Vol. V. Detroit Mich.: Gale Research Company, 1981: 333–346.

Brown, Gerald G., *A Literary History of Spain: The Twentieth Century.* London: Ernest Benn, Ltd, New York: Barnes and Noble, Inc., 1972: 45–53.

Brown, James F., "Gabriel Miró." In *Dictionary of the Literature of the Iberian Peninsula,* Germán Bleiberg, Maureen Ihrie and Janet Perez, eds. L-Z. Westport, CN: Greenwood Press, 1993: 1095–1097.

Coope, Marion G.R., "The Critics' View of *Nuestro padre San Daniel* and *El obispo leproso* by Gabriel Miró." In *University of British Columbia Hispanic Studies,* H.V. Livermore, ed. London: Tamesis, 1974: 51–60.

Coope, Marion G.R., "Gabriel Miró's Vision of the Garden as *Hortus Conclusus* and *Paraíso Terrenal. Modern Language Notes;* 1973; 68: 94–104.

Coope, Marion G.R., *Reality and Time in the Olezan Novels of Gabriel Miró.* London: Tamesis, 1984.

Guillén, Jorge, *Language and Poetry: Some Poets of Spain.* Cambridge, MA: Harvard University Press, 1961. "Adequate Language: Gabriel Miró,": 157–197.

Johnson, Roberta, *Crossfire: Philosophy and the Novel in Spain, 1900–1934.* Lexington, Ky.: University Press of Kentucky, 1993.

Johnson, Roberta, "The Genesis of Gabriel Miró's Ideas about Being and Language: The Barcelona Period (1914–1920). *Revista Canadiense de Estudios Hispánicos* 1984 Winter; 8 (2): 183–205.

Johnson, Roberta, "Miró's *El obispo leproso*: Echoes of Pauline Theology in Alicante." *Hispania* 1976; 59: 239–246.

Johnson, Roberta, "Time and the Elements Earth, Air, Fire and Water in *Años y leguas*. In *Critical Essays on Gabriel Miró*, Ricardo Landeira, ed. Lincoln, NE: Society of Spanish and Spanish-American Studies, 1979: 42–56.

King, Edmund L., "Gabriel Miró." In *Encyclopedia of World Literature in the 20th Century*, Steven Serafin, ed. Vol 3: L–R. Farmington Hills, Mich.: St. James Press: 271–272.

Johnson, Roberta, "Gabriel Miró Introduced to the French." *Hispanic Review*, 29, 1961 Oct: 324–332.

Johnson, Roberta, *El humo dormido* by Gabriel Miró, Edmund L. King, ed. New York: The Laurel Language Library, 1967. Introd. 11–53.

Johnson, Roberta, *Sigüenza y el mirador azul y prosas de El Ibero* by Gabriel Miró, Edmund L. King, ed. Madrid: Ediciones de la Torre, 1982. Introduction.

Johnson, Roberta, "Life and Death, Space and Time: "El sepulturero." In *Critical Essays on Gabriel Miró*, Ricardo Landeira, ed. Lincoln, NE: Society of Spanish and Spanish-American Studies, 1979: 107–120.

King, Willard, *Notes on the Value and Meaning of Sense Experience in the Novel: Montemayor to Miró*. In *Essays on Hispanic Literature in Honor of Edmund L. King*. Sylvia Molloy and Luis Fernández Cifuentes, eds. London: Tamesis, 1983: 141–149.

Landeira, Ricardo, *An Annotated Bibliography of Gabriel Miró (1900–1978)*. Manhattan, KS: Society of Spanish and Spanish-American Studies, 1978.

Landeira, Ricardo, *Critical Essays on Gabriel Miró*. Manhattan, KS: Society of Spanish and Spanish-American Studies, 1979.

Landeira, Ricardo, "Del Vivir." In *Gabriel Miró: Trilogía de Sigüenza*, Ricardo Landeira, ed. Chapel Hill, N.C.: Ediciones de Hispanófila, 1972: 33–59.

Landeira, Ricardo, "Three Quarters of a Century of Miró Criticism." In *Critical Essays on Gabriel Miró*, Ricardo Landeira, ed. Manhattan, KS: Society of Spanish and Spanish-American Studies, 1979: 1–12.

Larsen, Kevin S., "'A la manera del teatro ibseniano': Gabriel Miró and Henrik Ibsen." *Symposium: A Quarterly Journal in Modern Literature* 1984 Spring; 38 (1): 43–55.

Longhurst, C.A., *Gabriel Miró: Nuestro Padre San Daniel and El obispo leproso*. London: Grant and Cutler, 1994.

MacDonald, Ian R., "First-Person to Third: An Early Vision of Gabriel Miró's *Las cerezas del cementerio*," In *What's Past Is Prologue: A Collection of Essays in Honour of L.J. Woodward*, Salvador Bacarisse, Bernard Bentley, Mercedes

Clarasó and Douglas Gifford, eds. Edinburgh: Scottish Academic Press, 1984. xiv: 95–106.

Machen, Arthur, "Introduction." to *Our Father San Daniel* by Gabriel Miró, Tr. Charlotte Remfrey-Kidd. London: Ernest Benn Ltd., 1930: v–ix.

Madariaga, Salvador de, "Azorín, Gabriel Miró," In *The Genius of Spain and Other Essays on Spanish Contemporary Literature*. Oxford: Clarendon Press, 1923, Freeport, N.Y.: Books for Libraries Press, 1968: 148–164.

Miller, Yvette E., "Illusion of Reality and Narrative Technique in Gabriel Miró's Oleza-Orihuela Novels: *Nuestro Padre San Daniel* and *El obispo leproso*."In: *Critical Essays on Gabriel Miró*, Ricardo Landeira, ed., Lincoln, NEB: Society of Spanish and Spanish-American Studies, 1979: 57–65.

Norden, Ernest E., "Celestial Imagery in Gabriel Miró's *Dentro del cercado*." *Journal of Spanish Studies: Twentieth Century*, 1979; 7: 73–86.

Norden, Ernest E., "Man and the Mediterranean Landscape in the Works of Gabriel Miró," *Cuadernos de Aldeeu,* 1983 May–Oct; 1 (2–3): 385–391.

O'Sullivan, Susan, "Watches, Lemons and Spectacles: Recurrent Images in the Works of Gabriel Miró," *Bulletin of Hispanic Studies*, 1967 Apr.; 46 (2): 107–121.

Peers, Edgar Allison, *"Figures of the Passion of Our Lord." Bulletin of Spanish Studies* 2 (2) 1925: 140–141.

Schwartz, Henry C., "The Poetry of Nature in Gabriel Miró," In *Critical Essays on Gabriel Miró*, Ricardo Landeira, ed. Lincoln, NE: Society of Spanish and Spanish-American Studies, 1979: 17–41.

I

PALACE AND SCHOOL

PALACIO Y COLEGIO

1. Pablo

Se dejó entornada la puerta de la corraliza.

¡Acababa de escaparse otra vez! Y corrió callejones de sol de siesta. Se juntó con otros chicos para quebrar y amasar obra tierna de las alfarerías de Nuestra Señora, y en la costera de San Ginés se apedrearon con los críos pringosos del arrabal.

Pablo era el más menudo de todos, y al huir de la brega buscaba el refugio del huerto de San Bartolomé, huerto fresco, bien medrado desde que don Magín gobernaba la parroquia.

La mayordoma le daba de merendar, y don Magín, sus vicarios y don Jeromillo, capellán de la Visitación, le rodeaban mirándole.

Pablo les contaba los sobresaltos de su madre, el recelo sombrío de su padre, los berrinches de tía Elvira, la vigilancia de don Cruz, de don Amancio, del P. Bellod, ayos de la casa.

– ...¡Y yo casi todas las siestas me escapo por el trascorral!

– ¡Te dejan que te escapes!

Y don Magín se lo llevó a la tribuna del órgano.

Se maravillaba el niño de que por mandato de sus dedos – sus dedos cogidos por los de don Magín – fuera poblándose la soledad de voces humanas, asomadas a las bóvedas, sin abrir las piedras viejecitas. Siempre era don Jeromillo el que entonaba o "manchaba", gozándose en su susto de que los grandes fuelles del órgano se lo llevasen y trajesen colgando de las sogas.

Se enterraban en la cámara del reloj para sentirse traspasados por el profundo pulso. Allí latían las sienes de Oleza. Luego, otra vez, torciéndose por la escalerilla, llegaban bajo la cigüeña de las campanas; y desde los arcos, entre aleteos de falcones y jabardillos de vencejos, veían el atardecer, que don Magín comparaba a un buen vecino que volvía, de distancia en distancia, al amor de su campanario. Toda la ciudad iba acumulándose a la redonda. Su silencio se ponía a jugar con una esquila que sonaba, tomándola y deshaciéndola en la quietud de las veredas. Golpes foscos de aperador;

1. Pablo

The door to the yard was left partly open.

He had just escaped again! And he ran down narrow lanes bathed in mid-afternoon siesta sunlight. He banded together with other youngsters to break up soft clay from the potteries of Our Lady[1] and knead it into shape, and they and the besmirched urchins from the outskirts of town hurled them at one another on the slope of San Ginés.[2]

Pablo was the smallest one of all, and after he fled from the fracas he sought shelter in the garden of San Bartolomé,[3] a refreshing, thriving garden now that Don Magín was in charge of the parish.

The housekeeper gave him a snack and Don Magín, his vicars and Don Jeromillo, the chaplain of La Visitación, surrounded him and looked at him.

Pablo told them all about his mother's dread, his father's somber suspicions, his aunt Elvira's tantrums, the vigilance of Don Cruz, Don Amancio, Father Bellod, the tutors at his house.

"...And almost every day at siesta time I escape through the outer yard!"

"They allow you to escape!"

And Don Magín took him up to the organ loft.

The child was astonished to see that at a command from his fingers –Don Magín's fingers clasping his – human voices could pervade the solitude, reaching up high into the vaults without opening up the old stones above. Don Jeromillo was always the one who blew, or "manchaba" the bellows, taking pleasure in his fear that the great big bellows of the organ might carry him off and leave him hanging from the ropes.

They buried themselves in the room behind the clock so they could feel overpowered by the profound pulsation. Oleza's temples were beating there. Afterwards, they twisted their way once again up the narrow stairway till they came to a place under the crank of the bells; and from the arches, they could observe the afternoon coming to an end amidst the fluttering of the falcons and the swarming of the swifts, which Don Magín compared to a good neighbor pausing along the way as he returned to the love of his bell tower. The entire city kept gathering itself all around them. Its silence began to play with a ringing cowbell, taking hold of it and letting it go in the stillness of the footpaths. The sullen pounding of a wheelwright, the fresh

golpes frescos de legones; tonadas y lloros; el bramido del Segral. Arreciaba la bulla de las ranas.

– ¿Las oyes, Pablo? ¡Las chafaría todas con mis pies; pero con los pies descalzos del P. Bellod, poniéndomelos como botas para andar por los fangales! Oyendo un cántico se piensa en algo que está más lejos que ese cántico. Los grillos parecen de plata. En estas noches olorosas de cosechas se sienten como rebaños que pasturan a lo lejos, como cascabeles de una diligencia que viene por todos los campos. Un grillo, sólo un grillo, vibra en muchas leguas. Pasa un pájaro, y nos abre más la tarde. En cambio, principian a croar las ranas y no vemos sino agua de balsa.

Don Jeromillo se dormía. Solía dormirse en todo reposo, en cualquier rincón apacible de un diálogo; y al despertar se atolondraba de verse súbitamente despierto.

Revolvióse el párroco y con el codo tocó los bordes de la "Abuelona", la campana gorda, que se quedó exhalando un vaho de resonido.

– Deja tu mano encima y te latirá en los dedos la campana. Parece que le circule la sangre de las horas y de los toques de muchos siglos. ¿Verdad que tiene también su piel con sus callos y todo?

Pablo decía que sí, y palpaba los costados de bronce, calientes de sol. Se presentían los clamores en lo hondo de la copa enorme y sensitiva.

– Tienes miedo de que suene, y a la vez estás deseando empujarla. Todo el silencio del pueblo y de la vega es una mirada que se fija en tu mano y en tu voluntad. No nos atrevemos a remover la campana porque la tarde duerme dentro y se levantaría toda preguntándonos.

El niño miraba la "Abuelona"; se apartaba; volvía a tocarla despacito. En él se abría la curiosidad y la conciencia de las cosas bajo la palabra del capellán.

– ¡Ahora vámonos a Palacio!

Con don Magín entraba en Palacio un claror de vida ancha, como si siempre acabase de venir de viajes remotos. Le rodeaban los curiales, le saludaban los fámulos, le buscaban los clérigos domésticos, le consultaban los vicarios forasteros.

Si el prelado no salía a su ventana del huerto para llamarle, o no le

blows of the hoes, melodic airs and weeping: the roar of the river Segral. The tumult of the frogs kept growing louder.

"Do you hear them, Pablo? I would squash them all with my feet, even better, with the bare feet of Father Bellod, by putting them on like boots so I could walk around in the mud holes! When you hear a canticle you think of something far more distant than that canticle. Crickets seem like silver. On nights like these, fragrant with harvests, you hear them like herds grazing in the distance, like tinkling bells on a diligence spreading over all the fields. A cricket, just one cricket, vibrates for many leagues around. A bird passes by and opens up the afternoon even more for us. On the other hand, the frogs begin to croak and all we can see is the water in a stagnant puddle."

Don Jeromillo was asleep. He would doze off whenever he could, in any peaceful corner of a dialogue; and when he would wake up, he seemed astonished to find himself suddenly awake.

The priest turned around and touched the edges of the "Great big Grandmother," the potbellied bell, with his elbow, and it kept on exhaling a breath of reverberation.

"Leave your hand on top and the bell will throb in your fingers. It seems as if the blood of the hours and the ringing of many past centuries were circulating through it. Do you think it is true that it also has its own skin and its calluses and everything else?"

Pablo agreed and he palpated the bronze sides, warm with the sun. One was filled with a presentiment of a tolling for the dead in the depths of the enormous, sensitive cup-shaped bell.

"You're afraid that it will ring and, at the same time, you are anxious to push it. The complete silence of the town and the open plain is a glance staring at your hand and your will. We don't dare disturb the bell because the afternoon is asleep inside it and would rise up all at once to question us."

The child kept looking at the "Big Grandmother bell"; he drew back; he touched it again very slowly. Curiosity and an awareness of the things beneath the chaplain's words were opening up within him.

"Now let's go to the Palace!"[4]

A brightness from the wide world beyond entered the Palace with Don Magín, as if he were always coming back from far off journeys. The episcopal clerks all surrounded him, the house servants greeted him, the priests under the bishop's jurisdiction kept looking for him, the vicars from other parishes were consulting him.

If the prelate did not appear at the window facing the garden to call to

mandaba un paje convidándole a subir, el párroco se iba sin llegar a los aposentos del señor.

Algunas veces su illustrísima le sentaba a su mesa; pero antes había de internarse don Magín por las cocinas y despensas; y oyéndole, brincaban de gozo los galopillos, y era menester que el mayordomo se lo llevara para reprimir el bullicio.

Aprovechábase de su confianza ganando licencias, socorros, perdones y provechos para los demás. Era valedor, pero no valido, de la corte episcopal, porque no se acomodaba su desenfado ni con la disciplina del poder. El suyo no lo debía todo a la sangre que perdiera en el tumulto de la riada de San Daniel, sino principalmente a su mérito de humanidad en el corazón del obispo. Don Magín equivalía al diálogo, a salir su ilustrísima de sí mismo, descansándose en otro hombre. De manera que nunca pudo enojarse su ilustrísima de no poder enojarse, como Celio, que, harto de la mansedumbre de su cliente, tuvo que decirle: "¡Hazme la contra para que seamos dos!"

Al principio estuvo Pablo muy parado, sobrecogido del silencio del patio claustral, de la bruma de las oficinas diocesanas. Pronto llegaron a parecerle los techos de Palacio tan familiares como los de la parroquia de San Bartolomé. Se asomaba a los armarios del archivo, removía las campanillas, volcaba las salvaderas, se subía a los butacones de crin y a los estrados del sínodo. En el huerto ya le conocían los mastines, las ocas, los palomos; y hasta las mulas del faetón de su ilustrísima levantaban sus quijadas de los pesebres, volviéndose para mirarle.

Sus juegos y risas alborotaron todos los ámbitos. Y, una tarde, en la revuelta de un corredor, se le apareció un clérigo ordenándole respeto. Pero la voz de alguien invisible que mandaba más se interpuso protegiéndole:

– ¡Dejadle que grite, que en su casa no juega!

Todo lo corrió el hijo de Paulina, desde las norias hasta la torrecilla del lucernario.

Y otro día se perdió por un pasadizo mural que acababa en tres escalones de manises, con un portalillo como los del "Olivar de Nuestro Padre." Entró

him, or if he didn't send a page inviting him to come up, the parish priest would leave without going up to the lord bishop's rooms.

Sometimes His Excellency would have him seated at his table; but Don Magín first had to make his way into the kitchens and pantries; and when the kitchen help heard him, they would jump for joy and it was necessary for the majordomo to take him away in order to repress all the commotion.

He took advantage of his close, confidential relationship to acquire authority for permission for clerics to perform certain duties, for financial support, for indulgences and advantages for the others. He was a protector without being protected himself by the episcopal court, because his free and easy nature did not feel comfortable even with the discipline of power. He didn't owe his power completely to the blood he may have lost during the tumult at the time of the flooding at San Daniel's,[5] but principally to the awareness of his humanitarian qualities in the bishop's heart. Don Magín's presence was equivalent to dialogue, to allow His Excellency the opportunity to come out of his own self, resting for support on another man. So His Excellency was really never able to get angry at not being able to become angry, much like Coelius, who, weary of his client's meekness, felt obliged to tell him, "Favor me with your opposition so we may seem more like two persons!"[6]

In the beginning Pablo was quite diffident, intimidated by the silence in the cloister patio, by the murkiness of the diocesan offices. Soon the confines of the Palace came to be as familiar to him as those of the parish church of San Bartolomé. He would poke into the archival cabinets, shake the hand bells, overturn ink-drying sandboxes, climb up onto the big horsehair armchairs and the platform used by the diocesan synod. In the garden, the mastiffs, the geese and cock pigeons already knew him; and even the mules for His Excellency's phaeton would raise their jaws from the troughs, turning around to look at him.

His playfulness and laughter would fill every corner with excitement. And one afternoon, as he came to a turn in the corridor, a cleric appeared before him ordering him to show more respect. But the voice of an invisible person of greater authority intervened to protect him.

"Let him shout all he wants, because he can't play in his own house!"

Paulina's son ran about everywhere, from the draw wells to the small tower with the skylight.

And on another day he got lost along a passageway with walls on either side with three tile-surfaced steps leading up to a small door, just like those in "Our Father's Olive Grove." He went inside and found himself in a large

y hallóse en una sala de retratos de obispos difuntos. En el fondo había otros tres peldaños y otra puertecita labrada. Pablo la empujó y fué asomándose a un dormitorio de paredes blancas. Encima del lecho colgaba un dosel morado, como el de la capilla del Descendimiento de la catedral. Vió un reclinatorio de almohadas de seda carmesí, un bufete con atril, una mesa con libros y copas de asa y cobertera, copas de enfermo; y junto a la reja, un sacerdote demacrado, con una cruz de oro en el pecho, que le sonrió llamándole.

– No me tengas miedo. Sentí que venías y esperé sin moverme para no asustarte. Desde mi ventana te miro cuando juegas en el huerto.

El niño le contemplaba las ropas de capellán humilde. Su voz era la voz del que mandó que le dejasen jugar a su antojo.

– Yo te conozco mucho. Una tarde que llovía, tarde de las Ánimas, pasabas con tu madre por la ribera. Ibais los dos llorando...

– ¡Sí que es de verdad!

– Y al verme te paraste, y yo os bendije...

– ¡Sí que es de verdad!

– ¿Por qué llorabais?

– ¡Es el obispo!

Y el hijo de Paulina ladeaba su cabeza mirándole más.

Su ilustrísima lo llevó a la sala del trono, olvidada y obscura, con rápidos brillos envejecidos; le mostró el comedor, todo enfundado, aupándole para que alcanzase confites de los aparadores y credencias de roble; y en la biblioteca le derramó todo un cofrecillo de estampas primorosas.

Pablo las repasó y las contó sentadito en los recios esterones.

– Dime por qué llorabais.

– Yo no lo sé.

Y Pablo se encaramó al sillón de oro de la mesa prelaticia. Resbaló dulcemente, y quedóse sorprendido de tener todo el asiento para él y todo el escritorio para él. En su casa, la mesa del padre le estaba vedada como un ara máxima. Tendió sus brazos con las manos muy abiertas sobre la faz pulida de la tabla. ¡Toda suya! Y se reía.

room with portraits of dead bishops.[7] There were three more steps in the back and another ornately carved little door. Pablo pushed it open and made his way into a bedroom with white walls. A purple canopy was hanging over the bed, like the one in the chapel of the Descent from the Cross, in the cathedral. He saw a prie-dieu with cushions of crimson silk, a writing desk with a lectern, a table with books and goblets with handles and lids, goblets used for the ill; and next to the window grating sat an emaciated-looking priest with a golden cross over his breast, who smiled as he called to him.[8]

"Don't be afraid of me. I heard you coming and I waited here without moving so as not to frighten you. I often watch you from my window when you're playing in the garden."

The boy kept looking at a clergyman's humble garments. It was the same voice that had ordered them to let him play to his heart's content.

"I know you very well. You passed by me with your mother along the riverside when it was raining one afternoon, the afternoon of the Day of the Dead. You were both crying...."

"That's quite true!"

"And you stopped when you saw me and I blessed you both...."

"That's quite true!"

"Why were you both crying?"

"It's the bishop!"

And Paulina's son tilted his head to one side and stared at him even more closely.

His Excellency led him into the throne room, dark and forgotten, with sudden, brilliant flashes of faded splendor; he showed him the dining room, where all the furniture was covered over and he helped him up so he could reach the dainties in the oaken sideboards and credenzas; and in the library, he spread out the contents of a small chest filled with exquisite prints.

Pablo sat there comfortably on the heavy floor matting and looked through them and counted them.

"Tell me why you were both crying."

"I don't really know."

And Pablo climbed up onto the golden armchair of the prelate's table. He slid forward gently and seemed quite surprised to have the entire chair and the whole writing desk all to himself. In his own house, his father's table was forbidden to him as if it were a high altar. He stretched out his arms with his hands completely open over the polished surface of the wooden top. All his! And he laughed.

– ¿Y qué os dijo tu padre viendo que llorabais?

– Yo ya no lo sé.

Miraba el sello de lacrar; se apretó en los carrillos la hoja de marfil de la plegadera para sentir el filo de frío. Alzaba los ojos al artesón, y se quedaba pensando.

– En mi casa siempre llora la mamá. Es que la mujer y el marido parecen los otros dos.

Se distrajo con un pisapapeles de cristal, lleno de iris. Poco a poco la tarde recordada por el prelado se le acercó hasta tenerla encima de su frente, como los vidrios de sus balcones donde se apoyaba muchas veces, sin ver nada, volviéndose de espaldas al aburrimiento. Todo aquel día tocaron las campanas lentas y rotas. Tarde de las Ánimas, ciega de humo de río y de lluvia. La casa se rajó de gritos del padre. Ardían las luces de aceite delante de los cuadros de los abuelos – el señor Galindo, la señora Serrallonga –, que le miraban sin haberle visto y sin haberle amado nunca. Cuando el padre y tía Elvira se fueron, las campanas sonaron más grandes. Le buscó su madre; la vió más delgada, más blanca. Se ampararon los dos en ellos mismos; y entonces las luces eran las que les miraban, crujiendo tan viejas como si las hubiesen encendido los abuelos. Después, la madre y el hijo salieron por el postigo de los trascorrales. Todo el atardecer se quejaba con la voz del río. Caminaban entre árboles mojados, rojos de otoño. Pablo agarróse a una punta del manto de la madre, prendido de llovizna como un rosal. Ella no pudo resistir su congoja, y cayó de rodillas. Una mano morada trazó la cruz entre la niebla, y ellos la sintieron descender sobre sus frentes afligidas...

Entre sus ojos largos, un pliegue adusto le rompía la dulzura infantil. Vió una estampa con orla de acero al lado del velón. Sobre un fondo ingenuo de cipreses y lirios se reclinaba un niño; un avestruz le hincaba en la frente su pico abierto y voraz.

Su ilustrísima le acercó el grabado.

– Es San Godefrido, un niño siempre puro, que fué obispo. ¿Le tienes miedo a ese pájaro tan alto?

– ¡Yo no le tengo miedo! – lo dijo riéndose; pero se le plegó más la frente, como si se la rasgase el pico anheloso que atormentó los pensamientos de pureza de San Godefrido. – En mi casa hay un pájaro, de grande como una

"And what did your father say to you when he saw that you were both crying?"

"I don't know any more."

He looked at the wax seal and pressed the ivory blade of the paper knife against his cheeks so he could feel the cold edge. He raised his eyes to the decorative panel on the ceiling and sat there thinking.

"In my house it's my mother who's always crying. It's just that in my house, the wife and the husband seem to be the other two, my father and his sister."

He entertained himself with a paperweight of opalescent crystal. Little by little the afternoon the prelate had recalled kept drawing closer to him till it was right over his forehead, like the glass panes of his balcony windows where he would often lean his head, without seeing anything, turning his back on boredom. The bells kept ringing, slow and shattered, all day long on that day. The afternoon of the Day of the Dead, blind with the vapor from the river and the rain. The house was rent by his father's shouts. The oil lamps were burning in front of his grandparents' pictures– Señor Galindo and Señora Serrallonga– who stared down at him without ever having seen him or loved him. When his father and Aunt Elvira departed, the bells sounded even louder. His mother sought him out; he saw her ever so slender, ever so white. The two of them found solace in one another; and then the lamps were the ones that kept staring at them, crackling with old age, as if the grandparents had lit them. Then the mother and son left by the wicket to the outer yard. The whole of the late afternoon was moaning with the voice of the river. They walked between the damp trees, red with autumn. Pablo took hold of one end of his mother's cloak, adorned with the drizzle like a rosebush. She was unable to put up with her grief and fell on her knees. A purple-colored hand traced the sign of the cross within the mist and they felt it descend upon their afflicted foreheads....

A melancholy wrinkle between his wide-opened eyes broke his childish sweetness. He saw a print with a steel border beside the brass lamp. A child was reclining against the ingenuous background of cypress trees and lilies; an ostrich was sinking its open, voracious beak into his forehead.

His Excellency brought the engraving closer to him.

"It's Saint Godfrey,[9] an eternally pure child, who was a bishop. Are you afraid of that big tall bird?"

"I'm not afraid of it!" he said this with a laugh, but he wrinkled his brow even more, as if it were being torn open by the eager beak that tormented Saint Godfrey's thoughts of purity. "There is a bird in my house as big as a

paloma, y no es una paloma, es un perdigote, pero de bulto, gordo, con ojos que miran. Lo tiene tía Elvira de candelero y le pone una vela entre las alas. Y también hay un cuadro bordado de pelos de muertos, y es el nicho de abuelo y abuela que no sé quién son; y una Virgen de los Dolores con cuchillos, que está llorando; todo es de tía Elvira. ¿Quiere venir y verá?

— Yo estuve ya en tu casa del "Olivar" hace mucho tiempo.

— El "Olivar" sí que es de mi abuelo de veras, el que se murió, y mío. Tenemos una lámpara que es un barco de cristales que hacen colores, como esa bola de los papeles. A mí no me llevan al "Olivar".

De repente se le olvidó todo, complaciéndose en la graciosa anforilla del tintero de plata. Lo destapó y asomóse al espejo negro y dormido.

Un familiar entró las luces; y quedóse pasmado de que aquella criatura revolviese la mesa jeráquica. Y el señor, de pie, sonreía consintiéndolo todo.

Pasó por el huerto la voz de don Magín llamando al niño.

Fueron a la ventana; Pablo brincó como un cordero; y gritaba y se reía escondiéndose detrás de su ilustrísima.

2. Consejo de familia

Todavía de pañales el hijo, cerraron los condes de Lóriz su casa, trasladándose a Madrid. Ya podrían abrirse confiadamente las celosías de don Álvaro. Su calle se internaba de nuevo en un silencio de pureza; verdadero recinto suyo. Y en abril, casi todos los años en abril, volvía esa gente con sus criados señoriles y el ama del condesito, una pasiega grande, magnífica de ropas de colores de frutas y de collares, de dijes, de abalorios y dingolondangos. Parecía un ídolo rural. Elvira la miraba desde su persiana con rencor y con asco. De seguro que en aquellos pechos, tantas veces desnudos, y en aquellos ojos dulces de becerra se escondía la deshonestidad de una mala mujer. Más tarde, la nodriza se trocó en ama seca, y a su lado principió a caminar la cigüeña de un aya, cansada de idiomas y de virtudes antiguas.

dove, but it isn't a dove, it's a partridge, just a stuffed figure, real fat, with eyes that stare at you. Aunt Elvira uses it like a candlestick and puts a candle between its wings. And there's also a picture surrounded by dead people's hair, and it's a niche for grandfather and grandmother, but I really don't know who they are; and there's an Our lady of the Sorrows with all those knives around her, and she's crying; it all belongs to Aunt Elvira. Would you like to come and see it?"

"I've already been to your house at the "Olive Grove" a long time ago."

"The 'Olive Grove' is really and truly my grandfather's house, the one who died, and it's mine too. We have a lamp that's a boat made of crystal glass and it reflects colors like that ball for the papers. They don't take me to the 'Olive Grove.'"

He suddenly forgot everything, taking pleasure in the small, attractive vessel of the silver inkstand. He removed the lid and peered into the black, dormant mirror.

A familiar came in with the lamps; and he was astonished to see that small child upsetting the hierarchical table. And the Lord Bishop stood there, smiling, permitting it all.

Don Magín's voice passed through the garden calling to the boy.

They went to the window and Pablo jumped up and down like a lamb; and he shouted and laughed, hiding behind His Excellency.

2. Family Council

While their son was still in swaddling clothes, the Count and Countess of Lóriz closed up their house and moved to Madrid. Now Don Álvaro's lattices could be opened in full confidence. His street took refuge once again in a silence of purity; a truly confined space all his own. And in April, almost every year in April, those people would return with their haughty servants and the little count's nursemaid, a rather large wet nurse, magnificent in her fruit-colored clothes and necklaces, trinkets, glass beads and with flattery and pampering. She looked like a rustic idol. Elvira looked at her from behind her window blinds with rancor and disgust. She was certain that the indecency of an immoral woman was concealed in those breasts which had been exposed so many times and in those sweet calf-like eyes. Later on, the wet nurse was exchanged for a dry nurse and a stork-like governess, weary with languages and old-fashioned virtues, began to walk by his side.

Elvira la aborreció. ¡Qué perversidades no habría detrás de sus impertinentes laicos!

Don Álvaro y sus amigos también la miraban desde la reja del escritorio. En la pared, donde colgaba un trofeo y un retrato del "señor" desterrado, se estampaba el escandaloso resol de una vidriera de los Lóriz. De allí salía, como una fuente musical, la risa de la condesa.

– ¡Pero cuándo se irán! – clamaba don Álvaro.

Se iban; y la ausencia de esa gente de elegancias y claridades gozosas entornaba la vida de Oleza. Entornada y todo, la ciudad se quedaba lo mismo. Lo reconocía don Amancio *(Carolus Alba-Longa),* ordeñándose su barba nueva, lisa, barrosa. Lo mismo desde todos los tiempos, con su olor de naranjos, de nardos, de jazmineros, de magnolios, de acacias, de árbol del Paraíso. Olores de vestimentas, de ropas finísimas de altares, labradas por las novias de la Juventud Católica; olor de panal de los cirios encendidos; olor de cera resudada de los viejos exvotos. Olor tibio de tahona y de pastelerías. Dulces santificados, delicia del paladar y del beso; el dulce como rito prolongado de las fiestas de piedad. Especialidades de cada orden religiosa: pasteles de gloria y pellas, o manjar blanco, de las clarisas de San Gregorio; quesillos y pasteles de yema de la Visitación; crema de las agustinas; hojaldres de las verónicas, canelones, nueces y almendras rellenas de Santiago el Mayor; almíbares, meladas y limoncillos de las madres de San Jerónimo.

Dulcerías, jardines; incienso, campanas, órgano, silencio, trueno de molinos y de río; mercado de frutas; persianas cerradas; azoteas de cal y de sol; vuelos de palomos; tránsito de seminaristas con sotanilla y beca de tafetán; de colegiales con uniforme de levita y fajín azul; de niñas con bandas de grana y cabellos nazarenos; procesiones; hijas de María, camareras del Santísimo; Horas Santas; tierra húmeda y caliente; follajes pomposos; riegos y ruiseñores; nubes de gloria; montes desnudos... Siempre lo mismo; pero quizá los tiempos fermentasen de peligros de modernidad. Palacio mostraba una indiferencia moderna. Don Magín paseaba por el pueblo como un capellán castrense. Y esos Lóriz, de origen liberal, y otros por el estilo, se

Elvira detested her. What manner of perversities were probably lying behind her laic lorgnette!

Don Álvaro and his friends also watched her from the grating over the window in his study. On the wall, where a military insignia was hanging along with a portrait of the exiled "lord," the pretender,[10] the scandalous glare of the sun was imprinted, reflected from a glass window of the Lórizes. The countess's laughter kept emanating from there like a musical fountain.

"But when will they be leaving!" Don Álvaro exclaimed.

They were going away and the absence of those people with their pleasure-filled elegance and brilliance upset the life of Oleza. Upset or not, the city remained the same. Don Amancio (*Carolus Alba-Longa*)[11] recognized it, wringing his new, smooth, red clay-colored beard like an udder. Just the same as in all other times, with the aroma of orange trees, spikenards, jasmine bushes and magnolia trees, acacias and the China tree. The fragrance of vestments, of exquisitely delicate altar clothes fashioned by the novices of the Catholic Youth, the scent of honeycomb from the burning candles, the odor of transuded wax from past votive offerings. The tepid fragrance of the bakery and the pastry shops. Consecrated sweets, a delight to the palate and the kiss, the confectionary as a prolonged rite for holy days without obligation. Specialties of every religious order; ladylocks and puffs, or blancmange, from the Poor Clares of San Gregorio;[12] curds and egg-filled tarts from La Visitación; toasted custard from the Augustinians;[13] puffpastes from the Franciscan sisters of Santa Verónica;[14] cinnamon candy, nuts and soft-centered almonds from the church of Santiago el Mayor;[15] preserved fruits, honey and hemp seed taffy and small candied lemons from the mothers of San Jerónimo.[16]

Confectionery shops, gardens, incense, bells, organ, silence, the thunder of the mills and the river; the fruit market; closed window blinds; roof terraces of whitewash and sunlight; flights of ring doves; the passage of seminary students in short cassocks and taffeta sashes round their shoulders; schoolboys in uniforms of frock coats and narrow blue sashes; of young girls wearing fine scarlet ribbons and long, flowing hair; processions; Daughters of Mary;[17] Handmaids of the Holy Sacrament;[18] the Exposition of the Holy Eucharist;[19] warm, humid earth; pompous foliage; irrigation channels and nightingales; bright, heavenly clouds; barren mountains.... Always the same, but perhaps the times were in ferment with the dangers of modernity. The Palace showed a modern indifference. Don Magín strolled around town like a military chaplain. And the Lórizes, of liberal origins, and others of their

aficionaban al ambiente viejo y devoto como a una golosía de sus sentidos, imaginando suyo lo que sólo era de Oleza. En cambio, todo eso que nada más era de Oleza: sus piadosas delicias, su sangre tan especiada, sus esencias de tradición, el fervor y el olor vegetal, arcaico y litúrgico, se convertían para los tibios en elementos y convites de pecado. Los años aún no descortezaban los colores legítimos de la ciudad; ¡pero las gentes...! (Don Amancio, el P. Bellod, don Cruz, don Álvaro, preveían un derrumbamiento.) Las gentes, esas gentes de ahora, las nuevas; los hijos... Don Álvaro tenía un hijo: Pablo. ¡Y ese hijo...!

Pablo sentía encima de su vida la mirada de célibe y de anteojos de don Amancio; la mirada tabicada, unilateral, de tuerto, del P. Bellod; la mirada enjuta y parpadeante de don Cruz; la mirada huera del homeópata; la mirada de filo ardiente de tía Elvira; la mirada de recelo y pesadumbre de su padre. Ninguno le acusó de sus escapadas a Palacio y al huerto rectoral de don Magín, el capellán más relajado y poderoso de la diócesis. Muchas veces tuvo que recogerle la vieja criada de Gandía. Y nunca trataron de este asunto, porque no todas las desgracias pueden desnudarse. Lo pensaban mirándose; y don Cruz asumía la unanimidad del dolor elevando los ojos hacia las vigas del despacho de don Álvaro para ofrecer a Dios el sacrificio de su silencio.

No se resignaba el señor penitenciario a que un crío, y un crío hijo de don Álvaro Galindo, fuese la contradicción de todos, más fuerte que ellos, hasta impedirles la fórmula de su conciencia. Sus palabras y voluntades evitaban, como si trazaran una curva, el dominio de lo que con más títulos habrían de poseer. Esa criatura tan de ellos y tan frágil por ser el objeto de todas las complacencias de Paulina, se les resbalaba graciosamente entre sus manos. Sospechaban en la madre un escondido contento sabiendo que habían de quedar intactas las predilecciones de Pablo.

Don Cruz llegó a decir que las esposas como Paulina, por santas que fuesen, pueden ofrecer hijos a la perdición.

Reconcentróse don Álvaro bajo la sombra de su tristeza.

– No tan débil como se cree. ¡Nada tan resistente como sus lágrimas!

Don Amancio, dueño de una academia preparatoria, abría la esperanza:

ilk, took a fondness for the old-fashioned, devout atmosphere, as if it were a gluttony for their senses, imagining that what really belonged to Oleza was truly theirs. On the other hand, everything that belonged only to Oleza and to nobody else: its pious delights, its highly spiced blood, its essences of tradition, the archaic and liturgical fervor and vegetal aroma, was all converted into elements and invitations to sin for those lukewarm in spirit. The years had still not stripped away the legitimate colors of the city, but the Gentiles...! (Don Amancio, Father Bellod, Don Cruz, Don Álvaro, foresaw a collapse.) The Gentiles, the Gentiles of the present moment, the new ones; the sons.... Don Álvaro had a son: Pablo. And that son...!

Pablo felt Don Amancio's celibate, bespectacled glance encroaching on his life; Father Bellod's immured, unilateral, one-eyed glance; Don Cruz's scrawny, blinking glance; the homeopath's vacuous glance; the cutting edge of Aunt Elvira's glance; his father's mistrusting glance of affliction. None of them accused him for his escapades to the Palace and in the rectory garden of Don Magín, the ever so easygoing and most powerful parish priest in the diocese. The old maidservant from Gandía[20] would often have to go retrieve him. And they never dealt with this matter because not all misfortunes can be laid bare. They thought about it when they looked at one another; and Don Cruz assumed the unanimity of their sorrow when he raised his eyes to the rafters in Don Álvaro's study to offer God the sacrifice of his silence.

The canon-penitentiary could not resign himself to the fact that a small child, and a child who was Don Álvaro Galindo's son, should be the contradiction to everyone, should be stronger than they and even be able to restrain them from the formation of his conscience. His words and his willful desires, as if they were tracing a curve, prevented their domination over him, in spite of all the credentials they might possess. That child, who was so very much a part of them and so fragile because he was the object of all of Paulina's complaisances, was gracefully slipping through their fingers. They suspected a hidden sense of satisfaction in the mother at the knowledge that all of Pablo's inclinations would remain intact.

Don Cruz even reached a point where he said that wives like Paulina, no matter how saintly they might appear to be, are capable of offering their sons to perdition.

Don Álvaro withdrew into his thoughts under the shadow of his sadness.

"Not as weak as you think. Nothing as powerful as her tears!"

Don Amancio, the master of a preparatory academy, opened up their hope:

– De cera son los hijos, y podemos modelarlos a nuestra imagen. – y su calidad de célibe acentuaba su timbre pedagógico.

– ¿Pablo de cera? – tronaba el P. Bellod – . ¡Pablo es de hierro, y el hierro se forja a martillazos!

El homeópata propuso que esa difícil crianza le fuera encomendada a don Amancio.

– Mi casa no es herrería ni escuela de párvulos. Mi casa es academia.

Y como don Cruz se volviese con reproche a Monera, Monera, no sabiendo qué hacer, abrió y cerró la tapa de su gordo reloj de oro, y le cedió su butaca, como siempre a don Amancio. Entonces hablaron del internado en el colegio de "Jesús". La hermana de don Álvaro se compungió. Bien sabía que Pablo se encanijaba entre sus faldas. Muchas veces se confesó culpable de los resabios del sobrino. ¡Pero ya no podía más! ¡Para que Paulina siguiese viviendo en el dulce regaño de hija única, ella había de vivir en los afanes y trajines de ama y de sierva! ¡Arrancar a Pablo de la madre para encerrarle en "Jesús", imposible! Si Paulina les oyese, no acabarían sus lágrimas y sus gritos de desesperación. ¡Éste era su miedo!

– ¡Es usted un ángel!

Don Cruz llevaba muchos años repitiéndoselo; y se lo repetía como si dijese: ¡Es usted de Gandía, o está usted muy flaca!

Elvira se sofocó virginalmente.

– ¡Ya no puedo más!

No podía. Nunca sosegaba. Los armarios, las cómodas, el arcón de harina, las alacenas y despensa, todo se abría, se cerraba, se contaba bajo el poder, la vigilancia y las llaves de la señorita Galindo. En los vasares enrejados, las sobras de las frutas, de las pastas, de los nuégados y arropes iban criando vello; y las dos criadas, sin postres, lo miraban.

Ese estridor de llaves y cerraduras creía sentirlo Pablo hasta con la lengua, amarga por el relumbre del agua oxidada, agua de clavos viejos, que el padre y tía Elvira le obligaban a beber para que le saliesen los colores.

Elvira se abrasaba en la desconfianza como en un amor infinito. Si una puerta se quedaba entornada, temía el acecho de unos ojos enemigos.

"Children are made of wax and we can mold them in our image," and his celibate condition accented his pedagogical timbre.

"Pablo made of wax?" thundered Father Bellod. "Pablo is made of iron and you shape iron with a hammer!"

The homeopath proposed that the difficult task of educating the boy should be entrusted to Don Amancio.

"My house is not a blacksmith's shop nor a school for very little children. My house is an academy."

And since Don Cruz turned toward Monera with reproach, Monera, not knowing what to do, opened and closed the hinged lid of his bloated gold watch and ceded his armchair, as he always did, to Don Amancio. They then spoke of being a boarding student at the school of "Jesús."[21] Don Álvaro's sister was overcome with compunction. She knew very well that Pablo was growing up to be scrawny and sickly, so close to her skirts. She often confessed her responsibility for her nephew's bad habits. But there was nothing more she could do! She would have to live with all the burdensome tasks and plodding back and forth of a housekeeper and slave in order that Paulina could go on living in the sweet repression of an only daughter! Tear Pablo away from his mother and lock him up in "Jesús," impossible! If Paulina could only hear them, her tears and shouts of desperation would never end. This was her fear!

"You are an angel!"

Don Cruz had spent many years repeating it to her, and he would repeat it to her as if he were saying, "You are from Gandía," or "You look very thin!"

Elvira flushed like a virgin.

"I can't go on any more!"

She couldn't. She never rested. The closets, the chests of drawers, the flour bin, the cupboards and the pantry, everything was opened and was closed, was counted under the authority, the vigilance and the keys of Señorita Galindo. Leftover fruit, baked goods, nougats and fruit syrups were on the grill-covered shelves growing a coat of down on them, and the two housemaids, not permitted to have any dessert, could only look at them.

Pablo thought he could all but hear that strident sound of keys and locks with his tongue, which was bitter with the aftertaste of rusted water, a water with old nails in it, which his father and Aunt Elvira obliged him to drink so that he would have better color.[22]

Elvira was burning with a feeling of mistrust as one would with an infinite love. If a door were left ajar, she feared the spying eyes of her enemies. She

Retorcida por una prisa insaciable y dura. Prisa siempre. Y en cambio, Paulina recostaba su alma en el recuerdo de las horas anchas y viejas del "Olivar de Nuestro Padre". Una vez quiso mitigar ese ávido gobierno; y se puso muy dolida la hermana del marido.

– ¡Yo nada soy aquí! Lo sé; y me dejo llevar de mis simples arrebatos porque no tengo tu calma y tu primor. ¡Yo guardo para ese hijo vuestro! Que Álvaro te diga lo que se nos enseñó de pequeños. ¿Que se pudren y se pierden las cosas teniéndolas guardadas? Más se perderían dejándolas abiertas a todas las manos. Siento a ese hijo vuestro tan mío como de vosotros. ¡Y no me lo impediréis aunque mi mismo hermano me eche de esta casa!

Don Álvaro la tomó de los hombros, acercándosela con ansiedad devota. Elvira se acongojó y sus sollozos vibrantes la revolvían en crujidos... ¡Echar a esa hermana de supremas virtudes, la que se olvidó hasta de su recato de mujer, siguiéndole una noche, con disfraz de hombre, por guardarle de los peligros de "Cara-rajada"!

En presencia de don Cruz, de don Amancio, de Monera y del P. Bellod, supo Paulina el propósito de poner interno a Pablo en el Colegio de Jesús.

Elvira inclinaba la frente esperando los sollozos rebeldes de la madre.

Paulina nada más pronunció:

– Pablo no ha cumplido ocho años – después recogióse calladamente en su dormitorio.

La cuñada se quedó escuchando.

– ¡Es mi miedo, mi miedo a sus gritos, al escándalo de la desesperación!

No venía ni un grito ni un gemido. Y entonces tuvo ella que gemir y gritar; y llamó a Pablo.

Se asomó la vieja criada de Gandía.

– También se ha escapado esta tarde.

– ¡Ya no puedo más!

– ¡Es usted un ángel!

Y quedó acordada la clausura en "Jesús".

Anochecido llegó Pablo, y buscó enseguida a su madre para besarla. Después, en el comedor, sus ojos resistieron la mirada de tía Elvira sin

was twisted by an insatiable and unyielding sense of urgency. Always in a hurry. And Paulina, in contrast, found repose for her soul in the recollection of the protected, long past hours in "Our Father's Olive Grove." Once she tried to mitigate that avid governance of the household and her husband's sister was sorely grieved.

"I am nothing around here! I know it and I allow myself to be dominated by my simple outbursts of anger because I don't have your calm and your adroitness. I lay things by for that son of yours! Let Álvaro tell you what they taught us when we were little. Will things get rotten and be wasted if you keep them locked up? Even more would be lost if you left them open to every hand. I feel that child of yours is as much mine as he is yours. And you will not keep me away from him even if my brother himself throws me out of this house!"

Don Álvaro took her by the shoulders and brought her close to him with devoted anxiety. Elvira was deeply distressed and her vibrant sobs wrapped around her with a crackling sound.... Cast out a sister with supreme virtues, one who even forgot her womanly reserve and followed him one night, disguised as a man, just to protect him from the dangers of "Scar-face!"[23]

In the presence of Don Cruz, Don Amancio, Monera and Father Bellod, Paulina learned of the plan to send Pablo as a boarding school student to the School of Jesús.

Elvira bent her forehead down and awaited the mother's rebellious sobs.

Paulina only declared:

"Pablo isn't eight years old yet," and she then withdrew quietly to her bedroom.

Her sister-in-law remained there listening.

"It's my fear, my fear of her shouting, of the scandal of her desperation!"

Not a shout nor a moan was forthcoming. And then it was she who had to moan and shout and she called for Pablo.

The old maidservant from Gandía looked in.

"He ran away again this afternoon."

"I can't put up with this any more!"

"You are an angel!"

And the confinement in "Jesús" was agreed upon.

Pablo arrived after dark and immediately sought his mother to give her a kiss. Afterward, in the dining room, his eyes averted his Aunt Elvira's glance

esconder la luz de su felicidad, felicidad únicamente suya. Tía Elvira no pudo contenerse.

– ¡Aprovéchate de los veintisiete días que te quedan, porque el 15 de septiembre se acabó el holgorio! ¡Y veintisiete dias..., veintisiete días tampoco, que si quitas el de hoy y el de ingreso...!

Desde entonces, todas las noches, antes de la cena, le presentaba el arqueo de su libertad; y cada noche Pablo se acostaba aborreciéndola más...

3. "Jesús"

Espuch y Loriga, el curioso cronista de Oleza, tío de don Amancio, dejó inéditos sus *Apuntes históricos de la Fundación de los Estudios de Jesús.* Yo he leído casi todo el manuscrito, y he visitado muchas veces los edificios, cantera insigne de sillares caleños fajeados de impostas, con tres pórticos: el del templo, en cuya hornacina está el Señor de caminante con su cayada; el del Internado, de columnas toscanas y recantones, donde se sientan los mendigos que piden a las familias de los colegiales, y el de la Lección, con pilastras y archivoltas de acantos, por el que pasan y salen los externos. Tiene el colegio tres claustros; el de Entrada, con hortal; el de las Cátedras, con aljibe en medio; el de los Padres de arcos escarzanos y medallones cogidos por ángeles. Tiene huerta grande y olorosa de naranjos, monte de viña moscatel y gruta de Lourdes. Hay escalera de honor de barandal y bolas de bronce, refectorios y salas de recreación de alfarjes magníficos que resaltan en los muros blancos; capillas privadas, crujías profundas, biblioteca de nichos de yeso, y en un ángulo, una celda, cavada en cripta, prisión de frailes y novicios. De la viga cuelga el cepo, y en una losa quedan estos versos de un condenado:

Todo es uno para mi,
esperanza o no tenella;
pues si hoy muero por vella
mañana porque la vi.

without hiding the light of his happiness, a happiness that was uniquely his. Aunt Elvira could not contain herself.

"Take advantage of the twenty-seven days you have left, because the merriment will be over by the 15th of September! And twenty-seven days..., not even twenty-seven days, if you take away today and the day you enroll...!"

From then on, every night before dinner, she would present him with the gauging of his freedom, and every night Pablo would go to bed detesting her even more....

3. "Jesús"

Espuch y Loriga, the curious chronicler of Oleza, Don Amancio's uncle, left his *Historical Notes Concerning the Foundation of the School at Jesús* unpublished.[24] I have read almost the entire manuscript and I have visited the buildings many times; it is a renowned breeding ground of learning with limestone ashlars, banded with fascia, with three porticoes: the one to the temple with a vaulted niche with the Lord inside it, walking along with his shepherd's crook; the one for the Boarding Students with Tuscan columns and spur stones, where the beggars sit when they ask for alms from the schoolboys' families, and the one for the Lessons, with its pilasters and archivolts with acanthus leaves molded onto them, where the day students pass in and out. The school has three cloisters: the one for the Main Entrance, with a garden; the one for the Professorate, with a cistern in the middle; the one for the Fathers, with segmental arches and medallions held firmly by angels.[25] The school has a big, fragrant orchard with orange trees, a vineyard of muscatel grapes on a rising slope and a grotto of Lourdes.[26] There is a splendid stairway with a railing and bronze balls at the landings, refectories and recreation rooms with magnificently carved paneled ceilings which stand out beautifully over the white walls; private chapels, deep corridors, a library with plaster niches, and, in one corner, a cell, excavated in the form of a crypt, a prison for friars and novices. A pillory was hanging from a beam and these verses by a man who had been condemned are inscribed on a flagstone:

It's really all the same to me,
if hope there is or none perchance;
if now I die for just one glance,
tomorrow for I dared to see.[27]

En cuatrocientos mil ducados de oro tasa Espuch y Loriga el coste de la fábrica; y para que mejor se entienda y aprecie la suma, añade: "...que en aquel tiempo no pasaba de cinco ducados el cahíz de trigo, ni de uno un carnero, ni de dos reales el jornal de un buen operario".

Ese "aquel tiempo" es el del fundador, don Juan de Ochoa, pabordre de Oleza, que tuvo asiento en las Cortes de Monzón.

Los estudios – lo repite el cronista – se hermanaron en sus principios con los de San Ildefonso de Alcalá de Henares y los de Santo Tomás de Ávila. Como fray Francisco Ximénez de Cisneros y fray Tomás de Torquemada, don Juan de Ochoa está sepultado en su iglesia colegial. El sepulcro es de alabastro, de un venerable color de hueso; y encima de la urna, soportada por cuatro águilas negras, se tiende el pabordre con manto y collar. A un lado tiene la espada y el báculo, y al otro los guantes de piedra.

Por la desamortización pasó el colegio del poder de los dominicos al de la mitra, que después lo cedió a la Compañia de Jesús. Era obispo de Oleza un siervo de Dios, de quien se refiere que presentándose una noche en el tinelo, vio en la estera el caballo de espadas que se le cayó a un paje al esconder la baraja. Alzó su ilustrísima el naipe y preguntó el asunto.

– Es la estampa de San Martin!

El obispo la besó devotamente, guardándola en su libro de rezos. Rezando le cogió el estruendo de la revolución; y los RR. PP. de "Jesús" partieron expulsados.

Volvieron pronto; y entre las mejoras añadidas al colegio durante la segunda época, todos encarecen la del Paraninfo o *De profundis*. Solemnizóse la estrena con una velada. Espuch y Loriga recitó una prosa apolgética; y el P. Rector dio las gracias conmovidamente en lengua latina, con sintaxis de lápida. Y muchas señoras lloraron.

Le ciudad se enalteció. Los sastres, los zapateros, los cereros y todos los artesanos mejoraron su oficio. Los paradores y hospederías abrieron un comedor de primera clase. El Municipio trocó el rótulo de la calle de Arriba por el de calle del Colegio. Se comparaba la fina crianza que se recibía en "Jesús" con la que se daba en el seminario y en los casones de frailes

Espuch y Loriga appraises the cost of construction at four hundred thousand gold ducats, and so that one can better comprehend and appreciate the sum, he adds,"... for at that time nineteen bushels of wheat did not cost more than five ducats, nor the cost of one sheep, a single ducat, nor did the daily wages of a good laborer exceed two *reales*."[28]

"That time" refers to the time of the founder, Don Juan de Ochoa, the "pabordre" or provost of Oleza,[29] who held a seat in the Parliament of Monzón.[30]

The program of studies–repeats the chronicler–was attached in the beginning to the Colegio de San Ildefonso of the University of Alcalá de Henares[31] and the Colegio de Santo Tomás de Avila.[32] Like Fray Francisco Ximénez de Cisneros[33] and Fray Tomás de Torquemada,[34] Don Juan de Ochoa lies buried in his own school church.[35] The tomb is made of alabaster and is of a venerable bone color; and the provost is stretched out in his robe and his collar of office on top of the funerary urn, supported by four black eagles. He has a sword and a crozier on one side and stone gloves on the other.

Because of the disentailment of the church property, the school passed from the control of the Dominicans to that of the bishop, who later handed it over to the Society of Jesus.[36] The bishop of Oleza was a humble servant of God and they tell a story of his dropping in on the servants' dining room one night and seeing a "caballo" (queen of spades), that a page had dropped on the floor matting when he tried to hide the deck. His Excellency picked up the card and asked what it represented.

"It's a print of Saint Martin!"

The bishop kissed it piously and put it away in his book of devotions.[37] In the course of his prayers, he was overtaken by the turmoil of revolution and the Reverend Fathers of "Jesús" were expelled and forced to depart.[38]

They soon returned, and the Paraninfo, or the *De Profundis*[39] (Academic Assembly Hall) is extolled by everyone as being among the best additions to the school during this second epoch. The inaugural ceremonies were solemnized with an evening observance. Espuch y Loriga recited an apologetic in prose and the Rector Father gave thanks in the Latin language in a moving manner, using a pompous and funereal style. And many women wept.

The city was filled with exaltation. The tailors, shoemakers, candle makers and all the artisans improved their craft. The inns and hostelries opened first-class dining rooms. The Town Council changed the sign on the Calle de Arriba to the Calle del Colegio. They compared the fine training received at "Jesús" with the instruction given at the seminary and in the splendid houses of training

de sayal gordo. Los PP. ni siquiera se embozaban en su manteo como los
demás capellanes; lo traían tendido, delicadamente plegado por los codos,
y asomaban sus manos juntas en una dulce quietud devota y aristocrática.
Casi todos ellos habían renunciado a delicias señoriales de primogénitos:
capitanes de Artillería, tenientes de Marina, herederos de las mejores fábricas
de Cataluña...

Los olecenses cedían la baldosa y saludaban muy junciosos a las
parejas de la floreciente comunidad que paseaban los jueves y domingos.
Y antes de recogerse en casa – no decian colegio, estudios, residencia, sino
sencillamente casa – , solían orar un momento en la parroquia de Nuestro
Padre San Daniel, patrono de Oleza, y Oleza sentía una caricia en las entrañas
de su devoción.

Otro acierto de la Compañía fue que el Hermano Canalda, encargado de
las compras, vistiese de seglar: americana o tobina y pantalón muy arrugado,
todo negro; corbata gorda, que le brincaba por el alzacuello; sombrero duro,
y zapatones de fuelles. Con hábito y fajín de jesuita, no le hubieran tocado
familiarmente en los hombros los huertanos y recoveros del mercado de
los lunes. Saber que era jesuita y verle vestido de hombre les hacía sentir la
gustosa inocencia de que le contemplaban en ropas íntimas, casi desnudo,
y que con ese pantalón y tobina se les deparaba en traje interior, como
si dijesen en carne viva, toda la comunidad de "Jesús". Ni el mismo H.
Canalda pudo deshacer la quimera advirtiéndoles que los jesuitas usan, bajo
la sotana, calzón corto con atadera o cenojil y chaleco con mangas.

Cuando vino de la casa provincial de Aragón el primer mandamiento
de traslado, Oleza clamó rechazándolo. Todos aquellos religiosos eran
exclusivamente suyos. No habia más Compañía de Jesús que la del Colegio
de Jesús. Los reverendos padres trasladados tuvieron que salir de noche, a
pie, atravesando el monte de parrales de moscateles de casa.

Llegados los nuevos, Oleza confesó que bien podía consentir las
renovaciones y mudanzas de la comunidad de "Jesús". Todos los padres
y todos los hermanos semejaban mellizos, todos saludaban con la misma
mesura y sonrisa; todos hacían la misma exclamación: "¡Ah! ¡Quizá sí,

of friars in quality sackcloth. The Fathers hardly even covered their faces with their cloaks like the other clergymen; they wore them fully extended, delicately folded over at the elbows, allowing their hands, joined together, to protrude in a sweet, devout, aristocratic serenity. Almost all of them had renounced the lordly delights afforded primogenitors: Artillery captains, Navy lieutenants, heirs to the best factories in Catalonia....

The Olezans yielded the pavement to them and very judiciously greeted the pairs of clerics from the flowering Community when they went out for a stroll on Thursdays and Sundays. And before they would withdraw to their House– they didn't say school, institution of studies, the order's residence, but simply House– they would pray for a moment in the parish church of Our Father San Daniel, the patron saint of Oleza, and Oleza would feel a caress within the innermost core of its devotion.

Another accomplishment for the Society was the fact that Brother Canalda, assigned to doing the marketing, could dress in secular clothing. a sack coat or long jacket and very wrinkled pants, all black; a thick tie which bounded up from under his clerical collar; a stiff hat and soft, accordion-pleated shoes. If he had worn his Jesuit habit and sash, the fruit and vegetable farmers and poultry dealers on Monday market days would not have touched his shoulders with such familiarity. Just to know that he was a Jesuit and see him dressed like an ordinary man made them feel a pleasant innocence as if contemplating him in his underclothes, all but naked, and when he was wearing those pants and that long jacket, it seemed as if the entire Community of "Jesús" were presenting themselves before them in their undergarments, almost as if to say in the bare flesh. Not even Br. Canalda himself could dispel that illusion by pointing out to them that Jesuits wear short pants with support for the socks, like garters, with a long-sleeved vest under the cassock.[40]

When the first order for transfer came from the Residence of the provincial of Aragon, Oleza protested by rejecting it. All those members of the religious order belonged exclusively to them. There was no other Society of Jesus than the one at the Colegio de Jesús. The Reverend Fathers who were being transferred were compelled to depart at night on foot, crossing over the House's own muscatel grapevine bowers on the mountainside.

When the new ones arrived, Oleza confessed that they could easily accept the renovations and changes in the Community of "Jesús." All the Fathers and all the Brothers resembled twins; they all extended their greetings with the same gravity and smile; they all articulated the same exclamation, "Oh!

quizá no!" Y desde que Oleza no pudo diferenciar a la comunidad de Jesús, la comunidad de Jesús diferenció a Oleza en cada momento, en cada familia y en cada persona. Ya no fue menester que las gentes le cediesen la acera. El colegio se infundía en toda la ciudad. La ciudad equivalía a un patio de "Jesús", un patio sin clausura, y los Padres y Hermanos lo cruzaban como si no saliesen de casa.

Eran tiempos necesitados de rigor; y el rigor había de sentirse desde la infancia de las nuevas generaciones. Todavía más en una residencia que, como la de "Jesús", estaba tan poblada de alumnos internos y externos. Cada una de estas castas escolares podían traer peligros para la otra. "Y esto por varios conceptos." Así lo afirmaban los PP. Y las familias se persuadían sin adivinar, sin pedir y sin importarles ninguno de los varios conceptos.

Un P. Prefecto y un P. Ministro, de algún descuido y flaqueza en la disciplina, recibieron orden de pasar a una misión de Oriente. Ya salían con su maletín de regla bajo el manteo, cuando les llegó el ruido unánime y sumiso de suelas de las brigadas que iban al refectorio. Los dos desterrados se retrajeron en un cantón de la claustra para mirar por última vez a sus colegiales. Pero los colegiales, no sabiendo su partida, temieron que se escondiesen por acecharles. Los inspectores insinuaron un leve saludo de desconocidos.

Los dos jerarcas nuevos vinieron de la misma misión de Oriente. Después de la cena, pasearon por la sala de recreo de la comunidad. Predicadores, catedráticos, consiliarios, iban y volvían, en hileras infantiles, como de "Muchú, Madama, matarie, rie, rie", sin mudar de sitio, andando de espaldas los que antes fueran de frente, espejándose en los manises de pomos de frutas; los brazos cruzados, o las manos sumergidas en las mangas del balandrán; en la axila, el corte de oro de su breviario, y en el frontal, el brillo de hueso y de prudencia rebanado por el bonete corvo como una tiara.

Un Padre, de los antiguos, mencionó las procedencias de los contingentes académicos: provincias de Alicante, Murcia, Albacete, Ciudad Real, Almería, Cáceres, Badajoz, Cuenca, Madrid... Los dos forasteros, que ya lo sabían, principiaron a pasmarse desde Ciudad Real hasta Madrid, exhalando un ¡Aaah! que remataba menudito y fino.

Maybe yes, maybe no!" And since Oleza couldn't differentiate between the members of the Community of "Jesús," the Community of "Jesús" differentiated Oleza at every opportunity, in every family and in each person. It was no longer necessary to give them the right of way on the sidewalk. The school was taking deep root in the entire city. The city had become the equivalent of a patio at "Jesús," an uncloistered patio, and the Fathers and Brothers crossed every part of it as if they had never left their House.

These were times that required rigor; and that rigor had to be felt even during the infancy of the new generations. All the more so in a school setting which, like the one at "Jesús," was so populated with boarding and day students.[41] Each one of these student castes could bring dangers for the other. "And this for a variety of points of view." This was the Reverend Fathers' affirmation. And the families were persuaded without having to guess, without having to ask and without attaching any importance whatsoever to these various points of view.

A Prefect Father and an Administrative Father, somewhat lax in matters of discipline, received an order to transfer to a Mission in the Orient.[42] They were just departing with their standard satchels under their cloaks when the unanimous and submissive sound of the sandals of the brigades on their way to the refectory caught their ears. The two banished priests withdrew to one corner of the cloister to look upon their schoolboys for the last time. But the schoolboys, not knowing about their departure, were afraid that they were hiding there in order to spy upon them. The priest monitors extended a restrained greeting to them, as if they no longer knew them.

The two new hierarchs came from the same Mission in the Orient. After dinner, they strolled through the Community recreation hall. Pulpit orators, professors, house counselors kept moving back and forth in childish rows just as if they were singing, "Muchú, Madama, matarie, rie, rie,"[43] without moving from their places, those who had been facing before now turning their backs, all of them mirrored in the shining tile surfaces imprinted with clusters of fruit; their arms crossed or their hands buried in the sleeves of their cassocks, the golden edges of their breviaries under their armpits, and on their foreheads, the sheen of bone and prudence slashed by their curved clerical caps like a tiara.

One Father, one of the older members, mentioned the regional provenance of the academic contingents: the provinces of Alicante, Murcia, Albacete, Ciudad Real, Almería, Cáceres, Badajoz, Cuenca, Madrid.... The two outsiders, who already knew all about it, started to reveal their astonishment from the mention of Ciudad Real all the way up to that of Madrid, breathlessly uttering an Oooh! that so meticulously and finely put a finishing touch upon it.

– ¿También de la corte?

– Tenemos cuatro de Madrid, hijos de títulos; dos de El Escorial y uno de Aranjuez.

– ¡Aaah!

– Nunca hemos lamentado, en casa, amistades particulares entre internos, y queda así dicho que nunca las hubo entre internos y externos.

Aunque no las hubo, corrió una mueca de inquietud de boca en boca. Enseguida pasó. Todo pasaba rápidamente, y todo tenía el mismo acento de trascendencia: que hubiera alumnos de Ciudad Real, Almería, Cáceres, Badajoz, Cuenca, Madrid; que hubiera amistades particulares que nunca hubo.

Les pidieron los antiguos nuevas de los países de Oriente. En realidad, no les afanaba mucho saberlas: unos y otros irían y vendrían cuando Nuestro Señor y los superiores lo dispusieran.

Entonces, los recién llegados glosaron su travesía. Lo más doloroso era la intimidad atropellada, la promiscuidad de la vida de a bordo. (El P. Prefecto siempre decía nave.)

– Las señoras más honestas, los hombres más refinados, los religiosos, los niños, la marinería, todos en la nave acaban por adquirir un gesto de comarca densa y contribuyen al olor de pasaje. Olor de especie, de libertad de especie... Cada puerto va volcando en la nave los agrios de las razas, de los pecados, de las modas, que se confunden en el mismo olor... ¡Ah, ese Singapore!

– Es muy de agradecer – intervino ya el Padre Ministro – la solicitud de la Compañía Trasatlántica. Hace lo que puede por la decencia de las costumbres en el barco.

– Concedo. Hace lo que puede, pero puede muy poco. ¡Da pena el encogido carácter sacerdotal de los capellanes-marinos! ¡Son más marinos que capellanes!

– Claro que la oficialidad de los buques siempre acata nuestros advertimientos, y en la cámara de lujo y de primera llevamos el rosario, tenemos lecturas, pláticas, certámenes..., y así conseguimos que, poco a poco, se agravie menos a la modestia y a Dios.

El P. Prefecto porfiaba:

"Even from the Court?"

"We have four from Madrid, sons of titled families, two from El Escorial and one from Aranjuez."

"Oooh!"

"We have never discouraged personal relationships among the boarding students in the House, and it goes without saying that there have never been any between boarding students and day students."[44]

Even though there may not have been any, an uneasy grimace ran from one mouth to another. It all passed quite quickly, everything passed quickly and everything had the same note of transcendence: whether there might be students from Ciudad Real, Almería, Cáceres, Badajoz, Cuenca, Madrid; whether there may have been some personal friendships, which there never were.

The older members asked them for news about the countries in the Orient. They really weren't very anxious to know: one group or another would go away and return whenever our Lord and their superiors were disposed to order it.

Then the recent arrivals gave an annotated account of their ocean crossing. The most distressing part was the indiscriminate intimacy of life on board. (The Prefect Father always said "nave" for a ship.)

"The most decent ladies, the most refined gentlemen, clergymen, children, the ship's crew, everyone on the ship ends up acquiring the character of densely populated community and therefore contribute to the flavor of the passage. The flavor of the human species, the license of the species.... Each port keeps unloading the most distasteful elements of the races, of the sins, of the customs onto the vessel, and they are all confused into the same redolence.... Oh, that Singapore!"

"What is to be very much appreciated," the Administrative Father now interposed, "is the solicitude shown by the Transatlantic Company. They do whatever they can to maintain some air of decency of behavior on board ship."

"I grant that. They do what they can, but they can do very little. It is painful to see the subdued priestly character of the ship chaplains. They are more like sailors than chaplains!"

"Of course, the ship's officers always respect our observations, and we recite the rosary, we have readings, talks, literary competitions for the passengers in the deluxe and first class cabins..., and in that way we assure that, little by little, there is less offense to modesty and to God."

The Prefect Father persisted:

– De todas maneras, la vida en la nave es vida de sonrojo. Y ni los nuestros pueden impedir el extravío moral de los pasajeros en las pascuas y en los carnavales. No se contienen ni delante de los camarotes de los misioneros. ¡Ah, y con frecuencia aflige el espectáculo de frailes que fuman y se sientan subiéndose el sayal, cruzando las piernas ingle contra ingle!

– En casa – le interrumpió un Padre de los viejos – ya no hay un colegial que ponga una pierna encima de la otra. El último que lo hacía era Lidón y Ribes – José Francisco – , que había sido externo.

El P. Martí, profesor de matemáticas – de los dos cursos – , gordezuelo y pálido, apartó los doloridos asuntos estampándose una palmadita en la frente.

– ¡Aaah, conocerán sus reverencias al señor Hugo, nuestro maestro de Gimnasia, y a don Roger, nuestro maestro de Solfa! – y enseguida se reprimió la risa con la punta de los dedos, como un bostezo melindroso.

– ¿Señor Hugo? ¡Señor Hugo! Entonces ¿será sueco y rubio?

– ¿Será y rubio es? ¡Oh, cómo lo adivinaron!

Se alzó un coro de risas en escala. Y se deshizo la tertulia. Al recogerse en sus aposentos, cada Padre soportaba en sus gafas y en su frente toda la Compañía de Jesús.

...Otro día, el Prefecto y el Ministro recibieron el saludo del señor Hugo y de don Roger. El señor Hugo, muy encendido, muy extranjero, de facciones largas, de una longura de adolescente que estuviera creciendo, y crecidas ellas más pronto semejaban esperar la varonía; también el cuerpo alto, de recién crecido, y el pecho de un herculanismo profesional. Al destocarse, se le erizaba una cresta suntuaria de pelo verdoso. Erguido y engallado, como si vistiese de frac, su frac bermejo de artista de circo. Toda su crónica estaba contenida y cifrada en su figura como en un vaso esgrafiado: el origen, en su copete rubio; el oficio, en su pecho de feria; el nomadismo, en su chalina rozagante y en su lengua de muchos acentos forrados de castellano de Oleza; y la sumisión de converso, en sus hinojos y en su andar. Como a la misma hora – diez y media – se daban en "Jesús" las clases de Gimnasia y Música, que con las de Dibujo, constituían las "disciplinas de adorno", el señor Hugo

"At any rate, life on board the vessel is a life that makes you blush with shame. And not even our people can prevent the moral misconduct of the passengers at Easter time and the celebrations of Carnival. They can't even restrain themselves in front of the missionary's staterooms. Oh! How frequently the spectacle of friars smoking and sitting with their sackcloth skirts raised, crossing their legs, one thigh over the other, fills you with sorrow!"

"In our House," one of the old-time Fathers interrupted him, "we no longer have any students who put one leg over the other. The last one who did it was Lidón y Ribes – José Francisco – and he had been a day student."

Father Martí, a Mathematics teacher – for both of the academic years – chubby and pale, set these distressing matters aside, clapping his palm gently against his forehead.

"Oooh, Your Reverences will make the acquaintance of Señor Hugo, our Gymnastics teacher, and Don Roger, our Sol-fa teacher!" and he quickly suppressed his laughter with the tips of his fingers, as if it were a prudish yawn.

"Señor Hugo? Señor Hugo! Then he is probably Swedish and blond?"

"Swedish and blond he is! But, how did you guess?"

A chorus of laughter arose from one individual at a time. And the informal gathering broke up. As each one of the Fathers withdrew to the privacy of his room, he still sustained the entire Society of Jesus upon his eyeglasses and upon his forehead.

...On another day, the Prefect and the Administrator received the formal greeting from Señor Hugo and Don Roger. Señor Hugo, very high-colored, very foreign looking, with elongated features, lengthened like those of an adolescent who was still growing, and since they had grown all too quickly, they seemed to be waiting for him to attain full manhood; his body was also tall, like one that has only recently grown, and his chest was as herculean as a professional. When he removed his hat, a luxuriant crest of viridescent hair bristled on his head. Standing erect and haughty, as if he were wearing a full-dress coat, a bright red coat like that of a circus performer. His whole life story was contained and summarized in his figure, just like on a vase decorated with agraffito: his origins, in his blond pompadour; his occupation, in his side-show chest; his nomadism, in his long-ended bow tie and in his multi-accented language surfeit with Olezan Castilian; and the submissiveness of the convert, in his manner of kneeling and in his walk. Since classes in Gymnastics and Music, along with Drawing, constituted the "decorative disciplines," and were given at the same time – ten-thirty – at

llegaba al colegio con don Roger. Siempre se juntaban en la Cantonada de Lucientes.

Don Roger envidiaba con mansedumbre al señor Hugo. En "Jesús" no había más gimnasta que el sueco. Don Roger estaba sometido al P. Folguerol, maestro de capilla y compositor de fervorines, villancicos, dúos marianos, himnos académicos. En cambio, don Roger aventajaba al Señor Hugo en la nómina: sueldo y adehalas por profesor de solfeo y bajo solista. Todo ancho, redondo, dulce. Cejas, nariz, bigote, boca, corbatín y arillo, manos y pies muy chiquitines. El vientre le afollaba todo el chaleco de felpa naranja con botoncitos de cuentas de vidrio; los pantalones, muy grandes, le manaban ya torrencialmente desde la orla de su gabán color de topo, desbordándole por las botas de gafas y contera. Nueve años en la ciudad, y todos creían haberle visto desde que nacieron y con las mismas prendas, como si las trajese desde su principio y para siempre. Le temblaban los carrillos y la voz rolliza, como otro carrillo. Se ponía dos dedos, el índice y el cordal, de canto en medio de los dientes; los sacaba, y por esa hendedura le salía, de un solo aliento, un *fa* que le duraba dos minutos.

Los Padres de Oriente le probaron el rejo del *fa*. El Prefecto le atendía mirando su reloj, mirándole la cara, que pasaba del rosa doncella al lívido cinabrio; le estallaban las bolas de los ojos; criaba espumas. Olía a regaliz, a pastillas de brea y a humo de cocina frugal.

– ¡Un minuto y cuarenta y nueve segundos! Pero está bien. ¡Quizá demasiada voz!

– ¡Quizá, sí! – confirmó el P. Ministro.

Demasiada. Era verdad; y era desgracia de don Roger. Un coro de bajos reventaba en la garganta del solista. En los misereres, misas, trisagios, singularmente en los misereres, la voz de don Roger parecía descuajar la iglesia de "Jesús"; estremecía la bóveda como un barreno en una cisterna. Un temblor que desolaba a su dueño. Cuando más júbilo de artista principiaba a sentir, otro escondido don Roger le avisaba: "¡Desde ahora mismo estás ya excediéndote; calla, que te retumbas!" Y la voz implacable iba envolviéndole como una placenta monstruosa. No la resistió ningún tablado ni sala; y de

"Jesús," Señor Hugo arrived at school along with Don Roger. They always joined one another at the Lucientes Corner.

Don Roger envied Señor Hugo with a certain meekness. There was no other gymnast at "Jesús" than the Swede. Don Roger was subordinate to Father Folguerol, the choirmaster and composer of short ejaculatory prayers, Christmas carols, Marian duets, academic hymns. On the other hand, Don Roger had the advantage over Señor Hugo on the payroll listing: salary and perquisites as professor of solveggio and as bass soloist. He was entirely wide, round and sweet. Eyebrows, nose, mustache, mouth, bow tie and neck stock, tiny little hands and feet. His belly puffed out his entire orange-colored plush vest with its small glass bead buttons; his oversized trousers flowed outward like a torrent below the border of his mole-colored overcoat, inundating his boots with the round patches on either side as well as the ferrule of his cane. Nine years in the city and everyone thought that they had been seeing him ever since they were born, wearing the same articles of clothing, as if he had worn them from the beginning and forever. His cheeks trembled as did his rotund voice, as if it were another cheek. He would put two fingers, the index and middle fingers, sideways against the middle of his teeth; he would then pull them away and a *fa* would emerge from that cleft in one breath and last for two minutes.

The Fathers from the Orient tested the potency of his *fa*. The Prefect kept an eye on him as he glanced at his watch, looking right into his face, which changed from a maidenly pink to a livid cinnabar; the balls of his eyes were protruding; he was starting to foam at the mouth. He smelled of licorice, of tablets of gum rosin and the smoking interior of a frugal kitchen.

"One minute forty-nine seconds! That's quite good. Perhaps too much voice!"

"Yes, perhaps!" the Administrative Father confirmed.

Too much. It was true, and it was Don Roger's misfortune. A chorus of basses erupted in the soloist's throat. Don Roger's voice seemed to dissolve the church at "Jesús" in the Misereres, Masses, Trisagions, especially in the Misereres; the vault above trembled like a charge of powder in a cistern. A tremor that devastated its owner. Just as he was starting to feel greater joy as an artist, another Don Roger, hidden within him, would warn him, "From this moment on, you're starting to exceed yourself, so keep quiet, because you're beginning to reverberate!" And the implacable voice kept enveloping him like a monstrous placenta. Not a single stage or presentation room resisted it, and so he wandered from one itinerant company of performers to another, from

farándula en farándula, de catedral en catedral, paró en "Jesús". No era posible el dúo con don Roger; se quedaba solo su trueno, y él dejándolo salir de su boca de chico gordo y dócil.

Todas las mañanas se encontraban el señor Hugo y don Roger. El saludo del cantor equivalía a una topada suave, esférica, de globo. Su voz y su persona tocaban al gimnasta con un "Felices días" como un punto geométrico de su superficie curva.

El señor Hugo, todo el sueco, le correspondía con la gracia dinámica de su pirueta en el momento de una aparición en la pista, bajo la gloria de un velario con broche de banderas internacionales.

En el claustro se separaban sonriéndose. Don Roger se hundía en su aula, donde tocaban a la vez catorce colegiales en catorce pianos desgarrados. Pasaba entre hileras de atriles y de lecciones de Eslava; y de discípulo en discípulo, iba dejando el huracán de una enmienda.

Cerca de la gruta artificial de Lourdes estaba el gimnasio, umbrío como una bodega. Alumnos y Hermanos inspectores aplaudían al señor Hugo. Un brinco, una flexión de paralelas, todo lo acometido por el señor Hugo parecía una temeridad. En las ascensiones a pulso por las sogas, el señor Hugo llegaba, rápido y vertical, hasta la cuarta brazada. Desde allí, trenzando las rodillas, saludaba bellamente, como si sus manos esparcieran besos y flores.

Alumnos y Hermanos se emocionaban viéndole muy alto, muy alto. Y el señor Hugo caía en el lecho de arena con una sonrisa y elegancia de parada de minué, dando por acabados todos sus ejercicios con un ademán de tribuno que venía a significar: "¡Como esto que habéis visto pudiera yo hacerlo todo, por arriscado que fuese, y no lo hago porque yo he venido a este mundo del colegio para que lo hagáis vosotros!"

Pero, una mañana, un colegial casi párvulo se deslizó hacia arriba de las maromas, impetuoso y leve, torciéndose como uno de lizos de cáñamo. Llegó a las argollas de las vigas y se quedó colgando. Se le sentía resollar y reír.

– ¡Señor Galindo – gritó el Hermano inspector – , señor Galindo y Egea: baje usted enseguida!

Las piernas de pantalón corto del señor Galindo y Egea campaneaban gozosamente; y fue su vocecita la que bajó, hincándose como un dardo en el maestro:

– ¡Hermano, que suba por mí el señor Hugo!

one cathedral to another, till he ended up at "Jesús." It was impossible to do a duet with Don Roger, for his thunder stood all by itself as he stood there and let it emerge from his mouth as if it were that of a fat, docile little boy.

Every morning Señor Hugo and Don Roger would meet. The singer's greeting was very much like the gentle, spherical butt of a balloon. His voice and his person touched the gymnast with a "Joyful day to you" like a geometrical point from a curved surface.

Señor Hugo, every bit the Swede, responded with the dynamic grace of a pirouette at the moment of an appearance on the athletic field, under the glorious sky over a canopy-covered stand with a cluster of international flags.

They smiled at one another as they separated in the cloister. Don Roger would immerse himself in his classroom, where fourteen schoolboys were playing on fourteen battered pianos at the same time. He passed between rows of music stands and lessons by Eslava,[45] and as he moved from one pupil to the next, he would leave behind the hurricane of a correction.

The gymnasium, near the artificial grotto of Lourdes, was as umbral as a wine cellar. Students and Brothers serving as monitors applauded Señor Hugo. A leap, a flexure of the body on the parallel bars, everything undertaken by Señor Hugo, seemed like a reckless exploit. When climbing up the rope by the strength of his hands, Señor Hugo would reach the fourth knot rapidly and vertically. From there, he would intertwine his knees and wave his hand beautifully as if his hands were strewing kisses and flowers.

Students and Brothers were exhilarated when they saw him so high up, so very high up. And Señor Hugo would fall onto a bed of sand with the smile and elegance of a pause in a minuet, putting an end to all of his exercises with the gesture of a tribune, which had come to mean, "I could easily do everything that you have just observed, no matter how risky it might be, and I don't do it because I have come to the world of this school to have all of you do it!"

But one morning, a schoolboy who was little more than a child slid upward impetuously and effortlessly, all the way up the hemp rope, twisting round like one of those cane warps. He reached the large iron rings on the rafters and remained there hanging. You could hear him breathing heavily and laughing.

"Señor Galindo," the monitor Brother shouted, "Señor Galindo y Egea, come down here immediately."

Señor Galindo y Egea's legs in their short pants kept swinging back and forth delightedly, and it was his childish voice that came down instead and imbedded itself in the teacher like a dart:

"Brother, have Señor Hugo come up and get me!"

– ¡Señor Galindo, póngase de rodillas!

– ¡No puedo! ¡Es que no puedo soltarme! – y comenzó a plañir.

Todos se volvieron al señor Hugo mirándole y esperándole. Y hasta el mismo señor Hugo sorprendióse de su cabriola de bolero y de Mercurio de pies alados. Dejó en el aire una linda guirnalda de besos y se precipitó a las vigas, hacia las vigas, pero se derrumbó desde la quinta brazada, una más que siempre, reventándole la camisa, temblándole los hinojos, cayéndole la garzota de su greña rubia, su ápice de gloria, como un vellón aceitado por sudores de agonía.

Detrás, el señor Galindo y Egea, el hijo de don Álvaro, descendió dulce y lento como una lámpara de júbilo.

4. Grifol y su ilustrísima

Venía don Vicente Grifol de la Huerta de los Calzados, antiguo granero episcopal; y en medio de la calle de la Verónica – querencia de las sasterías eclesiásticas, de las tiendas de ornamentos, de los obradores de cirios y chocolates – le alcanzó la voz campechana de don Magín.

Aguardóse el médico. El capellán le puso su brazo robusto en los hombros viejecitos, y se lo fue llevando a Palacio.

Camino de Palacio, decía don Vicente:

– ...Casi todos los recados de enfermos de ahora me cogen en la calle, como si llamaran a un lañador o un buhonero que pasa. Oleza está lo mismo que cuando llegué de Murcia, el día de la Anunciación, hace cuarenta y dos años. Pero algunos olecenses se piensan que su pueblo se ha hinchado como un Londres. ¿Usted no ha ido a Londres? Yo sí que estuve, siendo mozo, como hijo de naranjero. Fui a vender las naranjas de mi padre, naranjas amargas para la confitura. A todas las gentes de los muelles, de los almacenes y lonjas, a todas las recordaba yo a mi gusto, por la noche, en mi cuarto. Pues a mí, de comida a comida, ni siquiera me reconocían los españoles que se albergaban en mi posada. Es una felicidad la insignificancia: no ser espectáculo para los demás y serlo todos para uno. Por eso, un mocito estudiante, no reparando en mí, se abrió las venas en mi alcoba. Pero se engañó. Yo le vi torciéndose

"Señor Galindo, get on your knees!"

"I can't! The fact is I can't let go!" And he began to wail.

Everyone turned toward Señor Hugo, looking at him and waiting for him. And Señor Hugo surprised even himself with a bolero caper like Mercury of the winged feet. He left a lovely garland of kisses in the air as he rushed headlong to the rafters, toward the rafters, but he plunged downward when he reached the fifth knot, one higher than usual, tearing his shirt, while his knees trembled and the plumage of his blond mop of hair, his apex of glory, fell down over his face like fleece oiled by the sweat of his agony.

Behind him, Señor Galindo y Egea, Don Álvaro's son, sweetly and slowly descended like a lamp of jubilation.

4. Grifol and His Excellency

Don Vicente Grifol was coming from the orchard of the Carmelite Friary,[46] a one-time episcopal granary, and in the middle of the Calle de la Verónica – a favorite site for ecclesiastical tailor shops, stores for religious ornaments, shops producing wax candles and chocolates – the hearty voice of Don Magín overtook him.

The doctor stopped. The priest put his robust arm around the weary old shoulders and started leading him off to the Palace.

On the way to the Palace, Don Vicente was saying:

"...Almost all my messages regarding sick people catch me in the street nowadays, as if they were calling a mender of crockery or a peddler who happens by. Oleza is just like it was when I arrived from Murcia, the day of the Feast of the Annunciation,[47] forty-two years ago. But some Olezans see fit to think that their town has swelled up like a London. You haven't gone to London? Well I was there when I was a young man, as the son of an orange dealer. I went there to sell my father's oranges, bitter oranges to use for preserves. At night, in my room, I would remember all those people from the docks, from the warehouses and markets at my pleasure. Well, between one meal and the next, the Spaniards who were lodging in my boarding house hardly even took notice of me. Insignificance is a joy: not to be a spectacle for others and have everyone be a spectacle for you. For that reason, a young fellow, a student, taking no notice whatsoever of me, opened up his veins in my room. But he made a mistake. I saw him twisting around on top of

encima de la cuajada de su sangre; le remendé los cortes, se los fajé y tuvo que matarse en otro sitio... Oleza se cree tan ancha, tan crecida, que ya no me ve. O me ve, y nada. Es decir, nada sí: algunos me miran y me sonríen por si acaso yo fuese yo. Y ahora, vamos a ver...

... Hablando, hablando, hallóse solo en la meseta alta de la escalera de Palacio, porque don Magín se lo dejó para prevenir a su ilustrísima. Grifol se puso a mirar la antecámara. Un eclesiástico descolorido escribía en su bufetillo de faldas de velludo rojo, sin sentir la presencia del médico. Lo mismo que todo el mundo.

Luego volvió don Magín, y entró a su amigo, colocándole delante del prelado.

Grifol besó una mano enguantada de seda violeta, una mano sin sortija. Y pensó: "Acabo de trastrocar mi beso de cortesia, o de reverencia, o de lo que sea; pero ya no he de enmendarlo tomándole la otra mano. ¡Y qué manos tan gordas! Debajo de los guantes no se le siente la piel, sino una blandura de hilas embebidas de aceites..."

Su ilustrísima se desnudó las manos. Don Magín fue descogiéndole los vendajes, y apareció el metacarpo, acortezado de racimillos de vesículas; las palmas estaban limpias y tersas. Su ilustrísima se miraba su carne llagada como si no fuese suya, y al hablar encogía apretadamente la boca.

El médico y el obispo se sonrieron con ternura de compasión y de compadecido.

– Vamos a ver: ¿y las noches? ¿Levantándose, acostándose, con un prurito de uñas, de pinchas? No acaban, no acaban esas noches, ¿verdad?

– Casi todas las noches sin sueño. Me lloran los ojos de dilatarlos. Una avidez de ojos, de oídos y hasta de pensamientos; y no es por el dolor que me quema concretamente un tejido, sino esperando que brote ese dolor en otro lado de mi cuerpo. Y me miro todo con una angustia que me hace sudar.

– Las manos. ¿Y en las rodillas, en la cintura, casi toda la cintura, y en las ingles?

– Donde usted dice; y además, entre los hombros, subiéndoseme. Pronto llegará a la nuca.

Don Vicente se quitó los anteojos, les puso su vaho, los estregó entre los

a puddle of coagulated blood, I patched up his incisions, wrapped them in bandages, and so he was obliged to kill himself somewhere else.... Oleza thinks it is so spread-out, so inflated, that it no longer sees me. Or that it sees me and pays me no heed whatsoever. That is to say, really nothing: there are some who look at me and smile at me just in case it happens to be me. And now, let's see...."

...As he kept on talking and talking, he found himself alone on the upper landing of the Palace staircase, because Don Magín left him there in order to prearrange things with His Excellency. Grifol started to look around the antechamber. A sallow-faced ecclesiastic was writing at a small desk with red plush skirts at its sides, and he hardly took notice of the doctor's presence. The same as everyone else.

Then Don Magín returned and led his friend inside, placing him in front of the prelate.

Grifol kissed a hand gloved in violet silk, a hand without a ring. And he thought: "I have just changed around my kiss of respect, or reverence, or whatever it may be, to the wrong hand, but I no longer have to rectify this by taking his other hand. What fat hands he has! You can't feel the skin under his gloves, only a softness of lint saturated with oil...."

His Excellency bared his hands. Don Magín kept unraveling the bandages and the metacarpus appeared, encrusted with small clusters of vesicles; the palms were clean and smooth. His Excellency stared at his ulcerated flesh as if it were not his own, and when he spoke, he contracted his mouth tightly.

The doctor and the bishop smiled at one another with a tenderness of compassion and commiseration.

"Let's see now: how about at night? When you get up and you lie down, you have an itching in the fingernails, a prickly feeling? They don't end, those nights don't end, am I right?"

"Almost every night without sleep. My eyes weep from dilating them. An eagerness of my eyes, ears and even my thoughts; and it's not on account of the pain that is specifically burning the tissue, but rather the waiting for that pain to erupt on another side of my body. And I look all over myself with an anguish that makes me sweat."

"Your hands. And how about the knees, the waist, almost the entire waist, and the thighs?"

"Exactly where you say; and in addition, between the shoulders, moving up my back. Soon it will reach the back of my neck."

Don Vicente took off his eyeglasses, blew his breath on them, rubbed

pliegues de un mitón. Volvióse hacia el ancho ventanal, y en sus espejuelos limpios se recogían y renovaban las miniaturas de la tarde campesina: un follaje, una yunta, un temblor del cáñamo verde, un trozo de horizonte...

Su ilustrísima miraba a don Magín. Y, de súbito, el viejecito le dijo:

– Pero vamos a ver: esto, este mal... – y se calló; hizo una tos pequeñita; sintió toda la mirada del obispo, y tuvo que seguir – : Este mal no aparece ahora en su ilustrisima...

Al obispo se le hincaron entonces los ojos de Grifol, y humilló los suyos. Enseguida esforzóse, y fue ya un enfermo jerárquico.

– No es de ahora mi mal. Pero ahora he principiado a estudiarme. Mi ministerio y mis aficiones me hicieron acudir a las Sagradas Escrituras. He recordado que si la piel presenta una mancha blanquecina, sin concavidades, el *lucens candor,* quedará el enfermo siete días en entredicho y observación. (Siete días estuve mirándome.) Si persiste, se aguardará otros siete días. (Yo aguardé.) Y si pasado este plazo, se ensombreciere la piel, no será lepra... Vi el *obscurior* en mi carne, y dije: ¡No es lepra!

Don Vicente respondió con una sonrisa pueril:

– ¡Todo eso, todo eso era en aquel tiempo!

Tan elemental resultaba su sonrisa, que el prelado le miró con un poco de desconfianza.

– Es verdad; todo eso era en aquel tiempo, lo sé; la lepra, "diagnosticada" por Moisés en el hombre, no sería únicamente lepra; sería este mal incurable y otros padecimientos de alguna semejanza.

Y el obispo mentó los eczemas, los herpes, el impétigo, la psoriasis y más denominaciones y estudios de la nosología de la piel. Semejaba muy persuasivo en las enfermedades leves. Agotó la memoria de sus lecturas, como si quisiera que el médico se descuidara de verle y de creerle enfermo.

Pero el viejecito se le acercó diciéndole:

– Yo mismo desnudaré a su ilustrísima...

El prelado inclinó su cabeza. Luego sonrió, y los dos pasaron al dormitorio, gozoso de sol y de naranjos que se asomaban desde el huerto.

Quedóse don Magín en la puerta, vigilando que nadie, ni el familiar de turno, viniese. Tosía; hojeaba libros con ruido para probar que no les escuchaba.

them between the folds of a fingerless glove. He turned toward the wide windows and the miniatures of the rustic afternoon were gathered and renewed in the clean lenses of his spectacles: the foliage, a team of oxen, a trembling of green hemp, a fragment of horizon....

His Excellency kept looking at Don Magín. Suddenly the tired old man said to him:

"So let's see: this thing, this malady...." And he stopped speaking; he coughed ever so weakly; he felt the bishop's eyes all over him and he had to continue, "This malady has not appeared only now in Your Excellency...."

Then Grifol's eyes thrust their way into the bishop and humbled his eyes. With an instantaneous effort, his he now became a hierarchical patient.

"My illness is not of recent origin. But now I have begun to study myself. My ministry and my inclinations made me turn to the Holy Scriptures. I remembered that if the skin shows a whitish spot, with no concavities, the *lucens candor*, the patient will remain under interdiction and observation for seven days. (I spent seven days examining myself.) If it persists, he should wait another seven days. (I waited.) And if, after this period of waiting, the skin should darken, it is probably not leprosy.... I saw the obscurior on my flesh and said, 'It isn't leprosy.'"

Don Vicente responded with a childlike smile:

"All that, all that was at that time!"

His smile turned out to be so elemental that the prelate looked at him with some lack of confidence.

"It's true; all that was at that time, I know; the leprosy 'diagnosed' by Moses in man was probably not only leprosy; it was most likely this incurable disease as well as other ailments of a similar nature."[48]

And the bishop mentioned the various forms of eczema and herpes, impetigo, psoriasis and other categories and studies of the nosology of the skin. He seemed very persuasive as he spoke of the less serious diseases. He exhausted the recollection of his readings as if he wanted the doctor not to take the trouble to see him or think he was ill.

But the little old man came over to him and said:

"I myself will undress Your Excellency...."

The prelate lowered his head. Then he smiled and the two went into the bedroom, which was joyous with sunlight and orange trees peeking in from the garden.

Don Magín remained at the door, watching that no one should come in, not even the familiar on duty. He kept coughing as he leafed through books noisily to show that he wasn't listening to them.

Un corro de canónigos y capellanes de la curia les esperaba en la claustra.

– Cuarenta y dos años en Oleza, y nunca había mirado la vega por el ventanal de su ilustrísima. ¡Me ha parecido todo el campo nuevo!

En el portal se paró el grupo del penitenciario, y destacóse el homeópata Monera, preguntándole.

Don Vicente desconoció a Monera. Enseguida se le precipitaron los recuerdos del padre de Monera, el sangrador de la calle del Garbillo.

– ...¡Un hombre de bien, del antiguo bien, de esos hombres que van quedando muy pocos! Aunque siempre decimos lo mismo, ¿verdad? ¡De modo que siempre nos queda alguno! Siendo yo un crío, cuando mi abuelo me contaba las virtudes de un viejo de su tiempo y decía: "¡Se acabó la simiente; ya quedan muy pocos de esos hombres cabales!", yo me volvía a pensar de conocido en conocido, y me daba mucha pena haber llegado a este mundo en "epoca tan ruin y desaborida. ¡Pero como cada tiempo es de uno! – y adelgazando su sonrisa, se apartó de todos, del brazo de don Magín.

– ¡Ni más ni menos! Uno no quiere morirse nunca, pero quiere vivir en su tiempo. Porque, vamos a ver: ¿a usted le agradaría vivir dentro de dos siglos? A mí, no. La felicidad de la vida ha de tener su carácter: el nuestro. Yo no leo libros de entretenimiento porque los hombres que por allí pasan no tienen carácter. (¡Diantre! El señor penitenciario y todos ésos se han quedado sin saber cómo sigue el enfermo.) Es decir: en esos libros cada carácter está ya formado desde antes de ocurrirle nada. Eso no es una creación. Hay que crear al hombre desnudo y que él se las componga. Le confesaré que yo nunca había tratado a un obispo. Después de todo, el fámulo que le calienta el agua para rasurarse todos los días – supongo que se afeitará todos los dias –, sigue siendo fámulo. Para mi, un obispo era un pectoral, un anillo con una piedra preciosa, un báculo y una mitra, todo entre cirios de un altar con los mejores manteles y floreros, o guardado y quietecito en su Palacio, que yo creí con poco sol, y no es verdad, porque los aposentos de su ilustrisima son magníficos de luces. Claros y limpios... Calle de la Aparecida. ¿Aún sigue usted pasando todas las mañanas por esta callejita de tapiales?

– Por esta calle y por la calle de la Verónica.

– ¡Ah, calle de la Verónica! ¡Ya no es la misma doña Corazón! – y Grifol se descabalgó los quevedos para enjugárselos.

A group of canons and priests serving as episcopal clerks were waiting for them in the cloister.

"Forty-two years in Oleza and I had never looked out upon the fertile plain from His Excellency's windows. The whole of the countryside seemed new to me!"

The group including the canon-penitentiary stopped in the entryway and the homeopath Monera made himself conspicuous by questioning him.

Don Vicente ignored Monera. The memories of Monera's father, the phlebotomist from the Calle del Garbillo immediately rushed to his mind.[49]

"...A man of his word, in the old-fashioned sense of the word, one of those men who are growing rarer and rarer! Although we always say the same thing, right? So there's always one left! When I was a small child, when my grandfather would tell me the virtues of some old man of his time, he would say, 'The seed has come to an end; there are no longer many of these faultless men around!' I would start thinking of one person or another whom I knew and it made me sad to have arrived in this world at so base and insipid a time. But since you have to be a part of your own time!" and he narrowed his smile and drew away from them all, holding Don Magín by the arm.

"No more and no less! One doesn't ever want to die, just to live in one's own time. So, let's see: would you like to live during two centuries? I would not. Happiness in life must have its own character: ours. I don't read entertaining books because the men who pass through them have no character. (The deuce! I left the canon-penitentiary and all the others not knowing how the ailing man was getting on.) That is to say, each character in those books is already formed even before anything happens to him. That's not a creation. You have to create a man naked and let him work things out. I will confess to you that I have never treated a bishop. After all, the house servant who heats his water so he can shave every day – I suppose he must shave every day – continues to be his servant. For me, a bishop was a pectoral cross, a ring with a precious stone, a crozier and a miter, all surrounded by wax candles on an altar with the very best altar cloths and flower vases, or else, tucked away so quiescently in his Palace, which I thought had little sunlight, and that isn't true because His Excellency's rooms are magnificent with light. Bright and clean.... Calle de la Aparecida. Do you still stroll along that little street with its mud walls every morning?"

"Along this street and the Calle de la Verónica."

"Oh, the Calle de la Verónica! She isn't the same Doña Corazón any more!" And Grifol unseated his pince-nez in order to wipe them clean.

– Yo no presencié la entrada de su ilustrísima en Oleza. ¡El dia 7 de este mes hizo años! No la vi porque estaba injertando un limonero agrio de limonero dulce. Quise producir un carácter frutal, y no pude. No prendió el injerto. Un obispo, nuestro obispo, enfermo. ¡Tengo delante al obispo, con llagas, con costras, con dolor de una dermatitis horrible o de lo que sea! Cuando me habló de Moisés y de enfermedades, yo pensé: ¡Diantre, quiere esconderse detrás de todo eso que dice! Lo mismo que todos. Después, al desnudarse, lloraba de pureza...

Y como don Vicente subía ya el umbral de su casa, el párroco le contuvo, pidiéndole que le dijera su parecer.

– ¿Mi parecer? No sé lo que tiene. Pero no se curará.

...Y el obispo mejoró. Se le fueron secando y descamando las cortezas. Ya no le quedaban sino unos rodales morenos sin rebordes, sin deformidad cutánea. Salió en coche. Hizo una visita pastoral y un viaje a Madrid.

Grifol no volvió a Palacio, y don Magín tuvo que buscarle para referírselo todo. Lo encontró adormecido en una butaca de recodaderos remendados. Tenía entre los dedos su cayada de ébano. Por el collarín se le torcía su breve corbata de luto, y le colgaban en medio de la pechera los lentes empañados.

–Aqui estoy, de día y de noche, visitándome a mí mismo. Nos engañamos sin querer. Lo digo ahora que no estoy solo, y así no me sentirá mi cuerpo de cañizo. Si se sorprendiese acostado, ya no le faltaría ni la postura para morir, y me moriría.

Le bromeó don Magín. Le dijo la mejoría de su ilustrísima, que se quejaba de su ausencia.

Grifol movió su cabecita afilada.

– ¿Su ilustrisima? ¡No se curará; tiene su mal en las entrañas!

"I was not present when His Excellency made his entrance into Oleza. The 7th day of this month many years ago! I didn't see it because I was grafting a sweet lemon onto a bitter lemon tree. I tried to produce a character of fruit and I didn't succeed. The graft didn't take. A bishop, our bishop, ailing. I have the bishop before me, with sores, with scabs, with the pain of a horrible dermatitis, or whatever it may be! When he spoke to me of Moses and diseases, I thought: The deuce, he wants to hide behind all that he is saying! The same as everyone else. Afterwards, when he disrobed, he was weeping with purity...."

And as Don Vicente was already stepping up to the threshold of his house, the parish priest stopped him and asked him to tell him his opinion.

"My opinion? I don't know what he has. But he can't be cured."

...And the bishop improved. The incrustations started drying up and falling off in scales. Only a few dark patches without rims around them seemed to be left now, without any cutaneous deformity. He started going out in his coach. He paid a pastoral visit and made a trip to Madrid.

Grifol did not return to the Palace and Don Magín had to seek him out to tell him all about it. He found him asleep in an armchair with elbow rest patches. He was holding his ebony walking stick between his fingers. His short black mourning tie was twisted around his collar and his blurred eyeglasses were hanging down the middle of his shirtfront.

"Here I am, day and night, visiting with myself. We deceive ourselves without intending to. I say that now that I'm not alone, and in that way my body won't feel like a hurdle of reeds. If I were to be caught by surprise while I was lying down, I would not even be lacking the posture for dying, and I would die."

Don Magín jested with him. He told him about His Excellency's improvement and how he was complaining about his absence.

Grifol moved his slender little head.

"His Excellency? He will not be cured; his ailment is rooted deep inside of him!"

II

MARÍA FULGENCIA

1. El señor deán y María Fulgencia

¡Para su buena salud y buen cuajo, el señor deán! – decían las gentes; y él no lo negaba.

Ni su memoria, ni su entendimiento, ni su voluntad, ni su corpulencia perdieron nunca su mensura. Ni un latido impetuoso, ni una borrasca en su frente, ni un paso más rápido de lo suyo, ni una costumbre nueva.

Presentósele en su casa un sobrino aventurero, capitán de tropas de Manila, lleno de ruindades y deudas. Comprendió el deán que ni su amor ni su consejo podrían enmendarle. Las cosas y los hombres eran según eran. Aceptada la premisa, no era ya menester el ahinco de los remedios. Es verdad que por la gracia de algunos santos y mujeres se alcanzaban conversiones difíciles; pero él no pecaría creyéndose santo. Entre las mujeres de dulces prendas, con casa de crédito y bienestar, ninguna en el pueblo como Corazón Motos, que heredaría un obrador de chocolates de seis muelas. Y el bigardo del sobrino dejó al canónigo por seguir a Doña Corazón.

Elegido vicario capitular de la diócesis, huérfana del anterior prelado, supo el señor deán quedarse inmóvil en todo su gobierno, guardando prudentemente la sede hasta la llegada del nuevo obispo. Volvió, después, a sus máximos afanes, primor de sus ojos y de su pulso: la caligrafía, arte gloriosamente cultivado por muchos varones de la Iglesia, como San Panfilio, San Blas, San Luciano, San Marcelo, San Platón, Teodoro el Studita, el patriarca Méthodo, José el Himnógrafo, el monje Juan, el monje Cosmas, el diácono Doroteo...

El deán de Oleza calcó viñetas, orlas y portadas, copió centones de pensamientos, compuso y minió pergaminos de gracias. No fue su pluma tan rápida como el ala de los ángeles, según se dijo de la del higumeno Nicolás; en cambio, mereció que se celebrase la clara hermosura de su letra aun después de muerto, como fue ensalzada, en su oración fúnebre, la letra del Studita.

El libro de San Nicón refiere que visitando un abad las Casas puestas bajo su obediencia, les pregunta a sus monjes el oficio que ejercen. Uno le responde: Yo trenzo cuerdas. Otro: Yo tejo esteras. Otro: Yo, lienzos. Otro:

1. The Dean-vicar and María Fulgencia

"For good health and composure, the dean-vicar!" people would say, and he didn't deny it.

Neither his memory, nor his intellect, nor his will,[50] nor his corpulence ever lost their sense of moderation. Not an impetuous beat, nor a tempest on his forehead, nor a more rapid step on his part, nor a new custom.

An adventurer of a nephew of his, a captain of troops stationed in Manila, a man replete with vicious habits and debts, appeared at his house. The dean understood that neither his love nor his good counsel could set him right. Things and men were what they were. If you accepted this premise, any zeal for remedies was no longer necessary. It is true that difficult conversions were often obtained through the grace of a number of saints and women; but he would never commit the sin of considering himself a saint. Among the women with sweet qualities, with a respectable and comfortable home, there was no one in town like Corazón Motos, who would inherit a chocolate-making establishment with six chocolate mills. And that rake of a nephew abandoned the canon to pursue Doña Corazón.[51]

Elected capitular vicar of the diocese, at that time bereft of the previous prelate, the dean-vicar learned how to remain motionless in all matters of governance, prudently protecting the ecclesiastical see until the arrival of the new bishop. Afterwards, he returned to what his heart most desired, the delight of his eyes and his steady hand: calligraphy, an art gloriously cultivated by many of the outstanding men of the Church, such as Saint Pamphilus, Saint Blaise, Saint Lucian, Saint Marcellus, Saint Plato, Theodore the Studites, the patriarch Methodius, Saint Joseph the Hymnographer, the monk John, the monk Kosmas, the deacon Dorotheus....[52]

The dean of Oleza traced vignettes, orles and title pages, copied centos of thoughts and composed and painted parchments of gratitude in miniature. His pen was not as swift as the wings of angels as was said of the pen of the hegumenos Nicholas;[53] on the other hand, he deserved to have the illustrious beauty of his script celebrated even after his death, just as the script of Studites was so extolled at the funeral oration for him.

The book of Saint Nicon[54] relates how an abbot, visiting the Houses placed under his authority, asks his monks the trade they exercise. One answers, "I braid rope." Another, "I weave mats." Another, "I, canvases."

Yo hago harneros. Otro: Yo soy calígrafo. El abad se apresura a decirle: El calígrafo sea humilde, porque su arte le inclinará a la vanagloria.

Por ese miedo de caer en la tentación del orgullo, los monjes calígrafos no firman sus obras, o lo hacen confesando sus flaquezas, encomendándose a las plegarias de los lectores, añadiendo a su nombre palabras de menosprecio. Así, el monje Leoncio se llama insensato; Nicéforo, desventurado y mísero; Cirilo, monje pecador.

El deán de Oleza puso ingenuamente su nombre junto al fecit y un gentil monograma. Quizá por eficacia venturosa del arte, si su gobierno diocesano y el capitán de Manila le dieron motivos de turbación, puede creerse que los mismos motivos, ello solos, ya cansados, le dejaron en paz.

Pero en el principio de su vejez se le acumularon los trastornos y cavilaciones de la noble casa de los Valcárcel de Murcia, donde había servido de mozo y recibido estudios y, finalmente, el valimiento que le exaltó al deanato de Oleza.

Una tarde, el señor deán presidió el entierro de don Trinitario Valcárcel y Montesinos. Iban los cleros de todas las parroquias de Murcia, y como el señor Valcárcel dejó mandas al Seminario, a los asilos, al hospicio y a muchos conventos, alumbraban sus despojos los seminaristas, los asilados, los hospicianitos y frailes. Llevaban el ataúd seis jornaleros de las haciendas de los Valcárcel, con sus duros trajes de paño, trajes de boda que guardan para su mortaja y se los ponen también para el luto de los amos. Entre responsos y el desfile del pésame cerró la noche. Quedó el cadáver en la grada de la capilla del cementerio, velándole sus labradores. Estaba vestido de frac, con dos bandas y placas de dos grandes cruces, todo de cuando estuvo de jefe político en Extremadura.

Los buenos hombres hablaban con sumisión. Callaban, bostezaban y se aburrían de mirar el amo muerto, los cirios, el Cristo del altar, Cristo de cementerio al que se encomienda que cuide de los difuntos depositados a sus pies mientras se duermen los que los guardan. Tanto bostezaban los seis labradores, que dos se fueron a mercar tortas y panecillos calientes de

Another, "I make sieves." Another, "I am a calligrapher." The abbot hastens to tell him, "The calligrapher should be humble because his art will likely incline him to vainglory."

Because of that fear of falling into the temptation of pride, the monk-calligraphers do not sign their works, or they do so while confessing their failings, commending themselves to the prayers of their readers, adding words of self-contempt to their names. In this way, the monk Leontius calls himself foolish; Nicephorus, faint-hearted and a wretch; Cyril, a sinful monk.[55]

The dean-vicar of Oleza ingenuously placed his name next to the fecit along with an elegant monogram. Perhaps because of the fortunate efficacy of the art, if his governance of the diocese and the captain from Manila gave him reasons for distress, one can believe that these very same reasons, by themselves, now tiresome, left him in peace.

But at the very beginning of his old age, the upheavals and the constant preoccupation with the noble house of the Valcárcels of Murcia, where he had served as a young man and had carried on his studies, piled up on him, as did finally the special favor that elevated him to the deanship of Oleza.

One afternoon, the dean-vicar presided over the burial of Don Trinitario Valcárcel y Montesinos. The clergy of all the parishes in Murcia attended, and since Señor Valcárcel left bequests to the Seminary, to the poorhouses, to the orphanage and to many convents and monasteries, the seminary students, the indigent, the little orphans and the friars all showed up to illuminate his mortal remains. Six day laborers from the farms belonging to the Valcárcels carried the coffin, all dressed up in their heavy woolen suits, their wedding clothes which they were saving to serve as a shroud, and which they also put on when in mourning for their masters. Night fell in the midst of the prayers for the dead and the procession of those offering their condolences. The dead body was left on the step in front of the cemetery chapel altar with the farm laborers sitting in wake over it. He was clothed in a full-dress coat with two sashes and insignia consisting of two large crosses, all dating back to the time when he had served as provincial governor in Extremadura.

The good fellows were conversing with a certain air of subservience. They would remain silent, yawn and appear bored as they looked at their dead master, the wax candles, the Christ on the altar, a kind of Christ found in cemeteries, whom you commission to watch over the deceased, deposited at his feet, while those entrusted with watching over him fall asleep. The six farm laborers were yawning so much that two of them went out to buy cakes

la cochura de madrugada, bacalao, vino y olivas. Todos juntos otra vez en la capilla, se hartaron, fumaron, despabilaron las luces y se acostaron en la estera.

Pasó tiempo. Las moscas chupaban en los ojos, en las orejas, en la nariz, en las uñas de don Trinitario, y de súbito zumbaron en un revuelo de huída. El cadáver había movido los párpados. Descruzó las manos, descansó los codos en los bordes del ataúd como en un cojín, fue incorporándose y se sentó. Debió de ser en la vida y en la muerte hombre socarrón y flemático. Estuvo mirándolo todo: sus gentes dormidas, los picheles de vino, los papelones pringosos de la cena, los cirios devorados, el Cristo delante, acogiéndole; un trozo de noche estrellada, con un panteón viejo y la fantasma de un ciprés...

– ¿Y no se murió usted del susto al despertarse allí? – le preguntó el deán cuando fue a Murcia para ofrecerle, un poco medroso, su parabién.

– No, señor – le dijo el resucitado – ; porque allí lo que más podía horrorizarme era el muerto, y al muerto no le veía porque precisamente era yo.

Don Trinitario bajó despacito de su tarima, le tomó la manta a un criado, envolvióse y salió.

Por el camino iba pensando en su muerte. No se acordaba de haber fallecido. Ya le parecía que debió morir en fecha remota; ya creía que acababa de jugar su tresillo con el brigadier y Montiña, el relator; no recordando si ganara o perdiera; de modo que jugando se moriría.

Le malhumoraba ir con la cabeza desnuda, de frac y condecoraciones – las sobredoradas, las económicas – y sin guantes, sin joyas, sin dinero, sin reloj: bolsillos de difunto – ¡qué concepto de ruindad, de miseria inspiraba un cadáver católico! – En cambio, le habían calzado unas botas nuevas, y se las pusieron rajándoselas, y se las abrocharon con un solo botón con un ojal que no se correspondían. ¡Qué prisa para el avío tan precario!

Llegó al blasonado portal de su casona. Llamó con el mismo repique de aldaboncillo de siempre. Silencio. Sueño de cansancio de desgracia.

and warm rolls from the morning's batch of dough, as well as codfish, wine and olives. When they were all together again in the chapel, they stuffed themselves, smoked, snuffed out the candles and lay down to sleep on the floor matting.

Time passed. The flies were sucking at Don Trinitario's eyes, ears, nose and fingernails, when suddenly they flew off in a swarm, buzzing as they rose. The corpse had moved its eyelids. He uncrossed his hands, rested his elbows on the edges of the casket as if it were a cushion, began to pull himself erect, and sat up. He must have been a crafty, phlegmatic man in life and in death. He remained there looking at everything: his sleeping workers, the pewter wine tankards, the greasy remnants of wrapping paper from the meal, the extinguished wax candles, the Christ in front of him, beckoning him, a patch of starry night along with an old mausoleum and the phantom of a cypress tree....

"And you didn't die of fright when you woke up there?" the dean asked him when he went to Murcia, somewhat fearfully, to offer him his congratulations.

"No, indeed," the resuscitated man said, "because what would most terrify me was the dead body and I didn't see the dead body there because it was actually me."

Don Trinitario stepped down from his dressing platform, took his shawl from a servant, wrapped himself up in it and left.

He kept thinking about his death along the way. He couldn't remember having passed away. It now seemed to him that he must have died at some remote time in the past and he now believed that he had just played a game of ombre with the brigadier and Montiña, the court reporter, and he could not remember whether he had won or lost, so that in all likelihood he must have died while he was still playing.

It put him into a foul humor to walk around with his head bare, wearing a full-dress coat and his decorations – the gold-plated silver ones and the ones of lower quality – and without gloves, without jewelry, without any money, without a watch: a dead man's pockets – a Catholic corpse inspired such a sense of stinginess and destitution! On the other hand, they had put a new pair of boots on him and they had split them when they put them on his feet and fastened them with a single button: a button and a buttonhole that didn't fit one another. What haste for such a precarious preparation!

He arrived at the emblazoned entryway to his ancestral house. He rapped on the door with the knocker repeatedly just as he usually did. Silence. The

En la esquina relumbró el farol del sereno. A lo lejos venía un estrépito de alpargatas. ¡Sus labradores! Entonces sí que se asustó el señor Valcárcel de que se le tuviese por un ánima en pena. Y a voces y manotazos consiguió que las mozas le abrieran un postigo, huyéndole despavoridas.

Para todos, y aun para sí misma, fue ya la mujer una ex viuda. De noche se creía acostada con el cadáver de su marido. Daba gracias a Dios por el milagro de la resurreccíon, uno de los pocos milagros que nunca se nos ocurre pedir. Se despertaba mirándole. Sin darse cuenta, le cruzaba las manos y, suavemente, le cerraba más los ojos...

Pertenecían los Valcárcel Montesinos a una de las familias más eminentes de Murcia por su rango y hacienda y por los títulos y méritos con que la ilustraron los dos linajes, en cuyas ramas florecieron guerreros, oidores, tribunos, un purpurado, dos azafatas, dos generaciones de primeros contribuyentes y, por último, don Trinitario, político de agallas, y don Eusebio, cónsul de muy adobada elegancia, que enviudó en Cette.

Don Trinitario se casó, ya maduro, con una labradora que le dio dos hijas; pero sólo una, María Fulgencia, vino al mundo bien dotada de salud y hermosura.

La otra hija nació convulsa y deforme. A los seis años fue sumergiéndose en una quietud de larva. Cuando murió, nadie lo supo. Estaba lo mismo que cuando vivía: mirándolo todo con la blanda fijeza de sus ojos de vidrio de color de ceniza.

Tan lindas ternuras puso María Fulgencia en el recuerdo y en la pronunciación de "mi hermanita", que hasta las amistades, que compadecieron y evitaron besar a la enferma, creían verla malograda en una graciosa infancia.

María Fulgencia se exaltaba y desfallecía llorando. El padre quiso que se la llevase su hermano al Consulado de Burdeos, pero ya el cónsul preparaba sus segundas bodas.

No resistía María Fulgencia su soledad infantil en la casa de Murcia. Y don Trinitario llamó a su ahijado, el deán de Oleza.

sleep of weariness and misfortune. The night watchman's lantern shone brightly on the corner. In the far distance you could hear the clatter of hemp sandals. His farm laborers! Then Señor Valcárcel really got frightened at the idea that he might be taken for a soul in purgatory. And so by shouting and clapping his hands, he succeeded in having the servant girls open the wicket for him, after which they ran off in terror.

For everyone and even for himself, his wife was now an ex-widow. At night she thought she was sleeping with her husband's corpse. She gave thanks to God for the miracle of his resurrection, one of the few miracles for which we never happen to ask. She would wake up looking at him. Without even realizing it, she would cross his hands and gently close his eyes even more....

The Valcárcel Montesinos belonged to one of the most eminent families in Murcia because of their societal rank and their property, as well as the titles and merits of the two family lineages which brought glory upon it, and within its branches there flourished warriors, judges of the *audiencia*, eloquent political orators, a cardinal, two ladies-in-waiting to the queen, two generations of prominent land-owning taxpayers, and finally, Don Trinitario, an intrepid political figure, and Don Eusebio, a consul of very seasoned elegance, who was widowed in Sète.

When Don Trinitario was getting on in years, he married a farm woman who gave him two daughters, but only one, María Fulgencia, came into the world well endowed with good health and beauty.

The other girl was born prone to convulsions and deformed. At the age of six, she started to immerse herself in a larva-like stillness. When she died, nobody knew about it. She was just the same as when she was alive: staring at everything with the bland steadfastness of her glassy, ashen-colored eyes.

María Fulgencia put such lovely tenderness into the memory and the pronunciation of "my little sister" that even the friends, who were filled with pity and avoided kissing the sick child, concluded that they saw her as having come to the sad end of a delightful childhood.

María Fulgencia was quite distressed and grew faint from weeping. Her father tried to get his brother to take her to the Consulate in Bordeaux, but the consul was already preparing for his second marriage.

María Fulgencia made no effort to resist the desire for her infantile solitude in her house in Murcia. And so Don Trinitario called upon his godson, the dean of Oleza.

– ¿Qué te parece que se haga con esta criaturita? ¿Cómo la curaríamos?

Ya se sabe que para su protegido las cosas y las personas no tenían remedio: eran según eran.

Don Trinitario se enfureció. Bajo su mando de jefe político de Extremadura todos los conflictos tuvieron remedio. Halló remedio entonces y después para todo, hasta para su muerte. ¿No lo habría para las congojas de María Fulgencia?

Y lo hubo encomendándosela al deán, que se la llevó a la Visitación de Oleza. No se conocía en muchas leguas a la redonda otro convento donde pudieran acogerse niñas educandas de algún primor de cuna.

Pasó María Fulgencia largos meses de lágrimas y desesperaciones pidiendo su hermanita, apareciéndosele su padre tendido en el féretro y al otro día sentado delante de su escritorio, repasando las cuentas de la funeraria. Domingos y jueves la visitaba el señor deán. Salían las monjas a contárselo todo, y él siempre decía:

– Eso es una crisis. ¡Ni más ni menos!

– ¿Y qué haríamos con ella?

El señor deán balanceaba pesadamente su cabeza redonda, inclinada, de calígrafo. Había una intención salvadora en sus ojos gordos. Por primera vez en su vida descubría remedio para un trance de apuro: devolver la mocita a su casa. Y no lo propuso, sintiendo que la gratitud sellaba su lengua.

Un jueves dejó de ir a la Visitación. Estaba en Murcia, porque don Trinitario haba muerto definitivamente. Fue humilde su entierro; ya no le velaron sus huertanos y sobranceros. La herencia se redujo a la casona con escudo en el dintel y a dos haciendas empeñadas, invadidas de hierba borde. La viuda se lo confió todo al señor deán. Le rodearon los acreedores, y él les escuchó y leyó sus documentos de letra procesal sin entenderlos, recordando con ternura a su bienhechor y diciéndose que no se debiera morir más de una vez en este mundo. Y como la viuda necesitaba, le trajo a María Fulgencia, y así pudo internarse en las delicias de sus membranas caligráficas. Cuatro meses de felicidad: un cuadro sinóptico de obispos y pastorales de la silla de Oleza, a tres tintas.

"What do you think we should do with that odd little child? How should we try to cure her?"

It is a matter of common knowledge that for his protégée, there were no remedies for things and for people: they were what they were.

Don Trinitario grew furious. Under his authority as provincial head of Extremadura, all conflicts had a solution. He found a remedy at that time and afterward for everything, even for his death. Couldn't there be one for María Fulgencia's anguish?

And there turned out to be one, entrusting her to the dean, who took her off to La Visitación in Oleza. No other convent for many leagues around was better known, where young girl students of splendid aristocratic lineage could be welcomed.

María Fulgencia spent long months of tears and desperation asking for her little sister, seeing her father appear before her stretched out on his bier, and on the very next day, seated in front of his desk going over the bills for the funeral. The dean visited her on Sundays and Thursdays. The nuns would come out in order to tell him everything, and he would always say:

"That situation is a crisis. No more and no less!"

"And what should we do with her?"

The dean-vicar would shake his round, tilted calligrapher's head wearily. There was every intention of deliverance in his big, round eyes. For the first time in his life, he was discovering a remedy in a critical moment of need: return the young girl to her home. And he didn't propose it because he felt that gratitude was sealing his tongue.

One Thursday he stopped going to La Visitación. He was in Murcia because Don Trinitario had really died. His burial was humble and now the regular farm laborers and those hired when needed did not watch over him. The inheritance was reduced to the ancestral house with the escutcheon over the door head and two mortgaged properties overrun with weeds. The widow entrusted everything to the dean-vicar. The creditors surrounded him and he listened to them and read their documents filled with legal formalities without understanding them, remembering his benefactor with tenderness and telling himself that one ought not to die more than once in this world. And since the widow needed company, he brought her María Fulgencia, and in this way, he succeeded in taking refuge in all of the delights of his calligraphic parchments. Four months of happiness: a synoptic illustration of the bishops and pastorals of the see of Oleza in three hues.

2. María Fulgencia y los suyos

María Fulgencia quedó huérfana también de madre. Alta, delgada, pálida; la boca muy encendida; las trenzas, muy largas, muy negras. Sola en el viejo casón, con criadas antiguas.

Desde su diócesis venía el señor deán a decirle palabras prudentísimas, y ella las recibía resplandeciéndole sus ojos de niña y de mujer, que siempre miraban a lo lejos.

Apareció tío Eusebio con la esposa casi nueva, una dama bordelesa, que hablaba un español delicioso y breve. Era toda de elegancias, en su vocecita, en sus mohines, en sus miradas y actitudes, como si su cuerpo, sus pensamientos, su habla y su corazón fuesen también obra de su modisto. Toda moda la consulesa y el cónsul también todo moda.

Los sastres de Murcia se asomaban al portalillo de su obrador para ver las galas de medio luto, de corte inglés, que paseó el cónsul por la Platería antes de visitar a su sobrina.

— *Voilà,* Fulgencia. ¡Aqui tienes a Ivonne-Catherine!

— ¿A quién?

— ¡Hija, tu tía! Pero nosotros no decimos tía.

La miraban, aceptando que fuese bonita a pesar de su encogimiento lugareño.

— ¿No me preguntas por Mauricio y Javier?

— ¿Mauricio y Javier?

— ¡Mis hijos! ¡Primos tuyos! ¡Claro!...¿Has visto, *Ivette,* qué primitiva cabellera?

Ivonne-Catherine tomó entre sus dedos las puntas de las trenzas de la sobrina.

— ¡Oh! ¡Mañificó!

María Fulgencia se pasmó de que lo hubiese dicho sin mover la boca, empastada tirantemente de carmín.

...Y otro verano vinieron Mauricio y Javier. Semejaban extranjeros, de tan parados y tan rubios. Los sastres de Murcia también salían de sus tiendas para verlos.

Destinado el cónsul al Ministerio, pasaba las vacaciones en sus heredades. Los hijos estrenaron uniformes de cadetes de Caballería. De tarde, paseaban por el viejo jardín de María Fulgencia. Ella, blanca, lisa y dulce. Ellos, rojos, desplegados, flameantes. Contaban maravillas de Burdeos y de Valladolid.

2. María Fulgencia and her Relations

María Fulgencia was made an orphan again by the death of her mother. Tall, slender, pale; her mouth very bright red, her braids very long and very black. Alone in the ancestral house with long-time servants.

The dean-vicar would come from his diocese to tell her very prudent words, and she would receive them with childish yet womanly eyes shining, always looking into the distance.

Uncle Eusebio appeared with his almost new wife, a lady from Bordeaux, who spoke a delightful, succinct Spanish. She was all elegance with her sweet little voice, with her facial expressions, with her glances and postures, as if her body, her thoughts, her speech and her heart were also the handiwork of her couturier. The consul's wife was all the fashion and the consul also all the fashion.

The tailors of Murcia looked out the narrow front doorways to their shops to see the finery of half mourning, of the English cut, when the consul would stroll along the Platería before visiting his niece.[56]

"*Voilà*, Fulgencia, here's Ivonne-Catherine to see you!"

"Who?"

"Your aunt, my child! But we don't say aunt."

They kept looking her over, accepting the fact that she was pretty in spite of her small-town self-consciousness.

"Aren't you going to ask me about Mauricio and Javier?"

"Mauricio and Javier?"

"My sons! Your cousins! Of course.... Have you ever seen such a primitive head of hair, *Ivette*?"

Yvonne-Catherine took the ends of her niece's braids between her fingers.

"Oh! Magnificent!"

María Fulgencia was astounded to see that she had said this without moving her mouth, which was tautly daubed with carmine.

...And Mauricio and Javier came another summer. They seemed to be foreigners because they were so spiritless and blond. The tailors of Murcia also came out of their shops to see them.

Since the consul's destination was the Ministry, he was spending his vacation on his country property. His sons showed off their Cavalry cadet uniforms for the first time. In the afternoon, they strolled through María Fulgencia's old garden. She, white, smooth and sweet. They, ruddy, expansive, flamboyant. They kept telling her of the wonders of Bordeaux

Mauricio siempre sonreía mirando a Murcia; porque no miraba un edificio, una calle, una torre, sino toda la ciudad con una sola mirada.

Contemplándole y oyéndole, recogía su prima una promesa de felicidad.

Y después. Después ya no vinieron hasta que Mauricio lució insignias y galas de teniente.

María Fulgencia estaba más descolorida, y sus cabellos negros, más frondosos, la dejaban en una umbría de ahogo apasionado, una umbría de mármol con hiedra, en el olvido de un huerto. Mauricio le besó los zarcillos de las matas de trenzas, y todo el mármol tembló sonrojándose, como si la estatua se viese a sí misma desnuda, llena de sol. Aquel invierno, Mauricio le escribió despidiéndose. Se marchaba lejos. Viaje de estudio; estudio comparativo de los más grandes ejércitos de Europa.

Toda la carta era una definición apologética de las virtudes del soldado. "Un buen soldado necesita saber cómo son los demás soldados. Este conocimiento es el origen de las gloriosas conquistas y resistencias. Un buen soldado ha de tener un espíritu internacional. Estas últimas palabras me las enseñó mi padre."

Si la carta no desbordaba de mieles de requiebros, en cambio era rica de firmes verdades. María Fulgencia la llevó en su pecho. Al acostarse la puso en el cofrecillo de sus joyas, y ya tuvo un perfume de galanía.

En esos días mostróse la huérfana con sobresaltos y deseos de soledad. Los pasaba en la profunda alcoba de los padres, quejándose y revolviéndose vestida en el lecho enorme, de baldaquino de damascos. Estuvo todo un domingo quietecita, ovillada. No quiso alimento; se fajó la frente con un terciopelo morado de una imagen.

Sus viejas criadas la besaban llorando.

– ¿Qué tendrás, nenica?

– ¡Ay, yo no sé! ¡Tendré calentura!

Todo amargo en su vida; sentía en su boca flores amargas; se le cerraban los ojos con un peso amargo; el agua que bebía era de hiel caliente. Su aliento y sus sienes abrasaban el hilo de los almohadones, dejándoles un olor de amargura.

Se avisó al señor deán, que acudió casi pronto.

and Valladolid. Mauricio was always smiling as he looked over Murcia; because he wasn't looking at a building, a street, a tower, but rather the entire city with a single glance.

As his cousin contemplated him and listened to him, she gathered a promise of happiness within herself.

And afterwards. After that, they didn't come back until Mauricio displayed a lieutenant's insignia and regalia.

María Fulgencia was even more pallid, and her black hair, now much thicker, left her in the shadows of passionate affliction, in the shadows of ivy-covered marble, in the oblivion of a garden. Mauricio kissed the small brambles of her mat of hair, fashioned into braids, and the whole of the marble trembled, blushing, as if the statue had seen itself naked, covered with sunlight. That winter, Mauricio wrote to her and bade her farewell. He was going off far away. A journey for study; a comparative study of the largest armies in Europe.

The entire letter was a definitive apologia concerning the virtues of a soldier. "A good soldier needs to know what other soldiers are like. This knowledge is the origin of glorious conquests and resistances. A good soldier must have an international spirit. These final words were taught to me by my father."

If the letter was not overflowing with the honey of flattery, it was, however, rich in firm truths. María Fulgencia carried it close to her bosom. When she went to bed, she would put it in her little jewel box, and it now carried a scent of gallantry.

During those days that followed, the orphan girl revealed that she was filled with sudden fears and a desire for solitude. She spent them in the deep bedroom that had belonged to her parents, fully dressed, moaning and twisting in the enormous bed with the damask canopy. She spent one entire Sunday there, ever so still, all curled up into a ball. She refused all nourishment and wrapped a purple velvet cape taken from a religious image around her forehead.

Her old maidservants kissed her as they wept.

"What can be the matter with you, sweet child?"

"Oh, I don't know! I must have a fever!"

Everything so bitter in her life; she tasted bitter flowers in her mouth; her eyes kept closing with a bitter heaviness; the water she drank was like warm gall. Her breath and her temples were burning up the fabric of her great big pillows, leaving an odor of bitterness on them.

The dean-vicar was notified and he came over almost immediately.

– ¿Y qué haríamos nosotras; nosotras y usted, señor deán?

– ¿Nosotros? Nada. Es un brinco para crecer. ¡De brinco en brinco vamos llegando a la palma de la mano del Señor, que un día, ¡zas! nos entra en la gloria! Es una crisis del crecimiento. Lleva ya muchas: la primera la tuvo cuando murió la hermanita...

Aquella noche empeoró. El médico de la casa pidió consulta. Reunidos en el escritorio del difunto don Trinitario, dijo el señor deán:

– No me cansaré de advertir que se trata del crecimiento...

– Es tifus. Tifus del peor en esas edades...

– ¿Tifus? Pero, bueno, el tifus lo tiene todo el mundo en Murcia; está siempre debajo de Murcia, a dos jemes de profundidad.

No murió María Fulgencia. El canónigo-ayo la visitó doce jueves. El jueves duodécimo habló complaciéndose en el triunfo de su diagnóstico.

– ¿No lo dije yo? El nuevo brinco de abajo hacia arriba. Has crecido. Vuelves a ser de carne blanca y no de tierra; porque parecías de tierra verdosa.

Y entre tanto un viejo peluquero cortaba las trenzas de la convaleciente. La dejó rapadita. En la luna del tocador de su madre se veía María Fulgencia sus ojos anchos, densos, como dos pasionarias húmedas, que, de súbito, se crisparon, porque allí, en el espejo, se le apareció Mauricio, todavía con uniforme de camino.

Ella se cubrió con las manos su cabecita raída. Alarmóse el deán; se desesperaron las criadas.

María Fulgencia se refugió dentro de un cortinaje, enrollándose toda entre los gordos pliegues, y desde allí salía su gemido.

El maestro apartaba con la punta de su bota los rizos y vellones. Después se aguardó, sin soltar su sonrisa y un frasco de loción.

Fue Mauricio el que sacó a María Fulgencia del fondo de las rancias telas, que crujieron desgarradas. La llevó junto a la ventana. La miró mucho y le dio unos blandos toquecillos en la nuca de cera.

– ¡No te apures, hija! ¡Ya te crecerá! ¡Y resultas muy bien! ¡Te pareces a Fernández Arellano, un compañero muy listo de mi promoción, el número siete, que ahora está en la Remonta!

"So what should we do, we and you, dean-vicar?"

"We? Nothing. It's a leap forward that is part of growing up. What with one leap and the next one, we keep moving closer to the palm of God's hand, and one day, wham! it opens our way into Heaven! It's a crisis of growing up. She's already had many others: she had the first one when her little sister died...."

That night she got worse. The family doctor sought another opinion. Gathered in the deceased Don Trinitario's study, the dean-vicar said:

"I shall not tire of informing you that it's simply a question of growing up...."

"It's typhus. Typhus of the worst kind at that age...."

"Typhus? Maybe so, but everyone in Murcia has typhus; it's always lying just beneath Murcia, a foot or so deep."

María Fulgencia didn't die. The canon-tutor visited her on twelve Thursdays. On the twelfth Thursday, he spoke with considerable pleasure of the triumph of his diagnosis.

"Didn't I tell you? The most recent leap from down below to up above. You have grown. You are once again like white flesh, not like earth, because you used to look like greenish earth."

And all the while an old barber kept cutting the convalescing girl's braids. He left her with closely cropped hair.[57] In the mirror of her mother's dressing table, María Fulgencia could see her wide, dark eyes, like two humid passion flowers, suddenly twitching, because there in the mirror, Mauricio appeared before her, still dressed in his traveling uniform.

She covered her closely cropped head with her hands. The dean grew alarmed and the maidservants were frantic.

María Fulgencia sought refuge inside a set of bed curtains, rolling herself up between its heavy folds, and her moan emanated from there.

The tutor parted the ringlets and sheared hair with the tip of his boot. Then he waited, without loosening his grip on his smile and a small bottle of lotion.

It was Mauricio who removed María Fulgencia from the depths of those rank-smelling linens that rustled as they were pulled apart. He brought her close to the window. He looked at her for a long time and touched her ever so gently on the back of her waxen-colored neck.

"Don't hurry, my dear girl! You will grow up soon enough! And you're turning out just fine! You're just like Fernández Arellano, a very clever companion of mine, who was promoted along with me, number seven, and is now with the Animal Procurement Department of the army!"

Enseguida le dijo que su padre, ya cónsul general, acababa de pedir la excedencia.

– Pero te advierto que, por su porte, sigue pareciendo en activo. Ahora viene a Murcia en busca de descanso.

En doce días descansó del todo tío Eusebio, y la víspera de su regreso a Madrid, él y su esposa tuvieron la ternura de visitar a la sobrina huérfana.

La miraban compadecidos, pero sin consentirle que se afligiese demasiado.

– ¡No! ¡Eso, no! *Kate* no puede con las tristezas. Es lo único que no resiste. Estás en lo mejor de la vida. Tienes en el buen deán padre, madre y hermano: toda una familia. ¡Es un agradecido! ¡Ah, *Kate,* si conocieras al deán! ¿Qué cumples, veintidós? ¡Como! ¿Nada más que diecisiete?

– ¡Un bebé! – suspiró *Kate* o Ivonne-Catherine por el esmalte de su boca inmóvil.

Debajo de aquella boca cromada, egipcia y hermética salía una respiración de bombones.

– Diecisiete? ¡No entiendo! ¡Entonces, entonces es Mauricio quien tiene veintidós!

– ¡Oh, qué *gafe!*

Y madama aplaudía, muy niña, con sus dedos ceñidos de mitones color de aromo.

El ex cónsul se reía con elegancia mirando a su mujer, mirándose sus zapatos de charol. Finalmente, colgó sus pulgares enérgicos de las sisas del chaleco de merino orillado de felpa.

Se levantó, porque no podía sufrir el ruido de una acequia que pasaba entre los naranjos y magnolios del jardín de la casona.

– ¿A ti, Fulgencia, no te desespera oír siempre ese agua? ¿Que no?

No. Cuando estuvo enferma le llegaba un alivio de esa estremecida frescura. Se creía caminar encima del riego, calentándolo con la brasa que soltaba su piel.

– Bueno; pero sería en el delirio de la fiebre... ¿Tuviste fiebre? ¿Mucha fiebre? ¡Entonces has resucitado, como tu padre! Pues en creciéndote el cabello, te vienes a Madrid con nosotros. ¿Verdad, *Gothon?*

He quickly told her that his father, now a consul-general, had just requested a temporary leave from his duties.

"But I must let you know that, because of his excellent bearing, he continues to appear quite active. He's coming to Murcia now seeking a bit of rest."

In twelve days, Uncle Eusebio was able to rest completely, and the night before his return to Madrid, he and his wife found it in their hearts to pay a visit to their orphaned niece.

They looked at her sympathetically, but without allowing her to become too distraught.

"No, not that! Kate can't stand sadness. It's the only thing she can't bear. Now is the best time in your life. You have a father, a mother and brother in the good dean, a whole family! You should be grateful. Oh, *Kate*, if you only knew the dean-vicar! How old are you, twenty-two? What! No more than seventeen?"

"A baby!" *Kate* or Ivonne-Catherine sighed through the enamel work of her motionless mouth.

A breath of bonbons emanated from beneath the chrome-covered, Egyptian, hermetic mouth.

"Seventeen? I don't understand! Then, then it's Mauricio who is twenty-two!"

"Oh, what a *gaffe*!"[58]

And madame applauded, like a child, her fingers fitted with fingerless gloves the color of yellow acacia.

The ex-consul laughed elegantly, looking at his wife, looking at his patent leather shoes. He finally hooked his energetic thumbs onto the darts of his woolen vest bordered with plush.

He stood up because he couldn't stand the noise of a water channel that ran between the orange trees and magnolia trees in the garden of the old ancestral house.

"Fulgencia, doesn't it drive you frantic always listening to the sound of that water? Doesn't it?"

No. When she fell ill, that shivery coolness brought her a degree of relief. She thought she was walking on top of the irrigation water, warming it with the fiery embers released from her skin.

"All right, perhaps it was amidst the delirium of the fever.... You did have a fever? Much fever? Then you were resuscitated, just like your father! Well, when your hair grows back, you'll come to Madrid with us. Right, *Gothon*?"

– ¡Oh, sí; unos días! – susurró Ivette, Kate, Gothon, Ivonne-Catherine.

– ¡Claro, unos días! No te faltarán partidos. Sabemos que pasó ya lo de Mauricio. No seríais felices. ¿Verdad, *Ivette?*

– ¡Oh, no!

Y se marcharon.

3. El ángel

El señor deán de Oleza recibió carta de un beneficiado de Murcia, muy sutil. Pero la sutilidad, la delgadez, el primor, era lo de menos. El señor deán abandonó las aristas y volutas del colofón de un códice. Las consultas, las crisis, los brincos de María Fulgencia le parecían siempre cosas pasadas, envejecidas. Ni siquiera había de meditar un consejo inédito. Le servían las mismas palabras, los mismos ademanes. Y he aquí que, de súbito, se topaba con lo inesperado: María Fulgencia quería comprar la imagen del Angel de Salcillo, aunque le pidieran en precio su casa y sus campos, que comenzaban a mejorar y producir.

¡Inesperado! Y una sorpresa para el señor deán era el vuelco de toda su vida. Ni se acordó de poner la frente entre sus manos para cavilar, sino que alzaba los puños y los miraba desde su sillón sin conocerlos. ¡Un sobresalto tan grande como el de la resurección de don Trinitario! ¡María Fulgencia era una Valcárcel!

Poco a poco el deán puso la lógica junto al desatino, el ungüento que adoba las inflamaciones.

¡Para qué quería esa infeliz el Ángel, ni dónde lo pondría, si por comprarlo se quedaba sin casa! Además de la lógica, estaba el consejo de familia, y además él. Pero ni él ni nadie podían ya impedir el alboroto de María Fulgencia y las zumbas de las gentes.

Una segunda carta del beneficiado de Murcia estremeció la corpulencia del señor deán. Todo el deán recrujía combándose hacia la decisión, mientras releía los principales conceptos:

"...Yo no he querido apartar de su locura a la señorita Valcárcel con destemplanza y malhumor, sino participando aparentemente de sus puericias,

"Oh, yes, for a few days!" whispered Ivette, Kate, Gothon, Ivonne-Catherine.

"Of course, a few days! There'll be no lack of prospective suitors. We know the business with Mauricio is over. You wouldn't be happy. Right, *Ivette*?

"Oh, no!"

And they departed.

3. The Angel

The dean-vicar of Oleza received a very subtile letter from an ecclesiastical beneficiary in Murcia. But the fact that it was subtile, delicate and elegant were the least part of it. The dean-vicar laid aside the sharp, curved edges and scrolls on the colophon of a codex. The consultations for María Fulgencia, her crises and her leaping up and down always seemed to him things of the past, now grown old. It was hardly necessary to meditate on some hitherto unwritten piece of advice. He could make use of the same words, the same expressions. And lo and behold, he was suddenly confronted with the unexpected: María Fulgencia wanted to buy the image of the Angel sculpted by Salcillo,[59] even though the price they were asking was her house and her fields, which were only now beginning to improve and produce.

Unexpected! The upheaval in all aspects of his whole life was a surprise for the dean-vicar. Nor did he remember putting his forehead between his hands to ponder, but he did raise his fists and stare at them from his armchair without recognizing them. A shock as great as the resurrection of Don Trinitario! María Fulgencia was a Valcárcel!

Little by little the dean put logic alongside folly, the ointment that treats inflammations.

For what purpose did that wretched girl want the Angel, and where would she put it if she were left without a house in order to purchase it! In addition to logic, there was the counsel of the family, and in addition to them, there was himself. But neither he nor anyone else could now stand in the way of María Fulgencia's agitation and other people's ridicule.

A second letter from the beneficiary in Murcia perturbed the dean-vicar's corpulence. The whole of the dean squeaked as he twisted his way toward the decision, as he reread the principal ideas:

"...I have not felt like turning Señorita Valcárcel away from her madness with intemperance and ill humor, but have chosen rather to share her childish

con el *similia similibus.* Esa talla – le dije – es magnífica. Si yo fuese obispo de Murcia, reclamaría el Ángel para mi palacio. Empresa imposible. Y, sin embargo, un obispo en su diócesis es y puede más, mucho más, que una señorita devota en su casa. Bien sé que esa imagen del Ángel es la que debemos amar entre todas las imágenes de todos los ángeles. Los que entienden de belleza dicen que el imaginero tuvo imspiración divina labrando un cuerpo hermoso que no fuese de hombre ni de mujer. No participa de nosotros, y pertenece a todos nosotros. Nos pertenece más a los murcianos por aparecerse junto a una palmera. El artista prefirió la palmera solitaria de nuestros jardines cerrados al olivo de la granja de Getsemaní. No quiso un ángel con espada, con laúd, con rosas. No un ángel de ímpetu, ni de suavidad ni de gloria: ángel fácil, de buena vida. Nos dejó el Ángel más nuestro y el que estuvo más cerca del dolor humano de Dios; el Ángel que descendió al huerto lleno de luna, para confortar al Señor en la noche de sus angustias. Ángel de los dolores... Lord Wellington pretendió, como usted, llevárselo. Ofreció dos millones y otro Ángel igual y nuevo. Y quedóse sin Ángel. Ni usted da tanto, ni yo soy ni seré obispo. A usted le queda un consuelo de ilusión: llamarse María Fulgencia, como la hija de Salcillo... La señorita Valcárcel me contestó inesperadamente que le importaba una friolera la hija de Salcillo... Yo nada más puedo hacer. Ella sigue consumiéndose. Compra todas las estampas del Ángel que encuentra y que le traen; y el precioso mancebo de Getsemaní se multiplica en la sala, en el dormitorio, en los libros y en el costurero de la señorita..."

Removióse el deán con un viejo estrépito de escabel y butaca.

Llegaba la hora de reclamar de sí mismo ante sí mismo. La protección de la casa de los Valcárcel no le pedía una perpetua mansedumbre a los antojos de una moza; no le obligaba a salirse de sus sendas tranquilas y pasar una vejez de trajines en el cabriolé de una diligencia. Ésta sería su jornada última de Oleza a Murcia.

Llegó y encaminóse a la noble casona. Ordenó que le abriesen y que alumbrasen el inmenso escritorio de don Trinitario, y desde allí llamó a la huérfana. En aquella estancia resultaría la entrevista de un eficaz entono.

Brincando compareció María Fulgencia. Ya tenía una graciosa cabellera de paje; ya le volvían los colores de la salud.

foolishness in an apparent manner with *similia similibus* (things are cured with like things).[60] That carved image – I said to her – is magnificent. If I were bishop of Murcia, I would reclaim the Angel for my palace. An impossible undertaking. And, nevertheless, a bishop in his diocese is and can do more, much more, than a devout young lady in her house. I know very well that the image of the Angel is one we should love among all the images of all the angels. Those who have an understanding of beauty say that the sculptor of the image had divine inspiration as he fashioned a beautiful body that was neither man nor woman. It doesn't partake of us and yet belongs to all of us. It belongs even more to us Murcians because it appears next to a palm tree.[61] The artist preferred the solitary palm tree of our enclosed gardens to the olive tree in the grange of Gethsemane.[62] He turned down an angel with a sword, with a lute, with roses. Not an angel of impulse, nor of softness or glory: a facile angel of a good life. He left us an Angel that is most ours, one that stands closer to the human suffering of God; the Angel who descended to the garden filled with moonlight to comfort the Lord on the night of his anguish. An Angel of suffering.... Lord Wellington,[63] like you, sought to take it away. He offered two million plus another Angel just like it and new. And he ended up without the Angel. Neither do you offer as much, nor am I, nor will I be a bishop. One consoling illusion remains to you: to be named María Fulgencia like Salcillo's daughter....[64] Señorita Valcárcel answered me unexpectedly saying she did not give a fig for Salcillo's daughter.... I can do nothing more. She continues being consumed. She buys every print of the Angel she can find and they bring to her, and the exquisite young man of Gethsemane keeps multiplying in the young lady's drawing room, in her bedroom, in her books and sewing room...."

The dean stirred with a timeworn scraping of footstool and armchair.

The hour was approaching for him to make greater demands of himself before himself. The protection of the Valcárcel house did not require a perpetual submissiveness on his part in the face of a young lady's whims; it did not oblige him to abandon his tranquil paths in order to spend his old age scurrying back and forth in the coupé of a diligence. This would be his last journey from Oleza to Murcia.

He arrived there, and he set out for the noble ancestral house. He gave orders for them to open and light up Don Trinitario's immense study, and from there he called in the orphan girl. The interview would turn out to have a more effective intonation in a room like that.

María Fulgencia made her appearance with a playful skip. She now had an attractive head of hair in a pageboy style, and the colors of good health were returning to her.

El enojado cánonigo no quiso oírla, porque él no había venido sino a imponer su seso y su voluntad.

— He venido a decirte que no puedes comprar el Ángel de Salcillo, entre otras razones, porque no puede venderse... ¡Y se acabó! ¡Ni más ni menos!

— Ya lo sabía...

— ¿Lo sabías?

— Sí, señor, que lo sabía. Lo que yo quiero ahora es ser monja suya, y así viviré a su lado.

— ¿Monja suya? ¡Tampoco, tampoco porque el Ángel de Salcillo no tiene monasterio!

— ¡Si no tiene monasterio, yo lo fundaré!

— ¿Que tú lo fundarás? ¿Tú?

— Con lo que yo tengo y lo que yo amo a mi Ángel...

— ¿Con lo que tú tienes? ¿Con lo que le amas?

¡Pero si él no era quien debía preguntar, sino quien debía decidir! Y el deán siguió preguntándole:

— ¿Pero hija, es que tú te piensas que se pueden cometer ni decir atrocidades y herejías?

— ¿Es una atrocidad que yo ame la imagen del Ángel de Nuestro Señor? ¡Mire que lo que usted dice sí que me parece una herejía!

Se precipitaba la contradicción sobre la roja frente del deán de Oleza. Y se puso a cavilar. ¿Podía él vedarle esas encendidas piedades sin caer en peligrosas apariencias iconoclastas? Enjugóse muy despacio los sudores, mirando a la señorita Valcárcel:

— ¿Tú le rezas al Ángel?

— ¿Yo? ¡Yo, no, señor!

— ¡Ya te tengo cogida!

Pero la soltó pronto. Resollaba cansándose de un diálogo tan preciso.

Las cosas eran según era. Nunca reparó en la imagen del Ángel, que no semejaba ni hombre ni mujer... ¡Claro que no lo sería! ¡Pues que se hartara de mirarla y de quererla! Enseguida se le deslizó una sospecha turbia, un barrunto miedoso que no lograba subir a las claridades de la proposición. La belleza de la imagen no sería de hombre ni de mujer; luego participaba de entrambos; y desde el momento en que María Fulgencia se encandilaba y derretía por el Ángel, el Ángel a pesar de su androginismo, ¿no se revelaría

The infuriated canon refused to hear her out because he had only come to impose his intelligence and his will.

"I have come to tell you that you can not buy Salcillo's Angel because, among other reasons, it can't be sold.... And that's all there is to it! No more, no less!"

"I already knew that...."

"You knew?"

"Yes, indeed, I really knew it. What I now want is to be one of his nuns, and in that way I will live by his side!"

"One of his nuns? Not that, not that either, because Salcillo's Angel does not have a convent!"

"If he doesn't have a convent, I will found one!"

"You will found one? You?"

"With all that I have and all that I love my Angel...."

"With what you have? With all that you love him?"

But he wasn't the one who should ask; he should rather decide! And the dean continued asking her:

"But, my child, do you really think that one can commit or say such atrocious and heretical things?"

"Is it so atrocious for me to love the image of the Angel of Our Lord? It looks to me as if what you are saying really seems to be heretical!"

The contradiction hurled itself headlong onto the flushed forehead of the dean of Oleza. And he began to ponder. Could he forbid her those inflamed acts of piety without falling into dangerous iconoclastic appearances? He wiped away his sweat very slowly as he kept looking at Señorita Valcárcel.

"Do you pray to the Angel?"

"I? No, indeed I don't!"

"Now I've caught you!"

But he quickly released her. He was breathing heavily, weary of so precise a dialogue.

Things were just as they were. He never took notice of the image of the Angel, which didn't resemble a man or a woman.... Well, of course it wouldn't! So let her have her fill of looking at it and loving it! All at once, a troubling suspicion slipped over him, a fearful conjecture which was unable to rise to the clarity of a proposition. The beauty of the image was probably neither that of a man nor a woman; and so it shared both; and from the moment María Fulgencia was dazzled and inflamed with passion for the Angel, wouldn't the Angel, in spite of its androgynous character, not reveal

para la huérfana con un espíritual contorno y hechizo masculino? Otra vez se quedó pensando el señor canónigo, y, de repente, le preguntó:

– ¿Y por qué no te marchas a Madrid, con tus tíos?

– ¿Con tío Eusebio y esa señora Ivonne-Catherine, Ivette, Kate y no sé qué más? ¡Ni los hijastros la resisten!

– Es que yo quiero que salgas de Murcia. ¡Y además de quererlo, tú lo necesitas!

– ¡Ahora mismo me marcharía de aquí!

– ¿Y adónde te llevaré? Estuviste en la Visitación... ¡Eras entonces una criatura! Allí, para verte, no había yo de viajar en diligencia...

– ¡Lléveme usted a la Visitación!

– ¡A la Visitación!...

Muchas cristianas doncellas fueron primorosas copistas de la biblioteca de Orígenes. En los monasterios de mujeres fue también la caligrafía labor honorable y deseada. ¡Ah, si María Fulgencia quisiera!

– ¡Lléveme enseguida a la Visitación, y allí me quedaré hasta que me canse!

– ¡Eso es lo peor; que te cansarás!

... Domingo por la tarde llegó al portal de las Salesas de Nuestra Señora un faetón estruendoso y polvoriento.

Acudió el mandadero, y él y el mayoral descargaron cofres, atadijos, cestos de frutas y pastas, ramos, cajas, combrillas, chales y una primorosa jaula de tórtolas.

Presentóse don Jeromillo, carne rural y alma de Dios, que se atolondraba y agoniaba de todo. Vio los equipajes, se agarró la cerviz, corrió hacia el cancel del convento, y desde allí volvió a la portezuela, socorriendo al señor deán, que no podía desdoblar sus hinojos y se quejaba, creyéndose cuajado y oxidado.

Asomó en la zancajera del coche un pie, un tobillo, un vuelo de falda... Y rápidamente se escondió todo dentro de la berlina. Venía una brigada de colegiales de "Jesús", la primera brigada, la de los mayores. Se oyó un grito de la señorita Valcárcel.

– ¡El Ángel!

El señor deán se revolvió consternado.

– ...Con galones de oro y fajín azul... ¡El último de la izquierda! ¡Es el Ángel!

itself to the orphan girl with the spiritual outline and enchantment of a male? The canon was left thinking once again, and he suddenly asked her:

"So why don't you go off to Madrid with your uncle and your aunt?"

"With Uncle Eusebio and that Señora Ivonne-Catherine, Ivette, Kate and I don't know what else? Not even her stepsons can stand her!"

"The fact is I want you to leave Murcia. And besides my wanting it, you need to leave!"

"I would leave here right now!"

"And where will I take you? You've already been to La Visitación.... You were only a small child then! I didn't have to travel in a diligence in order to see you there...."

"Take me to La Visitación!"

"To La Visitación!..."

Many Christian maidens were dexterous copyists of Origen's library.[65] In the convents for women, calligraphy was also an honorable and desirable labor. Oh, if only María Fulgencia were willing!

"Take me to La Visitación immediately and I'll stay there till I get tired!"

"That's the worst part; that you will get tired!"

...On Sunday afternoon, a rackety, dusty phaeton pulled up at the entrance to the Order of the Salesians of Our Lady.

The convent messenger came over and he and the coach driver unloaded trunks, loose bundles, baskets of fruits and pastries, bunches of flowers, boxes, parasols, shawls and an exquisite cage of turtledoves.

Don Jeromillo appeared, a man rustic of body and a soul of God, who always seemed to be bewildered and would agonize over everything. He saw the baggage, grabbed himself by the back of the neck, ran toward the convent storm door, and from there he went back to the carriage door to offer his help to the dean-vicar, who was unable to unbend his knees and kept complaining that he felt congealed and rusted.

A foot, an ankle, the flare of a skirt began to appear on the footboard of the coach.... And very quickly everything was hidden inside the closed compartment. A brigade of schoolboys from "Jesús," the first brigade, the one with the oldest boys, was coming by.[66] A shout from Señorita Valcárcel was heard.

"The Angel!"

The dean-vicar turned around in consternation.

"...With golden braid and a blue sash....[67] The last one on the left! It's the Angel!"

Don Jeromillo se aupó para mirar, se asustó sin entender nada, y saludó al Ángel.

– ¡Ese es Pablito, Pablito Galindo, hijo de don Álvaro, don Álvaro el que se casó con Paulina, la dueña del "Olivar de Nuestro Padre"!...

Pasaron al locutorio de la Visitación, y quedóse María Fulgencia entre las madres, que la besaban llorando y riendo.

Ella sentía un júbilo infantil. Corrió por los claustros, por el hortal, por la sala de labores y de capítulo. Todo lo preguntaba, y decía que de todo se acordaba. Lo creía todo suyo, en una posesión sentimental de sobrina heredera de Nuestra Señora. Abrió los cofres, los arconcillos, las cestas. Derramó sus ropas, sus sartales, sus brinquiños, sus esencias. Repartía flores y dulces; besaba sus tórtolas, meciéndolas en la cuna de su pecho. Quiso ver su aposento; lo engalanó. Pidió vestirse de novicia y profesar cuanto antes. Se llamaría Sor María Fulgencia del Ángel de Getsemaní. En verano se marcharía con toda la comunidad a sus haciendas de Murcia, que ya daban gozo...

La abadesa, blanda y maternal, la sonreía siempre con un dulce estupor de sus arrebatos.

La clavaria, grande, maciza, de ojos abismados por moradas ojeras, que le ponían un antifaz de sombra en sus mejillas granadas de herpes, la miraba con recelos, y hacía un grito áspero de ave en cada retozo de aquel corazón. ¡Cuánto dengue y locura! Se obligó a vigilarla; y se puso a su lado.

De noche en el coro, cuando la Madre dijo:

– Por la salud de nuestro reverendísimo prelado: *Pater Noster...*

María Fulgencia inclinóse hacia la clavaria, preguntándole:

– ¡Cómo ¿Qué le pasa al pobre señor? Será muy viejecito, ¿verdad? ¿Tiene sobrinas?

– ¡Calle y rece!

María Fulgencia no quiso recogerse sin hablar a solas con la Madre, para saber de su ilustrísima. El señor obispo llevaba mucho tiempo recluído en sus habitaciones privadas de Palacio. Le asistía un médico forastero; y aunque se ocultaba con rigor su mal, ya no era posible ignorarlo: su ilustrísima padecía una enfermedad horrible de la piel. Una desgracia para toda la diócesis de Oleza. La señorita Valcárcel imploró que le dieran pronto el hábito para ir a cuidar al venerable enfermo.

Don Jeromillo raised himself up to look, grew frightened without understanding anything and greeted the Angel.

"That's Pablito, Pablito Galindo, Don Álvaro's son, Don Álvaro, the one who married Paulina, the mistress of 'Our Father's Olive Grove'...."

They went into the locutory of La Visitación and María Fulgencia remained there among the mothers, who kept kissing her as they wept and laughed.

She felt a childish jubilation. She ran through the cloisters, through the garden, through the needlework room and the chapter meeting room. She asked everything and said she remembered everything. She thought everything was hers, with a sentimental possessiveness befitting the niece heiress of Our Lady. She opened the trunks, the small chests, the baskets. She spread out her clothes, her strings of beads, her trinkets, her perfumes. She dispersed flowers and sweets; she kissed her turtledoves, rocking them in the cradle of her bosom. She asked to see her room; she started to adorn it. She requested that she be dressed as a novitiate and be allowed to profess immediately. She would be called Sister María Fulgencia of the Angel of Gethsemane. In the summer she would depart with the entire Community for her properties in Murcia, which were then a joy to behold....

The abbess, tender and maternal, always smiled at her with a sweet show of amazement at her raptures.

The keeper of the keys, second in authority, big, solid, with violet rings beneath her sunken eyes, that put a shadowy mask on cheeks covered with herpes granules, kept looking at her suspiciously and would let out a harsh bird-like shout at every playful frolic of that heart. Such girlish affectation and madness! She felt obliged to watch over her and kept close beside her.

At night, in the choir loft, when the mother said:

"To the health of our most reverend prelate: *Pater Noster*...." M a r í a Fulgencia leaned over to the keeper of the keys and asked her:

"What do you mean! What's the matter with the poor man? He must be quite old and frail, am I right? Does he have any nieces?"

"Keep quiet and pray!"

María Fulgencia refused to retire without speaking to the Mother alone, in order to find out about more His Excellency. The lord bishop had been secluded for a long time in his private rooms at the Palace. A doctor from the outside was attending to him; and although his ailment was rigorously being kept secret, it was no longer possible to ignore it: His Excellency was suffering from a horrible disease of the skin. A misfortune for the entire diocese of Oleza. Señorita Valcárcel pleaded with them to grant her the habit quickly so she could go care for the venerable ailing man.

Sonrió la abadesa elogiando su propósito y pidiéndole que se acostara.

– ¿Pablo Galindo? ¿Quién es Pablo Galindo?

Sobresaltóse la Madre, principalmente porque acababa de aparecerse la clavaria, advirtiéndoles que ya reposaba toda la residencia.

A la madrugada, la señorita Valcárcel tuvo congojas. Y desde el segundo día de su ingreso se la vio sumirse en una vida espiritual, ganando en virtudes monásticas.

La clavaria desconfió más. Todas las noches desmenuzaba sus escrúpulos y avisos a la Madre.

– ¡Es menester probarla mucho! Es hija de casa principal, bien lo sé; pero tiene torbellinos en la sangre... Su padre resucitó, y no era ningún santo... ¡Yo no sé, no sé! Sólo digo que es menester probarla mucho.

Gozaba fama de prudente y sabidora en toda la Orden.

Y la abadesa la probó, quedando más confusa. La señorita Valcárcel subía a la virtud de las virtudes, al dejamiento de sí misma en Dios, según palabras del santo fundador. En el regazo divino se recostaba su alma. Pero algunas veces le parecía que el Señor la pusiese en tierra. La ejercitó en todo género de abnegaciones, imitando a Santa María Magdalena de Pazzis cuando fue maestra de novicias. La retiró del coro mandándola que fuese a contar los ladrillos de la sala de costura, y María Fulgencia los contaba haciendo tonada de escuela. La envió al huerto a coger hormigas, y ella las cogía con entusiasmo. La quitó de la oración más interna y sabrosa para que sacase agua del aljibe, y todas, menos la clavaria, la proclamaron humilde y hermosa como la Samaritana. Hasta se la obligó a servir en el refectorio, vestida de sedas de las galas que trajo del siglo, y también vieron todas en esa criatura la suma alegría de la mortificación.

Se supo que su ilustrísima había empeorado. Y la señorita Valcárcel redobló sus penitencias y sus preces.

Todo se lo dijo la Madre al señor deán. Y el señor deán respiró complacido.

– ¡Ya la tenemos encaminada! Hemos acertado. ¡Ni más ni menos!

The abbess smiled as she praised her intention and asked her to go to bed.

"Pablo Galindo? Who is Pablo Galindo?"

The Mother was startled primarily because the keeper of the keys had just appeared, informing them that the entire monastic residence had already retired.

Early the next morning, Señorita Valcárcel was overcome with anguish. And from the second day after her admission, she could be seen to immerse herself in spiritual life, gaining in monastic virtues.

The keeper of the keys grew even more suspicious. Every night she would unravel her scruples and her warnings to the Mother.

"She must be tested a great deal! She is a daughter from an influential house; and I know that very well; but she has whirlwinds in her blood.... Her father came back from the dead, and he was no saint.... I don't know, I don't know! I only say that she must be tested a great deal."

She enjoyed a reputation for prudence and wisdom throughout the entire Order.

And so the abbess tested her and became even more confused. Señorita Valcárcel rose up to the virtue of all virtues, to the abandonment of herself in God, according to the words of the holy founder. Her soul rested in the divine lap.[68] But sometimes it seemed to her that it was the Lord who put her on earth. She exercised her in all manner of abnegation, imitating Santa María Magdalena de Pazzis[69] when she was a teacher of novices. She removed her from the choir and ordered her to go to the sewing room to count the bricks, and María Fulgencia counted them singing a school melody. She sent her to the garden to gather ants and she gathered them with great enthusiasm. She withdrew her from the most inward and savory prayer so she could draw water from the cistern, and everyone, except the keeper of the keys, proclaimed that she was humble and beautiful like the Samaritan woman.[70] They even obliged her to serve in the refectory, dressed in the silks she chose from the finery she brought from the outside world, and all of them also saw the greatest joy in self-mortification in that child.

It was learned that His Excellency had taken a turn for the worse. And Señorita Valcárcel doubled her penances and prayers.

The Mother told all this to the dean-vicar. And the dean-vicar sighed with pleasure.

"Now we have her well on her way! We hit the mark. No more, no less!"

III

SALAS DE OLEZA

DRAWING ROOMS OF OLEZA

1. Vuelven los Lóriz

El conde abrazó a don Magín con elegancia; la condesa le tomó infantilmente las manos entre sus manos. Lóriz semejaba más menudo. Todos los Lóriz, en la madurez – según los lienzos de la sala familiar – , se quedaban cenceños y mínimos. Y este descendiente ya parecía un antepasado suyo, con empaque de reverdecida juventud, esa juventud de las decadencias adobadas por el ayuda de cámara.

– ¿Usted tenía ese lunar en el pómulo? ¡Pues ahora se lo veo!

– ¡Ahora, don Magín, acaba usted de verle a mi marido los ocho años que han pasado encima de nosotros!

Pero don Magín volvióse a la de Lóriz, y la proclamó más perfecta en su gracia que cuando, recién casada, vino a Oleza.

– Entonces era usted una dulce aspiración de la de ahora.

– ¡Ay, don Magín de mi vida, que se le ve su pobre lunar no viendo el mío! ¡Aunque sí que lo vio y demasiado que lo dijo; yo fui – ya no soy – una aspiración de mí misma! Lo más hermoso que se puede ser en este mundo.

Entró Máximo, el hijo. Y don Magín sintió la verdad del tiempo pasado; y ya no pudo valerse de galanas agudezas. En el heredero resalía otro Lóriz, un Lóriz del todo, sin puericias, un Lóriz en la carne y en el hueso; otro antepasado con su pliegue de orgullo y de cansancio en su boca delgada.

Se le quejó la señora de que tratase de *usted* a Máximo. Quería que fuese la escogida y provechosa amistad de su hijo.

– ¡Ya lo creo que seremos dos amigos ejemplares, dos amigos que se tratan de usted!

– ¿Y también le habla de usted al hijo de nuestros vecinos, los encerrados de enfrente?

– ¿A Pablo? Pablo todavía es un zagalillo. No sé aún si ha de quedar sellado con la semejanza del padre o de la madre. En cambio, Máximo ya es

1. The Lorizes Return

The count embraced Don Magín elegantly; the countess took his hands between her hands childishly. Lóriz appeared to be somewhat smaller. All the Lórizes, when they matured – according to the canvases in the family portrait room – eventually assumed a scrawny and diminished appearance. And this descendant already resembled one of his ancestors, with the countenance of an reinvigorated youth, a youthfulness common to physical decay restored through the services of a valet de chambre.

"Did you always have that mole over your cheekbone? Well, I can now see it plainly!"

"Don Magín, what you're just now seeing on my husband are the eight years that have passed over us!"[71]

But Don Magín turned toward the countess of Lóriz and declared that she was even more perfectly charming than when she came to Oleza, recently married.

"You were then but a sweet anticipation of what you are now."

"Oh, my very dear Don Magín, one can see his sad mole and can not see mine as well! And even if you did see it and repeated it: I was – I no longer am – an anticipation of what I am today! As beautiful as one can be in this world."

Their son, Máximo, came in. And Don Magín was aware of the truth of the time that had passed; and he was no longer able to make use of any tasteful witticisms to his advantage. Another Lóriz was emerging in the heir, a complete Lóriz, with no real experience of having had a childhood, a Lóriz in flesh and bone; another ancestor with his wrinkle of pride and weariness on his thin mouth.

The señora complained of his relating to Máximo with the formal *usted*. She wanted him to maintain a favored and advantageous relationship with her son.

"Of course we will be two exemplary friends, two friends who address one another using *usted*!"

"Do you also speak with the *usted* to our neighbors' son, those people who live all closed up across from us?"

"Pablo? Pablo is still a little fellow. I still don't know if he will have his father's or his mother's semblance imprinted on him. Máximo, on the other

todo él; se lleva años a sí mismo. ¡Acabará por ser mayor que su madre!

– ¿De modo que soy la madre de un hijo envejecido?

Lóriz les propuso bajar al huerto, donde murmurarían de Oleza. Necesitaban repasar la crónica antigua y saber la nueva para graduarse de vecinos; porque ahora lo serían hasta que Máximo saliese de "Jesús" con su diploma de bachiller.

– Es voluntad de mi mujer, que parece la descendiente de mis abuelos olecenses. Cuando ya me creí tranquilo en mi Círculo, se le ocurre acordarse de que tenemos fincas en Oleza, de que hay familias madrileñas que traen sus hijos a "Jesús" de Oleza. ¡Pues nosotros también; todos a "Jesús": Máximo, de interno, y yo, de externo! ¡La salvación, don Magín!

La hermosa señora le contuvo sonriéndole como a un hijo malcriado.

– ¡Si no la salvación, puede ser este retiro nuestra restauración!

El jardín de casa Lóriz estaba cerrado por un claustro de piedra morena; y de allí recibían las salas y las galerías de tránsito una claridad académica y un silencio estremecido por hilos de fuentes y cantos de mirlos. Árboles grandes trenzados de yedras; almenas y bolas de romeros; glorietas de rosales, de glycinas y jazmines con bancos y estatuas; hornacinas con lotos y lámparas de cuencos de cactos; medallones de bojes, y en medio un albercón de agua inmóvil y celeste, que duplicaba la arquitectura de piedra y de follajes. Se alzaban y venían los palomos parándose en los jarrones de las cornisas. Se soltaban las bayas de las simientes y se las oía caer mucho tiempo, dejando un olor maduro. Atravesaba la fronda un humo de sol y se producía un fresco amanecer en los troncos y en los escondidos paisajes de musgos.

Lóriz se cansó de pisar hojas que crujían como huesos. Los senderos y arriates siempre estaban en un otoño húmedo. Resonaba la voz de don Magín:

– Nos hemos quedado sin don Vicente Grifol, el viejecito más puro que teníamos. Estaba en su butaca jugando con sus anteojos y el bastoncito en sus rodillas, como si fuera a levantarse para dar su paseo por la calle de la Verónica, y se nos fue a pasear por la plaza del cielo. Murió también mosén Orduña, el arqueólogo. Había completado las papeletas de su *Iconografía*

hand, is already completely himself; he looks years older than he is. He'll end up looking even older than his mother!"

"So I am the mother of a son grown old before his time?"

Lóriz proposed that they go down to the garden where they could gossip about Oleza. They needed to review the old history and learn what was new in order to qualify as good neighbors; because that was what they were going to be until Máximo left "Jesús" with his baccalaureate diploma.

"It's my wife's inclination, because she seems to be the one descended from my Olezan grandparents. Just when I thought I'd found tranquility at my Club, she happens to remember we own farm property in Oleza, that there are families from Madrid who bring their sons to 'Jesús' in Oleza. Well, we have too; everybody to 'Jesús': Máximo as a boarding student and I as a day student! Our salvation, Don Magín!"

The lovely señora restrained him by smiling at him as if he were an ill-bred child.

"If not salvation, this retreat can be our restoration!"

The garden of the Lóriz house was enclosed by a cloister of dark stone; and it was from here that the drawing rooms as well as the galleries used as passageways received an academic brightness and silence perturbed only by the spurting of fountains and the singing of blackbirds. Tall trees braided with ivy; shrubs of rosemary cut in the shape of merlons and balls; bowers with rosebushes, wisteria and jasmine, with benches and statues; vaulted niches filled with lotus plants and lamps carved from hollowed out cactus; medallions formed out of boxwood, and in the midst of all this, a large pool of motionless, sky-blue water that reflected the architecture of stone and foliage. The ringdoves rose up into the air and returned, resting on the urns of the cornices. The fruits and berries kept breaking loose and dropping, and you could hear them falling for some time, leaving behind an aroma of ripeness. A streamer of sunlight crossed through a frond and produced a fresh dawn in the trunks and the hidden landscapes of moss.

Lóriz grew weary of stepping on leaves that crackled like bones. The paths and flowerbeds on the sides seemed as if they were in a perpetual humid autumn. Don Magín's voice resounded:

"We are bereft of Don Vicente Grifol, the purest little old man we had. He was seated in his armchair playing with his eyeglasses, with his favorite cane upon his knees, just as if he were going to stand up to go for a stroll along the Calle de la Verónica, and he departed from us to stroll along the heavenly plaza. *Mosén* Orduña, the archeologist, also died. He had completed his file cards for his research for his *Marian Iconography* of the diocese. I once

Mariana, de la diócesis. Yo conseguí que viese desnuda la imagen de Nuestra Señora de la Visitación. Encendimos toda la cera del altar mayor. Fue en la madrugada. La comunidad le miraba desde el coro. Una monjita le preguntó: "¿Verdad que la modelaron los ángeles?" Mosén Orduña volvióse y gritó tendiendo sus enormes brazos temblorosos: "¡Ese Niño, ese Niño es italiano; ese Niño no es su Hijo!" Mosén Orduña es el siervo de Dios que ha dicho más irreverencias en este mundo.

Entre dos pilares de murtas recortadas apareció el mayordomo, todo de paño negro y patillas blancas de contramaestre, y anunció que el chocolate estaba servido; el chocolate de casa rica del siglo xix.

Pero la señora antes de subir, les llevó a la sala del entresuelo. Después de la lumbre oriental de otro patio interior desnudo, la vieja estancia de artesones y tapices apagados quedaba en una fresca obscuridad de sótano.

– ¡Párese usted, don Magín, y mire la alfombra.

El párroco la obedeció. Poco a poco fue exhalando la mullida tiniebla unas rápidas luces, unas fosforescencias desgranadas.

– No sé lo que es, pero esos brillos deben de tener un tacto glacial.

Abrieron los postigos y persianas, y vio don Magín el hermoso fanal de una pecera.

– Aquí tengo peces del Jordán, del Nilo y de las fuentes del Vaticano.

Y el conde añadió:

– Una maravilla sagrada que hemos traído a cuestas desde Madrid, por orden de mi mujer.

Bendijo don Magín la abnegación de Lóriz; y subieron al gabinete, donde les esperaba la merienda española.

En aquel aposento se juntaban muebles de distintos estilos y épocas. Butacones de guadamecí y, como estrado, una banca tallada de presbiterio; una mesa camilla vestida de ropa de cachemira y detrás un pilar de retablo sosteniendo una Juno de piedra; un reloj de pesas, como un violoncello, entre un velador de taraceas y una consola con bernegales de cerámica dorada; lacrimatorios tan sutiles que sólo de hablar junto a sus bordes se quedaban vibrando con una dulce queja; y en una preciosa cómoda de olivo labrado como un mármol, dos vasos de Etruria, dos legítimos *vasi di bucchero nero*.

succeeded in having him see the unadorned image of Nuestra Señora de la Visitación. We lit up all the candles on the high altar. It happened at the break of day. The Community watched him from the choir loft. A young nun asked him, 'Is it true that the angels shaped it?' *Mosén* Orduña turned around and shouted, stretching out his enormous trembling arms, 'That Child, that Child is Italian; that Child is not her Son!' Mosén Orduña is the humble servant of God who has made the most irreverent remarks in this world."[72]

The major-domo appeared from between two basins filled with clipped myrtle, all dressed in the black woolen cloth and white pocket flaps of a boatswain, and he announced that chocolate was served; the chocolate typical of a wealthy household in the XIXth century.

But before they went up, the señora led them to the parlor on the entresol. After the oriental brilliance of another bare inside patio, the old room with its toned-down coffers and tapestries was possessed of the cool darkness of a cellar.

"Just stop and look at the rug, Don Magín!"

The priest obeyed her. Little by little, the soft, downy darkness began to breathe swift flashes of light, scattered particles of phosphorescence.

"I don't know what it is, but the brilliant flashes must feel glacial to the touch."

They opened the shutters and the blinds and Don Magín saw the beautiful glass covering of a fish tank.

"I have fish from the Jordan, the Nile and the Vatican fountains here."

And the count added:

"A sacred marvel that we have brought all the way from Madrid at my wife's insistence and with considerable difficulty."

Don Magín blessed Lóriz's abnegation; and they went upstairs to the sitting room where the Spanish style luncheon was awaiting them.

Furniture of varied styles and periods were gathered together in that room. Great big armchairs of embossed leather and, as sitting room furnishings, an elaborately carved bench from a presbytery; a round table with a brazier below and a cashmere covering draped over it and a pillar from a retable supporting a stone figure of Juno behind it; a grandfather's clock shaped like a violin cello, standing between a pedestal table with inlaid work and a console table with scallop-edged drinking cups of gilded ceramic ware; lachrymal vases so delicately made that just by speaking close to their edges, they would continue vibrating in a sweet lament; and two Etrurian vases, two legitimate *vasi di bucchero nero (vases of black earthenware),* on an exquisite commode made of olive wood carved like a piece of marble.

– Mi marido se ríe de esta almoneda; pero no importa. Pruebe usted esos concos de Inca. Oleza y Mallorca son los obradores de nuestra felicidad casera. En este cuarto he puesto lo que más me agrada. Mi marido es un crítico agrio, de esos críticos que delante de un cuadro, casi siempre mi cuadro predilecto, grita escandalizado: "Si esa figura que está sentada se levantase, se saldría del lienzo!" Yo no me apuro, porque sé que esa figura no se levantará. ¡Claro que yo no entiendo de estas cosas; pero a los aficionados no se nos va también a pedir que seamos inteligentes!

Lóriz la escuchaba recostado en sus almohadones y en su desgana de ese bullicio palabrero que le parecía muy de clase media de España y sus colonias. Tomó un sorbo de leche de almendras y suspiró:

– Cuéntenos usted más de este pueblo, porque no vale la pena de hablar de lo que nos va quedando. ¡La más humilde sacristía de Oleza nos aventaja en lujos y curiosidades!

La señora recordó el viaje a Madrid de su ilustrísima. Le tuvieron una tarde en su casa, y Lóriz le acompañaba en todos sus trajines para lograr el principio de las obras del ferrocarril.

– Estas gentes deben sentirse prendadas de nuestro obispo, que se cuida de abrirles caminos para el cielo y para el mundo.

Don Magín balanceó su testa imperial encanecida.

– El mundo de estas gentes no pasa de sus corrillos ni de sus haciendas; y ponen toda su gloria en vender la naranja, el aceite y el cáñamo en el bancal.

Lóriz le dijo confidencialmente:

– Su ilustrísima no se quitó los guantes ni la bufanda; guantes gruesos, bufanda rígida como una venda morada.

Pero don Magín se entretuvo rebañando infantil y eclesiásticamente su pocillo de soconusco sin reparar en la especulación suntuaria de Lóriz.

Lóriz sonrió para decir:

– Una pregunta indiscreta, que usted hará el milagro de que no lo sea: ¿Es verdad que nuestro obispo y los Padres de "Jesús" se tienen menos amor que usted y el penitenciario?

"My husband laughs at this auction sale accumulation of mine, but it makes no difference to me. Why don't you try one of those sweet egg muffins made by the sisters in the convent in Inca. Oleza and Mallorca are the workshops that have fashioned the happiness of our home. I have placed whatever pleases me most in this room. My husband is a bitter critic, one of those critics who is scandalized when he stands before a painting, almost always my favorite painting, and shouts, 'If that figure seated there were to get up, it would leave the canvas altogether!' I'm not at all worried because I know that figure will not get up. Of course, I don't understand these things; but they're not going to ask aficionados like us to be knowledgeable as well!"

Lóriz listened to her as he leaned back against the great big cushions, as he showed his distaste for all this wordy commotion that seemed to him so typical of Spain's middle class and its colonies. He took a sip of his sweet almond drink and sighed:

"Tell us more about this town, because it isn't worth our while to keep on talking about what we've been accumulating here. The humblest sacristy in Oleza has the advantage over us in luxurious items and curiosities!"

The señora recalled His Excellency's trip to Madrid. They had him at their house one afternoon and Lóriz accompanied him on all of his comings and goings in order to facilitate the inception of the construction of the railway.

"These people around here must feel captivated by our bishop, who is so careful to open the roads to heaven and to the world for them."

Don Magín rocked his imperial, gray-haired head.

"The world of these people here does not pass beyond their little coteries and their properties, and they put all their glory into the sale of the oranges, the olive oil and the hemp from their orchards and fields."

Lóriz confidentially said to him:

"His Excellency doesn't take off his gloves or his muffler; thick, heavy gloves, a stiff muffler like a purple bandage."

But Don Magín entertained himself by draining the last of his small cup of Mexican chocolate in a childish and ecclesiastical manner without taking any notice of Lóriz's sumptuous speculation.

Lóriz smiled as he said:

"An indiscreet question which you will miraculously turn into one that is not: Is it true that our bishop and the Fathers of "Jesús" have less love for one another than you and the canon-penitentiary?"

– El penitenciario y yo nos tenemos un amor literalmente evangélico. Y el confesor de su ilustrísima es un jesuita de "Jesús".

Recibieron los Lóriz una claridad de júbilo. "Jesús" se elevaba en jerarquía.

¿De "Jesús"? Será el Padre Rector, o el Padre Prefecto, o el Padre Espiritual, o el Padre...

– Es el P. Ferrando. De seguro que no lo conocen ustedes. Un viejecito humilde como un párroco de la huerta.

Y les contó que casi todos los días se paraba en el portón de los corrales del colegio un carro de heredad, o un labrador con su mula, y se llevaban al P. Ferrando dentro de sus adrales o encima del albardón. Le buscaban para confesar gentes pobres de la ribera; y al salir de la barraca del moribundo le llamaban de otras, aunque nadie estuviera muriéndose, para que también se dejase aviado al padre o al abuelo tullido o con tercianas. El P. Ferrando iba de senda en senda. Volvía a "Jesús" a la madrugada. El Hermano portero le recibía rojo de malhumor y de sueño. El P. Ferrando, encogido y sudado, le refería las faenas de la salvación de aquella viña que el Señor le tenía encomendada. ¡Qué duras, qué pesadas esas almas para soltarse de sus cuerpos; pero en el cielo resplandecerían lo mismo que los bienaventurados de las mejores familias! El P. Ferrando caminaba por los claustros, subía por escaleras de servicio, atravesaba salas, corredores, pasadizos, anda que andarás, para llegar a su aposento, el último de una crujía alta del patio de la tahona.

Y ese jesuita, que semejaba calzado y vestido con lo viejo de la comunidad, era el escogido entre todos los religiosos de la diócesis y entre todos los Reverendos Padres de la casa para penetrar en la conciencia del prelado. A sus pies se arrodillaba su ilustrísima. Teólogos, moralistas, predicadores, honra del confesonario, verdaderos especialistas de la medicina pastoral, no podían esconder su sonrisa y su asombro. "¿El P. Ferrando? Pero, ¿de veras el P. Ferrando? Bueno; ¡el P. Ferrando!" Y algunos eminentes de "Jesús" le daban palmadas en sus hombros, sacando de su hábito polvo y olor de pesebres. Semejaba un abuelo que vive recogido en casa de los hijos que han criado con holgura ya familia, y del que todavía pueden recibir algunos ahorros.

"The canon-penitentiary and I have a literally evangelical love for one another. And His Excellency's confessor is a Jesuit from 'Jesús'."

The Lórizes received a brilliant flash of jubilation. "Jesús" was rising hierarchically.

"From 'Jesús'? It must be the Rector Father or the Prefect Father or the Spiritual Counsellor Father or the Father who...."

"It is Father Ferrando. Of course you don't know him. A gentle, humble old man like a simple parish priest from cultivated plain."

And he told them that almost every day, a farm wagon or a farmer and his mule would stop at the gate to the school barnyard, and they would take Father Ferrando between the sideboards or on top of the saddle pad. They used to come looking for him so he could hear confession from the poor souls living along the river bank; and when he would leave the dying man's shack, they would call to him from other houses, even though nobody was dying, so that he might leave a father or a paralyzed grandfather or someone with tertian fever better prepared for what was to come. Father Ferrando would travel from one country road to another. He would return to "Jesús" very early in the morning. The Brother serving as gatekeeper would receive him ill-humoredly flushed and sleepy. Father Ferrando, timid and sweaty, would give him an account of the chores undertaken by him for the salvation of that vineyard the Lord had entrusted to him. How obstinate and weighty those souls were when they were compelled to abandon their bodies; but they would be ever so resplendent in heaven just like those blissful souls from the very best families! Father Ferrando would walk through the cloisters, ascend the service stairway, cross through all manner of rooms, corridors, passageways, moving determinedly, till he reached his own room, the last one along a hallway high up over the bakery patio.

And that Jesuit, who typified the oldest aspect of the Community in his shoes and clothing, was the one chosen from among all the clergymen of the diocese and among all the Reverend Fathers of the House, to penetrate the conscience of the prelate. His Excellency would kneel down at his feet. Theologians, professors of ethics, preachers, the very cream of the confessional, true specialists in pastoral medicine, could hardly conceal their smiles and their astonishment. "Father Ferrando? But really, Father Ferrando? All right then; Father Ferrando!" And several of the eminences of "Jesús" would slap him on the back, shaking out the dust and the odor of the fodder trough from his habit. He resembled a grandfather who lives withdrawn in his children's home after they have happily reared a family and who still entertain the hope of receiving some of his savings.

Don Magín proseguía su crónica menuda de Oleza:

– Murió la madre de "Cara-rajada", y como no pueden faltar amortajadoras en una buena república, tenemos a doña Nieves de las Agonías, que también ejerce oficio de santera, y no hay oración ni secreto que se le pase. Entra en todas las casas, participa de todas las tertulias, lo mismo de la de doña Corazón, que se nos quedó baldada, que de la de las *Catalanas,* dos solteronas con dineros y sin sobrinos, acosadas por la Monera y doña Elvira, las enemigas de doña Purita. Esta doña Purita, tan hermosa, que ustedes ya conocen desde mi herida de "San Daniel", ha de venir muy pronto a verles, porque quiere muy de verdad a la condesa.

– Nosotros – exclamó Lóriz en nombre de la casa – , nosotros también la queremos y la recordamos.

Ese tono de "nos" pastoral no pudo impedir que la condesa y don Magín le mirasen el lunar del pómulo, el lunar que crían los años.

El párroco se había levantado y hablaba paseando como si estuviese en su aposento rectoral. Verdadera falta de elegancia – según Lóriz – , resabio plebeyo de los célibes y de los capellanes y frailes españoles. Pero Lóriz se lo perdonaba todo a don Magín, que se detuvo en la vidriera y le envió su saludo a Paulina. Ella le sonrió inclinándose sobre su costura.

Se le acercaron los condes para mirarla. Y se empañó el cristal de la sala de don Álvaro con la cabeza lívida de Elvira.

– ¡Carne azul que morirás intacta! Aunque también puedan morir lo mismo criaturas admirables como Purita...

– ¿Doña Purita o Purita sigue...?

– Sigue soltera – anticipóse don Magín – . Y en que lo fuese siempre se obstinó su familia y todo este pueblo.

– ¿Pero es que este pueblo no da hombres para mujeres como ella?

– ¡Ay, señora, aquí los únicos célibes somos los capellanes y don Amancio, que se ha dejado la barba!

Y don Magín tomó y comió primorosamente una pella de las clarisas de San Gregorio. Lóriz tuvo que confesarse que ni en la Gran Peña, ni en la Nunciatura, ni en el Ministerio de Estado se comía el dulce con el patricio regodeo de don Magín.

Don Magín continued with his trivial chronicle of Oleza:

"'Scar-face's' mother died, and since there can be no shortage of enshrouders in any good republic, we have Doña Nieves de las Agonías, who also serves the function of bearer of the portable sanctuary, and there isn't a prayer or a secret that gets by her. She goes into everyone's house, participates in all social gatherings, whether it be at Doña Corazón's, who ended up crippled, or at the home of the *Catalan Sisters*, two spinsters with a great deal of money and no nieces or nephews, who are being relentlessly pursued by the Monera woman and Doña Elvira, Doña Purita's enemies. This Doña Purita, lovely as she is, whom you already know from the time of my injury at 'San Daniel,' must come to see you very soon because she truly has a great affection for the countess."

"We," Lóriz exclaimed in the name of his house, "we also love her and remember her."

That tone of a pastoral "we" could not prevent the countess and Don Magín from looking at the mole over his cheekbone, the mole that grows with the years.

The parish priest had gotten to his feet and went on speaking as he walked back and forth as if he were at his room at the rectory. A real lack of elegance – according to Lóriz – a bad plebeian habit common to celibates and Spanish priests and friars. But Lóriz forgave Don Magín for everything as he stopped in front of the glass windows and sent Paulina his greeting. She smiled at him as she bent over her sewing.

The count and countess came over to him in order to look at her. And the windowpanes of Don Álvaro's drawing room were blurred by Elvira's livid head.

"Virginal blue who will die untouched! Although admirable creatures like Purita may die like that too...."

"Doña Purita or Purita is still...?"

"She is still unmarried," Don Magín said anticipating her. "And her family and this whole town persisted in having her always remain that way."

"But is it possible that this town offers no man for women like her?"

"Oh, señora, the only celibate men here are the priests and Don Amancio, who has let his beard grow long!"

And Don Magín took a cream puff made by the Clares of San Gregorio and ate it fastidiously. Lóriz had to confess that not even on the Rock of Gibraltar, nor in the Nuncio's residence, nor in the Foreign Ministry did anyone eat a sweet with such patrician delight as Don Magín.

– Yo quiero a Purita tanto como a Paulina. Hace mucho tiempo, recién
ordenado, con ilusiones de llegar a organista de la catedral más grande,
salté un día de la banqueta de mi armonium y corrí a una casa vecina toda
alborotada. Había muerto un nene; pero ya estaba tan bien plañido, que yo
no esperaba que se recalentase el guayadero de las comadres hasta la hora
de enterrarlo. Y encontré un torbellino de mujeres gordas y de pelo colorado
que gritaban como si fuesen flacas. Eran las de López-Canci, las *Panizas,*
madre y cuatro hijas, y en medio, Purita, muy pequeña, vestida de sobrina,
con el niño muerto en sus brazos. La golpeaban y gritaban; y Purita, sin
comprenderlas, gemía: "Yo no lo romperé!" En la Purita de ahora se me
aparece la nena de entonces, jugando a dormir un hijo con un mortichuelo.
¡Y esa criatura se ha quedado soltera!

Sonó el estrépito de un carruaje sin alborozo de collerones, carruaje de
luto. Los Lóriz se asomaron como si ya fuesen lugareños de verdad. Era el
faetón del obispo. Iba un familiar acompañando a un médico forastero que
venía casi todos los meses.

Pero don Magín no lo dijo. Don Magín se acomodó en su butaca, porque
la condesa quería saber más de Purita.

– Creció y se hizo hermosa. ¿Y para qué había de llegar a mujer tan
garrida sino para casarse? Pero estaba recogida por su tía. De modo que
en la casa no había más mozas casaderas que las hijas. Lo menos que
podía hacer Purita era aguardarse y aguantarse. Así lo dispuso su tía y lo
quisieron sus primas y lo aceptaron las gentes. Tienen las mujeres días
en que parecen, o son de veras, más guapas que nunca. Purita los tuvo y
los tiene tan admirables, que hasta semeja emanar la belleza y la gracia
de su vida, esparciéndolas más allá de su persona. Yo lo he oido y lo he
pensado algunas veces viéndola en su ventana: "¡Madre mía, cómo está hoy
esa mujer!" ¡Todo en ella, cada instante de su cuerpo, coincidiendo para la
perfección, respirando hermosura!

Lóriz sentóse a su lado, diciéndole:

– Vive usted, don Magín, holgadamente debajo de su hábito...

– Sí, querido conde; llevé siempre la sotana sin sentirla, pero ajustada
como sí fuese mi piel, porque Dios me ha librado de que me pese como

"I love Purita as I do Paulina. A long time ago, when I had just been ordained and was entertaining the illusion of getting to be the organist in the greatest cathedral, I jumped up from the bench of my harmonium one day and ran to a nearby house that was in a high state of agitation. A baby had died, but they had already been wailed over it so well that I didn't expect excitement in the room reserved for weeping by the neighborhood women to die down until time for the burial. And I found a whirlwind of fat women with red-colored hair shouting so loudly that you would think they were skinny. The López-Canci women were there, with the *Panizas*, mother and four daughters,[73] and Purita in the middle, very small, dressed as a niece, with the dead child in her arms. They kept hitting her and shouting and Purita, without understanding them, kept moaning, 'I won't break it!' That little girl from way back then appears to me in today's Purita, playing at putting her baby to sleep with that poor little dead infant. And that creature has remained unmarried!"

The racket of a carriage without the merry jingling of a fancy horse collar could be heard, a funeral carriage. The Lórizes ran over to look outside as if they were already real town residents. It was the bishop's phaeton. A familiar was riding it, accompanying an out-of-town doctor who came almost every month.

But Don Magín didn't say so. Don Magín made himself comfortable in his armchair because the countess wanted to know more about Purita.

"She grew up and turned into a beauty. And why was it necessary to get to be so attractive a woman if not to get married? But she was forced into a cloistered existence by her aunt. So that there be no other marriageable girls in the house than the daughters. The least Purita could do was wait and put up with it. That's how her aunt decreed it and how her cousins wanted it and how people accepted it. There are days when women seem, or really are, more beautiful than ever. Purita had and still has such wonderful days, and it's as if she allowed beauty and grace to emanate from her life, strewing them far beyond her person. I've heard it and I've thought it a number of times when I saw her at her window: 'Good heavens, how beautiful that woman looks today!' Everything in her, every instant of her body, coinciding to attain perfection, breathing beauty!"

Lóriz sat down beside him and said:

"Don Magín, you live quite comfortably beneath your habit...."

"Yes, my dear count; I always wore my cassock without feeling its presence upon me, simply fitted, as if it were my skin, because God has

las vestiduras de plomo de los hipócritas de Dante... Pues decía que las primas de Purita, de las que se ha murmurado su afán de marido y su antojo de convento, las primas, viéndola tan hermosa, se revolvían erizadas: "¡No mira lo que hacemos por ella! ¡Será capaz de casarse antes que ninguna de nosotras!" Muchas familias participaban de sus recelos y agravios; y los posibles novios, tan moderados aquí, pasan de largo. Diálogos con varón en su casa no se le permiten sino con don Roger. Ya verán a don Roger en el Colegio de "Jesús". Figura nueva para ustedes. Un buen hombre que ha cantado óperas por esos mundos. Habla un poco de italiano y de francés. Le refiere a Purita sus jornadas en todos sus idiomas; y ésta es la última alarma de las mujeres y la imagen de perversidad de los hombres de aquí: que Purita pueda amar y pecar en español, en francés y en italiano.

Le interrumpieron las risas de los Lóriz.

– Y ya no queda qué decir; o queda lo mismo por muchos años: Purita o doña Purita no se casa. Y no se casa porque todavía tiene dos primas solteras, y porque es demasiado hermosa y demasiado señalada por la malicia. ¡Parece capaz de todo! Y yo la proclamo la más casta y la más virgen de todas las solteras de la diócesis; y doy la medida más grande de nuestra latitud de amor. Ahora hablemos de Paulina. Pero no hablemos más, porque alguien viene cuando sus vecinos, los facciosos, se asoman y acechan este portal!

Y don Magín se despidió, y dos Padres de "Jesús" se presentaron en visita de cortesía antes del ingreso de Máximo en el colegio. Ingresaba privilegiadamente ya mediado el curso académico.

Abrióse un balcón de los de Lóriz, y la condesa llamó a don Magín.

– ¡Que me traiga usted pronto a Purita!

Todo se sintió desde el escritorio del caballero de Gandía.

Don Amancio Espuch, el penitenciario, el P. Bellod, se prometieron los males de tanta tolerancia. Y llegarían dias peores.

freed me from having it weigh heavily upon me like the lead garments of Dante's hypocrites....[74] Well, I was saying that Purita's cousins, about whom it has been whispered that they long for husbands and have only a capricious desire for the convent, these cousins, when they see her so beautiful, twist and turn and bristle with envy and say, 'She doesn't appreciate how much we do for her! She's probably capable of getting married before any one of us!' Many families shared their misgivings and offended feelings, and so any possible suitors, so very limited in number around here, simply pass her by. A conversation with a man in her house is only permitted with Don Roger. You will soon see Don Roger at the Colegio de 'Jesús.' A new face for you. A fine fellow who has sung operas all over the world. He speaks a little Italian and French. He recounts his travels to Purita in all his languages, and this is the ultimate cause of alarm for the women and the image of perversity for the men around here: that Purita might love and sin in Spanish, in French and in Italian."

He was interrupted by the laughter of the Lórizes.

"So now there's nothing left to say; or it may just remain the same for many years to come: Purita or Doña Purita is not going to get married. And she's not getting married because she still has two unmarried cousins and because she is too pretty and malicious tongues allude to her all too often. She seems capable of everything! And I proclaim her the most chaste, the most virginal of all the unmarried women in the diocese, and I grant the greatest measure of latitude for our love. Now let's talk about Paulina. But let's not talk any more, because someone must be coming when your neighbors, those factious agitators, peer out their windows and spy on the doorway here."

And Don Magín took his leave of them and two Fathers from "Jesús" introduced themselves as part of a courtesy call before Máximo's enrollment at the school. He was entering as a privileged student, it now being the middle of the academic year.

A balcony window at the Lóriz house opened and the countess called to Don Magín:

"Please bring Purita to me as soon as you can!"

Everything was overheard from the study of the gentleman from Gandía.

Don Amancio Espuch, the canon-penitentiary and Father Bellod assured one another of the evils of so much tolerance. And worse days would follow.

Precisamente llegaba un ruido de azadas, no de azadas agrícolas, frescas, primitivas, sino un ruido de azadonazos rectos, unánimes, disciplinados que rajaban el campo para tender las traviesas y vías del ferrocarril.

Oleza parecía sobrecogerse escuchando a lo lejos.

2. Antorchas de pecado

Llegó una multitud. Había catalanes, andaluces, extremeños, valencianos y "gabachos". Ingenieros y sobrestantes franceses, grandes y rubios. Listeros, capataces, furrieles. Un ejército de invasión, con sus carros y toldos; y, como a todos los ejércitos, le seguía una nube de galloferos, de mercaderes y abastecedores de sensualidades. De Andalucia y de Orán venían mozas galanas, como la *Argelina* de tan curiosos afeites, olores y ringorrangos, que las pobres mujeres pecadoras del país se paraban y se volvían mirándola con ojos de mujeres honradas.

Cualquier bracero del ferrocarril comía y bebía con más rumbo que toda una família hidalga. Algunas cosas, entre ellas los dulces monásticos, encarecieron un poco. Se instalaron figones y botillerías, con tablado para cante; y de noche volcaban en Oleza el vaho de los ajenjos y frituras, el trueno del fandango, la brama de los refocilos.

Oraciones, labor de aguja, tertulias recogidas se contenían por oír los huracanes de la abominación. Y en el silencio se desgarraba una risa de mujer. Las señoras, entre ellas las *Catalanas,* que tuvieron tienda de tejidos, no se explicaban que esas infelices pudieran estar solas con tantos hombres.

Al amanecer, los ingenieros se bañaban desnudos en el río. Después, salían todos al trabajo; y Oleza se quedaba inocente y tímida bajo las campanas y esquilones de sus conventos y parroquias.

Don Cruz, don Amancio, el P. Bellod, lo miraban todo con amargura. ¡Se habían cumplido sus profecías!

Don Magín y el síndico Cortina les dijeron muy socarrones:

– ¡Todo pasa, y esas gentes también pasarán!

El P. Bellod, el mastín del rebaño blanco de las vírgenes de Oleza, redobló la furia de su castidad.

To be precise, there came a sound of hoes, not that of agricultural hoes, fresh and primitive, but rather a deafening sound of powerful strokes of hoes, straight, unanimous, disciplined, slicing through the countryside to extend the ties and the tracks of the railroad.

Oleza seemed to feel apprehensive as it listened in the distance.

2. Torches of Sin

A multitude arrived. There were Catalans, Andalusians, Estremenians, Valencians and "Frenchies." French engineers and foremen, big and blond. Roll takers, overseers, quartermasters. An army of invasion with its wagons and canvas tilts; and, like all armies, it was followed by a swarm of drifters, traders and purveyors of sensual pleasures. Young women of easy virtue came from Andalusia and Oran,[75] like the *Algerian woman*, with such curious make-up, scents and frippery that the poor local women of sin would stop and turn around to stare at her with the eyes of respectable women.

Any day laborer on the railroad ate and drank with greater extravagance than an entire family of noble descent. A number of things, among them the sweets made by monastic hands, grew a little more expensive. Cheap eating houses and refreshment bars were set up along with a stage for popular songs; and by night, the vapors of absinthe and fried foods, the thunder of the fandango, the roar of all that merriment disrupted the life of Oleza.

Prayers, needlework, quiet social gatherings were repressed when they heard the hurricanes of abomination. And a woman's laughter would rend the silence. The señoras, among them the *Catalan Sisters,* who owned a fabric store, could not understand how those wretched women could be by themselves among so many men.

At dawn, the engineers bathed naked in the river. Afterwards, they would all leave for work; and Oleza was left behind, innocent and timid beneath its church bells and large hand bells of its convents and parish churches.

Don Cruz, Don Amancio, Father Bellod looked at it all with bitterness. Their prophesies had come to pass!

Don Magín and Cortina, the syndic, told them somewhat in jest:

"Everything passes and those people will pass too!"

Father Bellod, the mastiff in charge of the white flock of the virgins of Oleza, redoubled the fury of his chastity.

– ¡Ya lo creo que se han de ir; pero cómo dejarán este pueblo!

De sus justas alarmas se comunicó el Círculo de Labradores y el colegio de "Jesús". Algunos corazones pusieron su confianza en Palacio.

Palacio callaba. Demasiada indiferencia habiendo contribuído a la venida de esas gentes. Ellas traerían el ferrocarril, un acierto, una mejora para algunas concupiscencias. Que a cambio de esas ganancias no se perdieran otros bienes: era el parecer de los amigos del penitencíario.

Por algo lo decían. Porque hubo familias que acogían ya en sus casas a los extranjeros, y les agasajaban. Algunas doncellas recatadas les miraban, les sonreían y acabaron por comparar esos hombres robustos y generosos con los reconcentrados de la Juventud Católica. Muchos viejos recordaban que, en otro tiempo, las mujeres de Oleza, tan tímidas y devotas, se habían montado a la grupa de los caballos de los facciosos, bendiciendo y besando a sus jinetes, colgándoles escapularios y reliquias, dándoles a beber en sus manos y ofreciéndoles frutas rajadas con su boca encendida.

Ese contraste del arrebatado fervor, de la pasión de la hembra olecense con su hurañía, su cortedad, su fácil sonrojo y la tristeza de su vida de clausura, lo atribuía también don Amancio Espuch a una irresistible herencia iberomusulmana.

Los más alborazados con los invasores fueron los del "Nuevo Casino", que para escarnio de las conciencias puras se fundó en la acera del puente de los Azudes, es decir, en recinto de la parroquia de Nuestro Padre San Daniel. En los ruedos de mecedoras y en torno de las mesas de billar se celebraba cada noticia de las jácaras y libertades de los bárbaros. El síndico Cortina elevó los brazos y se torció desperezándose. Como él era todo Oleza: un bostezo. El anterior obispo, andaluz y jinete, debió morir de murria. No había más pasatiempos que los aprobados por la comunidad de "Jesús" y por la comunidad del penitenciario. Procesiones de Semana Santa; juntas de las cofradías; coloquios de señoras con señoras, de hombres con hombres; tertulias de archivos; comedías de Navidad en el *De Profundis* de "Jesús". Allí, el público, de familias de alumnos, había de sentarse con separación de

"Of course they will have to leave eventually; but in what state will they leave this town!"

The Farmers' Club[76] and the school of "Jesús" made known their justifiable feeling of alarm to one another. A number of hearts placed their trust in the Palace.

The Palace remained silent. Too much indifference had contributed to those people's arrival. They would bring the railroad, a great accomplishment, an improvement for certain people's concupiscence. But in exchange for these gains, other advantages would surely be lost: that was the opinion of the canon-penitentiary's friends.

They had good reasons for saying it. Because there were families who were already welcoming the foreigners into their homes and entertaining them extravagantly. A number of modest young ladies kept looking at them and smiling at them and ended up comparing those robust and generous men with the withdrawn types in the Catholic Youth. Many old people recalled that, at another time, the Olezan women, so timid and devout, had mounted the rumps of the rebel soldiers' horses, blessing and kissing the riders, hanging scapulars and relics on them, giving them drinks in their hands and offering them slices of fruit, their mouths burning with passion.[77]

Don Amancio Espuch also attributed that contrast between the impetuous fervor and passion in the Olezan female and her customary diffidence, her shyness, her tendency to quickly blush and the sadness of her cloistered life to an irresistible Ibero-Muslim heritage.

Those most overjoyed with the presence of the invaders were the ones in the "New Club,"[78] which was established, as if to ridicule all those of pure conscience, on the very pavement of the Bridge of the Waterwheels, that is to say, in the area around the parish church of Our Father San Daniel. Every bit of news concerning the revelry and the liberties taken by the barbarians was celebrated in the coteries of rocking chairs and around the billiard tables. Cortina, the syndic, raised his arms, all twisted with desperation. All of Oleza was just like him: a yawn. The previous bishop, an Andalusian and a horseman, must have died of low spirits.[79] There were no pastimes permitted other than those approved by the Community of "Jesús" and the community around the canon-penitentiary. Holy Week processions, gatherings of the confraternities; colloquies of married women with other women, of men with other men; get-togethers of archivist clerks; Christmas plays in the *De Profundis*, the auditorium at "Jesús." There, the public, consisting of students' families, was required to be seated, the sexes separated,[80] as in

sexos, como en las primitivas basílicas, y bajo la vigilancia de un Hermano, que se deslizaba por el pasillo central como el inspector de una brigada extraordinaria. Entre los socios del Casino había antiguos colegiales que representaron *El martirio de San Hermenegildo* y *La vida es sueño,* con loas al colegio y sin "papeles de mujer".

El único solaz en sala cerrada y con mezcla de juventudes – hijas de María y luises, esclavas y caballeros de la Orden Tercera, camareras del Santísimo y seminaristas – lo traía Navidad, con el Nacimiento en los almacenes de "Chocolates y Azúcares de Nuestro Padre", de Gil Rebollo, proveedor del colegio; un Belén mecánico de lumbres y nieves, de molinos que rodaban y aguas que corrían por céspedes impermeables y torrentes de corcho.

En casa de Gil Rebollo podían sentirse cerca varones y hembras. Fuera de aquí, no; como no fuese en vísperas de boda o en la obscura soledad del pecado. Pero aun en la farsa sagrada de Gil Rebollo estaban presididos por Padres de la Compañía; y sin su presencia no comenzaban a moverse los pastores y rebaños, los ríos, la estrella, los camellos, los leñadores, los panaderos, las lavanderas, ni se iluminaba el retablo, que tenía la ingenuidad y abundancia de pormenores de un Evangelio apócrifo. En los descansos, un coro invisible de señoritas cantaba villancicos del P. Folguerol. La sociedad olecense subía a la esterada tarima de la presidencia, persuadiéndose entonces de que el rigor ignaciano podía compadecerse con sutiles donaires glosando los anacronismos del "Belén" de Rebollo. Festivos, asombradizos, sonrosados, no semejaban los Padres los mismos Padres del colegio. Pero pasaban días, y en una plática o junta de congregantes sentían algunos que se les enroscaba la palabra del predicador flagelando las deshonestidades de una gala demasiado atrevida, de un martelo demasiado ardiente dentro de la inocencia de una noche de Navidad. Hasta lo más profundo llegaban los ojos de los Ángeles de la Guarda de Oleza...

...Ahora, los del Nuevo Casino tenían ya el goce de ver cómo gozaban los forasteros. Y el síndico acabó dándose una puñada en su frente de tufos. ¡Estaban hartos del color de ceniza de su vida! Ellos eran otra Oleza! Y el

primitive basilicas, under the vigilant eye of a Brother, who glided up and down the central aisle like the monitor of an extraordinary brigade. There were former students among the members of the Club, who performed *The Martyrdom of Saint Hermenegild* and *Life is a Dream* with prologues of praise for the school and without "female roles."[81]

Christmas brought the only solace within a closed hall with mixing of young people of both sexes – Daughters of Mary and male members of the Marian Congregation of San Luis,[82] young women belonging to the Sodality of La Esclavitud de Nuestra Señora de la Merced and young men of a pious association of the Third Order,[83] women serving as caretakers of the altar of the Holy Sacrament along with seminary students – with Nativity Scenes presented in the warehouses of "Chocolates and Sugar Confectionary of Our Father," belonging to Gil Rebollo, one of the purveyors for the school; a mechanical Crèche with lights and snow, with mills that rotated and waters that ran through waterproof sod and torrents made of cork.

In Gil Rebollo's establishment, males and females were able to feel closer to one another. Outside of this place, it wasn't possible, unless it happened to be the night before a wedding or in the darkened solitude of sin. But even during Gil Rebollo's sacred farce, the Fathers of the Society kept watch over them; and without their presence, the shepherds and flocks could not begin to move, nor the rivers, the star, the camels, the woodcutters, the bakers, the washerwomen, and they couldn't light up the retable, which had all the ingenuousness and abundance of detail of an apocryphal Gospel. An invisible chorus of young women would sing the Christmas carols of Father Folguerol as they stood on the landings. Olezan society made its way up to the carpeted platform of the presiding officials, filled with the conviction that the rigor of the Ignatian order would sympathize with the subtle wit and gloss over the anachronisms of Rebollo's "Nativity Scene." The Fathers, festive, quite astonished, flushed, did not seem to be the same Fathers from the school. But after a number of days would pass, in the course of a homily or a gathering of congregants, there were some who felt the preacher's words were coiling themselves around them, flagellating them for the immodest activities of too daring a festive display or too ardent a flirtatious moment within the innocence of a Christmas night. The eyes of the Guardian Angels of Oleza reached one's innermost feelings.

...Now the people in the New Club had the pleasure of seeing how the outsiders enjoyed themselves. And the syndic ended up striking his fist against the forelocks over his forehead. They were fed up with the ashen color of their lives! They were another Oleza! And the group with the most

grupo de más brío se fue con el síndico Cortina a contárselo a don Magín.

Paseaba don Magín al sol de su huerto, leyendo en un volumen del Licenciado Cascales la epístola al Licenciado Bartolomé Ferrer Muñoz "Sobre la cría y trato de la seda".

Se lo dijeron todo, y el capellán sonreía escuchándoles.

– Tenemos Nuevo Casino, y tendremos comedias con mujeres, reuniones con mujeres, de todo con mujeres. Y a esas fiestas podrán asistir los sacerdotes y las familias de más remilgos, como a la sala de Rebollo y al salón de actos de los jesuitas, pero sin jesuitas. Eso para el invierno; y los ensayos para el verano, de noche, en la delicia de un jardín; ensayos y verbenas...

– ¡Así sea, aunque no me importe!

Le replicaron que le buscaban precisamente para que le importase y les encaminase a conseguir su propósito de divertirse sin tutela y en beneficio de enfermos y pobres de la diócesis.

– ¡Ah, vamos: la obra de caridad, la alcahueta de siempre! Pues ni por sus oficios alcanzaréis lo otro si no lo cobijáis en los jardines y claustros de "Jesús".

Oyendo a don Magín se marchitaban los ánimos de los fuertes. Todos ellos encontrarían en su mujer, en sus hermanas, en su madre, en su novia, una voluntad encogida, necesitada siempre de la consulta y legitimación de otras voluntades.

– Sobre todas las de la diócesis – gritó Cortina – está la voluntad de Palacio.

Palacio tuvo tiempos apacibles. El señor obispo mostraba una infantil complacencia en su salud. Bajaba a su huerto por la puerta de la Provisoría. Los curiales le veían conversar con el hortelano; acoger con risas los botes y cabezadas del mastín; daba de comer a los palomos; se sentaba y leía subiendo sus dedos para tomar el olor de una rama de limón.

Ofició en muchas solemnidades. En la del Corpus predicó un padre de "Jesús", que puso todos los tonos de su garganta, la pálida inmensidad de su frente teológica y la elegancia de sus manos, tan femeninas entre la riqueza de su roquete de Gonzaga, al servicio de una frondosa ciencia dogmática.

spirit went off with Cortina, the syndic, to tell Don Magín all about it.

Don Magín was strolling through the sunlit garden, reading from a volume of Licenciado Cascales, his epistle to Licenciado Bartolomé Ferrer Muñóz "On the breeding and handling of silkworms."[84]

They told him everything and the parish priest smiled as he listened to them.

"We have a New Club and we will have plays with women in them, gatherings with women, everything with women. And the priests will be able to attend those festivities along with the most prudish families, just as in Rebollo's hall and in the Jesuit assembly hall, but without any Jesuits. All that for the winter; rehearsals for the summer, at night, in the delightful atmosphere of a garden; the rehearsals and festive occasions on the eve of a saint's day...."

"So be it, although it makes no difference to me!"

They replied that they had come looking for him precisely because they wanted him to attach importance to it and show them the way to carry out what they intended to do, to enjoy themselves without chaperonage for the benefit of the sick and the poor in the diocese.

"Oh, I see now: the act of charity, the inevitable bawd! Well, not even with all your prayers and offices will you attain all the rest if you don't have it take place in the gardens and the cloisters of 'Jesús!'"

The spirits of the strongest in heart withered as they heard Don Magín. All of them would find a timorous will in their wives, their sisters, their mothers, their sweethearts, always requiring the consultation and legitimacy of other wills.

"The will of the Palace stands above all others in the diocese," Cortina shouted.

The Palace underwent peaceable times. The lord bishop was demonstrating a child-like satisfaction with his state of health. He would go down to the garden through the door of the Vicar General's Office. The curial clerks would see him conversing with the gardener; they would welcome with laughter the mastiff's jumping and butting; then he would feed the ringdoves; he would sit down to read, raising his fingers to savor the fragrance of a lemon tree branch.

He officiated at a number of solemn occasions. During the rites of Corpus Christi, a father from "Jesús" preached a sermon and put all the tones of his throat, the pale immensity of his theological forehead and the elegance of his hands, so feminine within the richness of his heavy Gonzagan rochet,[85] at the

Acabado el sermón, el señor obispo, sin dejarle tiempo de bajar del púlpito, fue comentando, desde su baldaquino, la institución eucarística, claro, dulce y lento, comparándola a la "luz prendida de otra luz". El cabildo, las autoridades y los fieles volvían la mirada, desde el prelado, que movió su báculo como sí quitase bondadosamente una niebla del ojo blanco de la radiante custodia, al jesuita que escuchaba inmóvil, con el bonete en el pecho y un dardo en cada cristal de sus gafas...

En esta época hizo su última visita pastoral; restauró algunos conventos; mejoró las casas parroquiales más pobres, y en una de un pueblo fragoso pasó el verano. Pidió que viniesen ingenieros, y con ellos caminó la comarca más amenazada del río, estudiando embalses y paredones que lo contuviesen, y a sus expensas se acabó el muro de Benferro. Logró el estudio del ferrocarril, y en Palacio se celebraron las primeras juntas para conciliar a los técnicos con los hacendados.

Poco a poco su ilustrísima volvió a sus soledades. Palacio vivía en voz baja. Una madrugada el paje de servicio oyó gemir al señor. Asomóse al dormitorio por la puertecita de la sala de los retratos, y le vio rajándose las llagas con un agujón de oro calentado en un fuego azul.

Lo supo don Magín y recordó las palabras de Grifol; "No se curará; tiene el dolor en las entrañas". Casi lo mismo, pero con más arrequives científicos que el difunto Grifol, dijo el médico forastero que venía a Oleza en el coche episcopal. Ese mal de la piel era como un mandato y la muestra de otro mal recóndito, de una etiología callada. Habló de sobresaltos y trastornos de emoción que predisponen a padecimientos que si no significan un peligro pueden ir fermentándolo.

Su ilustrísima nombró la lepra, y el médico apartó sus recelos con un ademán indulgente. Antaño se confundía y agrupaba la lepra con otras enfermedades; pero en estos tiempos cualquier curandero la reconocería desde sus principios. No se olvidó de decir el descubrimiento del bacilo, ni de nombrar a Hansen y a Neisser, ni la forma y las medidas del microbio por milésimas de milímetros, sin omitir los ensayos de remedios más audaces

service of a luxuriant display of dogmatic knowledge. When the sermon was over, the lord bishop, without even giving him time to come down from the pulpit, began a commentary from his place on the canopied dais, concerning the institution of the Eucharist, so clear, sweet and slow, comparing it to the "light set aflame by another light." The cathedral chapter, the authorities and the faithful turned their gaze from the prelate, who moved his crozier as if he were removing a haze from the white eye of the radiant monstrance in a good-hearted manner, to the Jesuit, who was listening motionless with his cap against his chest and a dart in each of the lenses of his spectacles....

He made his last pastoral visit during this period, he restored a number of convents and monasteries; he improved the poorest parish houses and then spent the summer in one of them in a rough, bramble-covered village. He ordered engineers to be brought in and walked with them through the section most threatened by the river, studying dams and heavy walls which might contain it, and the Benferro wall was completed at his expense. He brought about the survey for the railroad and the first meetings were held in the Palace to bring about a reconciliation between the technicians and the land owners.[86]

Little by little, His Excellency returned to his solitary ways. The Palace went on living in a low voice. One early morning, his personal page heard the lord bishop moaning. He looked into the bedroom through the small door of the portrait gallery and saw him tearing open his sores with a big golden needle heated over a blue flame.

Don Magín found out about it and remembered Grifol's words, "He will not be cured; his pain is rooted deep inside of him."[87] The out-of-town doctor, who used to come to Oleza in the bishop's coach, said almost the same thing, but with more scientific embellishments than the deceased Grifol. That skin disease was like a mandate and the sign of another hidden ailment of muted etiology. He spoke of emotional shocks and disturbances which predispose one to sufferings, which, even if they don't signify a particular danger, can keep on fermenting it.

His Excellency mentioned leprosy and the doctor pushed aside his misgivings with an indulgent gesture. In the distant past they had confused and grouped leprosy together with other diseases, but in current times, any healer would recognize it from its very inception. He didn't forget to mention the discovery of the bacillus, nor to mention the names of Hansen and Neisser,[88] nor the shape and the measurements of the microbe in thousandths of millimeters, without omitting the testing of the most daring remedies like

como el de inocular ponzoña de serpientes. También contó sus visitas a leproserías, donde murieron leprosos de pulmonía, de nefritis, de vejez, los cuales habían vivido más de veinte años con las llagas cerradas y secas, sin dolores, y con capacidad sensitiva hasta en la zona atacada, de modo que debieron ser rehabilitados sanitariamente; estaban limpios de su podre, y se les dejó morir entre los inmundos. Y el médico terminó con una bella frase de revista o conferencia dominical: "Si la medicina antigua tuvo carácter religioso, colocada entre el rito y el milagro, la medicina moderna participaba de la Ética y de la Sociología."

Era un dermatólogo de piel tan magnífica, de porte tan pulido, que todos sus enfermos se sentían realzados de ser el objeto de los estudios de ese hombre y hasta llegaban a no creer tan horrendos sus males tocándolos aquellas manos.

Para su ilustrísima la elocuencia del doctor objetivaba demasiado el mal. Escuchándole se veían las enfermedades separadas de la carne, contenidas y humildes bajo el poder de tanta sabiduría y elegancia. Después se soltaban por el mundo, y la suya se le escondía en la sangre y en los huesos, y se quedaba a solas con el dolor. Enfermo sin familia, con un pudor adusto de sus tristezas.

El cabildo, los familiares y domésticos recogían de sus ojos y de su silencio un veto de llegar a su intimidad. Enfermero y confidente de sí mismo, a sabiendas de que se hablaba de su padecer. No lo desnudaría con la palabra pronunciada. La palabra era la más preciosa realidad humana. Y el obispo se imponía esa ilusión de todos los que sufren de que el secreto existe, aun entre los que lo conocen, mientras la voz no lo abre.

Don Magín lo había aceptado. En sus conversaciones elegía asuntos y anécdotas que recrearan al pastor y al amigo y hasta contrariedades gustosas. Una de las más grandes la tuvo su ilustrísima cuando don Magín rechazó una canonjía de gracia.

— Serás canónigo por obediencia.

— Señor, ni por obediencia. ¡Huiré como un santo!

El señor obispo estuvo mirándole mientras le decía:

— ¡Mi pobre salud no ha de recibir ningún daño!

that of the inoculation of poisonous snake venom. He also recounted his visits to leprosaria, where those infected with leprosy died of pneumonia, nephritis, of old age, individuals who had lived for more than twenty years with their sores closed and dried up, without pain, and with the capacity for sensitivity even in the area that had been attacked, so that it became necessary for them to be rehabilitated by disinfection; they were free of all pus and were permitted to die among those who were contaminated. And the doctor ended with a beautiful sentence from a journal or from a Sunday academic lecture, "If ancient medicine had a religious character, situated between the rite and the miracle, modern medicine partook of Ethics and Sociology."

He was a dermatologist with so magnificent a skin, with so polished a bearing, that all his patients reached the point of not believing their ailments to be so horrendous, and felt fulfilled at being the object of that man's studies and even because those hands had touched them.

For His Excellency, the doctor's eloquence made his ailment too objective. If you listened to him, diseases would seem to be separated from the flesh, contained and humble beneath the power of so much wisdom and elegance. Afterward, they would be let loose upon the world and his particular ailment would remain hidden in his blood and in his bones, while he remained alone with his pain. A sick man with no family, with an austere modesty over his sadness.

The cathedral chapter, the familiars and domestic servants gathered that his eyes and his silence implied a refusal to allow them to penetrate his privacy. Nurse and confidant of his innermost self, fully conscious of the fact that they were talking about his suffering. He would not lay it bare with a word he might utter. The word was the most precious human reality. And the bishop imposed that illusion upon himself, one that is common to all those who suffer because the secret exists, even among those who know it, so long as the voice does not open it up.

Don Magín had accepted it. In his conversations, he chose subjects and anecdotes that might cheer up his pastor and friend, even including pleasant disagreements. His Excellency had one of the most important of these when Don Magín turned down an honorary canonry.

"You will be a canon out of obedience to me."

"My lord, not even out of obedience. I will flee like a saint."

The Lord Bishop kept looking at him as he said:

"No harm must come to my poor health."

Pero don Magín le replicó con maliciosa mansedumbre:

– Señor, que tampoco lo reciba la salud de las pobres criaturas como yo.

Y pidió la prebenda para un viejo capellán y el traslado a su rectoría de un vicario, los dos sometidos a la dura servidumbre del P. Bellod.

Pasó un doméstico anunciando a la Comisión del Nuevo Casino. Don Magín adelantó los intentos y supuestos de aquellos diputados. El familiar presagió temerosas discordias: "Jesús" no toleraría esos solaces; el penitenciario y los suyos, tampoco. Se culparía de todo a Palacio. Su ilustrísima hizo abrir la mampara, y desde su sillón bendijo cansadamente a los de fuera, diciéndoles:

– Si vuestra obra es buena, prometemos ir alguna vez y presidirla.

Salió don Magín con las gentes del Casino, que le llevaban abrazado.

Al atravesar el puente de los Azudes, cerca del Nuevo Casino, les atropelló uno de los socios corriendo y gritando como huido de una perdición:

– ¡Qué bárbaros! ¡Lo he visto, lo he visto yo!

Lo había visto y escapaba para contarlo. Los ingenieros, después de almorzar en las obras, habían desnudado a la *Argelina,* y desnuda del todo la colgaron entre dos naranjos en flor; ella cantaba, y los hombres la rodeaban campaneándola y dando bramidos. Una hoguera de carne. Tocaban acordeones, y parecía envolverles un viento marinero!

Desde la baldosa repitió a gritos la aventura para que llegase a los que salían del tresillo y del billar.

Así lo oyeron y se inflamaron todos los socios; los socios y la señorita de Gandía y la señora de Monera, que grifadas de honestidad, iban entonces muy de prisa, camino de casa de las *Catalanas.*

But Don Magín replied with malicious deference:

"My Lord, but even the good health of poor creatures like me need not receive it."

And he requested the prebend for a long-time priest and also the transfer of a vicar to his rectory, both these men now being subjected to harsh servitude under Father Bellod.

A domestic came by and announced the Commission from the New Club. Don Magín anticipated the intentions and suppositions of those representatives. The familiar foresaw frightful disagreements: "Jesús" would not tolerate such forms of pleasure; the canon-penitentiary and his friends wouldn't either. The Palace would be blamed for everything. His Excellency had them open up the folding screen and wearily blessed those on the other side as he sat in his armchair, saying to them:

"If your work is good, we promise to go there some time and preside over it."

Don Magín left with the people from the Club, who walked away holding him by the arm.

As they crossed the Bridge of the Waterwheels, near the New Club, one of the members ran into them as he ran and shouted, as if fleeing from perdition.

"What barbarians! I saw it, I really saw it!"

He had seen it and escaped to tell them about it. The engineers, after having lunch at the work site, had stripped the *Algerian* of her clothes and hung her up completely naked between two blossoming orange trees; she started singing, and the men surrounded her, swinging her back and forth as they roared with excitement. A bonfire of flesh. They were playing accordions and they seemed to be totally enveloped by a strong wind from the sea.

As he stood on the tiled pavement, he repeated the adventure in a loud voice so that it would reach those who were coming from the game of ombre and the billiard room.

That's how all the members heard it and were aroused; the members and also Señorita de Gandía and Señora de Monera, who, bristling with righteousness, were just then walking hurriedly along, on their way to the *Catalan Sisters'* house.

3. "Las Catalanas"

Eran dos. Menorquinas – mahonesas – de nacimiento, y comerciantes de Barcelona. El padre trajo a Oleza su negocio de tejidos de la calle de Puerta Ferrisa. Murió del cólera, y se alejaron veloces los años encima del mercader. Casi nadie se acordaba de su gabán color de aceite, de su gorro de punto de estambre con una borla morada que le caía cansándole la sien. Se le olvidó de manera que las huérfanas semejaban no serlo, no haberlo sido nunca ni necesitar de madre: *prolem sine matre creatam;* como si fuesen hijas de sí mismas, hechas de sí mismas. Según estaban, debieron de ser desde su principio y serían para siempre, aun después de muertas y sepultadas. No se las podía imaginar sino en su presente: altas, flacas y esquinadas; los ojos gruesos de un mirar compasivo, el rostro muy largo, los labios eclesiásticos, la espalda de quilla y, sobre todas las cosas, vírgenes. Sus lutos – todavía de retales de la tienda – nadie los creería de viudez ni de maternidad rota. Solteras. Estatura, filo y pudor de doncellez perdurable. Para ser vírgenes nacieron. Las dos hermanas se horrorizaban lo mismo del pecado de la sensualidad que nunca habían cometido, y casi tanto temían el de la calumnia, prefiriendo que fuesen verdaderas las culpas que se contaban en su presencia. Por eso, había de referirse todo menudamente, hasta quedar persuadidas de que el prójimo recibía su merecido nada más.

Luego de comer paseaban entre los cuatro limoneros y las dos palmeras de su huerto, el huerto del almacén de *Miseria;* los árboles y las dos hermanas se reflejaban deformes en las bolas metálicas de jardín colgadas de los arcos de un cenador de geranios y pasiones. Se cansaban y tosían a la vez, y entraban a sentarse en las butacas de lienzo puestas junto a la reja de la sala. Les quedaba un poco de dejo catalán; se acordaban con regaño de la plaza del Pino, de la calle de Puerta Ferrisa, de la Canuda y de su único viaje a Madrid, en 1850, donde una de ellas pudo ser la enamorada del dueño de un comercio de ropas de la calle de Atocha, que después no resultó dueño. Suspiraban, alzándose el pañuelo que les bajaba por las mejillas.

3. "The Catalan Sisters"

They were two. Minorcans by birth – from the city of Mahón – and merchants
from Barcelona. The father brought his fabric business to Oleza from the
Calle de Puerta Ferrisa. He died of cholera and the years swiftly removed
any vestige of the merchant's memory. Almost nobody remembered his
olive-colored overcoat or his worsted knitted cap with a purple tassel that
hung wearily over his temple. He was forgotten in much the same way that
orphaned girls often forget that they are bereft of their parents, nor ever
having been so, nor ever having wanted or needed a mother: *prolem sine
matre creatam (offspring born motherless)*[89]; as if they were daughters of
themselves, made by their own selves. Just as they appeared to be now, they
must have been like that from the very beginning, and so they would be
forever, even after they were dead and buried. You could only imagine them
just as they were in the present: tall, scrawny and angular; with the heavy-
lidded eyes of a compassionate glance, with very long faces, ecclesiastical
lips, bent backs and above all other things, virgins. Nobody would consider
their black mourning clothes – still made of remnants from their store – as
having anything to do with widowhood or miscarried maternity. Spinsters.
The stance, profile and modesty of everlasting maidenhood. They were born
to be virgins. The two sisters were horrified in the same way by the sin of
the sensual acts they had never committed and were almost as much afraid
of the sin of calumny, actually preferring the misdeeds related to them to be
true. For that reason, everything had to be narrated to them in great detail,
till they were fully persuaded that a fellow creature was receiving his just
deserts.

After they ate they would stroll between the four lemon trees and the
two palm trees in their garden, the garden belonging to *Miseria*'s wholesale
store; the trees and the two sisters were deformed in the reflection they made
in the metallic balls in the garden hanging down from the top of the arches
of a bower adorned with geraniums and passion flowers. They would grow
tired and cough at the same time, and go inside to sit down in the linen-fabric
armchairs set up next to the window grating in the drawing room. They still
had a trace of a Catalan accent left; they gruffly recalled the Plaza del Pino,
the Calle de Puerta Ferrisa, the Calle de la Canuda and their only trip to
Madrid in 1850, where one of them managed to become the sweetheart of
the owner of a clothing business on the Calle de Atocha, and who later turned
out not to be the owner. They would sigh as they raised their scarves that

Lo traían de seda de pita dentro de casa, y para fuera, manto. Y a esperar. Todo limpio, todo guardado. Sabían lo que habrían de sentir, comer, rezar, vestir y pensar en fechas memorables. De modo que a esperar al lado de la vidriera; a esperar que alguien viniese y empujase las horas hasta la de las oraciones. Ese alguien era siempre la mujer del homeópata Monera, y Elvira. Oyéndolas, no tenían más remedio las *Catalanas* que sobresaltarse. Pero la virtud de casada de la Monera y el furor de los ojos y de la lengua de la señorita Galindo, les curaban los escrúpulos. Sus amigas lo escarbaban y lo probaban todo, gracias a Dios. Y ya las dos hermanas podían respirar compadeciéndose de este mundo.

...Vinieron las de siempre. No pasaron juntas porque una celadora de la Adoración retuvo en el portal a la Monera. Elvira precipitóse en la sala y, sin besar a las dos viejas señoras, les refirió ella sola la depravación de los ingenieros.

Las *Catalanas* principiaron a toser y consternarse, diciendo que no era posible tanta inmundicia.

– Pero ¿desnuda? ¿Sin enaguas, sin pantalón de punto, sin medias? ¿Atada y colgando de dos naranjos? ¿Y ellos qué hacían, Dios mío?...

Entró la Monera. De sus ojos que le bailaban y del ansia de su resuello de mujer lardosa le salía el gozo de decir alguna noticia caliente. Pero Elvira no se dejaba vencer delante de aquellas solteronas sin herederos, y se olvidó de la *Argelina* para comentar el traslado de don Pío, vicario de "Nuestro Padre", a la parroquia de don Magín.

– ¡Atiende, que Dios los cría y ellos se juntan! -la interrumpió, ahogándose, la del homeópata.

– ¡Yo no sé si los criará Dios de ese modo; pero quien los junta me lo sé de sobra!

Aquí volvieron a su susto las *Catalanas*. ¿Es que don Pío no era un buen sacerdote?

Casi recién salido del seminario ingresó en la parroquia del P. Bellod. Descolorido, muy dulce, de tez de niña; resultó poeta. Ya en las veladas y concertaciones del Convictorio fue siempre el escogido para la oda o

kept dropping over their cheeks. Inside the house, they wore one made of a cheap silk fiber, and outside, they would wear a long, plain mantilla. And now it was time to wait. Everything clean, everything discreetly in place. They knew what they were supposed to feel, eat, pray, wear and think on memorable occasions. So now it was time to wait beside the wide windows; to wait for someone to come in and push the hours ahead until it was time for the Angelus. That someone was always the homeopath Monera's wife and Elvira. When they heard them, the *Catalan Sisters* had no alternative but to be startled. But Señora Monera's married woman's virtue and the furor in Señorita Galindo's eyes and tongue cured them of their scruples. Their friends picked at everything and sampled everything, thank God. And now the two sisters could breathe freely and feel compassion for this world.

...The usual ones arrived. They didn't come in together because a custodian of the association for the Nocturnal Adoration[90] detained Señora Monera in the entryway. Elvira rushed into the drawing room and, without even kissing the two elderly ladies, recounted the depravities of the engineers all by herself.

The *Catalan Sisters* started to cough and gave the appearance of being dismayed, saying that such filthy indecency was not possible.

"But, you mean naked? Without underskirts, without knitted drawers, without stockings? All tied up and hanging down between two orange trees? And what were they doing, good God?"

The Monera woman came in. The pleasure of reporting some spicy tidbit of news was dancing in her eyes and emanating from the anxious, heavy breathing of this lardaceous woman. But Elvira would not allow herself to be outdone in front of those two heirless spinsters, and the *Algerian woman* was quickly forgotten in order to comment on the transfer of Don Pío, the vicar of "Our Father," to Don Magín's parish church.

"Just listen to this; the fact is God rears them like that, and they seem to come together!" the homeopath's wife interrupted her, choking with excitement.

"I don't know whether God creates them that way; but I know only too well who brings them together!"

At this point, the *Catalan Sisters* reverted to their previous fright. Is it possible that Don Pío was not a good priest?

Almost as soon as he left the seminary, he entered Father Bellod's parish church. Pallid, very sweet, with a little girl's complexion; he turned out to be a poet. As far back as the evening literary presentations and contests in

disertación de honor, ofreciendo, como encanto separado de las virtudes literarias, la elegancia de su figura, de sus ademanes, de su sotana y la delicada belleza de su voz y de su mirar de adolescente.

– ¡Ahora habrá que oír y ver al curita poeta!

– ¡Si el Señor le ha dado gracia para eso! – dijo, compungida, una de las *Catalanas* en nombre de las dos,

– ¿Gracia para qué? ¿Para que en sus versos celebrando a las santas que se sabe que fueron muy lindas y de familia ilustre, y a las que pecaron a su gusto antes de la santidad, se sientan requebradas señoritas y señoras de este pueblo que no son para tanto?

Enrojeció la Monera en su amor olecense. Añadió Elvira que el P. Bellod ya tenía rebajados los vuelos de su vicario, y, un domingo, en el ofertorio de la misa conventual, se desmayó don Pío. Subieron en su socorro las Hijas de María. Quiso el P. Bellod adobar al dulce pichón. Pero su ilustrísima lo puso al lado de don Magín.

– ¡Pues, atiende, que muchas lloran su marcha! – y la Monera se relamió su boca gruesa de comadre.

– No se apure, que ya van en su busca, y el banquillo de su confesionario de San Bartolomé amanece como un tocador de novia, todo de flores, y entre las flores, cartas de pena, sin firma; allí se arrodillan las señoritingas y se las oye confesarse sollozando.

– ¿Y no será calumnia? Es mucho. ¡Ya verá!...

En seguida, la de Gandía fue sosegándolas. Su lengua iba descubriendo todas la intimidades de la ciudad, como si soltara los vendajes de un cuerpo llagado; y en cada revelación probada, ponía el ungüento de una protesta de ternura, porque no podía esconder que amaba ya este pueblo como suyo, y lo mismo les sucedería a sus amigas.

– ¡Lo mismo, lo mismo! ¡Ya verán! ¡Por eso nos duele lo que dicen!

Toda la Monera se removía en un tumulto de despecho, mientras agradecía y alababa tanto amor.

Elvira le sonrió con impertinencia. Ella bien sabía que en todos los tiempos hubo males y escándalos en Oleza. Lo sabía por don Amancio.

the student residence, he was always the one chosen to present the ode or the dissertation of honor, offering everyone, as a charming addition quite separate from the literary virtues, the elegance of his figure, his gestures, his cassock, and the delicate beauty of his voice and his adolescent expression.

"You ought to hear that precious little poet priest now!"

"But the Lord has granted him the divine gift to do that!" said one of the *Catalan Sisters* with compunction in the name of them both.

"The divine gift for what? So that when they hear his verses celebrating the female saints who were known to be very pretty and from illustrious families, as well as those who sinned quite freely before attaining sainthood, the young ladies and matrons in this town, who are not up to all of that, should feel flattered?"

Señora Monera was flushed with her Olezan love. Elvira added that Father Bellod had already reduced his vicar's flights of fancy, and that one Sunday, Don Pío fainted during the offertory during the conventual Mass. The Daughters of Mary ran up to help him. Father Bellod tried to set that sweet little bird straight. But His Excellency placed him at Don Magín's side.

"But listen to this; there are many women who are crying over his departure!" And Señora Monera licked her coarse, gossipmonger's lips.

"Don't you worry; they've already gone looking for him, and his confessional bench at San Bartolomé is beginning to take on the appearance of a bride's dressing table, all covered with flowers and unsigned letters filled with sorrow among the flowers; those brazen young hussies kneel down there and you can hear them sobbing during their confession."

"But isn't that probably just slanderous talk? It's too much, You'll see!..."

The woman from Gandía immediately began to calm them down. Her tongue went on revealing all the private affairs of the city, as if she were undoing the bandages of a lacerated body; and with each revelation she sampled, she would apply the ointment of a protest filled with tenderness, because she was unable to conceal her love for this town which she now considered her own, and she felt that the same would happen to her friends.

"The same thing, the same thing! You'll see! That's why it hurts us so much to hear what they say!"

The whole of the Monera woman was shaken in a tumultuous feeling of disgust while she showed her appreciation and gave praises for so great a love.

Elvira smiled at her impertinently. She knew very well that there had been evils and scandals in Oleza in all times. She knew it through Don

¡Qué saber de hombre! Desde que se dejaba la barba parecía más mozo: una barba lisa hasta el pecho, una barba preciosa de color de azafrán... Pero, en otros tiempos, no contaba Oleza con partidos como el que representaba su hermano don Álvaro, y más atrás, ni siquiera hubo obispo en Oleza. Ahora, en cambio, parecía no haberlo. Porque con un obispo enfermo, y un enfermo como ése, iba pudriéndose la diócesis.

Aquí Elvira les avisó de las últimas fugas del seminario: tres del curso de "teólogos", cinco del grado de "canonistas", un fámulo de refectorio... A otros se les oía llorar en sus aposentos; mordían la beca; se volcaban desnudos crujiendo en su márfega de forraje de panoja, sin poder contener sus deseos impuros. Si se refugiaban en la meditación de la castidad de algunos santos y santas, enseguida huían del remedio para no incorporar las imágenes inmaculadas a las imágenes de pecado. Dos "menoristas" pidieron a gritos convulsos que les abriesen la puerta para salir a la perdición del mundo. Vino don Magín, lector de Moral y Patrología, y los empujó contra una balsa, gritándoles: "¡Dejaos de perdición! No vale la pena. ¡Resistid vosotros los apasionados, no nos quedemos con los que no sirven ni para las tentaciones!"

Las señoras de Puerta Ferrisa sintieron generosas alarmas:

– ¡Ay, si todo esto lo supieran los enemigos de la Fe!

Se espantaban en vano, porque en Oleza no había ni un enemigo de la Fe. No lo eran los arrabaleros de San Ginés, que en su vivir andrajoso de muladar se respetaban sus machos, sus hembras y sus corralizas y cumplían con los preceptos de la Iglesia bajo la voz de don Magín. Tampoco lo eran los del Nuevo Casino, por muy audaces y aburridos que se creyesen. No faltaban a las conferencias cuaresmales, sintiéndose halagados cuando el predicador, casi siempre de Madrid o de Valencia, proclamaba encendidamente, al despedirse, que nunca había visto un espectáculo de piedad tan grande como el que Oleza ofrecía a los ojos de Dios y de los hombres. Íntegros y liberales, eran de la cofradía de "Jesús atado", y en la procesión matinal del Viernes Santo rodeaban el Prendimiento, vestidos de legionarios, sumisos al centurión don Amancio Espuch...

Amancio. How much that man knew! Ever since he had let his beard grow, he seemed more youthful: a smooth beard right down to his chest, a lovely beard the color of saffron.... But in other times Oleza couldn't count on parties like the one her brother Don Álvaro represented, and even further back, there wasn't even a bishop in Oleza. Now, on the other hand, it still seemed as if they didn't have one. Because, with an ailing bishop, an ailing one like him, the diocese was decaying.

At this point Elvira informed them of the latest flights from the seminary: three from the program of studies in "theology," five from the one in "canon law,"[91] a servant employed in the refectory.... You could hear others weeping in their rooms; they would bite into the sashes of their gowns, writhing, naked, making their mattresses of corn husks crackle, unable to contain their impure desires. If they sought refuge in meditation on the chastity of male and female saints, they would quickly flee this remedy so as not to incorporate the immaculate images into their own images of sin. Two young men studying for "minor orders"[92] pleaded and shouted for them to open the doors so that they could go out into the perdition of the outside world. Don Magín, lecturer in Ethics and Patrology, came over and pushed them up against a wine cask, shouting, "That's enough talk of perdition! It isn't worth the trouble. You who are so filled with passion, just try to resist, so we don't end up with only those who aren't even inclined to face temptation!"

The ladies from Puerta Ferrisa were overcome by generous feelings of alarm:

"Oh, if only the enemies of Faith knew all this!"

But their fright was in vain, because there wasn't even a single enemy of Faith in Oleza. There weren't any among those who lived in the outlying district of San Ginés, who respected one another's males, their females and their poultry yards, living out their raggedy existence in the dung heap they called home, and fulfilled the precepts of the Church under the authority of Don Magín. Nor were those in the New Club without Faith, no matter how bold and bored they might consider themselves. They did not fail to attend the Lenten apologetic dissertations[93] and felt flattered when the preacher, almost always from Madrid or Valencia, would ardently proclaim, as he took leave of them, that he had never seen a spectacle of piety as great as the one Oleza offered for the eyes of God and men. Upright and liberal, they belonged to the confraternity of "Jesus tied to the column,"[94] and they would surround the scene of the Seizure of the Lord during the morning of the procession on Good Friday, dressed as legionnaires, submissive to the centurion Don Amancio Espuch....[95]

No; no había en Oleza enemigos de la Fe. Lo dijo soflamándose la del homeópata.

– ¡No los habrá – arremetió Elvira – ; pero este bendito pueblo permite que se agravie a Dios y a la decencia!

– ¡Y ahora! ¡No diga eso!

– ¿Que no lo diga? ¡Si yo lo he visto! Hace un instante, don Magín no podía contener la bulla oyendo el escándalo de la *Argelina,* y con la boca llena como de un mal bocado, me saludó dejándome la baldosa para que yo sintiese aquella indignidad, que a buena crianza no hay quien le gane. En su casa, casa-rectoral, se regodean los ingenieros. No se santigüen, porque, después de todo, Palacio fue quien nos trajo esas cuadrillas de trueno, pidiendo, con las prisas de la salvación, que se hiciese el ramalico del ferrocarril. ¡Para qué querrá su ilustrísima el tren teniendo que pasar los años escondido arrancándose postemas! Palacio, sí, señoras; es decir, los dos palacios: ése y el de Lóriz, porque no hay quien me niegue que Lóriz puso dinero de la condesa en las obras, el poco que les va quedando; y a eso vino: a vigilarlas y, de paso, dejar interno en "Jesús" a su cría canija; hijo de vicioso, que le pegará sus resabios a los hijos de casas decentes. En la ropería del colegio no caben los cofres del ajuar del niño. Ni el de un novio. Lo sé. Cada presentación de la criatura es un alboroto. Recuerden las ayas, las nodrizas y aquel lujo del parto a todo pregón...

– ¡Lujo de parto... – balbució una de las *Catalanas,* mientras la otra elevaba con beatitud sus ojos – , lujo de parto el de la reina, el año 50, cuando nosotras estuvimos en la Corte!

– ¡La única vez que fuimos a Madrid!

– La única. ¡Eramos muy jovencitas!

Elvira y la señora Monera sonrieron delgadamente.

– En el Palacio Real se prepararon alcobas completas, con sus lavabos y armarios y todo, para los grandes de España y los ministros. Y arriba, en las terrazas, había guardias – nosotras los vimos – con banderas y fanales de colores para avisar de día o de noche si venía al mundo príncipe o

No, there were no enemies of the Faith in Oleza. The homeopath's wife said this, inflamed with passion.

"There probably aren't any," said Elvira taking the offensive, "but this cursed town permits God and decency to be offended!"

"Even now! Don't say that!"

"You don't want me to say it? But I've seen it! Just a little while ago, Don Magín was unable to restrain the uproar when everyone heard of the scandalous affair involving the *Algerian woman*, and even though his mouth was full, as with some distasteful morsel he wanted to relate, he greeted me, leaving the pavement clear for me so that I could see that indecent activity for myself, because there's no one superior to him when it comes to good manners. The engineers have a merry time at his rectoral house. Don't bother crossing yourselves, because, after all, it was the Palace that brought us those thundering crews, when, with all the urgency needed for salvation, it requested that they construct that contemptible branch line of the railroad. For what purpose can His Excellency possibly want the train when he has to spend the years hidden away, tearing at those festering abscesses! The Palace, yes, my dear ladies; that is to say, the two palaces: that one and the one belonging to Lóriz, because nobody can deny that Lóriz invested the countess's money in the construction works, what little money may be left to them; and that's why he came, to watch over it and, while doing so, to enroll his sickly brat as a boarding student in "Jesús;" The son of a reprobate, he'll end up forcing his bad habits onto the sons from decent homes. The trunks used for the boy's accoutrements can hardly fit in the school wardrobe. Not even a bridegroom could match it. I know. Every time that creature appears, there's a big commotion. Remember the governesses, the wet nurses, all that lavish outpouring of public announcements when she gave birth...."

"The lavishness of his birth..." one of the *Catalan Sisters* stammered while the other one raised her eyes beatifically, "the lavishness surrounding the time when the queen gave birth, in the year 50, when we went to the Court!"[96]

"The only time we went to Madrid!"

"The only time. We were so young and innocent!"

Elvira and Señora Monera smiled tenuously.

"They prepared fully furnished bedrooms in the Royal Palace with washstands and wardrobes and everything, for the grandees of Spain and the ministers. And upstairs, on the terraces, there were guards – we saw them – with flags and lanterns in many colors to announce whether a prince or a

princesa. Cañones, músicas, tropas; todo el pueblo en la calle para contar los cañonazos... ¡Lo estoy diciendo, y mírenme la piel cómo se me eriza!

La hermana también mostró su piel erizada. Elvira gritó:

– ¿De modo que forasteros, madrileños, soldados, todos sabían lo de la reina?

– ¡Oh! ¡Ya verá: es la reina! – convinieron las *Catalanas,* casi arrepentidas de sus predilectas memorias – . ¡Las reinas tienen que consentirlo!...

– ¡No lo sería yo por nada del mundo, y menos preñada! ¡Jesús"!

Nunca se le quitaría de sus oídos el grito de Paulina cuando parió. De no acudir la Monera, lo hubiese presenciado todo siendo soltera. Después estuvo lamiéndose la espumilla de sus labios, y preguntó:

– ¿Y qué hicieron esos palacianos, tanta gente y tanto cañon cuando nació la criatura?

Las *Catalanas,* confundiéndose más, dijeron:

– No sabemos... ¡La señora reina malparió!

– ¡Menos mal! A mi se me raya el hígado de ver esa vanagloria del vientre y ese embuste de disimularlo entre sedas y galas, estando todos en el secreto del disimulo; porque yo no puedo remediarlo: ¡yo me lo imagino todo!

Era verdad: Elvira se lo imaginaba todo con un ímpetu candente.

Las viejas señoritas de Mahón la miraban rendidas, tosian menudamente, sin cuidarse de la Monera, que no se resignaba al tono menor de segundona de la amistad en aquella casa. Y comenzó a decir:

– Ya no nos acordábamos de hablar del último escándalo. No lo adivinarán. ¡En cueros, como una perdida, y adrede!

– Lo conté yo cuando vine. Tuve que tirar la noticia de mi boca porque me quemaba.

– ¡Si usted, Elvira, tampoco lo sabe! Me lo dijo, cuando llegábamos, una celadora de la Adoración. ¡Una afrenta de mujer!

Las *Catalanas* se dejaron a Elvira, volviéndose con ansiedad a la Monera.

– ¿Y la conocemos nosotras? ¿Entra en esta casa?

princess had come into the world, be it by day or by night. Cannons, music, troops; the entire city in the streets to count the cannon shots.... Here I am telling it now, and just look at me, how my skin is just tingling!"

Her sister also showed them her tingling skin. Elvira shouted:

"So the outsiders, the Madrilenians, the soldiers, everyone knew all about the queen?"

"Oh! You'll see: she's the queen!" the *Catalan Sisters* agreed, almost repentant for their favorite memories. "Queens have to put up with that sort of thing!...."

"I wouldn't be one for anything in this world, and much less, pregnant! Good God!"

Paulina's scream when she gave birth would never leave her ears. If the Monera woman had not come to the rescue, she, an unmarried woman, would have witnessed it all. Then she started licking the light foam from her lips and asked:

"And what did the palace staff, all those people and all those cannons do when the baby was born?"

The *Catalan Sisters* seemed even more confused and said:

"We don't know.... The queen miscarried!"

"Thank God for that! It just turns my stomach to see all that vainglory over a big belly and all that deception by concealing it under silks and finery when everyone is in on the secret behind all the dissembling; since I can't do anything about it, I imagine it all!"

It was true: Elvira imagined it all with burning violence.

The old maids from Mahón looked at her wearily, coughed quietly, without taking note of the Monera woman, who refused to resign herself to a minor key in second place in her friendship in that home. And she began saying:

"We didn't remember to talk about the latest scandal. You'll never guess. Stark naked, like a wanton woman, and on purpose!"

"I told you all about it when I came. I just had to let the news fly right out of my mouth because it was burning in me."

"But, Elvira, you don't know it either! A custodian for the association for the Nocturnal Adoration told me all about it when we'd just arrived. A disgrace of a woman!"

The *Catalan Sisters* abandoned Elvira and turned toward the Monera woman anxiously.

"Do we know her? Does she come into this house?"

– La conocemos; pero no viene a esta casa ni a la mía...

– ¿Y de este pueblo? – suspiró Elvira – . ¡Es no acabar!

– ¡Purita!

– ¿Purita? ¿Doña Purita?

– Purita, o doña Purita, ha salido desnuda a su reja, cuando le daba toda la luna, para que el de Lóriz la viese desde la calle... ¡Lo puedo jurar!

Las *Catalanas* levantaron las manos y los ojos.

– ¡Si no es posible, Jesús! ¡Y delante del cielo! ¿Es que esa infeliz no pensaba en Dios, que todo lo ve? – las dos señoras se enrojecían mirándose su cuerpo tan virginal, tan guardado bajo sus ropas de lutos – . ¿Pero el de Lóriz la vio desnuda del todo? ¿Y qué hizo ese desdichado?

Y, afligiéndose más, suspiraron:

– ¡Esos padres, esos padres, qué cuenta han de dar a Dios!

4. Tertulia de doña Corazón

La tienda de Doña Corazón siempre tenía sueño y quietud de archivo, de archivo de sí misma. De tarde, dos potes de Manises goteaban rápidamente de sol. Después, todo parecía más interno y callado. En los vasares sudaban los tarros de astillas de canela, de libros y ovillos de cera, de estrellas viejecitas de anís, de gálbulos de ciprés y eucaliptos, de gomas de olor...

No latía el reloj de pesas, seco y embalsamado de silencio, con sus dos saetas plegadas entre las diez y las once, las dos juntas, sin medir ningún tiempo, como si nunca hubiesen podido caminar por el lendel de las horas. El calendario, liso, sin días, como una lápida de cartón de las fiestas desaparecidas. La estampa del Sagrado Corazón de Jesús se torcía casi descolgándose; y aunque el Señor tuviese entre los dedos su lis de llamas prometiendo "Reinaré," semejaba ofrecerlo y decirlo por divina costumbre, por infinita condescendencia con las casas de los hombres.

En el escritorio se volcaba un gato, y junto al cancel, una mujer enjuta,

"We know her, but she doesn't come to this house, nor does she come to mine either...."

"Is she from this town?" Elvira sighed. "Let's have it!

"Purita!"

"Purita? Doña Purita?"

"Purita, or Doña Purita, stepped out naked in front of her window grating when the moon was shining all over her, so that Lóriz could see her from the street.... I can swear to it!"

The *Catalan Sisters* raised their hands and their eyes.

"But dear God, it isn't possible! Before heaven itself! Wasn't that wretched woman thinking of God, who sees everything?" The two women blushed as they stared at their eternally virginal bodies, so protected beneath their black mourning clothes. "You mean that Lóriz fellow saw her completely naked? And what did that wretch do?"

And they sighed with even greater grief:

"Those parents, those parents, how are they going to give an account of themselves to God!"

4. Social Gathering at Doña Corazón's

Doña Corazón's store always possessed the drowsiness and stillness of an archive, of an archive concerning itself. In the afternoon, two ceramic pots from Manises[97] swiftly dripped with sunlight. Afterwards, everything seemed more inward and hushed. Jars of cinnamon sticks, flattened squares and balls of wax, of charmingly old star-shaped bits of aniseed, cypress and eucalyptus cones, fragrant gums all were sweating on the kitchen shelves....

The grandfather clock, dry and embalmed in silence, wasn't ticking, with its two hands folded over one another between the ten and eleven, the two of them together, without measuring any time, as if they had never been able to march around the rutted circle of the hours. The calendar, unadorned, without days, like a cardboard monument to disappeared holy days. The religious print of the Sacred Heart of Jesus[98] was all twisted, almost to the point of falling down; and although the Lord was holding his fleur-de-lis of flames between his fingers, promising, "I shall reign,"[99] he seemed to be offering it and saying it as if it were a divine custom, with infinite condescension for the homes of mankind.

A cat was turning over on its back on top of the writing desk, and a scrawny

una viuda pobre, miraba quietecitamente el mismo rodal de hierba menuda de la calle de la Verónica, donde brincaban los gorriones. Anochecido se cerraba el portal; arriba, se hincaban unas pisadas de madera; todo crujía; y luego iba pasando un coloquio de mujeres.

De mañana, muy temprano, volvían a sentirse los tacones de zancas. La mujer vestida de viuda dejaba entornado el postigo. Venían mozas de la vecindad; no mercaban nada; preguntaban por doña Corazón.

Doña Corazón seguía lo mismo: engordando y cuajándose en su sillón de anea, tullida de dolores; muy limpia, muy peinada, haciendo labor con un aleteo de manos de niña que dejaban luces de anillos arcaicos y aroma de bergamoto. Puesta en el ancho asiento, ella misma, con el ímpetu recogido en sus brazos mollares, lo hacía caminar de pata en pata, cansadamente, como una vieja cabalgadura. No quiso que le pusieran ruedecitas al mueble, miedosa de creerse ya baldada sin remedio.

De su alcoba de velos blancos a la ventanita florida. Ya no tenía más jornadas su vida. Cuidábala Jimena, la antigua mayordoma del "Olivar de Nuestro Padre", maciza y colorada y el pelo como el lino.

Le daban compañía muchas amistades. Labradoras, artesanas, señoras humildes, señoras de rango acudían a compadecerla y dejarle los regustos del mundo.

El funerario de Oleza quiso arrendar el obrador de chocolates. No lo permitió la dueña; pero, desde entonces, sus amigas se creían entre coronas y ataúdes, y le pidieron que quitase ya los despojos del comercio, transformándolo en pulido zaguán. Lo contradijo don Magín. Los cedazos, las cóncavas piedras, los rodillos inmóviles, todavía olorosos de la pasta de cacao, tenían para él una belleza arqueológica. Arrancar esos testimonios del ayer sería pecado de desamor.

– Sin ellos, sin ese ambiente, yo, lo confieso, yo no vendría a esta casa con tanto agrado y frecuencia...

Y don Magín se puso a mirar la tarde entre los tiestos de ciclamas y albahacas y el estrépito de los pardillos, que le festejaban desde los trapecios y cunas de sus jaulones.

Mediaba marzo. Olor de naranjos de todos los hortales. Aire tibio, y dentro

woman, a poor widow, was sitting next to the storm door, looking out ever so quietly at the same patch of meager grass on the Calle de la Verónica, where the sparrows were hopping about. At nightfall, they would close the main door; upstairs, the sound of footsteps digging into the wooden floorboards; everything creaked; afterwards, a conversation among women followed.

Very early in the morning, the sound of heels on the staircase boards could be heard again. The woman dressed as a widow left the wicket partly open. Young women from the neighborhood would come by; they didn't purchase anything and simply asked for Doña Corazón.

Doña Corazón was getting along as usual: growing fat and congealing in her rush-seated armchair, crippled with pains; very clean, very well groomed, doing her needlework with a fluttering of her child-like hands, which radiated flashes of archaic rings and the scent of bergamot. Seated in her wide chair, she herself, with a thrust gathered together in her soft, pulpy arms, would make it move along, one leg at a time, wearily, like an old riding horse. She refused to let them put small wheels on this piece of furniture, out of fear that she would then consider herself a hopeless cripple.

From her white-curtained bedroom to the flower-filled little window. Her life no longer had no other journeys. Jimena, the former housekeeper at the "Olive Grove of Our Father," a solid, ruddy woman with hair like flax, now took care of her.

Many of her friends kept her company. Farm women, craftswomen, humble women, ladies of some social standing came by to express pity for her and to leave the flavors of the real world with her.

The mortician in Oleza tried to rent the shop where the chocolate was made. The owner would have none of it; but, from that time on, her friends considered themselves to be among funeral wreaths and coffins, and they asked her to remove the remnants of the business once and for all and transform it into a neat-looking vestibule. Don Magín contradicted this point of view. The sieves, the concave stones, the motionless rolling pins, still fragrant with the cacao mix, possessed an archeological beauty for him. To tear away all that testimony of yesterday would be a sin of indifference.

"Without them, without that atmosphere, I, I must confess, would not come to this house with such pleasure and frequency...."

And Don Magín commenced looking at the afternoon between the pots of cyclamen and basil and the din of the linnets as they entertained him from the trapezes and cradles in their oversize cages.

It was the middle of March. The fragrance of orange trees from all the

de su miel una punzada de humedad, un aletazo del invierno escondido en la revuelta de una calle. Nubes gruesas, rotas, blancas, veloces. Azul caliente entre las rasgaduras. Sol grande, sol de verano. Más nubes de espumas. Otra vez sol; el sol, cegándose; y la tarde se abría y se entornaba, ancha, apagada, encendida, fría...

Doña Corazón elevó su sonrisa a Don Magín. Aunque nada quedara de sus tiempos, no le faltaría el palique de su capellán.

– ¡Adivine lo que ahora pienso!

La dulce señora se asustó sin querer.

Don Magín había cruzado sus brazos, dejándose una mano alzada donde descansar el medallón de su rostro como en una ménsula; y desde allí, mirándola, decía:

– Todos, todos en este mundo, hasta los que tienen entrañas puras, entrañas de azucenas como usted...

– ¡Ay, no lo diga!

– ¡Todos cometemos ingratitudes!

Se alarmó más la señora. Sus azucenas se doblaban dentro de la grosura de su cuerpo tullido bajo un poniente de memorias, que siempre había de ser don Magín quien lo trajera.

– ¿Piensa usted, don Magín, que voy olvidándome del pobre don Daniel? ¡Desde estas jamugas de mi borriquito – y tocaba su asiento con sus manos primorosas – miro yo a lo lejos los años de su desgracia y de la mía!...

– En cambio, ¿se acuerda usted de don Vicente Grifol? ¿Lo ha recordado usted hoy?

¿Hoy? ¡Precisamente hoy, no! Sin decirlo, lo confesaba compungiéndose.

Don Magín era como la conciecia de la apacible señora.

– Pues hoy, precisamente hoy, se cumple el año de su muerte, tan silenciosa como su vida. Todos, usted, usted y yo tambíen, fuimos crueles de desapegados con aquel hombre, que hasta para dar un golpezuelo de bastón en una losa miraba que no hubiese ni una hormiga que dañar. De todos nosotros, la única buena alma que le acompañó en su agonía fue doña Purita. Le veo morir en su butaca sin perder su sonrísa. Purita le tomó los quevedos; les puso su respiración de frutas; se los limpió con sus guantes, y el enfermo le pedía: "Guárdemelos en mi bolsillo del pecho para no dejármelos en este mundo." Cuando yo fui a reconciliarle, no quiso. "He

orchards. Tepid air and a prick of dampness within its honey, a flapping of the wings of winter, hidden at the turn of a street. Bulky, ragged, white, swift clouds. Warm blue between the rifts. A great big sun, a summer sun. More clouds of foam. Again the sun; the sun, blindingly bright; and the afternoon opened up and remained only partly open, wide, listless, aflame, cold....

Doña Corazón raised her smile toward Don Magín. Although nothing might remain of days gone by, she would not be lacking for a chat with her priest.

"Guess what I'm thinking now!"

The sweet woman grew frightened without intending to.

Don Magín had crossed his arms, leaving one hand raised, on which he could rest the medallion formed by his face, as if on a bracket; and he looked at her from that position and said:

"Everyone, everything in this world, even those who are pure of heart, with hearts like white lilies like you...."

"Oh, please don't say that!"

"We all commit acts of ingratitude!"

The woman grew even more alarmed. Her white lilies drooped within the bulk of her crippled body beneath a fresh wind of memories and it was always Don Magín who seemed to bring it.

"Don Magín, do you think that I keep forgetting poor Don Daniel? From this sidesaddle seat of my little donkey," and she touched the chair with her exquisite hands, "I look at the years of his misfortune and mine from afar!..."

"On the other hand, do you remember Don Vicente Grifol? Did you remember him today?"

Today? Precisely today, no! Without saying so, she was confessing it remorsefully.

Don Magín was like the conscience of the gentle woman.

"Well, today, precisely today, is the first anniversary of his death, which was as silent as his life. All of us, you, you and I, were also indifferently cruel to that man, who looked to see if there were even an ant he might injure before he would strike a flagstone gently with his cane. Of all of us, the only good soul who accompanied him in his death throes was Doña Purita. I can see him dying in his armchair, without losing his smile. Purita removed his pince-nez; she blew her fruit-scented breath on them; she cleaned them with her gloves, and the ailing man would ask her, 'Put them in my breast pocket for safekeeping so I don't leave them behind in this world.' When I went to offer

de morir riéndome de los cuentos de Purita; y si allí me lo quieren cobrar por irreverente, enhorabuena pase yo algo por esta criatura." De madrugada volví para ungirle, y ella seguía a su lado sonriéndole y enjugándole los sudores.

– ¡Y aquí me tienen ustedes! – y entró, riéndose, la mujer ensalzada que esparcía el júbilo y la claridad de su vida.

Don Magín se sofocó de que le hubiese sorprendido elogiándola.

– ¡Si used no pasa de párroco a obispo, ni yo de solterona, yo seré quien le cuide y le bizme, si lo necesita, en la vejez!

– ¡Usted, hija mía, me cuidará y me bizmará! ¡Porque used y yo haremos todo lo posible para no pasar de lo que somos!

– ¿De modo que no me casaré, no me casaré nunca? – y Purita lo dijo mirándose, desde su virginidad, sus pechos, sus brazos, sus caderas de diosa, de diosa casada; se los miraba dulcemente, como si fuesen de una hermana suya; y así murmuró:

– ¡Ya no están los ingenieros rubios!

– ¡Todavía han de volver algunos!

– ¡Qué se me da que vengan, don Magín, si para lo que ellos quisieran, por ser libres como extranjeros, yo soy decente, y para esposa, yo soy, según dicen, demasiado libre y ellos demasiado de Oleza! – y lo que pudo acabar en un gemido, se abrió en un alboroto de risa.

Era secretaria de muchas Juntas y de la Cofradía de la Samaritana. Su plenitud de treinta años le trajo el *doña* sin quitarle el diminutivo de su nombre, avenido con su soltería, con sus gracias y ligereza. "Eva deseando escaparse del Paraíso, todo un paraíso de manzanos, sin un primer hombre siquiera", según don Magín.

A don Magín se volvió, pidiéndole que se apartara porque tenía que hacer confesión de un pecado mortal.

– Aquí estoy para escucharla.

– No, señor; que para los pecados peores busco siempre la más grande inocencia, y vengo de confesarme con don Jeromillo.

him a summary confession of reconciliation, he refused. 'I have to die laughing at Purita's stories; and if they want to make me pay for being irreverent on the other side, then it's perfectly all right for me to undergo something because of this child.' I returned at daybreak to anoint him and she was still at his side, smiling at him and wiping the sweat from his brow."

"And here you see me!" and the woman being extolled, who spread her joy and the brightness of her life everywhere, came in laughing.

Don Magín flushed because she had surprised him while he was praising her.

"If you don't move up from parish priest to bishop, and I don't end my spinsterhood, it will be I who will care for you and put a poultice on you, if you need it in your old age!"

"My child, you say you will care for me and put a poultice on me! Because you and I will do everything possible so as not to change from what we are!"

"So I won't get married, I won't ever get married?" and Purita said this as she looked at herself, from her virginal state, at her breasts, her arms, her goddess-like hips, a married goddess; she looked at them all sweetly, as if they belonged to a sister of hers, and then she said:

"The blond engineers are no longer here!"

"Some may yet come back!"

"What difference does it make to me if they come, Don Magín, if for the kind of woman they have in mind, because they are free-thinking foreigners, I am too decent a woman, and to be a wife, according to what they say around here, I am too free in my style of life and the men are too much a part of Oleza!" and what could have ended in a sigh opened up into hilarious laughter.

She was secretary of many Church Societies and of the Sodality of the Samaritan Woman. The fullness of her thirty years brought her the title of *doña* without taking away the diminutive used with her name, which was in accordance with her unmarried state, her charms and her alacrity. "Eve, anxious to escape from Paradise, a paradise replete with apple trees, without even a first man," according to Don Magín.

She turned toward Don Magín and asked him to step aside with her because she had to confess to a mortal sin.

"Well, I'm here to listen to you."

"No, indeed, because for my worst sins I always seek the greatest innocence, and I have just come from taking confession with Don Jeromillo."

– ¿Y qué dijo don Jeromillo?

Contó doña Purita que, al principio, salió una mano del capellán estremeciéndose en el borde del confesonario; ella suspiró, y se doblaron dos dedos; pero el cordal, el índice y el pulgar porfiaban erguidos. La penitente se contuvo en la delicia de la contrición; toda la mano colgó madura. Y en acabando el "yo me acuso de que digan que me han visto desnuda del todo", don Jeromillo rebotó, golpeándose en la jaula, diciendo: "¡Leñe, qué ocurrencia!"

La dulce tullida parpadeó mucho, a punto de llorar. Don Magín quedóse rojo, y la Jimena, ronca y espantada, le gritó:

– ¡Doña Purita, Madre mía Santísima, Reina Soberana!

Doña Purita tomó las manos de doña Corazón; estuvo jugando con los viejos anillos de la señora, y en esta actitud de nena distraída, exclamó:

– Han de saber que esa "ocurrencia" la tenían picoteada en la tertulia de las *Catalanas*. La Monera y Elvira, la beata de Gandía, juraron que yo me quedé desnuda en mi reja para que el de Lóriz me viese... Todo me lo cuenta después la misma Monera, con celos de la otra.

Por el corpiño de doña Corazón subió un oleaje de pena y de ira que se le deshizo en un sollozo. La mayordoma se revolvía, prometiendo rebanar y pisar todas las lenguas de víboras.

Doña Purita la contuvo:

– ¡Es que hay verdad en lo que dicen! ¡Un poco de verdad!

Doña Corazón ya no tuvo más remedio que llorar, mientras don Magín no tuvo más remedio que reír.

– Yo me resigné a que esa "ocurrencia" fuese pecado porque las gentes lo decían, pero yo no pequé. Yo estaba acostada, sin sueño. (Lo de acostarme sin sueño vendrá de mi niñez de sobrina protegida.) A mi lado hay en espejo, lo único que heredé de mi casa, un espejo grande, donde me miro y me veo del todo; pero un espejo decente. Y me vi esa noche. Había luna llena, esta luna de marzo, la de la víspera de la luna de Semana Santa, cuando yo soy más feliz sintiéndome una María Magdalena virgen.

– ¿No tiene usted en su reja un rosal?

– Sí, don Magín de mi alma, un rosal, ahora ya tierno, que da gozo. Pues

"And what did Don Jeromillo say?"

Doña Purita recounted how, at first, one of the chaplain's hands emerged trembling on the edge of the confessional box; she sighed and two of the fingers bent; but the middle finger, the index finger and the thumb persisted in remaining straight. The penitent woman restrained herself in the delight of contrition; the whole hand hung down like ripened fruit. And as she finished saying, "I confess to what they say about seeing me completely naked," Don Jeromillo recoiled and struck himself inside the cage, saying, "Confound it, what an incredible thing to do!"

The sweet crippled woman blinked again and again and was at the point of breaking into tears. Don Magín turned red and Jimena, hoarse and startled, shouted at her:

"Doña Purita, Holy Mother of God, Majestic Queen!"

Doña Purita took Doña Corazón's hands; she started playing with the woman's old rings and exclaimed, very much like a small and distracted child:

"You ought to know that that 'incredible episode' was picked apart at the social get-together at the *Catalan Sisters*. The Monera woman and Elvira, that sanctimonious hypocrite from Gandía, swore that I stood naked at the window grating so that Lóriz fellow could see me.... The very same Monera woman, who's jealous of the other one, tells me everything about it afterwards."

A surge of sorrow and anger arose through Doña Corazón's bodice and overcame her in a sob. The housekeeper kept moving back and forth, promising to carve up and trample all those vipers' tongues.

Doña Purita restrained her:

"The fact is there's some truth in what they say! A small amount of truth!"

Doña Corazón now had no other recourse than to weep, while Don Magín had no other recourse than to laugh.

"I resigned myself to accepting that 'episode' as a sin because people said it was, but I didn't sin. I was lying in bed, unable to sleep. (This habit of going to bed without being able to sleep must come from a childhood living as a sheltered niece.) There is a mirror beside me, the only one I inherited from my home, a big mirror in which I can look upon myself and can see myself fully; but it is a decent mirror. I saw myself that night. There was a full moon, this March moon, the one just before the moon of Holy Week, when I am most happy and feel that I am a virginal Mary Magdalene."[100]

"Don't you have a rosebush at your window grating?"

"Yes, my very dear Don Magín, a rosebush still not in full bloom now,

me dio la gana de ver la noche entre mi rosal. Abrí los postigos, y entonces me aparecí en el espejo. Yo estaba sola, y me daba tanta luna, que quise verme como en un baño. ¡Ay, don Magín, nunca me he creído tan buena ni tan dichosa! Nos mirábamos la luna y yo en mi desnudez y en silencio. ¡Qué silencio de luz!... Dicen que me vieron. Yo cerré la ventana apenas me llegó el ruido, y me oculté y me cubrí, porque ya con sospecha de alguien no sentía yo la misma delicia. Ustedes me escuchan sonriendo y aceptándome. Yo no sé por qué las flacas, las feas, las de piel verdosa y ardiente como las Elviras!...

— Purita, por María Santísima!

— Doña Elvira sabe que yo la llamo verde, flaca y ardiente, y lo es. ¿Verdad, don Magín, que lo que yo digo es el Evangelio?

— No será precisamante el Evangelio, pero lo creo lo mismo!

— Pues yo no sé por qué las Elviras se enfurecen tanto de que las que no lo somos nos guste vernos, a la luna, blancas y hermosas. Sí, señor: blancas y hermosas, aunque me arrepienta enseguida de decirlo. Solas, desnudas, mirándonos. Yo, sola, mirándome y complaciéndome como si yo no fuese yo ni otra.

— ¿Pero la vieron a usted, la vio desnuda el de Lóriz? — le preguntó la Jimena con ansiedad.

Doña Purita se reía con exquisito pudor.

Y desde afuera vino una vocecita frágil, diciendo:

— Si a ella le agradara que la viese desnuda el de Lóriz, no sería por la ventana abierta, sino con la ventana cerradita, mis hijas.

Pasó doña Nieves la Santera, con su altarín de San Josefico, haciendo a todos sus comedimientos; y sentóse arrebujada en su manto, como si estuviese en las Cuarenta Horas. En doña Nieves se daban tres cualidades, por lo menos, de su nombre: blanca, fina y fría. El tono de su habla quebradiza semejaba a niña enferma y con regaño. Sus ojos, de un azul pálido y quieto, presenciaban insensibles los dolores y desventuras de casi todas las familias de Oleza. Asistía a los agónicos; amortajaba y velaba los difuntos sin admitir salario ni limosna, dejando los dineros para la que acudiese por oficio. Vio morir a sus padres, a sus hermanos, quedó sola en su casa, y nunca se le

but such a joy to behold. Well, I got an urge to see the night through my
rosebush. I opened the shutters and then I caught sight of myself in the
mirror. I was alone and the moon was shining so fully upon me that I made
up my mind to see myself like I do in my bath. Oh, Don Magín, I never
thought I could feel so good and so happy! The moon and I looked upon
one another silently in my nakedness. Such a silence of light!... They say
that they saw me. I closed my window as soon as I heard a noise, and I hid
myself and covered myself, because once I became suspicious of someone's
presence, I didn't feel the same delight. You both listen to me with a smile
and accept me. I don't know why the scrawny ones, the ugly ones, the ones
with greenish, feverish skin like the Elviras...."

"Purita, by the Holy Virgin!"

"Doña Elvira knows that I speak of her as green, scrawny and feverish,
and she is all that. Isn't that true, Don Magín, that what I'm saying is the
Gospel truth?"

"It's probably not precisely the Gospel, but I believe it just as you do!"

"Well, I don't know why the Elviras get so furious when those of us who
are not like that enjoy seeing ourselves in the moonlight, white and lovely.
Yes, indeed: white and lovely, although I may regret saying it very soon.
Alone, naked, looking at ourselves. I, alone, looking upon myself and taking
pleasure in myself as if I were not me nor any one else."

"But didn't they see you, didn't that Lóriz see you naked?" Jimena asked
her anxiously.

Doña Purita laughed with exquisite modesty.

A small, fragile voice came from outside saying:

"If it were her pleasure that Lóriz see her naked, it wouldn't have been with
the window open, but rather with the window closed really tight, my dears."

Doña Nieves, the Bearer of the Holy Image[101] came in with her miniature
altar for little Saint Joseph, and she offered everyone there her courtesies;
and she sat down all wrapped up in her shawl as if she were present during
the service of the Feast of the Forty Hours.[102] At least three qualities of
her name were evident in Doña Nieves: white, fine and cold. The tone of
her brittle speech was not unlike that of a sick little girl with a scolding
tone. Her pale, quietly blue eyes had impassively witnessed the sorrows
and misfortunes of almost all the families in Oleza. She would attend to
the dying; she would lie on the shrouds and keep vigil for the dead, without
ever accepting either remuneration or charity, leaving the money for anyone
whose occupation it was to serve. She saw her parents and her brothers and
sisters die; she remained alone in the house, but her expression never lost its

empañó su mirar. Para lavar a los muertos, les tomaba de los brazos, tan rígidos, de las piernas, tan grandes y duras; los zarandeaba con suavidad, con pocos crujidos, como si volviese muñecas primorosas, las muñecas con que jugaba aquella niña enferma que residía dentro de su vocecita.

Doña Purita la recibió aplaudiendo de júbilo.

– ¡Doña Nieves! ¡Doña Nieves ha de valerme! Doña Nieves ha de ser la prueba de mi negocio. Vean a doña Nieves: ella jamás habló a nadie, ni a nosotros, de su vida. Ella sale de su casa, cierra y se guarda la llave. Vuelve; abre, entra, cierra y se queda dentro sola. Nadie la ve; nadie la visita. ¿Quién pisó su alcoba? ¿Quién se asomó a su arca? Parece que doña Nieves no sea de bulto, sino lisa, estampada. ¿No es verdad? Ni ama ni odia, ni llora ni teme. Mírenla reír sin rebullirle los labios. Doña Nieves penetra en nuestras intenciones más que los ojos de Nuestro Padre. Ella sí que nos ve a todos desnudos, como si fuésemos cadáveres. Pero nosotros no pasamos de su ropa, como si detrás no hubiese más que el reverso de la tela. Doña Nieves es un misterio; debiera ser un misterio, y no lo es. En el Círculo de Labradores, en el Nuevo Casino, en San Ginés, en todas partes de Oleza se dice que doña Nieves, cuando se recoge, de noche, en su dormitorio, saca cuatro cirios amarillos, cuatro candeleros de madera, y se viste su mortaja de sayal de agustina; se la pone para dormir, como yo me pongo mi camisona; pero ella se añade la toca, las calzas de algodón, las alpargatillas, todo con una crucecita morada entre sus iniciales. ¿Es verdad, doña Nieves? Usted no lo ha contado, y lo sabemos. Ni usted tuvo la vanagloria de decirlo ni de mostrarse amortajada para dormir, ni yo de que me viesen desnuda. Y nos ven. Oleza tiene ojos de gato y de demonio que traspasan las paredes!

Doña Nieves había depositado en la consola su capilla. Hizo una genuflexión y, suspirando, abrió las hojuelas. Apareció San Josefico, muy lindo, con pelo de mujer, el tirso jovial de flores y las ropas ingenuamente bordadas, como si lo hubiesen vestido las niñas de Costura. Tenía a los lados floreros de cipreses con rosas de oro; el fondo, de bovedilla azul con avecitas, lúnulas, querubines, signos del zodíaco, atributos de labores artesanas y agrarias, y delante de sus sandalias miniadas, el vaso de la mariposa que cada

luster. In order to wash the dead, she would take them by the arms, ever so rigid, by their legs, so big and so hard; she would gently turn them one way and the other, with very little creaking, as if she were turning elegant dolls, the very same dolls with which that sick child residing within her soft little voice was playing.

Doña Purita received her by clapping her hands with joy:

"Doña Nieves! Doña Nieves has to defend me! Doña Nieves has to be the proof of what happened to me. Just look at Doña Nieves: she never spoke to anyone, not even to us, about her life. She goes out of her house, she locks it up and puts away the key. She returns, opens up, goes inside, locks up and remains inside alone. Nobody sees her, nobody visits her. Who ever set foot in her bedroom? Who ever looked inside her storage chest? It seems as if Doña Nieves had no physical substance, that she is only a flattened image. Isn't that true? She does not love, nor hate, nor weep, nor fear. Look at her laugh without even moving her lips. Doña Nieves penetrates our intentions more than Our Father's eyes. She really sees us all naked, as if we were cadavers. But we never go beyond her clothes, as if there were nothing else behind them but the other side of the cloth. Doña Nieves is a mystery; she really ought to be a mystery and she isn't. At the Farmers' Club, at the New Club, in San Ginés, everywhere in Oleza, they say that Doña Nieves, when she retires at night in her bedroom, takes out four yellow wax tapers, four wooden candle holders, and she dresses in her Augustinian sackcloth shroud; she puts it on to sleep just as I put on my nightdress; but she adds the headdress, the cotton stockings, the hemp sandals, all this with a small purple cross between the divine initials. Is that true, Doña Nieves? You haven't told anyone about it and yet we know it. Nor did you have the vanity to talk about it or show yourself enshrouded in order to go to bed, nor do I to let them see me naked. And yet they see us. Oleza has the eyes of a cat and the devil and that can penetrate walls."

Doña Nieves had deposited her chapel on the console table. She genuflected and opened the small, hinged leaves with a sigh. Little Saint Joseph appeared, very attractive, with a woman's hair, his thyrsus jovial with flowers and his clothes ingenuously embroidered, as if the little girls in the Sewing Class had dressed him. At the sides, it had flower stands with cypresses and golden roses; the background consisted of a small blue dome with little birds, crescent shapes, cherubs, zodiacal signs, attributes of the artisan and agrarian crafts, and in front of his miniature sandals stood the glass receptacle with the rush candle which every family filled with the very

familia llenaba del mejor aceite. Veinticuatro horas lo dejaba en su poder para que le rezasen y le pidiesen gracias y le alumbrasen, y al recogerlo, le daban socorro. Con él y sus recados ganaba su pan: recados de venta y trueque de joyas, telas, encajes, abanicos, bujería y olores. Corredora, medianera, consejera y amiga pobre, sin perder entono y señorío, de las principales casas de Oleza, cuyos hijos y criados la trataban siempre de doña, y ella tuteaba a todos, y sentábase a su mesa, comedida y ganadora de la confianza. En fin, su altarillo era su refugio, su alacena, su escudo y su llave para llegar a lo recóndito de todos los corazones y viviendas, y al lado de cada aflicción ajena sabía poner el dulce resumen de un suspiro.

Asomóse don Magín a la hornacina, y desde allí decia:

– Este San Josefico, tan aldeano y tan guapo, me impone más que la tremenda imagen de Nuestro Padre San Daniel. A Nuestro Padre se lo cuentan todo a voces; es santo de multitud. San Josefico se pasa una noche y un día en la intimidad de cada casa y se apodera hasta del olor de los ajuares. Lágrimas, murmuraciones, gritos, sonrisas y silencios se van quedando en esta cajuela. No se le puede mirar sin sentir como el pulso de algún recuerdo o confidencia de otro devoto. Aquí dentro está Oleza.

Doña Corazón le escuchaba mirando la menuda imagen. San Josefico presenció la olvidada agonía de don Vicente Grifol. A la otra tarde, doña Nieves le trajo el santo. Y hoy, que se cumplía el aniversario de la muerte, volvía San Josefico a pedir posada de piedad en su alcoba. San Josefico movía la rueda emocional de los tiempos y de los hogares. La imagen hablaba por la boca marchita de doña Nieves. Ella siempre advertía de dónde acababa de venir, y el diminuto huésped dejaba las encomiendas, las sensaciones y el vaho de la otra familia.

– ¡Ahora lo traigo del lado de Paulina!

Y doña Nieves suspiró y dejó que su San Josefico emanase la emoción de la ausente.

Todos callaron mirándolo; hasta que don Magín volvióse a la bizarra doña Purita:

– Ni ojos de gato ni de demonio, como usted dijo; sólo San Josefico

best oil. She would leave it in their care for twenty-four hours so they could pray to him, ask him for favors and light the lamp to him, and when she would come to pick it up, they would offer her some payment. She earned her living with this and with her running errands: errands and messages concerning sales, exchange of jewelry, cloth, lace, fans, cheap knickknacks and scents. Without losing a sense of haughtiness or imperiousness, she was message- bearer, go-between, advisor and poor friend of the most illustrious houses in Oleza, whose children and servants always addressed her as *doña*, and she would address them in the familiar *tú*, and sit at their tables in a courteous manner, worthy of their confidence. In short, her miniature altar was her refuge, her cupboard, her shield and her key used to reach the deepest recesses of all hearts and dwellings, and she knew how to put the sweet summation of a sigh beside every other person's affliction.

Don Magín peered into the niche and from there he said:

"This little Saint Joseph, so rustic and so handsome, impresses me far more than the awesome image of Our Father San Daniel. Everything they tell Our Father they say in a loud voice; he is the saint of a multitude. Our little Saint Joseph spends one night and one day in the intimacy of each house and he takes possession of even the aroma of the house furnishings. Tears, gossip, shouts, smiles and silences remain behind in that little box. One can not look at him without hearing something like the pulse of some memory or the confidential secret of another devout soul. Oleza is here inside."

Doña Corazón kept listening to him as she looked at the tiny image. Little Saint Joseph witnessed the forgotten death throes of Don Vicente Grifol. Doña Nieves brought him the saint on the following afternoon. And today, which marked the anniversary of his death, little Saint Joseph was returning to seek merciful shelter in his bedroom. Little Saint Joseph moved the emotional wheel of all times and all homes. The image spoke through the withered mouth of Doña Nieves. She would always announce where she had just been and the diminutive guest would leave behind the charges, the sensations and the life force of the other family.

"I'm just now bringing it from beside Paulina!"

And Doña Nieves sighed and allowed her little Saint Joseph to radiate the emotion of the absent woman.

They all remained silent and looked at it; until Don Magín turned toward the splendid Doña Purita:

"Neither the eyes of a cat or a devil, as you said; only little Saint Joseph

tiene poder para traspasar las paredes y averiguar el secreto de la casa de don Álvaro,

– ¡Yo también lo sé! – prorrumpió, encrespándose, la Jimena – , ¡A mí no me engañó esa gente! ¡Por algo mientras casaban a Paulina le pedí yo a Dios que me diera coraje y maldad para defenderla de todos!

Y don Magín sonrió.

– ¡Pero no siempre atiende Dios los ruegos de sus criaturas!

– Al pasar por aquella casa – gritó doña Purita – se tropieza una con el silencio y la obscuridad. Si veo cerrados sus balcones, me pregunto: ¿qué ocurrirá?, y si están abiertos, me digo: ¿qué habrá sucedido? Porque parecen balcones y rejas de salas, de dormitorios donde hubo un difunto, un difunto que nunca acaban de sacar. Y lo más horrible es que nunca pasa nada.

Entonces la vocecita endeble de doña Nieves exhaló como desde el pecho de San Josefico:

– Mis hijas; bien avisado iba don Magín: mi santo pequeño debe de saber más de Paulina que Nuestro Padre San Daniel. Mujer que no resista la mirada de Nuestro Padre, es mujer pecadora. Nuestro Padre no sabe sino que le llevan a Paulina bajo sus ojos. Pero San Josefico sabe más: sabe que Paulina puede resistir la prueba resistiendo cada noche los ojos de don Álvaro.

Alzóse Purita, y mientras se componía su tocado en el espejo de doña Corazón no paraba de hablar:

– ¡La frente de don Álvaro está rota por un pliegue como una herida abierta desde su alma! ¡Qué será ese hombre, que el hijo tutea a la madre y a él le habla de usted! ¡Hombre puro, que siempre tiene a Dios en su boca! ¡Dios de don Álvaro, Dios de doña Elvira!

– Ya es viejo el dicho – se interpuso el capellán – de que si los triángulos imaginasen a Dios, le darían tres lados. Pero por mucho que los hombres se afanen, y entre todos don Álvaro, en invocar a un Dios que se les parezca, Dios siempre es mejor que ellos, por fortuna para los bienaventurados.

– ¿Mejor? – revolvióse la Jimena santiguándose – . ¡Más puro y rígido el Dios de don Álvaro que el mismo don Álvaro! ¡Ay, don Magín, y qué Dios tan terrible! ¡Dios nos libre de ése!

has the power to penetrate the walls and find out the secret of Don Álvaro's home."

"I know it too!" Jimena burst out, bristling with anger. "Those people didn't fool me! For good reason I asked God to grant me the courage and the wickedness to defend her against everyone when they were marrying off Paulina!"

And Don Magín smiled.

"But God doesn't always heed the requests of those he created!"

"When you pass by that house," Doña Purita shouted, "you encounter the silence and the darkness. If I see its balcony windows closed, I ask myself: What can be happening? and if they are open, I say to myself: What can have happened? Because they seem to be balcony windows and window gratings of drawing rooms, of bedrooms where there was a dead person, a dead person whom they never really remove. And the most terrible part is that nothing ever happens."

Then the feeble little voice of Doña Nieves breathed forth as if from the breast of little Saint Joseph:

"My children, Don Magín was very well advised: my little saint must know more about Paulina than Our Father San Daniel. Any woman who can not bear Our Father's gaze is a sinful woman. Our Father knows only that they bring Paulina under his eyes. But little Saint Joseph knows more: he knows that Paulina can endure the test by enduring the gaze of Don Álvaro's eyes each night."

Purita stood up and did not stop speaking during the time she kept arranging her hair in Doña Corazón's mirror:

"Don Álvaro's forehead is split by a crease like an open wound that comes from his very soul! What can that man be like if his son speaks with the familiar *tú* to his mother and uses the formal *usted* to his father! A pure man, one who always has God on his lips! God of Don Álvaro, God of Doña Elvira!"

"The saying is quite old," the priest interrupted, "that if triangles could imagine God, they would give him three sides.[103] But no matter how much men, and especially Don Álvaro, may strive to invoke a God who would resemble them, God is always better than them, which is fortunate for simple, blessed souls."

"Better?" said Jimena, turning around and crossing herself. "Don Álvaro's God purer and more rigid than Don Álvaro himself! Oh, Don Magín, what a terrible God! God protect us from such a one as that!"

IV

CLAUSURA Y SIGLO

CLOISTERED AND WORLDLY LIFE

1. Conflictos

Las dominicas de Santa Lucía, las clarisas de San Gregorio, las salesas de Nuestra Señora enviaban al señor obispo potes de ungüentos maravillosos y redomas de aceites y aguas de bendición para las llagas.

Juntos salían de Palacio los demandaderos, diciéndose el cansancio y mohina que se les esperaba en sus monasterios. Pero el más caviloso era siempre el de la Visitación. Había de resistir los filiales fervores de la comunidad por su ilustrísima, y singularmente de la Madre y de sor María Fulgencia o la señorita Valcárcel. Nunca se saciaban de pedirle noticias. Querían saber si había visto al reverendo enfermo, o si pudo oír su voz y cómo la tenía; si le cuidaba en Palacio alguna religiosa de Oleza; quién le tomaba el recado; si supo algún alivio repentino; qué remedio tuvo más predilección, si el suyo, o los ofrecidos por las clarisas, o por las dominicas, o por las damas devotas; y, finalmente, cuando llegaba a la antecámara y decía: "De parte de la abadesa de la Visitación, y de toda la comunidad..." ¿Qué? Entraba, lo decía, ¿y qué?...

El donado movía resignadamente su esquilada cabeza de siervo, mirándose su gorra viejecita. No sabía nada. Entraba, lo decía, y nada. Un clérigo afilado les recogía a todos, de una vez, las pomadas, los bálsamos, los atadijos de hierbas y raíces. Se marchaba y volvía muy de prisa, repasando documentos, quitándose y poniéndose los anteojos, y de súbito se paraba:

– ¡Ah! Oigan: el señor da las gracias a la comunidad de, de eso..., de...

– ¿De las salesas? – le preguntaba muy encogido el recadero.

– Sí; de las salesas, de las salesas... Bueno. Y le pide que le encomiende en sus oraciones, y la bendice.

Se humillaba el abuelito para recibir esa benedición que había de llevar a las celestiales esposas, y se aguardaba. Los otros también.

El eclesiástico se ponía a leer en su bufetillo, mirándoles de reojo.

1. Conflicts

The Dominican sisters of Santa Lucía,[104] the Clares of San Gregorio, the Salesian sisters of the Order of Nuestra Señora de la Visitación sent the lord bishop jars of miraculous ointments and phials of oils and holy water for his sores.

The convent messengers left the Palace together, telling one another about the weariness and animadversion awaiting them in their convents. But the one from La Visitación was always the most captious. He had to put up with the sisterly fervor of the Community for His Excellency, and especially on the part of the Mother and Sister María Fulgencia or Señorita Valcárcel. They never tired of asking him for news. They wanted to know if he had seen the ailing Reverend Father, or if he was able to hear his voice and how it sounded; if some sister from Oleza was caring for him in the Palace; who took messages and ran errands; if he had learned of some sudden improvement, which remedy he most favored, whether theirs or the ones offered by the Clares, or by the Dominican sisters, or by some other pious ladies; and finally, when he reached the anteroom and said, "On the part of the abbess of La Visitación and the entire Community...." What happened? He went in, he said it, and then what?...

The lay brother moved his serf-like, shorn head in resignation and looked at his shabby old cap. He didn't know anything. He went in, said what he had to say and that's all. A sharp-featured cleric gathered together all their pomades, balms, loose bundles of herbs and roots at the same time. He marched off and returned very quickly, passing out documents, taking off his spectacles and putting them back on, and suddenly he stopped:

"Oh, one more thing: the lord bishop sends his thanks to the Community of, of, uh, uh..., of...."

"Of the Salesians?" the messenger asked him very timidly.

"Yes, of the Salesians, of the Salesians.... Good. And he asks them to remember him in their prayers, and he blesses them."

The little old fellow bent his head to receive that benediction which he was supposed to bring to the celestial spouses of Jesus and he waited. The others too.

The ecclesiastic started reading at his small desk, looking at them from out of the corner of his eye.

Ellos no se iban. Tañían horas los relojes de las salas. Y el fámulo de las dominicas osaba decir:

– Es que la priora quisiera saber si el agua santa del Jordán le probó a su ilustrísima.

– ¿Agua del Jordán? ...¿Agua del Jordán? ¿Era un frasquito verde con una cruz en el lacre?

– ¡Ay, no señor, que no era! ¡El mío tiene un San Juan Bautista en medio!

– El verde – mediaba el de las salesas – , el verde lo traje yo. Era de aceite de los olivos de Getsemaní. Lo tenía sor María Fulgencia o la señorita Valcárcel, porque se lo regaló un señor beneficiado de Murcia que estuvo en Jerusalén, y dicen...

El de las dominicas se expansionaba:

– Mire: el agua santa no venía en ningún frasquito, sino en un tarro de color de pan moreno; un pote de la misma tierra del pozo de Santo Domingo de Guzmán; de la tierra que hacen rosarios, que es tan milagrosa.

Y añadía el de la Visitación:

– ¡Si se lo preguntásemos al enfermero!...

Desaparecía el presbítero por la mampara de felpa amaranto cuyo escudo prelaticio de sedas de oro iba nublándose de huellas de manos sudadas.

Quedábanse los fámulos en silencio, sin moverse de los manises que les correspondían a sus alpargatas cenicientas.

Subían capellanes de la curia, criados de casas ricas preguntando por el enfermo. Volvía el familiar con fojas, con libros. Atendía a los recién llegados, sin acordarse de los otros, y alguno tosía. De repente les miraba con un frío de anteojos.

– ¡Ah! Me dicen que sí, que sí que le probaron a su ilustrísima: el agua y el aceite, el frasquito y el pote, los dos.

...Llevada de piadosos anhelos, la prelada de las salesas escribió a la Madre Ana de San Francisco, de la residencia generalicia de la Alta Saboya, pidiéndole el ostensorio de la Casa, que había sanado muchos enfermos de males empedernidos de la piel. Era una delgada bujeta de forma de libro, y entre dos hojuelas de esmeraldas se guardaban cinco limaduras del hierro con que la santa fundadora, Juana Francisca Frémyot, baronesa de Chantal, se grabó en el costado el nombre de Jesús.

They wouldn't go away. The clocks in all the rooms kept striking the hours. And the *famulus* for the Dominican sisters dared to say:

"The fact is the prioress would really like to know if they tried the holy water from the Jordan on His Excellency."

"Water from the Jordan?... Water from the Jordan? Was it a green little flask with a cross on the sealing wax?"

"Oh, no indeed, that wasn't it! Mine has a Saint John the Baptist in the middle!"[105]

"The green one," the man from the Salesian Order interrupted, "I brought the green one. It contained oil from the olive trees in Gethsemane. Sister María Fulgencia or Señorita Valcárcel had it, because it was given to her as a gift by a prebendary from Murcia who was in Jerusalem, and they say...."

The one from the Dominican sisters expansively said:

"Look here: the holy water did not come in any little flask, but in a jar the color of dark bread, a pot made of the same clay used for the wall of Santo Domingo de Guzmán,[106] of the clay with which they make rosaries and which is so miraculous."

And the one from La Visitación added:

"If we could only ask the clerical orderly!"

The priest disappeared past the amaranthine plush screen with a prelatic escutcheon of golden silks that was clouding over from the imprint of sweaty hands.

The *famuli* remained there in silence without moving from the glazed colored tiles corresponding to each of their ash-gray hemp sandals.

Priests from the clerical staff kept coming up, as well as servants from well-to-do households, inquiring about the ailing man. The familiar returned with legal papers, with books. He attended to the recent arrivals without remembering the others, and one of them coughed. He suddenly looked at them with the coldness of his spectacles.

"Oh, they tell me they did, that they did try them on His Excellency: the water and the oil, the small flask and the pot, both of them."

...Inspired by pious determination, the prelatess of the Salesian Order wrote to Mother Ana de San Francisco at the central residence of the order in Haute Savoie, asking her for the monstrance belonging to their House, which had cured many sick persons of indurated diseases of the skin. It was a slender wooden box in the shape of a book, with five filings of the piece of iron with which the sainted founder, Juana Francisca Fremyot, baroness of Chantal,[107] engraved the name of Jesus on her side, preserved between two small leaves adorned with emeralds.

Consintió la casa-madre en dejarlo a la casa de Oleza; pero temía los peligros y la irreverencia de confiar la preciosa reliquia al servicio de Correos entre estampas inmundas, impresos, cartas de herejes y pliegos de valores declarados de la banca judía difundida por todo el mundo.

La comunidad de Nuestra Señora horrorizóse imaginándolo. Durante algunos días vivieron consternadas las dulces religiosas.

Domingo de Quincuagésima, a punto de prosternarse María Fulgencia en la cratícula para comulgar, llegóse a la prelada, palpitándole la cruz de su pecho y resplandeciéndole de un regocijo de gloria sus hermosos ojos aterciopelados.

– ¡Ay, Madre, Madre, que Nuestro Señor me ilumina!

– ¡Comulgue, hija, y después hablará!

– ¡Si no puedo, Madre; si no puedo de la prisa de decirlo!

– ¿Pero tuvo alguna visión reveladora de impedimento?

– ¡Yo no sé; yo no sé!... – balbució la sor apasionándose.

Todas comulgaron. Mirábala la Madre sintiendo el apuro de su responsabilidad. Era un trance desconocido. En quince años de abadiato, la vida de claustro deslizóse siempre sosegada, sin trastornos ni sequedades de tentación, sin convulsiones ni arrobamientos místicos. ¡Y esa criatura de Murcia traía inesperadamente las alarmas de la santidad! Pues ¿qué haría ella con una santa en casa, una santa bajo su obediencia, una santa jovencita, con tránsitos ciegos, incomprensibles del gozo a las lágrimas, de las melancolías a los enfados pueriles? ¡Las santas, las santas no debieran manifestarse sino después de muertas, quietecitas en los altares! ¡Señor, arrobos, no! ¡Tan bien como se podía vivir siendo todas dóciles! – ¡la clavaria, la clavaria! – , ¡todas dóciles, todas buenas, muy buenas, y nada más!

Todavía insistió sor María Fulgencia:

– ¿No me oye, Madre?

Estremecióse la Madre.

– ¿Me oye? ¡Es el relicario, es el relicario que viene, que puede venir sin peligro!

Presintió la abadesa que iba a florecer la gracia de lo maravilloso.

The mother House consented to leaving it with the House in Oleza, but they feared the dangers and the irreverence if they entrusted the precious relic to the Postal Service, among all the filthy prints, printed matter, letters from heretics and sealed envelopes of certified currency of the Jewish banking establishment spread out all over the world.

The Community of Nuestra Señora was horrified just imagining it. For several days the sweet sisters lived in consternation.

On Quinquagesima Sunday before Lent,[108] María Fulgencia, just as she was about to prostrate herself at the small wicket through which she would take communion, came over to the prelatess, her cross over her bosom throbbing, and her lovely, velvety eyes shining with an exultation of glory.

"Oh, Mother, Mother, Our Lord is illuminating me!"

"Take communion, my child, and then you can speak!"

"But I can't, Mother, I just can't, because I'm in such a hurry to tell you all about it!"

"But did you have some vision of revelation cautioning us in some way?"

"I don't know, I don't know!..." the sister stammered, overcome with emotion.

They all took communion. The Mother kept looking at her, feeling the difficulty of her responsibility. It was an unprecedented peril. In fifteen years as abbess, cloistered life had always slipped by quietly, without any upheavals or acrimonious outbursts of temptation, without convulsions or mystical ecstasies. And now that creature from Murcia was bringing in unexpected alarms of saintliness! Well, what would she do with a saint in the House, a saint obedient to her, a frivolous young saint, passing blindly and incomprehensibly from joy to tears, from melancholy to childish outbursts of anger? Saints, saints ought not to manifest themselves until after their death, while lying ever so still on their altars! Oh, Lord, no need for outbursts of ecstasy, no! How well they could all live by being docile! – the Keeper of the Keys, the Keeper of the Keys! – all docile, all good, very good and nothing more!

Sister María Fulgencia still insisted:

"Don't you hear me, Mother?"

The Mother shuddered.

"Do you hear me? It's the reliquary, it's the reliquary that's coming, that can come without any danger!"

The abbess was overcome by the presentiment of a divine grace of the miraculous that was about to blossom.

– Pues ofrezcamos la comunión por tanta dicha. ¡Recójase, ande!

Acabado el oficio y rezo, y después de refectorio, juntóse la comunidad en la sala de costura. No quiso la prelada el coro ni la sala de Capítulo ni otro lugar de ceremonia, temerosa de los efectos extáticos. ¡Señor, arrobos, no! Un aposento apacible y claro, donde se habla con sencillez honestísimos júbilos, no había de invitar a demasiados prodigios. Por humilde olvidaba la Madre que el recinto del milagro es la simplicidad de los corazones. Llamado San Goar por su obispo, acude a Palacio; pasa la antecámera; no ve percha ni mueble donde dejar su capa, y la cuelga de un rayo de sol. De una devanadera podía temer la Madre que se quedaran prendidos como flores los anhelos de sor María Fulgencia. La miraron todas, y ella se puso colorada, y estaba más hermosa.

Palideció la Madre. ¿Exhalaría esa criatura la rara y celestial fragancia que dejan los cuerpos de los bienaventurados? ¡Ese dulce sofoco de su piel tan fina, ese temblor de su pecho!...

– Ya puede, ya puede decir... – le autorizó, suspirando.

Y la señorita Valcárcel dijo:

– Mi primo Mauricio está de agregado militar en la Embajada de Viena...

Se produjo una brisa de tocas, un oleaje de hábitos, de pecherines y lenzuelos.

La clavaria gritó:

– ¡María Santísima! ¡En el comulgatorio; en presencia de Nuestro Señor Jesucristo fue cuando pensó en el mundo!

Mostróse también la superiora con enojo de constitución, aunque sintiese un escondido alivio viendo remontarse el vuelo de lo extraordinario.

– ¡Ay! ¡Que siga!...

– Que siga su caridad... – pidieron muchas voces.

Revolvióse la clavaria murmurando que era demasiada impertinencia. Pero la Madre permitió que hablara la sor. De sus palabras podía originarse un bien para el amado enfermo.

– Mi primo Mauricio está de agregado militar...

"Well, let's offer our communion for such good fortune. Why don't you withdraw now, be off with you!"

When the office and the prayer were over, and after returning from the refectory, the Community gathered in the sewing room. The prelatess decided against using the choir loft or the Chapter meeting room nor any other ceremonial location because she was fearful of any ecstatic effects. Oh, Lord, outbursts of emotion, none of that! A peaceful, bright room where one could speak with simplicity and very proper jubilation would not invite too many prodigies. Due to her own humility, the Mother forgot that the ideal space for a miracle is the simplicity of the heart. When Saint Goar was called by his bishop, he came to the Palace; he passed by the antechamber; he didn't see a clothes rack or a piece of furniture where he could leave his cape, and so he hung it up on a sunbeam.[109] The Mother had good reason to fear that Sister María Fulgencia's yearnings might find themselves caught up like flowers on a winding frame. They all looked at her and she was flushed and looked more beautiful than ever.

The Mother turned pale. Could that creature be giving off the rare, celestial fragrance emitted by the bodies of the blessed? That sweet flush of her extremely fine skin, that trembling of her breast!...

"Now you can, now you can say it...," she authorized her with a sigh.

And Señorita Valcárcel said:

"My cousin Mauricio is serving as a military attaché in the Embassy in Vienna...."

This produced a breeze of headdresses, a swell of habits, starched shirt bosoms and linen handkerchiefs.

The Keeper of the Keys shouted:

"Most Holy Mother of God! At the very communion altar; in the presence of Our Lord Jesus Christ, that's where she thought of the outer world!"

The Mother Superior also revealed herself in the anger of her authority, although she felt a hidden sense of relief when she saw the flight of something extraordinary soaring away.

"Oh, dear! Let her go on!..."

"Let Her Charity go on...," many voices requested, using the order's form of address.

The Keeper of the Keys turned around muttering that this was too much impertinence. But the Mother permitted the sister to speak. Some good could originate from the words she spoke for the benefit of the beloved ailing man.

"My cousin Mauricio is serving as a military attaché...."

– ¡Ya lo sabemos! – le interrumpió la austera religiosa.

– ...En la Embajada de Viena, y ahora llegará a Murcia con permiso.

– ¿Y cómo lo averiguó su caridad? – se le interpuso de nuevo la clavaria.

– Yo nada averigüé. Me lo ha escrito tío Eusebio y tía Ivonne-Catherine...

– Cómo se llama esa señora?

– Ivonne-Catherine; pero tío Eusebio la llama Ivette, o Kate, o Gothon.

– ¡María Santísima!

– Me lo han escrito tío Eusebio y tía Ivonne-Catherine, que pasarán la Cuaresma y Semana Santa en sus haciendas de Murcia. La Reverenda Madre leyó la carta. Mauricio ha de detenerse en la Alta Saboya, mandado por su ministro. En Pascua llegará a Murcia, y trae licencia hasta la Asunción. Y yo me he dicho, sin duda movida por Nuestra Señora, que por qué no se le encomienda el venerando ostensorio. Su reverencia podría escribirle a la Madre Ana de San Francisco y esta pecadora a él...

Menos la clavaria, todas bendijeron el inspirado designio de la vía diplomática. Y quedó aprobado.

Camino de su celda, la Madre tuvo que soportar los buidos conceptos de su ministra.

– ¿No se habrá cometido ya un daño irremediable permitiendo que la sor dijese su parecer?

La Madre pudo valerse de San Pablo:

– El apóstol de las gentes ha escrito "que si alguno de los reunidos recibe una revelación, callará el que estuviere hablando".

– ¿Y fue revelación verdadera lo de la señorita Valcárcel? ¿No será sor María un peligro para la vida de suavidades de esta casa?

Humilló la abadesa su frente calva, como aceptando los males que pudiesen venir.

– Todas amamos a sor. Las educandas tienen un gozo de escogidas desde que ella vino a nuestro lado.

– ¡Es alegría y amor del mundo!

– En estas casas siempre hay una monja que trae la alegría. Ya lo dijo una santa: "El señor dotará de gracias a una hermana para que sea nuestra recreación". Aquí es sor María Fulgencia, que todavía no es sor, aunque se lo digamos.

"We already know that!" the austere nun interrupted her.

"...In the Embassy in Vienna, and he will be coming on leave to Murcia now."

"And how did Your Charity find that out?" the Keeper of the Keys interrupted her again.

"I didn't find out anything. Uncle Eusebio and Aunt Ivonne-Catherine wrote me about it...."

"What is that lady's name?

"Ivonne-Catherine, but Uncle Eusebio calls her Ivette, or Kate or Gothon."

"Holy Mother Mary!"

"Uncle Eusebio and Aunt Ivonne-Catherine have written to me saying they will spend Lent and Holy Week at their country property in Murcia.[110] The Reverend Mother read the letter. Mauricio is to stop over in Haute Savoie on a mission for his minister. He will arrive in Murcia during Easter and he has an authorized leave until the Feast of the Assumption.[111] Undoubtedly moved by Our Lady, I asked myself why we don't entrust the venerable reliquary to him. Your reverence could write to Mother Ana de San Francisco and I, this sinner, to him ...."

Except for the Keeper of the Keys, they all blessed the inspired plan for the diplomatic route. And so it was approved.

On her way to her cell, the Mother had to put up with the barbed opinions of her administrative assistant.

"Is it possible that irreparable harm has already been done by allowing the sister to offer her opinion?"

The Mother was able to avail herself of Saint Paul:

"The apostle to the gentiles has written 'that if any one of those gathered together should receive a revelation, then the one who might be speaking should remain silent.'"[112]

"Was what happened to Señorita Valcárcel a true revelation? Will Sister María not be a danger to the unruffled existence of this House?"

The abbess bent her bald forehead as if accepting the evils that might be forthcoming.

"We all love sister. Those who are still studying have the joy of feeling chosen ever since she came to live among us."

"It is the happiness and the love of the outer world!"

"In these Houses, there is always a nun who brings joy. A saint said it, 'The Lord will endow a sister with wonderful qualities so that she may be our source of recreation.'[113] In this place it is Sister María Fulgencia, who is still not a sister, although we call her that."

– Es que sus gracias pertenecen al siglo. ¿En qué probó quererlo renunciar?

– ¡Lo renunciará porque ha sufrido mucho!

– ¿En qué sufrió? ¿Qué dejará en el siglo si se deja el siglo? Nuestra santa fundadora se arrancó de sus padres y de sus hijos: dos hijas casadas y un hijo de quince años, y este hijo, recuérdelo su reverencia, este hijo se tendió en el umbral de la casa para que la madre retrocediera. La santa le miró, y pasó por encima del hijo, para bien de nosotras, sus hijas verdaderas.

– ¡No todos podemos ni debemos aspirar a la santidad!

Y oprimiéndose con dulzura los dedos, uno a uno, como si se los contase, recogióse en su celda. Allí elevó sus manos, y enseguida las descansó en un libro de cuentas, entre cuyas páginas dejara sus gafas desnudas. No se toleraba a sí misma ademanes de excelsitud y desesperación para no atraerse lo extraordinario. ¿No estaban bien todas? ¡Todas, no! La clavaria, no. ¿Y por qué no? ¿Por qué tan rígida señora había escogido esta orden, que no fue creada para duras penitencias? Todas las intenciones y palabras del sabio definidor, obispo y príncipe de Ginebra, San Francisco de Sales, fueron apacibles y misericordiosas. Así quiso ser ella, acogiéndose al que dijo: "Bienaventurados los corazones blandos, porque nunca se quiebran!"

Alcanzó de un vasar de yeso el *Directorio de Religiosas*.

En la huerta retallecida, bajo un envigado de rosales en flor, giraba un ruedo de hermanas jovencitas que cantaban, mirando la ventana de sor María Fulgencia:

Mari – ábreme la puer...
Mari – ábreme la puer...
¡Que vengo muy mal – heri!
¡Que ven – go muy mal – heri!...

Crujió la vidriera, y salió una tonadilla de párvula respondiendo:

No llaméis con tanto gri...
No llaméis con tanto gri...
que nos oye la clavá...
Que nos o – ye la clavá...

Y la Madre volvía las hojas rosigadas del libro, hasta que se detuvo, porque

"But the fact is her qualities belong to the outer world. In what way did she demonstrate that she wanted to renounce it?"

"She will renounce it because she has suffered a great deal!"

"In what way did she suffer? What will she leave behind in the outside world if she abandons the worldly life? Our sainted founder tore herself from her parents and her children: two married daughters and a son of fifteen, and this son, remember this, your reverence, this son stretched himself out on the threshold of the house so that his mother would go back. The sainted woman looked at him and stepped over her son, for the good of us, her true daughters."

"We can not all nor should we aspire to sainthood!"

And pressing her fingers together sweetly, one by one, as if she were counting them, she withdrew to her cell. There she raised her hands and quickly rested them on an account book where she had left her exposed spectacles between its pages. She did not tolerate any gestures of sublimity and desperation in herself in order not to attract the extraordinary. Weren't they all right? No, not all of them! Not the Keeper of the Keys. And why not? Why had so rigid a woman chosen this order, which was not created for harsh penance? All the good intentions and words of the wise definitor, bishop and prince of Geneva, Saint Francis of Sales, were peaceful and merciful. That's how she tried to be, taking refuge in the one who said, "Blessed are those who are tender of heart because they will never break!"

She reached up to take the *Guide for Nuns*[114] from a plaster shelf. In the garden, now in full bloom, beneath one of the rafters covered with flowering roses, a ring of sweet young sisters were singing as they looked up at Sister María Fulgencia's window:

Mari – open up the doo....
Mari – open up the doo....
For I come very sorely woun!...
For I co – me very sorely woun!...

The window creaked and a melodic childish ditty emerged in response:

Don't you call with such a shou....
Don't you call with such a shou....
For we'll be heard by the Keeper of....
For we'll be hea – rd by the Keeper of....[115]

And the Mother turned the moth-eaten pages of the book till she stopped,

tropezó en el capítulo que dice: "Qué es vivir conforme al espiritu?"

"...Si una hermana es dulce, agradable, y yo la amo con ternura, y ella también me ama, y hay amor recíproco, ¿quién no ve que la amo conforme a la carne, sangre y sentido?"

Se quedó mirando la rueda graciosa de educandas. Asomó muy tímida la señorita Valcárcel, presentándole la carta para su primo, y luego salióse.

La Madre siguió leyendo:

"...Si la otra tiene la condición seca y áspera, y con todo eso, no por el gusto que tengo, mas sólo por amor de Dios, la amo, la sirvo, la acudo, ése sí que es amor conforme al espíritu, porque no tienen en él parte la carne..."

Y sin querer, la abadesa pensó: "¡Siempre ha de salir gananciosa la clavaria!" Conforme al espíritu, la resistía y la amaba. ¡Y en cuanto a la señorita y sor, no era profesa, sino una avecita que se les entró asustada en este palomar de Nuestra Señora! ¡No, no se le quebraba el corazón!

Se puso a escribir, y apenas trazada la cruz de la cabecera, surgió la clavaria.

La Madre le dijo:

– ¡Mire qué linda carta de sor! ¡Parece que un ángel le haya llevado la pluma sobre el pliego!

– ¡Nunca fue la sor tan pulida en la letra como ahora!

Reparó más la prelada en la escritura con algún sobresalto. ¡Oh, Dios, y qué sufrir!

Y la monja se le apartó, acariciándose el cíngulo. Siempre decía muy sutiles advertimientos, y enseguida se retiraba, dejando a la Madre en la tribulación de la incertidumbre. ¡Pero en aquel difícil y piadoso negocio de la salud de su ilustrísima, tardar sería pecar! Y alentóse, escribió su misiva, bajó al locutorio, y avisó a don Jeromillo.

Todo se lo fue refiriendo, y cuando llegó al acomodo para traer al relicario brincó el capellán, gritando:

– ¡Leñe! ¡Y qué ingenio de moza!

– ¡Ay, don Jeromillo, no diga eso! ¡Toda la vida estamos pidiéndoselo!

Luego le entregó las cartas.

– Que no se aparten de usted hasta que usted mismo las lleve a la

because she came upon the chapter that says, "What is it to live in accordance with your spirit?"

"...If a sister is sweet, pleasant, and I love her tenderly, and she loves me too, and there is reciprocal love, who can not see her that I love in accordance with my flesh, my blood and my senses?"

She continued looking at the delightful ring of students. Señorita Valcárcel appeared very timidly before her and presented her with the letter for her cousin, and then she left.

The Mother continued reading:

"...If the other one has a withered, harsh disposition, and in spite of all that, I love her, I serve her, I show consideration for her, not for the pleasure I may have from it, but only for the love of God, that is truly love in accordance with one's spirit, because the flesh has no part in it...."[116]

And without intending to, the abbess thought, "The Keeper of the Keys always has to come out ahead!" In accordance with her spirit, she tolerated her and loved her. And as for the señorita and sister, she was not one who had professed, but rather a little bird who was frightened and came upon this dovecot of Our Lady! No, her heart was not going to be broken!

She started to write and hardly had she drawn the cross at the heading of the page than the Keeper of the Keys rushed in.

The Mother said to her:

"Just look how lovely the sister's letter is! It seems as if an angel had guided her pen over the sheet of paper!"

"The sister never had so polished a handwriting as she does just now!"

The prelatess now took greater notice of the writing with somewhat of a start. Oh, my God, what suffering!

And the nun withdrew from her presence, caressing the cingulum of her habit. She was always offering very subtle warnings, and then she would withdraw, leaving the Mother with the tribulation of her uncertainty. But in that difficult and pious question of the health of His Excellency, to delay would be to sin! So she took courage and wrote her missive, went down to the locutory and informed Don Jeromillo.

She kept explaining it all to him and when she came to the arrangements for bringing the reliquary, the priest gave a start and shouted:

"Confound it! What a talented young woman!"

"Oh, Don Jeromillo, don't say that! All our lives we keep asking for it!"

Then she handed him the letters.

"Don't let them out of your sight until you yourself bring them to the

diligencia, y mire que la diligencia sale a las cuatro del parador.

Abrióse el hábito don Jeromillo y se las puso en el seno.

La Madre entornó los ojos, porque la urdimbre del velo visitandino no impedía que se viese el rojo breñal de aquella carne de varón. ¡Ay, don Jeromillo era tan velludo como Esaú! ¡Quién lo pensara!

2. Miércoles y jueves

Miércoles Santo, dos Hermanitas de los Pobres, dos hormiguitas trajineras, con sus tocas cabezudas, le llevaron a Paulina la "tabla" de los turnos para la mesa petitoria de la catedral. Ella sonrió, aceptándolo todo. No era menester que la leyese. Nada más había que conciliar sus compromisos y devociones: en el oratorio de las clarisas, a las seis; en la parroquia de Nuestro Padre, a las siete, y la vela del Santísimo, de dos a tres, en la catedral. Pero las Hermanas, dulces y tercas, porfiaban que sí era menester; y Paulina leyó la hoja, y enseguida volvióse como si buscase aprobación y la temiese. Las monjitas se miraban, y ella salió del comedor, y luego vino Elvira y don Álvaro, que traía entre sus dedos el escrito.

– Aquí dice: "Santa Iglesia Catedral: De cuatro a cinco, condesa de Lóriz, señora de Galindo y doña Purita Canci". Y yo digo: ¿por qué juntaron ustedes estos nombres?

– Tres habían de ser, señor don Álvaro, y estos tres nos parecen de los más principales de Oleza – lo pronunció la Hermana joven con acento gascón y un fino parpadeo de inocencia y perplejidad.

– ¿Y por qué no podían ser la señora Monera, mi mujer y mi hermana doña Elvira?

– Bien podían haber sido – dijo entonces la monja más antigua – , si no viniésemos de hablar con los de Lóriz, generosos bienhechores de Casa; pero la condesa quiso que al lado de su nombre apuntásemos el de la señora Galindo y de doña Purita.

Otra vez se habían mirado las Hermanitas de los Pobres, y los hermanos de Gandía también, y entre ellos, Paulina estaba sola, inclinada, esperando.

diligence, and you are aware that the coach departs from the inn at four o'clock."

Don Jeromillo opened up his habit and put them close to his chest.

The Mother half-closed her eyes because the warp of the material of the veil of the order of La Visitación did not prevent her from seeing the ruddy thicket on his masculine flesh. Oh, Don Jeromillo was as hairy as Esau! Who would have thought it![117]

2. Wednesday and Thursday

On Wednesday of Holy Week, two Little Sisters of the Poor,[118] two little ants scurrying about on their charitable rounds, wearing their large-headed cornets, brought Paulina the "list" of the periods of duty of those who would serve at the petitionary table at the cathedral.[119] She smiled, accepting it all. It wasn't necessary for her to read it. It was only necessary to reconcile her appointments and her devotions: at the oratory of the Clares at six o'clock; at the parish church of Our Father at seven, and the vigil of the Holy Eucharist from two to three at the cathedral. But the sweet, stubborn Sisters insisted that it really was necessary; and Paulina read the page and quickly turned around as if she were seeking approval and yet fearing it. The little nuns looked at one another and she left the dining room, and then Elvira came in with Don Álvaro, who brought the piece of paper between his fingers.

"It says here, 'Holy Cathedral: From four to five, the Countess of Lóriz, Señora de Galindo and Doña Purita Canci.' And I say, 'Why were those names put together?'"

"There had to be three, Señor Don Álvaro, and these three seem to us the most illustrious in Oleza," the young Sister announced with a Gascon accent, as she daintily blinked with innocence and perplexity.

"And why shouldn't it be Señora Monera, my wife and my sister Doña Elvira?"

"It could well have been," the older nun then said, "if we hadn't just come from speaking with the Lórizes, the generous benefactors of our House; but the countess wanted us to put down Señora Galindo and Doña Purita's names alongside hers."

Once again the Little Sisters of the Poor had looked at one another, and the brother and sister from Gandía did as well, and, among them all, Paulina

Don Álvaro se mordía el silencio que se le enredaba en su boca, el silencío como si únicamente fuese suyo, pesándole como una barba de bronce.

Plácida y lisa, la monja vieja exclamó:

– Además de las señoras, estará una de nosotras en la mesa.

– Precisamente – dijo la francesita sonriendo –, Dios mediante, será una servidora quien les haga compañía en la catedral.

Elvira también sonrió mostrando sus encías.

– ¿Será usted? ¡Miren cómo la guardan para lo mejor! ¡Por algo se murmura en Oleza que pronto la tendremos de Buena Madre!

La Hermana puso toda su mirada de luz en los ojos enjutos de Elvira. En la monja asomaba la mujer virgen, y en la señorita de Gandía, la soltera.

– ¡Oh, guardarme para lo mejor! ¡Quizá sea verdad! Pero, si fuese usted de nosotras, también podría ser la elegida.

– ¿Y no siendo de ustedes, ya no puedo aspirar al rango de ese petitorio?

– No digo yo tanto. Fue la señora de Lóriz quien escogió los nombres.

– ¡Pues no sabe esa señora las gracias que le doy por que no se acordara del mío!

– ¿De veras? ¡Por Dios!

– ¡Qué "de veras" y qué "por Dios"!

Y ya estallaba su brío de descaro; pero se redujo, muy humilde.

– No tengo ingenio para remilgos de sociedad; yo soy de pueblo, y mi sitio será la mesa de una hermana de Monera, la que está al servicio del señor penitenciario.

– ¡Oh, es muy buena mujer!

Luego, la monjita volvióse a don Álvaro, dejándole exactamente a él la clara interrogación de sus ojos:

– ¿Entonces?...

Se entenebreció don Álvaro, sin contener el goce de mostrarse más rudo:

– Entonces, entonces... yo no me avengo a que esa señora condesa disponga de nosotros como de criados.

Se le movía la barba, se apretaba las manos y se aborrecía a sí mismo,

was alone, leaning over, waiting. Don Álvaro bit into the silence that was tangled up in his mouth, a silence he felt was uniquely his, weighing upon him like a bronze beard.

The old nun seemed placid and straightforward as she exclaimed:

"In addition to the señoras, one of us will be at the table."

"Precisely," the little French sister said with a smile, "God willing, it will be one of your humble servants who will accompany them in the cathedral."

Elvira also smiled, showing her gums.

"Will it be you? Just see how they save you for the best! For good reason do they gossip all over Oleza that we will soon have you as the superior Good Mother!"[120]

The Sister cast the whole of her light-filled glance at Elvira's dried-up eyes. The virginal woman revealed itself in the nun, while the spinster did so in the señorita from Gandía.

"Oh, save me for the best! It may very well be true! But if you were one of us, you could also be the one chosen."

"And since I am not one of you, I can no longer aspire to the high social rank for that petitionary table?"

"I wouldn't go that far. It was Señora de Lóriz who chose the names."

"Well that señora doesn't know how thankful I am to her for not remembering mine!"

"Really? Good heavens!"

"What do you mean 'really' and what do you mean 'Good heavens'!"

And now her spirit of insolence erupted, but it diminished quite quickly and changed to humility.

"I have no talent for society's affectations; I am a small-town woman and my place will be the table with a sister of Monera, the one who is in the service of the canon-penitentiary."[121]

"Oh, she's a very good woman!"

Then the little nun turned toward Don Álvaro, leaving the clear interrogation of her eyes precisely upon him:

"Well then?..."

Don Álvaro's face darkened and he was unable to contain the pleasure of showing how much ruder he could be:

"Then, then.... I can't reconcile myself to allowing that countess woman to treat us as if we were servants."

His beard began to move, he clenched his hands and detested himself

viendo que las Hermanítas se despedían de Paulina mirándola como si la compadeciesen. Y las paró con su grito:

– ¡Estoy harto de sentir mi voluntad empujada por la de todo este pueblo!

Ellas postraron sus frentes con aflicción.

– Mi mujer irá, pero yo también impongo y rechazo compañías.

La monjita buscó su lápiz entre los pliegues de la manga y esperó con un gracioso parpadeo.

Don Álvaro dictó:

– Señora de Lóriz, señora de Galindo y señora Monera.

– ¿De modo que hay que quitar a doña Purita?

Y fue repitiendo y escribiendo con mansedumbre: "Seño-ra Mo-ne-ra..."

– ¿Y usted admite la enmienda sin consultarla?

– ¡Es tan pobre cosa para esta vida!

Y se marcharon las dos hormiguitas del Señor.

Jueves Santo. La tarde se quedó inmóvil. Se oían los gorriones de toda la ciudad como en un huerto. El grito de una golondrina, las alas de un palomo rasgaban la seda del silencio. Arriba tableteaba huesuda y áspera la carraca de la catedral, y el clamor del río parecía del agua de la noria cansada de la torre. Sol y blancura de acacias en flor, de tapiales encalados. Todos los campos tiernos, acercándose a Oleza para ver al Señor, al Señor caminando por las cuestas de Jerusalén. Pero el Señor estaba tendido y desnudo delante del Monumento, entre los reclinatorios de la vela del Santísimo. Paulina le miraba los filos de hueso que le salían por la gasa morada: la nariz, las rodillas, los dedos alzados de los pies. Le buscó las uñas, las uñas azules del cadáver del Señor... Y llevóse a la boca su pañolito, que tenía manchas de sangre seca. Veía a su hijo, muy pequeño, con ella y don Álvaro. Don Álvaro, todo de negro, rígido y aciago. Se acercaban al Monumento. Fue en esta hora tan buena del principio de la tarde. Los únicos pasos, los suyos en las losas de la catedral. El niño tuvo miedo y buscó el arrimo de la madre. Sintióse caer un lagrimón de cirio en una arandela. Crujió la falda de Paulina entre los dedos del hijo. Se arrodilló don Álvaro, encorvándose para besar los pies llagados

when he saw the Little Sisters were taking leave of Paulina, looking at her as if they felt pity for her. And he stopped them with his shout:

"I'm fed up with feeling that my wishes are pushed aside by those of this whole town!

They lowered their foreheads with affliction.

"My wife will go, but I too can impose and reject those who will accompany her."

The little nun looked for her pencil within the folds of her sleeve and she waited as she blinked her eyes charmingly.

Don Álvaro dictated:

"Señora de Lóriz, Señora de Galindo and Señora Monera."

"So it's necessary to remove Doña Purita?"

And she meekly kept repeating and writing down,

"Se-ño-ra Mo-ne-ra...."

"And you accept the correction without consulting her?"

"It's such a little thing in this life!"

And the two little ants of the Lord departed.

Maundy Thursday. The afternoon stayed motionless. You could hear the sparrows from all over the city as if in a garden. The call of a nightingale, the wings of a ringdove tore through the silkiness of the silence. Up above, the bone-like wooden ratchet clackers of the cathedral rattled harshly[122] and the clamor of the river seemed like that of the water of the weary noria of the tower. Sun and whiteness of blooming acacias, of blanched walls. All the tender fields drawing closer to Oleza to see the Lord, the Lord walking up the slopes of Jerusalem. But the Lord lay stretched out naked in front of the improvised Easter altar, among the prie-dieux for the vigil of the Holy Eucharist. Paulina looked at the sharp edges of his bones which protruded through the purple gauze: the nose, the knees, the raised toes of the feet. She looked for his toenails, the blue toenails of the corpse of the Lord.... And she raised her small linen handkerchief with its stains of dried blood to her mouth. She saw her very small son with her and Don Álvaro. Don Álvaro, all in black, rigid and ill-fated. They were approaching the provisional Easter altar. It was at this wonderful hour of the beginning of the afternoon. The only footsteps on the flagstones of the cathedral were theirs. The child grew frightened and sought his mother's protection. You could hear the sound of a huge tear falling from a wax taper onto the disk round the candle-stand. Paulina's skirt rustled between her son's fingers. Don Álvaro kneeled down, bending over to kiss the lacerated feet of the image, and

de la imagen, y enseguida su mano enpujó a Pablo: "Bésalo", y Pablo cayó encima de las uñas del muerto. Ella lo recogió, enjugándole la boca con un lenzuelo de encajes, el mismo pañolito que todos los años traía en la vela del Jueves Santo. Lo aspiraba reverenciando aquella sangre viejecita como si fuese de las heridas de los pies de Jesús... De tiempo en tiempo entraba el plañir de los mendigos del portal: "Por la memoría de la Pasión y Muerte!" "Por las espadas de Nuestra Señora!" Gemían los muelles y la roldana del cancel forrado de cuero. Pisadas claras, exactas en la soledad. Lo mismo que entonces.

El Monumento esplendía sereno y profundo, como una constelación en la noche litúrgica. Terciopelos rojos y marchitos, oro viejo de los querubines del sagrario, oro de miel de las luces paradas, un crepitar de cera roída, un balbuceo de oraciones, un suspiro de congregantes, macizos de palmas blancas del domingo, floreros de rosas y espigas y los *mayos* de trigo pálidos con sus cintas de cabelleras de niñas alborozando de simplicidad aldeana el túmulo augusto y triste; olor ahogado, y la sensación del día azul rodeando los muros, la sensación de Jerusalén, blanca y tibia en el aire glorioso de Oriente.

Paulina sentía una felicidad estremecida en la quietud religiosa del Jueves grande: todo el día inmenso allí recogido como un aroma precioso en un vaso. Las luces la miraban como las estrellas miran dentro de los ojos y del corazón en las noches de los veranos felices de la infancia.

Alrededor del Monumento rezaban señoras humildes, esperando su guardia del Santísimo a esas horas quietas en que nadie puede ver sus vestidos mustios, nadie más que ellas mismas y el Señor desde la hostia rota de la urna radiante.

Paulina recordó las tardes del Jueves Santo, caminando desde el "Olivar" por las veredas de las mieses ya granadas, para visitar los sagrarios al lado de su padre y de Jimena. La mayordoma la contemplaba como criatura suya. Enmendaba un azabache de su ropa, le prendía mejor la mantilla, le vigilaba los broches de las joyas arcaicas que iban dejándole el viejo perfume de los Jueves Santos de la madre ya muerta...

...Levantóse de su reclinatorio extenuada y dulce. Llegábale ya el turno de la mesa de pedir de las Hermanitas. Pasó delante de capillas húmedas, desoladas y ciegas bajo el velo morado de Pasión, con las sacras y los candeleros caídos en el ara desnuda. Nada ni nadie en el altar. Los cielos de la

his hand quickly pushed Pablo, "Kiss them," and Pablo fell on top of the dead figure's toenails. She picked him up, wiped off his mouth with a lace-trimmed linen handkerchief, the very same handkerchief she brought every year for the vigil on Maundy Thursday. She breathed in its scent with a feeling of reverence for her son's precious old blood as if it were from the wounds on Jesus's feet.... From time to time the wailing of the beggars at the outside door would come inside, "For the memory of the Passion and Death!" "By the swords round Our Lady!" The springs and the sheave of the leather-lined storm door were groaning. Distinct, precise footsteps in the solitude. The same as then.

The provisional Easter Altar was shining serenely and profoundly like a constellation in the liturgical night. Red, withered velvets, the old gold of the cherubim in the sacrarium, the honeyed gold of the listless burning lights, a crackling of consumed wax, a babbling of prayers, a groan from the congregants, clumps of white palm leaves for Sunday, flower stands with roses and spikes and *May poles*[123] with pale wheat decorated with ribbons of little girls' hair gladdening the august and sad tumulus with rustic simplicity; a suffocating odor, and the sensation of the blue day surrounding the walls, the feeling of Jerusalem, white and warm in the glorious air of the East.

Paulina felt a tremulous happiness in the religious stillness of that glorious Thursday: the whole of the immense day cloistered there like a delightful aroma in a vase. The burning lights were looking at her just as stars look inside the eyes and heart on joy-filled summer nights of childhood.

All around the provisional Easter Altar humble women were praying, waiting to take their turn in the vigil of the Holy Eucharist during these quiet hours when nobody can see their pathetic dresses, nobody but they themselves and the Lord from the broken Host in the radiant urn.

Paulina recalled the afternoons of Maundy Thursday, walking from the "Olive Grove" through the pathways of the now ripened grain fields alongside her father and Jimena in order to visit the sacraria. The housekeeper would look upon her as if she were her own child. She would adjust some jet trinket that was part of her attire, fasten her mantilla more properly, check the clasps of the old-fashioned jewelry that kept pervading her with the onetime perfume of her long-dead mother's Maundy Thursdays....

...She arose from her prie-dieu extenuated and sweet. Her turn to serve at the little Sisters' alms table was fast approaching. She passed in front of the damp chapels, desolate and blind under the purple veil ever since Passion Sunday, with the sacring tablets and candlesticks lying flat on the bare altar. Nothing, nobody on the altar. The heavens of piety had been depopulated

piedad se habían despoblado y toda la liturgia se apretaba junto a los últimos momentos de la humanidad de Jesús. Principió a lucir el triángulo de cirios del tenebrario, y en su tronco labrado se quebraban dos grandes medallas de sol rural que caían desde el follaje negro de la piedra de la bóveda. Del continuo tránsito repicaba el cancel como la cítola de un molino. Destilaban las voces que iban cerrándose de las gentes que entraban, voces que se abrían a la lumbre de los pórticos. Familias artesanas y labradoras; juntas de cofradías; guardias civiles de zancas de algodón blanco; la oficialidad y los ordenanzas de la Zona de Reclutamiento; niños de un colegio pobre, esquilados, con botas gordas y trajecitos de huérfanos sin luto; mercedarios, carmelitas, franciscos, soltando un ruido de sandalias viejas, el mismo ruido de los pies de los discípulos cuando viniesen desde Bethanía para comer la pascua en el cenáculo; parejas de jesuitas, con el manteo tendido y el sombrero reclinado en el pecho; su doble genuflexión estricta, medida, como si oficiaran, postrándose, persignándose y alzándose a la vez, y enseguida, a otra visita de Monumentos, con su andar de viajeros de jornada piadosa, para volver pronto al oficio de Tinieblas de casa, el mejor de la diócesis...

La monja jovencita recibió a Paulina junto a la mesa de damascos de los Lóriz. También eran del palacio de Lóriz las bandejas y los candelabros de plata cincelada. En medio resplandecía una menuda imagen del Nazareno, imagen de fanal de consola, con cabellera de verdad, la túnica de lentejuelas y la cruz de filigranas. Llegó la Monera, redonda, sudada y el pecho repolludo de terciopelos, de azabaches, de blondas, de collares y cadenitas de joyeles. Se ahogaba del cansancio de traer sus galas por las iglesias, pero le reventaba el gozo. Subía sus manos para pulir su tocado, y se le enzarzaban los dijes con el rosario de nácar, con el abanico de concha, con el redículo lleno, con los broches de la "Semana Santa" de peluche, y jadeaba más.

Se retrajo la Hermanita para seguir las oraciones de su eucologio, y ya la Monera pudo hablar con holgura:

– ¡Atiende! ¿No se sienta usted en medio? Pues yo, sí, a lo menos hasta que se nos venga la de Lóriz. ¿Y no se tratan ustedes siendo vecinas? ¡Claro que tampoco nos tratamos nosotras como debiéramos teniéndose tanta

and the entire liturgy was now compressed alongside the final moments of Jesus's humanness. The triangle of wax tapers on the Tenebrae hearse started to shine, and the two large medallions of rustic sunlight coming from the black stone foliage of the vault overhead were breaking up on its wrought base.[124] The storm door resounded like the clapper in a mill with the constant coming in and out. Voices from outside filtered in, voices that would close themselves off from the people coming in, voices that would open up to the brightness of the porticoes. Families of artisans and farmers; confraternity councils; rural policemen wearing long white cotton stockings; officers and orderlies from the Recruitment Zone; young boys from a school for the poor, their hair cut short, wearing heavy boots and sad outfits befitting orphans without the mark of mourning; Mercedarians, Carmelites, Franciscans,[125] releasing a sound of old sandals, the same sound made by the disciples' feet when they came from Bethany to eat the paschal lamb in the Cenacle; pairs of Jesuits with their cassocks extended and their hats resting against their chests; their strict double genuflection, very measured, as if they were officiating at a service, prostrating themselves, making the sign of the cross and rising up at the same time, and quickly off to visit another provisional Easter Altar, with a gait not unlike that of travelers on a pious peregrination, so that they could soon return for the office of Tenebrae at their own House, the best service in the diocese....[126]

The sweet young nun received Paulina next to the damask-covered table of the Lórizes. The wrought silver trays and candelabra were also from the Lóriz palace. In the middle, a very small image of the Nazarene was shining, an image kept in a bell jar on a console table, with real hair, a sequin-covered tunic and a filagreed cross. The Monera woman arrived, round, sweating, her bosom plump with velvets, jet trinkets, blond lace, necklaces and slender chains with small jewels. She was smothering with weariness from having to drag around all her finery through the churches, but she was bursting with pleasure. She raised her hands to touch up her coiffure and her trinkets became entangled with her mother-of-pearl rosary, with her tortoise shell fan, with her stuffed reticule, with the clasps of her plush "Book of Prayers and Offices for Holy Week," and she started panting even more.

The little Sister withdrew in order to follow the prayers of her euchology and now the Monera woman could speak with ease:

"Just listen to this! Aren't you sitting in the middle? Well, I am, at least until the Lóriz woman deigns to come here to us. And aren't you on friendly terms since you're neighbors? Of course we aren't on as friendly terms with one another as we might be, considering the close relationship between our

amistad nuestros maridos! ¿Y ha sido ella, la condesa, quien nos escogió para este turno? ¿Usted lo esperaba? Yo, no; pero no se me encoge nada por eso. Bien han de morderse algunas cuando nos vean, y entre todas, doña Purita. ¿Es verdad que ha venido família forastera de los Lóriz? ¡Las vizcondesitas de no sé qué! ¿Pues cómo no las trajo? ¿Dejamos ya nuestra limosna porque no digan...o aguardaremos que llegue la señora condesa?

Paulina entornaba sus párpados, ya que no se cerraban los labios de aquella mujer.

"Tiene más orgullo que una noble sin serlo; un orgullo como si fuera feliz." Y, en tanto que la Monera lo pensaba, sonreía para seguir su comadreo:

– Dicen que el de Lóriz es un pillastre. Todas le encalabrinan, desde las mocosas de costura hasta los refajos de las huertanas y las piernas de pringue de las de San Ginés. Lleva dos dientes de oro. Una boca podrida de vicio. ¡Qué diferencia entre Lóriz y don Álvaro y el pobre del mío! ¿Y no ha venido también el hermano de la condesa?

Paulina se internaba dentro de su corazón. "Pasaré una hora de esta tarde, tan mía desde que era niña, al lado de la de Lóriz, la hermana de él."

Y se precipitó a mirar los canceles.

Prorrumpió la masa de los seminaristas, con estruendo de haldas y zapatones. "Filósofos" y "teólogos"; la granada juventud de Oleza, con sus lobas o sotanillas azules, recias, sin mangas, la beca encarnada que se tuerce en forma de corazón sobre el pecho, colgando las puntas por las espaldas con dos rollos de tafetán blanco. Se arrodillaron duros y polvorientos entre un vaho de camino. Se torcían los puños; hundían sus frentes de aldeanos. En los ojos de los sacerdotes inspectores había un trastorno que les secaba la oración.

Salieron despavoridos; y entonces surgió Elvira crispada, rápida, con los pómulos de cal, las sienes recalentadas, y entre las vedijas de crepé aparecían los calveros de la edad. Sus ropas, retorcidas a sus huesos como una piel; arrebatada y tirante, con un brillo húmedo en sus ojos ávidos, se puso a rezar, sin quitarlos de su cuñada, de la belleza de su cuñada. De pronto fue a la mesa, y Paulina se levantó.

husbands![127] And was it really she, the countess, who chose us for this turn at the table? You were expecting it? Well, I wasn't; but they don't choose me at all on that account. There are some women who are really going to burn with envy when they see us, and, among them all, Doña Purita most of all. Is it true that some of the Lórizes' family have come from out of town? Some silly viscountesses of somewhere or other! Well, how come she didn't bring them? Shall we leave our charitable contributions now so they won't say... or should we wait for that countess woman to arrive?"

Paulina half-closed her eyelids since that woman's lips were not about to close.

"She's haughtier than a noblewoman and she isn't even one; a kind of haughtiness befitting one who is truly happy." And all the while the Monera woman was thinking this, she smiled in order to go on with her gossiping:

"They say that Lóriz is a real scoundrel. Every kind of woman goes to his head, from the snotty-nosed seamstresses to the skirts of the farm girls from the cultivated plain and the greasy-legged girls from San Ginés. He sports two gold teeth. A mouth turned rotten from vice. What a difference between Lóriz and Don Álvaro and that poor husband of mine! And hasn't the countess's brother come too?"

Paulina took refuge within her heart. "I will spend an hour of this afternoon, so very much my own since I was a child, beside the countess of Lóriz, his sister."

And she hastened to look at the storm doors.

A crowd of seminarians surged in with the confused uproar of skirts and heavy shoes. Students in the "philosophy" program, students in the "theology" program; the outstanding youth of Oleza, with their soutanes or short blue cassocks, made of heavy cloth with no sleeves, with incarnadine sashes twisted over their chests in the form of a heart, the ends thrown back over their shoulders, with two rolls of white taffeta. Rough and dusty, with the fumes of the road, they kneeled down. They twisted their fists, they bowed their countrified foreheads down. There was an uneasiness in the eyes of the priest-monitors that dried up their prayers.

They seemed frightened as they departed, and then Elvira rushed in, her face contorted, moving swiftly, her cheekbones as white as lime, her temples inflamed and the bare patches of her aging appeared among the matted tufts of her false hair. Her garments twisted round her bones like an outer hide; flushed and tense, with a humid gleam in her avid eyes as she began to pray, without taking her eyes from her sister-in-law, from the beauty of her sister-in-law. She suddenly went over to the table and Paulina stood up.

– ¡No te asustes, hija! – y se arremolinó con la Monera – . ¿Los habéis visto? ¡Un bochorno que da grima y ganas de llorar! Esos, los seminaristas. A estas horas, los únicos que no lo sabéis sois tú y el señor obispo, tía Corazón y, claro, esa Hermana.

– ¡Ni yo tampoco! – rompió ahogándose la Monera.

– ¡Al lado de ésta, lo comprendo!

– ¡Nos están mirando todos! – suspiró Paulina.

– ¡Qué nos mire Dios con agrado, que los demás no me importan!

Luego soltó el lance escandaloso. Los seminaristas, por un podrido deseo de sus guías, atravesaron el callejón de la Balsa, el lupanar de Oleza.

– ¿Callejón de la Balsa? – y la señora Monera estrujaba los corcovos de espanto de su pecho.

– Corrieron los inspectores, y ya no tuvo remedio la indecencia. Desde los portales y ventanillos les llamaban las malas mujeres remangándose. Yo venía de Nuestro Padre, de ver el Lavatorio. Daba compasión el P. Bellod, tan viejo y tan sufrido, arrodillándose delante de aquellos pies, lavándolos, enjugándolos y besándolos. ¡Doce veces! Le reventaba la frente, le crujían los riñones ceñidos por la toalla. Eso se ahorra su ilustrísima...

No pudo seguir. Apareció la familia de Lóriz. La condesa y sus primas forasteras. Dejaban claridad, gracia, frescor y aroma de frutales finos en flor. Luz y goce de naturaleza. Sencillez de damiselas que fuesen a cultos humildes; cabelleras rubias replegadas levemente bajo la vieja suntuosidad de las blondas. Ritmos y contoneos de puerilidad, de ligereza. Delicias de carne recién comunicada de la tarde de abril. Aristócratas en el descuido selecto de una temporada de cortijo. Sin joyas; hasta los guantes blancos tenían una blancura de marfiles, los de la última comunión en Madrid o de misa temprana. Únicamente la condesa llevaba en medio del pecho un jazmín de diamantes antiguos. Ella y sus primas, de sedas negras, y parecían vestidas de blanco. Las miraban pasmadamente las damas y vírgenes de Oleza, obligadas a un esfuerzo y pesadumbre de vestidos brochados, de cuelgas de alhajas, de rigideces de lienzos interiores, de cinturas retorcidas

"Don't be frightened, my dear!" and she squeezed next to the Monera woman. "Have you seen them? A crying shame that is disgusting and makes you want to cry! Those boys, the seminarians. And at this moment, the only ones who don't know about it are you and the lord bishop, Auntie Corazón and, of course, that Sister."

"Well I don't either!" the Monera woman broke in, choking with interest.

"Sitting next to this one, I can understand why!"

"They're all looking at us!" Paulina sighed.

"May God look upon us with pleasure, for all the others don't count at all!"

She then let loose the scandalous episode. The seminarians, because of some rotten intention on the part of their guides, crossed the Callejón de la Balsa, where the brothel of Oleza is located.[128]

"The Callejón de la Balsa?" and Señora Monera squeezed the prancing leaps of terror in her bosom.

"The priest-monitors ran, but there was no longer any way to prevent the indecency. Those debased women tucked up their skirts and kept calling to them from the doorways and the openings in the windows. I was on my way back from Nuestro Padre from seeing the Maundy.[129] You couldn't help feeling sorry for Father Bellod, looking so old and long-suffering, kneeling down in front of those feet, washing them, wiping them and kissing them. Twelve times! His forehead was bursting, his loins with the towel wrapped round them were creaking. His Excellency is spared all that...."

She was unable to continue. The Lóriz family appeared. The countess and her cousins from out-of-town. They emanated brightness, charm, freshness and the aroma of lovely, blossoming fruit trees. The light and the pleasure of the natural. The simplicity of damsels on their way to humble worship; blond tresses gently folded back beneath the venerable sumptuousness of blond lace. The rhythms and the ostentations of puerilty, of lightness. The delights of flesh recently touched by the April afternoon. Aristocrats simply by their select indifference during a brief sojourn at a country estate. Without any jewels; even their white gloves had the whiteness of ivory pieces, worn at the last communion in Madrid or at an early Mass. Only the countess was wearing a jasmine flower of very old diamonds on her bosom. She and her cousins, dressed in black silk, seemed to be wearing white. The matrons and virgins of Oleza, obligated to undergo the exertions and the considerable burden of brocaded dresses, of bunches of hanging jewels, of the stiffness of linen undergarments, of contorted waists and breasts restrained inside a

y pechos retrocedidos entre el cañaveral de las ballenas. En cambio, de las forasteras se exhalaba la alegría de sus cuerpos con tanta gloria que casi se creía que fueran a brotar desnudas como de un baño.

— ¡Atiende! ¡Vienen de trapillo, pensándose que aquí no se viste!

Y la Monera se precipitó erizada de terciopelo a su silla, recelosa de que se la quitaran las de Lóriz. Detrás, Elvira lo acechaba todo. Parecía más flaca y su piel más verde entre las grietas de su yeso de arroz.

Paulina se había levantado acogiéndolas con una graciosa timidez. Sentíase muy infantil rodeada de esas gentes tan felices. Y de pronto se vió dentro de la mirada del hermano de la de Lóriz, siempre con traje de viajero. Semejante a la hermana, con los ojos más azules y amargos. Ya tenía hebras blancas en las sienes y en el oro de la barba.

— ¡Hace dieciocho años, Paulina, que no nos hablábamos! Era usted soltera. He visto a su hijo en el colegio. Lo he llamado para verle y besarle.

Por los mismos conceptos que decía: "verle y besarle" le miraba ella los ojos y después la boca. Se le apartó con suavidad, y bajó los párpados con un honrado temblor; y encima seguía descansándole la contemplación de aquel hombre. Como prueba de que no le pesaba, de que no había de huir ni de sonrojarse, volvió a subir su mirada y a recoger limpiamente la suya. Todo muy rápido como una luz. La misma fugacidad tuvo su pensamiento, el pensamiento que la traspasó y que estampaba distancias y tiempo: "Pude haber sido la mujer de ese hombre". Acababa de verse, toda virgen, tan blanca, en el viejo reposo del "Olivar de Nuestro Padre". Pudo ser su mujer. Pudo ser de ese hombre que descansaba en el silencio de la casa de Oleza como si se tendiese al amor de un árbol familiar, y aparecía por las aradas y huertas de don Daniel con su caja de pintor. Don Daniel no vio el elegido para Paulina como lo vio en don Álvaro. Cuando Máximo se despidió para seguir su camino, ella se dijo (se alzaban claramente los años, para ver la pronunciación de sus palabras): "Si nos quisiéramos, nos marcharíamos después de nuestra boda y recorreríamos el mundo." Y ahora, mirándose, reanudaba su pensamiento: "Ya llevaríamos diecisiete años casados desde entonces; diecisiete años..."

canebrake of whalebone, kept looking at them in astonishment. On the other hand, the joy of their bodies emanated from the out-of-town women with such glory that you would almost think they were going to suddenly emerge naked as if from a bath.

"Just look at that! They come here so simply attired, thinking that we don't get dressed up around here!"

And the Monera woman, bristling with velvet, rushed over to her chair, fearful that the Lóriz women would take it away from her. Behind her, Elvira watched everything carefully. She appeared to be even thinner and her skin looked even greener between the cracks in the layer of rice powder.

Paulina had gotten to her feet and welcomed them with a charming timidity. She felt very childish surrounded by those happy people. And suddenly she saw herself within the glance of the Countess of Lóriz's brother, as always in traveling clothes. Similar to his sister, with eyes that were bluer and more bitter. He already had threads of white at his temples and in the gold of his beard.

"It's been eighteen years since we talked to one another, Paulina! You were unmarried. I saw your son at the school. I called him so I could see him and kiss him."

For the same reasons that he said, "see him and kiss him," she looked into his eyes and then at his mouth. She drew away from him meekly and lowered her eyelids with an honest tremor; and the contemplation of that man continued to rest upon her. As if to prove that he wasn't causing her any sorrow,, that she didn't have to run away or blush, she raised her eyes again in order to sincerely recover his glance. All very quickly like a flash of light. Her thought had the same fugacity, the thought that pierced her and imprinted distances and times: "I could have been that man's wife." She had just seen herself, all virginal, so white, in the old tranquility of the "Olive Grove of Our Father." She could have been his wife. She could have belonged to that man who reposed in the silence of the house in Oleza as if he were stretched out beneath the love of a family tree, and who appeared among the plowed fields and the orchards belonging to Don Daniel carrying his painter's box. Don Daniel didn't see in him the one chosen for Paulina as he saw him in Don Álvaro. When Máximo said goodbye to her in order to go on his way, she said to herself (the years rose up clearly so she could see the precise pronunciation of her words), she said to herself, "If we loved one another, we could go off after our wedding and travel all over the world." And now, looking at herself, she renewed her thought, "We could already have been married seventeen years since that time, seventeen years...."

Y todo esto voló dentro de su frente, por el horizonte del "Olivar" de aquellos días deshojados, sin sobresaltos de casada perfecta. No se había complacido en otro amor, sino en otro matrimonio, otro matrimonio que le parecía referido a distinta mujer. Todo tan breve y tan ajeno que no dejó de oír ni de mirar a las aristócratas forasteras y de pagarles su sonrisa con la suya vigilada por la hermana de su esposo.

La de Lóriz la sentó a su lado con gentil llaneza; y volviéndose aturdida le dijo:

– ¡Cómo! ¿No es Purita nuestra compañera?

– ¡No, señora; no, señora, que soy yo! – respondió embistiéndose la del homeópata.

La de Lóriz se distrajo para confirmarle a Paulina que fue ella misma quien indicó este turno por verla y tenerla muy cerca. Su hijo siempre les hablaba de la mamá de Pablo, la mamá más hermosa del colegio. Ninguna sonreía y miraba como ella...

De un tarjetero de filigranas fragante y diminuto sacó una monedita de oro. Paulina, también. La Monera extrajo de su gorda faltriquera de mallas un escudo chapado, diez viejos reales, y pareciéndole escasa la limosna en presencia de tanto señorío de Madrid, desató de su pañuelo un rollo de menudos que se le reventó entre sus dedos enguantados, y los dineros botaron en las losas con el plebeyo ruido de la calderilla.

Se agobió buscándolos y estalló su rotunda cintura de agramanes.

Llegaba entonces la primera brigada de colegiales de "Jesús" con sus levitas ceñidas por el fajín de torzal azul, guante blanco, insignias y franjas de oro. En las últimas ternas iban juntos el hijo de Paulina y el de Lóriz, que se miraron avisándose. Máximo Lóriz, descolorido y frágil, la frente lisa, los ojos precoces, ya con elegancia y decrepitud de club. Pablo Galindo, alto, de una adolescencia dorada, pero con la infancia todavía en su sangre; la mirada de suavidad de la madre, y entre sus cejas, el fruncido adusto de don Álvaro.

Lejos, en los terciopelos descoloridos del sagrario, se reclinaba la cabeza fina y pálida del hermano de la de Lóriz. Desde allí contemplaba a Paulina

And all this flew around inside her forehead, over the horizon of the "Olive Grove" of those defoliated days, without any of the disquieting feeling of a perfect married woman. She had not taken pleasure in another love, but only in another marriage, another marriage that seemed to her to refer to a different woman. All of this so brief and so apart from her that she did not fail to hear nor look at the aristocratic out-of-towners and to return their smiles with her own, under the scrutiny of her husband's sister.

The Countess of Lóriz sat her down by her side with genteel candor; and she turned to her thoughtlessly and said:

"What! Purita is not our companion?"

"No, señora; no, señora, it is I!" the homeopath's wife responded aggressively.

The Countess of Lóriz paid no attention to her and turned toward Paulina and assured Paulina that it was she herself who specified this turn at the table, so that she could see her and have her close to her. Her son always spoke to them about Pablo's mother, the prettiest mother in the school. Nobody had a smile or a glance like hers...

She took a small gold coin from a tiny, scented filigreed card case. Paulina followed suit. The Monera woman extracted an out-of-date silver *escudo*, worth about ten old *reales*, from her heavy, meshed-fabric handbag, and since she felt that her charitable offering would seem quite meager in the presence of so many persons of quality from Madrid, she untied a roll of small change from her handkerchief and it burst out from between her gloved fingers and the coins bounced on the flagstones with the plebeian sound of copper coins.

She bent down to look for them and her rotund passementarie belt came apart.

The first brigade of schoolboys from "Jesús" was coming in just then, in their frock coats fastened round the waist with sashes of blue twist, wearing white gloves, gold insignias and fringes. Paulina's son and the Lóriz boy were walking together among the last groups of three, and their mothers looked at one another and pointed them out. Máximo Lóriz, pale and fragile, with a flat forehead, precocious eyes, already revealing the elegance and decrepitude of the elite clubman. Pablo Galindo, tall, at a time of golden adolescence, still maintaining his childhood qualities in his blood; his mother's gentle glance and Don Álvaro's sullen frown between his brows.

Some distance away, the fine, pale head of the Countess of Lóriz's brother reclined against the discolored velvet surfaces of the sacrarium. From there he contemplated Paulina as she passed her eyes over her son's forehead.

pasando sus ojos sobre la frente del hijo. Y otra vez se remontó para ella el vuelo de los años hacia el horizonte de su viginidad. Otra vez la imagen súbita de sus bodas con aquel hombre. Pero en medio se alzaba el hijo. El hijo no sería según era trocando su origen. Se le perdía la profunda posesión de Pablo, sintiendo en él otro hijo, es decir, otro padre. Este hombre, con quien podía haber sido dichosa, era él, en sí mismo, menos él que don Álvaro, tan densamente don Álvaro.

Ya salía la brigada de "Jesús". Los inspectores adivinaron el peligro para la devoción que emanaba de aquella mesa y del grupo femenino, más de festín de belleza y de ternura que de limosna de piedad; y se pusieron delante.

Quedó la iglesia en una quietud de aposento de enfermo. En el cancel surgió el tribunal enlutado de don Álvaro, *Alba-Longa* y Monera.

Paulina elevó su frente a la escintilación del Monumento. La de Lóriz y sus primas secreteaban con risas deliciosas. La Hermanita de los Pobres rezaba; la Monera se ahuecó entre las señoritas nobles que seguían de pie, y volvióse a su marido significándole con una mueca que ella no era como él; ella no cedía su asiento, ella no se levantaba por nadie... A lo último, Elvira, inmóvil, olvidada, sacrificada, recibía el saludo de su hermano, que dobló su cabeza de piedra.

Paulina tembló. Junto a su oído, los labios de Máximo el pintor, que acababa de aparecérsele, le decían:

– ¡Qué tarde tan immensa, Paulina! ¡Dios mío, la felicidad se pierde como la lluvia que cae en las aguas!... ¡Por qué lloverá sobre el mar!

Fuera, en el azul, rodaba de nuevo, áspera y vieja, la carraca de la catedral.

3. Viernes Santo

Por la mañana

La primera brigada de "Jesús" se internó, atropellándose un poco, en el ancho zaguán de casa Lóriz. En la calle se quedó la bulla de vendedores, de huertanos, de arrebaleros, entre humos crudos de sartenes de buñuelos y

And once again the flight of the years rose up before her toward the horizon of her virginal state. Once again the sudden image of her wedding with that man. But the son rose up in between. Her son would not be as he was by distorting his origins. She was losing her deep feeling of possession of Pablo as she kept sensing another son in him, that is to say, another father. This man with whom she could have been happy was that one, in himself, less he than Don Álvaro, so very intensely Don Álvaro.

The brigade from "Jesús" was now leaving. The priest-monitors foresaw the danger to religious devotion that emanated from that table and the feminine group there, more a feast of beauty and tenderness than of charity and piety; and so they placed themselves in front of them.

The church was left in the stillness of a sickroom. The tribunal in mourning black consisting of Don Álvaro, *Alba-Longa* and Monera appeared in the storm door.

Paulina raised her forehead to the scintillation from the provisional Easter Altar. The Countess of Lóriz and her cousins were conversing privately with delightful laughter. The Little Sister of the Poor was praying; the Monera woman was putting on airs among the noble young ladies who were still standing, and she turned to her husband, letting him know with a grimace that she wasn't at all like him; that she didn't give up her seat nor stand up for anyone.... At the very end sat Elvira, motionless, forgotten, sacrificed, receiving her brother's greeting as he bent his head of stone.

Paulina trembled. The lips of Máximo, the painter, who had just appeared near her, quite close to her ear, were saying:

"What a tremendous afternoon, Paulina! My God, happiness is lost like the rain that falls on the waters!... For what reason can it rain on the sea!"

Outside, in the blue, the wooden ratchet clacker of the cathedral, harsh and old, started turning again.

3. Good Friday

In the morning

The first brigade from "Jesús," occasionally shoving one another, moved inside the broad vestibule of the Lóriz house. The uproar of the vendors was left behind, of the farm people from the cultivated plain, those who lived in the outskirts of town, amidst the offensive smoke from frying pans filled

olores cansados de taberna que pringaban el aire fino de la madrugada.

El mayordomo, con su levita negra, maciza, como un tronco de carbón, inclinóse heráldicamente, besando la mano del P. Prefecto.

La segunda y tercera brigada – de alumnos "medianos" y "pequeños" – veían la procesión del amanecer desde los ventanales y azoteas del Ayuntamiento. Y la primera, la de los "mayores", la de los más ávidos y fáciles para los peligros del mundo, había de pararse en las calles, fermentadas por un trajín de feria y de bureo, oyéndolo y presenciándolo todo en el viernes de luto tan sagrado.

Siempre los obispos dieron ese día su Palacio a "Jesús". Domingo de Ramos, un familiar visitaba al rector del colegio, llevándole la invitación para las procesiones de Semana Santa. Y el de ahora dejó sus ventanas y balcones a la hierba rebrotada y a los vencejos y golondrinas que acababan de llegar a sus nidos de antaño. Sólo entre las rejas de las oficinas episcopales se apretaba el rebañito de las criaturas del Hospicio. Nadie comprendía la conducta de su ilustrísima. "Pero Dios – suspiraba la comunidad de "Jesús" – , Dios permite que hasta lo incomprensible sucede en Oleza, y que se olvide".

Lóriz les remedió de esa adversidad del Palacio cerrado, abriéndoles el suyo. Lo quiso su mujer, para gozo y vanagloria del hijo, que pertenecía a esa primera brigada. Y he aquí que el P. Prefecto venía también, calificando con su presencia la gratitud de Casa.

Lóriz y su cuñado Máximo les recibieron en la última meseta, y el conde les dió la bienvenida como si les diese las buenas noches para acostarse. Los colegiales iban subiendo los peldaños de losas con los brazos cruzados, como si fueran al estudio.

En la antesala. la condesa, sus primas y Doña Purita, claras y fragantes, exhalaban un júbilo gracioso de aves y flores que dan tan íntima sensación de mujer. Besaron a su colegial, y los besos se abrían con una frescura de rosas. Los inspectores se erizaron.

El huerto interior, retoñado, transpiraba hasta lo más profundo sus esencias húmedas.

– ¡Qué hermosa es la Semana Santa, Padre Prefecto! – suspiró la de Lóriz.

with crullers and the weary odors of the tavern that befouled the delicate air of early morning.

The major-domo, in his sturdy black frock coat, like a trunk made of coal, bent over heraldically and kissed the Prefect Father's hand.

The second and third brigades – made up of "middle-level" and "small" students[130] – watched the early morning procession from the wide windows and the rooftops of the Town Hall. And the first one, the one made up of "older students," the one consisting of the most eager, and vulnerable to the dangers of the outside world, was compelled to stop in the streets, bubbling with festive hustle and bustle and diversion, and they heard it all and witnessed it all on this very sacred Friday of mourning.[131]

The bishops always gave over their Palace to "Jesús" on that day. On Palm Sunday, a familiar would visit the school rector to bring him the invitation for the processions of Holy Week. And the one now in office left his windows and balconies to the newly sprouting grass and the swifts and swallows that had just returned to their nests of past years. A small flock of little children from the Orphanage were the only ones squeezed in among the window gratings of the episcopal offices. Nobody understood His Excellency's conduct. "But God," the Community of "Jesús" would sigh, "God permits even what is not incomprehensible to happen in Oleza, and that it then be forgotten."

Lóriz rescued them from the adversity of the closed Palace by opening up his own. His wife desired it for the pleasure and the vainglory of her son, who belonged to that first brigade. And so it is that the Prefect Father also came, attesting to the gratitude of the House by his presence.

Lóriz and his brother-in-law Máximo received them on the upper landing and the count welcomed them as if he were saying good night in order to go to bed. The schoolboys kept walking up the slabbed steps with their arms crossed as if they were on their way to the study hall.

In the antechamber, the countess, her cousins and Doña Purita, bright and fragrant, gave off a delightful and jubilant atmosphere of birds and flowers that offered so intimate a sensation of woman. They kissed their own schoolboy and the kisses opened wide with a freshness of roses. The priest-monitors were bristling.

The inside garden, now in bloom, transpired its humid essences to the very deepest recesses around.

"How beautiful Holy Week is, Prefect Father!" sighed the Countess of Lóriz.

El jesuita sonrió con misericordia, y sus ojos quisieron ser como manos que recogiesen los pensamientos de los adolescentes.

Le apartó el conde, hablándole como si le susurrara una confidente elegante. Le porfió mucho, dejándole un resplandor de sonrisas orificadas. En fin, el Prefecto dio una blanda palmada.

– *¡Deo gratias!*

Pero casi no resaltó la dispensa del silencio. Un criado, de frac doméstico, abrió las galerías, que ya principiaban a teñirse de los paisajes y cielos de las viejas vidrieras. Allí estaban paradas las mesas para un refrigerio escolar de natas, de fresas, de pasteles, de almíbares.

Este apuro lo resistieron severamente los Reverendos Padres. Antes de salir de casa estuvieron los colegiales en el refectorio; y ya bastaba.

– ¡De modo que los pobres chicos han de ayunar como santos!

¡Ese ilustre pecador no tenía ni concepto del ayuno! Y el Prefecto ladeaba su cabeza escuchando. Los relojes de las consolas, del comedor, del vestíbulo, todos tocaban sus campanitas de cristal, sus carillones infantiles, sus horas de órgano.

– ¡Las cinco! ¡A las cinco, qué infernal tumulto habría en el Pretorio!

– ¿Tan temprano? ¡Y nosotros, Padre, cayéndose de sueño en nuestro sofá! – Y Lóriz fue derrumbándose en los cojines de tisú. ¡No recordaba haber madrugado nunca!

El jesuita le amenazó con su índice blanco, prometiéndole un terrible castigo. Pero Lóriz se sentía perdonado.

– ¡Aaah, quién sabe! ¡Sí, sí; quizá no!

Lejos sonaban pífanos, tambores, alaridos. Se apretaron los colegiales en los damascos de los balaustres. Doce alumnos en cada balcón; el último para los fámulos. De pronto se volvieron hacia los salones. Dos camareras jovencitas les presentaban en canastillas de mimbres una volcada abundancia de frutas escarchadas, un júbilo de rimeros de cajas de chocolates, de almendras, de yemas...

– ¡Qué acepten siquiera esto! – Y Lóriz se gozaba de la dolorida resignación de los Padres.

Permitió el religioso el agasajo, pero recomendando, de grupo en grupo,

The Jesuit smiled with compassion and his eyes tried to be like hands that could gather up the thoughts of the adolescents.

The count took him aside and spoke to him as if he were whispering some elegant bit of confidentiality. He persisted for some time, leaving behind with him a gold-filled splendor of smiles. Finally, the Prefect clapped his hands in a restrained manner.

"Deo gratias!"[132]

But the dispensation to break the silence was barely evident. A servant wearing domestic livery opened up the galleries, just beginning to be tinged by the landscapes and skies from the old rows of windows. The tables were set up there for a scholastic refreshment consisting of whipped cream, strawberries, pastries and candied fruits.

The Reverend Fathers vigorously resisted accepting this compromising situation. Before leaving their own House, the schoolboys had been to the refectory, and that was enough.

"So the poor lads are going to have to fast like saints!"

That illustrious sinner had no idea what it was to fast! And the Prefect leaned his head to one side and listened. The clocks on the console tables in the dining room, in the vestibule, were all sounding their crystal little bells, their infantile carillons, their organ-like hours.

"Five o'clock! At five o'clock there must have been an infernal tumult in the Praetorial Tribunal!"[133]

"That early? And here we are, Father, falling down on our sofa overcome with sleep!" And Lóriz starting dropping back onto the cushions of tissue fabric. "I didn't remember ever having gotten up early!"

The Jesuit threatened him with his white index finger, promising him some terrible punishment. But Lóriz felt that he was forgiven.

"Oooh, who knows! Yes, yes; maybe not!"

The sound of fifes, drums and shouts could be heard in the distance. The schoolboys held on tightly to the damask-covered balusters. Twelve students on each balcony; the end one for the students who functioned as servants. Suddenly they turned their attention to the parlors. Two charming young maids were offering them a dizzying abundance of frosted fruits in small wicker baskets, a joyous bounty of heaps of boxes of chocolates, of almonds, of candied yolks....

"Let them at least accept this!" And Lóriz savored the pained resignation of the Fathers.

The cleric permitted the refreshment, but he went from group to group recommending to them that they hold on to it in order not to change the

que lo guardaran para no trocar la tristeza del Viernes en una apariencia
de convite de bautizo. Además, Oleza les miraba. Acababan de abrirse las
celosías de casa de don Álvaro Galindo. Salió el matrimonio Monera, y
después Paulina entre su esposo y Elvira. Detrás predominaba el cráneo
liso del penitenciario. La vieja Oleza se quedó mirando a la Oleza de los
Lóriz. Faltaban *Carolus Alba-Longa* y el P. Bellod. En ese día don Amancio
se despojaba de su levita jurídica y pedagógica para ceñirse de lumbres de
hierro de centurión, y el párroco de San Daniel empuñaba su maza de plata
de maestre de la cofradía del Ecce-Homo.

La condesa y Purita saludaron a Paulina con su sonrisa y sus manos
perfumadas de confites. Y los alumnos de "Jesús" ya no pudieron resistir la
tentación de las escarchas, de los chocolates, de las almendras, sintiéndose
más cerca de las deliciosas mujeres, comunicados de los mismos sabores,
dejando el mismo aliento que ellas en el tibio amanecer.

La disciplina de "Jesús" no alcanzaba al condesito. Máximo podía ir
de balcón en balcón, bromeando con todos los camaradas; apartarse con
sus predilectos y correr todo palacio. Les llevó al huerto, a las despensas, a
las cocinas; se deslizaron por puertecitas recónditas, por escaleritas súbitas;
brincaban por los desvanes despertando a los vampiros, los enormes
murciélagos colgados de la uña o de un ala triangular y satánica de las vigas
de troncos. Bajaron a las salas principales, se tendieron junto a la urna de
los peces sagrados para verlos nadar. Salón de retratos, oratorio, comedor.
El condesito era el guía de sus elegidos; dos madrileños rubios y zumbones,
Pablo Galindo y un mozallón de Aspe, de casa labradora, que no hacía sino
sonreír a los cortesanos, encogido entre las rancias suntuosidades. Confió
el rural que Pablo, por ser lugareño, quedase también pasmado; pero el hijo
de Paulina pronunciaba los nombres de las cosas de más estupenda rareza;
ánfora, lis, vitrina, lacrimatorio; sabía los secretos de los bargueños, de los
arcaces, de los relicarios, de algunas tallas, y habló de los muebles de su
casona del "Olivar de Nuestro Padre".

– ¿Y en tu casa de ahi enfrente?

Pablo humilló sus pensamientos recordando los lienzos grietosos del

sadness of this Friday and give it the appearance of a baptismal banquet. In addition, Oleza was looking at them. The blinds of Don Álvaro Galindo's house had just been opened. The Moneras, husband and wife, came out and then Paulina between her husband and Elvira. The canon-penitentiary's smooth skull was prominent behind them. The Oleza of the old ways was looking at the Oleza of the Lórizes. *Carolus Alba-Longa* and Father Bellod were missing. On that day, Don Amancio divested himself of his juridical and pedagogical frock coat in order to gird himself with the brilliance of a centurion's iron, and the parish priest of San Daniel was clutching his silver mace as grand master of the confraternity in charge of the Ecce- Homo.[134]

The countess and Purita greeted Paulina with their smiles and hands perfumed with confections. And the students from "Jesús" were no longer able to resist the temptation of the sugar-coated delicacies, the chocolates, the almonds, feeling themselves closer to the delightful women, sharing the same flavors, leaving the same breath as they did in the tepid early hour of morning.

The discipline at "Jesús" did not pertain to the young count. Máximo could go from one balcony to another, jesting with all his chums; he could even go off separately with his favorite friends and run all over the palace. He took them to the garden, to the pantries, to the kitchens; they slipped through small, secret doors and up short, unexpected stairways; they jumped around in the attics awakening the vampire bats, those enormous bats, hanging by their talons or from their triangular, Satanic wing from rafters fashioned from tree trunks. They descended to the principal drawing rooms, stretched out next to the tank where they kept the sacred fish so that they could watch them swim. The portrait room, the oratory, the dining room. The young count was the guide for his select friends; two blond, waggish lads from Madrid, Pablo Galindo and a robust young fellow from Aspe, from a farm family, who felt very self-conscious amid all that antiquated sumptuousness and did nothing but make the young boys from the court smile. The rustic lad was confident that Pablo, since he was from a small town, would also be astounded; but Paulina's son pronounced the names of the most extraordinarily rare things: amphora, fleur-de-lis, glass display cabinet, lachrymatory; he was familiar with the secrets of the ornate inlaid gilt cabinets, of the large chests, of the reliquaries, of various wooden carvings, and he spoke of the furniture in his ancestral home in the "Olive Grove of Our Father."

"And how about your house over there across the way?"

Pablo humbled his thoughts as he recalled the cracked canvases of Señor

señor Galindo, de la señora Serrallonga; el óvalo del panteón familiar de pelo de difuntos, la palmatoria de la perdiz embalsamada... El de Aspe se volvió con sobresalto al hijo de Lóriz, que se subía por los butacones de casullas haciendo vibrar las arandelas de las cornucopias, alcanzando los retablillos de ámbar y marfiles, las calabacillas de azabache de Compostela, los collares de amuletos, los vasos de aljófares...

– ¿Y no te dicen nada?

Pasaba el mayordomo, corpulento y ritual, y le sonreía y no le decía nada. Pasaba el conde, y le sonreía y tampoco le decía nada, asomándose a todas las ventanas del jardín interior, el *hortus conclusus,* según el P. Prefecto. Entre los romeros podados se alzaban las risas de doña Purita, que se apartó allí con las aristócratas, hartas ya de que las fisgonease la plebe.

Máximo y sus amigos corrían, dejándose al chico de Aspe, que gritaba llamándoles, con susto de tanto lujo solitario. Encima de las mesitas de taraceas, de los cofrecillos estofados, de las cornisas de las librerías, de las ménsulas, de las veloneras, había braseritos, vidrios catalanes, cuencos y platos de Alcora, llenos de rosas deshojadas. Pablo y Máximo sumergían sus manos en la frescura viejecita y sacaban entre sus dedos un olor muerto de jardines desaparecidos.

– ¿Hojas secas? – exclamaba el mozo de Aspe – . Hojas de rosas secas. ¿Y para qué?

Pablo dijo que en el "Olivar" había también copas y fruteros de alabastro con hojas de rosas y flores de espliegos. Su madre, siempre que pasaba, hundía la punta de sus dedos como en una pila sagrada; y sus vestidos y el aire se llenaban de un olor antiguo de huerto y de colina.

– ¿Y para qué?

– ¡Para nada! – le gritó Pablo – . ¡Para todo! ¡Porque sí!

Persiguiéndose llegaron a la salita de la condesa. Rodearon el pilar de la diosa de mármol, mirándole los pechos desnudos, los brazos redondos.

– ¡Así los tendrá doña Purita!

Todos se volvieron a Pablo.

Galindo, of Señora Serrallonga; the oval-framed picture of the family vault with the hair of the dead, the small candlestick with the figure of the stuffed partridge.... The boy from Aspe turned with a start toward the son of Lóriz, who was climbing up onto the large armchairs decorated with chasubles, making the socket pans of the mirrored sconces vibrate, reaching up to the small amber and ivory altarpieces, to the little gourd-shaped, jet eardrops from Compostela and used by pilgrims, the neck chains for amulets, the glasses holding small, irregularly-shaped pearls....

"And they don't tell you anything?"

The major-domo, corpulent and ceremonious, passed by, smiled at him and didn't say anything to him. The count went by and smiled at him and didn't say anything to him either, just peering out of all the windows facing the garden, the *hortus conclusus*, according to the Prefect Father. Doña Purita's laughter ascended from among the pruned rosemary shrubs as she withdrew from there with the aristocratic ladies, who, by now, were fed up with common people spying on them..

Máximo and his friends ran off, leaving the boy from Aspe by himself, and he kept shouting and calling to them because he was frightened in the midst of so much solitary luxury. On top of the small marqueterie-tables, the little gilded chests, the cornices for the bookshelves, the brackets, and the wooden candle shelves, there were small braziers, glass pieces from Catalonia, porcelain bowls and dishes from Alcora filled with defoliated roses. Pablo and Máximo submersed their hands in the fusty coolness and withdrew a departed scent of long vanished gardens between their fingers.

"Dried leaves?" the lad from Aspe exclaimed. "Leaves of dried-up roses. What for?"

Pablo said that there were also alabaster bowls and fruit dishes in the "Olive Grove" with rose petals and lavender blossoms. Whenever his mother would pass by, she would immerse the tip of her fingers as if in a holy water font; and her clothes and the air were filled with the very old aroma of a garden and a hillside.

"For what purpose?"

"For no purpose at all!" Pablo shouted at him. "For every reason! Just because!"

Chasing after one another, they reached the countess's private sitting room. They surrounded the pedestal used to support the marble goddess and stared at her bare breasts and rounded arms.[135]

"Doña Purita's are probably just like those!"

They all turned toward Pablo.

– ¿La viste tú así? – le preguntó Máximo.

Y el de Aspe se acercó a la escultura hasta sentir su aliento encima de los muslos de piedra. Y, de repente, estallaron las risas de los madrileños.

A su lado, inmóvil y negro, esperaba que acabase la contemplación un Hermano inspector.

– Yo estaba mirando, yo estaba...

– ¡Usted estaba mirando, señor Perceval! ¿Pero a quién? – Y se le arrojó, paralizándole y chafándole los ojos con los suyos, desglobados por los quevedos de miope – . ¿A quién, señor Perceval?

– ¡A doña Purita!

– ¿A doña Purita? – repitió estremecido el Hermano – . Y con la rapidez que tienen algunos justos para descubrir y sospesar el pecado, adivinó que aquella carne aldeana no lo cometía acercándose a las formas de una diosa, sino representándose en ellas las de una mujer, y de una mujer como doña Purita. Y bronco y ardiente de pureza (un Santo Padre ha dicho que el hábito de la castidad endurece las entrañas), gritó, tendiendo su brazo como una espada negra:

– ¡Es usted un depravado y un monstruo! ¡Váyase al balcón de los fámulos; el último, y en silencio!

Entonces, Pablo se arrebató y se puso delante, diciendo:

– ¡La hemos mirado todos; y Lóriz y yo más que él!

Perceval le oía sin entenderle. Un celeste furor hizo crujir los huesos del Hermano. Y en este difícil momento presentóse el mayordomo, avisándoles que ya estaba cerca la procesión.

Los huéspedes, la familia, los servidores de Lóriz acudieron a los colgados barandales.

Venían los timbaleros con sus capuces verdes, los tañedores de pífano con sus vestas moradas, los gonfalones y cruces de las parroquias, las lanzas de una Decuria, los sables y tricornios de la Guardia Civil... Y todavía pasaban gentes de Oleza, gentes forasteras y labradoras, grupos de señorío en busca de silla, de reja o de portal, y se dejaban los ojos en los balcones de Lóriz y singularmente donde estaba Purita. Era uno de sus días de plenitud de gracias y malicias, de los días proclamados por don Magín. No se olvidaba de prender su rehilete, su aguijón, su acento a los jóvenes olecenses que iban

"Did you see her like that?" Maximo asked him.

And the boy from Aspe moved closer to the piece of sculpture till he felt his breath right on top of her stone thighs. And, suddenly, the boys from Madrid exploded with laughter.

At their side, motionless and black, a monitor Brother waited for them to finish their contemplation.

"I was looking, I was...."

"You were looking, Señor Perceval! Well, at whom?" And he hurled himself upon him, paralyzing and squashing his eyes with his own, grossly dilated by his pince-nez of a myopic. "At whom, Señor Perceval?"

"At Doña Purita!"

"At Doña Purita?" the Brother repeated with a shudder. And with the rapidity that some righteous people have in discovering and in estimating the weight of sin, he guessed that this lump of rustic flesh was not committing it just by approaching the figure of a goddess, but rather by imagining the figure of a real woman in her, and a woman like Doña Purita. And so hoarse of voice and inflamed with purity (a Sainted Church Father has said that the habit of chastity hardens the heart), he extended his arm like a black sword and shouted:

"You are a depraved and monstrous boy! Go to the balcony for the student-servants; the one on the end, and keep silent!"

It was then that Pablo got carried away and stepped forward, saying:

"We all looked at her, Lóriz and I even more than he!" Perceval heard him without understanding him. A celestial rage made the Brother's bones creak. And the major-domo appeared at this difficult moment and let them know that the procession was now quite near.

The guests, the family, the Lóriz servants came over to the overhanging balustrades.

The kettledrummers were coming, wearing their green hooded capes, the fife players with their purple tunics, the gonfalons and crosses of the parish churches, the lances of a Decury, ten Roman soldiers, the sabers and three-cornered hats of the Rural Police....[136] And more inhabitants of Oleza still kept passing by, as well as people from out-of-town, farm women, groups of distinguished people in search of a chair, a window grating or an outer doorway, and they allowed their eyes to rest on the Lóriz balconies and specifically the place where Doña Purita was standing. It was one of her days of a plenitude full of charm and malice, one of those days proclaimed by Don Magín. She had not forgotten to assume her barbed remark, her sting, her emphatic tone, intended for the young men of Oleza who were coming and going, some of

y venían, algunos ya maridos humildes y malhumorados. Casí todos fueron cortejadores suyos, y si se detenían mirándola, ella les pagaba con su risa de chiquilla y un mohín delicioso de su lengua, que, traducido al romance, al romance de amor y bodas, equivalía claramente al "¡No sabes tú lo que te has perdido!"

Llegó el "paso" de la Samaritana. Una viña de luces, un pozo de brocal de oro, de rosas y lirios. Jesús sentado en una piedra de madera, desbordándole la túnica de brescadillo, con la cabeza hacia atrás, en medio de un sol de plata, dobla sus dedos pulidos, señalándose la fuente de aguas vivas que salta de su corazón. La mujer de Sickem le sonríe, mostrándole el cántaro que tiene en la dulce curva de su cadera. Sus vestiduras pesan tres mil libras de capullo-almendra, del que se hila la seda joyante, escaldada por devotos terciopelistas de la comarca que trabajan cantando: "¡Oh, María, Madre mía; oh, consuelo celestial!..."

Enfrente, Elvira Galindo acechó a la imagen como a una mujer viva.

– Mira al Salvador lo mismo que miraría a sus amantes. – Y volvióse a su cuñada y a los Monera para decir – : En este pueblo las damas que parecen más decentes se complacen en ataviar de pecadoras las imágenes de las arrepentidas, como si amaran en esas santas las deshonestidades que ellas no pueden cometer. ¡En cambio, la cofradía de la Dolorosa tiene cada perdida!

Le imploraba la Monera que callase, sin poder ni querer reprimir el júbilo que le encendía sus carrillos, mirando con inocencia a Paulina, que era de la Junta de "La Samaritana".

Y vino un rumor penoso de correas, de maderos, de yugo que crujía, de pies que se hincaban como el arado, de resollar de cuerpos tirantes... Y se paró el "trono" de la "Cena". Lo llevaban veinte huertanos de ropón bermejo, con la cola torcida a los riñones y la falda cazcarrienta de aplastársela con las esparteñas enfangadas; una mano de pezuña agarrándose al muñón de badana de las andas, que les partía los hombros, y la otra en la horquilla para los descansos.

them already humble and ill-humored husbands. Almost all of them had once courted her, and if they stopped to stare at her, she repaid them with her sweet child-like laughter and a delightful pouting of the tongue, which, translated into plain language, the language of love and marriage, was clearly the equivalent of "You don't know what you've lost!"

The portable platform with the Samaritan woman came by. A vineyard of burning lights, a well with a golden curbstone, with roses and lilies. Jesus seated on a stone carved out of wood, his tunic embroidered with silver twist, spread out all around him, his head thrown back, in the middle of a silvery sun, bending his exquisite fingers, pointing at the fountain of living waters pouring from his heart. The woman of Shechem is smiling at him,[137] showing him the jug she is carrying in the sweet curve of her hip. Her garments have the weight of three thousand pounds of elongated silk worm cocoons, from which they spin the glossy silk, after they have been scalded by the devout velvet weavers of the region who sing as they work, "Oh, Mary, dear Mother, celestial consolation!..."[138]

Opposite this, Elvira Galindo spied on the image as if it were a living woman.

"She looks at the Savior in the same way she would look upon her lovers." And she turned to her sister-in-law and the Moneras to say, "In this town the ladies who seem most proper are pleased to dress up the images of the repentant woman as sinners, as if they loved the indecent acts in those saints that they themselves can not commit. On the other hand, the sisterhood of the Sorrowing Mary has every kind of wanton woman in it!"[139]

Señora Monera implored her to be silent, though she was neither able nor willing to repress the jubilation that inflamed her cheeks as she innocently looked at Paulina, who belonged to the Council of the Sodality of the "Samaritan Woman."

And then came the labored sound of leather straps, of wooden poles, of a creaking yoke, of feet digging into the ground like a plough, of the heavy breathing of straining bodies.... And the "shrine" carrying the "Last Supper" stopped. Twenty men from the cultivated plain were carrying it, dressed in wide, loose-fitting vermilion gowns with the tails twisted round their waists and the skirts covered with mud splashes, because they had stepped all over them with their mud-spattered matweed sandals; one hoof-like hand clutching the sheepskin-covered trunnion supporting the portable platform, that was breaking their backs, and the other hand holding the pitchforks they used when they paused to rest.

Los doce apóstoles, en sillas Luis XV, y el Señor, más alto. Los discipulos, con barbas viejas asirias, menos San Juan, siempre juvenil y rubio. Todos mirándose, unánimemente pasmados, sin coincidir sus miradas, como los ojos de los ciegos. Judas, de codos, siniestro, rufo y sin nimbo, y debajo de la sandalia le salía la cabecita de una serpiente. Floreros, candelabros, picheles, manteles, peces, pollos, un cordero asado, frutas y verduras, y en la tarima, la jofaina y el jarro de la lustración; todo retemblando en su inmovilidad.

Monera sonrió.

– ¡Hasta lechugas, lechugas de nuestra huerta! Todos los años me lo digo: ¿Es que entonces había lechugas? ¡Y cómo se nos reirán los de Madrid!

El penitenciario le puso encima los ojos glaciales, y el homeópata, no sabiendo qué hacer, sacó su reloj de oro y apartóse para que se asomara más el penitenciario.

El mayoral de los "nazarenos" golpeó tres veces con su forca, previniendo el arranque. Bramaron los veinte huertanos aupando la carga, y pasó la "Cena", arremolinada como un navío, en una ráfaga de ropas, de brazos, de lumbres.

Máximo y Pablo aparecieron entre las primas de Lóriz y doña Purita.

Pablo sintió una delicia primaveral, como si floreciese de felicidad todo su cuerpo. Estaba mirándole Purita. No pudo él apartar sus ojos, y ella se los tomó en el regazo de los suyos, meciéndolos, llevándoselos. Tan poseída fue la mirada, que les pareció durar muchas horas. La Juno virgen, sonrosada pálidamente por la mañana de abril, se puerilizaba, ceñida toda por una caricia gloriosa y perversa, que fue quemándose hasta quedar en una claridad interior de aceites purísimos. Caricia de inocencia y de mortificación. Recordaba sus aflicciones y desamparos padecidos; y se hubiera ofrecido apasionadamente otra vez a todos sus dolores por acercarse a Pablo, renaciéndole una gracia de niña. Pero, mirándola el hijo de Lóriz, precoz y decrépito, regresaba a su esplendor sensual desconfiado.

Acababa de pararse el "Prendimiento". Jesús, atado con cordeles de seda

The twelve apostles in Louis XV chairs, and the Lord, up above them. The disciples wearing old-style Assyrian beards, except for Saint John, forever youthful and blond. All of them looking at one another, collectively dismayed, their glances not quite in focus, like the eyes of the blind. Judas, leaning on his elbows, looking sinister, with kinky red hair and without a halo, and the little head of a serpent was peeping out from under his sandal. Flower stands, candelabra, pewter tankards, tablecloths, fish, chickens, a roasted lamb, fruit and green vegetables, and the washbasin and the pitcher used for the lustration on the platform; everything shaking with immobility.[140]

Monera smiled.

"Even lettuce, lettuce from our own vegetable gardens! Every year I say to myself, 'Did they really have lettuce at that time? And how those visitors from Madrid must be laughing at us!'"

The canon-penitentiary laid his icy eyes upon him, and the homeopath, not knowing what to do, took out his gold watch and moved aside so the canon-penitentiary could have a better view.

The man in charge of the group of "Nazarenes" pounded three times with his two-pointed stick, preparing them to start up again. The twenty farm men from the cultivated plain roared as they raised up their burden, and the "Last Supper" moved by, all crammed with people as on a naval vessel, in a gust of garments, arms and blazing lights.

Máximo and Pablo appeared between the Lórizes' cousins and Doña Purita.

Pablo felt a springtime delight, as if his entire body were flowering with happiness. Purita was looking at him. He was unable to draw his eyes away, and she gathered them into her inner core, rocking them, taking them unto herself. So possessed was the glance that it seemed to last for many hours for them. The virginal Juno, rosy pale with the April morning, was assuming a childlike aspect, completely encircled by a glorious and perverse caress, that kept burning up till all that remained was an internalized brilliance of very pure oils. A caress of innocence and mortification. She remembered the sorrows and abandonment she had suffered, and she would have again offered herself passionately to all her grief just to draw nearer to Pablo, with the charm of the young girl reborn in her. But as the precocious and decrepit son of the Lórizes kept looking at her, she returned to her distrustful sensual splendor.

The platform with the "Arrest of the Lord" had just come to a stop. Jesus,

morada que terminan en bellotas de oro. Dos sayones alumbran la noche con hachos de llamas esculpidas. Todavía tiene Pedro la espada desnuda. Malko está derribado en el tronco de un olivo de Getsemaní, colgándole la oreja rebanada, lívida y dura. Rodeaban las andas los yelmos y picas de los legionarios. Delante, el señor Hugo, el insignia, alcanzando el "águila", estallándole su gallardía de circo, y después, jerárquicamente solo, el centurión: es decir, don Amancio, más don Amancio que nunca, más *Carolus Alba-Longa* que en sus paseos por la Glorieta, que en sus tertulias del Círculo de Labradores. Sus arreos y sus armas adquirieron transparencia para todos los ojos. Se le veía la calvicie de curial bajo el crestón de su casco de azófar; las rodilleras de los pantalones saliéndole de las grebas, la blanda americana estrujada por la cota, la esclavina de su carrik entre los aleteos de la clámide y su paraguas engordándole la espada.

A los madrileños y al menudo Lóriz les saltó la risa encima de Pablo.

– ¡El amigo de tu padre! ¡El amigo de tu padre! – Y rebotaron dos almendras de Alcoy en la coraza del centurión.

Apresuróse un Hermano a condenar la burla.

– ¡Piensen en la divinidad ultrajada! ¡Vean que no escarnios, sino elogios merece el piadoso entusiasmo de ese patricio!

Y prorrumpió la voz de colegiala de doña Purita:

– ¡Tía Elvira y el centurión no paran de mirarse! ¡Ay, qué ricos!

– ¡A mí tía Elvira no la quiere ni don Amancio!

Vióse doña Purita en tía Elvira, y se compadeció de todas las Puritas y las tías Elviras de este mundo. Pero las primas de la condesa dejaron libre su alborozo, y la magnífica doncellona se olvidó de sí misma para reír también.

Los penitentes, los anderos, los romanos, los vecinos se volvieron con agravio hacia la noble casa. El Salvador parecía quejarse con sus ojos cristalizados, y Pedro blandía vengadoramente su espada vieja.

Las gozosas mujeres se retiraron sofocadas, llevándose a Pablo a un túmulo de almohadones. Acudió el Hermano, les arrancó al culpable y lo puso entre los fámulos y el chico de Aspe. Desde allí las miraba el castigado.

tied with cords of purple silk with golden acorn-shaped adornments at the ends. Two confraternity members in purple tunics light up the night with torches of sculptured flames. Peter still holds his naked sword. Malchus lies prostrate against the trunk of an olive tree in Gethsemane, his livid, firm ear sliced from his head and dangling loose.[141] The legionnaires' helmets and pikes surrounded the portable platform. In front, Señor Hugo, the standard bearer, raising up the "eagle," his graceful bearing of a circus performer bursting from him, and behind him, hierarchically alone, the centurion: that is to say, Don Amancio, more Don Amancio than ever, more *Carolus Alba-Longa* than during his strolls through the Glorieta, than in his social gatherings at the Farmers' Club. His accessory adornments and weapons acquired transparency for all eyes. You could see the baldness of a lawyer under the crest of his brass helmet; the baggy knees of his trousers showing through the greaves round his lower legs, his soft jacket tightly squeezed by the coat of mail, the pelerine of his ample great coat between the flapping movement of his chlamys, and his umbrella making his sword seem even broader.

The laughter of the boys from Madrid and the young Lóriz swept over Pablo.

"Your father's friend! Your father's friend!" And two sugared almonds from Alcoy bounced onto the centurion's armor plate.

A Brother hastened forward to condemn this jocular behavior.
"Just think of the divinity you have offended! Can't you see that the pious enthusiasm of that patrician deserves praise and not scoffing!"

And the school girlish voice of Doña Purita burst out:
"Aunt Elvira and the centurion can't stop looking at one another! Oh, how wonderful!"

"Not even Don Amancio likes my Aunt Elvira!"

Doña Purita saw herself in Aunt Elvira and she felt sorry for all the Puritas and Aunt Elviras in this world. But the countess's cousins set loose their merriment and the magnificent confirmed virginal maiden forgot herself and laughed along with them.

The penitents, the platform bearers, the Romans, the local residents all turned toward the noble house as if they had been offended. The Savior seemed to be protesting with his crystallized eyes, and Peter vengefully brandished his old sword.

The carefree women were flushed with excitement and withdrew, taking Pablo away with them to a pile of large cushions. The Brother came over, pulled the culpable child away from them and placed him among the student-servants and the lad from Aspe. From there, the punished child

Las odiaba y se detenía, recogiendo con un dulce ahogo los perfumes que le habían dejado sus manos, sus mejillas y sus ropas. Y de repente les volvió la espalda con desdén porque ellas pedían su perdón al Prefecto.

...Cuando salió, el último, detrás de los fámulos, del portal de Lóriz, vio toda su casa silenciosa y cerrada. Y Pablo se replegó en una sombría indiferencia.

La brigada subió lentamente la calle de Palacio; cruzó la plazuela de la catedral...

En otro tiempo, después de la procesión, los colegiales esperaban allí al señor obispo, que pasaba con sus pajes y canónigos, dejando sonrisas y bendiciones, camino de su basílica para ofrecerse a la extenuación de la tremenda liturgia: las grandes plegarias, la adoración de la cruz, la misa de presantificados... Ahora, su ilustrísima se sepultaba en su biblioteca y en su dormitorio, y los oficios de la sede iban quedándose descoloridos y pobres.

Por fortuna para Oleza, la iglesia de "Jesús" y la parroquia de Nuestro Padre San Daniel mantenían las excelsitudes de las pompas sagradas.

Por la tarde

Acabado el Ejercicio de las Siete Palabras, había recreo, en silencio, a la sombra tenue de los olmos y de los parrales retoñados. Los balones y los zapatos de los colegiales retumbaban desoladamente.

Pablo no quiso jugar. Los inspectores aceptaban, esa tarde, como místicas mortificaciones, los apartamientos, tan reprobados siempre como indicios de melancolías peligrosas. Pablo reanimaba en su memoria el retablo de la agonía del Señor: la iglesia del colegio transformada en Calvario; peñas rojas y plomizas con tojos y retamares; veredas esclarecidas por quinqués ocultos; fondo de firmamento de paño de funeral; las tres cruces gigantes; los dos ladrones retorcidos, desriñonándose convulsos, aplastados por las ligaduras, y el de la derecha inclinándose ya un poco a Jesús, que colgaba liso, blanco, velazqueño; y bajo el divino horizonte de sus manos clavadas, la Madre y el discípulo: María, con manto azul y toca blanca bullonada; Juan,

kept regarding them. He hated them and paused and gathered to himself the perfumes left behind by their hands, their cheeks and their garments with a sweet breathlessness. And he suddenly turned his back on them in disdain because they were asking the Prefect Father to forgive him.

...When he left the entryway to the Lóriz house, the last one, behind the servants from the school, he saw his entire house silent and closed up. And Pablo fell back into a somber feeling of indifference.

The brigade slowly went up the Calle de Palacio; they crossed the small plaza in front of the cathedral....

On other occasions, after the procession, the schoolboys would wait there for the lord bishop, who would go by with his pages and canons, extending smiles and benedictions, on the way to his basilica to offer himself to the extenuation of the tremendous liturgy: the powerful implorations, the adoration of the cross, the Mass for the presanctified.... Now, His Excellency buried himself in his library and in his bedroom, and the liturgical offices of the see were left colorless and impoverished.

Fortunately for Oleza, the church of "Jesús" and the parish church of Our Father San Daniel still maintained the sublime beauty of the sacred ceremonies.

In the afternoon

When the Devotion of the Seven Words of Christ was over,[142] there was a period of recreation, in silence, in the subdued shade of the elm trees and the sprouting vine arbors. The footballs and the schoolboys' shoes resounded disconsolately.

Pablo had no desire to play. That afternoon, the priest monitors accepted the boys' withdrawal as a sign of mystical mortification, although it was generally regarded with reproval, as an indication of dangerous melancholy. Pablo revived the series of images of the agony of the Lord in his memory: the school church transformed into Calvary; red and leaden-colored crags with furze and Spanish broom; paths lit up by concealed oil lamps; a background of firmament made of funeral crape; the three gigantic crosses; the two thieves all twisted, their bodies cracked and convulsed, crushed by their bonds, and the one on the right now leaning a little toward Jesus, who was hanging there, smooth and white, as in a work of Velázquez; and beneath the divine horizon of his nailed hands, the Mother and the disciple: Mary wearing a blue cloak and a white veil adorned with puffs; John, in

con sayal color de vino y cíngulo negro, ladeaba su cabeza de adolescente hacia el mundo redimido. Ardían estopas en lámparas romanas de escayola, y sus llamas amarillas acostaban las sombras de los peñones de arpillera hasta el reclinatorio de Pablo.

Pablo se veía caminar de la mano de su madre por las afueras calientes de Jerusalén. Jerusalén, tostadita de sol como su Oleza. Un aire de follajes de huertos le ceñía como un vestido oloroso que crujía entre las cruces ensangrentadas. Después de la séptima palabra: "¡Padre: en tus manos encomiendo mi espíritu!", don Roger iba soltando el Miserere, tan apretado, tan espeso, que parecía negro.

Las tres en todos los relojes de Jerusalén. Las campanadas finas de los cuartos; las campanadas anchas de las horas, que sonaban lo mismo que las de un reloj de pesas del "Olivar" de su abuelo. En aquel tiempo – se decía Pablo – quizá no hubiera relojes ni campanarios; pero estas horas apócrifas que tocaban el Hermano Canalda, el Hermano Giner y Córdoba el sereno, con martillos en hojas de sierra, le emocionaban más que los lloros de las mujeres revolcadas de contrición y lástima en las tinieblas de las capillas, más que los gritos, ya roncos, del predicador, más que el terremoto bíblico. Los sollozos de mujer pudieron oírse en aquella tarde; los gritos imploradores pudo exhalarlos un discípulo afligido; y el terremoto era verdad evangélica, y ninguna de las posibilidades le angustiaba el corazón; en cambio, esos relojes falsos le precipitaban sus latidos en la dulce congoja de una verdad de belleza. Y subía sus ojos a la cruz del Señor.

Las fauces del Señor se hinchaban y se vaciaban de ahogo; le caían, cegándole, los cabellos, cuajados de sudores, de moscardas y de polvo podrido; se oía el golpear desesperado de su cabeza contra los maderos, y de pronto se le caía contra el pecho, crujiéndole la nuca, y se quedaba inmóvil, largo, resbaladizo, húmedo del helor de la agonía.

Muerto ya Jesús, Pablo iba perdiendo la emocionada ilusión de la Semana Santa. Otra vez el colegio de la Oleza contemporánea: oficio parvo, pláticas, examen de consciencia, liturgia menuda, desaromada; liturgia de diario. Para esta criatura, como para los más doctos Padres de la Iglesia, el origen y la cúspide del año litúrgico residía en las conmemoraciones de la Semana Santa.

Le llamó el Hermano portero para llevarle al salón de visitas. Este lego

wine-colored sackcloth and a black cingulum, was tilting his adolescent head toward the redeemed world. Bits of tow were burning in the Roman scagliola lamps and their yellow flames lay the shadows of the burlap peaks to rest all the way to Pablo's prie-dieu.

Pablo could see himself holding his mother's hand as they walked through the hot outskirts of Jerusalem. Jerusalem, gently baked by the sun like his Oleza. An air of garden foliage wrapped him round like a fragrant dress that rustled among the blood-covered crosses. After the seventh word, "Father, I commend my spirit to your hands!", Don Roger began sending forth the Miserere,[143] so tightly compressed, so thick, that it seemed black.

Three o'clock on all the clocks in Jerusalem. The soft sound of the bells for the quarter hours, the expansive sounds of the bells for the hours, that sounded just like the ones on a pendulum clock at his grandfather's "Olive Grove." At that time – Pablo said to himself – perhaps there weren't any clocks or campaniles; but these apocryphal hours tolled by Brother Canalda, Brother Giner and Córdoba, the night watchman, with their hammers on the blades of saws, filled him with greater emotion than the weeping of women wallowing in contrition and lamentation in the darkness of the chapels, more than the ever hoarser shouting of the preacher, more than the biblical earthquake. The sobbing of women could be heard that afternoon; a grieving disciple was able to utter the pleading shouts and the earthquake was an evangelical truth and none of these possibilities filled his heart with anguish; on the other hand, those false clocks precipitated their beating into the sweet anguish of a beautiful truth for him. And he raised his eyes to the cross of the Lord.

The Lord's fauces swelled up and drained out with affliction; his hair, coagulated with sweat, with blow flies and putrid dust, kept falling down and blinding him; you could hear the desperate pounding of his head against the boards, and it suddenly dropped down against his breast, making the back of his neck crack, and he remained there motionless, long, slippery, damp with the penetrating cold of his final agony.

Now that Jesus was dead, Pablo started to lose his emotion-filled illusion of Holy Week. Once again the school in contemporary Oleza: daily service in praise of Our Lady, informal talks, examination of conscience, inconsequential, tasteless liturgy; the liturgy of every day. For this child, as for the most learned Church Fathers, the origin and apex of the liturgical year rested in the commemorations of Holy Week.

The doorkeeper Brother[144] called him to take him to the visitors lounge.

tan viejecito, tan calvo y tan dotado de la gracia de la humanidad, tenía esa tarde un gesto desdeñoso. Los santos más desasidos, más ingenuos, más humildes, llegan algunas veces a conocer el valor de la insignificancia; y, entonces, un Hermano portero de la Compañía de Jesús, que ha consumido su vida imitando las obscuras virtudes de un San Alonso Rodríguez, también Hermano portero, se acuerda de que San Alonso ya no está ensartando rosarios en su jaula de una cancela de colegio, ni abriendo y cerrando el postigo, sino en su altar, un altar con azucenas y fanales de oro, un altar en cada iglesia de la Compañía, y la imagen tiene en sus manos el atributo de las llaves como la del príncipe de los apóstoles. A esta costosa cumbre únicamente puede subirse por los caminos de la humildad, de la renunciación de todos los afectos. ¡Pues cuán lejos de esa bienaventuranza las pobres gentes que ni siquiera Viernes Santo hacían el sacrificio de los apetitos y amores terrenales! Y cada vez que repicaba el esquilón de la portería – un esquilón como una quijada loca que se riese sacándole la lengua del badajillo-, el Hermano botaba de pesadumbre. ¡No podían vivir sin quererse, sin besarse, sin tocarse! ¡Oh qué engaños y peligros tenían los alumnos en sus familias; y singularmente en la madre, en la madre y en las hermanas!...

Llamaron. Abrió el ventanillo para mirar.

La señora Galindo. ¡La señora Galindo, tan piadosa y residiendo en Oleza! Acaso mereciese disculpa el celo de las familias forasteras; pero las otras, las de Oleza que, gozando de locutorio todos los jueves y domingos, apartaban a los colegiales del recogimiento del Viernes Santo, las de Oleza...

– Seremos muy pocos, ¿verdad?

– ¡De Oleza, nadie, por respeto al día!

– ¡Han castigado a Pablo, y yo quería verle y consolarle!

– ¿Y quién consoló a Jesucristo en esta tarde?

– Yo me marcharé pronto, pero tráigame a Pablo.

Lo trajo. Y Paulina y su hijo se quedaron en la claustra.

– ¿No viene nadie contigo? ¡Tú sola, sin tía Elvira! – Y la besaba y la miraba más.

– ¡Te han castigado, y tu padre ha sufrido mucho!

– ¡Me han castigado por ellas! Se han reído porque se ríen de todo... ¡Siempre están contentas! Y esa tía Elvira...

This kindly old lay brother, so bald and so endowed with the quality of humility, had a disdainful expression that afternoon. The most immaterial, the most ingenuous, the most humble saints sometimes come to know the value of insignificance, and then, a Brother doorkeeper of the Society of Jesus, who has spent his life imitating the obscure virtues of a Saint Alonso Rodríguez,[145] who was also a Brother doorkeeper, remembers that Saint Alonso is no longer stringing rosaries in his cage at the outer gate to the school, nor opening and closing the wicket, but rather he is on his altar, an altar with Madonna lilies and golden bell jars, an altar in every church of the Society, and his image has in its hands the attribute of the keys, like that of the prince of the apostles. One can only rise to this most difficult peak by taking the paths of humility, by the renunciation of all fondness for material things. Well, how distant from that state of bliss are all those poor souls who not even on Good Friday can make the sacrifice of their earthly appetites and loves! And every time the large call bell at the porter's lodge would ring – a big bell like a frenzied jawbone laughing as it stuck out its small clapper tongue at you – , the Brother would spring up in sorrow. Couldn't they live without loving one another, without kissing one another, without touching one another! Oh, how much deception and danger the students had in their families, and especially in the mothers, the mothers and the sisters!...[146]

Some one was knocking. He opened the small window to look out.

Señora Galindo. Señora Galindo, so pious and a resident of Oleza! Perhaps the zeal of the families that lived out-of-town could be forgiven; but the others, the ones from Oleza who enjoyed the use of the locutory every Thursday and Sunday and distracted the schoolboys from the intimate feeling of confinement on Good Friday, the women from Oleza....

"We are probably very few, am I right?"

"From Oleza, nobody, out of respect for the day!"

"They've punished Pablo and I wanted to see him and console him!"

"And who consoled Jesus Christ on this afternoon?"

"I'll leave right away, but please bring me Pablo."

He brought him. And Paulina and her son remained there in the cloister.

"Nobody came with you? You're all by yourself, without Aunt Elvira!" And he kissed her and looked at her even more.

"They've punished you and your father has suffered so much!"

"They punished me on account of those women! They burst out laughing because they laugh at everything. They're always happy! And that Aunt Elvira...."

– ¡Hasta nombrándola se siente tu desvío.

– ¡No la puedo ver! ¡No la quiere nadie!

– ¡Pero es hermana de tu padre!

– ¡De mi padre! ¡Tuya, no!

Se habían recostado en un pilar. Por las piedras calientes y tiernas de primavera subían los rosales. Entre los cipreses inmóviles se volcaban las golondrinas. Y en lo alto, dos vencejos coronaban la cruz de una cúpula fresca de aristas azules.

Caían hormigas y gusarapillos. Pablo los tomaba para verlos correr despavoridos en la mano de su madre; después se paraban y se ponían a tentar con el palpo, con las antenas, como si catasen las escondidas mieles de rosas de que estaban amasados los dedos de Paulina.

– ...Y esa tía Elvira no se ríe como ellas. No puede. ¡Pero me miraba riéndose cuando me castigaron!

La madre le pasó los dedos por los párpados para fundirle con su caricia la sequedad de sus ojos.

– ¡Se ha de sentir lástima por los que no tienen quien les quiera!

– ¡Que nos quieran también ellos!

– Tía Elvira te quiere.

– ¡Pues yo, no!

– ¡Tu abuelo quiso a todos, Pablo; sé como él!

– Y por qué yo no me llamo Daniel, como mi abuelo?... ¡Yo quisiera que el Señor hubiese muerto en Oleza!... Y cuando vinimos, me llevaron al aposento del Padre Prefecto. Me dio tanta rabia oírle, que yo acusé de todo a las de Lóriz y a Doña Purita, y entonces el Padre Prefecto me perdonó. Ahora me pesa. ¡Pero yo esta noche, en la procesión, no he de parar de reírme hasta que me castiguen otra vez!

Paulina le besaba. Y el Hermano portero les separó diciendo:

– ¡En esta tarde, Nuestra Señora no pudo besar a su Hijo sino después de muerto!

Por la noche

Toda la vida de Paulina se arrodillaba en esta noche del entierro del Señor. La luna de esta noche, la misma luna tan grande, que iba enfriándole de luz, su vestido, sus cabellos, su palidez, su vieja casa de Oleza, mojó de claridad el manto y la demacración de María y la roca de la sepultura del Señor. Como

"Even when you just say her name, one can feel your dislike!"

"I can't stand her! Nobody likes her!"

"But she's your father's sister!"

"My father's! Not yours!"

They were leaning back against a pillar. The climbing roses ran up the stones, warm and yellow with spring. The swallows were creating a commotion among the motionless cypress trees. And up above, two swifts were crowning the cross over a cool-looking cupola with blue arrises.

Ants and small water worms kept falling. Pablo would pick them up so that he could watch them run over his mother's hand in terror; then they would stop and begin to probe with their feelers, with their antennae, as if they were sampling the hidden rose nectar with which Paulina's fingers were imbued.

"...And that Aunt Elvira doesn't laugh like those other women do. She can't. But she kept looking at me and laughing when they punished me!"

His mother passed her fingers over his eyelids so that her caress might impart the dryness of her own eyes to his.

"One ought to feel sorry for those who have no one who loves them!"

"Let them love us in return!"

"Aunt Elvira loves you."

"Well, I don't!"

"Your grandfather loved everyone, Pablo; be like him!"

"Then why isn't my name Daniel, like my grandfather?... I would have wanted the Lord to have died in Oleza!... And when we came, they took me to the Prefect Father's room. It made me so angry to hear him that I blamed the Lóriz women and Doña Purita for everything, and then the Prefect Father pardoned me. Now I regret it. But tonight, in the procession, I'm not going to stop laughing until they punish me again!"

Paulina kissed him. And the Brother gatekeeper separated them saying:

"On this afternoon, Our Lady was not able to kiss her Son until after He was dead!"

At night

All of Paulina's life kneeled down on that night of the burial of the Lord. The moon that night, the same great big moon that kept chilling her dress, her hair, her paleness, her old house in Oleza with light, moistened Mary's cloak and her emaciated semblance with bright light, just as it did the stone

su hijo, ella también se sentía penetrada de las distancias de los tiempos. Evidencia de una pena, de un amor, de una felicidad que se hubiera ya tenido en el instante que se produjo y en que nosotros no vivíamos. Sentirse en otro tiempo y ahora. La plenitud de lo actual mantenida de un lejano principio. Iluminada emoción de los días profundos de nuestra conciencia, los días que nos dejan, los mismos días antepasados y conformados y que han de seguir después de nuestra muerte.

Y para ser del todo ella en aquel tiempo y siempre, había ya de acogerse al hijo; ella por hipóstasis del hijo, anegándose en él y conteniéndolo en su sangre. Ni podía recordarse niña ni sentirse hija sin él. Así llegaba hasta todos los horizontes; pero también en todos se tendía la sombra del esposo, acatado con obstinación como un dogma. Y amándolo en lo más obscuro de su voluntad le parecía haber llegado a madre siendo siempre virgen en su deseo y en la promesa de su vida.

...Y al volverse, le dio en los ojos la vieja relumbre de las vestiduras de San Josefico, que la míraba esperándola, bajo los óleos de los padres de don Álvaro: el señor Galindo, la señora Serrallonga.

La diminuta imagen, y los atributos y ornamentos pueriles del altarín, todo tenía un brillo dulce y turbio de pupilas socarronas que le pedían que fuese a recibir la emanación de su secreto poder. Anochecido lo dejó doña Nieves, más blanca y macerada, casi de celuloide, con su ajado vestido de Viernes Santo.

– Viene mi arquilla de la noble casa de Lóriz. No sabían aquellos señores ni aquellos criados en qué rincón obscuro ponerla. Y luego que les referí lo que mi San Josefico ve y oye y dice, y que desde allí había de traértelo, se lo llevó a su dormitorio el señor don Máximo, el caballero pintor. ¡A su lado pasó la noche; míralo, mi hija!

Paulina no pudo mirarlo. Los ojos infantiles de San Josefico eran más pavorosos que los ojos adivinos de Nuestro Padre San Daniel; y la llamaban como si quisieran que recogiese una culpable intimidad. San Josefico se parecía esa noche a doña Nieves...

Se reclinó en su ventana para ver el Entierro, y tembló dentro de la llama

of the sepulcher of the Lord. Like her son, she too felt that she was pervaded by the distances of other times. The evidence of a sorrow, of a love, of a happiness that one would already have lived through at the instant that gave rise to it and in which we were not living. To feel oneself in another time and in the present. The plenitude of the present moment sustained by a distant beginning. The illuminated emotion of the profoundest days within our consciousness, the days that leave us behind, the very same days, previous and adapted days, which have to go on even after our death.

And in order to be completely herself both in that time and forever, she now had to take refuge in her son: she herself, by the hypostasis of the son, drowning herself in him and containing him in her own blood. Nor could she remember herself as a child nor feel herself a daughter without him. In this way she was able to extend herself to every horizon; but the shadow of her husband, obstinately revered like a dogma, extended all over it as well. And by loving him in the darkest part of her will, she seemed to have become a mother while always remaining a virgin in her desire and in the promise of her life.

...And when she turned around, the age-old sparkle of little Saint Joseph's vestments caught her eye, for he was looking for her and waiting for her beneath the oil portraits of Don Álvaro's parents, Señor Galindo, Señora Serrallonga.

The diminutive image and the childish attributes and ornaments of the miniature altar all had a sweet and turbid brilliance like that of ironical pupils asking you to go and receive the emanation of their secret power. After night had fallen, Doña Nieves, whiter and more emaciated than ever, almost like celluloid, wearing her crumpled Good Friday dress, had left it there.

"This little box of mine has just come from the noble house of Lóriz. Neither those lordly people nor their servants knew into which dark corner they could put it. And after I explained to them what my little Saint Joseph sees and hears and says, and that I was supposed to bring it to you from their house afterwards, Señor Don Máximo, the gentleman who is a painter, took it away to his bedroom. It spent the night beside him; just look at it, my child!"

Paulina couldn't look at it. Little Saint Joseph's childlike eyes were more terrifying than the divining eyes of Our Father San Daniel, and they were calling to her as if they wanted her to gather in a culpable intimacy. Little Saint Joseph looked like Doña Nieves that night....

She leaned against her window to see the Burial[147] and she trembled within

negra de los ojos de don Álvaro, y ella refugió los suyos en el hijo. Lo tenían los de Lóriz en su balcón, complaciéndose en él, prefiriéndolo entre todos los colegiales. La delicada figura de Pablo, recortándose en el fondo de sedas antiguas, de arañas de cristal, de lámparas de cobre, era la de un príncipe dueño de todas las magnificencias de aquel palacio.

El esposo se apartaba lentamente alumbrando detrás de las andas de San Juan Evangelista. Y Paulina asomó más su cuerpo para seguir mirándole con obediencia, y sintió que la traspasaba como una luz la mirada de Máximo el pintor, que sonreía a Pablo con ternura. Recordó asustada, sin entenderla, la queja de ese hombre: "¡Por qué lloverá sobre el mar!" Entonces se miraron los dos, y ella se vio delante de todos, sola, iluminada calientemente, como si toda la procesión del Entierro de Cristo le hubiese acercado las velas para sorprenderle los pensamientos.

La calle recibía un tostado color de panal. Filas calladas de devotos con cirios ardientes. Un silencio de cielos campesinos que venían a tenderse encima de Oleza. Un pisar sumiso, y el plañir de los limosneros: "¡Por los que están en pecado mortal!"... Vibraban las monedas en las bandejas de hierro. Y de lo profundo salían más imploraciones: "¡Por la preciosa sangre de Cristo!... ¡Para Nuestro Padre San Daniel!"...

Pasó la Soledad, hueca y rígida de terciopelo negro; la faz de cera goteada de lágrimas; las manos de difunta sosteniendo un enorme corazón de plata erizado de puñales que se estremecían. Por antiguo privilegio, llevaban las andas, desnudas y ligeras, cuatro viejos militares, de uniforme, un uniforme de pliegues de cómoda, de categoría de mortaja. Y continuaban las hileras temblorosas de luces amarillas. Cirios y luto. A lo último, el resplandor helado del sepulcro de cristal, y bajo el sudario fosforescente de riquezas, el Señor muerto, el Señor, que se volvió para mirar a Paulina, lo mismo que la noche que le tuvo miedo a Nuestro Padre San Daniel...

De todos los balcones descendía una lluvia silenciosa de flores.

Se quedaba la luna sola en la calle, y más lejos iban abriéndose otros cauces quemados de velas y ondulados de silencio de oraciones del Entierro de Cristo.

De los campanarios caían las horas glaciales y largas.

A las diez se recogió Paulina, cumpliendo su turno de meditación de la Hora Santa para hacerle compañía a la Madre del Señor.

the black flame of Don Álvaro's eyes, and so she sought refuge for hers in her son. The Lórizes had him on their balcony, taking considerable pleasure in him, preferring him over all the schoolboys. Pablo's delicate figure, outlined against the background of very old silks, of crystal chandeliers, of copper lamps, was that of a prince, master of all the magnificent things in that palace.

The husband moved aside slowly, lighting up the space behind the portable platform bearing the image of Saint John the Evangelist. And Paulina leaned her body out even more in order to keep looking at him obediently, and she felt that the painter Máximo's glance pierced her like a light as he smiled at Pablo tenderly. She felt frightened as she recalled that man's complaint, even without understanding it, "Why should it rain on the sea!" Then the two looked at one another and she saw herself in front of everyone, alone, warmly illuminated, as if the entire procession of the Burial of Christ had brought the candles closer to her in order to surprise her thoughts.

The street was taking on the toasted color of honeycomb. Hushed lines of the faithful with long burning tapers. The silence of rustic heavens that were coming to extend themselves above Oleza. A submissive tramping of feet, the wail of the alms gatherers, "For those who are in mortal sin!..." The coins resounded in the iron trays. And more supplications rose up from the depths. "For the precious blood of Christ!... For Our Father San Daniel!..."

The representation of the Grieving Mary passed, featureless and rigid in black velvet; the waxen face dripping with tears, hands like those of a dead woman supporting an enormous heart, bristling with shivering daggers. Because of a long-standing privilege, four old soldiers in uniform, uniforms creased from lying folded in drawers, to be used later as shrouds, were carrying the bare, lightweight portable platform.[148] And the trembling lines of yellow lights kept coming. Tapers and mourning. At the very end, the frozen brilliance of the crystal glass sepulcher, and underneath the shroud, so phosphorescent with richness, the dead Lord, who turned to look at Paulina, just as he had the night she had been afraid of Our Father San Daniel... [149]

A silent rain of flowers descended from all the balconies.

The moon remained alone in the street and in the distance other channels were opening up, burning with candles and undulating with the silence of the prayers for the Burial of Christ.

The long, icy cold hours kept falling from the bell towers. At ten o'clock Paulina withdrew, to fulfill her obligation to take her turn at the meditation of the Holy Hour in order to keep the Lord's Mother company.[150]

La noche immensa se apoderaba de su vida, tocándola en el corazón como una mano de suavidad. Y se sonrojó de la delicia de sus lágrimas. A veces se descansaba en la ventana. Rodaba el río por las soledades tiernas de luna. Nadie en Oleza ni en los caminos. Luna y olor de felicidad de jardines abandonados.

"¡Por qué llovería sobre el mar!" ¡Aguas dulces y finas de las sierras descendiendo en las aguas amargas y desamparadas! Y sollozó, pidiéndole a Jesús muerto que lloviese en su vida el agua dulce y buena.

A su espalda se abrió la voz de su esposo:

– ¡No parece que llores por la muerte de Cristo, sino por ti misma!

Y don Álvaro estuvo mirándola en su frente y en su boca, y salió dejándole un vaho de cera de la procesión del Entierro.

4. Mauricio

Las oraciones y cartas de las vírgenes de la Visitación alcanzaron la gracia deseada. Y un día glorioso de mayo presentóse en el convento de Nuestra Señora don Mauricio Valcárcel, capitán de Húsares y agregado militar de la Embajada de España en Viena, portador del ostensorio de las Salesas de Annecy.

Le acompañaba el comandante de Infantería, Jefe de la Zona, que se calzó espuelas de rodajas oxidadas. Luego vino resollando el señor deán.

La prelada recibió por el torno el venerable atadijo, cuyas cintas se habían impregnado del fino olor de las maletas del húsar diplomático.

Toda la comunidad acudió al locutorio. A través de la jerga de sus cendales, las místicas palomas contemplaban las galas del mancebo. Su gallardía no era de este mundo. Hasta la clavaria creyóse en presencia de un enviado del cielo, de un arcángel resplandeciente. Iba el arcángel muy bizarro, todo de azul. Sus piernas, modeladas por los negros espejos del clarol de las botas de montar; su sable, cuajado de centellas; sus hombros, torrenciales de purísima plata, y culminando su figura, una cabeza de color

The immensity of the night was overpowering her life, touching her heart like a hand of softness. And she blushed from the delight of her tears. At times she would rest on the window. The river kept on rolling through tender, solitary and moonlit places. Nobody in Oleza nor on the roads. Moonlight and the aroma of the happiness of abandoned gardens.

"Why would it rain on the sea!" Sweet, gentle waters from the mountains, descending into the bitter, forsaken waters! And she sobbed, asking dead Jesus to rain the sweet, good water upon her life.

Her husband's voice opened wide behind her back:

"It doesn't seem that you're crying for the death of Christ, but rather for yourself!"

And there stood Don Álvaro looking at her forehead and her mouth, and then he went out, leaving behind with her a breath of wax from the procession of the Burial.

4. Mauricio

The prayers and letters from the virgins of la Visitación attained the favor they desired. And one glorious day in May, Don Mauricio Valcárcel, a light cavalry Hussar captain and military attaché in the Spanish Embassy in Vienna, bearer of the monstrance of the Salesian Order in Annecy, appeared at the convent of Nuestra Señora.

He was accompanied by the commandant of Infantry, Commanding Officer of the Recruitment Zone, who was wearing spurs with rusted rowels. They were followed by the dean-vicar who arrived breathing heavily.

The prelatess received the venerable parcel, the ribbons of which had been impregnated with the delicate scent of the diplomatic hussar's suitcases, through the revolving window at the wall.

The entire Community came over to the locutory. The mystical doves contemplated the young man's elegant regalia through the coarse woolen fabric of their humeral veils. His graceful bearing was not of this world. Even the Keeper of the Keys imagined herself in the presence of an emissary from heaven, a resplendent archangel. The archangel looked very dashing, all dressed in blue. His legs, molded by the black mirror-like surfaces of the patent leather of his riding boots; his saber, spangled as with flashes of light; his shoulders, torrents of the very purest of silver, and to put the finishing

de maíz, un leve bigote retorcido, los carrillos redondos, descansando en el bordado cuello, y la mirada y la boca con un asomo de sonrisa benévola y jerárquica, de alma placida de la simplicidad que le rodea sin perder el saboreo de sus magnificencias.

Rostro, jarcia, porte, brillos, armas, risa eran de militar; pero advertíase también en su continente un sutil misterio, un frío empaque, una elegancia de salones internacionales. Capitán y diplomático, con él habían entrado en la Visitación las milicias y las cancillerías de casi toda Europa. Y la abadesa y sus hijas le miraban, pareciéndoles recién venido de la Jerusalén celeste.

La prenda más clara de su distinción tal vez la ofreciese doblando el codo. Se lo notó el jefe de la Zona que, aunque de grado superior, estaba encogido, apoyándose en una pierna rígida y dejando la otra doblada, blanda, madura de rodilleras. Buen hombre, de piel bronca, de cráneo largo, vertical; pelo corto y gris, con el surco del ros, un ros enorme y duro, arrimado a su pecho en actitud de ordenanza.

De tiempo en tiempo, las dulces religiosas le dedicaban algunas palabras solícitas.

– ¿Usted ya le conocía?

– ¿Salió usted a recibirle en Murcia?

– ¿Sirve usted en su mismo escuadrón?

La más parladora era la señorita Valcárcel, pidiendo nuevas de cominerías deliciosas, que le velaban melancólicamente su vocecita rápida, aniñada; voz que al principio tuvo un tono piadoso y tímido de regla y después un gorjeo cálido de mujer entre nardos y claveles de una reja murciana.

– ¿Te has confesado en Viena y en París, Mauricio?

– ¡Agravian las preguntas de su caridad! – le reconvino la clavaria – . ¡El señor Mauricio es cristiano, y basta!

– Y en la Embajada, ¿coméis con las señoras?

– ¡Perdónela, señor Mauricio! – dijo la Madre.

El diplomático exhaló, entre el humo de su cigarrillo turco:

– ¡Oh!

– ¿Qué tienes en tu habitación? ¿Te llevaste la estampita calada que yo te regalé?

touch to his figure, a head the color of maize, a slight mustache turned up at the ends, rounded cheeks, all resting on a neck covered with embroidery, and eyes and mouth revealing a touch of a benevolent, hierarchical smile, belonging to a soul that felt placid within the simplicity surrounding him without his losing the ability to savor his own magnificence.

The face, the accouterments, the bearing, the brilliance, the side arms, the laughter were those of a military man; but you could also discern a subtle mystery, a cold presence, an elegance of international salons in his mien. Captain and diplomat, the military units and the chancelleries of almost all of Europe had entered la Visitación with him. And the abbess and her daughters looked at him and it seemed to them that he had just arrived from celestial Jerusalem.

Perhaps the clearest quality of his distinction was evident when he bent his elbow. The commanding officer of the Recruitment Zone noticed it and, though he was of higher rank, he appeared withdrawn, leaning on one rigid leg while leaving the other one bent, loose, ripe with bagginess at the knee. A fine fellow with rough skin, a long, vertical skull; short gray hair, with a furrow on his forehead made by his shako, an enormous stiff shako, which he now pressed close against his chest in a posture of military correctness.

From time to time the sweet sisters would offer him a few solicitous words.

"Did you already know him?"

"Did you go out to receive him in Murcia?"

"Do you serve in the same squadron as he?"

The most talkative one of all was Señorita Valcárcel, who kept asking him for news of delightful trivialities, which veiled her rapid, childish little voice in a melancholy way; a voice that at first had a pious, timid and proper quality, and then took on the warm trill of a woman among the spikenard and carnations of a Murcian window grating.

"Did you go to confession in Vienna and Paris, Mauricio?"

"Your charity's questions are offensive!" the Keeper of the Keys remonstrated her. "Señor Mauricio is a Christian and that is enough!"

"And in the Embassy, do you all eat with the ladies?"

"Forgive her, Señor Mauricio," said the Mother.

In the midst of the smoke from his Turkish cigarette, the diplomat exhaled:

"Oh!"

"What do you have in your room? Did you bring the little print of openwork embroidery I gave you as a gift?"

– ¡Hija, no me acuerdo!

– ¿No te acuerdas? ¡Si no es posible! Una del Arcángel San Miguel que hunde su espada en un dragón peludo. El animalito me miraba todas las noches cuando yo me desnudaba...

– ¡Su caridad! ¡Su caridad! Piense que ese animalito es Lucifer.

Mauricio les concedió su sonrisa de marfiles y oro.

Bajo las veladas cabezas de las Hermanas jóvenes pasaba un fragante oreo de los jardines del siglo.

Sor María deslizóse junto a la hornacina en que reposaba el doble calabacín de vidrio del reloj de arena, que mide el cuarto de hora de locutorio, y lo volvió para que principiase otra vez a contar el tiempo. Pero ya la clavaria susurraba en el oído de la priora. Sonoreó una esquila. Rebulleron los sayales y alas del palomarcillo. Sor María quedóse postrera.

– ¡Gracias al santo relicario te veo!

– ¡Yo ni por el relicario! Álzate ese velo del todo, ahora que la monja vieja habla con los curas. Tú no hiciste profesión, y te vales del velo como de un abanico.

Su prima, sin querer entenderle, le preguntó:

– ¿No has visto desde la diligencia las tapías de nuestra huerta y nuestras ventanitas? ¿Que no? ¡Pero si yo os veía muy bien! ¿Verdad que cojeaba el caballo de delante? Subiéndose en un poyo de la carretera, al lado del muro del río, se verá mi ventana. Una ventanita con una crucecita de palma... La quinta ventanita. Arriba tiene un nido y una teja rota; se rompió la tarde del Lunes Santo. Una ventanita...

– Sí, sí! Una ventanita como todas las ventanitas...

Sor María balbució con dejo monjil:

– ¡Nuestro Señor te ha colmado de la santa virtud de la indiferencia!

– Bueno, Fulgencilla o Fulgencica, como dicen en este país...

– ¡En este país hemos nacido tú y yo!

– Ya lo sé. ¡Pero quítate esa nube de abuela! Y, oye, cómo te pones esa toca con tanto primor, sin espejo?

La señorita Valcárcel soltó su risa de rapaza.

"My dear girl, I don't remember!"

"You don't remember? It just isn't possible! The one of the Archangel Saint Michael burying his sword in a hairy dragon. The little animal used to look at me every night when I undressed...."

"Your charity! Your charity! Just remember that that sweet little animal is Lucifer."

Mauricio granted them his smile of ivories and gold.

A fragrant breeze from the gardens of the outside world passed beneath the veiled heads of the young Sisters.

Sister María slipped over to a place next to the niche where the glass gourd-like double bulbs of the hourglass were resting, the one that measures the quarter-hours in the locutory, and she turned it over so it would begin to tell time once again. But the Keeper of the Keys was already whispering in the prioress's ear. A small convocation bell tinkled. The sackcloth vestments and the wings in the tranquil dovecot began to stir. Sister María remained to the last.

"Thanks to the blessed reliquary I am able to see you!"

"I can't see you even with the reliquary! Now that the old nun is talking with the priests, you can raise up that veil completely. You didn't even profess yet and you make use of the veil as if it were a fan."

His cousin, without trying to understand, asked him:

"Didn't you see the walls of our orchard and the little windows from the diligence? You didn't? But I saw you both very well! Isn't it true that the front horse was somewhat lame? If you climb up onto a stone bench alongside the road, long the wall by the river, you can see my window. A small window with a little palm leaf cross.... The fifth little window. There's a nest and a broken tile right above it; it was broken on the Monday of Holy Week, a little window...."

"Yes, yes! A little window like all little windows...."

Sister María stammered with a nun-like lilt:

"Our Lord has bestowed the blessed virtue of indifference upon you!"

"All right, Fulgencilla, or Fulgencica, as they say in this part of the country...."

"You and I were born in this part of the country!"

"I already know that. But why don't you take off that cloud covering your head, fit for a grandmother! And by the way, how do you manage to put on that headdress so skillfully without a mirror?"

Señorita Valcárcel burst out into girlish laughter.

– ¡Sí, sí que tenemos espejo! Hasta la clavaria lo tiene. Y después de vestirnos, lo cubrimos con una estampa, por modestia, para no mirarnos más en todo el día. Mi estampa es la del "Ángel". ¿No sabes, Mauricio? ¡Me crecieron las trenzas!

Mauricio sonrió con un poco de cansancio. En sus viajes y molicies había pensado en esta linda mujer, como si la viese y la sintiese en una presencia casi dolorosa de deseo. Y ahora, a su lado, la veía y la sentía con una desgana como si se hallase ausente.

La Madre puso término al coloquio. La comunidad había de hacer oración, con el relicario de manifiesto, antes que el señor Mauricio lo llevara a Palacio. Ya estaba prevenido su ilustrísima, que las autorizó para que pudiesen agasajar en casa al esclarecido viajero.

Y sor María y la prelada dijeron devotamente: "Ave María Purísima"; y las cortinas de azul nazareno cegaron la red.

Luego, en la fresca umbría de la iglesia monástica, corrió una fontanilla de plegarias. A veces se paraba en la revuelta de un salmo. Después, una monjita recitaba el canon de la súplica:

Per intercesionem Sanctae Joanna Francisca
Frémyot, concedar Reverendissimo Episcopo
salutem et pacem.

Cuando el jefe de la Zona levantó su cabeza de la almohadilla del reclinatorio, don Jeromillo hacía una genuflexión en el presbiterio y mataba las últimas abejitas de luz de los cirios.

– ¡De seguro que fue un acierto – iba diciéndose el señor deán – , un piadoso acierto, confiar la señorita Valcárcel al refugio de la Visitación!

Pero esta criatura, ¿no principiaba a complicar el acierto?

Soflamado y sudando llegó, entre el comandante y el húsar, a las grandes puertas entornadas de Palacio.

El sol, sol de siesta de pueblo, regolfaba en la baldosa. Ardían los viejos

"Yes, we really do have mirrors! Even the Keeper of the Keys has one. And after we get dressed, we cover it over with a religious print, out of modesty, so as not look at ourselves again for the rest of the day. My print is the one of the "Angel." Do you want to know something, Mauricio? My long braids grew back!"

Mauricio smiled a little wearily. In the course of his travels and his easy-going life, he had often thought of this pretty woman, as if he were seeing her and hearing her as a presence that was almost painful with desire. And now, as she sat beside him, he could see her and hear her with indifference as if she were not even there.

The Mother put an end to their conversation. The Community had to say a prayer with the reliquary in their presence before Señor Mauricio could take it to the Palace. His Excellency was already forewarned and he gave them the authorization to entertain the illustrious traveler at their House.

And Sister María and the prelatess said "Hail Mary Most Pure" with great devotion; and the curtains of Nazarene blue covered over the wire mesh netting.

Then a veritable fountain of prayers streamed forth in the cool shade of the convent church. Sometimes it would stop during the repetition of a psalm. Then a sweet young nun recited the canon of the prayer petition:

Per intercessionem Sanctae Joanna Francisca Frémyot, concedat Reverendissimo Episcopo salutem et pacem.

(By the intercession of Saint Jane Frances
Fréymot, grant the most Reverend Bishop
good health and peace.)

When the commanding officer of the Recruitment Zone raised his head from the small cushion of the prie-dieu, Don Jeromillo was genuflecting in the presbytery and extinguishing the last of the little bees of light of the wax tapers.

"It was most certainly a prudent step, the dean-vicar kept saying to himself, "a pious success, to entrust Señorita Valcárcel to the refuge of la Visitación!"

But this child, wasn't she beginning to complicate the success?

Overheated and sweating, he arrived at the big partly open doors of the Palace between the commandant and the hussar.

The sun, the midday small town siesta sun, accumulated on the flagstones.

llumasos, las bisagras y los aldabones; se golpeaban las moscas, zumbando por los calientes sillares. Era un portal de granja.

El recogido patio y la honda escalera repitieron mucho tiempo, como no creyéndolo, un ruido de espuelas vibradoras.

Asomóse un presbítero al barandal. Un fámulo de blusón negro agarró una enorme alcuza que goteaba en el desportillo de un peldaño, y escondióse en la mayordomía para mirar más desde allí la visita.

Mauricio dio su tarjeta. El comandante se limpió la frente corta y huesuda; el surco del ros parecía de labranza. El deán se derribó en la butaca del secretario.

Subían claros, exactos, los rumores de la abezara de la vega. La cortina, colgada sobre el huerto episcopal, se movía blandamente por una respiración perezosa de paisaje de verano.

Su ilustrísima estaba comiendo. Lo dijo un familiar, buscándose con su lengua los sabores interrumpidos, exprimiéndolos de los recodos de sus quijales. Vestía una sotanilla lisa y leve, sin alzacuellos. Taconeaba en la poma dorada de un mismo manís, y se daba golpecitos en las uñas con la elegante cartulina de Mauricio.

Dobló el húsar su codo izquierdo; adelantó la diestra, como sí prorrumpiese del manto de la diplomacia, y fue refiriendo su misión con tan bellas palabras que el señor deán las veía pronunciadas con letra redondilla.

Quizá se distrajo el eclesiástico doméstico, porque, mirándole con un destellar de anteojos que enfriaba el de las insignias y charreteras, le interrumpío:

– ¿Y pertenecen ustedes a esta guarnición?

Temblaron las espuelas del agregado de Embajada; se pasó los dedos entre su enrojecido pestorejo y el recamado del uniforme, y no dijo nada.

El comandante, doliéndose de la ignorancia del presbítero, le advirtió, como si leyese una orden de plaza:

– En Oleza no hay guarnición, sino Guardía civil: diez números de infantería, un sargento y dos oficiales, y siete de caballería del 15 tercio. Y en la Zona: un comandante, yo; un capitán, un sargento y dos cabos, y falta

The age-old ornamental ironwork, the hinges and the big doorknockers were burning hot; the flies kept making thumping noises as they buzzed among the warm ashlars. It was like the main entry to a farm building.

The secluded patio and the deep staircase repeated the sound of vibrating spurs for some time, as if they didn't really believe it.

A presbyter appeared at the balustrade. A servant wearing a long black blouse grabbed an enormous oil can dripping onto the chipped edge of one of the steps and hid himself in the steward's office so that he could better watch the visitors from there.

Mauricio presented his card. The commandant wiped his short, bony forehead; the furrow on his brow from wearing the shako was not unlike that acquired in doing farming. The dean tumbled into the secretary's armchair.

The sound of plowing out on the fertile plain rose up clearly and precisely. The curtain hanging over the window to the episcopal garden kept moving gently with the lazy breath of a summer landscape.

His Excellency was eating. A familiar told them this as he sought the interrupted flavors with his tongue, squeezing them out from the recesses of his jaws. He was wearing a short cassock, plain and light, without a stock. He kept tapping his heel against the design of a golden apple on the same floor tile as he gently flicked Mauricio's elegant Bristol board card against his fingernails.

The hussar bent his left elbow; he brought his right hand forward, as if he were breaking free from his diplomatic mantle, and he started explaining his mission with such beautiful words that the dean-vicar was able to see them pronounced as if in circular printed letters.

Perhaps the ecclesiastic grew inattentive, because, as he looked at him with a flash from his spectacles that chilled the officer with the decoration and epaulets, he interrupted him:

"And do you both belong to this garrison?"

The Embassy attaché's spurs trembled; he passed his fingers between the flushed nape of his neck and the raised embroidery of his uniform, and he said nothing.

The commandant was distressed by the presbyter's ignorance and, as if he were reading a military announcement, he informed him:

"There is no garrison stationed in Oleza, only a Rural Police force: ten infantry soldiers, a sergeant and two officers, plus seven cavalrymen from the 15th corps. And in the Recruitment Zone: a commandant, myself; a captain, a sergeant and two corporals; and they're missing a lieutenant, I'm not sure

un teniente, que no sé yo... Porque sí es que me dicen a mí que la plantilla de oficinas..., yo les podría decir...

No lo pudo decir, porque le interrumpió una voz apocada.

– De parte de la madre priora de Santa Lucía y de toda la casa, que cómo sigue su ilustrísima y que...

Sin volverse, repuso el secretario:

– Son horas privadas del señor. ¡También estos militares aguardan!

Mauricio le miró con aborrecimiento, y el donado de Santa Lucía quedóse muy complacido de la evangélica igualdad que en el seno de Palacio había para los clarísimos varones y para los pobretes.

Un paje anunció que el señor obispo, no queriendo retardar la especial audiencia, recibiría a los señores en el comedor.

– ¿En el comedor?

Y Mauricio sonrió compasivo.

El comedor de palacio era una pieza profunda, artesonada, de menaje barroco.

Pendía una gran lámpara de bronce, espejándose en una mesa redonda y desnuda. Un humo de años nublaba las pinturas de las paredes; llegaban hasta las orlas los sillones de cuero, de consistorio abacial; pero todo esto no pertenecía a nadie; nadie lo habitaba ni usaba; era como un rancio tapiz olvidado, y en su punta había renacido un fondo, un ambiente de sencillez.

Junto al ventanal, en un butacón de anea con almohadas blancas, de enfermo, delante de una mesita, el señor obispo se servía azúcar en su taza de infusión de hierbas.

Dos fámulos acercaron una banca que tenía un exprimido cojín atado al asiento.

Volvióse su ilustrísima, destacándose su busto en la lumbre gozosa. Su rostro quedó tan obscuro como los cuadros murales.

– ¡Sigue usted engordando, mi querido deán!

El deán, no sabiendo qué decir, se precipitó a besar otra vez el anillo prelaticio.

Su ilustrísima retrajo sus manos, gordas de hilas y de vendas moradas.

Y el húsar habló al principio, con el ardor, cifra y pompa de sus títulos.

why.... Because if they gave me a say concerning the personnel roster.... I could tell them...."

He was unable to tell him because a pusillanimous voice interrupted him.

"On behalf of the prioress mother of Santa Lucía and the entire House, as for the condition of His Excellency and as for...."

Without turning around, the secretary replied:

"These are the lord bishop's private hours. These military officers are also waiting!"

Mauricio looked at him with loathing and the lay brother from Santa Lucía felt very pleased with the evangelic equality that existed in the innermost recesses of the Palace for most illustrious men and for the poorest of souls.

A page announced that the lord bishop did not want to delay the special audience and would receive the gentlemen in the dining room.

"In the dining room?"

And Mauricio smiled compassionately.

The Palace dining room was a deep room with a caissoned ceiling and baroque furnishings.

A large bronze lamp was hanging there, mirrored on a round, bare table. The smoke of past years had clouded the paintings on the walls; the leather armchairs, for an abatial consistory, reached all the way up to the bottoms of the borders of the pictures; but none of this belonged to anyone; nobody lived here or used it; it was like a forgotten, long kept heraldic tapestry, and a background, an ambience of simplicity, had sprung up again in its needlepoint.

Next to the wide window, the lord bishop was seated in front of a small table in a large easy chair with a rush-bottomed seat, with white pillows, like those for an invalid, serving himself sugar in his cup of herbal infusion.

Two servants brought over a bench with a flattened cushion tied to the seat.

His Excellency turned and his bust was outlined in the pleasant warm light. His face remained as dark as the pictures on the walls.

"You keep getting fatter, my dear dean!"

The dean didn't know what to say and hastened to kiss the prelate's ring once more.

His Excellency withdrew his hands, bulky with lint and purple bandages.

And the hussar spoke at first with the ardor, precision and pomp of his

Si aludía a los afanes y preeminencias de la diplomacia, decía: nosotros; si a la Embajada: en casa. Después fue desjugándose y entibiándose.

El señor obispo le tomó la cajita del ostensorio. Estuvo sopesándola y mirándola. La dejó reclinada en el azucarero, y el familiar se la llevó.

En su respuesta no se cuidó de pagarle ninguno de los elogios protocolarios. Descansaba para beber su tisana olorosa. Recordó sobriamente que en su última *visita ad limina* conoció en Roma al nuncio de Austria. Hizo una pausa, mirando cómo se le caían los párpados al comandante.

– Monseñor era un numismático y paleógrafo insigne.

Mauricio, por deber de su carrera, tuvo que decir:

– Nuestro embajador también es muy listo. Todo un *gentleman*. ¡Sabe francés, portugués y no sé qué más!

...Cuando salieron a la antecámara, el mayordomo, desde una gradilla, encolaba un tejuelo al atadijo, y mientras lo acomodaba en el vasar de un armario, iba dictándole al paje de secretaría:

"Número 78. Tabla III. – Envío de las madres de la Visitación."

Y desde la puerta porfió el recadero de Santa Lucía:

– De parte de la madre priora y de...

...El señor deán y el jefe de la Zona se despidieron del agregado en el cancel del monasterio.

Ya estaba parada la mesa en el locutorio, limpia, primorosa, con un búcaro de azucenas y hierbaluisa.

Mauricio esperaba el convite en una sala colgada de damascos. Pero guardóse todo el rigor de la clausura. Comería él solo. Y detrás de la tupida reja aleteaban, blancas y cautivas, las manos de las esposas del Señor.

Le servía el donado. Hubo un instante de violencia, porque Mauricio sentóse sin hacer, al menos, la señal de la cruz. La Madre musitó el *Benedicite*, y la comunidad contestó en coro de dulzuras.

Comprendió el húsar su olvido, y alzóse con un temeroso estruendo de sable y espuelas.

– ¡Perdónenme, señoras! ¡Llevo recibidas tantas emociones!

titles. If he alluded to the efforts and preeminence of the diplomatic corps, he said: we; if to the Embassy: in house. Then the passion started draining from him and he began to grow lukewarm.

The lord bishop took the small box with the monstrance from him. He started balancing it in his his hand and looking at it. He left it resting on the sugar bowl and the familiar took it away.

In his response he was careful not to pay any of the protocolary forms of praise. He rested in order to drink his fragrant infusion. He soberly recalled that during his last "visita ad limina"[151] to Rome, he met the nuncio to Austria. He paused for a moment to watch how the commandant's eyelids were drooping.

"Monsignor was a renowned numismatist and paleographer."

Mauricio, out of duty to his career, felt obliged to say:

"Our ambassador is also very clever. Quite a *gentleman*. He knows French, Portuguese and I don't know what else!"

...When they went out into the antechamber, the steward was standing on a small stepladder, gluing a label onto the wrapped parcel, and while he was making room for it on a cabinet shelf, he kept dictating to the page from the secretariat.

"Number 78. Shelf III. – Shipment from the mothers of la Visitación."

And from the doorway, the messenger from Santa Lucía persisted:

"On behalf of the prioress mother of Santa Lucía and of...."

...The dean-vicar and the commanding officer of the Recruitment Zone bade farewell to the attaché at the storm door of the convent.

The table, clean and exquisite, was already set in the locutory, with a vase of white lilies and lemon verbena on it.

Mauricio was waiting for the feast to which he had been invited in a room with hanging damasks. But all the rules of cloistered life were maintained. He would dine alone. And the white, captive hands of the women wed to the Lord fluttered behind the closely woven screen.

The lay brother served him. There was a violent instant because Mauricio sat down without making, at the very least, the sign of the cross. The Mother mumbled the *Benedicite* and the Community answered in a chorus of sweet response.

The hussar realized his oversight and stood up with a frightful clatter of saber and spurs.

"Forgive me, ladies! I am overcome by so many emotions!"

Oyóse la vocecita cálida y apasionada de sor María:

– ¿Y se arrodilló su ilustrísima para coger el santo relicario?

– ¡Pues claro, hija! – exclamó la Madre.

– ¿Y tú, Mauricio, tú se lo colgaste? ¿Tú, mismo?

Mauricio sorbía la primera cucharada de un caldo de oro.

– ¡Lleva gallina y pichón; un pichón tan blanco, tan hermoso; un pichón tan rico!...

Algunas novicias se sofocaron. Sor María Fulgencia pronunciaba pichón blanco, pichón rico con una caricia tan fresca y encendida de su lengua, que la dulce ave parecía palpitar entre sus pechos, escapada del carro de Afrodita.

The warm, passionate little voice of Sister María was heard:

"Did His Excellency kneel down to take the blessed reliquary?"

"Why, of course, my child!" exclaimed the Mother.

"And you, Mauricio, did you hang it on him? You, yourself?"

Mauricio was sipping the first spoonful of a golden broth.

"It's made with hen and young pigeon, such a beautiful, white pigeon, such an exquisite pigeon!..."

A number of the novices choked with emotion. Sister María Fulgencia pronounced white young pigeon, exquisite pigeon with such a fresh and feverish caress of her tongue that the sweet bird seemed to palpitate between her breasts, as if just having escaped from Aphrodite's chariot....[152]

V

CORPUS CHRISTI

1. La víspera

Es difícil no toparse alguna vez con el éxito. Si no llega por el camino real, viene por el atajo. Si caminamos muy despacio, él nos esperará sentándose en una piedra. Bien puede suceder que nosotros corramos tanto que le pasemos, y, entonces, como no nos podemos parar, él no nos puede alcanzar.

Pero el homeópata Monera no salía de su andadura, y el éxito le puso campechanamente la mano en el hombro y le dio un vaso de buen vino. Sus aciertos clínicos crecían. El mismo penitenciario, aunque le tutease (una hermana del homeópata servía en casa del canónigo), celebraba la ascensión de Monera. Un día, Monera sanó a un loco. Enloqueció un seminarista del grado de teólogos, y dio en la manía de que cayendo en la tierra la lumbre del sol se quedaba el cielo a obscuras. Consideraba el caso de suma magnanimidad de Dios, y el consentirlo nosotros, de empedernida indiferencia. El teólogo veía la desgracia del firmamento y el desgaste del astro. Había sido dotado de ojos de águila. Podía mirar de hito en hito al sol. "Tengo los ojos de un águila, y soy de la provincia de Gerona". Vestido de negro, con alzacuello de reborde sudado, pasaba los días en su patio devolviendo a los cielos con un espejo la imagen de la redonda hoguera solar. Pero como eran sus ojos los que antes recibían la lumbrarada, principiaron a manarle como si se le hubieran podrido. Ni profesores, ni enfermeros, ni médicos viejos le remediaban. Llegó Monera, le limpió con colirios, le quebró el espejo, y además le dijo que no era ni águila ni de la provincia de Gerona, pues si lo fuese no pertenecería al seminario de Oleza. El loco, sin el espejo en sus manos y con la lógica de Monera a cuestas, sumergióse en su cama, donde murió reposadamente, pidiéndole a Dios que le diera en la otra vida la luz que en ésta le había él reexpedido con su ingenio.

El éxito lo confirman los demás, y quizá no consiste sino en los demás. Una tarde, la de la víspera de Corpus, el matrimonio Monera entró en la sala de las *Catalanas,* y la esposa, con un suave cansancio, suspiró:

1. The Day Before

It is difficult not to run into success every so often. If you don't get there by the highroad, then you come by the short cut. If we walk very slowly, it waits for us seated on a stone. It may very well happen that we run so fast that we pass it by, and then, since we are unable to stop, it can not catch up with us.

But Monera the homeopath did not depart from his customary walking pace and success good-naturedly put its hand upon his shoulder and offered him a glass of fine wine.[153] His clinical successes were growing. The canon-penitentiary himself, though he spoke to him with the familiar *tú* (a sister of the homeopath served in the canon's house), celebrated Monera's ascent. One day Monera cured a madman. A seminary student in theology studies went mad and developed a mania that made him believe that the sky would be left in darkness if the light from the sun should continue to fall on earth. He considered the situation to reflect the supreme magnanimity of God and our acceptance of it to be hard-hearted indifference. The theology student saw the misfortune of the firmament and the attrition of the star. He had been endowed with the eyes of an eagle. He was able to stare directly at the sun. "I have the eyes of an eagle and I am from the province of Gerona." Dressed in black, wearing a stock with a sweat-stained border, he would spend his days in his patio sending the image of the rounded solar bonfire back into the sky with a mirror. But since his eyes were the same ones that received the fiery brilliance before, they began to drain as if they had been putrefied. Neither learned professors, nor infirmary attendants, nor old doctors could offer a remedy. Monera came, washed out his eyes with collyrium, broke his mirror and told him, in addition, that he was neither an eagle nor from the province of Gerona, for if he were, he would not belong to the seminary in Oleza. The madman, without the mirror in his hands and with Monera's logic on his shoulders, immersed himself in his bed, where he died peacefully, asking God to grant him in the next life the light which he had sent ahead to him with his ingenuity in this one.

The others confirm the success and it may only consist for the others. One afternoon, the day before Corpus Christi,[154] the Monera couple entered the *Catalan sisters'* drawing room and the wife sighed with a gentle show of weariness:

– ¡Dios mío! ¡Me parece que estoy encinta!

Las de Menorca se volvieron a Monera, que les ofreció una sonrisa desconocida, reciente. Acababa de saber que ya sonreía con firmeza. Nadie le aturdía ni le negaba su voluntad. "He debido sonreír y he sonreído, y se acabó"...

En otros días la proclamación del embarazo hubiese alborotado el pudor de algunas amistades. Y ahora, no.

Lo repitió la señora acariciándose su anillo nupcial; lo dijo con gracia juvenil. Prometió criarse al hijo, y ella y sus amigas contemplaban sus pechos, tanto tiempo cerrados, como los de algunas mujeres insignes que, después de muchos años de matrimonio enjuto, los sintieron hincharse de generosa vida. No fue la Monera como esas casadas que se las ve todavía novias y a poco palidecen, se marchitan, andan despacio, y todo el mundo les sonríe diciéndose: "¡Qué prisa tenía esa mujer!"

Las de Puerta Ferrisa la miraban toda. No se "le conocía" en nada, y le acercaban el asiento más bajo y mullido. Pero los Monera les advirtieron que convenía más la silla alta y dura. Entonces ellas se sofocaron abundantemente disculpándose. ¡No podían atinar siendo solteras! Y después, las dos, se pusieron cavilosas. "¡Qué diría Elvira cuando lo supiese!"

En aquel momento Monera sonrió, y las dos hermanas se tranquilizaron. Monera sonreía por otra noticia que les dijo. La vida de Oleza se emocionaba. Este Corpus no se quedarían sin pompa pontifical.

– ¿Oficiará ya su ilustrísima?

Pero el obispo de Oleza no tenía salud para tanto. Ni salud ni humor con que resistir las solícitas bondades de su diócesis. Los muebles de su antecámara eran ya un curioso relicario, una farmacia y herboristería del cielo que daba un olor rancio de liturgia y de eternidad.

– No es nuestro pobre obispo, sino monseñor Salom. Un santo mártir. Parece que fue salvado a medio martirizar, con mutilaciones horribles. ¡Lo que ese hombre ha padecido y lo que ha visto!

– ¿Y está en Oleza?

– Llegará esta noche. Lo traen los Padres de "Jesús".

Quedó trastornada la gustosa plática, porque del huerto pasó una infantil algarabía. Y la señora Monera se impresionó mucho.

Su marido tuvo que decir:

"My God! It seems that I am pregnant!"

The sisters from Menorca turned to Monera, who offered them an unfamiliar, recently acquired smile. He had just found out that he now smiled resolutely. Nobody disconcerted him nor denied him his will. "I was supposed to smile and I smiled and that's all there is to it...."

At any other time, the announcement of the pregnancy would have disturbed the modesty of certain friendships. But not now.

The señora repeated it as she caressed her wedding ring; she said it with a certain juvenile charm. She promised to nurse her own child and she and her friends contemplated her breasts, closed up for so long, like those of certain prominent women, who after many years of barren marriage, felt them swell with generous life. The Monera woman was not like those married women who still seem to act like newlyweds and turn pale shortly after, wither, walk slowly, while everyone smiles at them and says, "That woman used to be in such a hurry!"

The ladies from Puerta Ferrisa looked her all over. You couldn't "know about her condition" in any way, and they brought over the lowest and softest chair. But the Moneras informed them that the high, hard chair would be better for her. Then the two ladies blushed with considerable embarrassment and asked to be forgiven. There was no way they could have known, being maiden ladies! And afterwards they both turned very pensive. "What would Elvira say when she found out!"

At that moment Monera smiled and the two sisters calmed down. Monera was smiling because of other news he gave them. Life in Oleza was all astir. This Corpus Christi they would not be left without pontifical pomp!

"His Excellency will now officiate?"

But the bishop of Oleza was not in good enough health for that. Neither the health nor the humor with which to put up with the solicitous kindness of his own diocese. The furniture of his antechamber was already a curious reliquary, a pharmacy and a heavenly herbalist's shop that gave off a rank odor of liturgy and eternity.

"It is not our poor bishop, but rather monsignor Salom. A sainted martyr. It seems that he was saved in the very act of being martyred and was horribly mutilated. What that man has suffered and seen!"

"And he is in Oleza?"

"He will arrive tonight. The Fathers at 'Jesús' are bringing him."

The pleasant chat was disrupted because a racket made by children reached them from the garden. And Señora Monera was deeply moved.

Her husband felt compelled to say:

– ¡Todo la enternece!

Después de decirlo, otra hubiera ido sosegándose. La Monera, no.

– ¿Tienen ustedes niñas en su jardín? ¡Yo nunca vi criaturas en esta casa!

Era una interrogación ávida y celosa. Seguramente sentía una inquietud de enferma, una irresistible crisis de su estado. Antes de que nacíese su hijo, esas dos solitarias sin herederos se habían complacido en otros niños; los tenían en su huerto, y quizá pretendieron ocultarlo.

Las tenían en el huerto. Eran niñas de la vecindad. Todo lo adivinaban los exaltados sentidos de la señora a través de sus recelos y de sus lágrimas. Estaba llorando.

Siete niñas: tres vestidas de ángeles, con los trajecitos blancos de primera comunión, alas doradas, tules y corona; bandejas de flores y una esquila de plata; y tres, de labradorcitas del país; traían zagalejos rojos y verdes con franjas de verdugado, pañuelo de cotón de colores, corpiño negro bordado de lentejuelas y en sus brazos canastillas de espigas. Las seis empolvadas. Les habían puesto muchos polvos, polvos de tienda humilde. Así irían al día siguiente en la procesión, delante del carro magnífico de la custodia; y como las mahonesas después de misa ya no dejaban la clausura de su casa, ni siquiera por la procesión del Corpus, las familias de las zagalicas, vecinas de la calle, las engalanaron, la víspera, para que las dos señoras las viesen. ¡Bien sabían embelecarlas esas comadres! Las seis. Pero ¿y la otra, la séptima niña? La otra era más menuda, y toda de luto, y de luto pobre.

Se le enconó la congoja a la Monera.

– Es una huérfana – le dijeron – . Al padre lo mató un barreno, y la madre ha muerto tísica el último día de mayo. La recogió una viuda sin hijos, y nos la trae para que juegue en el huerto.

– ¿Es huérfana?

Y la Monera quiso mirarla. Pero ya su marido se había apresurado a traérsela. Las tres ángeles y las tres labradorcitas les rodeaban.

La Monera se puso la huérfana en su regazo. Monera se estremeció; tendía sus manos ahuecadas para proteger el vientre precioso. Las *Catalanas*

"She is touched by everything!"

After he had said this, another woman would have started to calm down. But not the Monera woman.

"Do you have young girls in your garden? I never saw any children in this house!"

It was an avid and jealous interrogation. She surely felt the uneasiness characteristic of an ailing woman, an irresistible crisis because of her condition. Even before her child was born, those two solitary souls without any heirs had taken pleasure in other children; they had them in their garden and were perhaps trying to hide them.

They did have them in the garden. They were little girls from the neighborhood. The woman's exalted senses guessed it all through her misgivings and her tears. She was crying.

Seven little girls: three dressed as angels, wearing lovely white dresses from their first communion, golden wings, tulle veils and crowns; trays of flowers and a small silver bell; and three others were dressed in local peasant children's costumes; wearing red and green underskirts with fringed crinoline hoopskirts, cotton scarves in many colors, black bodices embroidered with sequins and little baskets of spikes in their arms. The six were bedaubed with powder. They had put many layers of powder on them, powder from humble shops. That is how they would appear in the procession on the following day, in front of the magnificent cart bearing the monstrance; and since the ladies from Mahon did not leave the confines of their house again after Mass, not even for the Corpus Christi procession, the families of all the sweet innocents, their neighbors on the street, dressed them up in their costumes the day before so that the two ladies could see them. Those crafty gossips really knew how to pull the wool over their eyes! The six little girls. But how about the other one, the seventh little girl? The other one was much smaller and all dressed in mourning, a quite impoverished mourning.

The Monera woman was overcome with grief.

"She's an orphan," they told her. "Her father was killed in a drilling accident and the mother died of consumption the last day of May. A childless widow took her in and she brings her to us so she can play in the garden."

"She's an orphan?"

And the Monera woman was anxious to look at her. But her husband had already hurried to bring her over to her. The three angels and the three young farm girls surrounded them.

The Monera woman put the orphan girl on her lap. Monera gave a shudder, stretching out his hollowed hands to protect the precious belly. The

también se asustaron. Habían cometido la ligereza de tolerar críos en su casa viniendo visitas como la señora Monera.

Lágrimas y besos. Deseperación de lágrimas y besos. Monera, de pie, a su lado, luchaba con su dolor por los dolores de la señora, que decía:

— ¡Ay, nena, nena! ¡Tú quisieras ir vestida como las otras!

La huérfana comenzó a balbucir, y la señora, para escucharla, le descansó encima de la boca su redondo carrillo.

— ¿Qué dices? ¿Que irás a la procesión? ¡Pobre ángel de luto! ¡Sin pensar en nada!

— ¡Ya pensará y ya llorará! — le prometió el marido, y quiso tomarle a la niña, pero su mujer la apretó con furor.

— ¡Con tu lazo en la trenza y tu chambrita limpia! ¡No, no muy limpia! ¡Y aquí, en la nuca, debajo de los polvos, y en las orejitas tienes mugre!

La señora, desconsolándose, la desabrochaba, le abría el delantal, escudriñándole el filo de la espaldita, el pecho, el vientre, tan frágiles, y le buscó en los oídos y en el pelo sin parar de gemir:

— ¿Te acuerdas de tu madre? ¿Dices que está lejos, pero que vendrá? ¿Que vendrá, dónde? ¿Para llevarte a la procesión? ¡Debieran raparla toda! Le he visto dos liendres. ¡Hija de mi alma! No vendrá tu madre. ¡Ya no la verás nunca!

La nena quiso desasirse. Toda arrugadita, la lazada deshecha, mojada de besos y lágrimas de compasión. Se afligió y le tuvo miedo. Entonces se sintió más aplastada contra aquel cuerpo rollizo, caliente y sudado. Ya no estaban las amiguitas. Tocaban las campanas de Oleza en el atardecer de la víspera del Corpus.

Adivinó Monera lo que estaba sufriendo su mujer. Lo adivinaba como esposo y médico. Y poderosamente le arrancó a la niña de los brazos, depositándola en el portal sin decirle nada, sin reprocharle nada, y volvióse a la sala. Pero subió el llanto, y Monera tuvo que salir y tomarla de un bracito y llevársela más lejos. Allí, aquella criatura hizo lo que Monera no esperaba: arrojarse en el suelo, llorar a gritos, estremecerse del berrinche. Cuando

Catalan sisters were also frightened. They had committed the indiscretion of permitting small children in their home when they were expecting guests like Señora Monera.

Tears and kisses. The desperation of tears and kisses. Monera kept standing by her side, struggling with his own suffering because of his wife's suffering, as she kept saying:

"Oh, my sweet child, my sweet child! How you must want to go around dressed like the others!"

The orphan girl started to babble and the señora, in order to hear her better, rested her rounded cheek right up against the girl's mouth.

"What are you saying? That you will go to the procession? You poor mourning angel! Without thinking of anything!"

"She will be thinking and weeping soon enough!" her husband promised her, and he tried to take the child from her, but his wife pressed her frenziedly closer to herself.

"With a bow in your braids and your clean little camisole! No, not so very clean! And you have grime here on the back of your neck, underneath the powder, and dirt in your little ears!"

The señora was very distraught, undid the child's clothes, opening her smock, scrutinizing the length of her delicate backbone, her chest, her belly, ever so fragile, and then she looked inside her ears and in her hair as she kept moaning:

"Do you remember your mother? You say she's far away, but that she'll come back? That she'll come back, where? To take you to the procession? They ought to cut off all her hair! I saw two nits there. Oh, my sweet child! Your mother is not going to come. You'll never see her again!"

The little girl tried to break free. All rumpled, her bow undone, drenched with kisses and tears of compassion. She became very distressed and was overcome with fear of her. Then she began to feel crushed against that plump, warm and sweaty body. Her little friends were no longer there. The bells of Oleza were tolling on that late afternoon of the day before Corpus Christi.

Monera guessed how much his wife must be suffering. He guessed because he was a husband and a doctor. And he tore the little girl from her arms with considerable force and deposited her in the entrance hall without saying a word to her, without reproaching her in any way, and then he returned to the drawing room. But the weeping increased and Monera was compelled to go out and take her by her little arm and lead her even further away. There, that small child did what Monera least expected: she threw herself on the ground, screaming and crying, shaking and throwing a

acudieron algunas mujeres, y entre ellas la viuda que había prohijado a la niña, el homeópata se la entregó con algún enojo diciéndole que malcriar a un huérfano era peor que desampararle.

Su mujer le recibió prendiéndose la mantilla. Necesitaba la tranquilidad de su casa. ¡Oh, lloraba esa nena con un brío que no parecía huérfana! Se colgó del brazo del esposo. Se miró sus brazaletes, su collar, su leontina de medallón rizado como una valva en cuyas hojuelas pronto llevaría la miniatura del hijo, y despidióse de sus amigas y les sonrió perdonándolas.

A poco de llegar, sosegada que estuvo la esposa, marchóse el marido a la tertulia de don Álvaro.

...Detrás de las frondosas rejas del caballero de Gandía pasaban los mozos con sus costales de álamo, de chopo y de mirto para enramar la calle, y todo se llenaba de un olor de Corpus y de felicidad de verano.

Conversaban de lo mismo que en casi todas las casas de Oleza: de monseñor Salom. Ya sabía don Amancio que monseñor había celebrado quince veces en la iglesia del Santo Sepulcro; que guió a los peregrinos españoles, portugueses y franceses por la *Vía Dolorosa;* que se quedó una noche del Jueves Santo, toda en oración, bajo los olivos de plata y los cipreses de ruiseñores y de la luna de Getsemaní; y que aquel silencio, rasgado por los sollozos del Salvador, crepitó de risas y besos de un francés y una española, y el justo se precipitó como un ángel terrible, arrojándolos de la tierra regada por la divina sangre.

Provechoso acierto de la comunidad de "Jesús" fue pedirle a este santo que viniese a Oleza. Hijo de casa labradora, había envejecido en misiones que dieron gloria al martirologio español. Vino a Europa para tratar con los legados de algunos países y con el Sumo Pontífice de una difícil reforma de los vicariatos apostólicos; y no quería internarse, quizá para siempre, en los remotos confines de su diócesis de Alepo sin despedirse de su pueblo natal. Y los Padres de "Jesús" fueron a su retiro de Bigastro para traerle a casa.

tantrum. When several women came running over, among them the widow who had adopted the child, the homeopath handed her over to them with a certain irritation, saying that bringing up an orphan badly was even worse than abandoning her altogether.

His wife received him as she was putting on her mantilla. She needed the tranquility of her own house. Oh, how that child wept with a determination that was so unlike that of an orphan! She clung to her husband's arm. She looked at her bracelets, her necklace, the watch chain holding her locket, rippled like the valves of a mollusk shell, where she would soon carry the miniature of her own child within its two small leaves, and she then said goodbye to her friends and smiled at them forgivingly.

Shortly after returning home, once his wife had calmed down, the husband marched off to Don Álvaro's social gathering.

...Behind the leaf-covered window gratings of the gentleman from Gandía, the young men kept passing by with their sacks of poplar, black poplar and myrtle in order to adorn the street with branches, and everything was filled with the aroma of Corpus Christi and summer happiness.[155]

They were having a conversation concerning the same topic being discussed in every house in Oleza: Monsignor Salom. Don Amancio already knew that the monsignor had celebrated Mass fifteen times in the church of the Holy Sepulcher in Jerusalem,[156] that he guided Spanish, Portuguese and French pilgrims along the *Via Dolorosa*,[157] that he spent the night of Holy Thursday totally absorbed in prayer under the silvery olive trees and the cypresses filled with nightingales and moonlight in Gethsemane; and that the silence, even now torn by the sobbing of the Savior, crackled with the laughter and kisses of a Frenchman and a Spanish woman, and that this just man threw himself upon them like a frightful angel and ejected them from that ground sprinkled with divine blood.

It was an advantageous accomplishment for the Community of "Jesús" to ask this saint to come to Oleza. The son of a farm family, he had grown old in the missions that lent their glory to Spanish martyrology. He came to Europe to confer with the legates of a number of countries and with the Supreme Pontiff concerning a difficult reform of apostolic vicarships;[158] and he didn't want to bury himself, perhaps forever, in the remote confines of his diocese in Aleppo without bidding farewell to his native town. And the Fathers at "Jesús" went to his retreat in Bigastro to bring him to their House. On the following day he would officiate in their church, hierarchically

Al otro día oficiaría en su iglesia, exaltando jerárquicamente el Corpus y el reparto de premios y término de curso.

Lo repetían, lo comentaban en el despacho de don Álvaro. Elvira sentábase un momento para escuchar; salía y reaparecía, dejando un suspiro. Ni ella ni su hermano podían cuidarse de fiestas.

Paulina había llegado a incomprensibles arrebatos. Revolvió roperos y cofres; encargó vestidos estivales, buscó en su escriño escogiendo las alhajas más hermosas para su adorno y una sortija de purísimos diamantes para Pablo. Quería solemnizar y premiar el principio de la nueva vida del hijo; vendría ya bachiller y a punto de cumplir los dieciséis años. Luego de unas semanas de descanso, en las que ella y el hijo pasearan su felicidad por Oleza, irían al "Olivar". Abrirían todos los armarios y arcas, se asomarían al pasado de todos los muebles, de todas las puertecitas; se mirarían en los mismos espejos de los abuelos, y esas lunas antiguas irían deshelándose al dar sus imágenes. Más de ocho años sin ese perfume y goce de su hacienda. Era menester reparar el abandono de aquellas salas, del comedor, del oratorio, de la panera. Las habitaciones de su padre, para el hijo. Y un sábado que vinieron los labradores, Paulina les encareció todos sus mandatos: avisar carpinteros, cristaleros, albañiles, colchoneros. Enjalbegar los corrales, desenfundar el comedor, vestir las alcobas, apartar las tres mejores cabras, embotellar todo lo que quedase del tonel de mistela que tenía su nombre esculpido a punta de navaja. Su hijo necesitaba cuidados primorosos. Para los postres de leche y de conserva repasaría el recetario de Jimena. ¿Y las tablas de fresas, y los perales espalderos, y los bergamotos, y los melocotoneros? ¡Por Dios, que no entrasen gusanos en sus frutales!

Cuando los labradores se marcharon y Paulina volvió a sus ropas y joyas, don Álvaro y Elvira la siguieron, mirándola en silencio; y como ella les pidiese su parecer y aguardase la confirmación de sus deseos, Elvira se le inclinó disminuyéndose:

– ¡Tú eres el ama de todo!

Don Álvaro, apenadamente, le dijo su miedo a esos ímpetus y apasionamientos que la consumían hasta enfermar. Ella exclamó:

exalting the Corpus Christi there, and he would distribute the prizes and mark the end of the school term.

They repeated it and commented upon it in Don Álvaro's study. Elvira sat down for a moment to listen; she would go out and reappear, leaving behind a sigh. Neither she nor her brother could be bothered with the holy days.

Paulina had reached a stage of incomprehensible fits of activity. She rummaged through wardrobes and trunks; she ordered summer dresses, she searched through her jewel case selecting the most beautiful pieces of jewelry to adorn herself and a ring of extremely fine diamonds for Pablo. She wanted to solemnize and reward the beginning of a new life for her son: he would now come home a baccalaureate and just about to turn sixteen. After a few weeks of rest, during which she and her son would parade their happiness all over Oleza, they would go to the "Olive Grove." They would open all the clothes closets and chests, they would peer into the past of all the furniture, of all the little doors; they would look at themselves in the same mirrors as their grandparents, and those antique mirror plates would keep melting away as they gave them back their images. More than eight years without that perfume and enjoyment of her country home. It was necessary to restore the abandoned state of the drawing rooms and parlors, of the dining room, the oratory, the grain storage. Her father's room for her son. And one Saturday, when the farm laborers came, Paulina emphasized the importance of all her orders: to notify the carpenters, the glaziers, the masons, the mattress makers. To whitewash the barnyards, remove the coverings from the dining room furniture, to dress up the bedrooms, separate the three best goats, bottle all that remained of the cask of sweet grape wine that had her name on it, carved with the point of a knife. Her son had to be treated with exquisite care. She would review Jimena's list of recipes for dairy desserts and preserves. And how about the stands of strawberries, the espaliered pear trees, the bergamots and the peach trees? God grant that the worms not get into her fruit trees!

When the farm workers departed and Paulina returned to her clothing and her jewels, Don Álvaro and Elvira followed her, looking at her in silence; and when she asked them for their opinion and waited for a confirmation of her wishes, Elvira bent her head in a demeaning way:

"You are the mistress of everything here!"

Don Álvaro dolefully told her of his fears concerning her impulsive activities and impassioned outbursts that were consuming her to the point of making her ill. She exclaimed:

– ...¡Seremos los padres más guapos de la fiesta de "Jesús"!

Su cuñada se les apartó sintiéndose excluída de toda porción de belleza, de toda fórmula de intimidad; y desde lejos miraba resignadamente a su hermano.

Y a medida que se acercaba el día prometido, iba todo sucediendo según la voluntad y la palabra de don Álvaro.

Elvira entornaba más los postigos y persianas; hablaba despacio, y si Paulina, afanada en los preparativos de sus adornos, no acudía puntualmente a la hora del rosario, la disculpaba siempre y pedía que se dispensase a la enferma de las devociones en familia. El canónigo y el P. Bellod toleraron que no saliese ni a la misa de precepto. Paulina principió a desfallecer de miedo a los augurios de los demás. Espió sus entusiasmos para contenerlos, y desconfió y guardóse de sí misma.

Llegó una carta del "príncipe", que desde su destierro volvía los ojos a sus viejos caudillos. Don Álvaro, tanto tiempo desganado de empresas políticas, revivió sus horas de tumulto juvenil, de furor de cruzado, leyendo en la tertulia la carta-circular ungida por la firma del rey. Una luz atravesaba la tierra para caer en su frente como una bendición. Y ese momento de júbilo no era recogido ni comprendido por su mujer. Cuando la llamó para leerle las magníficas palabras, ella se le precipitó con una sonrisa de sollozos.

– ¡Faltan cinco días nada más! ¡Yo no estoy enferma, yo no quiero estar enferma y no lo estaré! ¡Mírame, Álvaro!

El faccioso estrujó el documento en su bolsillo. Su hermana le alzó la frente pálida y dura.

Y el señor penitenciario presentaba sus manos tirantes, muy flacas. No era posible negar que sus amigos sufrían. Recordó la tarde que le había llevado al "Olivar" de don Daniel, la misma tarde que se iluminó su alma con la idea de un matrimonio de venturosas eficacias.

– ¡Yo, amigo mío – acabó con grande emoción – , yo creí y anhelé llevarles a la felicidad!

Lo pronunciaba como un ruego contrito de que volviesen la mirada a sus fallidas intenciones.

Elvira quiso esconder sus lágrimas y no pudo.

– ¡Es usted un ángel!

"...We will be the best looking parents at the celebration at 'Jesús!'"

Her sister-in-law withdrew from their presence since she felt excluded from any portion of beauty, of any form of intimacy; and she watched her brother in resignation from a distance.

And as the promised day drew nearer, everything was happening according to Don Álvaro's will and word.

Elvira kept the shutters and window blinds more and more partly closed; she would speak slowly, and if Paulina seemed overly busy with the preparation of her adornments and did not turn up promptly for the time for the rosary, she would always forgive her and ask that the ailing woman be excused from family devotions. The canon and Father Bellod even tolerated her not going out for Mass on days of obligation. Paulina began to lose courage because of her fear of other people's auguries. She kept close vigil on her moments of exaltation in order to better contain them; she grew distrustful and began to be on guard even against herself.

A letter arrived from the "prince,"[159] who was turning his eyes toward his former chieftains from his place of exile. Don Álvaro, who had been indifferent to political ventures for so long, revived his former moments of youthful enthusiasm, the crusader's fervor, as he read the circular letter anointed by the king's signature to his friends at the social gathering. A light was crossing the earth to fall upon his forehead like a benediction. And that moment of jubilation was neither welcomed nor understood by his wife. When he called her to read the magnificent words to her, she rushed headlong at him with a smile profuse with sobbing.

"It's only five days from now, no more! I am not ill, I don't want to be ill and I will not be! Look at me, Álvaro!"

The rebel sympathizer stroked the document in his pocket. His sister raised her pale, stern forehead toward him.

And the canon-penitentiary presented his tense, very skinny hands. It was impossible to deny that his friends were suffering. He recalled the afternoon he had brought him to Don Daniel's "Olive Grove," the same afternoon his soul had been illuminated with the idea of a marriage with advantageous consequences.

"I, my friend," he concluded with great emotion, "I believed and I sincerely longed to bring you both happiness!"

He pronounced these words like a contrite request for them to turn their eyes toward his failed intentions.

Elvira tried to conceal her tears without success.

"You are an angel!"

Y ella, retraída y humilde, subió al otro piso, previniéndolo todo, cerrándolo todo; encendió las mariposas de los Dolores, y se comió una yema de las que tenía escondidas en el segundo cajón de su cómoda.

Venía la hora de vigilancia y requisa. Desde abajo, Paulina siguió las pisadas en los techos, el quejido de las puertas. La casa iba penetrando en una sombra de encierro, sin el olor fresco de la tarde expulsada de todos los recintos como una mujer pecadora.

Una noche Paulina se dijo:

"Lunes: faltan tres días, y estoy enferma. Tenían ellos razón. Estoy enferma..."

Y se le reanudó el sufrimiento de su desnuda sensibilidad, sufrimiento de mujer que deja en todo lo que miran sus ojos y tocan sus manos una caricia de belleza, todavía intacta, la gracia única en cada instante sencillo; en un vaso con flores, en el doblez de un paño, en el adorno de un frutero, en un manjar, en un perfume, en un mueble; el rango, el modo estricto de fineza escondidos en cada cosa que esperaban sus dedos que lo revelasen, y que se perdían o se ocultaban en los decaimientos de ella, y entonces predominaban los cuidados tiesos, administrativos, la obscuridad de ceniza, el silencio de voz apretada, el sahumerio dormido en los rincones, y surgía la cabeza de Elvira entre los cortinajes, mirándola.

— ¡Estoy mejor; estoy casi bien!

Elvira le subía más las ropas y le cerraba más los maderos.

Así llegó la víspera del Corpus. Paulina madrugó. Se levantó enseguida que don Álvaro salió a misa de Nuestro Padre. Cuando la hermana asomóse templándole el alimento, Paulina se peinaba delante de su espejo con las ventanas de par en par.

— ¿Lo sabe Álvaro?

— ¡Qué ha de saberlo! Es mi sorpresa. Para mí misma ha sido un milagro de salud. Desayunaremos juntas en la mesita del huerto. Hasta del río viene un olor y una canción de Corpus, de víspera de Corpus. Pablo no me ha visto en "Jesús" hace tres domingos. Imagina su alegría de mañana; ¡yo ya la siento y palpito toda!

Su cuñada le dejó la taza de enferma y alejóse de puntillas; y a las criadas y a los mandaderos y cuantos venían les hablaba oprimiendo la voz,

Reserved and humble, she went upstairs to the second floor, making everything ready, closing everything up; she lit the night lamps for the image of the Sorrowing Virgin and ate up one of the candied egg yolks she kept hidden in the second drawer of her bureau.

The time for vigilance and inspection of the house was coming. From down below, Paulina followed the sound of the footsteps on the ceilings, the groaning of the doors. The house was infusing itself into a shadowy confinement, without the fresh aroma of the afternoon that had been expelled from every corner like a sinful woman.

One night Paulina said to herself:

"Monday: three days to go and I am ill. They were right. I am ill...."

And the suffering of her naked sensitivity was renewed, the suffering of a woman who leaves behind a caress of beauty, still intact, the only charm in each simple instant, in everything seen by her eyes and touched by her hands: in a vase of flowers, in the fold of woolen cloth, in the decoration of a fruit dish, in some tasty food, in a perfume, in a piece of furniture; the category, the strict mode of delicacy hidden in everything waiting for her fingers to reveal them, and which were then losing themselves or hiding themselves in her moments of dejection; and then all the rigid, administrative preoccupations would predominate, the darkness of ashes, the silence of a tight voice, the dormant incense in every corner, and Elvira's head would suddenly appear between the curtains and stare at her.

"I am better; I am almost well!"

Elvira would pull the bedclothes even higher and close the shutters even further.

And so the day before Corpus Christi came. Paulina awoke early. She got up right after Don Álvaro left for Mass at Our Father. When his sister looked in while she was warming the food for her, Paulina was combing her hair in front of her mirror and the windows were wide open.

"Does Álvaro know this?"

"Why should he know it? It's my surprise. For me alone it's been a miraculous return to good health. You and I will have breakfast together at the little table in the garden. An aroma and a song of Corpus Christi, of the day before Corpus Christi is even coming from the river. Pablo hasn't seen me at 'Jesús' for three Sundays. Just imagine his joy tomorrow. I can feel it and touch it all even now!"

Her sister-in-law left the sickbed cup with her and withdrew on tiptoe; and she spoke to the maidservants and the errand boys and anyone else who

mitigando todos los rumores como si en lo profundo alguien sufriese.

El hermano decidiría. Pero don Álvaro comió reservadamente con el P. Bellod y el penitenciario para tratar de la ejemplaridad de ir ellos también a Bigastro.

Recelando las murmuraciones de su viaje, no fueron; y al atardecer se juntaron para tratar de la fiesta, en el escritorio de don Álvaro. Se asomaba la hermana dolorida, hasta que ya no pudo contenerse.

– ¡No acaban, no acaban Paulina y las costureras! Tu mujer se extenúa. Es una fiebre que se contagia. Hemos comido también en el huerto. Quiso levantarse...

Y bajó los párpados arrepentida de la condescendencia, de la lenidad de su custodia.

Alba-Longa profirió:

– ¡La maternidad! ¡Santa fuerza de la maternidad!

Se llenó el cielo de campanas, y él tendía su mano señalando hacia la gloria de las torres.

– ¡Corpus! ¡El hijo, el goce del hijo; las vacaciones!

El señor canónigo abrió con holgura sus brazos para recoger y disciplinar este instante.

– ¡Santa fuerza de la maternidad, goce del hijo, ha dicho inspiradamente nuestro don Amancio; pero también pasión, y la pasión que se obedece siempre llega a ser costumbre, y la costumbre que no se resiste se trueca en necesidad!... Son palabras de San Agustín. Y lo veo en nuestra naturaleza. No nos negamos nunca. ¡Por eso veo siempre en Paulina a su pobre padre!

Se volvió a don Álvaro para recibir su aprobación. Don Álvaro sentía un desaliento que le secaba la boca y una brusca conciencia de su cansancio de aquella gente.

Llegó Monera.

– ¡Ya le tenemos! – murmuró el canónigo.

Y Monera sonrió. Se le aguardaba; y a punto de sacar su reloj de oro para mirarlo sin gana, contuvo ese ademán de su pasada incertidumbre.

De nuevo pasó tímidamente Elvira. Se habían ya marchado las costureras, y Paulina llevaba las galas que le habían traído.

– No descansará si tú no las ves, Álvaro. ¡Nunca me ha parecido tan hermosa! ¡Mañana se la comerán todos los ojos!

came by in a tight voice, mitigating all the sounds as if deep down someone were really suffering.

Her brother would decide. But Don Álvaro ate privately with Father Bellod and the canon penitentiary in order to discuss the exemplarity of their also going to Bigastro.

Fearful of the gossip their trip might arouse, they didn't go; and they got together in Don Álvaro's study in the late afternoon to deal with the feast day. His sister kept looking in, appearing to be very aggrieved, until she could no longer contain herself.

"There's no end to it, there's no end to Paulina and the dressmakers! Your wife is exhausted. It's just like a contagious fever. We've also eaten in the garden. She insisted on getting up...."

And she lowered her eyelids as if repentant for her condescending manner, for the leniency of her vigilance.

Alba-Longa offered these words:

"Motherhood! The blessed power of motherhood!"

The sky was filled with bells, and he extended his hand and pointed toward the glory of the towers.

"Corpus Christi! The son, the enjoyment of the son; the vacation!"

The canon opened his arms expansively to gather in and discipline this instant.

"Our Don Amancio has said so inspirationally the blessed power of motherhood, the enjoyment of the son; but also passion, and the passion that is always obeyed gets to be custom, and the custom that can not be resisted is converted into necessity!... Those are the words of Saint Augustine.[160] I see it in our nature. We never deny ourselves. That's why I always see her poor father in Paulina!"

He turned to Don Álvaro to receive his approbation. Don Álvaro was overcome by a feeling of discouragement that left his mouth dry, as well as a brusque awareness of his weariness with those people.

Monera arrived.

"We finally have him here!" the canon muttered.

And Monera smiled. They were waiting for him; and just as he was about to take out his gold watch to look at it with no particular purpose in mind, he restrained that gesture of his former uncertainty.

Elvira timidly came by once again. The dressmakers had already departed and Paulina was wearing the finery they had brought her.

"She won't be able to rest if you don't go see her, Álvaro. She's never looked so lovely! Everyone will just devour her with their eyes tomorrow!"

Don Álvaro se arrojó en su alcoba.

¡Tan hermosa! Se paró delante de ella mirándola. La claridad de la tarde la esculpía en las sedas negras y ligeras que le palpitaban por la brisa del río y se le ceñían a su cuerpo; palidez dorada de sol de junio que le glorificaba los cabellos; los ojos con el goce de sí misma; se embebía de luz su boca de flores húmedas y sensuales en su castidad. Toda hermosa, pero de una hermosura apasionada y nueva; un principio de plenitud de mujer que se afirmaría y existiría muchos años más, cuando él fuese alejándose por los resecos caminos de la senectud. Nunca había poseído ese cuerpo de mujer en su mujer. Y la miraba con rencor amándola como si Paulina perteneciese a otro hombre. Se inclinaba todo él a la caricia desconocida y brava. Y otro don Álvaro huesudo y lívido le sacudió con su grito llamando al médico.

Vio que Monera la miraba extrañamente. La encontraba mejor de lo que podía esperarse. ¡Únicamente ese pulso, ese pulso que no tenía medida!

Don Álvaro clamó delirante:

– ¡No tiene medida! ¡Es eso! ¡No tiene medida, no tiene medida! ¡Acuéstate, desnúdate, acuéstate!

Se le torcía la boca con un temblor de poseído. Y agarró los cristales de la ventana del huerto y los cerró con un ímpetu espantoso. Después, cuando se pasó las manos por su frente, se dejó una frialdad húmeda de difunto.

Monera y Elvira habían desaparecido.

Paulina principió a desnudarse; y en el aire cerrado iba esparciéndose una blanca suavidad de ropas íntimas, un fino perfume de cuerpo de mujer. Por el aturdimiento de su obediencia bajo la furia del esposo, se desnudaba sin recatarse, de pie, inclinándose, curvándose, alzándose para descalzarse, y prorrumpían sus formas desceñidas, la cadera opulenta y firme, los pechos trémulos y perfectos, la espalda, los muslos... Así se contemplaría ella a sí misma todas las noches, todas las mañanas. Así la vería y la desearía un amante, otro marido; y se le obstinó el pensamiento celoso de ella por ella; ella mirándose, sabiéndose hermosa, pensando en ella y en quien la poseyese en todo su temperamento, todos los días, todas las noches; y él por única vez. Le sobrecogió una acometida de sensualismo abyecto que le brincaba flameándole por toda la piel, golpeándole las sienes, el cuello y el

Don Álvaro rushed into her bedroom.

So lovely! He stopped in front of her and stared at her. The brightness of the afternoon sculptured her in the light black silks that shivered all over her in the breeze from the river and clung to her body; the golden paleness of the June sunlight glorified her hair; her eyes were filled with the pleasure of her own being; her humid and sensually flowered mouth was drenched with light within her chastity. All so beautiful, but of a passionate, new beauty; a beginning of womanly plenitude that would affirm itself and continue to exist for many years more, while he would be drawing further away along the parched pathways of old age. He had never truly possessed that womanly body in his wife. And he kept looking at her with rancor, loving her, as if Paulina belonged to another man. And all of him bent over toward the unfamiliar, magnificent caress. And another Don Álvaro, bony and livid, shook him as he shouted out and called for the doctor.

He saw that Monera was looking at her strangely. He found her to be better than could be expected. The only thing was that pulse, that pulse that had no limit!

Don Álvaro cried out deliriously:

"It has no limit! That's it! It has no limit, it has no limit! Go lie down, take off your clothes, go lie down!"

His mouth was twisted with the tremor of someone possessed. He took hold of the windowpanes that opened onto the garden and closed it with frightening violence. Afterwards, when he passed his hands over his forehead, he felt a damp chill, the characteristic of a dead man.

Monera and Elvira had disappeared.

Paulina started to remove her clothes; and a white silkiness of her intimate garments, and the fine perfume of a woman's body kept pervading the stuffy air. Because she was stunned into obedience in the face of her husband's fury, she undressed without reserve, standing up, leaning over, bending down, rising up to take off her shoes, and her unloosened form, her opulent, firm hips, her perfect trembling breasts, her back, her thighs, all burst into view.... That was how she must have contemplated herself every night, every morning. That was how a lover, another husband would see her and desire her; and her own jealous thought of herself persisted; she looking at herself, knowing that she was beautiful, thinking about herself and the one who might possess her in all the fullness of her temperament, every day, every night; and he for the one and only time. She was overcome by an onslaught of abject sensuality that bounded over her, inflaming her all over

costado. ¡Si hubiera podido hablar con su voz, la suya, para decir su nombre y amarla como ahora; pero llamarla hubiera sido desconocerse a sí mismo y espantarla a ella; a ella – otra vez, Señor –, ella que se complacería en su solitaria belleza con unas calidades de sensibilidad de las que don Álvaro no fué dotado!

Acababa de tenderse en la cama, y le miraba con ojos anchos y atónitos. Estaba ya vestida por la castidad de su desnudo entre lienzos blancos.

Fue abriéndose la puerta del dormitorio, y apareció Elvira.

– ¿Ya está? – y les sonrió.

Ya estaba todo irreparablemente como antes, como siempre.

– Se han ido sin querer llamarte. Os reuniréis en el vestuario de "Jesús" para la ceremonia de monseñor. Y no os apuréis por Pablo ni por nada. ¡Dios mío! ¿No me tenéis, no soy de vosotros? Pues servíos de mí. ¡Yo os traeré a vuestro hijo!

Enseguida abrió el armario que dejaba su esencia de cedro; buscó las mejores ropas del hermano; su levita, su chaleco de orillas. Pasó los topacios de don Daniel por los ojales bordados de la camisa finísima.

– Has de ir muy galán, por ti, por todos y porque la gente no murmure de tu abandono como si fueses un viudo, ¿verdad?

Don Álvaro se paseaba por la sala, ya del todo él, pálido, compacto y desgraciado.

2. Monseñor Salom y su familiar

Corpus vino aquel año en la plenitud de junio, como una fruta tardana del árbol litúrgico, olorosa de frutas de verdad: cerezas, pomas, albaricoques... La ciudad, con sus cobertores, sus toldos, sus altares a la sombra de tabernáculos de follajes para la procesión eucarística, daba una respiración agraria, inocente y devota; pero además, arrabalera con la crecida de forasteros, con estruendo y bullanga de diligencias, tílburis, galeras, faetones y calesines; gritos de vendedoras de almendras verdes, de alábegas y rosas, de peroles

her skin, pounding at her temples, her neck and her side. If only he had been able to speak with his own voice, his very own, to say her name and love her as she was now; but to call her by name would have meant not following his true inclination and frightening her; her – once again, oh Lord – she who would take pleasure in her solitary beauty with qualities of sensitivity with which Don Álvaro was not endowed.

She had just stretched out on the bed and kept looking at him with wide, astonished eyes. She was now dressed in the chastity of her nakedness between the white sheets.

The bedroom door slowly opened and Elvira appeared.

"Is everything all right now?"

Everything was irreparably as before, as always.

"They've gone away because they didn't want to call you. You will all get together in the dressing room at 'Jesús' for the ceremony for the monsignor. And don't you worry about Pablo or anything else. My God! Don't you have me; am I not one of you? Well, make use of me. I will bring your son to you!"

She immediately opened the wardrobe that gave off a scent of cedar; she looked for her brother's best clothes: his frock coat, his vest with the selvedged borders. She slipped Don Daniel's topaz studs through the buttonholes of the extremely sheer shirt.

"You must go very handsomely dressed, for your own sake, for everyone else, and so that people don't gossip about your neglecting yourself as if you were a widower. Am I not right?"

Don Álvaro was walking back and forth in the drawing room, now completely himself, pale, compact and wretched.

2. Monsignor Salom and his Familiar

Corpus Christi came that year in the plenitude of June, like a belated fruit of the liturgical tree, fragrant with true fruits: cherries, apples, apricots.... The city, with its covered stands, its awnings, its altars in the shade of leaf-covered tabernacles for the Eucharistic procession, gave off an agrarian breath, innocent and devout; but somewhat coarse at the same time, because of the increased number of out-of-towners, along with the clatter and the racket made by diligences, tilburies, covered wagons, phaetons and light chaises; the shouts of women selling unripe almonds, leaves of basil and

de quesillos, de lerchas de ranas desolladas, de pastas de candeal y gollerías, plagios humildes de los dulces monásticos.

A veces, por un callizo, por una cantonada entraba la frescura de las arboledas del río, la lumbre de los campos segados con los ejidos llenos de garbas, la quietud de los olivares en las tierras rojas. Y la ciudad subía en el azul como una vieja custodia de piedra, de sol y de cosechas, estremecida de campanas y palomos.

Nunca pareció tan adusto y desolado el palacio de su ilustrísima, ni tan pobre y obscura la catedral con el trono del obispo dentro de su funda lisa color de violeta.

El culto, el júbilo, el atuendo, la felicidad se juntaban en el colegio de "Jesús". ¡Qué mezclas de hábitos, de galas, de olores, de cortesías y cordialidades en aquellos salones y jardines! Aristocracia de Madrid y de provincia, hacendados, mercaderes, órdenes religiosas, el cabildo, cuatro caballeros santiaguistas, el comandante de la Zona...

Y todos salieron a los claustros, y se tendió un silencio reverente como un paño precioso. En la puerta labrada del refectorio de los Padres apareció monseñor Salom rodeado de la comunidad. Más que hombre era la imagen viva de un santo de los primitivos siglos de la Iglesia. Vestía un hábito negro con cíngulo bermejo como una cicatriz de toda su cintura; le colgaba por pectoral un rudo crucifijo con orla de toscos granates; era su sombrero redondo, duro, sin felpa; su piel, de breña, y sus barbas, de crin. Hambres, trabajos, vigilias, rigores de climas y de penitencias habían plasmado en piedra volcánica aquel cuerpo de justo. Se le vio enseguida la señal de su martirio: una mano mutilada bárbaramente. Le quedaban dos dedos: el pulgar y el índice; los otros se los cercenaría el hacha, el cepo, el brasero, las púas, los cordeles, el refinado ingenio de los suplicios en que tanto se complacen los pueblos idólatras. También le miraban los zapatones, que se pisaban y levantaban en gordos pliegues las haldas mostrándose sus suelas, moldes de tantas leguas de santidad. Y el apóstol de Oriente se volvía de una fila a otra del concurso y en sus órbitas parecía que se asomasen dos diminutos anacoretas en cuevas recremadas. A su lado, el Rector y el Prefecto, silenciosos y pulcros, con los ojos vaciados en la luz de sus gafas, iban

roses, pots of artichoke hearts, reeds strung with skinned frogs, white wheat pastries and all manner of exquisite delicacies, humble imitations of convent-made sweets.

At times the fresh breeze from the groves along the river, the warm glow of the harvested fields with their common lands filled with sheaves of wheat, the stillness of the olive groves in the red-colored earth would find their way onto a narrow street or along a corner. And the city rose up into the blue like an aged monstrance of stone, sunlight and crops, trembling with church bells and ringdoves.

His Excellency's palace never seemed so gloomy and desolate, nor the Cathedral so impoverished and dark with the bishop's throne all wrapped in its smooth, violet-colored covering.

The worship, the jubilation, the pomp, the happiness were joined together in the school of "Jesús." What a mixture of habits, finery, scents, graciousness and cordiality in those reception rooms and gardens! Aristocrats from Madrid and from the provinces, land owners, merchants, religious orders, the chapter council, four knights of the Order of St. James,[161] the commanding officer of the Recruitment Zone....

And they all went out into the cloisters and a reverent silence spread out like a precious cloth. Monsignor Salom appeared in the decoratively carved doorway of the Fathers' refectory surrounded by the Community. Even more than a man, he was the living image of a saint from out of the primitive centuries of the Church. He was wearing a black habit with a bright red cingulum like a scar all around his waist; a rough crucifix with a border of unpolished garnets hung round his neck as a pectoral cross; his hat was round, hard, without any plush; his skin was weather-beaten and his beard like horsehair. Hunger, hardships, vigils, the rigors of harsh climates and penances had molded that righteous man's body into volcanic rock. Almost immediately you could see the marks of his martyrdom: a hand barbarously mutilated. Two fingers remained: the thumb and the index finger; an axe, a pillory, a stake, iron barbs, whip thongs, the refined ingenuity of the tortures in which idolatrous peoples take such pleasure, had most likely lopped off the others. They also looked at his big, heavy shoes, which would tread heavily upon his skirts and then raise them in thick folds, revealing his soles, molds of so many leagues of saintly movement. And the apostle from the Orient turned from one row to another among those gathered round him, and it seemed as if two diminutive anchorites in murky caves were peering out of his eye sockets. The Rector and the Prefect were at his side, silent and fastidious, their eyes hollow in the light on their spectacles, dispersing their

dejando su sonrisa. Si ellos, los hijos de San Ignacio, admitiesen dignidades, sus prelados serían como éste, con las mismas virtudes de sacrificio; como éste, pero más limpios, más cuidadosos de su persona. Y erguían las corvas alabardas de sus bonetes. El cortejo, como todos los cortejos de este mundo, se sentía ya particionero de la gloria del elegido.

Los invitados, singularmente las mujeres de más elegancia y belleza, eran tan dichosos que se sobresaltaban de serlo, y no sabiendo qué hacer ni qué pensar, daban gracias a Dios. ¡Nunca olvidarían este Corpus! Pórtico del verano, tan azul, tan esenciado de emociones. Todos reunidos como una familia en un huerto de abuelos señoriales. ¡Qué ligereza, qué ímpetu y qué dulzura en sus ojos y en su sangre! Hasta tenían un mártir para su adoración: un obispo mutilado, venido de Oriente. Podían abrirse todas las rosas de los pensamientos y de los deseos bajo la gracia emitida por este buen pastor, que perdonaba la felicidad perecedera que él no conocía. Estaba todo: el goce en ellos y el padecimiento en el fuerte.

Detrás iba el Padre Ferrando, el confesor de su ilustrísima; detrás y solo, como el caudatario que llevase la cola de la magnificencia de la comitiva; el último, el más viejecito, de faz gruesa, morena y blanda de madre labradora, olvidada en la fiesta de suntuosidades. Pero, acaso se le dejaba respetuosamente el último. He aquí el hombre que veía en su desnudez la más alta conciencia de la diócesis y con sus manos rollizas atraía el perdón sobre la frente humillada del obispo enfermo. Y como iba el postrero, pudo pararse y hablar con el comandante de la Zona sin entorpecer el tránsito. Enseguida tomó carrera y se juntó con el séquito.

Refirió el comandante las maravillas que acababa de oír. Monseñor Salom no había sido mártir de los infieles, sino de sí mismo, y lo sería hasta su muerte. Estaban cabales sus manos; pero desde que ingresó en el sacerdocio hizo voto de llevar dentro de la diestra una imagen de bronce de Nuestra Señora. Había envejecido con su mano devotamente crispada. Oficiando, comiendo, predicando, durmiendo, bendiciendo; en camino, en oración, en peligro, en reposo, siempre, siempre, siempre con sus dedos encogidos trenzando la figurita de la Virgen que iba penetrándole en la carne, comunicándose de ella, y le criaba una llaga callosa y verde en la palma.

smiles all around them as they walked. If they, the sons of Saint Ignatius, were to permit positions of honor, their prelates would be like this man, with the same virtues of self-sacrifice; like this man, only cleaner, more concerned with their personal appearance. And they raised up their curved halberd-shaped caps. The cortege, like all corteges in this world, already felt that it was participating in the glory of the one who had been chosen.

The invited guests, especially the most elegant and beautiful women, were so overcome with happiness that they were startled to feel that way, and as they didn't know what to do or think, they gave thanks to God. They would never forget this day of Corpus Christi! A gateway to summer, so blue, so intimately wrapped in emotions. All of them gathered together like a family in a garden of aristocratic ancestors. Such lightness of spirit, such animation and sweetness in their eyes and in their blood! They even had a martyr for them to adore: a mutilated bishop who had come to them from the Orient. All the roses of their thoughts and desires could be opened wide in the presence of the grace emitted by this kindly shepherd, who forgave them the transient feeling of happiness which he himself did not know. It was all there: the pleasure in themselves and the suffering in the strong one.

Behind them came Father Ferrando, His Excellency's confessor; in the rear and all alone, like the ecclesiastic who carried the train of the bishop's robe, now carrying the train of the magnificence of the whole retinue; the last one of all, so old and pitiful, with the heavy, dark and bland features of a farm mother, forgotten in the midst of this fiesta of sumptuosities. But perhaps they let him walk at the very end out of respect. For here was the man who saw the loftiest conscience of the diocese in all his nakedness, and who drew forgiveness upon the humbled forehead of the ailing bishop with his plump hands. And since he was able to walk at the very end, he could stop and speak to the commanding officer of the Recruitment Zone without obstructing the movement. He quickly took to his heels and joined the retinue.

The commandant recounted the wonders he had just heard. Monsignor Salom had not been a martyr to the infidels, but to himself, and he would be so until he died. His hands were perfectly normal; but ever since he entered the priesthood, he made a vow to carry a bronze image of Our Lady inside his right hand. He had grown old with his hand devoutly clenched. While celebrating the Mass, eating, preaching, sleeping, consecrating; when on the road, in prayer, in time of danger, in repose, always, always, always with his fingers contracted, plaiting the tiny figure of the Virgin while it continued penetrating his flesh, communicating with it and finally forming a callous green sore on his palm.

Se conmovió la multitud. Algunas mujeres exquisitas llegaron a creer suya la penitencia del santo, y se amaron más a sí mismas. Era un estado de inocencía, de ardor, de beatitud, de voluptuosidad.

Inflamado el P. Bellod, se puso los puños en los riñones, y así gritaba:
— ¡Viva monseñor!

Y un hidalgo corpulento, de paño gordo, de botas de ternera, sombrilla verde y un palillo en su boca, se hincó de rodillas, sollozando:
— ¡Viva Corpus Christi!

Era el padre del colegial de Aspe y contratista de obras públicas. Don Roger, que llegaba con su cañuto de solfa, y un fámulo de la ropería, tuvieron que sosegarle. En aquel momento se abría el *De Profundis* o paraninfo. La multitud, con docilidad canónica, se acomodó según la pragmática de los espectáculos de "Jesús": las señoras, a la izquierda, y los caballeros, a la derecha del estrado. Estrado con fondo de banderas bordadas, con friso de epigrafías de oro, candelabros de tulipas, mesa de terciopelo para los dos secretarios, jovencitos y pálidos, detrás de las grandes escribanías de plata, de las que no habían de servirse, y de bandejas de medallas, de cintas, de bandas, de mazos de diplomas...

Bajo, se abrían las gradas de alumnos. Un torzal rojo y ondulante separaba los internos de los externos. Enfrente, el dosel del obispo de Alepo; y de allí descendía un anfiteatro alfombrado, consistorial, de sillones Imperio, Luis XVI, Enrique II, de bancas de felpa y asientos de rejilla. Todo se pobló de sayales, de manteos, de mucetas, de levitas; y se afirmaron las cornisas de solideos de borla, de bonetes, de calvas, de cerquillos de tonsuras; y en lo último, el tupé lírico del señor Hugo y el cráneo recto y gris del comandante de la Zona.

Una voz atenorada, de evangelista y anagnostes, iba recitando la memoria académica, que todos los años comenzaba con tono y dejos de anales de Roma: "...*Quod felix faustumque sit rei litterariae omnibusque nostri gymnasii alumnis proemia sequenti ordine consecuti sunt*"; y en el

The multitude was stirred. Several exquisite women reached the point where they believed that the saintly man's penance was theirs, and they loved themselves even the more for it. It was a state of innocence, of excitement, of beatitude, of voluptuousness.

Father Bellod grew so impassioned that he put his fists against his loins and shouted thus:

"Long life to the monsignor!"

And a corpulent hidalgo in a heavy brown woolen suit, calf boots, carrying a green sunshade and with a toothpick in his mouth, bent down on his knees sobbing:

"Long live Corpus Christi!"

It was the father of the schoolboy from Aspe, who was a public works contractor. Don Roger, who arrived with his tube of sofeggio musical notations, along with a *famulus* from the cloakroom, had to calm him down. At that very moment, they opened up the *De Profundis*, or assembly hall. The multitude, with canonical docility, settled down according to the pragmatic sanction prevalent at all presentations at "Jesús": the ladies to the left and the gentlemen to the right of the platform. The platform with a background of embroidered flags, with a frieze with epigraphy in golden letters, candelabra with glass globes in the shape of tulips, a velvet-covered table for the two very young, pale secretaries, who were sitting behind silver ornamental inkstands which they did not have to use, and trays full of medals, ribbons, sashes, bunches of diplomas....[162]

Below the platform, the tiers of seats for students opened out. A red, undulating silk twist separated the boarding students from the day students. Facing them, the dais for the bishop from Aleppo; and a carpeted, consistorial amphitheater descended from there, with Empire style, Louis XVI and Henry II style armchairs, with plush covered benches and wickerwork chairs. It was all crowded with sackcloth, long cloaks, mozettas, frock coats; and the cornices were secured by tasseled zucchettos, ecclesiastic caps, bald patches, fringes of hair round a tonsure; and in the very back, the lyrical forelock of Señor Hugo and the erect, gray skull of the commanding officer of the Recruitment Zone.

A tenor-like voice of a gospel chanter and dinnertime reader kept reciting the academic account that began every year with the same tone and lilt as the annals of Rome: "...*Quod felix faustumque sit rei litterariae omnibusque nostri gymnasii alumnis proemia sequenti ordine consecuti sunt, (...So that it may be happy and prosperous for letters and for all the students of our school, the awards were earned in the following order),*" and at a closing or

cierre o en la curva de un párrafo, en una demostración sinóptica, los Padres sonreían y levantaban sus gafas y su frente a la bóveda, reprimiendo su emoción de maestros.

Iban espesándose las esencias sutiles de ropas de mujer; los abanicos aventaban los perfumes de los tocados, de las mejillas, de los pechos entre olores de verano tierno, de maderas y lacas. En los altos ventanales, las cortinas carmesí con el monograma de Jesús se combaban en un vuelo redondo; caía la lumbre y el aliento de las huertas verdes con sol. Era el paisaje como un ave infinita que de cuando en cuando moviese sus alas de cultivos. Los alumnos miraban ya indómitos a sus familias; las señoras y los caballeros se inclinaban enviándose parabienes; salía un temblor de cuerda de violín, una nota de armonium; otra vez las cortinas colgaban sin brisa, y pasaba la calma del mediodía; todo alrededor del eje de la palabra latina del secretario, tronco de elocuencia en que florecían los títulos y leyendas de laurel: *"Quod in studiis optime profecerit; honoris causa; Dominus..."* y brotaban los nombres, también en latín, de los laureados: *"Vicencius, Josephus, Emmanuel, Ludovicus...".* Y dentro de esta onomástica de príncipes, de pontífices, de santos, se sentían glorificadas muchas familias, y paladeaban las mieles de la crianza en "Jesús".

"Pietate, Modestia, Diligentia...: Dominus, Victorinus Messeguer et Corbellá"; un interno robusto y sordo al que tuvieron que avisar a codazos. Y antes de que pudiese postrarse en la alfombra de la presidencia, le ganó el doméstico de monseñor, arremolinado de esclavina y faldas, cetrino y peludo, con retumbos de botas viejas. Se puso a conversar con su dueño, rascándose la quijada tupida, volviendo los ojos de relumbres minerales a la ceremonia. Monseñor le atendía desalentado. Una gota de sol se quebraba en su frontal recocido. Después quedóse inmóvil, como si acabara de subirse definitivamente al cojín de piedra de un pórtico románico.

Messeguér y Corbellá les miraba aguardando el premio y la bendición. Y en los bancos de los alumnos y en las sillas del público pasó un leve rebullicio; y cuando el familiar bajaba del trono, una voz fisgona le llamó con el nombre latino del sordo: *¡Victorinus, Victorinus!*

turn of a paragraph, as a synoptic demonstration, the Fathers would smile and raise their spectacles and their foreheads toward the vault above, repressing their emotions as teachers.

The subtle scents of women's clothes were getting thicker; the fans were wafting the perfumes of their coiffeurs, their cheeks, their breasts amidst the aromas of gentle summer, of wooden boards and lacquers. In the tall wide windows, the crimson curtains with the monogram of the Jesuits bulged out in rounded fullness; the warm light and the breath of the green, sun-drenched gardens and orchards fell upon them. The landscape was like an infinite bird moving its wings of cultivated fields every so often. The students now looked at their families without submission; the ladies and gentlemen leaned forward sending congratulations to one another; the shivering of a violin string, a note from the harmonium emerged; once again the curtains hung down without a breeze and the calm of midday passed; all of this encircling the axis of the secretary's Latin word, a trunk of eloquence in which the degrees and the accounts of academic achievement flourished: "*Quod in studiis optime profecerit; honoris causa; Dominus... (For having advanced at the highest level in their studies, Señor... are worthy of honor)*," and the names of the laureates poured forth, also in Latin: "*Vicencius, Josephus, Emmanuel, Ludovicus....*" And within this omnasticon of princes, of pontiffs, of saints, many families felt that they were covered with glory and they savored the honey of the training at "Jesús."

"*Pietate, Modestia, Diligentia...: Dominus, Victorinus Messeguer et Corbellá (For his piety, modesty, diligence... : Señor Victoriano Messeguer y Corballá)*"; a robust and deaf boarding student whom they had to inform by nudging him with their elbows. And before he could prostrate himself on the rug of the main platform, he was overtaken by the monsignor's manservant, in a whirl of his short cape and skirts, sallow-complexioned and hairy, his well-worn boots resounding as he moved. He took up a conversation with his master, scratching his thick jaw, turning the mineral-like sparkle of his eyes toward the ceremony. Monsignor listened to him dispiritedly. A droplet of sunlight was breaking upon his overheated forehead. Then he stood there motionless, as if he had just arisen definitively to the stone cushion of a Romanesque portico.

Messeguer y Corbellá kept looking at them, waiting for his prize and blessing. And a slight commotion spread among the students' benches and the chairs for the public; and when the familiar came down from the throne, a mocking voice called out to the deaf boy with his Latin name: "*Victorinus, Victorinus!*"

Atravesó el lego la sala y los claustros, y salió de "Jesús" a seguir su jornada bajo el sol de Corpus de Oleza. Monseñor necesitaba un coche de alquiler que le llevase a Murcia, a poco precio. Y él corría, de nuevo, hostales y paradores. ¡Qué ánimo tan encogido para la tierra tenían algunos santos tan valerosos para el cielo! Nada más que monseñor hubiese dicho: "Tráiganme un carruaje", le hubiesen llevado los mejores de la comarca. Pero el apóstol nada pedía, y los R.R.P.P. de "Jesús", que tan afanosos le buscaron, ya no se cuidaban sino de sus solemnidades y vacaciones.

Y entró el lego en el mesón de San Daniel. Criados, recaderos, mayorales, banastas de aves y frutas, atadijos, cofres de internos, colchones forrados de lona con el escudo del colegio. Carros cosarios, ruedos de caminantes, de huertanos, de mozos que gritaban, que se pasaban las calabazas de vino, las rebanadas de pan, las escudillas y ollas humeantes de condumio; y en el suelo de cortezas se arrufaban los perros, retozaban los gatos devorando mondaduras, aleteaban las gallinas picando entre los costales y a veces salían las palomas de lo profundo de las cuadras. El familiar preguntó a los cuadreros. Los caballos y mulas le miraban compendiándole en sus ojos húmedos; les crujía el pienso roto entre sus quijales, y, al volverse, el viento de sus morros levantaba el pajuz del pesebre. Coches y acémilas estaban ya comprometidos para familias de alumnos.

Se marchó el lego con sus zapatones gordos de estiércol y la cara hilada de colgajos de arañas. ¡Y monseñor se estaría en su baldaquino, con la ilustre comunidad que tenía jardines, salas artesonadas, huertas, refectorio, claustros, aposentos, sin importarle los alquileres de mulos ni galeras, sin cuidarse de nada, gracias a su voto de pobreza que les libraba de padercerla! En cambio, él y monseñor viajaban con la conciencia de su escasez. "¡Qué bien se vivirá en el palacio de Oleza, monseñor!", le había dicho, por la mañana, mientras le entraba las calzas y le abrochaba los hebillones de los zapatos. Monseñor le sonrió. "Hay que marcharse pronto, y ahorra lo que puedas, que hemos de atravesar el mundo, y un mundo costoso, antes de

The lay brother crossed the hall and the cloisters and departed from "Jesús" in order to continue his journey beneath the Olezan sun of Corpus Christi. Monsignor needed a coach for hire to take him to Murcia for a very low price. And he was running once again to hostelries and inns. What a faint-hearted spirit for earthly affairs some saints possessed when they were filled with such zeal for the heavenly! All the monsignor would have had to say was, "Bring me a carriage," and they would have brought him the finest ones in the whole region. But the apostle asked for nothing and the Reverend Fathers at "Jesús," who had sought him so eagerly, no longer were concerned with anything but their ceremonies and their vacations.

And so the lay brother entered the San Daniel Inn. Servants, messengers, stagecoach drivers, hampers with birds and fruits, all manner of bundles, boarding students' trunks, mattresses lined with canvas, with the school coat of arms. Carters' wagons, circles of travelers, farm people from the cultivated plain, porters, all shouting, passing gourds of wine, slices of bread, bowls and pots steaming with all manner of food back and forth among one another. And on the ground covered with crusts and rinds, dogs kept snarling, cats romped about devouring the peelings, hens flapped their wings as they pecked among the sacks and the doves would occasionally emerge from the depths of the stables. The familiar made inquiries among the stable boys. The horses and mules looked at him as they summarized him in their moist eyes; the crushed feed crackled between their jaws and, as they turned around, the stream of air from their snouts lifted the half-rotted straw in the cribs. Coaches and beasts of burden were already reserved for students' families.

The lay brother marched off, his big, clumsy shoes heavily coated with manure and his face spun over with tatters of spider webs. And Monsignor would most likely now be under his baldachin along with the illustrious Community, which had gardens, caissoned parlors, orchards of fruits and vegetables, a refectory, cloisters, lodgings, and which couldn't attach any importance to the renting of mules and covered wagons, which didn't really care about anything, thanks to their vow of poverty, which freed them from suffering from it. He and the monsignor, on the other hand, were traveling with full awareness of their deprivation. "How well one must live in the palace of Oleza, monsignor!" he had said to him that morning as he helped him on with his stockings and fastened the large buckles of his shoes. Monsignor smiled at him. "We have to depart quickly and you must save whatever you can, for we have to go across the world, and a very costly

llegar a nuestros pobres conventos". "¡Si se muriese ese obispo llagado y nombraran a monseñor!" Pero el apóstol cerró los párpados, quemados por la luz y los relentes de Siria, y apretó más la imagen de bronce en su mano encogida.

Calle del Olmo, calle de la Corredera, plazuela de Gosálvez... Todo lleno, todo enramado. Sensación de los campos dentro de la ciudad vieja. Y desde el día siguiente hasta el otoño, Oleza se quedaría callada, quietecita; toda la ciudad en vacaciones, toda cerrada, respetando el sosiego de los señores de "Jesús". ¡Qué deleitoso verano en esta sede dormida al amor de las alamedas del Segral, fresca y olorosa de naranjos y cidros, como la antigua Jaffa! Y el doméstico se hundió en la Posada Nueva. Le rodearon los arrieros, los mozos, los compadres y galloferos que beben de fiado y viven de la bulla de los que pasan. ¿Un coche con regateo y en día de ganancia? Le miraban a lo socarrón. Un mayoral tuerto que picaba verónica con su faca consintió en alquilarles, en setenta reales, una diligencia arrumbada que le decían la *mascota* por su semejanza con el carro de lonas negras que recogía los cadáveres del último cólera. Salió una oveja preñada, llevándose delante gallinas y pavos, que se subieron con alboroto por las galgas de una carreta. La hostelera amasaba un lebrillo de patatas y maíz para sus cerdos. La pocilga estalló de guañidos candentes que se retorcían. Un pollastre se plantó encima de una corambre. Pompa blanca de manto de santiaguista y cresta de boina; aleteó con bizarría, mirando de reojo al misionero, y soltó su clarín de metal magnífico. Balaba la cordera; zumbaban avispas y moscardas de pesebre. Un labrador forastero disputaba con el mayoral muy en sigilo. Por fin, el tuerto se arrimó al fraile, y sin dejar su risa humilde, pidióle perdón y le negó la *mascota*. Aquel hombre le daba siete duros por otro viaje. El cántico del gallo fastuoso le taladraba sus sienes. Y marchóse de allí tan desesperado, que las gentes se le reían compadecidas. A botes y zancadas se precipitó en "Jesús", y cuando llegaba al Paraninfo, el lector entonaba su invocación postrera, grito de júbilo y de aliento, últimas palabras que todos

world, before we arrive at our impoverished convents." "If that ulcer-ridden bishop were to die and they should name monsignor!" But the apostle closed his eyelids, burned by the light and the damp evening dew of Syria, and he squeezed the bronze image in his clenched hand even more firmly.

The Calle del Olmo, the Calle de la Corredera, the Plazuela de Gosálvez.... All filled up,, all adorned with branches. The sensation of the countryside within the old city. And from the following day until the fall. Oleza would remain silent, ever so quiet; the whole city on vacation, all closed up, out of respect for the tranquility of the masters at "Jesús." What a delightful summer in this dormant episcopal see so very close to the poplar groves by the Segral, fresh and fragrant with orange trees and citrons, like ancient Jaffa! And the servant plunged into the Posada Nueva. He was surrounded by mule drivers, porters, chance acquaintances and unsavory idlers who drink on credit and live off the confusing bustle of those who pass through. A coach at a bargain rate and on such a profitable day! They stared at him mockingly. A one-eyed coachman, who was chopping up some speedwell leaves with a large curved knife, agreed to hire out a diligence to them for seventy *reales*, one that was not regularly used and which they called the *mascot, (the talisman)*[163] on account of its similarity to the wagon with the black canvas top that picked up the corpses after the last outbreak of cholera. A pregnant ewe came out with some hens and turkeys in front of her, and they climbed up onto the hub brakes of a cart making a considerable racket. The innkeeper's wife was mixing up an earthenware tub full of potatoes and corn for her pigs. The pigsty erupted into heated grunting and twisting about. A young rooster planted itself on top of a pile of hides. The white splendor of the cloak of a knight of the Order of Saint James and the crest as a beret; it flapped its wings gallantly, looking at the missionary out of the corner of its eye and blared out with its magnificent metal-like clarion. The lamb was bleating; wasps and blue bottle flies from the manger were buzzing all around. An out-of-town farmer was arguing with the coachman in a very furtive manner. Finally the one-eyed man came up close to the friar and, without abandoning his humble smile, he asked him to forgive him and refused him the mascot. That other man was offering him seven *duros* for another trip. The song of the fatuous rooster was drilling into his temples. And he marched off from there in such desperation that the people laughed at him with compassion. With leaps and long strides he rushed into "Jesús," and just as he reached the Assembly Hall, the lector was intoning his final invocations, a cry of jubilation and encouragement, the last words that all the students knew by heart and kept pronouncing syllable by syllable at the

los alumnos se sabían y las iban silabeando a la vez: *"Macti, o juvenes, hodie dignis proemia diribentur quos vero spes fefellerit animum ne despondeant, sumant vires, audeant aliquid dignum patria in annum proximum"*. Y alzóse el Rector para cerrar la ceremonia con su discurso de gracias, mientras la comunidad se quitaba los negros torreones de sus bonetes.

– Reverendísimo prelado y misionero, insigne...

– ¡*Victorinus, Victorinus* vuelve! – Y saltó la zumba de banco en banco. Los inspectores se atirantaban mirando a los que ya no podían contener en esas últimas horas escolares, y sus ojos de ascuas santísimas retaban al público, como si quisieran ponerlo de rodillas, con los brazos en cruz.

El doméstico escaló la tribuna estrujando el tapiz, dejándole las huellas de los establos, y se hincó de codos en los tisús de la mesa. El Padre Rector subía la frente, y su boca se plegaba con resignación. La comunidad esperaba compungida. Algunos profesores se volvieron hacia ese diálogo, tan poco afortunado, del que caían nombres de hostales, precios de alquiler, tres duros y medio, siete duros, mayoral tuerto...

Con la dulzura de las apariciones, presentóse un Hermano descolorido junto al trono de monseñor; hizo una mesura de rúbrica litúrgica, y se llevó al doméstico hasta la fila del señor Hugo, y allí, sonriéndole, lo empujó con buen puño por los hombros, sentándole a su lado. Entonces derramóse otra vez, clara y pulida, la palabra del Padre Rector:

– Reverendísimo prelado y misionero insigne.

3. Monseñor, su cortejo y despedidas

Se acabó la disciplina. Sala de visitas y canceles abiertas y joviales. Patio de la lección silencioso, aulas desamparadas. Algunas señoras se asomaban, y se sentaron y todo en las cátedras, contemplando el obrador de la sabiduría de sus hijos; los padres se vanagloriaban de aquellos ámbitos, como de una herencia de familia.

same time: "*Macti, o juvenes, hodie dignis proemia diribentur quos vero spes fefellerit animum ne despondeant, sumant vires, audeant aliquid dignum patria in annum proximum (Courage, oh youths, today the prizes will be distributed to those worthy of them, but let not the spirit flag for those whom hope deserted; let them recover their strength and dare to realize something for their native land in the following year.*" And the Rector rose to close the ceremony with his speech of thanks, while the Community removed the black fortified towers that were their caps.

"Most reverent prelate and illustrious missionary...."

"*Victorinus, Victorinus,* come back!" and the jest leapt from bench to bench. The priest monitors grew taut as they stared at those whom they could no longer restrain in those final scholastic hours, and their eyes, like the holiest of embers, challenged the public, as if they wanted to force it to its knees, with arms outstretched.

The manservant climbed up to the platform, crushing the carpeting, leaving his tracks from the stables upon it, and he sank down on his elbows on the lamé surface of the table. The Rector Father raised his forehead and his mouth was creased in resignation. The Community was waiting in sorrow. Several professors turned toward that very unfortunate dialogue, in which the names of inns, the rental prices, three-and-a-half *duros*, seven *duros*, a one-eyed coachman kept dropping....

With the sweetness of apparitions, a pale Brother made his appearance beside the monsignor's throne; he offered the customary liturgical reverence and led the servant off to the row where Señor Hugo was seated, and there he smiled at him and pushed him by the shoulders very hard with his fist, and sat him down beside him. It was then that the word of the Rector Father spread out once again, clear and polished:

"Most reverend prelate and illustrious missionary."[164]

3. Monsignor, his Cortege and Farewells

The scholastic period of rigorous discipline had ended. The visitors' lounge and the storm doors open and cheerful. The classrooms abandoned, the courtyard outside the instructional area wrapped in silence. Several ladies were looking in and even went so far as to sit down in professors' chairs, contemplating the workshop for their sons' acquisition of knowledge; the parents boasted of these surroundings as if they were a family legacy.

Elegancias, risas y galanías en los jardines. Las madres, las hermanas de los alumnos cortaban un heliotropo, un azahar, un clavel, y después de acariciarlo, se lo prendían en el pecho.

El Hermano portero balanceaba con lástima su cráneo redondo, con lástima de las flores. Sus ojos y su pensamiento buscaban el refugio de San Alonso Rodríguez, arca de su piedad y consuelo, y depósito de recados, de avisos, del bolsón de cuentas y de agallones para ensartar rosarios.

Los colegiales, al salir, le disparaban por la cerbatana de su diploma:

— ¡*Deo gratias, Deo gratias!*

El hermano abría despacito, queriendo retardar el instante de abrirles las puertas de la perdición.

— ¡Acuérdense del "Bendita sea tu pureza!"

— ¡No se apure, Hermano!

Le sonreían como a un santo de escaso poder; y el santo les veía alejarse con un celoso furor. Los grandes peligros de las vacaciones anidaban dentro de las familias: vestidos. olores, risas. Para todas era menester un internado perpetuo.

— ¡Qué solitos se van quedando ustedes!

Y el Padre Rector, el Padre Prefecto, el Padre Ministro inclinaban la cabeza con exquisito apenamiento, enviando su gravedad de estirpe a las corvas almenas de sus bonetes, mientras se sometían a los menudos cuidados de recibir y devolver parabienes, de dar consejos para la holganza veraniega, de refirir un viaje — ¡hacía ya mucho tiempo! — a la misma comarca de la familia que estaba despidiéndose — una anécdota, un episodio de aquel viaje que sobresaltaba a todos — . Pero venían más grupos; y el Rector, o el Prefecto, o el Ministro, abrían sus brazos, encogían sus hombros, elevaban los ojos significando que no se pertenecían; y después de unos pasitos hacia atrás destocándose brevemente, se apartaban muy súbitos. Las señoras adivinaban que el Padre Rector, o el Padre Ministro, o el Padre Prefecto se marchó tan rápido porque ya no podía contener su emoción, y se volvían a mirarle, diciéndose que al fin ellos eran tembién criaturas humanas.

El Padre Rector, el Padre Prefecto, el Padre Ministro quedaban enseguida rodeados, haciendo los mismos ademanes, las mismas exclamaciones, el mismo sorbo de risa, retirándose con los mismos melindres que antes, porque se emocionaban otra vez; y así iban pasando de despedida en despedida.

Displays of elegance, laughter, shows of gallantry in the gardens. The mothers, the sisters of the students would cut a heliotrope, an orange blossom, a carnation, and after caressing it, they would pin it to their bosom.

The Brother gatekeeper kept rocking his round skull with compassion, filled with pity for the flowers. His eyes and his thought sought the refuge of San Alonso Rodríguez, the coffer of his pity and consolation and a depository for messages, announcements, for the large bag of ordinary beads and large, wooden beads used to string rosaries.

As the schoolboys were leaving, they held their diplomas to their mouths like blowguns and fired off:

"*Deo gratias, Deo gratias (Thank God)!*"

The brother opened up ever so slowly, anxious to delay the moment for opening the gates of perdition for them.

"Remember the prayer 'Blessed be your purity!'"[165]

"Don't you worry, Brother!"

They smiled at him as if he were a saint with meager powers; and the saint was filled with a jealous furor as he watched them draw away. The great dangers of vacations nestled within the families: dresses, scents, laughter. For all of them a perpetual confined environment was necessary.

"How very much alone you will all be left!"

And the Rector Father, the Prefect Father, the Administrator Father bent their heads with exquisite sorrow, sending the solemnity of lineage to the curved merlons that were their caps, while they submitted to the petty concerns of receiving and returning their congratulations, giving advice concerning summer idleness, referring to a trip – oh, so very long ago! – to the same region where the family bidding them farewell happened to live – an anecdote, an episode during that trip that startled everyone. But more groups kept coming; and the Rector, or the Prefect or the Administrator opened their arms, shrugged their shoulders, lifted their eyes to signify that they did not belong there, and after a few short steps backward, curtly removed their caps and swiftly moved away. The ladies assumed that the Rector Father, or the Administrator Father or the Prefect Father had walked off so quickly because they could no longer contain their emotion, and so they turned to look at them, saying that, after all, they were also human beings.

The Rector Father, the Prefect Father, the Administrator Father were quickly surrounded, making the same gestures, the very same exclamations, swallowing their laughter in the same way, withdrawing with the same affectation as before, because they were overcome with emotion once again, and so they moved from one farewell to another.

Doncellitas, damiselas y mamás jóvenes se secreteaban, celebrando un donaire del Rector, o sofocándose, besándose, ciñéndose la cintura, dejándose su mano como una paloma en la cadera de una amiga. Atravesaban legos y fámulos atrajinados, y desde un cantón de la claustra, desde una revuelta se paraban mirándolas.

Entre los follajes y vides de la huerta de Casa aparecían y se ocultaban monseñor y su séquito: el P. Neira, de Física; el P. Martí, de Matemáticas; el P. Bo, de Filosofía, y a lo último, el familiar.

En sus penosas jornadas de vicario apostólico, monseñor había llegado a penetrar los secretos de los bosques, las alucinaciones de los desiertos y de las soledades talladas en las rocas, los vapores de las marismas, los alaridos de los vientos y de las bestias, la intención de los ojos y de los recónditos idiomas de los infieles; y ahora se quedaba sin entender al P. Neira, al P. Martí, al P. Bo. ¡Qué agonías por alcanzar un poco de las sutilezas de la plática en ese paseo académico al amor de los árboles!; paseo y gay-parlar que duraría hasta que se fuesen los colegiales; y después, a refectorio, al festín en su honor, con sexteto y discursos.

El catedrático de Matemáticas le hablaba bellamente de Euclides.

– ¡Ah, monseñor! ¡He tenido la gloria de sentir en mis manos la edición princeps!

– ¿Princeps? ¡Muy bien, muy bien!

– La de Ratdolt. En casa está la romana con los *Elementos,* la *Specularia* y *Perspectiva.* Se nos han perdido los *Fenómenos.*

– ¡Es una lástima! Los libros... Claro es que nosotros, allá en Oriente, ¿verdad? – Y volvíase a su doméstico y apretaba la imagen de Nuestra Señora.

El P. Neira dijo:

– También tenemos, monseñor, las *Vulgares:* la de José Zaragoza, 1673, y la inglesa de Roberto Simson, en cuarto, 1756...

Y añadió el P. Martí:

– No hemos podido encontrar las *Opticas,* traducción de Pedro Ambrosio Ondériz, con gráficos, de 1585. Pero poseemos, en manuscrito, el *Tratado de algunas dificultades de las definiciones de Euclides,* de Omar Ibu Ibrahim El Khayyâm.

Sweet young maidens, pretentious damsels and young mothers whispered confidentially to one another, praising a witticism on the part of the Rector, or blushing, kissing one another, encircling one another's waists, resting a dove-like hand on a friend's hip. Lay brothers and servants made their way through the crowd, loaded down with refreshments, and they stopped to look at all of them from a corner of the cloister, from a turn in a passageway.

Monsignor and his retinue appeared and then were hidden among the foliage and grapevines of the garden and orchard belonging to the House: Father Neira, in Physics, Father Martí, in Mathematics, Father Bo, in Philosophy, and last of all, the familiar.

In the course of the arduous journeys of his apostolic vicarship, monsignor had come to penetrate the secrets of the forests, the hallucinations of the deserts and the solitary confines carved into the rocks, the mists of the marshes, the howling of the winds and the beasts, the true significance of the eyes and the recondite languages of the infidels; and he now found himself unable to understand Father Neira, Father Martí, Father Bo. What an agony to undergo to grasp even a little of the subtleties of the conversation during that academic stroll in proximity to the trees; a stroll and high-flown talk that would last until the schoolboys left; and afterwards, to the refectory, for the banquet in his honor, with a sextet and speeches!

The professor of Mathematics was speaking to him beautifully about Euclid.

"Oh, monsignor! I've had the good fortune to hold the *princeps* edition in my hands!"

"The *princeps*? Very nice, very nice!"

"The one by Ratdolt.[166] The one in Latin with the *Elements*, the *Specularia* and the *Perspectiva* is in this House.[167] We seem to have lost the *Phaenomena*."[168]

"That's too bad! The books.... Of course, we out there in the Orient, you understand?" and he turned to his servant and squeezed the image of Our Lady.

Father Neira said:

"Monsignor, we also have the *Vernacular editions*: the one by José Zaragoza, 1673, and the one in English of Robert Simson, quarto, 1756...."[169]

And Father Martí added:

"We haven't been able to find the *Optics* in the translation by Pedro Ambrosio Ondériz, with diagrams, of 1585.[170] But we do possess a manuscript of the *Treatise on Some of the Difficulties of Euclid's Definitions* by Omar Ibu Ibrahim El Khayyâm."[171]

– ¡Qué memoria tienen ustedes! Claro es que nosotros allí, tan escondidos... Las costumbres de nuestros diocesanos... ¡Oriente, Oriente!

El matemático exclamó:

– Oriente, monseñor, Oriente nos traza una profunda proyección en nuestra disciplina. Damasco fue también un camino de luz científica para nosotros. He pensado que Oriente realzó las imaginaciones geométricas de nuestro sabio. Damasco guardó en sus blancuras la infancia de Euclides, prestándole la claridad de sus demostraciones.

Monseñor quedóse gratamente sorprendido.

– A un ingenio de Damasco se le debe un descubrimiento de nuevas proposiciones euclidianas...

– ¡Es muy meritorio!

– Y una completa traducción...

– ¿Y cómo se llama?

– ¡Otomán, monseñor!

– ¿Otomán? – Y se lo repitió a su lego – : ¿Otomán, Otomán?

– Se le cree del siglo X – apuntó el P. Neira.

Y el P. Martí, remendando los desafíos académicos de sus alumnos, se le precipitó:

– ¡Corrige, corrige! Del siglo XI.

¡Ah Santísimo Dios, del siglo diez y aunque fuese del once! – suspiraba monseñor Salom.

De la huerta pasaron al jardín de Lourdes; y cuando se internaban en la gruta, se levantó del banco del estanque un grupo de invitados a la comida de honor: el juez de Oleza, flaco y teñido, el comandante de la Zona, don Magín, el Padre Francisco de Agullent, guardián de los capuchinos de Oleza y docto botánico, corpulento, de barba bellida.

Sentóse monseñor, respirando con delicia el frescor de roca y agua, y dio su permiso para fumar.

Los tres jesuitas se grifaron ante esa condescendencia de santo de Oriente y decaído; los tres se irguieron, sintiéndose apartados con la pureza helada del agua de la gruta.

Menos ellos, todos encendieron los cigarros que les dio don Magín. El familiar se frotaba las manos como un jornalero, y decía:

– ¡Tuviese yo ahora mi narguile, monseñor!

El P. Francisco de Agullent recordó con júbilo de mocedad sus horas en el Sinaí, secando y coleccionando plantas olorosas. De trece hierbas

"What a memory you people have! Of course, we out there, so hidden away.... The customs of those in our diocese..., the Orient, the Orient!"

The mathematician exclaimed:

"The Orient, monsignor, the Orient draws a profound diffusion for us in our discipline. Damascus was also a road filled with scientific light for us. I've thought that the Orient enhanced the geometrical imaginations of our savant. Damascus sheltered Euclid's childhood in its white ambience and lent him the clarity of his proofs."

Monsignor was left pleasantly surprised.

"We owe a discovery of new Euclidian propositions to a genius from Damascus...."

"That's very praiseworthy!"

"And a complete translation...."

"And what is his name?"

"Otomán, monsignor!"

"Otomán?" And he repeated it to his lay brother: "Otomán, Otomán?"

"It is believed that he is from the Xth century." Father Neira pointed out.

And Father Martí, imitating the academic challenges of his students, pounced on him:

"Correction, correction! Of the XIth century."

"Oh, Holy God, whether the tenth century or even of the eleventh century!" Monsignor Salom sighed.

They moved from the orchard into the garden of Lourdes; and when they made their way into the grotto, a group of guests who had been invited to the dinner in his honor stood up from the bench next to the pool: the judge of Oleza, a skinny man with dyed hair; the commanding officer of the Recruitment Zone, Don Magín, Father Francisco de Agullent, superior of the Capuchin Order in Oleza[172] and a learned botanist, a corpulent man with a handsome beard.

Monsignor sat down, breathing in the coolness of rock and water with delight, and he granted everyone permission to smoke.

The three Jesuits were appalled by this indulgent attitude on the part of this crestfallen saint from the Orient; the three of them felt inflated with righteousness, feeling isolated with the icy purity of the water in the grotto.

Everyone but they lit up the cigarettes Don Magín gave them. The familiar rubbed his hands together like a day laborer and said:

"I wish I had my narghile pipe with me to smoke now, monsignor!"

Father Francisco de Agullent recalled his time spent in the Sinai with youthful jubilation, when he was drying and collecting fragrant plants. He was able

aglutinaba combustible para su pipa hasta que la caravana de San Juan de Acre le abastecía de tabaco confitado.

El P. Neira odiaba esas sensuales memorias, y murmuró con voz muy delgada:

– Repare, monseñor, en el P. Francisco de Agullent: tiene la barba roja, como Judas.

El capuchino tocó suavemente sus vellones bermejos, y dijo con simplicidad:

– ¿De veras, de veras que resulta comprobado que Judas fuese rojo? ¡Quién sabe, Dios mío! No hallé ningún texto que lo afirme. Ni si era flaco, ni menudo, ni orondo: ¡nada! Lo único cierto es que Judas perteneció a la compañía de Jesús.

El P. Martí, el P. Neira, el P. Bo se levantaron llevándose a monseñor, que distraído y dulce repetía:

– ¡Muy gratas personas, muy gratas personas!

En el patio enlosado, donde estaba el gimnasio y las mosteleras, los zapatones de monseñor retumbaban multiplicadamente.

Le convidaron a recogerse en la biblioteca, en el oratorio, en algún aposento, cátedra o sala donde preparar su discurso de gracias.

– ¿Mi discurso? ¡Un discurso! – Y de pronto anheló volver a la obscuridad de su vicariato; y colgó su mano cerrada en un hombro de su doméstico, preguntándole:

– ¿No tiene ya remedio lo del carruaje?

– ¡Señor, no tiene remedio!

– Un prelado – intervino el P. Neira – , cuando levanta su báculo para caminar, ve sometidas todas las voluntades y todas las sendas. Pero los caminos de monseñor se reúnen ahora en "Jesús" y en la diócesis olecense.

Llegó la Junta de los Luises con su caudillo, el P. Espiritual, pidiéndole a monseñor que no les desamparase. Plegóse el frontal de monseñor que no les desamparase. Plegóse el frontal de monseñor. Un congregante dijo:

– ¡Monseñor: no tenemos prudencia, la prudencia necesaria para las lides del mundo; pero tenemos caridad!

Y el P. Espiritual adelantóse como si se ofreciese al sacrificio:

– No la caridad inspirada por las tinieblas de las Logias, condenada en encíclicas y pastorales, sino la caridad contenida en el vaso ardiente de la fe.

Monseñor asentía y se maravillaba mucho.

to agglutinate combustible material for his pipe from thirteen herbs until the caravan from Saint John of Acre provided him with sweetened tobacco.

Father Neira hated those sensual memories and muttered in a very thin voice:

"Take a good look at Father Francisco de Agullent, monsignor: he has a red beard, just like Judas."

The Capuchin gently touched his vermilion fleece and simply said:

"Is that so, so they've really proved that Judas was red-headed? My God, who really knows! I could not find any text that affirms it. Nor if he were skinny, or small in frame, or pot-bellied: nothing at all! The only thing certain is that Judas belonged to the Society of Jesus!"

Father Martí, Father Neira, Father Bo all stood up and took Monsignor away while he kept repeating distractedly and sweetly:

"Very pleasant people, very pleasant people!"

In the courtyard paved with flagstones, where the gymnasium and the storage area stacked with sheaves of grain were located, monsignor's heavy shoes resounded, multiplied again and again.

They invited him to retire to the library, to the oratory, to some private chamber, classroom or parlor where he could prepare his speech of acknowledgement.

"My speech? A speech?" And he was suddenly anxious to return to the obscurity of his vicarage, and he draped his closed hand over his servant's shoulder and asked him:

"So there is no solution to the business of the carriage?"

"No, sir, there's no way to resolve it!"

"A prelate," Father Neira interceded, "when he raises his crozier to walk, sees every will and every path as being submissive to him. But monsignor's roads all join together now at 'Jesús' and in the diocese of Oleza."

The Council of the Marian Congregation of Luises arrived with their leader, the Spiritual Counselor Father, and they asked monsignor not to abandon them. Monsignor's forehead wrinkled. One of the congregants said:

"Monsignor: we do not have prudence, the prudence necessary for the struggles of the world; but we do have charity!"

And the Spiritual Counselor moved forward as if to offer himself for the sacrifice:

"Not the charity inspired by the darkness of Masonic Lodges,[173] condemned in encyclicals and in pastoral letters, but the charity contained in the fervent vessel of faith."

Monsignor assented and seemed quite astonished.

– No tenemos prudencia, ha confesado uno de mis congregantes más dilectos. Y yo digo – y el índice del Padre parecía llegar al cielo – . Y yo digo: no quiero ser prudente, sino ciego y arrojado. Es la hora evangélica de decir al Maestro: ¡Baje fuego y consuma Samaria! Que os lo diga, monseñor, el P. Bellod, el señor penitenciario, el caballero Galindo. Yo pido que baje fuego. Que mis superiores, si conviene, impongan el comedimiento, que me contengan y me someteré – . Y habiéndolo dicho, bajó su dedo y lo tendió a los suyos, dándoles la vez para que fuesen refiriendo las abominaciones.

Sentóse monseñor en un banco del claustro; delante, se doblaban los racimos de flores de las acacias, y a su vera le decían:

"... La tolerancia de los de arriba trajo el dolor de los fuertes, la vacilación de los tibios, la vanagloria de los flacos." (Frases del señor penitenciario.)

Crónica de *Alba Longa*:

Se había fundado el "Recreo Benéfico", que celebraba veladas, comedias, tómbolas, coros, jiras... Algunos sacerdotes apadrinaban los fines de la fundación: remediar a los perjudicados en las riadas, llevar la enseñanza y la salud a los críos del arrabal de San Ginés, socorrer a los enfermos y desvalidos... Todo a costa de júbilos y licencias, de perdición y de lágrimas. De lágrimas, porque había maridos liberales que obligaban a sus mujeres a participar de esas fiestas nefandas, prohibidas por su confesor de "Jesús"; y había hermanas y novias, vírgenes locas, aborrecidas y repudiadas por sus hermanos y prometidos.

"La sensualidad, los rencores, las discordias desanillaban sus sierpes en las familias de Oleza." (De un luis.)

Todos se volvían a monseñor. Volaban los palomos por el huerto claustral; bullían los gorriones en los follajes y cornisas. Y él recordaba sus viajes por la escondida sede; su descanso en el monasterio de San Sabas; la verja erizada de cráneos amarillos de mártires; los monjes esparciendo grano en las terrazas donde acuden las palomas descendientes de las primeras palomas domésticas que trajo Herodes al "país del Señor"; encima de los muros suben las rocas verticales, esponjas ardientes de sol que maduran precozmente los higos; la palmera del fundador, la que lleva dátiles sin hueso, de carne rugosa de azúcar; la cueva donde meditaba Sabas y a su lado jadeaba un viejo león

"We do not have prudence, one of my most beloved congregants has confessed. And I say," and the Father's index finger seemed to reach up toward heaven. "And I say: I do not want to be prudent, but rather blind and bold. It is the evangelical moment to say to the Master: Bring down fire and let Samaria be consumed! Oleza is Samaria. Let Father Bellod, the canon-penitentiary, the honorable Señor Galindo tell you, Monsignor. I ask for fire to be brought down. Let my superiors, if they see fit to do so, impose accommodation, let them restrain me and I will submit." And having said this, he lowered his finger and extended it toward his people, giving them the opportunity to go on reporting the abominations.

Monsignor sat down on a bench in the cloister; in front of him, the clusters of blossoms on the acacias were bending over, while those beside him were saying:

"...The tolerance of those at the top brought about the affliction of the strong, the vacillation of the lukewarm, the vainglory of the weak." (Words of the canon-penitentiary.) The Chronicle of Alba-Longa: The "Benevolent Recreational Association" had been founded, and it presented evening entertainments, plays, *tombolas*, choruses and picnics.... A number of priests supported the goals of the foundation: offering help to those who were victims of floods, bringing instruction and better conditions of health to the small children of the outlying district of San Ginés, succoring the sick and the destitute.... All this at the cost of encouraging merriment and licentious behavior, of perdition and tears. Of tears, because there were liberal-minded husbands who obliged their wives to participate in those nefarious festivities that were prohibited by their confessor at "Jesús;" and there were sisters and sweethearts, virginal young women all but driven mad, detested and repudiated by their brothers and their fiancés.

"Sensuality, rancor, discord uncoiled like serpents among the families of Oleza." (From one of the Confraternity of Luises.)

They all turned toward monsignor. Ringdoves were flying above the cloister garden; sparrows were swarming in the foliage and in the cornices. And he remembered his journeys through the isolated see; his stopover at the monastery of Saint Sabas;[174] the grating bristling with the yellowed skulls of martyrs; the monks scattering grain along the terraces where the doves gather, doves that are descended from the first domestic doves that Herod brought to the "land of the Lord";[175] vertical rocks rise above the walls, fiery sponges of sunlight ripening the figs prematurely; the founder's date palm, the one that bears dates without pits, with a wrinkled, sugary flesh; the cave where Sabas meditated with an old lion panting at his side, following him

que le seguía por el huerto y por los caminos, meneando la cola, lamiéndole sus manos como un lebrel! ...Y fueron entornándose los ojos del obispo, y la imagencita de la Virgen rodó sonoramente por las losas.

Muchas manos quisieron recogerla, pero a todas pudo el hidalgo de Aspe, que se la entregó de rodillas. De hinojos se puso también su mujer, mujer garrida con hermoso jubón, sayas muy anchas, pañuelo de cachemira, arracadas de almendrillas, el cabello negro trenzado en la nuca, y con raya luciente partiendo la crencha tirante.

El apóstol les bendijo. En aquel momento se detuvo la familia de Lóriz, acompañada por el P. Rector. El de Aspe le besó dos o tres veces la diestra.

– ¡Todo muy bien, P. Rector, diga que sí, todo muy bien! ¿Pero quiere que le hable con franqueza?

Su reverencia volvióse hacia los Lóriz, elevando la mirada, encogiendo sus hombros y mirándole como si dijese: ¡Hábleme con franqueza, si no hay otro remedio; pero me da lo mismo!

– Pues nos ha faltado nuestro prelado. ¡Qué lástima!

– ¡Felices vacaciones! – le interrumpió el jesuita, y llevóse dos dedos al bonete, reduciendo la cortesía.

Iba delante Máximo con doña Purita. Parecía imcreíble que esta mujer no se sintiese rechazada por todo los corazones de "Jesús". Era la primera en asistir a las fiestas y comedias benéficas, y en un reciente ensayo no bajó de las tablas por la gradilla, sino de los brazos del galán y le soltó su risa en medio de la boca, como si lo rociase de besos. Se sabía en "Jesús". Y el Rector dolióse con los condes de la perniciosa generosidad en las amistades, y Purita le atendía, brillándole en la mirada una lucecita de insolencia.

– Quiera Dios que acertemos en nuestro designio. Pero, es verdad: ¡qué lástima! – según dijo el buen señor de Aspe – . Yo me pregunto si por mi sangre aragonesa no seré demasiado súbito. Nos faltó el prelado... ¡Siento la herida en medio de mi alma, y en mi herida deben sentirse todos heridos!

Lóriz hizo una grave mesura que afirmaba la solidaria herida en nombre de toda una raza; pero no le inquietaban las palabras del P. Rector, y casi no las entendía ni las atendía. Ligero y adobado, se complacía en el contorno de doña Purita. Esta bella doncellona de pueblo le inquietaba ya como una endiablada mujer del gran mundo.

through the garden and along the roads, wagging its tail, licking his hands like a whippet....[176] And the bishop's eyes started to partly close and the tiny image of the Virgin rolled noisily over the flagstones.

Many hands tried to pick it up, but the *hidalgo* from Aspe beat them all to it, and he handed it over to him on his knees. His wife also got to her knees, a good-looking woman in a lovely jerkin, very ample skirts, a cashmere scarf, almond-shaped pendant earrings, black hair braided in back of the neck and a gleaming part dividing the tightly-combed hair on either side.

The apostle blessed them. At that very moment the Lóriz family stopped by, accompanied by the Rector Father. The man from Aspe kissed his right hand two or three times.

"Everything just right, Rector Father, you must agree, everything just right! But do you want me to speak frankly?"

His Reverence turned toward the Lórizes, raised his eyes, shrugged his shoulders and regarded him as if to say: "Speak to me frankly, if there is no other way, but it's all the same to me!"

"Well, we were missing our prelate. What a pity!"

"Have a pleasant vacation!" the Jesuit interrupted him and raised two fingers to his cap, reducing the degree of courtesy.

Máximo was walking in front with Doña Purita. It seemed incredible that this woman should not feel rejected by all hearts at "Jesús." She was the first one to attend the charity festivities and plays, and at a recent rehearsal, she didn't come down from the stage by the steps, but in the arms of the leading man, and she sent forth her laughter into the middle of his mouth, as if she were spraying him with kisses. This was well known at "Jesús." And the Rector spoke with regret to the count and the countess about the pernicious generosity in friendships, and Purita took notice of what he was saying with a subtle gleam of insolence shining in her glance.

"God grant that we achieve our purpose. But it is true: what a pity! – according to what the good gentleman from Aspe said. I wonder if I may not be too impetuous because of my Aragonese blood. We missed the prelate.... I feel his wound to the very depths of my soul, and everyone ought to feel wounded within my wound!"

Lóriz bowed very deeply in respect to affirm the solidarity of his wound in the name of the entire race; but the Rector Father's words did not disturb him, and he barely understood them or paid any attention to them. Fickle and smartly dressed as he was, he took pleasure in being around Doña Purita. This beautiful, small-town maiden lady disturbed him now as if she were a devilish woman of high society.

Infantil y graciosa, prometió la condesa, en nombre del bachiller su hijo, regalar al colegio el magnífico acuarium de peces del Vaticano, del Nilo y del Jordán. Lo aceptó el Rector por el gabinete de Historia Natural. Pero la condenación que disparaban los arcos de sus gafas deshizo la gratitud. Purita se reía deliciosamente con don Roger y el señor Hugo. Don Roger la miraba embelesado. El señor Hugo caracoleaba con todas sus viejas bizarrías de circo.

El P. Prefecto los veía desde la sombra del séptimo pilar del claustro. Y ya no fue menester que el P. Rector les viese.

También lo vio todo la señorita Elvira Galindo que pasaba, y tuvo bascas de pureza.

4. Pablo, Elvira, don Álvaro

Las ventanas del salón de estudio, de par en par. Azul de mediodía estremecido y maduro de azul; anchura cortada por la rotonda de la enfermería; la torrecilla y las dos setas de cobre del reloj con sus mazuelos, que cada cuarto de hora se apartan tirantemente y tocan lo mismo que en los días angostos, lo mismo que siempre. Un trozo de monte plantado de viña; los naranjos, los olmos, la noria y las tapias de casa; la llanada de las huertas de Oleza, una curva del río; sierras finas, de color caliente... Todo eso fue para Pablo la promesa de una felicidad, la lejanía, el principio de un mundo de cuento; y ahora, por haber terminado el curso y seguir delante de su pupitre, todo aquello era lo de todos los días, era paisaje escolar, la renovada conciencia del año de clausura.

Quedaban en el salón nueve colegiales. En la tarima, un Hermano con gafas negras, las gafas del disimulo de todo el año, repasaba una *Lectura Popular*. ¡La *Lectura Popular*, con su olor de imprenta húmeda; el periódico que les repartía el cuestor de estudios a la hora en que comenzaban a subir del patio los olores de cocina! Y dentro del ruido de aquellas fojas entre los dedos del Hermano se les perdía la sensación del Corpus. Se recodaban en sus pupitres sin asignaturas, mirándose su uniforme de paño recio y de oro escomido, con un cansacio de jornada ya cumplida. Todo esto, todo eso era

The countess, childish and charming, promised that she would present her magnificent aquarium of fish from the Vatican, the Nile and the Jordan as a gift to the school in the name of her son, the graduate. The Rector accepted it on behalf of the Natural History museum. But the condemnation discharged by the bows of his spectacles undid the gratitude. Purita was laughing delightedly with Don Roger and Señor Hugo. Don Roger kept looking at her in fascination. Señor Hugo kept caracoling around her with all his old circus gallantry.

The Prefect Father saw them from the shade of the seventh pillar of the cloister. And it was no longer necessary for the Rector Father to see them.

Señorita Elvira Galindo also saw it all as she passed by and she felt almost nauseous with purity.

4. Pablo, Elvira, Don Álvaro

The windows in the study hall, wide open. Midday blue trembling and ripe with blue; the wide open space rent by the rotunda of the infirmary; the small tower and the two copper hands of the clock with its little hammers, which tautly draw apart every quarter hour and chime just as they do on days of mourning, just as they always do. A patch of mountain planted with vineyards; orange trees, elms, the draw well and the walls around the House; the flat plain of the cultivated gardens of Oleza, a bend in the river; delicate mountain ranges, warm in color.... For Pablo, all that was the promise of happiness, the far off, the beginning of a storybook world; and now, because the school term had ended and the fact that he still remained there in front of his desk, all that was like every other day, a school landscape, the renewed awareness of the year of confinement.

Nine schoolboys remained in the room.[177] A Brother wearing black spectacles, the glasses representing the dissimulation of the entire year, was on the platform leafing through a copy of *Popular Reading*.[178] *Popular Reading* with its smell of damp newsprint; this was the newspaper that the student quaestor in charge of study materials distributed to them at the very moment when the aromas from the kitchen were just beginning to rise up from the courtyard! And the very sensation of Corpus Christi was lost for them within the sound of the sheets of paper between the Brother's fingers. They leaned their elbows on their desks, now devoid of course assignments, looking at themselves in their rough-textured woolen uniforms with worn-

lo mismo que si se sentaran en un banco de andén de estación para esperar después de llegar. Y se volvían de pronto a la puerta de la sala. Saludos de los que se iban; jovialidad de Reverendos Padres; y esos Reverendos Padres, si se asomaban, recuperaban la cautela y el canon de la plena observancia.

Pablo se precipitó en el pasillo. Tía Elvira le llamaba desde el fondo moviendo un mitón vacío.

¡No te canses mirando a lo lejos, que no viene nadie más por ti!

– ¿Y a mi madre?

– ¡La pobre no puede soportar mis trajines! Pero, anda, hijo, y despídete y vámonos, que estoy sola para todo.

La obedeció Pablo; y luego vino arrancándose las insignias y medallas y estrujando su gloria dentro del bolsillo de su casaquín. Sus labios se apretaban en una curva de sollozo y de ímpetu contenidos.

Cuando salieron a la escalera apareció en el quicio de la sala de recreación de la Comunidad un grupo de sacerdotes y de seglares eminentes. Empujó tía Elvira al sobrino, y Pablo inclinóse y besó la mano de su padre.

Tierra, calles, sol de Oleza. Oleza ya suya del todo, sin que la viese ni la sintiese desde "Jesús" ni en los paseos en ternas. Oleza, olorosa de ramajes para la procesión; vaho de pastelerías y de frutas de Corpus; aleteo de cobertores, aire de verano; goce de lo suyo, de lo suyo verdaderamente poseído, con perfume de los primeros jazmines, de canela y de ponciles. Todo el pueblo, todos los árboles, todas las gentes parecía que perteneciesen a la heredad de Nuestro Padre; todo le acogía como si él volviese de profundas distancias.

Y entró en su portal llamando a su madre. Gritaba para remover el viejo silencio de su casa entornada; y grítaba para oír su grito, grito único, sin el plural del griterío de los patios escolares. Quiso tía Elvira impedir tanto alboroto, y el bachiller se le escapó al dormitorio de su madre. Abrió los maderos y celosías y subióse al lecho de la enferma. Las blancas paredes y

out gold trimming, with the weariness of a journey now completed. All this, all this was just the same as if they were seated on a bench on the platform of a train station, having just arrived and still having to wait. And they suddenly turned toward the door to the room. Best wishes from those who were departing; the joviality of the Reverend Fathers; and those Reverend Fathers, if they did happen to look in on them, recovered their caution and the canon of strict plenary observance.

Pablo rushed into the corridor. Aunt Elvira was calling to him from the far end, moving an empty fingerless glove back and forth.

"Don't wear yourself out looking further down, because nobody else is coming for you!"

"How about my mother?"

"The poor thing can't put up with my running back and forth! But, come on, my boy, and say goodbye to everyone and let's be on our way, because I am alone and have to do everything by myself."

Pablo obeyed her; and then he came after her, pulling off the insignia and religious medals and squeezing the cream tart inside the pocket of his short cassock. His lips were clenched into a curve of restrained sobbing and impetuosity.

When they went out to the stairway, a group of priests and prominent laymen appeared in the doorway of the Community recreation hall. Aunt Elvira pushed her nephew forward and Pablo bent over, and kissed his father's hand.

Earth, streets, sun of Oleza. Oleza now completely his, without his having to see it or feel its presence from "Jesús," nor during their supervised walks in groups of three. Oleza, fragrant with clusters of branches for the procession; the aromas of the pastries and fruits of Corpus Christi; the fluttering of the stall coverings, the air of summer; the enjoyment of what was his, truly possessed by him, with the perfume of the first jasmine, cinnamon and citrons. The whole town, all the trees, all the people seemed to belong to the ancestral estate of Our Father; everything welcomed him, as if he were returning from immense distances.

And he came into the entryway to his house calling to his mother. He was shouting so that he could stir the long-standing silence of his half-closed house, and he was shouting in order to hear his shout, his very own shout, without the collectivity of the shouting in the courtyards at school. Aunt Elvira tried to restrain all that uproar and the baccalaureate escaped from her and rushed to his mother's bedroom. He opened the shutters and the blinds and climbed up onto the bed of the ailing woman. The white walls and curtains grew bright with

cortinas se encendieron de día grande, y en las almohadas se volcó un trigal de trenzas y de sol. El humo azul del braserillo de espliegos se apretaba en los rincones de la alcoba.

    – ¡Levántate para comer conmigo!

    – ¡Conmigo y con tu padre también!

    – Mi padre? ¡Mi padre come hoy con monseñor y todos ésos!

    – ¡Ay, hijo, y qué bien aprendiste la graciosa crianza del niño de Lóriz! – Y tía Elvira les apartó, porque se sonrojaba de verlos abrazados y tendidos bajo los velos de la cama de su hermano.

    Paulina pidió sus ropas, y el hijo se levantó brincando y aplaudiendo.

    – ¡Así quieres a tu madre! – clamó tía Elvira – . ¿Y tú, te vestirás sin saberlo Álvaro? ¿Te vestirás delante de tu hijo?

    La enferma se recostó sumisa y, sonriendo, le dijo a Pablo que abriese las vidrieras del comedor para verle y tenerle cerca mientras comían. Se resignó él, y sentóse vestido de uniforme.

    Tía Elvira le trajo una blusa de colegio.

    – ¿Ésa?

    Había de ser su madre quien le diese y le vistiese las ropas suyas, las de hijo; porque para enfundarse con delantal de internado, bien estaba con su levita, su fajín y hasta con gorra. Prefería creerse del todo en "Jesús" y que aún hubiera de venir el júbilo de la primera comida de vacaciones. Y no comer con tía Elvira nada más. ¡Sopa de puchero de enfermo, y casí a oscuras! ¡Más claridad había en el refectorio!

    – ¿Ropas tuyas, preparadas por tu madre para ti? ¡No tengo su primor; pero tú tienes blusa que ponerte porque yo me cuidé de aviártela!

    – ¿Ésa? ¿La vieja, con volantes de añadidos? ¡Por ella se me rieron en clase, y yo lloré, y el P. Neira, comiéndose su risa, nos recordaba: "los que lloran serán consolados; los que se humillan serán ensalzados!" En recreo me llamó el Hermano Buades; estuvo tocando los remiendos, y decía: "¡Blusa

the fullness of the daylight and a veritable wheat field of tresses and sunlight poured out onto the pillows. The blue smoke from a small lavender-filled brazier gathered in the corners of the bedroom.

"Get up so that you can eat with me!"

"With you and with your father too!"

"My father? My father is eating today with monsignor and all those other people!"

"Oh, my child, how well you've learned all those charming manners of the Lóriz boy!" And Aunt Elvira separated them because she was embarrassed to see them embracing as they lay stretched out under the curtains of her brother's bed.

Paulina asked for her clothes and her son got up with a jump and applauded.

"So that's how you love your mother!" Aunt Elvira cried out. "And you, you're going to get dressed without Álvaro's knowing about it? You're going to get dressed in front of your son?"

The ailing woman lay down again submissively and smiled as she told Pablo to open the wide windows in the dining room so that she could see him and have him close to her while they were eating. He resigned himself to this and sat down dressed in his uniform.

Aunt Elvira brought him a school blouse.

"That one?"

It should have been his mother who gave him his own clothes and dressed him with them, in the clothes of a son; because if he were going to wrap himself up in a boarding student's apron, he would do just as well in his frock coat, his sash and even with his cap. He preferred to consider himself completely at "Jesús," and that the joy of the first vacation meal was yet to come. And not have to eat with Aunt Elvira any more. A plain stew without vegetables like they feed the sick, and in virtual darkness! It was even brighter in the refectory!

"Your own clothes, prepared by your mother just for you? I don't have her skill; but you do have a blouse to put on because I took the trouble to mend it for you!"

"That one? The old one with the flounces sewed on? They laughed at me in class on account of it and I started to cry, and Father Neira suppressed his laughter and reminded us: 'those who weep will be consoled; those who humble themselves will be exalted!'[179] During recreation, Brother Buades called me over; he started touching the mended part and said: 'A blouse that

crecedera! ¡Tira nueva en lienzo viejo, hasta en los Evangelios se prohibe!"
¡Entonces yo me la desgarré!

– ¡No la rasgarías como yo! – Y tía Elvira se la arrebató; sus dedos
crujieron como un cardizal, y sus lágrimas gotearon el mantel.

Pablo pidió los fruteros, y desbordándole las manos de cerezas, volvióse
al dormitorio.

– ¡Aunque sea pecado jurar, yo te juro que no cometeré nunca la simpleza
de llorar delante de ti!

La congoja rompía las palabras de tía Elvira.

Pablo acostóse al lado de su madre. Desde allí miraba los álamos y
salgueros del río, la planicie hortelana con las coordinaciones de los verdes
jugosos; los campos de siega en un vaho azul traspasado por una palmera,
por un ciprés, y en la cerámica rosada de una colina florecía el lirio de un
santuario.

– Ya tengo tu olor – gritaba Pablo jugando con las trenzas de su madre
– . Los demás huelen a vestidos, a gente y a olores. ¡Tú sola, tú nada más,
hueles a tí!

Ella se lo atrajo más; le puso la cabeza en su brazo desnudo y le sonrió.

– Siendo como eres, ¿por qué has de hacer sufrir? ¡Tía Elvira ha
llorado!

– Quiero más a don Amancio que a ella.

– ¡Quiérela por tu padre!

– ¿Por mi padre? Y además, es que no te quiere; no nos quiere a nadie.
¡En "Jesús", todos los días, menos los jueves, cocido! ¡Pues hoy, jueves,
Corpus, primera comida de vacaciones, cocido también en mi casa!

– ¡Desde mañana yo seré tu cocinera, y tú me darás de salario el ser
dulce para todos, y habrá siempre alegría en esta casa!

– ¿Alegría en esta casa, que si no fuera por ti, yo...?

– Por mí y por tu padre, Pablo, por tu padre...

– ¿Mi padre?

– ¡Tu padre, tu padre! – Y Paulina incorporóse angustiada y miraba con
ansiedad la frente ceñuda y pálida y los ojos magníficos y adustos de su
hijo.

Poco a poco se le suavizó la faz. En el silencio semejaba verse el clamor
del río enrollándose frescamente en la alcoba como un viejo mastín de la
casa.

allows for growth! A new strip of cloth on old linen, that's even forbidden in the Scriptures!'[180] That's when I tore it off!"

"You wouldn't tear it off like I would!" And Aunt Elvira snatched it away from him; her fingers crackled like a field full of thistles and her tears dropped onto the tablecloth.

Pablo asked for the fruit bowls and returned to the bedroom with his hands overflowing with cherries.

"Even though it may be a sin to swear, I swear to you that I will not commit so foolish an act as to cry in front of you!"

Anguish cracked Aunt Elvira's words.

Pablo lay down beside his mother. From there he could look at the poplars and willows near the river, at the flatness of the cultivated plain with neatly arranged patterns of luscious green; the harvested fields in a blue haze, pierced through by a date palm, by a cypress, and an iris-shaped sanctuary blossoming on the rose-colored ceramic shape of a hillside.

"I now have your fragrance," Pablo shouted as he played with his mother's tresses. "The others smell of clothing, of people and aromas. You alone, you and nobody else, smell of yourself!"

She pulled him closer; she put his head on her bare arm and smiled at him.

"Being like you are, why do you make others suffer? Aunt Elvira has been crying!"

"I love Don Amancio more than I do her."

"Love her for your father's sake!"

"For my father's sake? And besides, the fact is she doesn't love you; she doesn't love anyone. At 'Jesús,' every day but Thursday, stew! Well, today, Thursday, Corpus Christi, my first meal of vacation, also stew, in my own house too!"

"Starting tomorrow I will be your cook, and you will repay me by being sweet to everybody, and there will always be happiness in this house!"

"Happiness in this house; do you know that if it weren't for your sake, I...?"

"For my sake and for your father's, Pablo, for your father's...."

"My father?"

"Your father, your father!" And Paulina sat up in anguish as she anxiously looked at her son's frowning, pale forehead and the magnificent, sullen eyes of her son.

Little by little his features softened. In the silence, seeing the clamor of the river refreshingly winding the bedroom was similar to an old house mastiff.

– Esta noche lo sentiré desde mi cuarto, lo mismo que cuando le tenía miedo. ¿Tú no te acuerdas? Tú hablabas del río como de un abuelo que cantaba para que todos los niños se durmiesen temprano; y yo me dormía viéndole y queriéndole...

Tronó una puerta al cerrarse por el vendaval de un codazo de la señorita de Gandía. Pablo se crispó de rabia.

– ¡He sentido el golpe en las sienes!... Pues yo se lo dije una noche a ella, a tía Elvira, y me dijo que lo tuyo era todo embuste; que el río retumbaba tanto de noche porque salían a las orillas las ánimas en pena. ¡Yo no podía dormirme; me persignaba y lloraba, y las ánimas me tocaban, gordas y mojadas como sapos!

Paulina le abrazó. La madre y el hijo se fueron quedando dormidos bajo la evocación de aquellos años, en una quietud profunda y clara como una bóveda de firmamento; y la tarde de junio les envolvía de suavidad; la tarde, allí tan parada encima de la vega, tenía la pureza y la fragilidad de un vidrio sagrado, y a veces, se rompía de aleteos de campanas y músicas del Corpus. Y en la tarde tan ancha se traslucía otra tarde muy remota, ciega de nieblas que iban creciendo del río. Campanas de Todos Santos. Paulina y su hijo caminaban abriendo el humo de la lluvia; y al pasar por el huerto de palacio se arrodillaron para recíbir la piedad de una mano que les bendecía y de unos ojos tristes que les acompañaron desde lejos.

De pronto, Paulina se revolvió sobresaltada, y sus latidos le resonaron en todo el dormitorio.

Venía la voz del esposo:

– ¡Pablo, Pablo!

El hijo se le apretó más, mirando a lo profundo de la casa, ya obscura.

– ¡Pablo!

Apareció el padre, y detrás la silueta de su hermana.

– ¡Pídele perdón a tía Elvira!

Obedeció Pablo, humillándose sin mirarles.

– ¡Pablo, bésala!

Tía Elvira puso su pómulo grietoso en la boca de Pablo.

Y él acercóse, y no la besó.

– ¡Bésala! – Y temblaba de imperio la cabeza de don Álvaro.

Los labios de Pablo palpitaban por el ímpetu de un sollozo mordido; y

"I will hear it from my room tonight, just like when I used to be afraid of it. Don't you remember? You used to talk about the river as if it were a grandfather who would sing so that all the children would fall asleep early; and I used to fall asleep seeing him and loving him...."

A door thundered as it was closed by the violent gust of a shove by the señorita from Gandía's elbow. Pablo was contorted with rage.

"I felt the blow in my temples!... Well I told Aunt Elvira all about it one night and she told me that everything you said was a lie, that the river thundered like that at night because the souls in Purgatory came out onto the banks. I couldn't fall asleep; I made the sign of the cross and I cried and the souls, fat and wet like toads, kept touching me!"

Paulina embraced him. Mother and son started falling asleep beneath the evocation of those years, in a deep, bright stillness like a vault of the firmament; and the June afternoon wrapped them in its gentleness; the afternoon, so motionless out there above the plain, had the purity and fragility of a sacred stained-glass window, and it would occasionally break out with the fluttering of church bells and the music of Corpus Christi. And another afternoon, one very remote, blind with mists rising up from the river, showed itself through the full amplitude of the afternoon. The bells of All Saints' Day. Paulina and her son were walking along, opening up the mist from the rain; and as they passed the Palace garden, they kneeled down to receive the pity of a hand that blessed them and of saddened eyes that accompanied them from a distance.

Paulina suddenly turned around startled, and the beating of her heart resounded all through the bedroom.

Her husband's voice came to her:

"Pablo, Pablo!"

Her son pressed closer to her, staring into the depths of the house that was now dark.

"Pablo!"

His father appeared with his sister's silhouette behind him.

"Ask Aunt Elvira to forgive you!"

Pablo obeyed, humbling himself without looking at them.

"Kiss her, Pablo!"

Aunt Elvira put her chapped cheek against Pablo's mouth.

And he moved closer to her, but he didn't kiss her.

"Kiss her!" And Don Álvaro's head trembled with authority.

Pablo's lips were palpitating with the urgency of a choked sob, and his

el padre agarró la nuca del hijo, y lo empujó apretándolo en la mejilla de su hermana.

Pablo sintió el hueso ardiente de tía Elvira. Y no la besó.

Los ojos de don Álvaro daban el parpadeo de las ascuas. Y esos ojos le acechaban como la tarde del Jueves Santo, en que la boca del hijo sangró hendida por los pies morados del Señor. Paulina dio un grito de locura. ¡Sangre por el Señor, la ofrecía como martirio suyo; pero sangre de herida abierta por el hueso de aquella mujer la llagaría y marcaría siempre su vida! Y saltó desnuda del lecho, amparando al hijo. Pablo levantó su frente entre los brazos de la madre, y gimió desesperado:

– ¡No puedo, y no la beso!

Paulina le mojaba con su boca en medio de los ojos, queriendo derretirle el pliegue de dureza, el mismo surco de la frente de piedra de don Álvaro.

Y como si estuviese muy remota, muy honda, percibióse la voz del padre:

– ¡No puede! – Y se estrujó su barba entre sus manos pálidas de santo.

5. Final de Corpus

Fervorines. *Tantum Ergo*. Bendición y reserva. Solos del nuevo Himno eucarístico del Padre Folguerol! ... Jornada gloriosa para don Roger. El señor Hugo le felicitó, cogiéndole atléticamente de las muñecas:

– ¡Y ahora, un buen verano! – Y lo soltó con elegancia, como si lo dejara caer a la pista desde un trapecio.

El Padre Prefecto les aguardaba en la puerta del coro; y de sus manos recibieron las cesantías de sus cátedras.

– ¿Cesantes? ¿Y en vacaciones y para siempre? – exhaló el solfista, con voz ténue por primera vez en su laringe.

– ¡Quizá, sí!

– ¡Pero Padre Prefecto!...

El Padre Prefecto suspiró un "¡Aaah!" pequeñito, y se les apartó rápidamente.

father grabbed his son by the back of the neck and squeezed him tightly as he pushed him against his sister's cheek.

Pablo could feel the feverish bone on Aunt Elvira's face. And he didn't kiss her.

Don Álvaro's eyes blinked like burning embers. And those eyes kept watching him just as they had on the afternoon of Holy Thursday, when the son's mouth bled after it was split by the purple feet of the Lord. Paulina screamed out frenziedly. Blood on account of the Lord, he could offer that as his own kind of martyrdom; but blood from an open cut made by the bony cheek of that woman would injure him and leave a mark upon his life forever! And she jumped up from the bed naked in order to protect her son. Pablo raised his forehead between his mother's arms and moaned in desperation:

"I can't; I won't kiss her!"

Paulina moistened the space between his eyes with her mouth as she tried to melt away the severe crease there, the very same wrinkle as on the stone-like forehead of Don Álvaro.

And the father's voice could be detected, seeming very remote, very deep:

"He can't!" And he squeezed his beard between his pale, saintly hands.

5. The End of Corpus Christi

Short prayers. *Tantum Ergo*. The benediction and the Preservation of the Blessed Sacrament. Solos for the new Eucharistic Hymn of Father Folguerol....[181] A glorious day's accomplishment for Don Roger. Señor Hugo congratulated him, seizing him athletically by the wrists:

"And now, a good summer to you!" And he released him elegantly, as if he were letting him fall to the circus ring from a trapeze.

The Prefect Father was waiting for them at the doorway to the choir loft, and they received the dismissals from their teaching posts from his hands.

"Dismissed? And on vacation and forever?" the sol-faist teacher breathed heavily with a delicate voice in his larynx for the first time.

"Perhaps, yes!"

"But Prefect Father!..."

The Prefect Father sighed a very muted "Oooh!" and quickly withdrew from them.

Don Roger y el Sr. Hugo, que entraban juntos en "Jesús" todos los días, a las diez y media, salieron también juntos esa tarde. En el pórtico se pararon, mirando la hornacina donde está el Señor con su cayada de caminante. ¡Qué hermosura fuera vivir como el Señor, sin más impedimenta que un cayado!

Campaneo de las parroquias, de los monasterios, de la catedral, música de la procesión; estampidos ardientes del "Sacre", el dragoncillo de San Ginés atorado de pólvora gorda; aliento de los jardines y de la vega de junio... Y al bajar los escalones creyeron descender a una ciudad torva y desconocida.

Lo primero que dijo el Sr. Hugo lo pronunció en su lengua natal. Plegó los brazos y se tocó los biceps. ¡Para qué los quería en Oleza! Luego, como casi todas las criaturas, necesitó que alguien tuviese la culpa de su desgracia.

– ¡Ha sido por doña Purita; por la amistad de doña Purita!

¿No bendecían los ancianos de Troya la belleza de Elena, aunque les trajese la ruina de sus hogares, el incendio y la muerte? Así, don Roger, que al lado de la queja y de la acusación del Sr. Hugo, puso el elogio a la beldad menospreciando las pesadumbres del mundo:

– ¡Qué guapa estaba hoy! ¡Dios la bendiga!

Después, de su pecho de cantor, precisamente del suyo, tan apacible y no del arrogante gimnasta, salió la nota viril:

– ¡Qué hacemos! ¡Es menester luchar!

– ¿Luchar? ¡Muy bravo, cuando a los sesenta y tres años se tiene más voz que a los veintitrés!

Don Roger llevóse sus dedos enguantados al garguero. Hasta en silencio se presentía y casi se palpaba la fortaleza de su órgano. Pero fue generoso, y fue justo, diciendo:

– ¿Y yo, yo qué hago aquí con tanta voz cerrándome "Jesús" sus puertas?

– ¿Nos ha perdido la amistad de doña Purita? ¡Vayamos a ella y luchemos!

Y el Sr. Hugo tendía bizarramente su mano en la cantonada de la calle de la Verónica.

El profesor de solfeo ensalzaba y bendecía a la hermosa mujer; pero escogía un itinerario de más prudencia; "Jesús", "Jesús" por la mediación de don Álvaro Galindo y de otras casas de grande valimiento.

Don Roger and Señor Hugo, who used to enter "Jesús" together at ten-thirty every day, also left together that afternoon. They stopped at the entrance and looked at the niche where the Lord stands, walking along with his shepherd's crook. How beautiful it would be to live like the Lord with no other impedimenta than a shepherd's crook!

The ringing of the bells from the parish churches, from the monasteries and convents, from the cathedral, the music of the procession; blazing explosions from the cannon called the "Saker," the ancient gun from San Ginés stuffed with heavy gunpowder; the breath of the gardens and the open plain in June.... And as they went down the steps, they thought they were descending into a grim, unfamiliar city.

The first thing that Señor Hugo said, he uttered in his native language. He folded his arms and touched his biceps. For what purpose would they want them in Oleza! Then, like almost all other creatures, he needed someone whom he could blame for his misfortune.

"It was because of Doña Purita; because of our friendship with Doña Purita!"

Didn't the ancient Trojans bless the beauty of Helen, even though she brought about the ruin of their homes, the conflagration and even death?[182] Because of this, in the face of Señor Hugo's complaint and accusation, Don Roger offered his praise to beauty, scorning the sorrows of the world:

"How beautiful she looked today! May God bless her!"

Afterwards, a virile note emanated from the singer's chest, precisely from his very peaceable self and not from the haughty gymnast:

"What are we going to do? We must fight!"

"Fight? Very heroic, when at sixty-three one has more voice than at twenty-three!"

Don Roger brought his gloved fingers to his windpipe. Even in his silence one had a presentiment, one could almost touch the strength of his vocal organ. But he was generous and he was just and he said:

"As for me, what am I going to do here with all that voice if 'Jesús' closes its doors to me?"

"Our friendship with Doña Purita was our ruination, wasn't it? Let's go to her and let's carry on the fight!"

And Señor Hugo extended his hand gallantly at the corner of the Calle de la Verónica.

The sol-faist teacher extolled and blessed the beautiful woman, but he chose a more prudent itinerary: "Jesús," "Jesús" through the mediation of Don Álvaro Galindo and other houses of considerable prestige.

Persuadióse Hugo, y bien avenidos llegaron a los dinteles del caballero de Gandía.

Se pasmó la vieja criada de ver dos hombres tan nuevos allí y de tan desemejante catadura: uno, rotundo y dulce; otro, de un verticalismo acrobático, aunque entrambos hiciesen una misma sonrisa juiciosa y sometida.

No les recibió don Álvaro, sino su hermana, que, mirándoles mucho, les aconsejó que visitaran a los Lóriz, a don Magín y otras gentes parejas. ¡El mundo era muy ancho!

– ¡Tan ancho – le respondió el Sr. Hugo – , y nos tropezamos siempre!

– ¡Huy, no será conmigo!

Y la señorita de Gandía les llevó al portal y cerró duramente la cancela.

– ¡Usted con toda su voz y yo con todos mis bríos, y usted se ha callado y yo no aplasté a la señorita contra el escritorio!

Y el Sr. Hugo arqueó con fiereza su pecho; hizo una flexión de brazos y apartóse de su camarada.

Partían los caminos: él, al palacio de su ilustrísima para pedirle misericordia; y don Roger, al palacio de los Lóriz.

Conmovióse halagadoramente el músico recibiendo el saludo de una gentil doncella. Se lo hubiera contado todo en el zaguán para que lo transmitiese a la señora; y prendido de la graciosa sonrisa de la camarista pasó al patio de entrada, deslumbrante de blancura, y de aquí a un aposento entornado, que olía a magnolias. Se quedó solo y comenzó a decirse: "No veo, pero se adivinan las magnificencias. Las alfombras deben ser preciosas; las alfombras, porque de seguro que hay más de una y de dos para que el suelo resulte tan mullido. Me dormiría de pie. Casi es increíble que yo sea un pobre hombre sin acomodo sintiéndome tan ricamente en esta sala"... De súbito le asustó más saber que se hallaba esperando a los condes de Lóriz, que pensar en su desventura. "¡Dios mío, ya me sudan las manos! Los guantes se me van embebiendo de sudor angustioso. Parece que el único remedio de los sudores es olvidar que se suda. ¡Pues lo olvidaré! ¡Qué tibieza y olor de lujo! Todavía no se me olvida. Quizá no haya tanta suntuosidad como yo imagino. Es que no veo. ¿Tendré un síncope sin saberlo? ¡Me sudan las

Hugo was persuaded and they arrived at the doorstep of the estimable gentleman from Gandía in complete agreement.

The old maidservant was astonished to see two unknown men there, men who looked so different from one another: the one, rotund and sweet, the other, so vertically acrobatic, although both offered the same judicious, submissive smile.

Don Álvaro did not receive them, but rather his sister, who looked at them for a long time and advised them to visit the Lórizes, Don Magín and other people of that kind. The world was very wide!

"So wide," Señor Hugo replied to her, "and we always seem to bump into one another!"

"Good grief; not with me!"

And the señorita from Gandía led them to the outer door and shut the iron grating with a crash.

"You with all your voice and I with all my vigor and you kept silent and I didn't squash that woman against the desk!"

And Señor Hugo expanded his chest fiercely; he flexed his arms and walked away from his companion.

They parted ways: he to His Excellency's Palace to ask him for mercy, and Don Roger to the palace of the Lórizes.

The musician was moved and flattered to receive a greeting from a charming housemaid. He would have explained everything to her in the vestibule so that she could transmit it to the lady of the house; and he was very taken by the delightful smile of the maid-in-waiting, he walked into the outer patio, so dazzlingly white, and from here into a semi-darkened room that smelled of magnolias. He was left alone and started to say to himself, "I can't see very well, but one can sense the presence of magnificent things. The rugs must be beautiful; I say rugs because there are surely more than one or two for the floor to feel so soft. I could fall asleep standing on my feet. It's almost incredible to think that here I am, a poor fellow with no position, and I feel so very richly welcomed in this room...." He was suddenly more overcome with fright to think that here he was waiting for the count and countess of Lóriz than to think of his misfortune. "My God, now my hands are sweating! My gloves are getting soaked with sweat from sheer anguish. It seems that the only remedy for sweating is to forget that you are sweating. Well, I'll forget it! What a pleasant warmth and aroma of luxury! I still can't forget it. Perhaps it isn't as sumptuous as I imagine. The problem is that I can't see. Can I be having a fainting spell and not know it? My hands,

manos, la frente y las rodillas! Es que llego de ese patio de sol y de piedra, y esta obscuridad me venda los ojos con una cinta de seda perfumada. Es muy probable que tarden los señores en aparecérseme. Primero se presentará un criado con luces; encenderá la lámpara, no una lámpara, sino una o dos arañas de cristal. Arañas de Venecia, de ese color marino, de vislumbres de perla"... Pues ese lacayo no había de encontrarle inmóvil y encogido.

Y don Roger se animó y se puso a pasear con algún tonillo. De repente le reventó en la contera de sus zapatones un estrépito vibrante de esquilas de vidrio, un estallido hidráulico. Se le cuajó la conciencia y la sangre. Únicamente dijo: "¡Estoy sudando!" El sudor le bañaba los pies y le salía y empapaba el tapiz como lluvia en un prado. Ladeóse un poco, y todo el prado crujió. Creyó que se le caía el corazón a pedazos, y cada trozo le rebotaba en la alfombra golpeándole en los carcañales. Fue doblándose, doblándose, y entre sus manos enguantadas sintió, rebullirle no un fragmento, sino todo el corazón, palpitante y glacial, y le saltó, dejando una rápida lumbre. Dentro de la blanda quietud del recinto se oía un brincar cansado, gelatinoso, un húmedo aleteo. Don Roger se arrancó un guante con los dientes; encendió una torcida de muchos fósforos.

– ¡He roto algo! qué habré yo roto?

Había roto la pecera regalada al Padre Rector de "Jesús".

Los peces del Nilo, del Jordán, del Vaticano agonizaban mirándole y estremeciéndose, sagrados y magníficos.

Don Roger, todo don Roger era una branquia que latía. Fue retrocediendo; alzó un cortinaje, salió al patio, abrió una verja, después un postigo, y escapóse de la casa de Lóriz sin volver la cabeza.

my forehead and my knees are sweating! The fact of the matter is that I've come from that patio filled with sunlight and stone and this darkness is like a blindfold over my eyes made of a perfumed silk band. The master and the lady of the house will probably take some time to appear here. First a servant will make an appearance with some lighted candles; he will probably light the lamp, no, not a lamp, but one or two crystal chandeliers. Chandeliers from Venice, of that sea color, with glimmers of pearl...." Well, that lackey shouldn't find him here motionless and fainthearted.

And Don Roger took courage and began to move about with a bit of self-confidence. Suddenly a vibrating crash like that of small glass bells, an hydraulic explosion burst from the tips of his heavy shoes. Both his consciousness and his blood curdled. The only thing he could say was, "I'm sweating!" The sweat was bathing his feet and pouring out of him and soaking the rug like rain on a meadow. He leaned to one side a little and the whole meadow rustled. He was convinced that his heart was falling from him in pieces, and that each piece was bouncing onto the rug and striking him in the heels. He started to bend over, bending over, and he felt not a fragment, but his whole heart, palpitating and icy, stirring between his gloved hands, and it jumped away from him, leaving behind a swift flash of light. Within the bland stillness that surrounded him, you could hear a weary, gelatinous leaping, a moist fluttering. Don Roger tore off a glove with his teeth; he lit a wick fashioned from many matches.

"I must have broken something! What can I have broken?"

He had broken the fish tank given as a gift to the Rector Father at "Jesús."

The fish from the Nile, the Jordan, from the Vatican were in their death throes as they stared at him and shuddered, sacred and magnificent.

Don Roger, all of Don Roger, was a gill that kept throbbing. He started backing away, he lifted a set of curtains, went out into the patio, opened a door grating, then a wicket and escaped from the house of the Lórizes without turning his head.

VI

PABLO Y LA MONJA

PABLO AND THE NUN

1. Tribulaciones

Don Jeromillo se descansó en los viejos travesaños del locutorio, mojándolos del sudor de sus dedos. Se le movían las quijadas y las sienes, dentellando por el trabajo de entender los conflictos de la Madre.

La Madre apartóse un poco de la red.

– Quiso la clavaria que todo se lo contásemos al señor penitenciario y al P. Bellod; y el penitenciario nos dijo que no encontraba en la señorita Valcárcel a sor María Fulgencia...

– ¡Leñe, que no!

– Ella estaba delante. El P. Bellod refería ejemplos de mucho espanto. Sor le miraba sin respirar. Daba compasión, y la llevé a recreo para que se consolase con las Hermanas jóvenes, y allí sacó del pecherín una bolilla de cera, y en la bolilla, Jesús mío, en la bolilla vimos el rostro del P. Bellod, que la sor estuvo labrando con sus uñas mientras él nos angustiaba con su palabra.

– ¡Buena moza de Murcia!

– ¡Yo quisiera que acudiésemos a su ilustrísima!

– ¡Vaya que sí! ¡Su ilustrísima es un sabio!

– Por ser quien es, le pido que usted le visite y le hable.

– ¿Que yo le visite? ¡Su ilustrísima está enfermo, todo vendado!

– ¡Ay, don Jeromillo!

– ¡Ni para qué su ilustrísima, teniendo a don Magín! ¡Don Magín es un sabio!

– ¡Muchos son los sabios y ninguno nos remedia!

– ¡A don Magín se lo traigo yo a rempujones!

Y don Jeromillo escapóse, brotando del contento de escapar.

Le recibió en la calle una lluvia traspasada de sol. Oleza se le ofreció tierna y olorosa como un huerto de piedra.

Corría tan aturdido, que no pudo pararse donde iba.

– ¿Qué te recome que ni siquiera miras estos portales?

1. Tribulations

Don Jeromillo rested against the well-worn crossbars of the grating in the locutory, dampening them with the sweat from his fingers. His jawbones and temples were in constant movement, chattering from the effort to understand the Mother's conflicts.

The Mother drew back somewhat from the screen.

"The Keeper of the Keys tried to have us tell everything to the canon-penitentiary and to Father Bellod; and the canon-penitentiary told us that he couldn't find a Sister María Fulgencia in Señorita Valcárcel...."

"Holy God, that isn't so!"

"She was there before him. Father Bellod kept recounting some very frightening examples. Sister was looking at him without breathing. You couldn't help but feel sorry for her, so I took her off to recreation so that she could find solace with the younger Sisters, and there she took a little ball of wax from out of her shirt front, and in that little ball, sweet Jesus, in that little ball we saw Father Bellod's face, which the Sister had been fashioning with her fingernails while he was busy distressing us with his words."

"That's one fine Murcian girl!"

"I would like us to avail ourselves of His Excellency!"

"Yes, indeed! His Excellency is a wise man!"

"Because he is who he is, I'm asking you to visit him and speak to him."

"I visit him? His Excellency is ailing, all covered with bandages!"

"Oh, Don Jeromillo!"

"There's really no need for His Excellency since we have Don Magín! Don Magín is a wise man!"

"There are many wise men and none of them can solve our problem!"

"I'm going to bring Don Magín here if I have to drag him all the way!"

And Don Jeromillo escaped, bubbling with joy at being able to escape.

A rain shower soaked with sunlight received him in the street. Oleza offered itself to him, tender and fragrant like a garden of stone.

He was so bewildered as he ran that he couldn't even stop at the place where he was going.

"What can be consuming you so that you hardly even look at this doorway?"

Y don Magín, acodado en su ventanal, le mostró su hermosa tabaquera desbordante de una espuma de algodones.

– ¡Sube y llégatela al oído, y la sentirás como una caracola!

Arremangóse el hábito don Jeromillo para brincar mejor por la escalera, y desde la colaña le gritó el párroco:

– ¡Pues en acabando la lluvia la abriremos entre mis rosales y verás la volada de mis palomicas de la seda, y después merendaremos!

Se apuñazó don Jeromillo su frente pecosa, y fue diciendo el recado de la Madre.

Don Magín se complacía en su cajuela conmovida de un recóndito zumbo, pero apiadóse del apuro y renunció a las delicias prometidas.

No iba tan ahina como era menester, porque a todos saludaba y a todos se volvía, y se estuvo mirando la nube que se descortezó y se rajó como una piña de ascuas.

Los follajes del jardín monástico se hinchaban nuevos y rotundos en el azul, y el hastial de la Visitación se regocijó de sol poniente.

Del deslumbramiento de la tarde de julio pasaron a la penumbra malva del locutorio, quietecito y fresco como una cisterna. Arrimó don Magín su paraguas a una consola que tenía dos floreros planos de rizos de oro, un quinqué de bronce, un álbum de muestras de randas de bolillos y un jarro de loza con su haz de azucenas. Se recostó en un butacón de funda planchada y puso su frontal dentro de sus manos tan sensuales, tan elocuentes. Así se entregó a las tribulaciones de la monja.

– ...Ya me da miedo la duda de si Nuestro Señor ha querido castigar nuestra vanagloria. ¡Fue demasiada! Siempre diciéndonos que nuestro ostensorio sería la reliquia de mejores efectos en la salud del señor obispo. Será posible que hasta de lo sagrado se aproveche el enemigo para nuestra perdición?

Don Magín alcanzó delicadamente un bohordo de azucenas.

– El P. Bellod nos culpa de frecuencia de locutorio. Nos repitió, con muchos santos, que aquí es donde peligran los ojos, los oídos y la lengua de las religiosas.

Levantó don Magín la faz enharinada de amarillo.

– Pero, Madre, ¿estas azucenas son del huerto de ustedes?

And Don Magín, propped on his elbow in the wide window, showed him his attractive snuffbox overflowing with a cottony foam.

"Come up and put it next to your ear and you'll hear it just as if were a conch!"

Don Jeromillo tucked up his habit in order to jump up the staircase better, and the parish priest shouted down to him from the guardrail on the stairway:

"Well, after the rain is over, we'll open it up among my rose bushes and you'll see the flight of my silk moths, and we'll have lunch afterwards!"

Don Jeromillo struck his freckled brow with his fist and started repeating the Mother's message.

Don Magín was taking great delight with his small box, stirring with a recondite buzzing sound, but he felt pity for the difficult situation and gave up the pleasures he had promised himself.

He was unable to walk as quickly as was necessary because he kept greeting everyone and turning toward everyone, and he stopped to look at a cloud that stripped off its outer surface and split apart like a cluster of embers.

The foliage in the convent garden swelled up rotundly new in the blue of the sky and the gable wall of la Visitación rejoiced in the setting sun.

They passed from the dazzling glare of the July afternoon into the mauve penumbra of the locutory, now so still and cool like a cistern. Don Magín leaned his umbrella against a console table upon which were standing two smooth-surfaced flower vases with golden curlicues, a bronze oil lamp, an album with samples of bobbin lace trimmings and an earthenware pitcher with a bunch of white lilies. He leaned back in a big easy chair with an ironed slipcover and put his forehead between his very sensual, very eloquent hands. In this way did he hand himself over to the nun's tribulations.

"...It frightens me now to question whether the Lord has decided to punish our vainglory. It was excessive! Always telling ourselves that our monstrance would be the relic with the best effect on the health of the lord bishop. Can it be possible that the enemy takes advantage even of what is most sacred in order to bring about our perdition?"

Don Magín reached out discreetly to touch a scape of white lilies.

"Father Bellod blames us for excessive use of the locutory. He cited many saints when he repeated to us that it is here where the eyes, the ears and the tongues of the nuns are in greatest danger."

Don Magín raised his face now besprinkled with yellow.

"But, Mother, are these white lilies really from your garden?"

– Sí, señor, que lo son. Está el jardín muy lindo desde que sor María lo cuida y le da sus lecciones al hortelano. No lo vio cuando vino la señora Infanta, que hubo dispensa de clausura? ¡Ay, no; bien recuerdo que no entró usted, sino el P. Bellod! Cortamos una vara de nardos para cada uno del cortejo.

– ¡Yo digo azucenas!

– Azucenas, azucenas; pero también los nardos le agradarían; la flor bendita del perfume con que la santa mujer ungió los pies del Salvador. ¡Lástima que luego quebrara el vaso, que ahora podría servir de relicario precioso!

Este asunto exaltó a don Magín.

– ¡Ha caído usted en pobres errores!

– ¡Ay, don Magín!

– Aquel ungüento se hacía del nardo indio y siriano; así lo llama Dioscórides, según se criara la planta en la vertiente del monte que se inclina a la India o en la que se vuelve a la Siria. ¿Piensa usted que ya no hubo más especies de nardos? Pues, sí, señora; pero la legítima era el *nardum montanum, nardum sincerum.* El aceite más fino y fragante lo hacían en Tarsis, aprovechando las espigas, las hojas y las raíces. Usted hablaba de la flor. Engañosa apariencia. De las raíces, de las raíces salía el mejor ungüento, y dice Plinio que alcanzaba el precio de las perlas: cuatrocientos denarios la libra de perfume; y ese tan rico fue el que mercó aquella hermosa mujer; porque sín duda era hermosa la que sabía tanto de olores. Guardábase en pomos o redomas de alabastro, que es la substancia que no deja que transpiren y se pierdan los aromas, y tenían un gollete sellado. ¡Dígame cómo había de verter el ungüento sino quebrando el tarro! De modo que no lo rompió por antojo de hembra delirante ni pródiga. Ese nardo de su huerto será una degeneración del índico. ¿De flor doble jaspeada? ¿De veras? El jacinto índico: *Nardus polyanthes tuberosa.* Suele decírsele vara de Jessé. ¡La vara de Jessé en las manos del P. Bellod! ¿Qué hubiese dicho el ilustre señor de Lecour? – Y levantóse y compuso su manteo.

– ¿Es algún monseñor, algún príncipe de la Iglesia?

– No, señora; es un floricultor de Holanda que pasó recios afanes para

"Yes, indeed, they truly are. The garden looks very lovely ever since Sister María has been caring for it and she is giving lessons to the gardener. Didn't you see it when Her Royal Highness[183] the Infanta came here and the restrictions on confinement were set aside? Oh, no; I remember very well that you didn't come in, only Father Bellod! We cut a scape of nards for everyone in the entourage."

"I say white lilies!"

"White lilies, yes, white lilies; but nards would also please you; the blessed flower for the perfume with which the sainted woman anointed the Savior's feet.[184] What a pity that she later broke the jar, for it could now serve as a precious reliquary!"

This subject excited Don Magín.

"You have fallen into pitiful errors!"

"Oh, Don Magín!"

"That unguent was made of Indian and Syrian nards; that's what Dioscorides calls it,[185] depending on whether the plant was grown on the mountain slope facing India or the one that turns toward Syria. Do you really think there were no longer any other kinds of nards? Well, there were, my dear señora, but the genuine one was the *nardum montanum, nardum sincerum*. The finest, most fragrant oil was made in Tarshis, making use of the spikes, the leaves and the roots.[186] You were talking about the flower. A deceptive appearance. The best unguent came from the roots, from the roots, and Pliny says that it attained the price of pearls: four hundred *denarii* per pound of perfume;[187] that was the very precious kind that beautiful woman purchased; because anyone who knew so much about fragrances was undoubtedly beautiful. It was stored in alabaster phials or flasks, because that material does not allow the aroma to transpire and be lost, and they also had a sealed neck. Tell me how one could pour out the unguent except by breaking the jar! So you see that she didn't break it out of whimsy because she was a delirious or prodigal woman. That nard from your garden is probably one that has degenerated from the Indian one. Did it have a double jaspered flower? Am I right? The Indian hyacinth: *nardus polyanthes tuberosa*. It used to be called Jesse's rod, the tuberose. The tuberose in the hands of Father Bellod! What would the illustrious Señor de Lecour have said?"[188]

And he stood up and rearranged his cloak.

"Is he some monsignor, some prince of the Church?"

"No, señora, he is a floriculturist from Holland who toiled with vigorous

criar la verdadera cebolla del nardo doble. Rodeó sus jardines de tapias muy altas, como un marido celoso. Antes que dar una de sus flores hubiese chafado todos sus planteles. ¡Y el P. Bellod, sin olfato, se lleva un racimo! – Y don Magín cogió su magnífico paraguas de Génova y su teja vislumbrante.

Apareció muy gozoso don Jeromillo, tomando incienso de una orza vidriada y desgranándolo en las navetas.

– ¿Ya está? ¡Bien se lo prometí yo, Madre!

Volvióse el párroco suspirando; dejó su canalón y su paraguas, y gimíeron otra vez los muelles del asiento bajo su pesadumbre.

– ¡Siga, Madre, siga!

La Madre siguió:

– Por mi culpa, por mi grandísima culpa de acoger tan pronto a la sor nos vienen los desabores y sustos. Sor o la señorita Valcárcel se aprovecha de todas las vidrieras para mirarse, y hasta del portapaz se ha servido, al besarlo, como de un espejo. La vio la clavaria. Pero sus noches, sus noches son irresistibles. Se siente el río y el viento como criaturas en pena que se paran llamándonos en cada celosía. Sor María Fulgencia y otras tres Hermanas no duermen o gimen con pesadillas. Dicen que un arcángel se pasea por los dormitorios mirándolas...

– ¡Duerman con luz!

– Con luz dormimos, don Magín. ¡A obscuras no sosegaríamos, porque a obscuras lo ven mejor!

– ¿A quién?

– ¡Al arcángel! El jueves se consumió la lámpara y tuvimos que rezar a gritos, mientras la clavaria, que es la más valerosa, se levantó enferma y desnuda para encender los cirios de la hornacina del santo fundador. ¿Es vida de religión o de condenación?

Pasábase don Magín los dedos por los párpados, por los carrillos, por la nuca, por las sienes, como si quisiera despertar y abrir sus entendederas; pero el olor de la navecilla, que se dejó el capellán de la casa junto al búcaro de la consola, podía más que la confidencia de los trabajos y adversidades. Tomó un grumo; lo deshizo entre sus palmas, y aspirándolas, prorrumpió:

zeal to grow the true bulb of the double spikenard. He surrounded his gardens with very high walls, like a jealous husband. He would have crushed his entire nursery of plants before he would have given away one of his flowers. And Father Bellod, with no sense of smell, walks off with the whole bunch!" And Don Magín grabbed his magnificent umbrella from Genoa and his dazzling priest's shovel hat.

Don Jeromillo seemed quite overjoyed and took some incense from a glazed crock and let them drop one at a time into the censers.

"Is everything taken care of now? Didn't I promise you, Mother?"

The parish priest turned around with a sigh; he put aside his shovel hat and umbrella, and the springs of his chair groaned under his weight once more.

"Continue, Mother, continue!"

The Mother continued:

"It is my fault, my very grievous fault, for having welcomed the sister so quickly that all these distressing and frightening events have come upon us. Sister or Señorita Valcárcel takes advantage of every pane of glass to look upon herself and has even made use of the pyx, using it as a mirror when she kisses it. The Keeper of the Keys saw her. But her nights, her nights are irresistible. You can hear the river and the wind as if they were creatures in torment who stop and call to us in every window blind. Sister María Fulgencia and three other Sisters do not sleep or moan, beset by their nightmares. They say that an archangel wanders through the sleeping rooms looking at them...."

"Let them sleep with the light on!"

"We do sleep with the lights on, Don Magín. We would have no repose whatsoever in the dark because they see him better in the dark!"

"Whom?"

"The archangel! The lamp burned out on Thursday and we had to pray at the top of our voices, while the Keeper of the Keys, who has the most courage, got up, even though she was sick and unclad, in order to light the wax tapers in our sainted founder's niche. Is this a life of religion or damnation?"

Don Magín ran his fingers over his eyelids, over his cheeks, over the back of his neck, over his temples, as if he were trying to awaken and open up his brains; but the aroma from the censer left there by the House chaplain next to the odorous clay jar on the console table was more powerful than the revelations concerning the ordeals and adversities. He picked up a small cluster, broke it into bits between his palms, sniffed them and burst out:

– Este incienso, Madre, este incienso no es del mismo que se quema en las otras iglesias de la diócesis. Es legítimo orobias, generoso en el brasero y en la mano; el que arde con humo inmaculado, tupido, vertical, de oblata pontificia.

– ¿Y no será del que usted le regaló a don Jeromillo?

– ¡Ya respiro!

– ¿Cuándo respiraremos nosotras con holgura? Porque sor nos mira como si entre sus ojos y los nuestros hubiese alguíen, ¡así como si siempre le viera!

– ¿A quién?

– ¡A él, al señor Mauricio, al señor capitán!

– ¿Pero es que ese señor Mauricio, ese capitán es el arcángel?

– ¡Ése, don Magín, ése! En sueños pronuncia sor su nombre y lo repiten las educandas. ¿Intentará el sacrilegio de subir, y ellas lo saben?

– El P. Bellod les diría que todo eso se impide con una navaja. Así lo remedió la abadesa Ebba cuando las hordas cercaron enardecidas el monasterio de Collinham. Juntó Santa Ebba el capítulo – todas sus monjas eran muy guapas – , y sacando de su túnica un cuchillo, les gritó: ¡Aquí tenéis con qué libraros de la insolencia de los hombres!

– ¿Se mató? ¡No es posible, Jesús mío! ¡Lo condenan los Santos Padres!

– No se mató: lo que hizo fue desnarigarse y rebanarse también los labios; y la imitaron sus hijas. Acometieron y asaltaron los enemigos la casa, y ni tocaron el sayal de las pobres mujeres, pero quemaron el convento con todas las castas criaturas. Tal vez la belleza hubiese ablandado el corazón de aquellas gentes.

– ¡No podemos, don Magín, penetrar en los designios del Señor! – Y luego de un suspiro, dijo – : Es que algunas tardes toca la esquila del locutorio y se nos aparece el señor Mauricio en el rayo. ¡Cómo rechazarle siendo un enviado de tan altas prerrogativas! Mirándole y oyéndole se nos transfigura en un ser sobrenatural.

Don Magín recordó lo que cuenta Eusebio de Constantino en su *Historia de la Iglesia.* Constantino, de humilde y encendido creyente, va subiendo a una substancia y significación sagradas. Ya no es posible en el Imperio la religión dogmática y orgánica sin la voluntad, sin los mandamientos, sin

"This incense, Mother, this incense is not the same kind that they burn in the other churches in the diocese. It is a genuine fine grained incense, superior in the burner and in the hand; the kind that burns with immaculate, dense, vertical smoke, of the kind for a pontifical oblation."

"Isn't it possibly the kind you gave Don Jeromillo as a gift?"

"Now I can breathe!"

"When will we be able to breathe with ease? Because Sister looks at us as if there were someone between her eyes and ours. Just as if she were always seeing him!"

"Whom?"

"Him, Señor Mauricio, the captain!"

"But do you mean that Señor Mauricio, that captain, is the archangel?"

"That's the one, Don Magín, that's the one! Sister pronounces his name in her dreams and the students repeat it. Will he attempt to commit the sacrilege of climbing up here, and do they know about it?"

"Father Bellod would tell them that all of that can be prevented with a knife. That's how the Abbess Ebba resolved it when the inflamed hordes besieged the monastery at Coldingham.[189] Saint Ebba gathered the chapter together – all her nuns were very pretty – and she pulled out a knife from her tunic and shouted at them, 'Here you have the means to free yourselves from the insolence of men!,"

"She killed herself? sweet Jesus!, it's not possible! The Holy Fathers of the Church condemn it!"

"She didn't kill herself: what she did was to cut off her nose and also slice off her lips, and her daughters imitated her. Their enemies attacked and stormed the House, but they never even touched the sack cloth habits of those poor women, but they did burn down the convent with all those chaste creatures inside. Perhaps beauty had softened the hearts of those people."

"Don Magín, we can not penetrate the designs of the Lord!" And after a sigh, she said, "The fact is that the bell for the locutory rings on a number of afternoons and Señor Mauricio appears before us, framed in the bright light. How could we turn him away when he is an envoy of such privileged authority! Just looking at him and hearing him, transfigures him into a supernatural being before us!"

Don Magín remembered what Eusebius of Caesarea related concerning Constantine in his *History of the Church*.[190] Constantine, a man of humble and impassioned belief, keeps rising to a sacred importance and significance. Dogmatic and organic religion is no longer possible in the Empire without

la presencia del príncipe; él sabe y decide desde lo cominero y servil hasta lo jerárquico y teológico. Vienen a palacio los obispos de su Consejo, los obispos áulicos y los obispos de las diócesis más remotas, tan encogidos algunos como nuestros capellanes rurales. Las magnificencias de la corte les deslumbraban. El emperador, cubierto de púrpura, recamado de joyas, es una imagen celeste. No es un hombre, no es un obispo como ellos: es un ángel del Señor que les anticipa el goce del reinado de Cristo.

Parecida ilusión pudo exaltar a las buenas mujeres del monasterio de Nuestra Señora. Por primera vez en su encerrada vida contemplan un señor Mauricio, vestido de azul, con lumbres de plata, que ha caminado por las lejanías del mundo con una reliquia en sus manos. No es como don Jeromillo; no es como el hortelano ni el mandadero, no es como ningún hombre de Oleza. ¿Será un arcángel? ¡Es un arcángel! Y diciéndole arcángel, y repitiéndolo, la palabra infundía un estado fervoroso.

Un estado fervoroso contenido, de tiempo en tiempo, por otra menor categoría celestial: la de ángel.

— Sor habla con mucha pasión del ángel de Murcia. Dice que lo ha visto en Oleza y que trae uniforme de interno de "Jesús".

Levantóse don Magín muy malhumorado.

— ¡Que se decida ya esa moza!

Viéndole tan ceñudo y tan harto, se desconsoló más la Madre.

— ¡Ay, don Magín! ¿Es que ya se nos vino la perdición? ¿Ha de condenarse la sor para siempre, siempre? Santa Margarita de Cortona, después de haber sido pasto de no sé qué fuego, trocóse en un Etna de amor de Dios en la Tercera Orden de San Francisco. Santa Pelagia, de mala mujer, acabó coronada de virtudes en Monte Olivete, con hábito de religioso y nombre de Pelagio. María, sobrina del santo abad Abraham, engañada por un falso y perverso monje, se abandonó a una vida de infamia; y su tio, disfrazado, la buscó y la restituyó con mucho ingenio al claustro y a la castidad más perfecta... Pues nuestra sor no ha caído para que no podamos esperar en la gracia. Bien me duele que todavía tenga gustos del mundo y ponga demasiadas ternuras

the will, without the commands, without the presence of the prince; he knows and decides everything from the trivial and base to the hierarchical and theological. The bishops of his Council come to the palace along with the bishops of his court and the bishops from the remotest diocese, some of them as reserved as our own rural priests. The magnificence of the royal court dazzles them. The emperor, covered with purple, embroidered with jewels, is a celestial image. He is not a man, he is not a bishop like them; he is an angel of the Lord who anticipates the enjoyment of the kingdom of Christ for them.

A similar illusion succeeded in exalting the good women of the convent of Our Lady. For the first time in their sheltered existence, they contemplate a Señor Mauricio, dressed in blue, with flashes of silver, who has traveled through the far distant corners of the world with a relic in his hands. He is not like Don Jeromillo; he is not like the gardener or the messenger, he is not like any man in Oleza. Can he be an archangel? He is an archangel! And by calling him an archangel and repeating it, the word infused a fervent state of mind in them.

A contained fervent state of mind, every once in a while, for another lesser celestial category: that of an angel.[191]

"Sister speaks with great passion of the angel of Murcia. She says she has seen him in Oleza and that he wears the uniform of a boarding student at 'Jesús.'"

Don Magín arose very ill-humoredly.

"Let that girl make up her mind once and for all!"

When she saw him frowning like that and so fed up with it all, the Mother grew even more disconsolate.

"Oh, Don Magín! Has perdition finally come upon us? Must Sister be damned forever and ever? Saint Margaret of Cortona,[192] after having been fuel for I know not what fire, changed into a veritable Etna of love for God in the Third Order of Saint Francis. Saint Pelagia,[193] once a woman of evil ways, ended up crowned with virtues on the Mount of Olives, wearing the religious habit of a man and with the name Pelagius. Mary, a niece of the sainted abbot Abraham,[194] after she was deceived by a false, perverse monk, abandoned herself to a life of infamy; and her uncle, in disguise, sought her out with considerable ingenuity and brought her back to the cloister and to the most perfect chastity.... Well, our Sister has not fallen so far that we can not place our hope in divine grace. It truly grieves me that she still holds on to the pleasures of the outside world and shows too much tenderness

en lo perecedero. A veces la he sorprendido compadeciéndose más de sus tórtolas que del prójimo: más que de la clavaria. ¡Oh Jesús, y cómo las ama, y las besa, y las acaricia!...

– ¿Tórtolas?

– Dos tórtolas que trajo de su casa de Murcia. El P. Bellod nos aconsejó que las hirviésemos, y el señor penitenciario nos dijo que esas aficiones eran un peligro para la vocación. Prometió volver con don Amancio, de quien alaba su doctrina. ¡Ay, yo no sé! ¡Si ahora tuviésemos el relicario donde se guarda el corazón de Nuestro Padre San Francisco para ponérselo a sor en el costado!

– Eso las consolaría mucho; pero recojan el otro y devuélvanselo al señor capitán, ¡y se acabó el arcángel! – Y don Magín encendió un cigarro y fue oprimiéndolo con sus tenacillas de plata. Luego abrió la puerta de la sacristía, y en aquel instante presentóse don Jeromillo.

– ¡No se lo dije, Madre! ¿Ahora sí que ya está?

– Para que así sea te necesito: vete a Palacio y que te den el ostensorio que trajo el señor capitán.

– ¿Y que me den el ostensorio? ¿A mí?

Y don Jeromillo miraba a la Madre con agonía.

Ella sobresaltóse.

– ¿Osaremos pedirlo y devolverlo? ¿Y es lepra, lepra de verdad lo que aflije a su ilustrísima? ¡Y dicen que por los pecados de la diócesis! ¿No le quitaremos el remedío? ¿No impediremos el milagro?

Don Magín frisaba y sobaba su teja, y antes de cubrirse respondió:

– No se apure; que si la reliquia le probó al enfermo, ya no es menester; y si no le remediaba, ¿para qué la quiere? Las gracias emanadas de las cosas santas no suelen retardarse... ¡Anda, Jeromillo, aviva!

Salió don Jeromillo. Brincaba por los aguazales de la lluvia. Se atolondró tanto que había de cogerse a los cantones para no rodar en las revueltas.

Y cuando estuvo en presencia del familiar, se amohinó, diciéndose que para qué habría llegado tan súbito donde no hubiera querido llegar.

for things that are transitory. I have surprised her at times showing greater compassion for her turtledoves than for her fellow beings: more than for the Keeper of the Keys. Oh, sweet Jesus, how she loves them and kisses them and caresses them!...."

"Turtledoves?"

"Two turtledoves she brought from her house in Murcia. Father Bellod advised us to boil them and the canon penitentiary told us that such fondness was a danger to her vocation. He promised to return with Don Amancio, whose doctrinal knowledge he praised. Oh, I just don't know! If we now had the reliquary where we keep the heart of Our Father Saint Francis so we could place it against Sister's side!"

"That would console them a great deal; but why don't you pick up the other one and return it to the captain, and that will be the end of the archangel!" And Don Magín lit a cigarette and started squeezing it with his silver smoking tongs. Then he opened the door to the sacristy and Don Jeromillo appeared just at that moment.

"Didn't I tell you, Mother! Isn't it all taken care of now?"

"So that it can all be resolved, I need you; go to the Palace and have them back give you the monstrance that the captain brought."

"They should give me back the monstrance? Me?"

And Don Jeromillo looked at the Mother with anguish.

She seemed startled.

"Shall we dare ask for it and return it? And is it leprosy, really leprosy that afflicts His Excellency? And they say it's because of the sins of the diocese! Won't we be taking the cure away from him? Won't we be preventing the miracle?"

Don Magín kept frizzing and fondling his shovel hat and, before putting it on his head, he replied:

"Don't you worry, because if the relic was tried on the ailing man, it's no longer necessary, and if it didn't do him any good, why would he want it? The favors emanating from holy objects are not generally delayed.... Be on your way, Jeromillo, get a move on!"

Don Jeromillo went out. He kept jumping over the puddles from the rain. He was so rattled that he was compelled to grab hold on at the corners so he wouldn't tumble over when he made a turn.

And when he was standing in the presence of the familiar, he was vexed with himself and told himself that he could not see why he had come here so quickly considering that he hadn't even wanted to come.

Los anteojos congelados del clérigo doméstico le apresuraban las palpitaciones; esos anteojos parecían medirle el trastorno de su sangre, exhalando una lumbre afilada y renovada en cada aliento suyo.

No supo cómo dio el mensaje, pero lo dio; y en acabando, al sentir su silencio, se le velaron los ojos y se agobió. De un momento a otro se abriría la roja mampara, y participaría de oficios solemnes, de rúbricas incomprensibles. En la quietud crujía un oleaje de folios. Y alzó poco a poco la frente.

El familiar devoraba las notas de un libro-registro muy viejo, hasta que respiró y dijo:

– Número 78. Tabla III. Envío de las Madres de la Visitación.

Luego puso una gradilla junto al armario, alcanzó del tercer vasar el atadijo de las salesas de Annecy; lo protegió con un *Boletín Diocesano,* le pegó dos obleas, le pasó un cordel, y en tanto que le hizo la baga, decía:

– El Señor agradece paternalmente este consuelo de la comunidad de la Visitación, a la que bendice con especial cariño.

¡Ya estaba todo! Y con la reliquia en sus brazos se le incorporó a don Jeromillo un ímpetu de victoria.

Denodado, arrogante y gozoso entró en el convento.

– Récenle, si quieren, antes de llevársela al señor Mauricio.

– ¿Vendrá la perdición? – porfió la Madre.

...Diez de agosto, día de San Lorenzo, vino la perdición.

El señor deán se agarraba desesperadamente a la reja pidiendo calma. Don Jeromillo saltaba por el locutorio. La Madre gemía. La clavaria se torcía el ceñidor. La señorita Valvárcel levantó el grito y la jaula de las tórtolas.

– ¡Ha sido ella, la clavaria! ¡Lo mató apretándole el corazoncito con las uñas! ¡Me ha matado el macho! ¡Acababa yo de besarlo y lo dejé precioso! ¡Ha sido ella; yo la vi salir!

– ¿A mí? ¿El macho, dice? – Y la clavaria se quedó mirándola – . ¿El macho? ¿De modo que había un macho?

– ¡Sí, señora; como en todas las parejas, hasta en la de Adán y Eva!

– ¡Su caridad, su caridad! – le imploró la Madre.

The domestic cleric's congealed spectacles sped up his palpitations; those spectacles seemed to be measuring the upheaval in his blood, emanating a sharp, renewed glow with every breath he took.

He didn't know how he was able to deliver the message, but he did; and when he finished, he was aware of the silence and his eyes dimmed and he felt exhausted. From one moment to the next, the red screen would open wide and he would participate in solemn offices, in incomprehensible flourishes. A surge of folio pages crackled in the stillness, and little by little he raised his forehead.

The familiar was devouring the notations in a very old registry book, until he breathed heavily and said:

"Number 78. Shelf III. Shipment from the Mothers at La Visitación."

Then he placed a small ladder next to the book shelves, took down the package sent by the sisters of the Salesian Order in Annecy from the third shelf; he wrapped it in a copy of the *Diocesan Bulletin* to protect it, stuck two wafers on to seal it, and as he tied it with twine, he said:

"The lord bishop is paternally thankful to you for this gift of consolation from the Community of La Visitación and he blesses them with special affection."

Now it was all taken care of! And with the relic in his arms, Don Jeromillo was overcome by an outburst of victory.

He entered the convent, intrepid, arrogant and joyful.

"Pray to it, if you wish, before taking it back to Señor Mauricio."

"Will perdition be coming?" the Mother persisted.

...On the tenth of August, St. Laurence's Day, perdition came.

The dean grasped the grating in desperation and asked for calm. Don Jeromillo was jumping all over the locutory. The Mother was moaning. The Keeper of the Keys kept twisting her sash. Señorita Valcárcel raised a cry and the cage for her turtledoves.

"It was she, the Keeper of the Keys! She killed him by crushing his little heart with her fingernails! She killed the male that was mine! I had just kissed him and left him looking so wonderful! It was she; I saw her going out!"

"Me? The male, she says?" And the Keeper of the Keys stood there looking at her. "The male? So you mean there was a male?"

"Yes, señora, as in all couples, even in that of Adam and Eve!"

"Your Charity, your Charity!" the Mother implored her.

– ¡Déjenmela, que quiero que me diga su caridad cómo supo lo de macho y hembra! ¡Para mí nada más eran dos tórtolas!

– ¡Señora, usted es tonta y mala!

Arreció el alboroto. Y lo deshizo milagrosamente la señorita Valcárcel.

– ¡Yo me voy de aquí, señor deán!

– ¿Que te vas? ¿A Murcia?

– Me marcho con usted. Y me casaré...

– ¿Que te casarás?

– ...¡Y me casaré con el primero que se me presente!

2. Jesús y el hombre rico

Verano de calinas y tolvaneras. Aletazos de poniente. Bochornos de humo. Tardes de nubes incendiadas, de nubes barrocas, desgajándose del azul del horizonte, glorificando los campanarios de Oleza.

Las mejores famílias – menos la de don Álvaro – se fueron a sus haciendas y a las playas de Torrevieja, de Santa Pola y Guardamar. La ciudad se quedó como un patio de vecinos. El palacio de Lóriz semejaba ya mucho tiempo en el sueño de su soledad; el del obispo, en el ocio de los curiales, que fumaban paseando por la claustra; "Jesús" y el seminario, entornados en el frescor de las vacaciones. Las hospederías, los obradores, las tiendas callaban con la misma modorra de sus sueños sentados a la puerta, cabeceando entre moscardas. Los árboles de los jardines, de la Glorieta, de los monasterios, hacían un estruendo de vendaval de otoño, o se estampaban inmóviles en los cielos, bullendo de cigarras como sí se rajasen al sol. El río íba somero, abriéndose en deltas y médanos de fango, de bardomas, de carrizos; y por las tardes, muy pronto, reventaba un croar de balsa. Se pararon muchos molinos de pimentón y harina; y entraban las diligencias, dejando un vaho de tierras calientes, un olor de piel y collerones sudados. Verano ruin. No daba gozo el rosario de la Aurora y tronaba el rosario del anochecido. Fanales de

"Let me at her, because I want her Charity to tell me how she found out about the male and the female! To me they were nothing more than two turtledoves!"[195]

"Señora, you are stupid and evil!"

The uproar grew worse. And Señorita Valcárcel miraculously put an end to it.

"I'm leaving here, dean!"

"You're leaving? For Murcia?"

"I'm going away with you. I'm going to get married...."

"You're going to get married?"

"...I'm going to get married to the first man who comes along!".

2. Jesús and the Rich Man

A summer of haze and dust storms. The flapping of the westerly wind. The sultry morning vapors. Afternoons of incandescent clouds, baroque clouds, breaking off from the blue of the horizon, glorifying the bell towers of Oleza.

The best families – except for Don Álvaro's – departed for their country properties and the beaches of Torrevieja, Santa Pola and Guardamar. The city was left like an enclosed neighborhood patio. The Lóriz palace for some time now took on its appearance from the somnolence of its solitude; the bishop's, from the idleness of the palace clerks, who strolled through the cloister smoking; "Jesús" and the seminary, mostly closed up in the refreshing interlude of its vacations. The hostelries, the workshops, the stores were silent with the same drowsiness displayed by their owners as they sat in the doorways, their heads nodding amidst the blowflies. The trees in the gardens, in the Public Square, in the monasteries and convents, made an uproar like an autumn gale, or else they stood motionless, engraved against the skies, swarming with cicadas just as if they were splitting in the sunlight. The river ran shallow, opening up into deltas and muddy sandbanks, heaps of muck and ditch reeds; and in the afternoon, a croaking from a pool of water would suddenly break out. Many red pepper and flour mills stopped working; and the diligences kept coming in, leaving behind fumes smelling of warm earth, an odor of sweaty skin and horse collars. A vile summer. The Rosary to the Virgin at Dawn was unpleasant and the rosary at nightfall

velas amarillas alumbrando el viejo tisú de la manga parroquial, hileras de hombres y mujeres colgándoles los rosarios de sus dedos de difunto; capellanes y celadores guiando la plegaria; un remanso en la contemplación de cada misterio, y otra vez se desanillaban las cofradías y las luces por los ambages de las plazas, por los cantones, por las callejas, por las cuestas. De trecho en trecho caía con retumbos dentro de las foscas entradas el "¡Mira que te mira Dios, – mira que te está mirando, – mira que te has de morir, – mira que no sabes cuándo!". Y, según adelantaba el tránsito, se les venían más gentes a rezar.

Penetraba en casa de Pablo ese río de oración, más clamoroso que el Segral. A lo lejos, era de tonada de escolanía, de pueblo infantil que, no sabiendo qué hacer, conversaba afligido con el Señor. Y, ya de cerca, articulado concretamente el rezo en su portal, por cada boca, sentía Pablo un sabor de amargura, de amargura lívida. Alzaba los ojos al cielo de su calle. De tanto ansiar se reía de su desesperación; y palpaba su risa. Tocaba sus gestos como si tocase su alma desnuda. Vivía tirantemente. El júbilo de las vacaciones se le quedó seco y desaromado. Pasó los primeros días siempre en diálogo con su madre. Tía Elvira alababa la suerte de su cuñada por tener un hijo tan hija. No fuera tan enmadrado y enfaldado si trajese faldas de verdad. Y convidó al sobrino a sus tertulias de las *Catalanas* y de la Adoración. Después mudó de chanza, santiguándose y mirándole todo el cuerpo.

– ¡Se te siente medrar! ¡Ni las sayas de tu madre ni las ropas de tu padre te aprovecharían! ¡Con esa cara de mujer guapeta y esa figura de ángel talludo, habrá que colgarte evangelios!

...En agosto todavía estaba la família de don Álvaro en su casa de Oleza.

Ni ruegos de la esposa, ni enojos ni postraciones del hijo removieron la voluntad del padre. El cansancio, la molicie y el calor le solicitaban también a la holgura campesina y a olvidarse flojamente de la contienda de Oleza. Pero él resistiría; porque la contienda de la pobre Oleza significaba la del mundo. Desde su destierro, el príncipe les recordó palabras de un esclarecido

sounded like thunder.[196] Glass shades over the yellow candles lighting up the worn-out lamé manga of a parish church, lines of men and women with rosaries dangling from their lifeless fingers; priests and custodians leading the prayer; a backwater in the contemplation of every mystery, and once again the confraternities and the lights wound their way through the ambages of the plazas, past the corners, along the narrow streets, up the slopes. Every so often one could hear, "Be wary, for God looks upon you, – be wary for He is watching you, – be wary, for you must die, – be wary, for you don't know when!" the words of the song falling resoundingly from within the gloomy entryways.[197] And as the moving lines kept making their way forward, more and more people came to join them in prayer.

That river of prayer, more tumultuous than the Segral, penetrated into Pablo's house. While still at a distance, it was like a choirboy's air, like a community of little children who, not knowing what to do, conversed with the Lord in their affliction. And now that it was closer, the prayer being concretely articulated at the doors of his house, coming from every mouth, Pablo felt a taste of bitterness, of livid bitterness. He raised his eyes to the sky over his street. Because of all his yearning, he could laugh at his own desperation; and he palpated his laughter. He touched the expressions on his face as if he were touching his naked soul. He was living under tension. The jubilation because of his vacation now turned dry and flavorless. He spent the first days in constant dialogue with his mother. Aunt Elvira praised her sister-in-law's good fortune in having a son who was so like a daughter. He couldn't be any more attached to his mother and tied to her skirts if he actually wore skirts. And she invited her nephew to the social gatherings at the *Catalan sisters* and the Society of the Adoration. Afterwards she changed her jocular tone, crossing herself and looking up and down his body.

"One can see you're growing up! Neither your mother's skirts nor your father's clothes would be of any use to you! With that silly, pretty woman's face of yours and that figure of a carved angel, they'll have to hang little books with Scripture round your neck!"[198]

...In August, Don Álvaro's family was still in their house in Oleza.

Neither his wife's entreaties nor his son's anger or prostration could move the father's will. His weariness, his easygoing way of life and the heat seemed even to him to be an invitation to the pleasant activity out in the country where he could lazily forget the conflict in Oleza. But he would resist; because the conflict in poor Oleza represented the very same thing in the outside world. From his place of exile, the prince recalled the words

purpurado: "Preferible es el impío al indiferente." En aquellos días, León XIII dijo a los hombres: "Cumplid vuestros deberes de ciudadanos." Ahora la santa causa no peleaba con estrépito humeante de armas, sino con el fuego de la doctrina, con la espada de las intenciones, con el ejemplo de las virtudes. Como en el mundo, las dos mítades de Oleza, la honesta y la relajada, se acometían para trastornar la conciencia y la apariencia de la vida. "Jesús" esforzaba a los olecenses puros. Ya no se temía la discordia como un mal, sino que era un deber soltarla en lo íntimo de las amistades y de las famílias. El Recreo Benéfico, con su mote masónico de caridad, iba pudriendo las limpias costumbres. Muñía bailes, jiras, cosos, tómbolas, comedias y verbenas, que "Jesús" condenaba implacable, repudiando a los luises que participaron de las abominaciones. Y Palacio se retrajo con el silencio de las tolerancias. Se dijo que, creyéndose menoscabado por las censuras de "Jesús", su ilustrísima le devolvió al Rector la medalla de oro de presidente honorario de la Congragación de San Luis.

¡Baje fuego y consuma esta Samaria! Y los legionarios del Padre Espiritual, en vez de subir los ojos imprecando el castigo, los volvían con recelo a Palacio. La mitra procuraba los edificios de "Jesús"; la mitra se los entregó a la Compañía, y la mitra tenía poder para confiarlos a otra comunidad religiosa.

La población escolar iba creciendo, a mayor gloria de Dios. El último censo había llegado a cifras consoladoras: 227 internos, 195 externos. ¿Se malograría una empresa tan fecunda en bienes espirituales? Y cundió el sobresalto entre los recoveros, zapateros, sastres y todos los abastecedores de casa.

En esa hora confusa, el dedo de Dios indicó el camino de la salud: la tierra de la tradición, el "Olivar de Nuestro Padre". De la antigüedad de sus olivos y de sus generosas oleadas recibe nombre Oleza; de una de las oliveras está labrada la imagen de Nuestro Padre San Daniel, y en la raíz del árbol cortado brota milagrosamente un lauredo. Tierra de veneraciones y prodigios. He aquí el solar pingüe y académico de la futura residencia de teólogos, de misioneros, de maestros; si la desgracia empujase a la Orden fuera de los recintos de "Jesús".

of an illustrious cardinal for them, "The impious man is preferable to the indifferent one." In those days, Leon XIII said to all men, "Fulfill your duties as citizens."[199] Now the holy cause wasn't struggling with the smoking crash of arms, but rather with the fire of doctrine, with the sword of intentions, with the example of virtues. Just as in the outside world, the two halves of Oleza, the honorable one and the dissolute one, were attacking one another in order to disrupt the conscience and the appearance of life. "Jesús" kept encouraging the pure Olezans. It was no longer feared that discord would be an evil, but rather a duty to be unleashed within the intimacy of friendships and families. The Benevolent Recreational Association, with its Masonic motto of charity, was bringing about the decay of wholesome customs. It was arranging dances, picnics, outdoor public spectacles, charity raffles, plays and fairs, all of which "Jesús" implacably condemned, reprimanding the young men who belonged to the Marian Congregation of San Luis and who participated in such abominable affairs. And the Palace remained withdrawn in its silence of tolerance. It was said that His Excellency, feeling discredited by the censure from "Jesús," returned the gold medallion of honorary president of the Congregation of San Luis to the Rector.[200]

Let fire come down and consume this Samaria! And the Spiritual Counselor Father's legionnaires, instead of raising their eyes and imprecating punishment, turned them toward the Palace with suspicion. The miter took possession of the buildings of "Jesús," the miter handed them over to the Society, and the miter had the power to entrust them to another religious Community.

The student population kept growing, for the greater glory of God. The last census had attained comforting numbers: 227 boarding students, 195 day students.[201] Would an enterprise so fertile in spiritual rewards come to naught? And the shock spread among the poultry dealers, the shoemakers, tailors and all those who supplied the House.

In that confused hour, the finger of God indicated the salutary road: the tract of land of tradition, the "Olive Grove of Our Father." Oleza received its reputation from the antiquity of its olive trees and its abundant olive harvests; the image of Our Father San Daniel is carved from one of its olive trees, and a laurel tree miraculously sprouts from the roots of the hewn tree. A tract of land of miracles and prodigies. Here stands the bountiful academic site for the future scholarly residence of theologians, missionaries and teachers in the event that misfortune should happen to drive the Order outside the present confines of "Jesús."

Y la legítíma Oleza depositó todas sus inquietudes y todos los remedios en don Álvaro Galindo, dueño del "Olivar".

En llegando don Álvaro a "Jesús", le subían al aposento del Rector sin espera en la sala de visitas. El Rector dejaba su estudio, su recreo, su oración, acogiéndole con apenada sonrisa. Hundía la pinza del tabloncillo de su puerta en el epígrafe "Ocupado", y al regresar a la almohada de su sillón doblaba la frente delante del crucifijo para elevarla con súbita firmeza, ofreciéndose a todos los dolores. Porque no temía el dolor, sino el error.

– ¡Quién adivinará el término de la jornada! ¡Amigo y dueño: nosotros llevamos siempre la cintura ceñida, y no traemos alforja ni muda!

Otra sonrisa, de prudencia y de renunciación, rubricaba su faz.

Callaba don Álvaro. Callaba siempre, con su ceño hundido y los ojos puestos en sus manos de estatua de sepultura.

El Rector esperaba. Esperaba también siempre.

Y una tarde, el caballero de Gandía dijo:

– ¡Si ese "Olivar" fuese mío, únicamente mío!

Para salir a la gran escalera habían de caminar el largo corredor de las tribunas del templo. Se detuvo el jesuita; abrió una de las puertas de roble tallado, y entre las celosías les llegó el silencio de los profundos ámbitos tan sensitivos. En el firmamento místico de los retablos lucían inmóviles y dulces las estrellas de los lamparines. Por la rosa de vidrios del coro pasaba el sol poniente, estampándose en el sepulcro del fundador Ochoa, y ardía la piedra encarnada y estremecida como un enorme corazón.

– ¡Eternamente recogerá esa urna el último rayo de sol de la tarde!

– ¡Si el "Olivar" fuese sólo mío!

– ¡Sea suya la voluntad de hacer el bien!

La víspera, una carta del Provincial de Aragón le avisaba que no creía en las posibilidades de un fracaso del Colegio de Oleza. No creía; es decir, no quería... Se alejaron los pasos recios de don Álvaro y vinieron otros pasos chafados, viejecitos. ¡Ah, el Padre Ferrando! Acabaría de dejar el calesín, el carro, el albardón de la cabalgadura que le volviese de salvar almas rurales.

And the legitimate Oleza deposited all of its uneasiness and its possible solutions upon Don Álvaro Galindo, proprietor of the "Olive Grove."

As soon as Don Álvaro arrived at "Jesús," he was led up to the Rector's room without having to wait in the visitor's lounge. The Rector abandoned his hour of study, his time for relaxation, his time for prayer, welcoming him with a pained smile. He inserted the peg on the small board on his door next to the inscribed word "Occupied,"[202] and when he returned to the cushion on his armchair, he lowered his forehead in front of the crucifix and then raised it with sudden resolution, offering himself to all possible sorrows. Because he did not fear pain, only error.

"Who can guess where is the end of our journey! Friend and master: we always travel with belts tightened in obedience, and we humbly bring neither provisions nor change of clothes!"[203]

Another smile, of prudence and renunciation, inscribed itself on his features.

Don Álvaro remained silent. He always kept silent, knitting his brow, his eyes fixed on his hands, resembling a mortuary statue.

The Rector was waiting. He was always waiting.

And one afternoon, the gentleman from Gandía said:

"If only that 'Olive Grove' were mine, mine alone!"

In order to walk out to the main stairway, they had to go down the long corridor with the upper level balconies. The Jesuit stopped; opened one of the carved oak doors, and the silence of the profound, ever so sensitive surroundings reached them through the latticework. The star shapes in the lamp rings shone motionless and sweet in the mystical firmament of the retables. The light from the setting sun passed through the rose-tinted windows of the choir, imprinting itself upon the sepulcher of the founder Ochoa, and the incarnadine, trembling stone seethed like an enormous heart.

"That urn will gather in the last ray of afternoon sunlight forever!"

"If the 'Olive Grove' were only mine!"

"May the will to do good be yours!"

The day before, a letter from the Provincial of Aragon let him know that he did not believe in the possibilities of a failure of the School at Oleza.[204] He did not believe, that is to say, he didn't want to.... Don Álvaro's firm footsteps moved away and other subdued, timid, aging footsteps approached. Oh, Father Ferrando! He must have just left the light chaise, the cart, the large saddle of the mount that had just brought him back from saving rustic souls.

¡Buena vida la del mínimo Padre confesor de su ilustrísima! Y el Rector dióse una palmadita en la curva sudada de su frontal. Se llevó al P. Ferrando y, sonriendo lo preciso, le encomendó el negocio de las paces con el difícil penitente.

Porque "se acabó el aceite y ardían las torcidas".

Fue asomándose Pablo al huerto episcopal. Todo lo recordaba por suyo, como si hubiese sido suyo. En otro tiempo corría entre las bardizas, saltaba las acequias, regaba, le gritaba a Ranca el hortelano; por todo rebullía y todo lo gozaba sin pensar que fuese suyo ni ajeno. Era dueño con los ímpetus de su antojo y con la complacencia del señor obispo que le miraba desde su estudio, y él no lo sabía. Ahora Pablo iba subiendo los ojos a todos los ventanales, siempre cerrados.

— ¿Y Ranca?

Volvióse un viejo que llenaba una espuerta de estiércol.

— Ranca ya no está.

— ¿Y por qué no está ya Ranca?

— No está porque le dio la perniciosa y nos lo llevemos; y nos lo llevemos porque se murió.

¡Ranca había muerto, y el huerto se quedaba! Ranca se ponía a fumar su verónica encima de la gleba recién volcada, y él, a la aúpa de sus riñones hasta colgársele de los hombros, le mandaba que le llevase al salón del obispo. Ranca, sin mujer, sin família, salió en el huerto como una hierba borde. Era todo vegetal, y vegetal de allí: de terrones, de cortezas, de raíces, de sol, y de olor y de aire. Viéndole por Oleza, se sentía todo el hortal en su pellejo arado, en sus uñas de mantillo, en su voz que sonaba como un calabazón del andaraje de la senia. Le dio la terciana, y se murió, y el huerto seguía...

— ¿Y el obispo qié dice?

— ¿El obispo? Qué dice de qué?

— ¡De Ranca!

— ¿De Ranca? – y el hortelano vertió la espuerta en la almajara y se puso a escardar.

A fine life for this insignificant Father confessor for His Excellency! And the Rector slapped his palm lightly against the sweaty curve of his frontal bone. He led Father Ferrando off, smiling as much as he felt necessary, and entrusted him with the business of a peaceful arrangement with the difficult penitent.

Because "the oil had been used up and now the wicks were starting to burn."[205]

Pablo kept glancing into the episcopal garden. He remembered everything as being his, as if it had really been his. At another time, he used to run among the encircling reed enclosures, jump over the irrigation channels, sprinkle water all over and shout at Ranca, the gardener; he would make his way through everything and enjoy everything without thinking whether it was his or someone else's. He was master of all the impulses of his caprice and he possessed the indulgence of the lord bishop, who watched him from his study, without his even knowing it. Now Pablo kept raising his eyes to all the wide windows, which were always closed.

"And Ranca?"

An old man turned around as he filled a two-handled frail with manure.

"Ranca isn't here any more."

"And why isn't Ranca here any more?"

"He isn't here because he caught a pernicious intermittent fever and we had to take him away; and we took him away because he died."[206]

Ranca had died, and the garden remained! Ranca used to start smoking some speedwell leaves on top of a mound of recently turned over earth, while he, riding high up on him, his legs round his loins, till he was hanging from his shoulders, would order him to carry him to the bishop's reception room. Ranca, without a wife, without a family, emerged in the garden like an wild plant. He was completely vegetal, of the vegetation of that very place: of the clods of earth, of the bark, of the roots, of the sun and the aroma and the air. Whenever you saw him around Oleza, you had a feeling of the whole garden itself in his furrowed skin, in his manure-filled fingernails, in his voice that resounded like a large wooden bucket on the wheel of the water mill. He caught tertian fever and he died, and the garden went on....

"And the bishop, what does he say?"

"The bishop? What does he say about what?"

"About Ranca?"

"About Ranca?" And the gardener turned the basket over onto the hotbed and started to pull out the weeds.

¿Es que el obispo ya no rezaba ni leía bajo su limonero? ¡Tanto tiempo estaba ya el hortal en ese abandono que hasta pasó la muerte muy callando entre los árboles! Pablo sintió el vuelo de los años encima de su corazón. Y todo lo que se quedó coordinado y dormido en su primera infancia, le resalía ahora con sensación de presencia.

Lejos y hondo, en lo último del huerto, detrás de los vidrios de Provisoría, comenzó a fraguarse el rostro llano de don Magín, como un recuerdo; un recuerdo que le miraba, que le llamaba, que se le apareció en el aire diáfano.

– ¿Ya no te consienten que vengas a Palacio ni a mi casa? ¡Te han temblado los ojos, y por tu frente pasa también temblando la verdad con el sofoco de los que todavía son buenos!

Le entró en las oficinas. Allí los capellanes fumaban con zumbas y albardanías de tertulias de archivo, y algunos se hablaban con grave sigilo de capítulo.

De la escalera les llegaba una quietud de casa de enfermo. Pablo le dijo:

– Fue mi madre la que quiso que viniese aquí en su busca. Anoche la cena acabó con gritos. Mi madre lloraba. Dicen que el "Olivar" de mi abuelo ha de ser colegio de "Jesús".

Un paje les avisó con muchos melindres las nuevas de arriba. ¡El P. Ferrando pedía ver a su ilustrísima desde las diez! Vino el P. Ferrando luego de celebrar su misa de la Virgen, la que rezan los sacerdotes de cansada edad y de ojos enfermos. Vino bajo la guardia de un Hermano ávido en oír y ver con lisa apariencia.

– Está en la saleta. ¡Llegó a las diez; ya dieron las once, y nada! – Y escapó santiguándose.

Desde la jaula negra de su negociado un clérigo decía:

– ¡Sí, sí!...¡Sí, sí! – Semejaba el cuco que sale al ventanillo del reloj.

Dos ofiales no pudieron contenerse; y recatándose por escalerillas y por pasadizos, se acercaron a la cámara. En aquel instante el P. Ferrando, muy apocado, imploraba:

– ¡No soy yo, no es el P. Ferrando el que pide audiencia; es el confesor de su ilustrísima!

Could it be that the bishop no longer prayed nor read under his lemon tree? The garden had been in such a state of abandonment for so long a time that even death passed very quietly between the trees! Pablo felt the flight of the years over his heart. And everything that remained coordinated and dormant in his early childhood emerged now with the sensation of present time.[207]

Deep and far away, at the very end of the garden, behind the glass windows of the Pantry, the frank countenance of Don Magín began to take shape, like a memory; a memory that looked at him, that called to him, that appeared to him in the diaphanous air.

"Don't they permit you to come to the Palace or to my house any more? Your eyes were trembling and the truth also passes trembling over your forehead, revealing the chagrin of those who still are good!"

He brought him into the offices. There the priests were smoking in a manner more typical of the jesting and clowning of a gathering of archivists, and some of them were talking to one another with the grave reserve expected at a chapter meeting.

A stillness like that of a sickroom came down to them from the stairway. Pablo said to him:

"It was my mother who wanted me to come here to look for you. Last night, dinner ended with shouting. My mother was crying. They say that my grandfather's 'Olive Grove' is going to be the school for 'Jesús.'"

A page informed them of the news from upstairs in a very affected manner. Father Ferrando had been asking to see His Excellency since ten o'clock! Father Ferrando came here just after he finished celebrating his Votive Mass for the Virgin, the one offered by priests getting on in years and with poor eyesight.[208] He arrived under the watchful eye of a Brother with a plain appearance, anxious to hear and see.

"He's in the small antechamber. He arrived at ten o'clock; it's already past eleven and nothing has happened!" And he crossed himself as he escaped from there.

From the black cage of the department where he served, a cleric said:

"Yes, yes!...Yes, yes!..." He resembled the cuckoo that is coming out of the small window of a clock.

Two clerks could no longer contain themselves; and, moving stealthily up narrow stairways and along the corridors, approached the chamber. At that very moment Father Ferrando was very diffidently imploring:

"It is not I, it is not Father Ferrando who is requesting an audience; it is His Excellency's confessor!"

El lego transpíraba un helor azul. Y el doméstico resignóse a llevar el recado, y al volver, sus anteojos eran de ráfagas de lumbres.

– ¡Su ilustrísima tampoco puede recibir a su confesor!

Los de la curia corrieron a las oficinas para referirlo. Y el capellán enjaulado movía fajos procesales diciendo:

– ¡Sí, sí!...

En la tarima del escritorio que fue del difunto mosén Orduño, un eclesiástico rubio se soltó el collarín y presagió, frotándose las manos:

– ¡El estallido!

Le rodearon algunos escribas, sobándose también las suyas como si las lavasen en el sol. ¡Que viniese ya el estallido! Ese era el concepto que estaba mudo en su conciencia, y acababa de revelar el archivero. Sentían por delegación el denuedo suficiente para que estallasen los dos poderes: la mitra y "Jesús". Ellos pertenecían a la mitra, y desde sus asientos de delantera iban a presenciarlo todo. El archivero Orduña, en sus éxtasis históricos, no se habría dado cuenta de la actualidad. El de ahora, con sus claros sentidos, tentaba lo porvenir, aunque, por su oficio, se mantuviese de ejemplos de las crónicas episcopales:

– En mil seiscientos veinticinco, el mayordomo del obispo va de casa en casa pesquisando si los olecenses comen carne en la Cuaresma. Impone multas y otras penas de más aflicción. El Justicia quiere impedirselo. Excomulga al obispo al Justicia. El Justicia, en venganza, manda pregonar: que puesto que los clérigos, con excusa de ir de noche a sus iglesias, promueven escándalos, ninguno salga, desde el toque de oraciones, sin llevar luces. Se suceden los encarcelamientos, las contiendas, los tumultos. Un criado del Justicia golpea a un fámulo del mayordomo, que huye, y apostándose bajo los pilares de la catedral, aguardó al otro y, al pasar, le arremete, lo acuchilla y se acoge al asilo sagrado. El Justicia lo arranca de los brazos de los canónigos y lo cuelga del cancel. El obispo fulmina excomunión contra toda la ciudad, y no se celebran oficios divinos ni sacramentos.

En mil setecientos quince, un prelado junta caudales para construir otra catedral, que ha de ser gloria de Oleza. Los planos y estudios se hacen en

The lay brother transpired an intense blue cold. And the servant resigned himself to bring the message, and when he returned, his spectacles were like gusts of glowing light:

"His Excellency can not receive his confessor either!"

The episcopal clerks ran to their offices to report this.

And the caged priest kept moving bundles of legal papers as he said:

"Yes, yes!..."

On the platform with the desk that once belonged to the deceased *Mosén* Orduña, a blond ecclesiastic unfastened his stock and rubbed his hands together as he said with foreboding:

"The explosion!"

Several scribes surrounded him, massaging their own hands also as if they were washing them in the sunlight. Let the explosion come then! That was the thought that lay silent in their consciousness, which the archivist had just revealed. In their official capacity they felt sufficiently intrepid to hope that conflict would break out between the two powers: the miter and "Jesús." They belonged to the miter and they were going to witness it all from their front row seats. The archivist Orduña, in his historical ecstasies, would not have even been aware of the present state of affairs. The present one, with his alert senses, was dealing with what was yet to happen, although, because of his position, he had to support his point of view with examples from the episcopal chronicles:

"In sixteen hundred and twenty-five, the bishop's steward goes from house to house inquiring as to whether Olezans are eating meat during Lent. He imposes fines and other punishments even more distressing. The Magistrate tries to prevent him from carrying this out. The bishop excommunicates the Magistrate. The Magistrate, seeking vengeance, orders this to be proclaimed: that since clerics promote such scandalous behavior with the excuse of having to go to their churches at night, none of them shall go out after the Angelus bells without bearing lanterns. Incarcerations, altercations and turmoil ensue. One of the Magistrate's servants beats one of the steward's domestics, who then flees, stations himself under the pillars of the cathedral, waited for the other one to pass by, and attacks him, stabs him with a knife and takes sanctuary in a sacred place of refuge. The Magistrate snatches him from the arms of the canons and hangs him from the gate. The bishop fulminates and threatens the entire city with excommunication, and no divine offices or sacraments are practiced.[209]

"In seventeen hundred and fifteen, a prelate gathers together a great fortune to construct another cathedral, which is going to be the glory of

su palacio. Trae los mejores canteros, alarifes, fusteros, artífices. Pero el cabildo entorpece sus designios de magnificencias. Le oprime, le cansa, le desespera. Y el obispo consume todos los dineros de la catedral en un cuartel de Caballería, más tarde lonja y después convento.

En mil setecientos noven...

– ¡Sí, sí...Sí, sí! ¡Se quedarán ustedes sin el estallido de ahora!

Le dejaron todos para ver al confesor, que bajaba.

Bajaba llorando. Le llovían las lágrimas por sus carrillos de labradora, empañándole las gafas. Se estrujaba el manteo y lo soltaba para cogerse al barandal. Su hipo de sollozos resonó en la cupulilla de la escalera. Y a su lado, el Hermano agobiaba los hombros como si recibiese la cruz de los agravios para llevarla integra a "Jesús". Pero, en la claustra, quiso que, antes de salir, redujese el Padre su congoja; lo apartó, lo arrimó al balaustre de un arco, frente al terebinto que trajo de Palestina una piadosa familia romera. Y el P. Ferrando, sin querer, leyó tres veces la lápida: "Tendí mis ramas como el terebinto, y mis ramas lo son de honor y gracia!" Y se precipitó más su lloro. El viejo confesor hacía como esas criaturas que aflojan su berrinche y de súbito aprietan y se encorajinan más. Lo tomó el Hermano entre sus brazos enjutos de constitución. Así desfalleció más el afligido. Acudieron capellanes y fámulos. Fue socarrándose el lego de ver que el trance se derramaba y atraía la compasión de las gentes antes que en casa. ¡Y eso sí que no!

Gritó el secretario llamando al jesuita, porque su ilustrísima venía en su busca. Llegó hasta la segunda meseta, descansándose en el brazo de don Magín y en el hombro de Pablo. Los oficiales de la curia le veían después de mucho tiempo. Creyéndole roído por el mal, torciéndose encima de su podre, como Job; y se les apareció con un cansacio y delgadez de convaleciente, sin otros indicios de la enfermedad recelada que las vendas de sus manos y de su cuello. Abrazó al P. Ferrando con dulzura filial, pero jerárquica. Subieron juntos, y el obispo se paraba porque su confesor había de enjugarse

Oleza. The plans and surveys are prepared in his palace. He brings the best stonemasons, architects, carpenters and artisans. But the cathedral chapter obstructs his designs for magnificence. It oppresses him, it wearies him, it drives him to desperation. And so the bishop uses up all the money intended for the cathedral on a Cavalry barracks, later used as a warehouse, and finally ending up a convent.[210]

"In seventeen hundred ninet...."

"Yes, yes...Yes, yes! You will have to do without the explosion for the time being!"

They all left him to go see the confessor who was coming downstairs.

He came down weeping. The tears were pouring down his cheeks, more properly those of a farmwoman, blurring his spectacles. He was squeezing his cloak and let go of it in order to grab hold of the banister. His choked sobbing echoed in the small dome over the stairway. As he walked beside him, the Brother's shoulders seemed overly burdened, as if he were receiving the cross of the Savior's humiliation in order to bear it intact to "Jesús." But once he reached the cloister, the Brother tried to have the Father moderate his anguish; he drew him aside and leaned him against the baluster supporting an arch that faced the terebinth that a pious family had brought back from a pilgrimage to Palestine. And Father Ferrando, though he did not wish to do so, read the tablet three times: "I spread my boughs as a terebinth tree and my boughs are full of honor and grace!"[211] And his weeping grew even more intense. The aged confessor was acting like those small children who allow their tantrum to subside and then suddenly grow tense and fly into an even greater rage. The Brother took him into his constitutionally skinny arms. For this reason the bereaved man grew even weaker. Priests and clerical servants came running. The lay brother started simmering with anger when he saw that the crisis was spreading and drawing the compassion of people other than those of the House. And that could not be permitted in any way!

The secretary shouted as he called to the Jesuit, because His Excellency was coming down to look for him. He got as far as the second landing, resting on Don Magín's arm and on Pablo's shoulder. The clerks on the bishop's staff were seeing him after a very long period of time. They had thought that he would be consumed by his ailment, writhing over his purulence like Job, and he appeared before them with a weariness and emaciation like that of a convalescent, with no other indications of his suspected malady than the bandages on his hands and his neck. He embraced Father Ferrando with filial if hierarchical sweetness. They went upstairs together and the bishop stopped

y sonarse, y doblar y guardarse su gordo pañuelo azul de ropería S. J.

Pasaron al oratorio. El sol de septiembre recalentaba el oro viejo del altar, la lámpara de cobre, las paredes desnudas, los floreros de paño, todo de un júbilo ingenuo y solitario de ermita de aldea. Su ilustrísima se postró en una vieja almohada; el P. Ferrando, desde su butaca, le puso la cinta de la Congregación de San Luis. Y un familiar juntó la puerta.

Se sentían los relojes de las salas, los ruidos agrarios del huerto episcopal. Y el Hermano trenzó sus dedos como si cogiese un estandarte de gloria para llevarlo íntegro a "Jesús".

...A mediodía llegó Pablo a su casa gritando:

— ¡Ya no se pierde, ya no se vende el "Olivar" del abuelo!

Su madre le besó cohibida bajo la mirada del esposo.

Todos callaban; y levantóse como una llama roja la voz de don Álvaro:

— ¡Irás siempre conmigo! ¡Siempre! – y se mordió su labio convulso.

¿Por qué chillaría su padre con ese odio entre tanto silencio y sumisión? Y acabada la comida, se apartó a la solana y estuvo mucho tiempo mirando los follajes del río. Por qué le gritó su padre, y por qué volvió él tan contento y ya no lo estaba? Había visto llorar a un jesuita como si no fuese un jesuita; al obispo arrodillado delante del confesor, lo mismo que él se arrodillaba. Todos los hombres se sometían a las medidas de los niños.

Se cansó de la ribera; y desde la sala, de un ambiente de recinto ajeno, contempló el cerrado palacio de Lóriz. Jardín de claustro; caricia de los sofás, de los aromas, de las sedas; las risas de las primas de Lóriz..., todo iba recordándolo como prendas suyas desaparecidas que no supo tener. Y ahora venía el agobio del invierno en su casa; y el palacio de Lóriz sin nadie.

Gimieron las bisagras de su postigo. De la sombra morada de la calle subían los pasos duros de su padre. Asomóse y le miró la espalda robusta, el bastón de espino negro con puño de oro entre sus dedos pálidos, las botas, el contorno de toda su figura...

Iba don Álvaro recogido en sus cavilaciones.

to allow his confessor to wipe his brow and blow his nose and then fold and put away his coarse blue handkerchief from the Society of Jesus linen room.

They went on into the oratory. The September sun generously warmed the old gold of the altar, the copper lamp, the bare walls, the flower holders made of fabric, everything, with the ingenuous, solitary jubilation of a village hermitage. His Excellency prostrated himself on an old cushion; Father Ferrando, from where he was seated in his armchair, placed the ribbon of the Congregation of San Luis upon him. And a familiar partly closed the door. You could hear the clocks in the large rooms, the rustic sounds from the episcopal garden. And the Brother braided his fingers as if he were taking hold of a banner of the Glory to carry it to "Jesús" intact.

...Pablo arrived home at midday shouting:

"It won't be lost now, they're no longer going to sell grandfather's "Olive Grove!"

His mother kissed him though she was somewhat restrained by her husband's glance.

They were all silent; and Don Álvaro's voice rose up like a red flame:

"You will always go with me! Always!" and he bit his lip convulsively.

Why should his father be screaming with such hatred amid all that silence and submission? And when the meal was over, he withdrew to the sun parlor and remained there for a long time looking at the foliage along the river. Why did his father shout at him and why did he himself come back so happy and now no longer felt that way? He had seen a Jesuit weeping as if he were not a Jesuit, and the bishop kneeling in front of his confessor the same way that he would kneel. All men surrendered themselves to the measure relevant for children.

He grew tired of the riverside; and contemplated the closed-up Lóriz palace from the drawing room, from the environment of a space that was alien to him. He kept remembering it all; the cloister garden, the caress of the sofas, the aromas, the silks; the laughter of the Lóriz's cousins..., as if they were precious things that belonged to him and had disappeared when he could no longer hold on to them. And now the oppressive feeling of winter in his house was coming upon him and there was nobody in the Lóriz palace.

The hinges on the wicket groaned. His father's firm footsteps rose up from the purple shadows of the street. He looked out and observed his father's robust back, the blackthorn cane with the golden head between his pale fingers, his boots, the outline of his whole figure....

Don Álvaro was walking along engrossed in his deep thoughts.

Ya no se vendía el "Olivar". ¡Qué gozo tuvieron su mujer y su hijo! Hasta ellos lograban ser enteramente ellos según eran, sin el padecimiento confinado y obscuro de serlo. Se les encendía la luz de su voluntad. "¡Ya no se vende, ya no se pierde el Olivar!" Es decir, ya no sufrían ellos, ni a él le dejaban padecer. Capacitado para el dolor, como otros nacen dotados para las delicias, se le empujaba y se le apartaba siempre de su camino. Le estaban negadas todas las complacencias, hasta la de sacrificarse...

...Anochecido llegó don Álvaro a la portería de "Jesús". Le dejaron en una silla de Vitoria del salón de visitas; y tuvo que esperar. Tardó el Rector, disculpándose con sus afanes del comienzo del curso académico. Prosperaba el número de internos, muchos, muchos de familias ilustres. Y como don Álvaro insinuara el asunto del "Olivar", el Rector sorprendióse delicadamente. Don Álvaro pronunció la palabra sacrificio...

Y el jesuita le sonrió con indulgencia:

– ¡Oh, a veces Dios no lo permite y envía sus ángeles para impedirlo! Un ángel detuvo el brazo de Abraham cuando ya su cuchillo tocaba la garganta de Isaac. ¿No nos habrá enviado Dios al P. Ferrando? Otras veces, cuán costosas son las decisiones que pueden trastornar las regaladas costumbres; quizá sea más difícil para el cristiano la renuncia de su bienestar que el acometer las más arriesgadas empresas. ¡Quizá, sí! Nos lo dice San Marcos en aquel commovedor episodio de su evangelio: Un hombre rico le pregunta al Salvador: "Maestro, ¿Qué haré para conseguir la vida eterna?" El Señor le responde: "Cumple los mandamientos." Y él añade: "Los he guardado desde mí juventud." Y Jesús puso en él los ojos (así los ponemos nosotros). Y le mostró agrado – *dilexit eum* – (también como nosotros hacemos), y le dijo: "¡Una cosa te falta: vende cuanto tienes y entrégalo a los pobres y tendrás un tesoro en el cielo; y ven y sígueme!" Pero el hombre rico afligióse y se apartó de Jesús... ¡Qué lástima!

The "Olive Grove" would no longer be sold. How overjoyed his wife and son had been! Even they succeeded in being entirely themselves, just as they really were, without the confined, gloomy suffering for being like that. The light of their willpower showed them the way. "They're no longer going to sell it, the Olive Grove won't be lost now!" That is to say, they would no longer suffer, nor would they allow him to be distressed. Though he was given the capacity for suffering, just as others are born endowed with the ability to enjoy delights, he was forever being pushed and held back from his natural bent or held back from it. He was denied every satisfaction, even that of self-sacrifice....

...Don Álvaro arrived at the gatehouse of "Jesús" after night had fallen. He was left seated in a rush-bottomed chair from Vitoria in the visitors' waiting room; and he was compelled to wait. The Rector was late and excused himself referring to the responsibilities of the beginning of the academic term. The number of boarding students was flourishing, many, many of them from illustrious families. And since Don Álvaro brought up the matter of the "Olive Grove," the Rector acted tactfully surprised. Don Álvaro uttered the word sacrifice....

And the Jesuit smiled at him indulgently:

"Oh, sometimes God does not permit it and sends his angels to prevent it! An angel stayed Abraham's arm just as his knife was about to touch Isaac's throat.[212] Didn't God probably send us Father Ferrando? At other times, how costly are the decisions that can upset our comfortable customary way of doing things; it may perhaps be more difficult for a Christian to renounce his well being than to undertake the riskiest of enterprises. Maybe so! Saint Mark tells us this in that moving episode in his Gospel: A rich man asks the Savior, 'Master, what can I do to achieve eternal life?' The Lord answers him, 'Fulfill the commandments.' And the man adds, 'I have observed them since my youth.' And Jesus fixed his eyes upon him (that is how we fix them). And he showed him his pleasure – *dilexit eum* – (as we also do), and said to him, 'One thing dost thou lack: sell whatever thou hast and handeth it over to the poor and thou shalt have a treasure in heaven; and now cometh and followeth me!' But the rich man was much grieved and departed from Jesus....[213] What a pity!"

3. Estampas y graja

"¡Y me casaré con el primero que se me presente!"

El primero que se presentó, que le presentaron a la señorita Valcárcel, fue don Amancio Espuch.

— ¡Quítese usted eso, esa barba, por Dios! — y María Fulgencía se reía, cubriéndose la faz con su rebociño de tules.

El señor penitenciario intervino gravemente:

— He de advertirle, hija mía, que este caballero tiene bufete de jurista y academia de estudiantes de Facultad; escribe libros muy doctos, y en su periódico *El Clamor de la Verdad* encubre su nombre con el precioso seudónimo de *Carolus Alba-Longa*...

— ¡Sí; pero que se quite, que se rape todas esas barbas de cuero!

Alba-Longa se afeitó la barba, y sin ella parecía haberse fajado las secas mejillas con piel apócrifa.

La señorita Valcárcel se quedó pasmada y arrepentida, y tuvo que reírse otra vez. El señor Espuch la miraba con amargura.

— ¡Ay, no se apure usted, que sí que nos casaremos!

Se casaron y se fueron a sus haciendas de Murcia. La novia, como un naranjo en flor; el marido, como un cayado de ébano. Boda muy escondida.

Por eso resonó tanto en las zarandas de los maldicientes. La tertulia de doña Corazón bramaba contra los casamenteros. Dõna Purita juró que los novios habían hecho voto de vivir como hermanos, imitando a muchos matrimonios.

Don Magín dictó con suavidad:

— Como San Valeriano y Santa Cecilia, como San Galación y Santa Epistema, como San Paulino y Therasia...

La mayordoma invocaba:

— ¡También los hubo casados y padres!

— Sí, señora, como San Marcelo, que tuvo doce hijos, y de ellos, siete, según dicen, se los dio su santa mujer de un solo parto.

...En la sala de las *Catalanas* desmenuzó Elvira la crónica nupcial. Todo lo tenía sabido y contado: desde las galas hasta los pensamientos categóricamente conyugales de la "Monja". Las dos viejecitas de Mahón

3. Prints and Chough

"And I'll marry the first man who comes along!"

The first one who appeared, who was introduced to Señorita Valcárcel, was Don Amancio Espuch.

"Take that thing off, for God's sake, that beard!" and María Fulgencia started laughing, covering her face with her fine white tulle shawl.

The canon penitentiary intervened with considerable gravity:

"I must warn you, my child, that this gentleman has a law office and an academy for students preparing for the professions; he writes very learned books and he conceals his name with the delightful pseudonym of *Carolus Alba-Longa* in his newspaper *The Outcry of Truth....*[214]

"Yes, but let him take it off, let him have all those leathery whiskers shaved off."

Alba-Longa shaved off his beard, and without it, he seemed to have swathed his dried-up cheeks with apocryphal skin.

Señorita Valcárcel was left astounded and repentant, and she had to laugh again. Señor Espuch looked at her bitterly.

"Oh, don't you worry, we're really going to get married!"

They got married and went off to her country property in Murcia. The bride, like an orange tree in blossom; the husband like an ebony shepherd's crook. A very well-concealed wedding.

For that very reason it reverberated so much as it sifted through the mouths of those given to calumny. The social gathering at Doña Corazón's bellowed against the matchmakers. Doña Purita swore that the bride and groom had sworn to live as brother and sister, thus imitating many married couples.

Don Magín gently suggested:

"Like Saint Valerianus and Saint Cecilia,[215] like Saint Galatian and Saint Episteme,[216] like Saint Paulinus and Therasia...."[217]

The majordomo's wife alleged:

"There were even some who were married and even parents!"

"Yes, señora, like Saint Marcellus,[218] who had twelve children, and of that number, according to what they say, his sainted wife gave him seven in one single childbirth."

...In the *Catalan sisters'* drawing room, Elvira shredded the nuptial account to bits. She knew it all and everything was accounted for: from the bridal trousseau to the categorically conjugal thoughts of the "Nun."

devoraban con susto el curioso anecdotario. Días de triunfo para la señorita Galindo en aquella casa. Pero, una tarde, suspiró la señora Monera:

– ¡Dios mío, yo no estaba encinta!

Lo dijo con una sofocación tan dulce, que semejaba entonces estarlo.

Se adolecieron las *Catalanas* contemplándola. La Monera ya tenía un bondadoso descuido en su talle, un amplio regazo. Pudo estar encinta, y no lo estaba. No cabía más honestidad.

Y palideció la gloria de Elvira Galindo en aquella casa sin herederos.

...Pues en la de don Álvaro decía el canónigo don Cruz:

– Poco se me da de las murmuraciones en siendo feliz nuestro don Amancio, que ni por su felicidad de novio se olvida de sus deberes. Hoy escribe que le tarda el volver a su puesto. ¡Oleza está en peligro, en peligro aún con la victoria y todo de "Jesús"!

El P. Bellod rugía, subiéndose una calza de pliegues morenos:

– La gusanera del Recreo Benéfico se revuelve bajo nuestro pie. ¡Esa tropa jura que ha de celebrar desgarradamente la inauguración del ferrocarril!

Después salieron, y al lado del padre iba Pablo. Llegaron a los olmos del camino de Murcia para ver los edificios nuevos de la estación de Oleza, y de retorno por el puente de los Azudes, fueron al Círculo de Labradores. Dejó don Álvaro a su hijo en la sala de lectura, y él se sumió con sus amigos en el aposentillo mural, donde se juntaban los mejores eclesiásticos y seglares de la "causa". Casi siempre permanecían callados, y en el silencio ardían más sus propósitos.

Pablo pisoteó los esterones traspasados de la humedad de los ladrillos. Luego se sentó en la reja del patio, un patio hondo con cortezas de verdín. El ábside de la parroquia de Nuestro Padre cuajaba la sombra de una rinconada de ortigas.

Salía el conserje, vestido de negro, con botas de paño, a darle de comer a una graja manera.

Pablo alzó los ojos al óvalo del cielo como si lo mirase desde una cárcava. Se precipitaban torbellinos de vencejos. Vencejos libres, y no volaban en la anchura del "Olivar" ni encima del río ni en los jardines de familias de

The two little old ladies from Mahon devoured the prying collection of anecdotes with alarm. Days of triumph for Señorita Galindo in that house. But one afternoon Señora Monera sighed:

"My God, I really wasn't pregnant!"

She said it with such sweet embarrassment that it seemed that she really was in such a condition at that moment.

The *Catalan sisters* were extremely grieved as they contemplated her. The Monera woman now had a generous feeling of indifference for her figure, an ample lap. She could very well have been pregnant, and she wasn't. You couldn't ask for more honesty than that.

And Elvira Galindo's glory paled in that heirless house.

...But in Don Álvaro's house the canon Don Cruz was saying:

"All that gossip makes little difference to me as long as our Don Amancio is happy, because he seems not to have overlooked his duties even though he is so happy as a bridegroom. He writes today that he can't wait to get back to his post. Oleza is in danger, in danger in spite of the victory of 'Jesús' and all of that."

Father Bellod was bellowing as he pulled up a dark-creased stocking:

"That worm pit of a Benevolent Recreational Association keeps crawling under our feet. That pack of evil doers swears they're going to celebrate the inauguration of the railroad shamelessly!"[219]

Then they went out and Pablo walked alongside his father. They came to the elm trees on the Murcia road so they could see the new buildings at the Oleza station, and on their way back, by way of the Bridge of the Waterwheels, they went to the Farmers' Club. Don Álvaro left his son in the reading room while he buried himself with his friends in the small private room, where the best ecclesiastics and laymen of the "cause" would get together. They would almost always remain quiet and their intentions would burn even brighter in the silence.

Pablo trampled all over the coarse floor matting permeated with the dampness of the bricks. Then he sat down at the grating to the patio, a deep patio encrusted with patches of moss. The apse of the parish church of Our Father congealed the shadow of a growth of nettles in one corner.

The porter came out, dressed in black, wearing heavy cloth boots, in order to to feed a tame female chough.

Pablo raised his eyes to the oval shape of the sky as if he were looking at it from a deep ditch. Whirlwinds of swifts hurriedly flew around. Swifts that were free, and they weren't flying over the breadth of the "Olive Grove," nor

colegiales que tenían hermanas tan hermosas. Pero sí que volaban en el azul del "Olivar", del río y de los huertos, y como iban tan altos, los veía desde su brocal del patio del Círculo, y el encerrado y el oprimido era él.

Pasó delante de los nichos de los armarios, leyendo los títulos de los volúmenes como si fuesen lápidas: *Teologías, Botánicas, Ordenanzas de Riegos,* colecciones de *El Año Cristiano,* de *El Clamor de la Verdad,* de *La Lectura Popular,* del *Mensajero del Sagrado Corazón.*

La graja croaba tan erizada, que se le veía el pellejo roído de miseria. Y el P. Bellod, desde la puerta del patio, blandía un puño peludo, diciendo:

– ¡Yo te apañaré!

Pablo volvióse a los tejuelos: *El Episcopologio Olecense, Anales de la diócesis de Oleza,* las *Actas de los Mártires,* el *Arte de pensar o Lógica admirable,* por el doctor sorbónico don Antonio Arnaldo, la *Respuesta fiscal sobre abolir la tasa y establecer el comercio de granos,* por don Pedro Rodríguez Campomanes; la *Historia de la Tercera Orden de San Francisco,* por fray Juan Carrillo; *Historia y estampas de los trajes de las Órdenes religiosas,* del abate Tirón...

Brincó la graja por la fenestra, mondándose su pico pringoso de color de calabaza en la rajadura de un vidrio. De pronto le temblaron sus alones secos y escapó, dejando su gañido y una borra de pluma de buche.

– ¡Yo te apañaré!

Pablo quitó la colanilla de la biblioteca; sacó los dos tomos de la "Obra dedicada al eminentísimo cardenal Lambruschini" y abrió en el atril de bufete de hule el libro de las láminas.

Religiosa de San Isidoro: muy jovencita, con sayal pardo, asomándole una guedeja rubia por el griñón; arrodillada en una grada de dibujo lineal, modelándosele los muslos y las piernas y saliéndole de los pliegues académicos un pie descalzo. Pablo se lo acarició.

Religiosa Armenia: topas ornamentales, hinchadas por una brisa matinal, y en su mano un cesto de mimbres. Alta, colorada, ardiente y ceñuda; la boca gordezuela, los ojos muy castos, rechazando una tentación asidua. Pablo la hubiese besado de rabia.

above the river nor in the gardens of families of schoolboys with such pretty sisters. But they were truly flying in the blue of the "Olive Grove," of the river and the gardens, and since they were flying so high, he saw them from where he was sitting on the well curbstone in the Club patio, and it was he who was confined and oppressed.

He passed in front of the recesses with the bookcases, reading the titles of the volumes as if they were inscribed tablets: *Theologies, Botanicals, Statutes on Irrigation*, collections of *The Christian Year*,[220] *The Outcry of Truth, Popular Reading, The Messenger of the Sacred Heart*.[221]

The chough kept croaking and was bristling in such a way that you could see her wretched, mangy skin. And Father Bellod, standing in the doorway to the patio, blandished a hairy fist and said:

"I'll get hold of you yet!"

Pablo turned back to his book labels: *Biographies of the Bishops of Oleza*,[222] *Annals of the Diocese of Oleza*,[223] the *Acts of the Martyrs*,[224] the *Art of Thinking or Admirable Logic* by M. Antoine Arnald, Doctor of the Faculty of the Sorbonne,[225] the *Fiscal Response Concerning the Abolition of Assessments and the Establishment of the Grain Trade* by Pedro Rodríguez Campomanes;[226] the *History of the Third Order of Saint Francis* by Fray Juan Carrillo;[227] *History and Prints of the Vestments of the Religious Orders* by the Abbé Tirón....[228]

The chough jumped through the window and scraped her grimy pumpkin-colored beak on a cracked pane of glass. Suddenly her great big dried-up wings trembled and she escaped, leaving behind the sound of her cawing and a fluff of crop feathers.

"I'll fix you yet!"

Pablo slid back the small bolt to the library door; he took out the two volumes of the "Work dedicated to the most eminent Cardinal Lambruschini"[229] and opened the book with the plates on the lectern on the oilcloth-covered writing table.

Nun of the Order of Saint Isidore:[230] very young and sweet, wearing brown sackcloth, a long blond tress peeking out from under her wimple; kneeling on a step as in an instrumental drawing, the shape of her thighs and legs clearly outlined and a bare foot sticking out from under the academic folds of her habit. Pablo caressed it.

Nun of an Armenian Order: ornamental vestments, swelling out in the morning breeze, with a wicker basket in her hand. Tall, of ruddy complexion, passionate and frowning; a full-lipped mouth, very chaste eyes, resisting a persistent temptation. Pablo could have kissed her frenziedly.

Religiosa de la Anunciación ¡qué pureza, qué cortedad, qué remilgos, y con pechos de casada, aunque se los apastase el percherín rígido y el corsé! Llevaba corsé y miriñaque bajo su jubón y la saboyana escarlata; las mangas eran azules, la capa blanca, la toca de almidón y el velo con pico en la frente. Sus manos tiernas tenían un libro muy lindo, sin estrenar. Pablo se hubiese dormido sintiendo la dulzura de esas manos en sus ojos. Ella humillaba los suyos; pero esos ojos serían de los que dijo, una tarde, doña Purita, de los que se abren y miran mucho cuando se aleja el que estuvo mirándolos.

La *Religiosa de la Orden del Verbo Encarnado* miraba con asombro, sin ver concretamente más que a sí misma. Capuz de lana, manto de ceremonia con cauda grande, bermeja como el escapulario, y en el seno la corona de espinas, el corazón, los clavos y la cifra de Jesús; el brazo en asa y la diestra en el talle, como una chula, y con la otra mano se pellizcaba la cola. Pablo ya la conocía. La vio en las salas del "Olivar" de su abuelo y en las de Lóriz, dentro de óvalos dorados, daguerrotipos y óleos de señoras austeras, de ojos negros y esquivos y cejas altas, que les ponen una tilde de pasmo y frialdad; reclinan el codo en un mueble, y siempre tienen una cajuela de marfiles, un cofrecillo de orificia que únicamente pueden abrir ellas cuando están solas.

Detrás de sus hombros le dijo el P. Bellod:

— Pasaste sin ver la estampa de San Basilio, y la del Penitente de Jesucristo, y la del Fuldense, y la del Hospitalario. No te paras más que en las de las monjas. ¿Ha vuelto la graja?

Luego se fue.

El último claror de la tarde se lo embebía el techo de vigas; un vaho de pozo salobre iba cayendo por la reja. Todo el casón semejaba desamparado. Pablo se acordó del conserje que se quedaba de noche en el sótano de la botillería, solo, con la graja dormida en un travesaño. Y angustióse del horror de ser él ese hombre de luto. Poco a poco le fue mirando una lececita como la de los cuentos de los niños que se pierden por los campos. Pero los niños

Nun of the Order of the Annunciation: what purity, what timidity, what primness, and the breasts of a married woman, even though her stiff shirtfront and corset tended to flatten them down! She was wearing a corset and a crinoline petticoat under her tight-fitting jerkin and scarlet outer skirt; the sleeves were blue, her cape white, her headdress starched and the veil with a peak in the front. Her tender hands held a very lovely book, unopened till now. Pablo could have fallen asleep feeling the sweetness of those hands on his eyes. She kept her eyes lowered in humility, but those eyes would probably be like those Doña Purita spoke of one afternoon, like those that open wide and keep on looking for a long time as the one who kept looking at them draws away.

The *Nun of the Order of the Incarnate Word* had a look of astonishment without seeing anything concretely other than herself. A woolen cowl, a ceremonial robe with a long train, bright-red like her scapular, and the heart, the nails and the monogram of Jesus in the bosom of the crown of thorns; her arm bent and her right hand at her waist, just like a saucy wench, and she was pinching the train of her gown with the other hand. Pablo already knew her. He saw her in the parlors of his grandfather's "Olive Grove" and at the home of the Lórizes, inside the gilded oval-shaped frames, the daguerreotypes and oil paintings of austere ladies, with black, disdainful eyes and arched eyebrows, which give them a semblance of astonishment and coldness; they are leaning their elbows on a piece of furniture and always have a small case of carved ivory pieces, a little jewel box of inlaid gold which only they can open when they are alone.

Father Bellod spoke to him from behind his shoulders.

"You passed through it without seeing the print of Saint Basil, and the one of the master of the Confraternity of the Penitents of Jesus Christ, and the one of the Cistercian monk from Fulda, and the one of the Knight Hospitaler.[231] You only stop at the ones of nuns. Has the chough come back?"

Then he went away.

The rafters forming the roof soaked up the last brilliance of the afternoon; a vapor like that of a brackish well kept falling over the grating. The big unpleasant house in all its entirety seemed forsaken. Pablo remembered the porter who remained by himself in the basement of the refreshment café at night with the chough asleep on a crossbeam. And he was overcome with horror at the thought of being that man dressed in mourning black. Little by little a point of light as in stories of children lost in the open countryside started looking at him. But the children in the stories walk beneath the

de los cuentos caminan bajo los bosques y los cielos, y él estaba inmóvil, entre vasares y muros. La lucecita venía de la parroquia, de la lámpara de Nuestro Padre San Daniel, la misma lámpara que palpitó sobre la frente de su madre la noche de su terror en la capilla del santo.

Y huyó Pablo por las soledades del Círculo, que olían a gentes que ya no estaban.

En el portal, el conserje miraba las losas con el ahinco que otros ojos miran las estrellas.

— Tu padre y los demás siguen allá dentro.

— ¡Es que yo estaba a obscuras!

— Ellos también.

Pablo prefirió su encierro. En el patio, todo negro, temblaba el ruido leñoso de la graja. Sintió tan cerca la parroquia, que recibía en su piel el unto de la lámpara, el tacto de los exvotos, la sensación de las imágenes. Entre las cornisas, el aire se abría y se plegaba blandamente por el vuelo de los murciélagos.

Olor de sotana del P. Bellod. Fue acercándosele su fantasma, que rascó un fósforo en la estera y encendió el velón.

— ¿Ya te escondes de la graja? ¡Está endemoniada, y te aborrecerá! ¡Guárdate de hacerle mal, aunque te aoje! ¡Te chafaría su amo! Ahora nos estará guipando ella desde las ortigas. Si te aburres, yo te daré un libro.

Escogió un volumen de las *Actas de los Mártires,* y dijo:

— Aquí tienes el cyfonismo Fíjate.

Arrimó una silla, se puso de hinojos y torcióse para mirar con su ojo entero. Iba señalando el asunto con el dedo cordal, y lo explicaba como si dictase la receta de una confitura:

— Se toma al mártir y se le encaja entre dos artesas o esquifes. ¿Sabes lo que son esquifes? ¿Y artesas?... Pues dos artesas bien clavadas, pero dejándoles huecos para sacar las piernas y los brazos; como una tortuga al revés. Arriba hay una trampilla que se abre encima de la boca, y por allí se le embute leche y miel, y se le deja al sol. Más leche y miel, y al sol; más leche y miel, y al sol. Se le paran las moscas, las avispas. Y leche y miel, y sol. El mártir se corrompe. Pero dura mucho tiempo. Siente que le bulle la carne, deshecha en una crema. Dicen que el cyfonismo está tomado del escafismo de los persas, que son muy ingeniosos.

forests and the skies and he was here motionless between the shelves and the walls. The small light was coming from the lamp in the parish church of Our Father San Daniel, the same lamp that throbbed over his mother's forehead the night of her terror in the saint's chapel.

And Pablo fled through the lonely confines of the club, which smelled of people who were no longer there.

At the entryway, the porter was looking at the flagstones with the eagerness with which other eyes look at the stars.

"Your father and the others are still inside there."

"Actually I was in the dark!"

"They are too."

Pablo preferred his confinement. The ligneous sound of the chough kept trembling in the total darkness of the patio. He was so aware of the parish church's proximity to him that he received the anointing of its lamp upon his skin, the touch of its votive offerings, the sensation of its images. The air opened wide between the cornices and was gently folded back by the flight of the bats.

The odor of Father Bellod's cassock. His phantom started approaching him and scraped a match against the floor matting and lit the oil lamp.

"So now you're hiding from the chough? It's bewitched and it probably abhors you! Be careful you don't do it any harm even if it casts an evil eye on you! Its master would squash you! Right now it's probably eying us from the nettles. If you get bored, I'll give you a book."

He selected a volume of the *Lives of the Martyrs* and said:

"Here you have siphon torture. Take a good look at it."

He brought over a chair, got on his knees and twisted around in order to look at it with his whole eye. He kept pointing out the material with his middle finger and explained it as if he were dictating the recipe for a fruit preserve:

"The martyr is taken and encased between two troughs or skiffs. Do you know what skiffs are? And troughs?... Well, two troughs nailed together solidly, but leaving hollow places for the legs and arms to stick out; like a turtle in reverse. There is a trapdoor on top which opens just over the mouth, and through it you stuff him with milk and honey and you leave him out in the sun. More milk and honey and back out in the sun; more milk and honey and again out in the sun. Flies and wasps alight on him. And milk and honey and out in the sun. The martyr starts to decay. But it lasts a long time. He feels his flesh seething, melting into a cream. They say that siphon torture is taken from the scaphism torture of the Persians, who are really very ingenious."

Iba cayendo sobre Pablo el resuello del ayo; sus ojos seguían obedientes los intinerarios y las insistencias del dedo trémulo, de uña roblada; su nuca había de doblarse agarrotada por la horquilla de la otra mano del capellán.

– ¿Qué dice ahí, en el margen de la estampa?

– Está escrito con tinta.

– Con tinta; ¿pero qué dice?

Pablo leyó: "Puede verse lo mismo en el tomo III, capítulo IV, de los *Viajes de Antenor por Grecia y Roma". – E.L.*

– Eso lo anotaría el Sr. Espuch y Loriga, tío de don Amancio; y no nos importa.

Estuvo volviendo páginas con su pulgar; buscaba precipitándose encima del folio, y su ojo abierto relucía de delirio algolágnico.

– ¡Aquí es! Aquí tienes los tormentos inventados por los hugonotes. Tampoco están mal. Tienden al católico, lo abren, le ladean con cuidado las entrañas para hacer sitio; se lo llenan de avena o de cebada y ofrecen este pesebre a sus jumentos.

La inminencia del verbo en tiempo presente encrudecía la óptica de los martirios.

– Están también los ultrajes y suplicios de muchas vírgenes cristianas, que de ningún modo debes ver. Y vámonos, que acabó la junta.

Durante la cena, el silencio de don Álvaro refluía en el silencio de la familia. El trueno del Segral se enroscaba por los muros. Pablo se acostó.

A las diez le llegó la jaculatoria de tía Elvira:

Señor, a dormir voy.
Confesión pido;
Oleo Santo,
perdón
del Espíritu Santo.

...Y a la otra tarde buscó las estampas prohibidas. Se contuvo mirándose sus dedos, que se le estremecía como los del P. Bellod. Vio santas empaladas, trucidadas, enrodadas, rotas a martillo. En el tormento de la virgen Engracia leyó con avidez los versos de Prudencio:

Tú sola vences la muerte;
vives palpando el hueco

The tutor's heavy breath was falling on Pablo's neck; his eyes obediently followed the insistent itineraries of the trembling finger, of the clinched fingernail; he was forced to bend the back of his neck as it was held in a throttling grip by the priest's other forked hand.

"What does it say here in the margin of the print?"

"It's written in ink."

"Yes, in ink, but what does it say?"

Pablo read, "You can see the same thing in volume III, chap. IV of the *Travels of Antenor Through Greece and Rome*." – *E.L.*[232]

"That annotation was probably made by Señor Espuch y Loriga, Don Amancio's uncle, but it's of no importance for us."

He kept turning pages with his thumb; he all but pounced onto the folio as he kept on looking and his open eye was shining with algolagnian delirium.

"Here it is! Here you have the tortures invented by the Huguenots.[233] They aren't bad either. They stretch out the Catholic, they open him up, they carefully push aside the entrails to make room, they fill him with oats or barley and offer this rack of fodder to their donkeys."

The imminence of the verb in the present tense made the optical apprehension of the martyrs even more irritating.

"The outrages and tortures upon many Christian virgins are also here, but you should in no way be permitted to see them. So let's go, because the meeting is over."

During dinner, Don Álvaro's silence flowed back into his family's silence. The thundering of the Segral coiled along the walls. Pablo went to bed.

At ten o'clock, Aunt Elvira's brief ejaculatory prayer reached him:

Lord, I go to sleep.
I ask confession;
Holy chrism,
forgiveness
of the Holy Spirit.[234]

...And on the following afternoon he looked for the prohibited prints. He restrained himself as he looked at his fingers, which were trembling like Father Bellod's. He saw sainted women, impaled, torn to pieces, subjected to torture on the wheel, their bodies shattered by hammer blows. In the torture of the virgin Engracia,[235] he avidly read the verses of Prudentius:

You alone conquer death;
you live fingering the hollow space

de tu arrancada carne.
Una mano inmunda
desgarró tu costado;
rebanados los pechos,
se vio tu corazón desnudo.
La gangrena roía tus médulas;
agudos garfios arrebataron
tus entrañas a pedazos.

Venía un grañido tan ansioso, que Pablo dejó su lectura; y vio que se escapaba del patio el P. Bellod; y él aguardóse un poco y salío. Estaba la graja apiolada con una atadera roñosa de media; tenía los alones desgoznados; se le hinchaba y vaciaba el buche como un fuelle; y un clavo le desencajaba las dos mitades del pico. Como si se hubiera pregonado su agonía, acudieron moscas bobas, hormigas chiquitinas y hormigas cabezudas de buenas tenazas, gusarapillos y lombrices del arbollón. Se le subían al pardal impedido, corriéndole por el borde y el telo de los ojos, por las boqueras, por el paladar; se le entraban y salían; algunos se quedaban cogidos en las calientes crispaciones de la sustancia. Toda la graja se retorció por el feroz prurito del insaciable tránsito de las sabandijas.

Pablo se inclinó y le arrancó a la victima la cuña del martirio. Entonces alzóse un alarido de grajo descomunal. Y las manos y las botas del conserje lo rechazaron contra los muros del ábside.

Vinieron asustados los capellanes y devotos de la junta. La graja se doblaba de sacudidas; se tendió y fue quedándose inmóvil.

Todos rodearon a Pablo: y don Álvaro se lo llevó. Se miraron, y el padre se dijo:

"No ha sido él y ni siquiera se disculpa. ¡No le importa tener razón!"

En la calle recibieron la delicia del aire de octubre, dulce de cosechas.

of your torn flesh.
An impure hand
has rent your side;
your breasts sliced away,
your naked heart now seen.
Decay gnawed away your marrow;
sharp hooks carried away
your innards in bits and pieces.[236]

Such an anguished croaking reached him that Pablo abandoned his reading; he saw that Father Bellod was escaping from the patio; and so he waited a moment and went out. The chough had its legs tied together with a filthy stocking garter; her large wings were disjointed, her crop kept swelling and emptying like bellows; and a nail had dislocated the two halves of her beak. As if her agony had been publicly announced, bot flies, tiny ants and large headed ants with powerful pincers, small flatworms and earthworms came swarming from the drain in the patio pool. They climbed up onto the disabled bird, running over the edges and inner membranes of her eyes, along the open wounds of her mouth, along the palate; they kept going in and coming out; some remained behind, attached to the warm, pulsating substance. The whole of the chough was writhing from the fierce itching caused by the insatiable movement of the nasty little insects.

Pablo bent over and tore out the wedge causing the victim's martyrdom. Then an infernal shrieking arose from the chough. And the hands and boots of the porter drove it all up against the walls of the apse.

The priests and pious laymen came running with fright from their meeting. The chough lay there contorted and shaking; finally it stretched out and remained there motionless.

They all surrounded Pablo; and Don Álvaro took him away. They looked at one another and the father said to himself:

"He wasn't the one who did it and he won't even make excuses for himself. It isn't important for him to be right!"

In the street they were met by the delightful October air, sweet with harvests.

4. La Monja

Octubre trajo el buen tiempo. Pasó el ahogo de los nublos y calinas que apretaban la ciudad. El verano desgreñado de vendavales, de cielos de remiendos, de mala color arrabalera, se trocó en un oroño alto, fino, miniado. Y entonces se cerró más la vida de Pablo. Sentíase retenido en la vigilancia de tía Elvira como en el centro de una lente que le precisaba cada uno de sus pensamientos para entregárselos al padre.

Los ojos de don Álvaro relucían de un dolorido rencor.

La madre, de una blancura lunar, de una tristeza sin lágrimas, le pidió al hijo que no la buscase tanto, que no la quisiese más que al padre.

— Te lo ha dicho "él"?

Y su mirada la repochó de blanda y medrosa.

Ella la soportaba renunciando a sus abandonos y goces pueriles de madre, para que Pablo creciese labrado por su voluntad y la del esposo. Lo quería hijo cabal, de las dos sangres. Hijo únicamente de su complacencia, sería reducirlo y menoscabarse a sí misma en los términos de su amor. Por eso alzóse su corazón cuando se rebeló Pablo con firmeza de Galindo diciéndole a *él:*

— ¡Yo no iré más allí!

Don Álvaro le miró dentro de los ojos.

Muchas veces le sorprendió Paulina acechándole.

Y una noche le avisó que al otro día, muy temprano, fuese a la academia de don Amancio.

— Todos los días, por la mañana, por la tarde. ¡Todos los días!

Y esforzaba su mandato mirándoles densamente. Ni su hijo ni su mujer se quejaban. ¡Ojalá se le arrebatasen y se le interpusiesen para tener razón de aborrecerlos! Ese "tener razón" que desperdiciaba su hijo.

Estuvo esperando la hora exacta de la salida de Pablo. Se incorporaba para ver el reloj de oro descolorido de su mujer; quiso que la hora puntual y disciplinaria la señalese el reloj de la madre. Y cuando llegó, como Pablo no se despertaba, don Álvaro precipitóse en su dormitorio y le arrancó las ropas. Se le hinchaba de furor la garganta. Y el hijo levantóse con graciosa ligereza diciendo:

— ¡Ya es otra vida!

4. The Nun

October brought good weather. The oppressiveness of the cloudy skies and the haze that beset the city came to an end. The disheveled summer of strong winds from the sea, of patchy skies, of offensive, coarse colors, changed into an uplifted, fine, delicately painted autumn. And then Pablo's life grew even more confined. He felt that he was restrained within Aunt Elvira's vigilance as if in the center of a lens, which meticulously defined every one of his thoughts in order to hand them over to his father.

Don Álvaro's eyes glowed with a pained rancor.

His mother, with a lunar-like whiteness, with a sadness bereft of tears, asked her son not to seek her out so often, nor to love her more than he did his father.

"Did 'he' tell you to say that?"

And his glance reproached her for being so compliant and fearful.

She put up with it, renouncing her childish abandonment and motherly pleasure, so that Pablo would grow up molded by her will and that of her husband. She wanted him to be a perfect son, of the two blood lines. To make him a son only to her complaisance would be to reduce him and diminish herself in terms of her love. For that reason her heart was uplifted when Pablo rebelled with the firmness of a Galindo when he said to him:

"I won't go there any more!"

Don Álvaro looked into the depths of his eyes.

Many times Paulina surprised him by spying on him.

And one night he informed him that he would be going to Don Amancio's academy very early the next day.

"Every day, in the morning, in the afternoon. Every day!"

And he intensified his command by looking at them impenetrably. Neither his son nor his wife complained. If only they would get carried away with anger and intervene to oppose him, so that he could have good reason to detest them! That "being right" that his son failed to use against him.

He kept waiting for the exact time for Pablo to depart. He kept sitting up in bed in order to see his wife's faded gold clock; he wanted the boy's mother's clock to mark the precise disciplinary hour. And when it came and Pablo still hadn't gotten up, Don Álvaro rushed into his bedroom and tore off the bedclothes. His throat was bursting with anger. And his son got up with affable rapidity, saying:

"So now it's another life!"

Y se vistió y se marchó cantando.

Olor de nardos recién abiertos; la ribera transparentaba lejanías con promesas de felicidad; los árboles del río incendiaban el azul con sus follajes de oro. La misma limpidez y fragancia del aire tenían los pensamientos de Pablo cuando pisó el umbral de don Amancio.

Portalón enlosado y húmedo, con cancela de hierro. Una moza quitaba los cerrojos para que saliese otra con cesta de mercado apoyada en el albardoncillo de la cadera.

– ¡Éste es nuevo, atiende!

Pablo, sonrojándose, les dijo que venía a la lección.

– Arriba está el chepudo.

Le salió un jorobado, con blusa larga y alpargatas grises, mordiendo un cañote de pluma de palomo.

Por la reja del vestíbulo aparecía una corona de cielo en las sienes viejecitas de la catedral. Aleteó el címbalo anunciando que alzaban a Dios.

Pablo imaginó anchura de campos, países desconocidos, barcos de vela en mares de Oriente, lo mismo, lo mismo que en su pupitre de los Estudios de "Jesús" cuando tocaban estas campanitas matinales.

El mozo de escaleras se le puso de través.

– Don Amancio y los discípulos no vienen hasta que acabe la misa mayor.

– Me manda mi padre...

– ¿Y quién es tu padre?

Enseguida que lo supo el giboso, descolgóse su reloj de hierro, se quedó calculando la espera y le convidó a pasar. Le dejó en una sala de sillería de lienzo rizado, con estampas agronómicas y devotas. Un velador de Manila y encima una bandeja de prendas íntimas de mujer y camisas de marido, recién planchadas, sin lustre. En un cojín del sofá se recostaba una linda muñeca con briales de labradora. Daba la ventana al huerto. Sol en los naranjos, en las celindas, en los heliotropos y rosas. Un ruido fresco de alberca; un gozoso estrépito de palomar.

Pablo cogió la muñeca en sus brazos; le compuso el vestido, le cerró las rodillitas, la asomó al huerto; y cuando quiso volverla a su almohada, aturdióse

And he got dressed and went off singing.

The fragrance of newly opened spikenard; the river bank revealed far off places with promises of happiness; the trees along the river set the blue of the sky afire with their golden foliage. Pablo's thoughts had the same limpidity and fragrance of the air when he stepped over Don Amancio's threshold.

A large entryway, paved with flagstones and damp, with an iron gate. A housemaid was drawing back the bolts so that another one could go out with her market basket resting against the small protective pillow against her hip.

"This one is a new one, mark my word!"

Pablo blushed and told them that he had come for his lesson.

"The crookback is upstairs."

A hunchback, wearing a long blouse and grey hemp sandals came over to greet him while he kept gnawing at the heavy shaft of a ringdove feather.

Through the vestibule grating a crown-shaped patch of sky appeared on the aging temples of the cathedral. The fluttering of the small bell was announcing that they were elevating the Host.

Pablo imagined the breadth of the fields, unknown lands, sailing ships on the seas of the Orient, just the same, the same as when he was at his writing desk in his Course of Studies at "Jesús," when they would ring these small matinal bells.

The all-around menial stood in front of him blocking his way.

"Don Amancio and the students won't be back until High Mass is over."

"My father sent me...."

"And who is your father?"

As soon as the gibbous lad found this out, he took off the iron clock hanging round his neck, stood there calculating how long he would have to wait and invited him to come in. He left him in a sitting room with a set of chairs of rippled linen, with agronomic and religious prints on the walls. A pedestal table from Manila,[237] and on top of it a tray with women's undergarments and a husband's shirts, recently ironed, with no starchy gloss. A pretty doll wearing rich silk peasant skirts was reclining on a sofa cushion. The window opened onto the garden. Sunlight in the orange trees, in the syringa, in the heliotropes and roses. A refreshing sound from a pool of water; a joyful din from a dovecot.

Pablo took the doll in his arms; he rearranged her dress, brought her little knees closer together, had her look out into the garden; and when he

porque una señora, con mantilla y devocionario, estaba mirándole.

La creyó una visita de consulta y encogióse junto a la vidriera.

Pero la señora se le acercó más, y siempre mirándole mucho le preguntó rápidamente:

– Es usted de Murcia? ¿Ha visto usted el "Ángel"? ¿Es que busca usted a mi marido?

Pablo le sonrió con sencillez. Según iba desprendiéndose la mantilla quedábase tan jovencita que se la hubiese llevado de la mano a jugar con la muñeca, entre los rosales.

– Yo no sé quién es su marido.

– ¿No sabe quién es y viene usted aquí?

– ¿Entonces usted será la...?

– Puede decirlo del todo: la "Monja". En la Visitación yo era la señorita Valcárcel, y en el siglo me llaman eso, la "Monja". De modo que sí que soy la mujer de don Amancio.

– ¡La mujer de don Amancio!... ¡Si es usted como yo! ¡Y yo tengo diecisiete años!

Ella, por ocultarse a sí misma su confusión, subía sus manos acariciándose los cabellos; y sobresaltóse más porque el Ángel la miraba en la boca, en el pecho, en la dulce angustia de su vida. Toda la mirada se le fue quedando encima de sus ojos... ¡Ahora, Señor, ahora se le aparecía de verdad su "Ángel"!... "¡Es usted casi como yo, y yo tengo diecisiete años!" Y repitiéndoselo volvió a mirarla confiada. El aparecido lo había pronunciado con alegría infantil. Era de una adolescencia pálida y hermosa; tenía frente de orgullo, y los labios y los ojos de pureza, de placer y de infortunio.

Sintiéronse pisadas humildes por los desnudos corredores, como el tránsito de colegiales por la claustra de "Jesús".

Desapareció la mujer de *Alba-Longa*. Y una mano grande y flaca tocó los hombros de Pablo.

– ¿Qué hacías?

– ¡Yo! Yo no lo sé. Me dijo el jorobado que aguardase.

– El jorobado se llama Diego, y es mi sobrino. Ven al escritorio.

Sala de paredes de yeso azul con friso de manises; mesas negras, mapas y quinqués; un vasar de rollos de causas y carpetones de documentos; el

tried to return her to her cushion, he was amazed to see that a lady wearing a mantilla and holding a prayer book was looking at him.

He thought she was a visitor coming for legal consultation and shrank back next to the wide window.

But the lady came closer to him and kept her eyes fixed on him for some time as she quickly asked him:

"Are you from Murcia? Have you seen the 'Angel?' Or is it that you are looking for my husband?"

Pablo smiled at her ingenuously. As she started to remove her mantilla, she ended up looking so very young that you could have taken her by the hand to play with the doll among the rosebushes.

"I don't know who your husband is."

"You don't know who he is and yet you've come here?"

"Then you must be the...?"

"You can say the whole thing: the 'Nun.' In La Visitación I was Señorita Valcárcel, and in the outside world that's what they call me, the 'Nun.' But I really am Don Amancio's wife."

"Don Amancio's wife!... But you're just like me! And I'm just seventeen years old!"

In order to hide her confusion from herself, she raised her hands to caress her hair; and she was even more startled because the Angel kept looking right at her mouth, at her bosom, at the sweet anguish of her life. His entire glance kept fixing itself right over her eyes.... Now, oh Lord, now her "Angel" was really appearing before her!... "You're just like me, and I am seventeen years old!" And as she repeated it to herself, she looked at him again confidently. The apparition had uttered it with childish joy. His was a pale and beautiful adolescence; his forehead was one of pride and his lips and eyes of purity, pleasure and misfortune.

Humble footsteps could be heard along the bare corridors, like the movement of schoolboys along the cloister at "Jesús."

Alba-Longa's wife disappeared. And a big, skinny hand touched Pablo on the shoulders.

"What were you doing?"

"I! I don't know. The hunchback told me to wait."

"The hunchback is named Diego, and he is my nephew. Come to my office."

A large room with blue plastered walls and a tiled frieze; black tables, maps and oil lamps; a shelf full of rolled-up sheaves of lawsuits and big portfolios of

bufete de don Amancio, y detrás un retrato suyo, de toga, con fondo de cortinón de grana. Dos balcones con reparos de maderos contra las lluvias. Luz amarilla reflejada por los sillares de la catedral. Siete alumnos que hacían de amanuenses; y del folgo de piel de borrega que desbordaba por el escañuelo del maestro, salió cojeando un gato cebrado.

– ¡Tonda!

Tonda era bizco y gordo.

– ¿Me oyes, Tonda? Enfrente de ti se sentará Pablo Galindo.

Vino Diego con un alcuza y llenó de tinta morada las ampolletas de vidrio, antiguos bebederos de jaulas de gafarrones. Se persignaron; y *Alba-Longa* repartió pliegos procesales.

– ¡Tonda! Tonda: "Epsilón" te pide que lo subas a la mesa.

Agarró el bisojo al gato del pellejo, y el animal se ovilló entre las escrituras.

A poco sonó en los ladrillos un golpe de carroña.

– ¡Tonda, tienes entrañas de hiena!

Al chico se le quedaron los ojos blancos y en su boca le asomaba la bulla.

– ¡Yo estaba escribiendo!

– ¡Tú estabas escribiendo, y con el codo le diste hasta derribarlo!

"Epsilón" se lamía la pata lisiada, y las centellas verdes de sus ojos se le enconaban de mirar al bizco.

Volteaba el cencerrete del cancel. Subían curiales, recaderos, escribanos, labradores, mujeres. Si alguna moza principiaba a gemir su desgracia, el licenciado la recogía en lo último de la sala, por sigilo de honestidad; y de amanuense iba Tonda, cuya catadura le fiaba de peligrosas tentaciones. Entonces le dictaba tratándole de usted.

– Tonda, escriba usted sin fijarse.

No se sentían las plumas ni el resuello de los demás, que se atirantaban escuchando. Y don Amancio se inflamaba de virtud y de odio.

A mediodía, bajo el campaneo de todas las torres de Oleza, rezaron

documents; Don Amancio's writing desk and behind it, a portrait of him, wearing a lawyer's robe, against a background of heavy scarlet curtains. Two balcony windows with protective shutters against the rains. Yellow light reflected by the ashlars of the cathedral. Seven pupils who were serving as amanuenses; and a striped cat came out limping from the lambskin leg-warming bag that was sticking out over the teacher's footstool.

"Tonda!"

Tonda was cross-eyed and fat.

"Do you hear me, Tonda? Pablo Galindo will sit in front of you."

Diego came with an oil bottle and filled the small glass vials, formerly used as drinking containers in cages for linnets, with purple ink. They crossed themselves and *Alba-Longa* distributed some legal papers.

"Tonda! Tonda: 'Epsilon' is asking you to lift him up onto the table."

The cross-eyed boy grabbed the cat by its skin and the animal curled up into a ball among the written documents.

Shortly thereafter the thudding sound of putrid flesh resounded against the bricks.

"Tonda, you have the soul of a hyena!"

The boy's eyes assumed a look of innocence and a look of confusion began creeping over his mouth.

"I was writing!"

"You were writing and you pushed him with your elbow till you knocked him off the table!"

"Epsilon" was licking his injured paw and the green sparks from his eyes seemed inflamed as he stared at the cross-eyed boy.

The small cowbell on the gate outside kept ringing loudly. Clerks from the bishop's offices, messengers, notaries, farmers and women kept coming upstairs. If some young woman began to bemoan her misfortune, the lawyer would seclude himself with her at the far end of the room, to maintain some air of confidentiality for her modesty; and Tonda would go over to serve as amanuensis because his appearance was a guarantee against dangerous temptations. He would then dictate to him addressing him with the formal *usted*.

"Tonda, write it down and don't pay any attention to what you're writing."

You couldn't hear the pens or the heavy breathing of the others as they strained to listen. And Don Amancio was inflamed with virtue and with hatred.

At noon they prayed the "Angelus"[238] under the constant ringing of the

el "Angelus" y salieron los estudiantes, menos Pablo, que se quedó convidado.

– Aquí tienes, María Fulgencia, al hijo de don Álvaro Galindo y Serrallonga.

Ella y Pablo se contemplaban en silencio; y como se les pasó el instante de decir que ya se habían visto en la salita de la muñeca, se miraron más y les pareció que, sin querer, consentían en un secreto.

Sentados a la mesa, comentó don Amancio sus métodos de enseñanza. Por la mañana, las prácticas de procedimientos. Por la tarde, la teórica y lección de elocuencia, de historia, de humanidades y otras disciplinas de Facultad mayor. Puede que alguien le malsinara creyendo que se aprovechaba de sus alumnos como de aprendices que le hacían los traslados de balde. ¿Y es que en cambio de esa faena no les guardaba? ¿No les servía la ciencia del mundo que habían de vivir, formándoles hombres expertos y cristianos?

Don Amancio disertaba y hacía platos. María Fulgencia prevenía lo más primoroso; enmendaba un leve descuido del servicio, dejaba su caricia en las flores del centro. Pablo reparó en el ajuar del comedor, tan mezclado de muebles de domicilio de célibe y de familia de abolengo, de objetos canijos y suntuarios, de vejez y de gracia. Manifestábase allí el marido y la mujer, juntos y distantes, las dos casas, las dos edades, las dos vidas.

Se le paraban encima las gafas azules de *Alba-Longa,* y él inclinaba sus ojos, y no sabiendo qué hacer, iba trazando rasgos con el marfil de su cuchillo en la labrada blancura de los manteles adamascados, de realces de pavones y cuernos de abundancia.

– ¡Este mantel se parece a los que tiene mi madre en los roperos del "Olivar"!

Y la señora dijo con un hilo de su vocecita:

– Es de mi casa de Murcia.

Su contorno se cincelaba en la gloria del ventanal. Y mirando Pablo a María Fulgencia recordó el pie desnudo de la "Religiosa de San Isidoro", la boca encendida de la "Religiosa Armenia", el pecho de la "Religiosa de la Anunciación", el exquisito recato de la "Religiosa del Verbo Encarnado".

bells from all the towers in Oleza, and the students all departed, except for Pablo, who was invited to remain and eat with them.

"María Fulgencia, we have here the son of Don Álvaro Galindo y Serrallonga."

She and Pablo contemplated one another in silence; and since the time had passed for them to say that they had already seen one another in the small parlor with the doll, they stared at one another even longer and it seemed to them that they were unwillingly agreeing to keep a secret.

When they were seated at the table, Don Amancio expounded on his teaching methods. In the morning, training in legal proceedings. In the afternoon, theory and instruction in eloquence, history, the humanities and other disciplines in university studies in Theology, Law and Medicine. It may very well be that someone could be spreading around the nasty idea that he was taking advantage of his students by using them as apprentices to do his copying without remuneration. But isn't it true that he kept them there in exchange for doing that task? Did he not offer them the knowledge of the world in which they would have to live, molding them into expert and Christian men?

Don Amancio kept on discoursing and preparing dishes. María Fulgencia took charge of the more exquisite aspects; she corrected any slight oversight in the service, leaving her caress on the flowers of the centerpiece. Pablo took notice of the furnishings in the dining room, such a mixture of a bachelor's household furniture and that of an ancestral family, of objects colorless and sumptuous, of things old and charming. The husband and the wife were manifest there, together and distant from one another, the two houses, the two ages, the two lives.

Alba-Longa's blue spectacles came to rest upon him and he lowered his eyes, and not knowing what to do, he started tracing strokes with the ivory part of his knife on the embroidered white surface of the damask tablecloth with the embossed peacocks and horns of plenty.

"This tablecloth is similar to the ones my mother has in her linen closets at the 'Olive Grove'."

And the señora said with a thread of her soft voice:

"It's from my house in Murcia."

Her outline was chiseled into the glory of the wide window. And when Pablo looked at María Fulgencia, he remembered the naked foot of the "Nun of Saint Isidore," the bright red mouth of the "Nun of the Armenian Order," the bosom of the "Nun of the Order of the Annunciation," the exquisite modesty of the "Nun of the Order of the Incarnate Word."

El maestro se llevó al alumno. Ya tañía el esquilón de la catedral llamando a coro.

En el azafate del pan quedaba casi todo el que María Fulgencia cortó para Pablo. Y estuvo tocando los trozos. Y al retirar sus copas, también casi intactas, vio los signos del mantel. Eran letras... Eran nombres. Fue leyéndolos, y fue temblándole sonoramente el corazón... "María Fulgencia..." "María Fulgencia..." "María Fulgencia y Pablo..."

La señorita recogió de prisa las ropas de mesa.

Sonaba el cimbalillo de los canónigos. En el sol de la plazuela iba saliendo poco a poco la sombra y después todo el señor deán muy reposado. Antes de llegar al pórtico se paró; volvióse a los viejos balcones de don Amancio Espuch, y suspiró complacido:

– ¡En fin, ya está María Fulgencia encaminada! Ahora sí que acertamos; y se acabó. ¡Ni más ni menos!

5. Ella y él

Pablo vio un zapato de María Fulgencia. Lo vio, lo tomó y lo tuvo. No lo había soltado el pico de un águila desde el cielo, como la sandalia de la "Bella de las mejillas de rosa" del cuento egipcio, sino que lo cogieron sus manos de la tierra. Tampoco era un zapato, sino un borceguí de tafilete. Y no vio un borceguí, sino el par. Se había quedado solo en el estudio haciendo una copia, y al salir asomóse a la sala. La muñeca del sofá le llamó tendiéndole sus bracitos; y en la alfombra del estrado estaban las botinas de la "Monja". ¡Qué altas y suaves! Muy juntas, un poco inclinadas por el gracioso risco del tacón. Sumergió su índice en la punta; allí había un tibio velloncillo. La señora necesitaba algodones para los dedos; y el suyo salió con un fino aroma de estuche de joyero. Pies infantiles; y arriba, la bota se ampliaba para ceñir la pierna de mujer. Se acercó el borceguí a los ojos, emocionándose de tenerlo como si la señora, toda la señora, vestida y calzada, descansase en sus manos. Y de repente se le cayó. La señora estaba a su lado, mirándole.

The teacher led the student away. The large bell at the cathedral was already tolling, calling the worshippers to the Choir service.

Almost all the bread María Fulgencia had cut for Pablo remained in the flat breadbasket. And she started touching the pieces. And as she cleared away his glasses, also almost untouched, she saw the marks on the tablecloth. They were letters.... They were names. She started reading them and her heart began trembling resoundingly.... "María Fulgencia...." "María Fulgencia...." "María Fulgencia...." "María Fulgencia and Pablo...."

The señora gathered up the table linen hurriedly.

The small bell of the canons was ringing for entry into the choir. In the sunlight of the small plaza, first the shadow and then the whole of the dean himself, looking very reposed, started coming out little by little. He stopped just before he reached the portico; he turned around toward Don Amancio Espuch's old balconies and sighed with satisfaction:

"At long last, María Fulgencia is now well on her way! We really hit the mark this time, and it's all taken care of. No more, nor less!"

5. She and He

Pablo saw one of María Fulgencia's shoes. He saw it, he picked it up and he held it. An eagle's beak hadn't dropped it from the sky as it had dropped the sandal of the "Beauty with the Pink Cheeks" in the Egyptian tale,[239] but rather his hands had picked it up from the ground. Nor was it an ordinary shoe, but rather a half-boot of morocco leather. And he didn't see one half-boot but the pair. He had remained alone in the office making a copy and as he was going out, he looked into the parlor. The doll on the sofa beckoned to him, extending her little arms, and the "Nun's" ankle boots were on the parlor rug. How high and smooth they were! So close together, leaning ever so slightly to one side by the charming height of the heel. He buried his index finger in the toe; there was a warm soft fleece inside it. The señora needed cotton wadding for the toes, and his finger came out with the fine aroma of a jewel case. Childlike feet; and in the upper part, the boot widened to fit round the leg of a woman. He brought the half-boot closer to his eyes and was very moved as he held it, as if the señora, the whole of the señora, all dressed and wearing her shoes, were resting in his hands. And suddenly it fell from his hands. The señora was at his side, looking at him. She had

Le había sorprendido como la primera mañana de lección. Para disculparse le mostró en su solapa una gota de tinta, y dijo que entró buscando agua y un paño...

– ¿Tinta? ¡Y aquí también, en esa mano! Tráigame usted mismo un limón. No es menester que baje al huerto. Hay cuatro o cinco muy hermosos en los fruteros.

Fué Pablo al comedor y vino con un limón como un fragante ovillo de luz.

– ¿Y para partirlo? No vaya. No vaya otra vez.

Y María Fulgencia hundió sus uñas en la corteza carnal. Saltó más fragancia.

– ¡No puede usted!

– ¿No puedo? ¡Sí que puedo!

Y mordía deliciosamente la pella amarilla.

Pablo se la quitó. Les parecía jugar en la frescura de todo el árbol.

– ¡Tampoco puede usted!

La fruta juntaba sus manos y sus respiraciones. Recibían y transpiraban el mismo aroma, pulverizado en el aire húmedo y ácido de su risa. Y entre los dos rasgaron los gajos sucosos. María Fulgencia los exprimió encima de la mancha y de los dedos de Pablo. Pero tuvo que llevarle al tocador.

Allí él se aturdió más y quiso crecerse diciendo:

– ¡Yo me lavaré; yo solo!

La señora le sonrió. ¡Claro que él se lavaría! Y no se lavaba. No se lavaba divertido en mirarlo todo: los grabados antiguos de fiestas de pastores, de ceremonias nupciales de los reyes de Francia; las muselinas de rosa pálido del balcón del huerto; los frágiles silloncitos dorados. Más hondo, el dormitorio: el *suyo*, pequeño, inocente y claro; su cama, camita de soltera, de novicia, con su velos de lazada también de un rosa descolorido de flor de frutal. Su celda de *sor* y señorita Valcárcel. Y ella entornaba los ojos y le resplandecía su boca con el jugo de la cidra. En su belleza y en su acento se afirmaba un brío y tono de voluntad. Y a él le halagó mucho que entre las cejas de la señora se hiciese un gracioso fruncido.

– ¡Nos parecemos!

surprised him just as she had the morning of his first lesson. In order to excuse himself he showed her a drop of ink on his lapel and said that he had come in looking for water and a piece of cloth....

"Ink? And here also, on that hand! You yourself go and bring me a lemon. It isn't necessary for you to go down to the garden. There are four or five very lovely ones in the fruit bowls."

Pablo went to the dining room and came back with a lemon like a fragrant clew of light.

"Now how to split it? Don't go away. Don't go away again."

And María Fulgencia buried her fingernails in the fleshy rind. Even more fragrance leaped out.

"You can't do it!"

"I can't do it? Of course I can!"

And she bit into the yellow round mass in a delightful manner.

Pablo took it away from her. It seemed as if they were playing in the coolness of the entire tree.

"You can't do it either!"

The fruit joined together their hands and their breaths. They received and transpired the same aroma, pulverized in the humid, acid-like air of their laughter. And between the two of them, they tore off the juicy slices. María Fulgencia squeezed them over the stain and over Pablo's fingers. But she had to take him over to her dressing table.

There he seemed even more bewildered and he tried to assume greater independence by saying:

"I can wash myself; I can do it alone!"

The señora smiled at him. Of course he would wash himself! And yet he didn't wash himself. He didn't wash himself because it amused him to look at everything: old prints of shepherds' festivities, of the wedding ceremonies of the French sovereigns; the pale pink muslin over the balcony window facing the garden; the small, fragile gilt armchairs. Further back, the bedroom: *hers*, small, innocent and bright; her bed, the small bed of an unmarried woman, a novice's bed, with its bed curtains decorated with bows, also in the faded pink shade of a fruit tree blossom. Her cell, that of a *sister* and Señorita Valcárcel. And she partly closed her eyes and her mouth was shining with citron juice. A high spirit and a tone of willfulness was affirmed in her beauty and the expression in her voice. And he was quite flattered to see a charming frown forming between the señora's eyebrows.

"We are like one another!"

María Fulgencia escogió las toallas de mejor frisa, sus jabones, sus esencias.

Se lavó solo. Ella fue estregándole la tinta; pudo marchitarla y empalidecerla, pero la difundía más; y enojábasese de su torpeza; y él creyó que le había prendido en la solapada un pomo de flores brotadas de sus dedos.

Aquella noche tía Elvira le dijo:

– ¿Te han perfumado, sobrino? ¡Llevas perfume y tinta!

...Despertóse muy de mañana; y acostado veía las viejas alamedas otoñales estremecidas dentro del río. "Ella" también miraría el agua, los árboles, el cielo, y diría: río, árbol, cielo. Cuando saliesen los palomos de su terrado a volar por las huertas, ella los vería y pronunciaría: palomos, aire, sol... Así se afanaba Pablo en pensar y regalarse con las palabras que María Fulgencia tuviera en sus labios, como si le tomase una miel con los suyos. Todas las que le escuchó adquirían forma reciente y sonido precioso; y, repitiéndolas, participaba de su pensamiento, de la acomodación de su lengua, de sus actiudes interiores, coincidiendo sus vidas.

Fue tan pronto al estudio, que tuvo que aguardar en el peldaño hasta que una moza le abrió la cancela. Desde su pupitre se absorbía inhalándose del silencio profundo para recoger las leves pisadas, el habla, la brisa del roce del vestido de ella. Y el techo, los muros, todo el ámbito le cerraban en una bóveda sensitiva, palpitante del temblor de sus pulsos.

Luego de comer salió sin volverse a su madre, que, como todas las tardes, le despedía desde la solana.

Ya tocaba el esquilón del coro. Corrió mucho para pasar pronto de las tapias de Palacio. Y desde allí vio que *Alba-Longa* se hundía en la catedral, a su siesta de la banca del crucero.

Rodeando la casona, asomóse Pablo al postigo de la corraliza; y de la vid del lavadero brotó la algarabía de los alumnos y criadas.

El sobrino del amo se le humilló haciendo gentiles meneos y reverencias de juglar.

– ¡Con tantos dengues y bien suspiste arrejuntarte a nosotros!

María Fulgencia chose her best frieze towels, her soaps and her scents. He washed himself. She kept trying to scrub the ink from him; she succeeded in making it fade and seem paler, but that spread it even further; and she grew angry at her clumsiness and he ended up believing that she had fastened onto his lapel a bunch of flowers that had sprouted from her fingers.

That night Aunt Elvira said to him:

"Has someone put perfume all over you, nephew? You give off the aroma of perfume and ink!"

...He woke up very early in the morning; and from where he was lying he could see the old autumnal poplar groves shivering on the surface of the river. "She" too was probably looking at the water, the trees, the sky, and she was probably saying: river, tree, sky. When the ringdoves departed from the roof terrace to fly over the cultivated plain, she most likely saw them and pronounced the words: ringdoves, air, sun.... In this way Pablo occupied himself by thinking and rewarding himself with the words that María Fulgencia would likely have on her lips, as if he were taking a bit of honey from hers with his own lips. All the words he heard her say acquired a recent form and an exquisite sound; and as he repeated them, he shared her thought, the arrangement of her tongue, her innermost attitude, and their lives merged together in this fashion.

He went to the law office so quickly that he had to wait at the doorstep till a servant girl opened the iron door grating for him. From his writing desk he absorbed himself in inhaling the deep silence so that he might gather in the light footsteps, the speech, the breeze from the contact with the dress that was hers. And the ceiling, the walls, the entire ambience enclosed him in a sensitive dome, palpitating with the shivering of his pulses.

After he had eaten, he left without going back to his mother, who bade him goodbye from the sun porch as she did every afternoon.

The big bell calling worshippers to choir service was already ringing. He ran as hard as he could so he could quickly pass by the walls round the Palace. And from there he saw that *Alba-Longa* was plunging into the cathedral for his siesta on the bench in the transept.

Pablo circled round the big house and peered through the postern into the poultry yard, and a terrible racket erupted from the students and the housemaids under the grapevines in the washing area.

The master's nephew humbled himself before him with genteel shaking and wiggling, bowing like a buffoon.

"With all your prissy manners, you sure figured out how to get so chummy with us!"

– Yo vine para subir al estudio por el patio.

Diego se cogió los ijares con los pulpos azules de sus manos, moviéndose fachendoso:

– ¡Por aquí no se sube, y el portón de la calle no lo abro hasta que no me salga de la chepa!

Y su sombra de camello retozaba en el sol de la balsa.

Pablo se fue a la margen del río y recostóse en una olma. El giboso no le dejaba; le caracoleó contoneándose, y el espolón de su espalda se triangulizaba en el azul. Pablo tuvo que sonreír recomido de furia.

– ¡Ya te ablandas, entecao! ¡Eres como mi tía, que así hace pucheretes como brinca de gusto!

– ¿La señora?

– Señora y tía de este pobretico. Se está toda una tarde de rodillas, y si a mano viene deja los rezos para vestirse que da gloria, y no sale ni a la reja.

Diego se volvía riéndose, porque le silbaban desde el trascorral.

– Aquéllos me chiulan porque quieren que te diga lo de mañana.

Hizo recrujir las cabezotas de sus dedos y le dijo:

– ¿Pero tú me atiendes a qué?

Pablo recibió en los ojos la lumbre lívida y untada de sus ojos.

– Mañana se van a Murcia tu padre y tu madre y mi tío. Ellos saben para qué, y yo también me lo supe. ¿Tú, no? Pues ellos se van, y aunque la "Monja" se quede, se irá a la Visitación o se encerrará en su alcoba y nosotros nos estaremos en el amasador con la "Bigastra" y la cocinera. La "Bigastra" quiere catarme... – y Diego puso su belfo en el oído de Pablo, que al huirle dejó caer fuera lo que faltaba del secreto – : ¡Y ha de ser delante de vosotros! Cada uno vendrá con lo que robe de sus casas para el jollín. ¿Qué nos traerás tú?

"I only came this way to go upstairs to the office by way of the courtyard."

Diego grabbed himself by the loins with his blue octopus-like hands, moving about ostentatiously:

"No one goes upstairs this way, and I won't open the main door to the street till I get rid of this confounded humpback!"

And his camel-like shadow romped about in the sunlight reflected on the pool of water.

Pablo went over to the river's edge and leaned back against a wide, leafy elm tree. The gibbous boy wouldn't leave him alone; he moved round him in caracoles, wriggling his hips, and the ridge on his back took on a triangular shape against the blue of the sky. Pablo had to smile even though he was consumed with fury.

"You're turning soft now, you sissy! You're just like my aunt, who screws up her face like this or else jumps up and down for joy!"

"The señora?"

"The señora and aunt of this poor devil. She can spend a whole afternoon on her knees, and if something should happen to come up, she abandons her prayers and gets all dressed up so nice your heart would leap, and she won't go out at all, not even to the window grating."

Diego turned around and laughed because they were whistling to him from the outer courtyard.

"Those fellows are whistling at me because they want me to tell you about what's going to happen tomorrow."

He cracked the club-headed ends of his fingers and said to him:

"Are you paying attention to me or what?"

Pablo received the livid, unctuous glow of the boy's eyes in his own eyes.

"Your father and your mother and my uncle are going off to Murcia tomorrow. They know very well why, and I found out about it also on my own. You don't know? Well, they're going, and even though the 'Nun' is remaining, she'll either go off to La Visitación or she'll lock herself up in her bedroom and we'll be left to ourselves in the kneading room with 'La Bigastra,' the housemaid from Bigastro, and the cook. 'La Bigastra' wants to have a go at me...." and Diego placed his blubber lips against Pablo's ear, and when Pablo ran away from him, he allowed whatever remained of the secret to fall out in the open: "And it's going to be in front of all of you! Every one of you will come with whatever you can steal from his house for the wild party. What are you going to bring for us?"

Pablo, enrojecido, volvióse al patio, y Diego le seguía resonándole su llavero en el anca.

– ¡Aunque quiebres el aldabón no te abrirán! – y a los estudiantes les guiñó de ojos conteniéndoles – : ¡Dejadme con él!

Se pararon en una vieja puerta clavonada.

– ¡Si tú no abres, yo llamaré hasta que la señora salga!

– ¿La señora? ¡Llévale ya los limones para la tinta de hoy!

A Pablo le ardieron las mejillas y le tembló la voz.

– ¡Quiero recoger lo mío y marcharme de aquí!

– ¿Marcharte? ¡Yo te abro! ¡Pasa; pero yo también, porque no te suelto! – y lo empujó por el pasadizo del amasador y del horno de la colada que acababa dentro de la cancela. Pablo comenzó a subir, y el ímpetu de su sangre orgullosa y pura se cohibía por el helor de la risa del jorobado que le recordaba su fisga: "¡Llévale los limones!..." Y sintió miedo de niño y miedo de amor por la señora tan desvalida en aquella casa, bajo el acecho de ruines.

El estudio le dio ahogo. No tenía más claridad que la ensangrentada por la piel de los nudos de los maderos. Aspiraba el olor de legajos, de obleas, de pasta de los gropos; le crujía el calzado en los manises ásperos de arenillas de salvaderas, y en la quietud se soltaba el vaho de todas las gentes que pasaron por el escritorio, de sus documentos, de sus ropas, de su intimidad. ¡Se marchaba para siempre! Y se sentó en su pupitre, y no se decía: ¡Aquí estoy!, sino: ¡Aquí estuve!

Diego desdobló los grandes postigos estruendosos de decrepitud. Apareció el gato por la zalea de la tarima; rodeó a Pablo, pasándole y hopeándole, y él se lo puso en las rodillas y se le incorporó un ronquido caliente y recóndito. Se complacía en todas las humildades y repugnancias de la servidumbre escolar por voluptuosidad ascética, pensando en la belleza de la señora. ¡Y él se iba! Le rebajaban y le desesperaban los estudiantes, el chepudo, el maestro. ¡Se iba para siempre! Y ella se quedaba para siempre. Y repitió: ¡Siempre, siempre, siempre!

Pablo was all flushed, turned toward the courtyard and Diego followed him, his ring of keys resounding against his haunch.

"They won't open for you even if you break the doorknocker!" and he winked at the students with his eyes to restrain them. "Leave me with him!"

They stopped at an old door decorated with nails.

"If you don't open up, I'll yell until the señora comes out!"

"The señora? Go bring her the lemons for today's ink!"

Pablo's cheeks were burning and his voice trembled.

"I want to pick up what's mine and get away from here!"

"Go away? All right, I'll open up for you! Come on in; but I'll go with you because I won't let you out of my sight!" and he pushed him along the passageway to the kneading room and the furnace used for the washing area, which ended just inside the door grating. Pablo started to go upstairs and the rush of his proud and pure blood was inhibited by the intense cold sensation of the hunchback's laughter that reminded him of his words of ironic ridicule, "Go bring her the lemons!..." And he felt the fear of a child and the fear of his love for this utterly helpless señora in that house, under the constant scrutiny of despicable people.

The study room was stifling him. The only brightness coming in there was the blood-red light from the surface of the knots in the wood of the shutters. He breathed in the aroma of bundles of legal papers, of wafers used for sealing, of the mash of the gauze used in the inkwells; his shoes crunched on the tiles which were gritty from the fine sand in the boxes used to dry the wet ink, and the breath of all the people who passed through this office was released into that stillness, of their documents, their clothes, their intimate essence. He was going away forever! And he sat down at his writing desk and he did not say to himself, "Here I am!, but rather, "Here I was!"

Diego opened wide the large shutters that were noisy with decrepitude. The cat appeared over the undressed sheepskin on the footstool; it walked around Pablo, passing by him and rubbing its tail against him, and Pablo put it on his knees and he felt pervaded by a warm, recondite snort. He took pleasure in all the acts of humility and repugnant activities of the school servants out of a feeling of ascetic voluptuousness, as he kept thinking of the beauty of the señora. And now he was going away! The students, the humpback, the teacher made him feel humiliated and drove him to desperation. He was going away forever! And she was remaining forever. And he repeated, "Forever, forever, forever!"

Encima del bufete del licenciado se balanceó la cabeza y la joroba de Diego.

– ¿No viste en el patio a Ballester, que le decimos "Calavera" por su cara de muerto? Pues a "Calavera" lo despachó mi tío; y ya vuelve. Cogiste al gato por antojo. ¡Eso no vale! Lo cogerás cuando te lo grite el viejo. "Calavera" se hartó, como ya se harta Tonda, y fue y le traspasó una pata con plumas que se le endeñaron.

Pablo se quedó mirando a "Epsilón". Gato del giboso y de don Amancio. Tenía la querencia a los pies del maestro, sin comunicarse nunca del primor de la señora. Y se arrancó a "Epsilón" y alzóse juntando sus libros.

– ¡Te piensas que te vas! ¡Qué te has de ir! ¿Qué le contarías a tu padre?

– ¡Me marcharé a mi "Olivar", o lejos!

– ¡A *tu* "Olivar", A *tu* "Olivar", o lejos! ¡Si pareces un Lóriz! ¿A que si te apuro, lloras? – el chepudo le hincó su mirada, sacó su brazo y se tocó la giba con un gesto de burdel – . ¡Yo la llevo y no me la siento, y a tí te va saliendo otra con *tu* "Olivar" que ya sentiréis! Pregúntaselo a tu madre. ¡Señoritingo del "Olivar", y que te lave la "Monja"! – y escapó con un corcovo.

Principiaron a subir los alumnos y destrás el licenciado.

Fue muy poca la lección. Cuando los muros de la catedral se inflamaron de sol poniente y la sala recibía una llama dolorosa, don Amancio puso el rosario entre los dedos de Pablo.

Rebulleron las mujeres de la casa en un aposentito empanado. Todos se persignaron.

Pablo vacilaba en el rezo, escuchándose como si mirase su voz que había de llegar a María Fulgencia.

Antes del anochecer soltó don Amancio a los chicos, y en la cantonada del tapial alcanzó Diego a Pablo y le pasó las sogas de sus brazos por los hombros, hablándole muy lagotero:

– El viejo se calló su viaje para no dejarnos respiro; pero yo le avisé la tartana. ¡Tú agarra lo que puedas de tu casa!

Pablo corrió, y creía escaparse de su niñez. Nunca había sentido tan triste y tan frágil su intimidad de criatura.

Diego's head and hump swung back and forth above the lawyer's writing desk.

"Didn't you see Ballester in the courtyard, the boy we call 'Death's Head,' because he has such a cadaver-like face? Well my uncle dismissed 'Death's Head' and now he's back. You grabbed the cat because you just felt like it. That's not allowed! You'll grab it only when the old man shouts for you to do so. 'Death's Head' got fed up, just as Tonda is now fed up, and he went and stuck some pens into the cat's paw and it got infected."

Pablo remained there looking at "Epsilon." The gibbous boy and Don Amancio's cat. It had its favorite spot at the master's feet, without ever becoming aware of the señora's loveliness. And "Epsilon" was pulled away from him and he stood up to gather his books.

"You really think you're going away! What do you mean you have to go! What would you tell your father?"

"I'm going away to my 'Olive Grove' or simply far away!"

"To *your* 'Olive Grove'! To *your* 'Olive Grove' or simply far away! Why you're acting like a Lóriz! I bet if I start annoying you, will you start to cry?" the humpback fixed his gaze upon him, reached out his arm and touched his hump with an obscene gesture. "I carry this and I don't even feel it and another one is growing out on you with *your* 'Olive Grove,' and you're really going to feel it! Go ask your mother about it. Fancy little momma's boy from the 'Olive Grove;' and you can have the 'Nun' wash you!" And he escaped with a prance.

The students began coming upstairs and behind them came the lawyer.

There wasn't much of a lesson. When the cathedral walls turned red with the setting sun and the room captured a dolorous flame, Don Amancio put the rosary between Pablo's fingers.

The women of the house began to stir within a small dark, unventilated room. They all made the sign of the cross.

Pablo hesitated in his prayer, listening to himself as if he were looking at his own voice that was intended to reach María Fulgencia.

Don Amancio let the boys go before nightfall, and Diego caught up with Pablo at the corner of the garden wall and put his rope-like arms around his shoulders and spoke to him very ingratiatingly:

"The old man kept quiet about his trip so as not to give us a breathing spell; but it was I who let the trap driver know. You grab whatever you can at your house!"

Pablo ran and he thought he was escaping from his childhood. He had never felt the intimacy of his early years to be so sad and fragile.

...Arrinconado en el comedor, iba mirando los aparadores y alacenas por el mandata que se le quedó de las palabras del giboso. Y después, mientras cenaba, sentía en sus párpados la mirada de la madre. No pudo resistirla, y levantó su frente, y entonces le buscaron los ojos del padre. Hubiese preferido que le gritasen, que le conturbasen. La quietud, la suavidad y el silencio le avergonzaban, dejándole a solas con el desabor de la tarde.

Todos se recogieron. Y desde su alcoba vio a tía Elvira encender su vela en las luces de los Dolores. Las manos pajizas de la beata se llevaron la claridad al rostro, y la sombra del candelero de la perdiz embalsamada apeonó en el yeso de la pared, enorme como un buitre vivo rajado por la candela. Las odió tanto, que le repugnó menos la tentación del chepudo.

Ya casi dormido, parecióle que la imagen de la Dolorosa se dulcificaba perteneciéndole y que venía a su cabecera mirándole. Empezó a gotear el susurro cada vez más tenue de su madre. Se le prendían algunas palabras: Murcia, hipoteca, "Olivar"..., todo dentro de una niebla tibia; y todo, hasta su amor, se iba quedando a distancias viejas y azules; y él sumido en una Oleza sin río; porque no se sentía el río y, en cambio, sonaba la vocecita de la imagen como una fuente diminuta, y encima de todo el techo del mundo volaba un cirio que salía de la carcasa de una perdiz.

...Despertóse con sobresalto, encerrado en la caracola del Segral clamoroso, que ardía de sol.

Se habían ido sus padres, y tía Elvira estaba en sus devociones de la parroquia.

Enseguida que salió de su dormitorio le miraron oblicuamente los retratos de sus abuelos: el señor Galindo, la señora Serrallonga; y desde su fanal también le miró Nuestra Señora de los Dolores, mostrándole el erizo de espadas de su corazón de plata. Huyó de la sala, y sin querer volvióse hacia el aposento de tía Elvira; en el fondo le esperaban las pupilas de vidrio de la perdiz, preguntándole: "¿Vas a robar?" Pablo la derribó, y rebotando por la estera, seguía diciéndole: "¿Vas a robar?".

Pablo se descalzó; las pisadas de sus pies desnudos resonaban en todo el

...Forsaken and alone in the dining room, he kept looking at the sideboards and cupboards in accordance with the command that still persisted from the gibbous boy's words. And afterwards, while he was eating dinner, he felt his mother's glance upon his eyelids. He was unable to resist it and raised his forehead, and then his father's eyes sought him out. He would have preferred that they shout at him, that they upset him. The tranquility, the forbearance and the silence made made him feel ashamed, leaving him alone with the tastelessness of the afternoon.

They all retired. And from his bedroom he saw Aunt Elvira light her candle from the flame of the one for the image of Mary of the Sorrows. The straw-like hands of the fanatic woman brought the brightness nearer to her face, and the shadow of the candlestick with the stuffed partridge moved swiftly over the plastered wall, as enormous as a living vulture split in half by the candle. He hated them so much that even the humpback's temptation seemed less repugnant to him.

Almost asleep now, it seemed to him that the image of the Sorrowing Mary grew sweeter, belonged to him and that she had come to the head of his bed to look at him. His mother's ever more tenuous whisper began to drip. Several words seemed to stick in his mind: Murcia, mortgage, "Olive Grove"..., all within a tepid mist; and everything, even her love, was being left behind at old and blue distances, and he was immersed in an Oleza without a river; because he could not hear the river, and on the other hand, the small voice of the image sounded like a diminutive fountain, and above the whole roof of the world, a wax candle, rising up from the carcass of a partridge, kept flying around.

...He awoke with a start, enclosed in the conch that was the turbulent Segral, that was burning with sunlight.

His parents had gone away and Aunt Elvira was busy with her devotions at the parish church.

No sooner had he left his bedroom than his grandparents' portraits stared down obliquely upon him: Señor Galindo, Señora Serrallonga; and from under her bell glass, Our Lady of the Sorrows was also looking at him, showing him the thistly cluster of swords on her silver heart. He fled from the parlor and then reluctantly turned toward Aunt Elvira's room; in the back, the partridge's glass pupils awaited him, asking him, "Are you going to steal?" Pablo knocked it over, and as it bounced on the floor matting, it kept saying to him, "Are you going to steal?"

Pablo took off his shoes; the footsteps of his bare feet echoed through

ámbito y las repetía cada ladrillo y cada viga, y al entrar en el escritorio de
su padre, le golpearon sus pasos debajo de toda su piel, como sí su sangre
fuese un pie muy grande de bronce que le hollaba todo su cuerpo. Se apretó
el costado y las sienes, porque sus latidos hacían temblar las vidrieras.

Todos los muebles estaban cerrados. Se precipitó en el gabinete de su
madre. Perfume leve y bueno de sus ropas; el olor que buscaba en el colegio
besando sus hombros, su mantilla, sus cabellos, su manos; olor antiguo de
pureza, y parecióle que regresaba desde tiempos muy hondos protegiéndose
a sí mismo, pequeñito y débil. Y se acercó al tocador de caoba. Le salió
su palidez en un espejo de libro; allí dentro estaban sus ojos con la mirada
materna, y entre los ojos el ceño duro de los Galindo. De una frutilla de
marfil del mueble pendía el collar de seda de las llavecitas de la madre, y las
tocó y se le fue comunicando su frío. Tan menudas, tan infantiles, y le abrían
todos sus pensamientos. ¡Pero vio los cajoncillos confiadamente entornados,
y se sonrojó, y tuvo miedo, y refugióse en su cuarto!

En aquella soledad de paredes blancas el tiempo corría con el ímpetu
de sus palpitaciones. Habría comenzado ya el regocijo encanallado de los
alumnos con las mozas; y arriba, María Fulgencia se afligiría rezando y
engalanándose cautiva y gloriosa.

Tornó a salir, y todavía pisaba sin ruido. El señor Galindo y la señora
Serrallonga le dijeron desde las cortezas de óleo de sus lienzos: "Puedes
andar sin esconderte, porque no has robado. No has robado nada. La llaves
eran de tu madre... ¡Si hubiesen sido de tu padre!..."

¡Qué ancha y qué intima la mañana en la ribera! Abría con sus pies la
margen tierna y aparecía un agua fina, nuevecita, que empapaba la seroja de
los álamos; tocaba los troncos húmedos y recogía el sentido de la circulación.
El Segral se llenó de una nube blanca como una vestidura fresca, y él estuvo
contemplándola hasta que la corriente se quedó en la intacta desnudez del
cielo...

Le arrancaron de su gozo los muchachos de la academia. Diego no traía
blusón de fámulo. Era todo sobrino, con botas hinchadas y luto viejo del
tío.

the whole of his surroundings and each brick and each rafter repeated them, and as he entered his father's study, his footsteps pounded beneath all of his skin, as if his blood were a huge bronze foot trampling upon his entire body. He squeezed his side and his temples, because their throbbing was making the glass in the windowpanes shake.

Each piece of furniture was enclosed. He rushed into his mother's boudoir. The delicate, fine perfume of her clothes; the scent that he would seek at school when he kissed her shoulders, her mantilla, her hair, her hands; the long-time aroma of purity, and it seemed to him that he was returning from the depths of distant time, protecting a self that was so very small and weak. And he walked over to the mahogany dressing table. His paleness struck him in the mirrored surface of a book; his eyes were there inside with his mother's glance and the stern Galindo frown between his eyes. The silken cord with his mother's tiny keys was hanging from an ivory rosary bead on this piece of furniture, and he touched them and the cold within them was transmitted to him. So very small, so child-like, and yet they opened all his thoughts for him. But then he saw the small drawers candidly half open and he blushed and was overcome with fear and sought refuge in his room!

In the solitude of those white walls time raced on with the impulse of his palpitations. The debased merriment of the students with the maidservants must have already begun; and upstairs, María Fulgencia was probably overcome with distress as she prayed and was dressing herself up in all her finery within her captivity and her glory.

He went out again and his footsteps still made no sound. Señor Galindo and Señora Serrallonga spoke to him from the oily encrustation of their canvases, "You can walk by without hiding because you haven't stolen. You haven't stolen anything. The keys were your mother's.... If they had belonged to your father!..."

How wide and how intimate the morning at the river bank! He opened the water's tender edge with his feet and a fine water, quite new, appeared and it saturated the dried-up leaves that had fallen from the poplar trees; it touched the damp trunks and gathered the direction of the circulation. The Segral was filled with a white cloud, like a fresh vestment, and he stood there contemplating it until the current finally ended up like the untouched nakedness of the sky....

The boys from the academy snatched him from the midst of his pleasure. Diego wasn't wearing the loose-fitting shirt of a servant. He was all the nephew, with pompous boots and his uncle's old mourning clothes.

Lleváronse a Pablo, revolviéndole, estrujándole para que diese su escote.
Y bajo el cobertizo del lavadero exprimió sus bolsillos; y entre los menudos,
relumbraron algunas monedas de plata.

– ¿Las robaste?

Pablo se inflamó de vergüenza y de ira.

– ¡Yo no robé! ¡Es mío, de mi ahorro, de lo que me sobra de los
domingos!

No le atendían los demás, arremolinados con las criadas. La "Bigastra"
gimió de dolor furioso mordida por Tonda en las calientes axilas. "Calavera"
se lo descuajó zamarreándole; encima de todos orzaba la corcova de Diego,
y con un tumulto de faldas y carnes retrenzadas que cruijían se revolcaron
por las losas del amasador.

– ¡Ay, señorito Pablo, venga, usted que es bueno y decente! – y se
desgarró una risa de retozo de brama.

Acudió Pablo mirándoles con avidez torturada de verlo todo y de
escaparse del vaho del refocilo que le quemaba las mejillas. Se vio y se
sintió a sí mismo en instantes de sensualidad primorosa. (Mañana del
último Viernes Santo. Palacio de Lóriz. Huerto florecido en la madrugada
de la Pasión del Señor. Rosales, azucenas, cipreses, naranjos, el árbol del
Paraíso goteando la miel del relente. Hilos de agua entre carne de lirios. Y,
dentro, salones antiguos que parecían guardados bajo un fanal de silencio; la
estatua de doña Purita en un amanecer de tisú de retablo; mujeres que sólo
al respirar besaban. Y por la noche, la procesión del Entierro; temblor de
oro de luces; rosas deshojadas; la urna del Sepulcro como una escarcha de
riquezas abriendo el aire primaveral, y él reclinado en suavidades: damascos,
sedas, terciopelos; ambiente de magnificencias, aromas de mujer y de
jardines; tristeza selecta de su felicidad; la luna mirándole, luna redonda,
blanca, como un pecho que le mantenía sus contenidos deseos con delicia
de acacias). Y viose más remoto, más chiquito delante de una estampa de
la mesa de estudio del prelado enfermo: la estampa de un niño cuya frente,
de pureza eucarística, resiste el pico anheloso de un avestruz, y ese niño,
ya hombre, atormentado por voraces tentaciones, murió virgen y puro. La

They carried Pablo off, turning him around, pressing him to hand over his share. And so he squeezed out his pockets under the protective covering above the laundry area; and several silver coins were shining brightly amid the small change.

"Did you steal them?"

Pablo was inflamed with shame and anger.

"I didn't steal them! It's all mine, from what I save up, from what's left over from my Sunday church money!"

The others paid him no heed, because they were milling around the housemaids. "La Bigastra" moaned with a raging pain when she was bitten by Tonda in her warm armpits. "Death's Head" tore him off of her, knocking him about; Diego's crooked back projected above all of them, and they rolled about upon the flagstones in the kneading room amidst the tumult of crackling skirts and bare flesh all entwined.

"Oh, Master Pablo, why don't you come over here, you who are so good and decent!" And a playful, ruttish laughter burst forth.

Pablo drew closer and looked at them with the tortured eagerness of having to see it all and with a desire to escape from the hot breath of delectation that was burning his cheeks. He saw himself and he heard himself during moments of exquisite sensuality. (The morning of last Good Friday. The Lóriz palace. The flowering garden in the early morning of the day of the Passion of the Lord. Rosebushes, white lilies, cypresses, orange trees, the China tree dripping with the honey of the evening dew. Trickles of water between the flesh of the irises. And inside, very old sitting rooms that seemed to be preserved under a bell glass of silence; Doña Purita's statue at a dawn like the gold woven tissue of an altarpiece; women who kissed just by their breathing. And by night, the procession of the Burial of Jesus; the golden trembling of burning lights; roses stripped of their petals; the glass casket containing the image of the dead Jesus, like a hoarfrost of riches opening up the spring air, and he, Pablo, reclining on all manner of smoothness: damasks, silks, velvets; an atmosphere of magnificent things, the aromas of a woman and of gardens; the choice sadness of his happiness; the moon looking down upon him, the round, white moon, like a breast preserving its restrained desires for him with the delight of acacias.) And he saw himself more remote, ever so much smaller, in front of a print on the study table of the ailing prelate: the print of a young boy whose forehead, out of Eucharistic purity, resists the avid beak of an ostrich, and that small child, now a man, tormented by voracious temptations, died virginal and

frente de Pablo ardía desgarrada por pensamientos inmundos. Era menester un prodigio que le subiese a la gracia de su complacencia sin el tránsito penoso de los arrepentidos. Acogióse al recuerdo de lecturas y cuadros de apariciones de ángeles que refrescan con sus alas las frentes elegidas; de vírgenes coronadas de estrellas que mecen sobre sus rodillas, en el vuelo azul de su manto, las almas rescatadas...

Pablo pidió el milagro de su salvación. Y el milagro le fue concedido; y llegó por una vereda celeste de resplandores como todos los bellos milagros. La franja de sol otoñal se hizo carne y forma. Una voz, que parecía emitida de la luz y exhalar luz, pronunció el nombre de Pablo.

¡La señora!

Pablo se apartó de los réprobos, y siguió las claridades y fragancias de la aparecida.

Traspuso el portalillo del jardín, y allí, en una soledad de limoneros en flor, María Fulgencia, sin gloria ni fortaleza de santa, sino toda de lágrimas y de dulzuras de mujer, gemía.

– ¡Pablo, Pablo: usted entre ellos; usted, que era el "Ángel" mío que tiene la mano tendida hacia el cielo!

Pablo se acongojó de pena y de rabia. Ella también lloró, y llorando se besaban en los ojos y en la boca...

pure. Pablo's forehead was burning as it was torn by unclean thoughts. A miracle would be required to elevate him to the grace of his complaisance without having to go through the painful passage of repentance. He sought refuge in the memory of readings and pictures about the appearances of angels who refresh the brows of the chosen with their wings; of virgins crowned with stars who rock the souls of the redeemed upon their knees in the blue flare of their mantles....

Pablo asked for the miracle of his salvation. And the miracle was granted to him; and it came along a celestial path of resplendence like all beautiful miracles. The fringe of autumnal sunlight became flesh and form. A voice that seemed to emanate from the light and to exhale light uttered Pablo's name.

The señora!

Pablo withdrew from the reprobates and followed the brilliance and the fragrance of the apparition.

He disappeared behind the small garden gate, and there, in a solitude of blossoming lemon trees, María Fulgencia, without saintly glory or strength, with only womanly tears and sweetness, kept moaning:

"Pablo, Pablo; you together with them; you, who were the 'Angel' that was mine, who have your hand stretched out toward heaven!"

Pablo was distressed and overcome by sorrow and rage. She too wept, and as they wept, they kissed one another on the eyes and on the mouth....

VII

LA FELICIDAD

HAPPINESS

1. Un último día

La ventana abierta del todo. Sol de las huertas silenciosas; sol de domingo de noviembre que pasaba desde la cavidad perfecta y azul. Daba el río un frescor de claridades. El río no semejaba correr por las espaldas remendadas de Oleza, sino por una ciudad de mármol y por tréboles tiernos.

Oleza callaba. Oleza debía de estar oyendo misa en monasterios y parroquias. Quietud y limpidez de otoño. Vuelos de palomos; crujidos de las ropas que lavaba una mujer en su piedra de la orilla; y los lienzos lavados en la calma del domingo parecían esparcir su olor de blancura nueva.

Pablo sentíase dichoso y bueno, y el sol entraba a dormirse dócilmente en sus brazos. La madre le acercó más el desayuno; y como él no acababa de soltarse de la pereza, le sumergía las rubias pastas en el tazón, hondo y fino como una magnolia, y luego se las ponía, emblandecidas de leche, en la boca.

– ¡No eres como todas las mañanas!

Pablo, sonriendo, decía que no.

– No eres como todas las mañanas. ¡Te ríes y parece que te hayas olvidado de reír con tu risa de antes!...

El hijo parpadeó y se puso a beber con voracidad de niño. Paulina le fue contando las últimas pesadumbres por la santa causa. Pero cuando el príncipe viniese a sentarse en su reino, las mejores recompensas serían para los que le hubieren confesado en la desgracia. Todos se lo prometían. El "Olivar" había sido gravado, y la mitad de los dineros de la hipoteca se derramó en los Comités facciosos mortecinos, con beneficio para el semanario de *Alba-Longa*. Si algún sobresalto tuvo Paulina al poner su firma en la escritura, se lo quitó el ver a su esposo incorporarse de su cerrada torvedad.

– ...¡Y vosotros redimiréis las tierras y la casa del abuelo Daniel!

Nada dijo Pablo, como si en ese "vosotros" no se sintiese junto a su padre.

Siempre, en los trastornos, en las aflicciones, siempre buscaba Pablo a don Magín; y después, de las palabras que el hijo le traía, iba recogiendo la madre un calor de refugio, de guarda, de remedio de la distante amistad

1. One Last Day

The window completely open. The sunlight of the silent cultivated plain; a Sunday sun of November passing down through the perfect, blue concavity. The river emitted a refreshing brilliance. The river did not seem to run past the shabby patches in back of the Olezan houses, but rather through a city of marble and tender clover.

Oleza was silent. Oleza must have been hearing Mass in monasteries and parish churches. The stillness and the limpidity of autumn. Flights of ringdoves; the crackling sound of laundry washed upon a stone by a woman at the river bank; and the linens washed in this Sunday calm seemed to disperse their aroma of new whiteness.

Pablo felt happy and good, and the sunlight entered docilely to sleep in his arms. His mother brought his breakfast closer to him; and since he had not yet abandoned his indolence, she immersed the light-colored pastry in his bowl for him, deep and delicate like a magnolia, and then, after softening them with milk, she put them in his mouth.

"You're not the same as you are every morning!"

Pablo smiled and said that he wasn't.

"You're not the same as you are every morning. You laugh, but it seems that you've forgotten how to laugh the way you did before!..."

Her son blinked and began to drink with childlike voracity. Paulina kept telling him the latest sorrowful events for the holy cause. But when the prince returned to take back his throne in his realm, the best rewards would be for those who had professed their loyalty to him during his time of misfortune. They all promised that this would happen.[240] The "Olive Grove" had been encumbered and half the money from the mortgage had been lavished on the dying Committees of the rebels, with some benefaction for Alba-Longa's seminary. If Paulina felt somewhat shocked as she put her signature on the papers, it disappeared when she saw that her husband had been roused from his pent-up grim disposition

"...And you will redeem grandfather Daniel's lands and house!"

Pablo didn't say anything, just as if he did not feel at all united with his father in that use of the plural "you."

Pablo would always seek out Don Magín in times of upheaval and affliction; and afterwards, his mother would gather from the words her son brought back to her a warm feeling of refuge, of protection, of assistance

del párroco y de doña Corazón, de la brava ternura de Jimena y, más alta, la promesa del sostén ilustre del obispo. Ahora, Pablo la escuchaba como si ya no amase su "Olivar" y, no amándolo, tampoco temiese perderlo.

Paulina le habló del obispo. Y Pablo volvió sus ojos, ocultándose de sus remordimientos. En todas las iglesias de la diócesis se rezaba por el llagado. El Señor la había elegido para salvar a Oleza. Y Oleza ya se cansaba de decirlo y oírlo. Oleza recordaba que el anterior prelado, de una mundana actividad de agente de negocios espirituales, no necesitó sufrir para obtener los bienes de su apostolado. Pues el otro pobre obispo de Alepo siquiera padecía por su perfección de santidad y no por redimir a nadie. ¿Ni redimir a estas horas de qué? Los hombres rubios pecadores, los extranjeros del ferrocarril, ya no estaban; y para los pecados del lugar no era menester una víctima propiciatoria.

La víctima llevaba mucho tiempo escondida, sin audencias, sin oficios ni galas; invisibles sus atributos, escasas las noticias de sus dolores. Y hasta los más consternados por la laceria de Palacio habían de esforzarse para imaginarla y agradecerla.

De los santos queda el culto, la liturgia, la estampa y la crónica de su martirio. Del obispo leproso no se tenía más que su ausencia, su ausencia sin moverse ya de lo profundo de la ciudad, y el silencio y esquivez de su casa entornada. Y al pasar por sus portales, las gentes los miraban muy de prisa.

– ¡Cuántas veces, Pablo, te habrá bendecido sin que tú te volvieses a su reja ni a su huerto, ese huerto tan tuyo cuando eras chiquito!

Pablo hundió su sonrojo en la almohada.

Paulina recordó una lejana visita del prelado al "Olivar". Fue la tarde que don Álvaro la pidió por esposa. El penitenciario, don Amancio y Monera rodeaban a su padre, el abuelo Daniel, tan desvalido, tan frágil, en el ancho sofá de la sala. Don Álvaro, de pie, muy pálido, tenía en su mano un pomo de rosas, su junco y su sombrero; el sol de los parrales le circulaba por la frente. Apareció su ilustrísima, cuyos ojos escudriñaban los corazones. A

because of the remote friendship of the parish priest and of Doña Corazón, of the brusque tenderness of Jimena, and, at an even higher level, the promise of the eminent support of the bishop. Now Pablo was listening to her as if he no longer loved her "Olive Grove," and if he didn't love it, he might no longer fear losing it.

Paulina spoke to him of the bishop. And Pablo turned his eyes away, hiding from his remorse. They were praying for the ulcerated prelate in all the churches of the diocese. The Lord had chosen him to save Oleza. And Oleza was growing weary of saying it and hearing it. Oleza remembered that the previous prelate, one concerned with worldly activity, like that of a salesman of spiritual business, had no need to suffer in order to attain the benefits of his apostolate. Well, that other poor soul of a bishop from Aleppo at least suffered in order to perfect his holiness and not to redeem anyone. And what was there not to redeem at this particular time? The blond, sinful men, the foreigners from the railroad, were no longer there; and a propitiatory victim wasn't really necessary for the sins of the town.[241]

The victim kept himself hidden away for a long time, without any audiences, without religious services or any other display of pomp; his attributes were invisible, the news concerning his suffering very sparse. And even those most dismayed by the wretched situation at the Palace were compelled to make considerable effort to imagine it and be grateful for it.

The cult, the liturgy, the religious print and the chronicle of their martyrdom remain behind for saints. As for the leper bishop, they had nothing more than his absence, his absence without requiring him to move in any way from the depths of the city, and the silence and aloofness of his virtually closed-up house. And as they passed by the entrance, the people would look at it very hurriedly.

"How many times must he have blessed you, Pablo, without your turning to the grating at his window or his garden, that garden that was so much a part of you when you were very little!"

Pablo buried his flushed face in his pillow.

Paulina recalled a long-past visit of the prelate to the "Olive Grove." It was the afternoon Don Álvaro had asked for her as his wife. The canon-penitentiary, Don Amancio and Monera were all surrounding her father, grandfather Daniel, who seemed so helpless, so fragile, on that wide sofa in the drawing room. Don Álvaro, so very pale, was standing there, holding a bouquet of roses, his slender cane and his hat in his hand; the sunlight from the vine arbors kept circulating over his forehead. His Excellency appeared and his eyes were able to scrutinize every heart. He smiled at her and at her

ella y su padre les sonrió, dedicándoles las palabras del escudo del primer obispo de Oleza: "Llamad y se os abrirá".

Pablo preguntó la hora, y enseguida quiso vestirse.

Cuando salió sonaba muy alto, encendiéndose de azul, el cimbalillo de la catedral. Entró por el pórtico de la plaza, y fue pasando verjas de capillas húmedas, rinconadas de imágenes de nicho, las palmeras de piedra del ábside. Volvió por la vía-sacra. En el pináculo de un facistol, la paloma de la Trinidad abría su vuelo de oro roído delante del trono enfundado; y en el altar mayor, el señor deán iba miniando su misa de diez con primorosa tardanza de calígrafo.

No estaba María Fulgencia.

Pablo empujó el cancel del Sacramento. El arco del pasadizo episcopal le apagó el día. Asomóse a Palacio. – quizá María Fulgencia le esperaba ya en su huerto, como todos los domingos – . Y aquí, en este patio, árboles, pilares, sol y cielo cerrados, todo para los gorriones que brincaban por las cornisas ye se espulgaban en la rama cimera del terebinto; y de pronto, estrujaron el silencio con sus alas rapadas. No se asustaban de los curiales y fámulos, y huían de él, que venía a tientas, conteniéndose, lo mismo que la mañana que quiso robar y no robó.

Pisó una losa rajada que le salían hormigas. La losa del hormiguero que miró y tocó cuando llegaba de la mano de don Magín. Nueve años sin acordarse de ella. Pero de la mano de don Magín pasó por esta claustra el día que lloraba el confesor del obispo. ¡Después de todo, no hacía tanto tiempo! Se lo dijo para que callase su pensamiento que le propuso: "Si no te contentases con mirar las oficinas!" – estaban abiertas siendo domingo – . "¡Si fueses al lado del enfermo!..." Olor viejo de escritorios; sol en un rodal de estera, en una bisagra de armario. "¡Si no te impacientases por salir al huerto y buscar la puertecita del río!..."

Se impregnó de la respiración tranquila y madura condensada entre tapias blancas. – Cuando María Fulgencia le besara bajo su limonero, él

father, dedicating the words inscribed on the coat of arms of the first bishop of Oleza to them: "Knock and the way shall be opened unto you."

Pablo asked for the time and made up his mind to get dressed right away.

When he went outside, the cathedral minor bell was ringing way up high, lighting itself with the blue of the sky. He entered by way of the portal facing the plaza and kept passing by the grilles leading into the damp chapels, the corners with images in their niches, the stone palm trees in the apse. He came back along the Via Crucis. On the top part of a lectern, the dove of the Trinity held its wings of corroded gold open in flight in front of the ensheathed throne; and on the high altar, the dean went on delineating a miniature version of his ten-o'clock Mass with the exquisite leisureliness of a calligrapher.

María Fulgencia wasn't there.

Pablo pushed open the outer storm door of the chapel of the Blessed Sacrament. The arch over the episcopal passageway closed out the daylight for him. He looked out at the Palace. – Perhaps María Fulgencia was now waiting for him there in her garden, as she did every Sunday, And here, in this patio, trees, columns, sunlight and sky closed off, all of this for the sparrows that hopped about on the cornices, ridding themselves of fleas on the uppermost branch of the terebinth tree; and suddenly they crushed the silence with their cropped wings. They were not frightened by the bishop's clerks and servants, but they were only fleeing from him, who came here groping his way, restraining himself, just as he had the morning he tried to steal and he didn't steal.

He stepped on a cracked flagstone with ants crawling out of it. The very same flagstone with the swarming ants that he had observed and touched when he had come holding Don Magín by the hand. Nine years without remembering it. But it was when he was holding Don Magín by the hand that he passed through this cloister the day the bishop's confessor was crying. It wasn't such a long time after all! He said this to himself to quiet his thought, which was postulating to him, "But you weren't satisfied just to look at the offices!" – they were open since it was Sunday, "But you walked alongside the ailing man!..." A very old odor of writing desks; sunlight on a small patch of floor matting, on a cabinet hinge. "If only you were not so impatient to go out into the garden and look for the little door to the river!..."

He was impregnated with the tranquil, mature breath condensed between the white garden walls. – When María Fulgencia kissed him under the lemon

podría decirse: "Pero yo estuve en casa del que sufre, y sufrí" – . ¡Pobre huerto, sin el goce de la balsa llena de agua clara y azul; sin el frescor de los cósioles de geranios, de malvarrosas, de alábegas! Ahora se hinchaba la cuaja verde del fondo... Y al revolverse del borde de yeso, se le apareció don Magín, rezando en su breviario, y con el índice tendido le mostraba a su ilustrísima, reclinado en un almohadón, al pie del limonero de sus antiguos recreos y oraciones.

El niño de antes aleteó en Pablo, y le pudo. Se dejaba llevar de aquella interior criatura mientras su frente se le endureció pensando: "¡Si yo no hubiese venido!" Y tuvo que inclinarse para pasar la bóveda olorosa. Le daban en las mejillas y en los hombros los follajes del peso de los limones. – Dormitorio de María Fulgencia, de candidez de virgen y de flor de limón. Fruta que acercó sus manos, su risa, su boca... La espalda, el pecho, la garganta de ella siempre con fragancia de su limonero – . Y en el aire parado de este árbol, como el *suyo,* se derretían, y se volatilizaban los aceites balsámicos de la carne padecida, carne del hombre puro que le miraba.

Le miraba esperándole:

– ¡No me tengas miedo! ¿Te acuerdas, Pablo? Así te hablé la primera vez que, corriendo y jugando por todo Palacio, te asomaste a mi aposento. Te miraba jugar desde mi ventana. Aquella tarde sentí que venías, y ni me moví de mi sillón. Ahora también me estuve muy quieto para que tampoco me tuvieses miedo.

La misma voz de entonces, pero más afligida. ¿No era como la voz del Señor cuando reconviene al que se aparta de su gracia? Todo niño se postró Pablo en la tierra del tronco como antaño en la alfombra de la biblioteca. Un piar filial descendía de los árboles envolviendo de inocencia el balbucir de sus secretos; y, según los confesaba, iba sumergiéndose su corazón en el azul del domingo de otoño.

– ¡Tú quisiste robar, tú lo quisiste, y por otro pecado contra tu pureza!

– ¡Pero yo no robé! – y el orgullo de Pablo se deshizo en congoja, una congoja tan dulce de ser todavía infantil cuando ya se quedaba sin infancia.

Subió el obispo sus manos para perfumárselas en las hojas tiernas del

tree, he could say to himself, "But I was in the house of someone who is suffering, and I suffered." Poor garden, without the pleasure of the small pool full of clear, blue water; without the refreshing presence of the earthen tubs full of geraniums, hollyhocks, basil! Now the green coagulated mass at the bottom was swelling up.... And as he turned away from the plastered edge, Don Magín appeared to him, praying from his breviary, and he extended his index finger and pointed out His Excellency, reclining on a large cushion at the foot of the lemon tree of his long-past diversions and prayers.

The child of that past time fluttered within Pablo and took possession of him. He allowed himself to be carried away by that child within him while his forehead hardened as he thought, "If I hadn't come!" And he had to bend down in order to pass through the fragrant vault. The foliage, bent by the weight of the lemons, touched him on the cheeks and on the shoulders. – María Fulgencia's bedroom, full of virginal candor and lemon blossoms. A fruit that brought her hands, her laughter, her mouth closer to him.... Her back, her bosom, her throat always with the fragrance of her lemon tree, And in the motionless air of this tree, as in hers, the balsamic oils of the suffering flesh, the flesh of the pure man who was looking at him, were melting and volatilizing.

He kept looking at him and waiting for him.

"Don't be afraid of me! Do you remember, Pablo? That's how I spoke to you the first time when you looked up at my room while you were running around and playing all over the Palace. I was watching you play from my window. I felt that you were coming that afternoon and I hardly moved from my armchair. Just now I remained very still too so you wouldn't be afraid of me."

The same voice as then, only more afflicted. Wasn't it like the voice of the Lord when he reproaches someone turning away from his divine grace? Completely the child, Pablo prostrated himself on the ground near the tree trunk as he had done long ago on the library carpet. A filial chirping descended from the trees wrapping him with innocence as he blurted out his secrets; and as he continued confessing them, his heart was submerging itself in the blue of the autumnal Sunday.

"You tried to steal, you tried to, because it would be another sin against your purity!"

"But I didn't steal!" and Pablo's pride dissolved in anguish, an anguish that was so sweet because it was still that of a child, at a time when he found himself without his childhood.

The bishop raised his hands in order to perfume them in the tender leaves

limón; y las vio llagadas, y no quiso tocar la hermosura del árbol; y después, sin acercarlas, puso su bendición sobre la frente del hijo de la mujer en quien pensaba, tantos años, sin sonrojarse de ninguno de sus pensamientos.

Pablo se lo confesó todo al obispo; y creció su gracia y su fortaleza. Felicidad nueva. Todo rodeándole para que él lo poseyese. Así contemplaría el primer hombre la creación intacta delante de sus ojos y de sus rodillas. Y se compadeció de María Fulgencia, que estaba sola, sin el goce suyo.

Corrió a su huerto, y le recibieron sus brazos y sus labios. Temblaba encendida y se le alzaba el pecho anhelante y glorioso.

– ¡Tú tardabas, y llegas contento, y yo me moría de no verte! – y no se pudo contener en su amor, como siempre hizo hasta el retiro del ancho limonero, sino que, en medio de un vial de jazmines, lo abrazó besándole, besándole; y luego se lo apartaba para mirarle, y lo besaba más, como los niños que miran la fruta después de morderla.

Apretado encima de su boca, pudo decirle Pablo:

– Vengo tarde y vengo contento porque se lo dije todo al obispo. ¡Acabo de ser perdonado, y yo te comunico mi alegría!

– ¡Tu alegría la recibo así! – y se besaron delirantemente, y ella quiso la caricia más suya: desnudarle el pecho y contemplarlo para atinar con su boca en la punta de su corazón. Pero se quedó muy blanca y ciñó a Pablo, amparándole.

– ¡Nos ha visto Diego! ¡Nos está mirando! – y dio un brinco de pájaro y le besó en las pestañas.

Bajo los frutales pasó la risa del giboso como un alarido.

María Fulgencia volvióse hacia lo profundo del jardín, y oprimiendo con dulzura los hombros de Pablo, fue llevándoselo hasta la puertecita. Miraba las rosas, los jazmines que se abrían a su lado, y parecía mirar a lo lejos.

– ¡Se ha ido! ¡Pero se ha ido en busca de su tío, que estará con tu padre!

of the lemon tree, and he saw that they were ulcerated, and he didn't try to touch the tree's beauty; and afterwards, without bringing his hands closer, he placed his blessing upon the brow of the son of the woman about whom he had been thinking for so many years, without blushing over any of his thoughts.

Pablo confessed everything to the bishop; and his grace and his fortitude grew. A new happiness. Everything surrounding him was meant for him to possess it. That was how the first man must have contemplated creation intact before his eyes and his knees. And he felt sorry for María Fulgencia, who was alone, without his feeling of pleasure.

He ran to her garden and her arms and her lips received him. She was trembling with a burning passion and her eager, glorious breast rose up toward him.

"You were late and you came here happy, and I was dying from not being able to see you!" and she could not contain herself in her love, as she always did till they reached the seclusion of the broad lemon tree, but now, in the middle of a lane of jasmine bushes, she embraced him and kissed him and kissed him; and then she held him away from her so she could look at him, and she kissed him again, like children do when they look at the fruit after they have bitten into it.

Though Pablo was being held, pressed tightly to her mouth, he succeeded in telling her:

"I've come late and I've come back happy because I told the bishop everything. I have just been forgiven and I am communicating my happiness to you!"

"I receive your happiness like this!" and they kissed one another deliriously and she tried to make the caress even more a part of her: to bare his chest and contemplate it so she could touch the exact place with her mouth on the nipple over his heart. But she turned very pale, and put her arms around Pablo, protecting him.

"Diego has seen us! He's watching us!" She hopped up like a bird and kissed him on his eyelashes.

The laughter of the gibbous boy spread out under the fruit trees like a howl.

María Fulgencia turned toward the far end of the garden and, squeezing Pablo's shoulders sweetly, she kept leading him toward the small gate. She looked at the roses, the jasmine bushes that opened up beside her and she seemed to be looking into the distance.

"He's gone away! But he's gone off in search of his uncle, who is probably with your father!"

En el tapial, ella se lo separó.

– ¡No te acerques más, pero mírame mucho!

De pronto le tomó de una mano, le sonrió y le despidió diciéndole:

– ¡Bendito seas!

Entró Pablo, recatándose, por el postigo del hortal. Su casa seguía en el buen silencio del domingo. La mesa, ya parada; y en el mantel, en las vajillas y frutas brincaba con regocijo el sol. Ni siquiera se sentían las pisadas de tía Elvira. ¡Qué lástima que se trastornase esa quietud, tan gustosa hoy!

Apareció su madre; y supo que había venido Diego buscando atropelladamente a don Amancio, y como no estaba, se fue, y tía Elvira se le juntó en la calle.

– ...¿Es algo tuyo, Pablo¿ Es algo de allí?

¿Por qué diría ese *"allí"* que empujaba tan lejos la casa de María Fulgencia?

Quiso Pablo aquietarla con su sonrisa, y no pudo, recordando que ya no sonreía como antes.

Tantos años lisos de infancia entre paredes; tantos años para ir subiendo a la faz oreada de su júbilo, y en unas horas se le escombró la vida...

Se acercaban tía Elvira y su padre. Y volvióse rápidamente a todo. Le dio vergüenza de lo que iba a suceder; le dio miedo ya de hombre, el miedo que después se vuelve miedo de niño. Tía Elvira le quemaba con los ojos.

– Tienes hambre, sobrino? ¡Pues a comer..., por si acaso!..

No había revelado nada; y así era la fuerte, la poderosa entre ellos.

Pablo mordía el pan, y lo dejaba. Tomó su copa, y el agua le amargó la lengua. Tía Elvira ya no se fijaba en él, sino en todo lo que tocaban sus manos.

"¿Y María Fulgencia?... ¿Y María Fulgencia?..." Se lo preguntó muchas veces a sí mismo, y su culpa de grande hinchaba hasta desencajarle su recóndita sensibilidad infantil.

– ¿Qué tiene esa criaura que no atina ni a comer ni a mirarnos?

She separated from him at the garden wall.

"Don't come any closer, just keep looking at me more!"

She suddenly took him by the hand, smiled at him and bade him farewell saying:

"May you be blessed!"

Pablo came in surreptitiously by the wicket to the garden. His house was still pervaded by a pleasant Sunday silence. The table was already set; and the sunlight leaped for joy upon the tablecloth, on the table service and the fruits. You couldn't even hear his Aunt Elvira's footsteps. What a pity that all this stillness, that was so especially cheerful today, should have to be upset!

His mother appeared; and he learned that Diego had come by hurriedly seeking Don Amancio, and since he wasn't there, he left and Aunt Elvira joined him in the street.

"...Does it have something to do with you, Pablo? Is it something that happened there?"

Why should she say "there" like that, which only served to push María Fulgencia's house even further away?

Pablo tried to calm her down with his smile, but he couldn't do so, recalling that he no longer smiled like before.

So many unruffled years between these walls; so many years so that he could rise up to the refreshing face of his jubilation, and in just a few hours life had cleared a way for him....

Aunt Elvira and his father were approaching. And he quickly turned to face it all. He was ashamed for what was going to happen; he was afraid as a man now, with a fear that would later turn to that of a child. Aunt Elvira burned into him with her eyes.

"Are you hungry, nephew? Well, how about eating something..., just in case!..."

She hadn't revealed anything; and in this way she was the strong one, the powerful one between the two of them.

Pablo bit into the bread and set it aside. He picked up his glass and the water tasted bitter on his tongue. Aunt Elvira was no longer taking notice of him, and only watched what his hands were touching.

"And what about María Fulgencia?... And María Fulgencia?..." He asked himself this many times and his feeling of guilt as a grown-up expanded till it dislocated his hidden, childish sensitivity.

"What can be the matter with that creature that he can't manage to eat or even look at us?"

– ¿Yo? – tan breve esta palabra, y tropezó pronunciándola.

Su madre le tocó la frente y se la descansó en la suya.

Pablo quiso desasirse, y la buscaba más, cegándose en el dulce refugio, porque tía Elvira dijo con desgarro:

– ¡Déjalo, que se ahoga de pena! ¡Déjalo, mujer, que principia a llorar como los viejos pecadores!

Se levantó pálido y feroz.

– ¿Verdad, azucena, que me estrangularías? – y tía Elvira precipitóse y pudo alcanzarle en el vestíbulo.

Pablo la rechazó a puntapiés y puñadas como a una perra, y tía Elvira se le agarró de la cintura, torciéndose a sus brazos y a sus muslos, crepitando como el sarmiento en la lumbre, sonriendo bajo su respiración de odio, dándole la suya rota y caliente.

– ¡No te arrancarás así de la "Monja" cuando ella se te embista!

Apasionado de rencor, centelleándole magníficos los ojos, Pablo le aplastó en la frente una palabra inmunda, y ella le miró con locura, y casi derribada por la rodilla del sobrino, pudo apretarle de los riñones, se lo volcó encima, onduló acostada, y le besó en la garganta buscándole la boca.

Resonó un grito desconocido de don Álvaro, y Elvira escapóse de su condenación.

Paulina vio en su hijo y en su esposo un acento de estupor y de tristeza que les unía con una semejanza que nunca tuvieron; como si Pablo fuese viejo, como si don Álvaro fuese niño. Y adivinó que acababa de partirse la jornada inmutable de su hogar; y se encendió de piedad por todos.

Buscó a Elvira, y no pudo abrir la puerta de su alcoba. La llamó, y de la cerradura, cegada con un paño, salía silencio, y del silencio un gemir mordido. Quiso acogerse al lado de ellos. Bajó, y ya no estaban.

La afligía toda la casa. En el comedor vio la mesa abandonada. Subió, y estuvo esperando en el dormitorio de Pablo.

Así fue anocheciendo aquel domingo de otoño, como un último día de una época suya toda de sed por la misma cuesta...

"I?" Such a short word and he stumbled as he pronounced it.

His mother touched him on the forehead and rested it against hers.

Pablo tried to pull away and he only sought her even more, blinding himself within the sweet refuge, because Aunt Elvira boldly said:

"Leave him alone, let him choke with his anguish! Leave him alone, woman, because he's starting to cry like long-time sinners do!"

He stood up pale and fierce.

"Isn't it true, you mother's darling, that you would strangle me?" Aunt Elvira rushed out and succeeded in catching up with him in the vestibule.

Pablo pushed her away, kicking and punching at her as if she were a dog, and Aunt Elvira seized him by the waist, twisting herself round his arms and his thighs, crackling like a vine shoot in a burning fire, smiling under his hate-filled breath, giving him back her own breath, licentious and hot.

"You probably don't pull back like that from the 'Nun' when she goes after you!"

Filled with passion and rancor, his eyes flashing magnificently, Pablo crushed a filthy word right into her forehead, and she looked at him wildly, and though she was almost knocked over by her nephew's knee, she was able to grab him by the loins, she pulled him over on top of her, undulated her hips as she lay there, and kissed him on his throat as she sought his mouth.

An uncustomary shout from Don Álvaro resounded and Elvira escaped from his condemnation.

Paulina saw in both her son and her husband a sign of amazement and sadness that joined them together in a common feeling they had never had before; as if Pablo were the older one, as if Don Álvaro were a small child. And she foresaw that the immutable journey in the life of her family had just been ruptured; and she was stirred to pity for everyone.

She went looking for Elvira and was unable to open the door to her bedroom. She called to her and only silence emerged from the keyhole of the lock, covered over by a piece of cloth, and out of the silence a stifled moan. She decided to take refuge beside her loved ones. She went downstairs, but they were no longer there.

The whole house filled her with grief. In the dining room she saw the abandoned table. She went back upstairs and sat there waiting in Pablo's bedroom.

In this way did night begin to fall on that Sunday in autumn, like one last day of an epoch that was all hers, athirst for what life offered, descending along the same slope....

2. La salvación y la felicidad

Levantóse Paulina de madrugada. Don Álvaro tenía los ojos abiertos, inmóviles en lo alto del muro.

Nunca se habían sentido tan cerca, sin haberse mirado. No se miraban para no verse en el fondo antiguo de sus ojos. Y él murmuró:

– ¡Déjala!

Paulina le respondió:

– Es a él. Quiero ver a Pablo.

El hijo dormía entristecido y puro; pero se despertó bajo le ternura de la madre, como nos despierta la claridad en los párpados, y volvióse su alma hacia el día que acababa de pasar. Por primera vez en la mañana recién abierta le pesaban los pensamientos viejos. Eso sería no ser ya niño: no principiar del todo las horas que siempre se le ofrecieron intactas; discos nuevos y resbaladizos de las horas entre sus dedos. Sol, árboles, olores matinales de la creación; mundo acabado siempre de nacer para los ojos y las manos que juegan descuidadamente con la virginidad del momento. Eso sería no ser ya niño: depender del pasado sentir, de su memoria, de sus acciones, de su conciencia, de los instantes desaparecidos; proseguir el camino, rosigar el pan de la víspera, acomodar la hora fina y tierna con la hora cansada: sol, árboles, azul, aire del día nuevo, todo ya con el regusto de nosotros según fuimos...

Pablo sintió en su carne el beso y el ardor desesperados de tía Elvira, y se compadeció con desdén, pero se compadeció de ella. Eso sería ser ya hombre: apiadarse y menospreciar; sentir por los demás y hacia los demás; resonarle humanamente el corazón.

Sentóse su madre en la orilla de la cama; y él ya no temió sonreírle, y se lo fue contando todo; todo menos lo de tía Elvira. Eso sería ser ya hombre: verse desnudo; ver la desnudez de los otros.

...Y cuando acabó, le besó su madre, prometiéndole:

– ¡Yo te salvaré!

– ¿Que tú me salvarás? ¿A mí? ¿Y a María Fulgencia?

Buscó dentro de su alma peligros concretos que temer. Se había confesado con el obispo y con su madre. Ella y Dios lo sabían ya todo, y fue perdonado. Entonces, ¿qué faltaba para que aún fuese necesaria su salvación? Lo sabía

2. Salvation and Happiness

Paulina got up at daybreak. Don Álvaro had his eyes open, motionlessly fixed on the uppermost part of the wall.

Without having even looked at one another, they had never felt so close to one another. They didn't look at one another because they didn't want to see themselves in the onetime background of their eyes. And he murmured:

"Leave her be!"

Paulina answered him:

"It's him. I want to see Pablo."

Her son was asleep, saddened and pure; but he awoke under his mother's tenderness, just as the bright light on our eyelids awakens us, and his soul turned toward the day that had just passed. For the first time in the newly opened morning, the old thoughts were weighing heavily upon him. That would be to no longer be a child: not to make a complete beginning for the hours always offered to him intact; new and slippery disks of the hours between his fingers. Sunlight, trees, matinal aromas of creation; a world that is over, yet always recently born for the eyes and the hands that carelessly play with the virginal aspect of the moment. That would be no longer being a child: depending on past feeling, on his memory, on his actions, on his awareness, on moments that have disappeared; to continue on his way, to nibble at the bread of the day before, to accommodate the fine, tender hour with the exhausted hour: sunlight, trees, the blue, the air of a new day, everything now with the aftertaste of ourselves as we once were....

Pablo felt Aunt Elvira's desperate kiss and passion in his flesh and his pity for her was tinged with disdain, but he did pity her. That would be to be a man now: to be filled with pity and disdain; to feel for others and toward others; to have a heart that resonated in a humane way.

His mother sat down on the edge of his bed; and he was no longer afraid to smile at her, and he began telling her everything; everything except what Aunt Elvira had done. That would be to now be a man: to see himself naked, to see the nakedness of others.

...And when he finished, his mother kissed him and promised him:

"I will save you!"

"You will save me? Me? And how about María Fulgencia?" he searched for concrete dangers within his soul. He had confessed to the bishop and to his mother. She and God now knew everything and he was forgiven. Well then, what was missing that his salvation should still be necessary?

su madre; lo sabía Dios. Pero es que, además de ellos, lo sabrían las gentes: el P. Bellod, Monera, el penitenciario, "Jesús", Oleza... ¡Y don Amancio, su maestro!

Y don Amancio, su maestro, era precisamente el dueño de María Fulgencia. ¿Consistiría la salvación en no ver y en no amar a María Fulgencia?

Su madre se le apartó repitiéndole:

— ¡Yo te salvaré!

Pablo atravesó los corredores, el gabinete, la sala, y abrió el viejo balcón para mirar a su madre. Le pareció transfigurada. Muy pálida; pero no era por eso. No se puso mantilla, sino manto; pero tampoco era por eso. ¿Qué tenía su madre hoy, desde hoy, que nunca tuvo, que él no vio ni presintió? La miraba mucho. La llamó para que ella se volviese. Y de repente, lo supo: su madre tenía edad. Más joven que su padre, pero ya tenía edad esa vida de mujer que antes se hallaba fuera del tiempo de las otras mujeres; una edad suya que iría desgastándose como un oro, como un marfil; edad de madre siéndolo de un hijo que había cometido el mal, que hizo sentir el dolor y que sufría. Su deleite y su amor caían en el pecado desde que lo averiguaron y lo escarbaron los demás, desde que era desgracia para otros.

Se curvó para asomarse, y tocó la palma del último Domingo de Ramos, seca y atada entre los hierros. ¡Qué inmediato y leve aquel día de los "¡Hosanna, Hosanna!" La rama amarilla de palmera, tan fría y jugosa en sus manos. Su palma de un gentil latido en su punta. Su palma más recta que la de Aparici y Castro. (Aparici y Castro era de El Escorial, y decía azufaifas en vez de gínjoles. Aparici ya estaría estudiando para ingeniero agrónomo.) Su palma más alta que la de Perceval y la de Lóriz. (Perceval se habría matriculado de Farmacia en Barcelona, y Lóriz se marchaba a un colegio de Inglaterra.) ¿Por qué, Señor, había de recordarles en estos momentos? ¡Ni Aparici, ni Perceval, ni Lóriz necesitaban de salvación como él! Revolvióse hacia la puerta del dormitorio de tía Elvira. ¡La pobre mujer! Y se avergonzó. ¿Pensarían ya todos de él lo mismo que él pensaba de la pobre mujer? ¡Eso, no! María Fulgencia, no. Hoy, a las doce y media, llevaría veinticuatro horas sin besarla. ¡Mañana, dos días; y después, más días y meses y meses!...

His mother knew it; God knew it. But the fact is that, in addition to them, other people would know it: Father Bellod, Monera, the canon-penitentiary, "Jesús," Oleza.... And Don Amancio, his teacher!

And it was Don Amancio, his teacher, who was precisely María Fulgencia's master. Would salvation consist of not seeing and not loving María Fulgencia?

His mother moved away from him repeating:

"I will save you!"

Pablo passed through the corridors, the sitting room, the drawing room and opened the old balcony window to look at his mother. She seemed transfigured to him. Very pale, but it wasn't for that reason. She didn't put on a mantilla, but rather a shawl; but it wasn't for that reason either. What was going on with his mother today, ever since today, that was never so before, that he didn't see or foresee? He kept looking at her for a long time. He called to her so that she would turn around. And suddenly he knew: his mother had maturity. She was younger than his father, but that life as a woman that found itself outside the time of other women before, now had maturity; a maturity that was hers alone, that would go on wasting away slowly like a piece of gold, like a piece of ivory; the maturity of a mother, which she was by having a son who had committed a wrong, who made others feel pain and who suffered himself. His delight and his love had fallen into sin ever since others found out about it and poked their noses into it, ever since it was a disgrace to others.

He bent over to look outside and touched the palm branch from last Palm Sunday, all dried up and tied to the iron bars. How immediate and frail that day of the "Hosanna, Hosanna!" The yellow branch of the palm tree, so cold and succulent in his hands. His palm branch with a pleasant throbbing at its point. His palm branch straighter than Aparici y Castro's. (Aparici y Castro was from El Escorial and used to say *azufaifas* instead of *gínjoles* when referring to jujube candies. In all likelihood, Aparici was studying to be an agricultural engineer at this time.) His palm branch was taller than Perceval's and Lóriz's. (Perceval was probably enrolled in the School of Pharmacy in Barcelona, and Lóriz was going off to a school in England.) Why, oh Lord, did he have to remember them in moments like these? Neither Aparici, nor Perceval, nor Lóriz needed salvation as he did! He turned around toward the door of Aunt Elvira's bedroom. The poor woman! And he was overcome by shame. Would everyone now think about him the same as he was thinking about the poor woman? No, not that! Not María Fulgencia. Today at twelve-thirty, he would have gone twenty-four hours without kissing her. Tomorrow, two days; and after that, more days and months and months!...

Su madre desapareció por la plazuela de la catedral, buscando la salvación...

Según se alejaba, se le perdían a Paulina los contornos de su propósito, como si esa salvación únicamente pudiera dársele al lado del hijo. Lo salvaría de los hombres, de su mismo dolor y del poder de María Fulgencia; y pronunciando este nombre le saltó de su pecho una dulzura de madre por ella.

Volvióse para saber si la veían; llegó a su portal y tiró de la esquila de la verja.

Se abrió un ventanillo de la pared, y el jorobado, lívido en su blusón de hopa, estuvo mirándola mucho, con una sonrisa villana.

– ¡Esto se acabó! ¡Colorín, colorado! ¡Ahora la mamá, y ayer el señoritingo del hijo toda la tarde de ronda como un gato!

Un codazo rechazó al chepudo, y presentóse la "Bigastra", que saludó con mucha crianza; y, relamiéndose y sonriendo, le dijo que don Amancio y la "Monja" se fueron a su casa de Murcia; que el penitenciario y el P. Bellod vinieron a despedirles; que *ella* iba muy blanca...

Paulina se refugió en el claustro de la catedral. El ciprés más afilado de Oleza, los viejos laureles, el pozo entre hierba quemada por las escorias de los incensarios, los lagartos soleándose en las baldosas. Altar de San Gregorio, con su cofre de basalto que guardaba las entrañas de un rey; y se paró, como su padre hacía todas las siestas del 28 de junio, leyendo los escomidos signos del epitafio. Altar de San Rafael y Tobías, con el único exvoto que le quedaba: un pie de cera morena.

Se hundió por un portalillo húmedo. La gran nave tibia y profunda. Fue rodeando el deambulatorio, escondiéndose de las viejecitas rezadoras que ya sabrían la culpa de su hijo. Cómo le salvaría? Ella necesitaba decir: "Mi hijo engaño a su maestro, amigo de su padre. La casa del maestro fue la de su iniquidad. A estas horas las gentes de Oleza – Oleza que tanto nos amó – esas gentes se ríen de nosotros. ¡Cómo le mirarán cuando él pase! Por ruin que haya sido el pecado, son más ruines los que con él se gozan. ¿Verdad,

His mother disappeared along the small plaza in front of the cathedral, seeking salvation....

As she drew further away, Paulina began losing the contours of her purpose, as if that salvation could only be granted her at her son's side. She would save him from men, from his own pain and from the power of María Fulgencia; and as she uttered this name, a sweet feeling of motherliness toward her leaped from her bosom.

She turned around to see if she could be seen; she reached her gate and pulled at the bell on the grating.

A small window in the wall opened up and the hunchback, looking livid in his loose-fitting cassock, remained there for a long time looking at her with a coarse smile.

"Well, that's the final touch! That's the end of the story! Now it's the mamma and yesterday that spoiled little darling of a son of hers prowling around the house all afternoon like a he-cat!"

The humpback was elbowed out of the way with a shove and "La Bigastra" appeared and greeted her with considerable courtesy; gloating and smiling, she told her that Don Amancio and the "Nun" had gone off to her house in Murcia, that the canon-penitentiary and Father Bellod had come to bid them farewell; that she was looking very pale....

Paulina found refuge in the cloister of the cathedral. The most sharp-pointed cypress in Oleza, the old laurel trees, the well surrounded by grass that had been charred by the scoria emptied from the censers, the lizards sunning themselves on the flagstones. Saint Gregory's altar with its basalt coffer containing the bowels of a king; and she stopped, just as her father used to do at siesta time each afternoon on the 28th of June, reading the worn-away inscription on the epitaph. Saint Raphael and Tobias's altar with the only votive offering remaining, a dark waxen foot.

She plunged into a damp little doorway. The great nave, tepid and deep. She continued walking round the ambulatory, keeping herself hidden from the inconspicuous old women praying there, who probably already knew about her son's sin. How could she save him? She needed to say, "My son deceived his teacher, a friend of his father. His teacher's house was the place for his iniquity. At this time of day the people of Oleza – the Oleza that once loved us so much – those people are laughing at us. How will they look at him when he passes by! No matter how base his sin, the ones who take pleasure over it are even viler. Isn't that so, oh Lord? They will also laugh

Señor? Se reirán también de don Amancio. A mí me da más lástima su mujer pecadora que él. "¡Yo te salvaré!" Y mi hijo me pidió que la salvase a ella. Pablo es generoso, y es todavía puro. Pureza y dolor después de pecar. ¡Qué infancia ha tenido mi hijo con ellos! Entre ellos está su maestro escarnecido. ¡Yo me quejé de la risa de las gentes; y aún no pensaba en el furor de ese hombre y de Álvaro! Seré yo sola para amarle; yo y la que no debe quererle. Yo quiero a mi hijo más que antes; y me compadezco de Elvira como nunca me había compadecido de esa mujer, y no puedo imaginarla desdichada sin ver – lo veo realmente – lo que hizo con Pablo. ¡Señor: acúerdate de mi vida en mi casa viejecita del "Olivar"!... ¡Cómo se ha trastornado todo para que no sea yo feliz! "¡Yo te salvaré", le he prometido a mi hijo. Y no es posible salvarle sin salvar a María Fulgencia, sin salvar a Elvira, sin salvarnos todos. ¡Es que han sido ellos! ¿Serán ellos, Álvaro y el marido, los que tienen la culpa?..."

Y Paulina corrió porque todo lo estaba diciendo en la capilla del Señor del Sepulcro, el Señor que se adoraba el Jueves Santo, tendido en la alfombra del Monumento, y en cuyos pies desollados y duros sangró la boca inocente de Pablo. Y no podía decírselo a esa imagen ni acudir a la de Nuestro Padre San Daniel, que se parecía a don Álvaro; ni el P. Bellod, de tan horrenda castidad; ni al Penitenciario...

Se llenó de sol en el pórtico. ¿Dónde buscaría la salvación? Estaba delante de la casa del justo, que padecía también por el daño que Pablo cometió, y en las vetustas puertas se le aparecieron las palabras de misericordia: "Llamad y se os abrirá." He aquí la hora de llamar y pedir su consejo. Y pasó rápida y sobrecogida.

El cansancio del último día y la mañana de afán le pesaban según iba subiendo los escalones de losas. Soledad de casa de enfermo sin cuidados de mujer.

En un quicio de la saleta colgaba un rótulo: "Suspendidas todas las audiencia", descolorido y viejo, como si ya no tuviese validez. La antecámara, tan honda, de armarios barrocos, de bancos y bufetes de velludo, tan fría y rigorosa con la figura del familiar de los anteojos de nieve, estaba únicamente habitada por una avispa que rodeó todo el torcido cordón de la lámpara. Salió por el abierto ventanal a los follajes de los naranjos, y

at Don Amancio. I feel sorrier for his sinful wife than for him. 'I will save you!' And my son asked me to save her. Pablo is generous and he is still pure. Purity and suffering after having sinned. What kind of childhood did my son have with them! And among them is his mocked teacher. I complained about people's laughter; and I still wasn't thinking about the fury of that man and of Álvaro! I will be alone in loving him; I and the one who ought not to love him. I love my son more than before; and I feel sorry for Elvira like I had never felt sorry for that woman before, and I can not imagine her unfortunate without seeing – I actually see it – what she did with Pablo. Oh, Lord, remember my life in my sweet old house at the 'Olive Grove!' ...How everything seems to have been overturned just to make me unhappy! 'I will save you!' I've promised my son. And it isn't possible to save him without saving María Fulgencia, without saving Elvira, without saving us all. The fact is that it was they! Can it possibly be they, Álvaro and the husband, who are really to blame?..."

And Paulina ran because she was saying it all in the chapel of the Lord in the Sepulcher, the Lord who was worshipped on Holy Thursday, stretched out on the carpet of the Temporary Altar, and on whose flayed, hard feet Pablo's innocent mouth bled. And she couldn't tell it all to that image nor resort to the image of Our Father San Daniel, which looked like Don Álvaro; nor Father Bellod, who was so horrendously chaste; nor the canon-penitentiary....

The portico was filled with sunlight. Where would she look for salvation? She was in front of the house of the just one, who was also suffering because of the wrong committed by Pablo, and the words of mercifulness, "Knock and the way shall be opened unto you,"[242] appeared before her on the ancient doors. Here then was the moment to call to him and ask for his advice. And she was overcome by fear as she hastily went inside.

The weariness of the last day and the morning of anxiety weighed heavily upon her as she kept climbing the stone steps. The solitude of an ailing man's house without the attentions of a woman.

On a frame of the door of the antechamber a sign was hanging, "All audiences suspended," and it looked faded and old, as if it were no longer in force. The antechamber, so very deep, with baroque cabinets, with benches and writing desks covered with plush, so cold and severe with the figure of the familiar wearing spectacles like snow, was occupied only by a wasp that circled the entire twisted wick of the lamp. It went out through the open windows onto the leaves of the orange trees and moved over straight away

enseguida vino y palpó el racimo de una talla. Ella contemplaba los rumbos
de la avispa, que de un gracioso vaivén se coló por la sala de recepciones, y
enseguida volvió a las claridades de la secretaría. Pero Paulina, no; Paulina
se quedó bajo el reproche de un grupo de ensotanados; los unos con la faja
colorada de los pajes, los otros con su lisura pobre y negra de los fámulos, y
el familiar con su esclavina como las telas flojas de un paraguas, todos junto
a la puertecita del dormitorio del obispo, como si aguardasen el mandato
de precipitarse dentro. Se llegaron a Paulina para contenerla. Le hablaron
con un susurro, con un asombro y ademanes de gentes enfaldadas. El señor
había tenido un ataque y acababan de acostarlo. ¡Ya no podía más! Abrióse
la alcoba y apareció don Magín. Paulina se le cogió de las manos. Pero el
enfermo se removía quejándose, y don Magín entró y le alzó la cabeza, que
le colgaba por el borde del lecho para mirar entre el ahogo del vendaje.

El olor de los bálsamos, de los aceites, de los inhaladores de hierbas, olor
de otero, de anchura, de salud era, allí, aliento de enfermedad.

Tuvo que esperarse, porque el llagado hablaba saliéndole un soplo de su
laringe podrida.

Nadie le entendió.

...Cuando Paulina traspuso los umbrales de Palacio, tampoco llevaba la
salvación del hijo.

Y en su casa, al descansar sus manos, tan pálidas, tan pueriles, en
los hombros de don Álvaro, recogieron el temblor íntimo de su hueso; y
comenzó a presentirla.

Elvira ya no estaba. La dejó su hermano en la diligencia de Novelda, y
de allí seguiría en tren hasta Gandía.

Don Álvaro inclinó la frente para decir:

– ¡Y nosotros nos encerraremos en el "Olivar"!

Tenía la mirada húmeda, los pómulos azules, su barba comenzaba a
envejecer.

Su mujer sonrió a la promesa de felicidad. Miraba los viejos muebles de
los padres de Elvira y de don Álvaro, y los muebles también la miraban. ¿La
felicidad? Pero ¿y ellos, y lo que fueron criando y dejando con su presencia?
¿Qué haría en este mundo la perdiz embalsamada si ya no se hacía de

to palpate a cluster of blossoms on a single stalk. She kept contemplating the wasp's movements as it slipped into the reception room, elegantly flitting up and down, and just as quickly returned to the brightness of the secretary's office. But Paulina didn't; Paulina remained under the reproachful eyes of a group of men wearing cassocks, some with the red-colored sashes of the pages, others with the pitiful black simplicity of the house servants, and the familiar, with his pelerine like the limp folds of an umbrella, all of them next to the small door to the bishop's bedroom, as if they were waiting for the command to rush inside. They came over to Paulina to forestall her. They spoke to her in whispers, with the air of astonishment and the gestures of frocked people. The lord bishop had had an attack and they had just put him to bed. He would be unable to put up with anything more! The bedroom opened and Don Magín appeared. Paulina grasped him by the hands. But the ailing man was stirring and moaning and Don Magín went inside and elevated his head, which was hanging over the edge of the bed, in order that he might look inside the suffocating bandage.

The odor of the balms, of the oils, of herbal inhalers, the aroma of the hillock, of open expanses, of good health, in this place, was the breath of sickness.

They were compelled to wait because the sore-ridden man was speaking with a puff of breath emerging from his suppurating larynx.

Nobody understood him.

...When Paulina walked out beyond the confines of the Palace, she still didn't possess her son's salvation.

And once she was home and rested her very pale, child-like hands on Don Álvaro's shoulders, they gathered in the intimate tremor of his inner core; and he began to have a presentiment about her.

Elvira was no longer there. Her brother left her on the diligence to Novelda, and from there she would continue by train to Gandía.

Don Álvaro bent his forehead to say:

"And we will enclose ourselves in the 'Olive Grove!'"

His glance was moist, his cheekbones blue, his beard just beginning to show signs of aging.

His wife smiled at this promise of happiness. She looked at the old family furniture of Elvira and Don Álvaro's parents and the furniture also looked at her. Happiness? But what about them and what they continued to nurture and leave behind with their presence? What could the stuffed partridge do in this world if it could no longer make itself be detested simply because it

aborrecer por ser de Elvira? Sus ojos redondos, embusteros, de botones de vidrio, que contemplaron las muecas íntimas, la soledad, las horas de vigilia de la beata y hasta sus horas de nobleza y de dolor de no haber sido nunca dichosa ni en trueque de la desgracia de los otros, ¿presenciarían los tiempos de la felicidad venidera? Y Nuestra Señora de los Dolores, con su terciopelo tirante y ajado, sus lágrimas heladas, su corazón transido de siete puñales de plata, esa Virgen que no consoló a Paulina, Virgen de la especial devoción de una casa tan remota y ajena de su pasado, ¿podría convertirse en una Nuestra Señora quietecita y suya, que acoge todos los años el dulce septenario de familia?

¿Y ésos, el Sr. Galindo, la señora Serrallonga, que miraban a la nuera y al nieto sin amarles, les miraban rápidamente y se aprovechaban de esa fugacidad para saber que tampoco les habían amado a ellos? ¿Y el óvalo del panteón de pelo de muerto, y los butacones, y el brasero de los sahumerios?

Pero Paulina no había de recelar de ese menaje que volvería para siempre a la casa originaria de los Galindo.

En el "Olivar" les esperaban los muebles suyos: las cómodas de olivo, los armarios de ciprés, los lechos de columnas de caoba, los candelabros de roca, los espejos románticos, las consolas, los relojes, los alabastros... Y según iba recordando sus contornos, sus calidades, y pronunciándolo, adquirían configuraciones y semblante de vacilación. Todo aquello y los muros y envigados de los ámbitos de la casona y los árboles, la tierra y el aire y el silencio, todo pertenecía a su legítimo pasado, a su sangre y, por tanto, a su hijo; todo estuvo aguardando la felicidad de la heredera desde antes que ella naciese. Y todo quedó en un olvido de repudio por la voluntad de don Álvaro, el amo nuevo. El "Olivar" se desaromó de su recogimiento; se cerró el casalicio, fraguándose el ambiente del desamparo, conformándose en la desgracia. ¿Se despertaría jubiloso ahora, uniéndose a una súbita felicidad que no era de allí?

Paulina se asomó al balcón para ver Oleza, verlo todo sin la vigilancia de Elvira.

Palacio de Lóriz, la catedral, los campanarios, las azoteas, los palomares, Oleza, también toda Oleza, se quedó mirándola con asombro: "¿De veras

belonged to Elvira? Its rounded, deceitful eyes, made of buttons of glass, that once contemplated the intimate grimaces, the solitude, the hours of vigil of the fanatic woman, and even her moments of nobility and suffering at never having been happy even in exchange for the misfortune of others, would they witness the moments of happiness that were now to come? And the image of Our Lady of the Sorrows, with its taut, withered velvet, with its frozen tears, with its heart pierced by seven silver daggers, that Virgin who had never consoled Paulina, a Virgin of special devotion in a house so remote and alien to her past; could it be converted into an image of Our Lady who was very still and all hers, who welcomes the sweet family Septenary celebration every year?

And how about the others, Señor Galindo, Señora Serrallonga, who looked down on the daughter-in-law and grandson without loving them, looked at them rapidly and took advantage of that fugacity to discover that they hadn't been loved either? And how about the oval-shaped picture in the shrine with the hair of the dead, and the big easy chairs and the incense burner?

But Paulina had no need to distrust all that household furniture that would return forever to the Galindo family home from which it had come.

Her own furniture was waiting for her at the "Olive Grove": the olive wood bureaus, the cypress wardrobes, the beds with mahogany posts, the rock-crystal candelabra, the romantic mirrors, the console tables, the clocks, the alabaster pieces.... And as she kept remembering their outlines, their qualities, and kept repeating them, they acquired configurations and a semblance of vacillation. All that and the walls and rafters of the compass of the big old house, and the trees, the land, and the air and the silence, all that belonged to her legitimate past, to her blood, and therefore, to her son; all that was there waiting for the happiness of the heiress since even before she was born. And all that remained in an oblivion of repudiation because of the will of Don Álvaro, the new master. The "Olive Grove" withdrew its protective aroma of withdrawal; the present house was closed up, solidifying the atmosphere of abandonment, resigning itself to its misfortune. Would it now awaken in jubilation, unifying itself with an unexpected happiness that didn't even belong there?

Paulina looked out of the balcony window to see Oleza, to see it all without putting up with Elvira's vigilance.

The Lóriz palace, the cathedral, the bell towers, the roof terraces, the dovecots, Oleza, yes, all of Oleza too, lay out there looking at her in

que ya está decidida vuestra felicidad? ¿No tiene eso remedio? ¿Estonces no servirá de nada lo pasado, lo padecido, lo deshecho? ¿Qué servirá para la plenitud de vuestro goce? No sabemos. Todavía no sois sino lo que fuisteis, y la prueba te la da tu memoria ofreciéndote como un perdido bien aquel "Olivar" de tu infancia y aquella felicidad que te prometías bajo los rosales. ¿Te bastará la improvisada felicidad de rebañaduras? Resultasteis desgraciados; una lástima, pero así era. ¿Vais ahora a dejar de ser lo que sois? ¿Y nosotros, y todos?".

Pero Paulina no había de atender sino a su vida. La felicidad no era un propósito de la juventud. Y se internó en sí misma, escuchándose transverberada por los ojos, por las palabras, por el silencio de su esposo y de su hijo. En aquellos días, ¡qué pasmo, qué corazón asustado delante de la felicidad! ¡Cómo sería esa felicidad, una felicidad que, para serlo, había de desvertebrarse de la felicidad que cada uno se había prometido!

Y una tarde paró en el portal la vieja galera, la misma galera en que vino don Daniel todos los 28 de junio para comer con su prima doña Corazón y asistir a las horas canónicas de la vigilia de San Pedro y San Pablo, la misma galera que trajo a Paulina para su boda en el alba del 24 de noviembre, día de San Juan de la Cruz. También era de noviembre aquella tarde. Se cerró la cancela y la puerta. Y en los ladillos de badana del carruaje se acomodaron Paulina, don Álvaro y su hijo. Casi a la vez se soltaron tres toques de la espadaña de Palacio. Se puso a retumbar un campanón obscuro, siempre dormido en su alcándara de la catedral; luego se removió todo el campanario, y a poco cabeceaban las campanas de las parroquias, de la Visitación, de Santa Lucía, de San Gregorio, de "Jesús", de los Calzados, del Seminario, de los Franciscos... Y el campaneo se volcaba roto en las calles, en las rinconadas, en las azoteas, en los huertos, en el río... Todas las campanas doblaban por el obispo, que acababa de morir.

Paulina, don Álvaro y su hijo se persignaron, y siguieron silenciosos, sin mirarse, camino de la felicidad.

astonishment, "Is your happiness definitively decided now? Is there no way out of that? Then what is past, what has been suffered, what has been undone, will all serve for nothing? What will serve to offer you the plenitude of your pleasure? We don't know! You are not yet anything more than what you once were, and the proof lies in your memory that offers you, as a lost possession, that 'Olive Grove' of your childhood and that happiness you promised yourself under the rosebushes. Will that improvised happiness of gleanings be enough for you? You all ended up being quite wretched; that's too bad, but that's how it was. Are you now going to stop being what you are? And we, and everyone else?"

But Paulina had only to attend to her own life. Happiness was not a goal for youth. And so she withdrew into herself, listening to herself, transfixed by the eyes, by the words, by the silence of her husband and her son. What a feeling of astonishment in those days, what a frightened heart in the face of that happiness! What would that happiness be like, a happiness that would have to break the very backbone of the happiness that one had promised oneself, in order to be that!

And one afternoon, the old four-wheeled covered wagon stopped at the entryway, the same covered wagon in which Don Daniel would come every June 28th to eat with his cousin Doña Corazón and attend the services of the canonical hours for the vigil of Saint Peter and Saint Paul, the same covered wagon that brought Paulina to her wedding at dawn on November 24th, the day of Saint John of the Cross. That afternoon also belonged to November. The outside gate and the door were closed. And Paulina, Don Álvaro and their son settled down against the dressed sheepskins on the side panels of the coach. Almost at the same time, three peals rang out from the bell gable at the Palace. A great big bell, tucked away, always asleep on its perch in the cathedral, began to resound; then the entire bell tower began to stir, and shortly after, the bells in the parish churches, of La Visitación, of Santa Lucía, of San Gregorio, of "Jesús," of the Calced Carmelites, of the Seminary, of the Franciscans all began to shake.... And the constant ringing erupted furiously and disjointedly in the streets, on the corners, on the roof terraces, in the gardens and in the river.... All the bells were tolling for the bishop, who has just died.

Paulina, Don Álvaro and their son crossed themselves and remained silent, without even looking at one another, on their way toward happiness.

3. María Fulgencia y Pablo

María Fulgencia le escribió a Paulina:

"...Les han dicho que yo no estaba en mi casa de Murcia, sino en mi hacienda, y que sería inútil que pretendieran visitarme. Y sí que estaba. Yo sola. Los he visto desde que aparecieron por la esquina del aperador. Miraban ustedes mucho mís balcones. Les aguardé hasta sentirles en la escalera, y entonces corrí a esconderme en mi alcoba, la de mis padres, donde yo estuve muy enferma de tifus. En todos mis miedos me refugié aquí. Le vuelvo la espalda a todo el caserón porque me pongo en la ventana para mirar el huerto; todo lo miro muy bien; voy contando los limones que han salido en una rama, o las veces que acude la misma abeja al mismo albaricoque, o rompo papeles y los dejo ir para ver los trocitos que caen dentro de la acequia y se van a caminar por el agua, y yo me digo que estoy muy distraída, que al miedo me lo dejé perdido por la casa tan grande, y que no soy precisamente yo la preocupada y la temerosa. Eso quise hacer cuando ustedes iban subiendo. Me puse a la ventana para mirarlo todo, para contarlo todo, y nada me importó. Porque yo no quería volverme de espaldas a mí misma ni persuadirme de que no era yo quien huía de la sala donde usted y don Álvaro acabarían de llegar. Sí que era yo y eran ustedes, y entré hasta quedarme detrás de los cortinajes. Sentía la respiración de usted y la media con mi latido. ¡Qué cerca estábamos; qué cerca yo de la madre de Pablo! Yo no le tenía miedo. Lo comprendí enseguida de mirarla. Nunca le había mirado tanto. ¡Si hubiese venido usted sola! Si usted hubiese venido sola, tampoco hubiera yo salido a besarla... Y yo les esperaba todos los días, desde que supe que quiso usted verme en Oleza. Y me dije: Me escribirá o vendrá. Todos se imaginan que estoy recluida en el campo como una penitente. Pero ella me buscará y preguntará por mí en esta casa. ¡Y huí de usted! Es que ustedes, por ser generosos, no podían venir sino a consolarme. Y yo no quiero que me consuelen. ¡Si nos hubiéramos tratado; si nos hubiésemos querido allí, en Oleza! ¡Si es que allí no se quiere nadie! El grupo de nuestros maridos no necesitaba que fuéramos amigas nosotras. Les bastaba con tener ellos asuntos. No es que me queje. No me quejo de nadie ni de mí misma. Como

3. María Fulgencia and Pablo

María Fulgencia wrote to Paulina:

"... They've told you that I was no longer in my house in Murcia, but in my country property, and that it would be useless for you to try to visit me. And that's where I really was. All by myself. I saw you from the moment you appeared, coming round the corner at the wheelwright's place. You kept looking up at my balcony windows for quite a while. I waited for you till I heard you on the stairs, and then I ran and hid in my bedroom, the one which once was my parents', where I once fell ill with typhus fever. Whenever I was afraid, I sought refuge here. I turn my back on the whole rambling old house because I stand at the window and look out on the garden; I look at everything very closely; I keep counting the lemons that have appeared on a single branch, or the number of times the same bee goes over to the same apricot, or else I tear up some papers and let them float away just to see the little pieces falling into the irrigation channel and start moving away over the water, and I tell myself that I am very absentminded, that I've left fear behind me, lost in that great big house, and that it is not exactly I who am preoccupied and frightened. That's what I tried to do when you were coming upstairs. I went over to the window to look out at everything, to count everything and nothing made any difference to me. Because I didn't want to turn my back on myself nor persuade myself that it wasn't I who was running away from the drawing room where you and Don Álvaro had probably just arrived. But it really was I and it was you, and I went inside so I could hide behind the curtains. I was aware of your breathing and I measured it against my own heartbeat. How close we were; how close I was to Pablo's mother! I wasn't afraid of you. I understood this as soon as I looked at you. I had never looked at you for so long. If you had only come alone! Even if you had come alone, I still wouldn't have come out to kiss you.... And I waited for you every day, ever since I discovered that you tried to see me in Oleza. And I said to myself, 'She will write to me or she will come. Everyone imagines that I am staying in seclusion in the country like a penitent. But she will look for me and ask for me in this house.' And I fled from you! The fact is that, because of your generosity, you could come only to console me. And I don't want to be consoled. If we had only had some kind of relationship with one another; if we had only cared for one another, there in Oleza! The fact is that nobody loves anybody else there. Our husbands' group didn't need us to be friends. It was enough for them to have their own matters of consequence. It's not that I'm complaining. I'm not complaining

es mi vida, es mía y la quiero mía. Hace un instante acusé a nuestros maridos de su amistad sin nosotras. Pero, ¿tratarnos, vernos, querernos nosotras? ¿Cuándo pude yo ir a usted, si enseguida se me apareció Pablo? Tuve que pararme a lo lejos. Y ahora, todavía más. Usted es su carne, su sangre, las manos de él son como las suyas, y la boca, y los cabellos, y la ansiedad de los ojos. ¡Qué vida tan profunda de mujer debe sentirse siendo la madre de él! Al principio de verme aquí sola me aconsejaba a mí misma: "Ya no he de recordar nada, porque ya no hay remedio." Pero, por eso, porque ya no hay remedio, no se me olvida nada. De veras le juro que no hay remedio, no se me olvida nada. De veras le juro que no hay remedio; él no me verá nunca. Renuncio a lo más gustoso: a ser mirada por él; pero no renuncio a verle, verle sin que él lo sepa.

"Cuando me di cuenta de que Diego nos había sorprendido – perdóneme – aquella mañana en el jardín, adiviné que yo, como casi todas las mujeres comprometidas, podía valerme de habilidades para encubrir la verdad. Pude *remediarlo* con embustes, y hasta se me ocurrieron y todo, y no quise. Y no quise fingir porque "él y yo solos", sin pensar en los demás, no caíamos en ninguna vergüenza; pero pensar en los otros hasta tener que engañarles era ya sentirse desnudos, como dicen que se vieron nuestros primeros padres en el Paraíso. Y anticipándoseme ese sonrojo, tuve el presentimiento de que mi paraíso estaba ya cerrado. Y si no había de entrar, ¿para qué entonces había de mentir? Cogí de la mano a su hijo y lo llevé hasta la puertecita de la ribera. Quise que me mirase mucho. Sabía que era la última vez que me miraba. Nada más nos mirábamos. Y cuando oí que me llamaban, entonces solté a Pablo, y rodeando las tapias me presenté a mi marido y dije la verdad, como si mi marido no fuese para mí sino un don Amancio Espuch. No es menester, ni debo contarle, nuestra pobre entrevista. Las gentes se han quedado sin drama ni comedia.

"Aquella mañana, cuando Diego nos sorprendió, yo sentí un alivio muy grande, imponiéndome la renunciación. Acepté mi sacrificio con un poco de gracia de generosidad; lo acepté para no acatarlo algún día con malas actitudes. ¡Se acabó – como suele decir el señor deán – , se acabó el *Ángel!* Fue la promesa de mi felicidad. Yo lo buscaba, yo lo adoraba; quise ser su velada o su santera. Nunca me propuse que las cosas fuesen mías, sino

about anyone, not even myself. Whatever my life is like, it's mine and I want it to be all mine. A moment ago I accused our husbands of having a friendship that did not include us. But getting to know one another, seeing one another, loving one another? When could I have gone to see you if Pablo showed up right away? I had to stop at a distance. And now, even more so. You are his flesh, his blood; his hands are like yours, just as his mouth and his hair and the anxiety in his eyes. What a profound sense of womanly life you must feel by being his mother! In the beginning, when I saw myself here alone, I advised myself, 'I no longer have to remember anything because there's no longer any way out.' But for that reason, because there's no longer any way out, I can't forget anything. I truly swear to you that there's no way out; he will never see me. I give up whatever it is that gives me most pleasure: to be looked upon by him; but I don't give up seeing him, seeing him without his knowing it.

"When I realized that Diego had surprised us – forgive me – that morning in the garden, I guessed that I, like all compromised women, could avail myself of my abilities to cover over the truth. I could resolve it with lies and some even occurred to me, and all that, but I refused. I decided not to pretend because 'he and I alone,' without even thinking of the others, had not fallen into anything shameful; but to think of the others to the point of having to deceive them would be to now feel naked, just like they say our ancestors saw themselves in Paradise. And as I anticipated that embarrassment, I had a presentiment that told me that my paradise was already closed to me. And if I was not going to enter, then why would it be necessary to lie? I took your son by the hand and led him to the little door by the riverbank. I wanted him to look at me for a long time. I knew that it was the last time he would look at me. We did nothing more than look at one another. And when I heard them calling me, that's when I let go of Pablo; and after I went around the garden walls, I faced my husband and told him the truth, as if my husband were nothing more to me than a Don Amancio Espuch. It isn't necessary, nor ought I to tell you all about our sad interview. The people concerned have been left with neither a dramatic nor a comic conclusion.

"That morning, when Diego surprised us, I felt a tremendous sense of relief and imposed an act of renunciation upon myself. I accepted my sacrifice with somewhat gracious generosity; I accepted it so that I wouldn't look upon it some day with great respect and a bad attitude. It's all over – as the dean is accustomed to say – it's all over with the Angel! He was the promise of my happiness. I sought him out, I adored him; I wanted to be either his bride or his custodian. I never really intended for things to belong

yo de ellas. Por eso parezco tan antojadiza. Me rodeaba de estampas y de recuerdos de mi *Ángel,* y el *Ángel* fue la promesa de Pablo.

"Principian a tocar las campanas del Sábado Santo. Tocan lo mismo que antes de marcharme a la Visitación. ¡Antes de ir a Oleza, cuánto había de sucederme! ¡Tocan las mismas campanas, y, ya está todo!

"Ya no voy a ver el *Ángel.* Ahora todos los días me asomo a mi terrado para mirar el tren de Oleza, el que sale de Murcia a Oleza. Tan lejos se quedó mi Oleza, que ya tiene tren, y con las mulas de mi labranza y un faetón de mis abuelos fui de este casón a la felicidad. Si su hijo también subiese a la ventanita más alta para ver el otro tren, el que viene a Murcia, no se enfade usted ni me aborrezca. Ya no pasará nada. Se lo juro, porque ahora ni su hijo podría volverme a la felicidad de antes".

Buena sonaja de los molinos; olor de harinas y salvados; olor de almazaras; olor de higueras, de naranjos, de maíces y cáñamos; los bancales de cáñamos donde pudo guarecerse toda la facción de Lozano en los tiempos heroicos. Llegaba de la vega el aliento del Segral, allí río crecido, del todo agrícola y caminante.

Casas de hacenderías. Casalicio de los señores. Porches y pilares con cuelgas de mazorcas. Estufas de capullos de la seda. Cañizos de almijar. En los zafariches se enjugaban los trigos, las ñoras, las cebadas. Al sol de las eras secaban sus meollos los calabazones de odre, las calabacillas bocales, las calabazas rotundas de cortezas de callo.

Viejos cipreses de aguja húmeda de cielo; su sombra, aceitada de antigüedad, y en el cerrado follaje el ruiseñor de todas las primaveras.

Romeros, jazmines, laureles; el aljibe con toldo de rosales. Jabardillos de palomas y golondrínas que vuelan redondamente y algunas descansan en las mismas socarreñas, en las mismas gárgolas de las palomas y golondrínas de antaño.

Calma de los insignes olivares. Sembradío, almendros y viñar que suben los oteros y bajan los barrancos; y en las lindes, los setos de granados agrios;

to me, but rather that I should belong to them. That's why I may seem to be so capricious. I surrounded myself with religious prints and memories of my *Angel* and the *Angel* was the promise of Pablo.

"They're starting to ring the bells for Holy Saturday. They're ringing the same way they rang before I went off to La Visitación. Before going to Oleza, so much was to happen to me! The same bells are ringing and that's all there is to it now!

"I no longer go see the *Angel*. Every day now I look out over my roof terrace to look at the train for Oleza, the one that leaves from Murcia for Oleza. My Oleza, which now has a train, remained so very far away, and I departed from this big old house to seek happiness with my farm mules and a phaeton that used to belong to my grandparents. If your son would also go upstairs to the small window, way up high, to see the other train, the one coming to Murcia, don't you be angry or detest me. Nothing will happen any more. I swear to you, because now even your son couldn't bring me back to the happiness I had before."

The pleasant jingling sound from the mills; the aroma of wheat meal and bran; the aroma from the oil presses; the aroma of the fig trees, of the orange trees, of corn stalks and hemp plants; the terraced fields of hemp where the whole of Lozano's rebel band successfully took shelter in those heroic times.[243] The breath of the Segral rose up from the fertile plain, a swollen river in that place, wholly agricultural and meandering.

The houses and outbuildings of the farms. The imposing house of the land owners. The porches and stone posts with ears of corn hanging from them. Stoves to keep the silk cocoons heated. Wattle screens for drying figs. The wheat, the Guinea peppers, the barley were drying on the pitcher shelves. The big bottle gourds used to store wine and oil, the small narrow-mouthed gourds and the rounded thick-skinned calabashes were drying out their inner core in the sunlight of the threshing floors.

Old cypresses with needles damp with sky light; their shade anointed with antiquity, and every spring's nightingale within the enclosed foliage.

Rosemary, jasmine shrubs, laurels; the cistern with an awning of rose bushes. Noisy swarms of pigeons and swallows flying round and round, and some coming to rest in the same hollows, on the same gargoyles as the pigeons and swallows of long years past.

The calm of renowned olive groves. Fields ready for sowing, almond trees and vineyards that climb the hillocks and descend down to the ravines; and at the margins, hedges of sour pomegranate bushes; aroma trees with

de aromos con su leña de púas y sus cabezuelas de pelusa fragante; las pitas, con sus espadones dentellados y sus candelabros de tortas en flor; las chumberas, retorciendo sus codos de rebanadas verdes que dan en el borde los erizos de los higos.

De mañana y de tarde, a la misma hora, venía por el azul el silbo del tren de Oleza, y enseguida el estrépito del puente de hierro. Aquel ámbito de jácenas y tirantes roblonados parecía estrujarse, vaciándose de un temblor encendido que se descalfaba en las aguas dulces del Segral; y después, el silencio tan liso, tan desnudo en todo el campo.

Muchos días, de mañana y de tarde, vio Paulina a su hijo en la ventana cimera del desván contemplando ese tren, y no lo miraba cuando partía de Oleza para entrar en la comarca de Murcia, donde la mujer que le amó vivía retirada y sola; miraba el tren que de Oleza iba dejando la vega por los saladares, el que llegaba al mar y a las estaciones de enlace, principio de las líneas poderosas de ferrocarriles, los fuertes brazos que abrían las puertas del mundo lejano.

En el atardecer se desprendía el olor de los jazmines, de los naranjos, de los cipreses, que principiaban a enfriarse dentro del olor ancho y humedecido del horizonte.

Los jazmines, las rosas, los naranjos; los campos, el aire, la atmósfera de los tiempos de las viejas promesas; olor de felicidad no realizada; felicidad que Paulina sintió tan suya y que permanecía intacta en los jazmines, en el rosal, en los cipreses, en los frutales; la misma fragancia, la misma promesa que ahora recogía el hijo. El cielo se combaba glorioso sobre sus tierras, sobre los olivares extáticos. Un cántico balbuciente de agua que pasaba como entonces. Una nube blanca, pomposa, que dejaba un acento de alegría en la heredad.

La huerta, la labor, lo yermo, toda la heredad iba mirando don Álvaro, toda la corría en su ocio de caballero confinado, sin empresa ni designio que sentir ni consentirse. Se asomaba a los molinos, a las trojes, a los patios y alhorines. Buscaba su casa, hundiéndose por las salas, por los dormitorios, por las escalerillas de servicio. Llegaba a los sobrados, prenderías del tiempo: cribas, orzas, libros, cofres; la espada, las botas de espuelas y el casaquín de brigadier carlista de un tío de Paulina, y en lo alto, el estudio

spine-covered wood and flower heads of fragrant down; pita plants with their serrulated, sword-shaped leaves and their cake-like flowering candelabra; prickly pear cactuses, twisting the green elbow-like slices of their branches which grow bristly pear-like fruit at the edges.

In the morning and in the afternoon, at the same time, the whistle of the train to Oleza came blowing through the blue, and immediately made the racket from the iron bridge. That ambience of support beams and riveted tie rods seemed to squeeze together, emptying itself with an incendiary trembling that scattered all over the sweet waters of the Segral; and afterwards, silence, so smooth, so naked over the entire countryside.

Many days, in the morning and in the afternoon, Paulina would see her son at the very highest window in the attic, contemplating that train, and he didn't look at it when it departed from Oleza to make its way to the region around Murcia, where the woman who loved him lived all alone, in seclusion; he was looking at the train that was leaving behind it the fertile plain of Oleza by a route through the salt marshes, the one that reached the sea and the stations that were junctions, the beginning of the mighty railroad lines, the powerful arms that opened the doors of the distant world. In the late afternoon, there emanated a fragrance of jasmine, of orange trees and of cypresses that were starting to turn cold within the expansive, dampened fragrance of the horizon.

The jasmine, the roses, the orange trees; the fields, the air, the atmosphere of the times of old promises; the aroma of unfulfilled happiness; the happiness that Paulina felt was so very much her own and which remained intact in the jasmine, in the rose bush, in the cypresses, in the fruit trees; the same fragrance, the same promise that her son was now gathering to himself. The sky curved over the land below, over the ecstatic olive groves in all its glory. A babbling canticle of water that kept passing by just as it had then. A white, magnificent cloud that left behind a trace of joy all over this country property.

Don Álvaro kept looking over the irrigated plain, the tillage, the barren land, the entire country estate, roaming all over it in his idle status of a confined landed gentleman, without anything to undertake nor a project to judge or to authorize. He would look in on the mills, on the barns, on the yards and the granaries. He would look all over his own house, burying himself in the drawing room and parlors, in the bedrooms, on the service stairways. He would find his way up to the attics, time's second-hand shops: sieves, crocks, books, chests; the sword, the boots with the spurs and the short dress coat of a Carlist brigadier that had belonged to one of Paulina's

de astronomía del buen faccioso, con su butacón de terciopelo, el atril y la esfera de meridianos de arañas.

De la luz ancha de los desvanes a la clausura de los salones, al escritorio, al herbario, y de nuevo pasaba por las vides de su puerta, caminando sin goce, porque de todo lugar, de todas las cosas en que hubiese querido complacerse: del rosal del aljibe, que coronó a Paulina novia, cuando ella le esperaba sonriéndole de amor; de la noche, aquí tan intima, tan nupcial; de todo motivo de ternura y delicia, y de sus recuerdos y de su cansancio; de donde quisiera reclinar el corazón le salía una voz, la voz de sí mismo, empujándole con el "Anda, anda, anda" del maldecido.

Don Álvaro se recostaría en los más grandes dolores sin una queja. ¿No repudió a la hermana? ¿No se apartó de su único camino: del ardor de la causa, del odio y de la amistad y del mundo suyó? Sería capaz del mal y del bien, de todo menos de entragarse a la exaltación y a la postración de la dulzura de sentirse. No se rompía su dureza de piedra, su inflexibilidad mineralizada en su sangre. Siempre con el horror del pecado.

A veces quiso leer. Abría viejos documentos y volúmenes de los abuelos de Paulina. Una noche leyó en las *Ordenanzas de Castilla* la ley XXI, donde se manda "que todas las barraganas de los clérigos de todas las ciudades, lugares y villas traigan por señal un prendedero bermejo, tan ancho como tres dedos, encima de las tocas, pública y continuamente..." Recordó el beso delirante de Elvira a Pablo. La que besó de esa manera ¿no pudo traer la faja de ignominia?

En la *Crónica de Oleza* encontró un pregón del Justicia que decía: "que se hiciese requisa en las casas de los capellanes, llevando a la mancebía las mujeres que tuvieran amagadas..."

¿Se hubieran llevado también a su hermana? Y se avergonzó de su pensamiento.

Horror del pecado. Horror de la desgracia que podía suceder.

Otra noche quiso un libro. Lo abrió por el capitulo XV. Y leyó:

"No hay nadie que tema más el infortunio que aquellos cuya mísera vida les habría de dejar a salvo del miedo y que debieran decir como Andrómaca:

– *¡Pluguiera a los dioses que yo temiese!* Hay en Nápoles cincuenta mil hombres que se alimentan de hierba, que se cubren con harapos, y

uncles; and at the very top, the studio used for astronomy by the kindly rebel sympathizer, with its velvet-covered easy chair, its lectern and a hanging meridional celestial sphere.

From the ample light of the attics to the confinement of the parlors, to the study, to the herbarium, and he passed once again by the grapevines at the doorway, walking along joylessly, because no matter from what place, nor from all the things in which he might have taken pleasure: from the rosebush at the cistern, which was used to crown Paulina his bride when she waited for him smiling with love; from the night, so intimate and nuptial here; from every reason for tenderness and delight, and even from his memories and his weariness; from wherever he might wish to rest his heart, a voice would come forth, his very own voice, pushing him on with the "Keep on going, keep on going, keep on going" of the accursed one.[244]

Don Álvaro would seek repose in the very greatest kind of suffering without a complaint. Didn't he repudiate his sister? Didn't he withdraw from his one and only path: from his ardor for the cause, from hatred and friendship and from his whole world? He could be capable of evil and of good, of everything except handing himself over to the exaltation and prostration of the sweetness of feeling. His stony rigidity, his inflexibility petrified in his blood, remained unbroken. Always with the dread of sin.

Sometimes he tried to read. He would open old documents and volumes belonging to Paulina's grandparents. One night he read law XXI in the *Ordinances of Castile*, where it is ordered "that all the concubines of the clerics of all cities, villages and towns shall wear as a sign a bright reddish fillet, at least three fingers wide, on top of their headdresses, in public and at all times...."[245] He remembered Elvira's delirious kissing of Pablo. One who kissed like that, wouldn't she have worn the band of ignominy?

In the *Chronicle of Oleza*, he found a proclamation by the Magistrate that said, "that an inspection should be made of priests' houses, and that any women kept hidden away there under threat should be carried off to the brothel...."[246]

Would they have taken his sister away also? And he was overcome by shame at this thought.

The dread of sin. The dread of the misfortune that could occur.

On another night he sought a book. He opened it to chapter XV. And he read:

"There is nobody who fears misfortune more than those whose wretched lives should have left them safe from fear and who should say like Andromache:

Would to the gods that I were afraid!' There are fifty thousand men in Naples who feed on grass, who cover themselves with rags, and these

estas gentes se horrorizan a la más leve humareda del Vesubio. Tienen la simplicidad de temer que puedan llegar a ser desgraciados".

4. F.O.C.E.

El ferrocarril de Oleza-Costa-Enlace dejaba la emoción y la ilusión de que toda la ciudad viajase dos veces al día: en el correo y en el mixto; o de que toda España viese a Oleza dos veces al día. Oleza estaba cerca del mundo, participando abiertamente de sus maravillas.

La estación, de ladrillos encarnados y andenes de eucaliptos y acacias, era por las tardes sala de familias, horizonte diario de la mocedad, alivio de los afanados, solaz de canónigos y caballeros, feria de flores – en ramos, en haldadas y canastos – y de las sabrosas especialidades de masa y confitura: pasteles de gloria de las clarisas de San Gregorio, costradas de yema de la Visitación, hojaldres de las verónicas, limoncillos y arropes de las madres de San Jerónimo... Muchos sábados se voceaba también *El Clamor de la Verdad,* y los jueves *La Antorcha* – semanario liberal – . *La Antorcha* se complacía de esta abundancia de productos olecenses. *Carolus Alba-Longa,* no. *Alba-Longa,* desde sus fondos titulados "Alerta", daba el aviso de fraudes funestos para el merecido renombre del dulce de Oleza. No era posible que todo lo que se vendía y se facturaba en la estación saliese de los obradores de las comunidades. De seguro que lo apócrifo se mezclaba cautelosamente con lo legítimo. *La Antorcha* publicó su réplica: "¿Y qué?", epígrafe de arremangada impertinencia. Probó, a la fría luz de la estadística, que la cochura de pastas y compotas no había menguado en los hornos monásticos. Domingos y fiestas, las clarisas, las salesas, las jerónimas, las verónicas no podían satisfacer todos los pedidos. Al mismo tiempo doblaban sus tareas las confiterías seculares, tareas no clandestinas, porque las casas estampaban su marca, y ni en aprovecharse de las advocaciones de los dulces monjiles había engaño, sino uso lícito de una onomástica tradicionalmente ineludible.

people are terrified at the very slightest puff of smoke from Vesuvius. They are naïve enough to fear that misfortune may befall them."[247]

4. F.O.C.E.

The *ferrocarríl de Oleza-Costa-Enlace* (Oleza-Coastal-Connection Railroad Line)[248] left you with the emotional impression and illusion that the entire city was traveling two times per day: on the mail train and on the combined freight and passenger train; or that all of Spain was seeing Oleza twice a day. Oleza was close to the world, openly participating in its wonders.

The station, with its incarnate bricks and its platforms with eucalyptus and acacia bushes, was a sitting room for families in the afternoon, a daily horizon for young people, a place of alleviation for the distraught, a place of relaxation for canons and gentlemen, for a flower market – in bouquets, in burlap bags and in baskets – and for the delicious specialties of pastry and confectionery: cream tarts from the Clares of San Gregorio, candied seedcakes from the sisters at La Visitación, puff pastes from the Franciscan sisters at Santa Veronica, small candied lemons and syrups from the mothers at San Jerónimo.... On many Saturdays, they would also hawk *The Outcry of Truth*, and on Thursdays, *The Torch* – a liberal weekly.[249] *The Torch* was extremely pleased with this abundance of Olezan products. But *Carolus Alba-Longa* wasn't. *Alba-Longa*, from his editorials entitled "Beware," released the warning concerning the baneful frauds against the deserved reputation of Olezan confectionery. It wasn't possible that everything that was sold or listed for shipment at the station could come from the workshops of the religious Communities. Most certainly the apocryphal was cautiously being mixed with the legitimate. *The Torch* published its reply, "So what about it?", an epigraph of resolute impertinence. By the cold light of statistics, it demonstrated that the preparation of pastries and sweetmeats had not diminished in the monastic ovens. On Sundays and holidays, the Clares, the nuns of the order of La Visitación, the nuns of the order of San Jerónimo, the Franciscan sisters of Santa Veronica, were not able to satisfy all the orders. At the same time, the secular confectioneries doubled their work output, in no way a clandestine output, because these houses imprinted their trademarks; nor was there absolutely any deception in their taking advantage of appellations ascribed to the confections from the religious orders, but rather a legitimate use of a traditionally inevitable

Si los viajeros del ferrocarril de Oleza-Costa-Enlace compraban hojaldres y bizcochos laicos, creyéndolos amasados en las artesillas "de las hacendosas abejas de los panales del cielo" – verdadera galantería liberal – , ¿qué culpa tenía el gremio de dulceros? ¿Qué se confunden las castas de dulces? ¿Y qué? Si el dulce del siglo resultaba tan gustoso como el del claustro, ¿negaría *Carolus Alba-Longa* las eficacias del progreso, los beneficios públicos de la competencia?

De este pleito se apartaba el señor penitenciario, amargo de realidades diocesanas; el P. Bellod, de broncos sentidos, y el homeópata Monera, sin ninguna voluntad para los gustos de este mundo.

Pesábale al canónigo que *Alba-Longa* se disipara en naderías, necesitándose de tanto ahínco para otras difíciles empresas. Por ejemplo.

Cuando pronunció "por ejemplo" ocurriósele al homeópata decir:

– Sin don Álvaro, todos habíamos de confiar en don Amancio; don Amancio se tiene por el caudillo. ¡Se llama a sí mismo el *Juan* de la Causa!

– ¿Juan? – preguntó el P. Bellod soltando su risa – . Juan ¿qué?

– Por ejemplo – insistió recremándose el señor penitenciario – : siete meses está Oleza sin pastor, siete meses huérfana, y nadie parece sentir la expectación aflictiva de otros tiempos de sede vacante. ¡Cómo se encendía entonces don Amancio pidiendo nuestro remedio! Su generosa palabra no fue oída en Madrid, por fortuna para mis sienes...

El P. Bellod sonrió con boca marrullera, mirándoselas con su único ojo.

– ¡Mis sienes, que no hubieran resistido la pesadumbre de la mitra! Y ahora...

Monera necesitó interrumpirle otra vez. Después del apartamiento de don Álvaro Galindo y del fracaso conyugal y tibieza política de don Amancio Espuch, Monera podía creerse el seglar eminente del corro. Y Monera dijo:

– Ahora no es entonces; ahora ya tiene Oleza candidato seguro, candidato de "Jesús" y de los liberales: monseñor Salom.

– ¡Monseñor Salom! ¡Pobre monseñor Salom!

Y el penitenciario y el P. Bellod se reían de Monera.

onomastic process. If the travelers on the Oleza-Coastal-Connection Railroad Line bought laic puff pastes and biscuits, in the belief that they had been kneaded in the troughs "of the industrious bees of the heavenly honeycomb" – a true liberal compliment, – what blame did the confectioners' guild have for that? And if the lineage of the confections were confused? So what? If the confections of the outside world turned out to be as tasty as those from the cloisters, would *Carolus Alba-Longa* deny the effectiveness of progress, the public benefits of competition?

The canon-penitentiary, embittered by realities of the diocese, kept his distance from this dispute; Father Bellod, with his coarse sensibilities, and Monera, the homeopath, had no inclination for the tastes of this world.

It grieved the canon that *Alba-Longa* should dissipate himself in such trivialities, when he was so desperately needed for other difficult undertakings. For example.

When he expressed the words "for example," it occurred to the homeopath to say:

"Without Don Álvaro, we were all obliged to trust in Don Amancio; Don Amancio is regarded as the chief. He even calls himself the *John* of the Cause!"[250]

"John?" Father Bellod asked as he burst into laughter. "John what?"

"For example," the canon-penitentiary insisted, getting more inflamed, "Oleza has been without a pastoral head for seven months, seven months an orphan, and nobody seems to feel the distressing sense of expectancy felt at other times when the see was vacant. How impassioned Don Amancio felt at that time when he asked us for our resolution! His generous words went unheeded in Madrid, fortunately for my temples...."

Father Bellod smiled with a cajoling expression on his mouth as he looked at those temples with his one good eye.

"As for my temples, they would never have been able to bear the considerable weight of the miter! And now...."

Monera found it necessary to interrupt him again. After Don Álvaro Galindo's withdrawal and Don Amancio Espuch's conjugal failure and his lukewarm political interest, Monera could consider himself the outstanding layman of the circle. And Monera said:

"Now is not then; Oleza now has a sure candidate, the candidate of 'Jesús' and of the liberals: Monsignor Salom."

"Monsignor Salom! Poor Monsignor Salom!"

And the canon-penitentiary and Father Bellod laughed at Monera.

(Es difícil escaparse del éxito. Pero el éxito se descabulle de todas las manos. Es arcaduz que ya sube colmado, ya baja vacío. Por la mañana, Monera no supo cómo aplacar a su mujer, que poco más o menos le gritó: "Tráeme tazas y picheles de las alfarerías de Nuestra Señora, barro bendito que vuelve fecundas a las estériles. ¡Venga un hijo, hija o hijo, yo lo que quiero es quedarme embarazada!". Y por la tarde, Monera no supo cómo resistir la burla y los ojos del penitenciario, y miró sin gana su reloj, gordo como una naranja de oro, lo mismo que hacía en sus poquedades de antaño.)

Tenía razón el canónigo: Oleza no se desesperaba por su orfandad. Pasaba el tiempo, y pasaba el tren divirtiéndola de su luto.

Desde la Glorieta hasta la estación, el antiguo y arbolado camino de Murcia convirtióse en alameda con bancos, baldosas, faroles, podas y riegos municipales. Tránsito y rebullicio de mocitas y viejas del arrabal y de la huerta, vestidas de pendones y mugres, flacas y descalzas, pero sin faltarles en su moño la brasa de un clavel o la peina estrellada de diamelas. Llevaban pomos de rosas, manojos de clavelones y nardos, biznagas de jazmines, ramos de figura de jarrón, ramos de tres pisos de forma de ánfora con un leve temblor de nebulosas y estelarias; las asas, de hierbacinta; la boca de azucenas y de azahar o de magnolias abriéndose en el nido de follaje de laca de su árbol, y el mazo de los tallos zumosos atado sabiamente con tomiza fresca...

Los beneficios del ferrocarril para los floricultores y floristas no los negaría *Alba-Longa*. Los cosecheros de naranja, de pimentón, de aceite, de hortalizas y cáñamo, los terciopelistas, los aperadores, los alfareros exportaban ahora lo suyo en los trenes mixtos y mercancías; pero antes tampoco se les malparaban las cosechas y las industrias agrícolas, porque todo hallaba salidas con los cosarios y arrieros que iban a los mercados de la provincia y de la Mancha y a los muelles de Alicante, de Torrevieja, de Cartagena y Águilas. Pero las flores, no: las flores renacían, se multiplicaban y se ahogaban dentro de Oleza. Oleza había sido un jardín cerrado y

(It is difficult to escape from success. But success can slip right through all our hands. It is a bucket that first comes up overflowing and then goes down empty. In the morning, Monera could find no way to placate his wife, who, more or less, shouted at him, "Bring me cups and mugs from the potteries of Nuestra Señora, the blessed clay that makes sterile women fertile. It's time for me to have a child, be it a daughter or a son; what I want is to find myself pregnant!" And in the afternoon, Monera could find no way to withstand the canon-penitentiary's mockery and his eyes, and so he looked at his watch, as fat as a golden orange, without any desire to even do so, just as he had done in his pusillanimous moments in the past.)

The canon was right: Oleza was so filled with despair because it was orphaned. Time kept passing and the train kept passing through, diverting it from its time of mourning.

From the gardens of the Square to the station,[251] the old tree-lined road to Murcia was now converted into a public walk, with benches, flagstones and street lamps, and the pruning and watering was done by the municipal authorities. The passing back and forth and the tumult of young girls and old women from the outlying district and the cultivated plain, dressed like slatterns and filthy, skinny and barefooted, but never failing to wear the fiery red of a carnation or a high, tortoise shell comb spangled with Arabian jasmine in the topknots of their hair. They were holding bouquets of roses, bunches of marigolds and spikenards, bell-shaped bouquets of jasmine, floral arrangements in the shape of vases, bouquets arranged in three tiers in the form of an amphora, with a delicate quivering of lady's mantle and starwort; the handles were made of ribbon grass; the mouths of white lilies and orange blossoms or of magnolias, opening up wide in the nest of shiny, lacquer-like foliage in their tree, and the whole cluster of juicy stalks cleverly tied together with strands of fresh esparto grass....

Alba-Longa could not deny the benefits of the railroad for the flower growers and flower vendors. Those who produced crops of oranges, red peppers, olive oil, vegetables and hemp, the velvet makers, the wheelwrights and the potters, were now exporting all they produced on the passenger-freight trains and the freight trains; but even before, their crops and agricultural products had not gone to waste, because everything found a market by using the carters and mule drivers going to the markets throughout their own province and in La Mancha and the piers of Alicante, Torrevieja, Cartagena and Aguilas. But not the flowers: the flowers kept being reborn, they multiplied and were smothered right inside Oleza. Oleza had been an

abandonado. Las flores se criaban entre las habas y las fresas, en los tablares de lechugas, en las lindes del panizo. Cuadros de coles con orillas de alhelíes, de rosales de francesillas, de carraspiques y dalias; senderos de lirios, de margaritas, de hierbaluisa; cañar de alubias con espalderas de heliotropos y de celindas; rebordes de noria plantados de girasoles y geranios, arrimo y puerta de barraca a la sombra de un olmo y del árbol del Paraíso; blancas campánulas y galán de noche entre la higuera y la vid, y no había corral sin dondiegos y cidro, balcón sin claveles, azotea sin jazmín, leja ni cantarero sin albahaca, sin vaso de flores. Flores en los altares, en el mostrador, en la sala, en el burdel, en el corpiño y en los cabellos de la mujer de manteleta y de la andrajosa.

Si no se engorda con las flores, daban un jornal menos duros que menando soga o recogiendo estiércol del camino.

Fueron conocidos los ramos de Oleza, y subió la fama de sus dulcerías y tahonas.

Pero las familias de rango no aceptaban otros manjares de postre de santos y fiestas que los modelados por dedos místicos. Cundía la preferencia entre muchos golosmeadores forasteros, con lo que creció tanto la demanda de las especialidades legítimas, que ni quebrantando el horario regular lograban las abejas del cielo abastecer la parroquia de este mundo, y tuvieron que valerse de labores profanas. Así fue perdiéndose la virtud de la emulación, cantada por *La Antorcha.* Y todos fueron unos. Aunque fuesen unos, don Magín siempre quiso los dulces monásticos; pero los ensalzaba todos. Proclamaba la importancia del dulce por lo que recuerda y sugiere y por su valor folklórico; afirmaba también que era un indicio del carácter, de las virtudes y de los pecados de toda una época. Y se dolía de no ser tan docto en disciplinas históricas como *Alba-Longa,* y más aún de no serlo como el tío de *Alba-Longa:* el difunto Espuch y Loriga; pues, siéndolo, juntaría papeles y estudios para escribir un comentario de la cocina y artesa de la antigua Corona de Aragón, desde los últimos confines de la diócesis de Urgel hasta los primeros términos del obispado de Cartagena-Murcia. En esta obra, con apéndices de parcelas filológicas, se vería que el horno y el

enclosed and abandoned garden. Flowers were grown among the beans and the strawberries, in the beds of lettuce, at the edges of a field of millet. Beds of cabbages with borders of wallflowers, of rose bushes, of turban buttercups, of candytuft and dahlias; footpaths with irises, daisies, lemon verbena; a field of cane with French beans and trellises of heliotrope and syringa; the borders of a draw-well planted with sunflowers and geraniums; a supporting wall and doorway of a cabin in the shade of an elm tree and a China tree; white bellflowers and night jasmine between the fig tree and grapevines, and there wasn't a yard without marvels-of-Peru and citron bushes, a balcony without carnations, a roof terrace without jasmine, a shelf or storage area without basil, without a jar of flowers. Flowers on the altars, on the counter, in a drawing room, in the brothel, on the bodice and in the hair of a woman in a fancy mantelet and one in rags.

If one doesn't prosper from flowers, at least they gave you a wage less taxing than if you were winding esparto fiber or picking up manure from the road.

The bouquets of flowers from Oleza were widely known and the reputation of its confectioneries and bakeries was on the rise.

But the families of quality accepted no delicacies for dessert on saint's days and holidays other than those molded by mystical fingers. This preference was spreading among many out-of-towners possessed of a sweet tooth, and so the demand for legitimate specialties increased to such a degree that the heavenly bees were no longer able to provide for the parish in this world even by breaking their regular schedule, and they were forced to resort to the use of profane labor. In this way the virtue of the imitation, praised by *The Torch* was beginning to lose its force. And so they were all the same. Even though they might be the same, Don Magín always preferred monastic confections; but he extolled them all. He proclaimed the importance of sweets for what they recall and suggest and for their folkloric value; he also affirmed that they were a sign of the character, the virtues and the sins of a whole epoch. And he was grieved at not being so learned in historical disciplines as *Alba-Longa*, and even more at not being the equal of *Alba-Longa*'s uncle: the deceased Espuch y Loriga; for if he were, he would gather papers and studies in order to write a commentary on the kitchen and the baking trough of the old Crown of Aragon, all the way from the furthest corners of the diocese of Urgel right up to the nearby boundaries of the bishopric of Cartagena-Murcia.[252] In this work, with appendices of philological subdivisions, one would see that the oven and the kneading

amasador van medrando al abrigo de la liturgia y de la hagiografía, y que la Corona de Aragón comprendía las tierras más emocionadas de tradiciones y devociones; la más rica en artes populares, en variedad de culturas estéticas y agrarias y en condimentos, suculencias, conservas, masa de huevo, de manteca y aceite. Deduciéndose de todos los datos y doctrinas que una buena gollería, un buen saborete de abolengo responde siempre a un estado categórico civil y eclesiástico de la vida y del idioma.

Retozaban las risas, y todos decían:

– ¡El don Magín de siempre!

– ¡Si todo se muda, a todo se acomoda! ¡Tañe el esquilón y duermen los tordos al son!

– ¡Y siempre tordos son! ¡Y don Magín siempre es don Magín!

Pero ¿de verdad era don Magín el mismo don Magín? Como siempre, seguía su itinerario mañanero por las calles de Oleza, ceñido un lado del manteo y el otro cayéndole a pliegues; el canalón, en la nuca, le dejaba la frente al sol; sus dedos, con la caricia de una hoja tierna, de un copo de gramínea. Se volvía hasta sin querer a todas las rejas donde floreciesen nardos, clavellinas, doncellas bordadoras, y descansaba en el portal de algunos obradores de chocolates para recoger el generoso vaho. Corredora de San Daniel, con trajín de recuas de molino; calle de los Caballeros, de casones blasonados; calle de la Aparecida, con unbría de tapias y frutales y ruido de acequias; plazuela de Gosálvez, con su álamo de aldea, cargas de encendajas para las tahonas, y, en medio, el farol de aceite, que le decían el "Crisuelo".

– ¡Ya viene don Magín!

– ¡Atienda, don Magín!

– ¡Eso no será sin don Magín!

Lo mismo que siempre. ¿Lo mismo? Ya no estaban los de Lóriz en su palacio, que tampoco era palacio, sino lonja de contrataciones de las industrias de sedas y cáñamos. Ni se asomaba don Magín al huerto y biblioteca del obispo, acabó su diálogo de amistad, amistad sin desencanto, sin llaneza de camaradas que se quedan en mangas de camisa y precipitadamente se ponen la muda de paño nuevo de domingo. Don Magín y el prelado nunca se

room keep thriving under the protection of liturgy and hagiography, and that the Crown of Aragon comprised regions most moved by traditions and devotions; the richest province in popular arts, in the variety of esthetic and agrarian cultures and in condiments, succulent foods, preserves, dough made of eggs, butter and oil. It can be deduced from all the data and lore that a good delicacy, a fine and delicate ancestral flavor always responds to a civil and ecclesiastical categorical civil state of life and language.

There was rollicking laughter and everyone said:

"Don Magín is the same as always!"

"Even if everything changes, he accommodates himself to everything! The big bell keeps ringing and the thrushes keep sleeping without fear of the sound!"[253]

"And they'll always be thrushes! And Don Magín is always Don Magín!"

But was Don Magín really the same Don Magín? As always, he kept up with his early morning itinerary along the streets of Oleza, one side of his long cloak clinging to his waist and the other dropping down in folds; his shovel hat pulled down over the back of his neck, left his forehead open to the sun; his fingers with the caress of a tender leaf, of a tuft of grass. He turned, almost without intending to, toward all the window gratings where spikenard, pinks and maidenly embroiderers were blooming, and he paused to rest in the entryways of some chocolate-making establishments in order to gather in the generous aroma. The Corredera de San Daniel, with its back and forth movement of droves of mules from the mills; the Calle de los Caballeros, with its vast mansions with their heraldic shields; the Calle de la Aparecida, shaded with walls and fruit trees and the sound of water channels; the Plazuela de Gosálvez, with its age-old village poplar, piles of kindling wood for the bakeries, and in the middle, the old-time oil street lantern everyone called the "Crisuelo (The Dripping Pan)."

"Here comes Don Magín!"

"Wait up, Don Magín!"

"That can't be without Don Magín!"

The same as always. The same? The Lórizes were no longer in their palace, and it was no longer a palace, but a trade exchange for the silk and hemp industries. Nor did Don Magín ever show up at the bishop's garden and library; his dialogue of friendship was over, a friendship without disillusionment, without the straightforwardness of close friends who stand about in shirtsleeves and quite suddenly change into their best Sunday clothes. Don Magín and the

desnudaron del señorío de sus calidades ni tuvieron que añadirse de pronto vuelo de almidón. Oleza se encogía de hombros al pasar por el Palacio episcopal, entornado y vacante. Desapareció la "Monja". Se cerró la casa de don Álvaro... Todo se quebrantaba y aventaba en el ruejo y en la intemperie de los años.

Y don Magín seguía siendo don Magín. Capellán de cuerpo entero y bien entero. Afirmativo y consustanciado de la Oleza clásica; comunicado del aire y sal de humanidad de todos los tiempos. Se hablaba de él y se le sentía hasta por tradición, como el clima, las campanas, el edificio histórico de un lugar. Pero el clima de una tierra y de sus ánimas mejor lo siente el forastero que el lugareño; las campanas le suenan y retiñen al vecino cuanto más se aleja de su parroquia, y el edificio famoso quedó para eso: para fama, y no se ha de meditar en lo que de todas maneras ya tiene su concepto sellado. Así don Magín en Oleza.

Como ya se sabía que don Magín era don Magín, no se sabía de él ni su pecado, su pecado concreto, lo más conocido de todos los clérigos y seglares. Por su brío y sensualidad podría cometer los peores con la misma elegancia que llevaba su manteo y su paraguas de Génova.

Las flaquezas de los demás serían en don Magín robusteces. Finalmente, no se le perdonaba la paradoja de que, siendo, según era, fuese puro.

Meditaciones primarias de don Magín: "No aspires, alma mía y alma de mi prójimo, a demasiada perfección; no grandes sacrificios, no fuera que lo costoso de estos actos te disculpe de cumplirlos. Acepta las humildes bondades, que el gusto y la ternura que les siguen nos convidan a otras mejores. El Kempis dice: "Tentación es la vida del hombre sobre la tierra. El fuego prueba al hierro y la tentación al justo". Yo te digo: toda la vida del hombre es un sacrificio, y se asusta cuando se le impone estrictamente alguno. Después de todo, el sacrificio es una virtud resolutoria. ¿Que no puedes poseer lo que apeteces? Sacrifícate a no tenerlo. Luego ¿deberá aceptarse el sacrificio más a sabiendas y pronto para que sus provechos se ocasionen antes? Dejemos a los sacrificios con sus desabrimientos y dolores, y así, y por lo menos, serán sacrificios, y el hombre tendrá que agradecerse algo y que ofrecer a Dios, ya que nunca se le ofrecen los goces. Y si los

prelate never stripped themselves of the dignity of their qualities, nor did they ever find it necessary to suddenly add starched lace ruffles to their manners. Oleza shrugged its shoulders as it passed by the episcopal palace, now partly closed and vacant. The "Nun" disappeared. Don Álvaro's house was closed up.... Everything was breaking down and blowing away in the millwheel that was life and the inclemency of the years.

And Don Magín continued being Don Magín. A full-fledged priest, really full-fledged. An affirmative and consubstantial part of classical Oleza, in communication with the air and the wit of the humanity of all times. They would speak about him and have feelings about him almost out of tradition, like the climate, the bells, the historic building of a particular place. But the outsider rather than the town dweller often better grasps the climate and the spirit of some place; the bells ring and keep resounding for the native all the further that he draws away from his own parish, and the famous building remained standing for that very purpose: for its fame, and one needn't meditate upon that which already has the conception established anyway, sealed within it. So it was with Don Magín in Oleza.

Since it was already known that Don Magín was Don Magín, not even his sin was known about him, his concrete sin, what was best known about all clerics and laymen. Because of his high spirit and sensuality, he could commit the worst sins with the same elegance with which he wore his long cloak and carried his umbrella from Genoa.

Other people's weaknesses would be strengths in Don Magín.

Finally, he could not be pardoned for the paradox in him, that he could still be pure in spite of being how he was.

The principal meditations of Don Magín: "Do not aspire, my soul and the soul of my fellow man, to too much perfection; no great sacrifices, lest the costliness of such acts excuse you from fulfilling them. Accept acts of humble kindness, for the pleasure and tenderness that follow them invite us to do even better ones.[254] Thomas à Kempis says, 'The life of man upon earth is temptation. Fire puts iron to the test and temptation the just man.'[255] I say to you: all of a man's life is a sacrifice, and he becomes frightened when one is strictly imposed upon him. After all, sacrifice is a virtue that leads to resolution. So what if you can not possess what you crave? Make the sacrifice of not having it. Then, ought we not to accept sacrifice knowingly and quickly so that we may occasion its advantages earlier? Let us set aside sacrifices with their unpleasant aspects and their pain, and in that way, at least, they will truly be sacrifices, and man will have to be grateful for something and will have to make an offering to God,

sacrificios no fueren soluciones, que sean siquiera un sufrimiento, y serán algo, aunque no sean afirmativamente nada".

Algunos decían que en don Magín se daba el difícil primor de esconder lo mismo sus pecados que sus virtudes. Y para eso hubiera tenido que vivir siempre cerrado, con luz artifical y bajando el resuello. Y él no renunciaba al grito ni a la holgura, y así pudo responderle a doña Purita, que le quiso picar y recelar por desaparecer de las amistades:

– ¡Yo, hija de mi alma, lavo, tuerzo y tiendo mi vida al sol!.

– ¡No será al de la ventana de doña Corazón, donde ya no se le ve ni por lástima de aquella impedida!

Al separarse, no pensaba don Magín: "¡Cómo está hoy esa mujer!", sino: "¡Qué tendrá esa criatura!" En la mirada de la gentil doncellona había una quietud de lejanía.

Y aquella tarde aparecióse en la sala de la tullida señora. A la Jimena se le reverdeció y alborotó el enfado de la ausencia del capellán con tan súbita presencia.

Con ellas estaba una celadora del Santísimo, y nadie más. Poco fue lo que se devanó: que una de las *Catalanas* – la mayor o la menor – había muerto, y los bienes quedaron para la otra, de la que pasarían – según testamento de entrambas – a dotar tres capellanías en Barcelona, menos su casa y tierras de Oleza, legadas a Nuestro Padre San Daniel, y mil reales a una niña huérfana de su vecindad. Que don Roger y el Sr. Hugo, después de mirar un día con tristeza a doña Purita, dejaron ya de mirarla, y se volvieron, dóciles y arrepentidos, a "Jesús", y "Jesús" los aceptó misericordiosamente.

...Y doña Purita no venía, y doña Nieves tampoco.

Agotado el hilo, recordóse la Jimena de la beata de Gandía y de don Álvaro. Llegó a decir que había sido de justicia aborrecerles tanto y que en fuerza de ser tan justos con ellos iban aborreciéndoles menos.

since he is never offered any pleasures. And if sacrifices were not solutions, let them at least be a form of suffering, and they'll be something, though, in a positive sense, they may be nothing."

Some said that in the case of Don Magín, one had an example of this most difficult skill of hiding his sins as well as his virtues. And in order to do that, he would have had to live in confinement all the time, with artificial light and holding his breath. But he wasn't renouncing being able to shout out loud nor enjoying life fully, and for that reason he could respond to Doña Purita, who tried to pique him and was suspicious of his having disappeared from their close friendship:

"I, my very dear child, wash and wring my life and put it out to dry in the sun!"[256]

"But it certainly won't be at Doña Corazón's window, where nobody ever sees you any more, not even out of pity for that poor crippled woman!"

When they separated, Don Magín wasn't thinking, "How attractive that woman looks today!", but rather, "What can possibly be the matter with that creature!" There was a quietude of remote distance in the glance of that charming maiden lady.

And he made his appearance in the parlor of the crippled woman that very afternoon. Jimena's anger over the priest's absence followed by his sudden presence sprouted anew and stirred her up even more.

One of the women who served as a guardian of the Holy Sacrament was with them and nobody else. Very little was spun there: that one of the *Catalan sisters* – either the older one or the younger one – had died, and that the estate had been left to the other one, from whose hands it would pass – according to a will made by both – to the endowment of three ecclesiastic beneficent funds in Barcelona, except for their house and the lands in Oleza, bequeathed to Our Father San Daniel, and a thousand *reales* to a little orphan girl in their neighborhood. Also that Don Roger and Señor Hugo, after looking sadly at Doña Purita one day, had now stopped looking at her, and had turned back toward "Jesús" docilely and repentantly, and "Jesús" had accepted them back in all its mercy.

...And Doña Purita didn't come, nor Doña Nieves.

Once the thread had been used up, Jimena remembered the sanctimonious woman from Gandía and Don Álvaro. She ended up saying that it had been quite justifiable to detest them so much and that by virtue of being so just with them they could now be detested less.

En el regazo de doña Corazón y entre sus manos pulidas y perfumadas de sebillo de bergamota se dormían los años viejos de Oleza, y a la vez rodaban las mudanzas de los tiempos.

– Ay, todo pasa, todo pasa volando, don Magín!

Don Magín penetró en la segunda morada de su conciencia:

"¡Era verdad; todo pasaba volando después de haber pasado! Pero ¿y antes de pasar? En las delicias y en las adversidades pocos escapan de decirse: ¡Eso no lo pude gozar! ¡Esto no lo podré resistir! Pues aguardemos, y dentro de algunos años: diez, quince, veinte años, todo se habrá derretido. Escondida tentación de mujer: ¿Es aqélla? ¿Es esta mujer? – ¿pensaría entonces don Magín en doña Purita? – . Ella tiene treinta años y yo cincuenta. ¡Dentro de veinte más! Todo pasa, inclusive lo que no pasó."

Pues que vemos lo presente
Que en un punto se es ido
Y acabado,
Si juzgamos sabiamente
Daremos lo no venido
Por pasado.

¿También lo no pasado lo daremos por pasado? Todo pasa. ¿Todo? Pero ¿qué es lo que única y precisamente pasará sino lo que fuimos, lo que hubiéramos gozado y alcanzado? Y si no pudimos ser ni saciar lo apetecido, entonces ¿qué es lo que habrá pasado? No habrá pasado la posibilidad desaprovechada, la capacidad recluída? ¿Y nuestro dolor? También nuestro dolor. ¿Y no quedará de algún modo lo que no fuimos ni pudimos, y habremos pasado nosotros sin pasar? Dolorosa consolación la de tener que decir: ¡Todo pasa, si morimos con la duda de que no haya pasado todo: la pasión no cumplida, la afición mortificada!...

Sin doña Purita se desganaba la charla, quedándose en porciones. Verdaderamente habían pasado también los tiempos de la tertulia de doña Corazón.

Y el capellán levantóse y se fue a su banco de la alameda, frente a los huertos; allí fumaba y tragaba el aire del atardecer, que venía embebido de olor de campo tierno; desde allí recogía el silbo y estrépito del tren, que le dejaba la promesa de distancias, más claras y grandes en las losas de su

The bygone years of Oleza lay asleep in Doña Corazón's lap and between her hands, smoothed and perfumed with bergamot-scented soap, and at the same time the changes in the times kept rolling on.

"Oh, everything passes, everything passes so swiftly, Don Magín!"

Don Magín penetrated into the second mansion of his own consciousness:[257]

It was true; everything was passing so swiftly after having passed! But what about before it passed? In delights and adversities, few escape telling themselves, "I wasn't able to enjoy that! I won't be able to resist this! So let's wait, and within a few years: ten, fifteen, twenty years, everything will have melted away." A hidden temptation for a woman, "Is it that one? Is it this woman?" – Would Don Magín be thinking about Doña Purita then? – "She is thirty years old and I am fifty. Within twenty more! Everything passes, including what did not pass."

For we see the present
How it has gone in a flash
And is over,
If we judge wisely
We shall deem what has not come
As having passed.[258]

Shall we also consider what has not passed as having passed? Everything passes. Everything? But what is it that solely and precisely will pass but what we once were, what we may have enjoyed and achieved? But if we did succeed in being or satisfying what we craved, then what is it that must have passed? Will it not be the unfulfilled possibility, the shackled capacity that must have passed? And our sorrow? Our sorrow too. And what we were not able to be nor to do, will that not remain in some way, and will we have passed without passing? A sorrowful consolation having to say, "Everything passes, if we die doubting that everything may not have passed: unfulfilled passion, mortified affection!..."

Without Doña Purita, the conversation lost any positive quality and remained in fragments. In truth, the times of Doña Corazón's social gatherings had also passed.

And so the priest stood up and went off to his bench on the public walk, facing the gardens; there he smoked and drank in the late afternoon air, which came in soaked with the aroma of the tender countryside; from there he was able to gather in the whistle and the din of the train which left him with the promise of distant places, brighter and larger on the slabs of his favorite

banco predilecto que en los andenes ferroviarios donde se ve con exactitud al maquinista y el número de la máquina; y después, en su aposento rectoral, dentro de la corona de luz de su velón de aceite, se abrían los horizontes de su mundo y se apretaba su soledad, tan yerma sin el obispo leproso.

...Estruendo y polvo de un coche amarillo, con muestra verde de la "Fonda de Europa", antiguo parador de Nuestro Padre.

Mandaderos, mozas, anacalos y aprendices con bandejas, cuévanos y tablas de hornos y pastelerías.

Trallazos, colleras, herrajes y tumbos del coche del "Mesón de San Daniel".

Familias de Oleza, menestrales de las sederías, arrabaleros de San Ginés, viajeros rurales, frailes, socios del Casino...

Mujeres con ramos de flores, de cidras y naranjas. Una vendedora, toda vibrante y dura como un cobre, le dio a oler a don Magín su esportilla de magnolias húmedas. Y el capellán entró todo su rostro en las carnales blancuras suspirando: "¡Ay, sensualidad, y cómo nos traspasas de anhelos de infinito!".

Alameda callada; don Magín solitario; y comenzó a sentirse el tren que venía de Murcia. Entonces, bajo el toldo de los árboles, surgió, al galope de botes de mula, una tartana de alquiler con cestos, atadijos, y a la zaguera un cofre. Volvióse don Magín para mirarla, y vio entre los equipajes un bulto repulgado y una graciosa silueta que le envió un adiós cohibido.

Don Magín olvidóse de su edad, de su hábito, de su sosiego, y se atolondró y corrió como un don Jeromillo.

La visera de cinc de la marquesina y el lomo del tren cerraban la tarde; y dentro hervía la folla de viajeros, de ociosos, de mendigos, de ferieros...

La vieja ciudad episcopal palpitaba en las orillas del universo. Desde las portezuelas, comisionistas de azafrán y cáñamo, técnicos ingleses de las minas de Cartagena, viajantes catalanes, mercaderes valencianos de sedas, familias castellanas de alumnos de "Jesús", cogían en brazos las flores, los manojos de limas, de naranjos, de ponciles... Tanto se condensaban los aromas que don Magín tuvo angustia. Los vagones le parecían capillas de

bench than on the railroad platforms, where one could see the engineer and the number of the engine with great precision; and afterwards, in his room at the rectory, inside the crown of light from his oil lamp, the horizons of his world opened up and his solitude pressed in upon him, now so barren without the leper bishop.

...The uproar and dust of a yellow coach with a green sign, from the "European Inn," the one-time inn of Our Father. Messengers, servant girls, bakers' deliverymen and apprentices with trays, panniers and serving boards from the bakeries and the confectioners.'

The cracking of whips, the sounds of horse collars and iron fittings and the jolting of the coach from the "San Daniel Inn."

Olezan families, artisans from the silk factories, people from the outlying district of San Ginés, rural travelers, friars, members of the Men's Club....

Women with bouquets of flowers, from citron and orange trees. A vendor, ever so vibrant and as hard as nails, let Don Magín smell her small basket of moist magnolias. And the priest immersed his whole face inside the carnal whiteness sighing, "Oh, sensuality, how you prick us with the longing for the infinite!"

A silent public walk; Don Magín all alone, and you began to hear the train coming from Murcia. Just then, beneath the awning of the trees, a light hired carriage suddenly appeared, accompanied by a hurried and frolicsome bounding of mules, with baskets and bundles inside and a trunk tied to the rear. Don Magín turned around to look at it and he saw a huddled and twisted shape amidst all the baggage, as well as an attractive silhouette that was sending him a restrained farewell.

Don Magín forgot his age, his habit, his tranquility, and he felt bewildered and started to run like a Don Jeromillo.

The zinc visor over the locomotive cab and the roof of the train closed off the afternoon light; and inside, a hodgepodge of travelers, idlers, beggars and market vendors were swarming about....

The old episcopal city was palpitating on the shores of the universe. From the doors of the coaches, commission merchants of saffron and hemp, English technical experts from the mines in Cartagena, Catalan traveling salesmen, Valencian silk merchants, Castilian families of students from "Jesús," were grabbing flowers, handfuls of blossoms from sweet lime, orange and bitter lemon trees in their arms.... The aromas condensed to such an extent that Don Magín was overcome with anguish. The train coaches seemed to be like chapels for a wake for the dead or else bridal altars. A

vela de difunto y de altares de novia. Olor nupcial. Olor de muerte. No paraba la barbulla de huertanas ofreciendo ramos a peseta, a seis reales, a nueve reales... Y al segundo toque de la esquila ferroviaria, vino la baja de los precios del mercado floral. ¡A seis, a nueve y doce *perros jordos!*

En el estribo de un segunda, un buen hombre, todo inflamado, devoraba una pella de San Gregorío, torcida la gorra, saliéndosele los puños postizos de porcelana; y se reía y ahogaba de manjar defendiéndose de las floristas.

Se le embistió una rapaza con dos espigas de nardos y dos magnolias entornadas, las dos más altas y frías del árbol. ¡Todo por siete perricas!

— ¡Quiere decir!

— ¡Cinco!

— ¡Obsolutamente! (Era de Granollers).

Se apartó para que bajase una viejecita de manto.

¡Doña Nieves!

Vio la santera de San Josefico a don Magín, y santiguóse diciendo:

— ¡Estaba de Dios! ¡Aquí lo tienes, mi hija!

Y apareció doña Purita. ¡Se marchaba de Oleza escondiéndose, como si huyese!

— ¿Hasta cuándo?

— ¡No lo sé, don Magín!

Y rápidamente le contó que su hermana casada en Valencia la llamaba. Medraron los asuntos del marido; crecía la casa. A nadie más que a doña Nieves se lo dijo. De nadie más quiso despedirse. Doña Nieves lo presenciaba y resistía todo sin una lágrima.

El último toque. Estrépito de portezuelas.

— ¡A cuatro perricas!

Don Magín tomó los nardos, las magnolias. Y subieron los valores.

— ¡A peseta, don Magín!

Le rodearon las vendedoras; y él les arrebataba rosas ardientes, rosas pálidas, capullos de naranjo, broches de jazmines, y todo lo volcó en el asiento y en el regazo de la viajera.

Ella le besó la mano, y cortó un nardo y también lo besó y se lo dio diciéndole:

nuptial fragrance. A fragrance of death. The hubbub among the women from the cultivated plain would not stop as they kept offering bouquets of flowers for a *peseta*. for six *reales*, for nine *reales*.... And after the railway bell rang for the second time, the prices in the flower market started to fall. For only six, nine and twelve *perros jordos* (10 cent pieces)![259]

A fine-looking man was standing on the step of a second-class coach, quite flushed, and he was devouring a pastry puff from the convent of San Gregorio; his cap was askew and his detachable porcelain cuffs protruding; he laughed and choked on his delicacy and defended himself against the women selling the flowers.

A young girl accosted him with two spikes of nards and two half- closed magnolias, the two that were highest and coldest on the tree. All that for just seven paltry coppers!

"So that's your best price!"

"Five!"

"*Obsolutely*!" (He spoke this way because he was from Granollers).

He moved aside so that a sweet old lady in a cloak could step down.

"Doña Nieves!"

The custodian of Saint Joseph's miniature chapel saw Don Magín and crossed herself as she said:

"It was God's will! Here he is, my child!"

And Doña Purita appeared. She was departing from Oleza surreptitiously, as if she were running away!

"Till when?"

"I don't know, Don Magín!"

And she quickly told him that her married sister in Valencia had sent for her. Her husband's business affairs were prospering and her household was growing. She hadn't told anyone else but Doña Nieves about it. She made no effort to say goodbye to anyone else. Doña Nieves was witnessing and bearing it all without a tear.

The final ringing of the bell. The slamming of coach doors.

"Four measly coppers!"

Don Magín took the spikenards, the magnolias. And the prices went up.

"One *peseta*, Don Magín!"

The vendors surrounded him; he snatched up flaming red roses from them, along with pale roses, orange blossoms, bouquets of jasmine and he piled them all up on the seat and into the traveler's lap.

She kissed his hand and cut off a spikenard, kissed it too and gave it to him saying:

– Cuando yo iba de corto, usted me dijo que me parecía a un nardo. ¡Tómeme chiquitina!

Descubrióse don Magín, y se inclinó en silencio.

Silbó la máquina, retumbó todo y comenzó a salir el correo de Oleza.

– Adiós, don Magín; adiós, doña Nieves! ¡Ya no me quedo para vestir imágenes, voy a vestir y lavar y besar sobrinos que dan gloria!

...Vientecillo fino, crujidor, que le alborotaba los rizos y el velo. Anchura de campo. Purita se asomó más. En la primera acacia de la estación permanecía don Magín con la cabeza desnuda, plateada; una mano caída y la otra elevando la flor besada. Don Magín, de lejos – de lejos para siempre –, parecía envejecido y más solo que ella. Y a su lado, muy quietecita y disminuída, doña Nieves, con el pañolito en los ojos impasibles.

El tren arremolinaba la hojarasca de las cunetas. De cada cruce de vereda, de cada barraca se alzaba un vocerío enseguida remoto. Un rugido de agua. Calma y silencio. Carretas de bueyes. Senderos entre maizales. Humos de ribazos. Pozas y agramaderas de cáñamo. El paso a nivel de la carretera con sus olmos corpulentos. Dos jesuitas que miraban el correo y después siguieron su vuelta a "Jesús". Ruedas de menadores en un camino hondo de tapias. Más silencio. Más pequeña Oleza, recortándose toda en las ascuas de poniente. Racimos de campanarios, de cúpulas, de espadañas – ruecas y husos de piedra – en medio de lienzos verdes, de barbechos tostados, de hazas encarnadas, de cuadros de sembradura. Palmeras. Olivar. Todo giraba y retrocedía bajo la comba del azul descolorido. Cipreses y cruces entre paredones. El Segral solitario. Lo último de Oleza: la torre de Nuestro Padre; el cerro de San Ginés... Se adelantó un monte con las faldas ensangrentadas de pimentón. Nieblas y cañares. Y se quedó sola en el campo una colina húmeda con una ermita infantil. Encima temblaba la gota de un lucero...

"When I was still a little girl, you told me that I resembled a spikenard. Think of me now as if I were still a little girl!"

Don Magín took off his hat and bent over in silence.

The engine whistled, everything started to rumble and the mail train began to depart from Oleza.

"Good-bye, Don Magín; good-bye, Doña Nieves! I'm not staying on here any longer just to dress religious images; I am going to dress and wash and kiss the most wonderful nieces and nephews!"

...A gentle, fine, crackling breeze that ruffled her curled hair and her veil. The broad expanse of the countryside. Purita stuck her head even further out of the window. Don Magín remained there close to the first acacia tree at the station with his head bare and silvery; one hand fallen down and the other raising the flower she had kissed. Don Magín, from afar – from afar forever – seemed aged and more alone than she. And by his side, Doña Nieves, so very still and diminished, with her little shawl over her impassive eyes.

The train whirled the fallen leaves in the ditches round and round. A shout rose up at every road crossing, from every thatched cabin, only to die away in the distance. A roaring of water. Calm and silence. Ox-drawn carts. Paths among the cornfields. Smoke along the embankments. Pools of water for retting and brakes of hemp. The grade crossing with the highway with its corpulent elm trees. Two Jesuits who kept looking at the mail train and then continued on their way to "Jesús." Silk winders' wheels on a far-extending road of low walls. More silence. Oleza smaller now, completely outlined in full against the embers of the setting sun. Clusters of bell towers, of cupolas, of bell gables – like distaffs and spindles made of stone – in the midst of canvases of green, browned fallow land, red-colored beans, squares of seeded fields. Palm trees. An olive grove. Everything was revolving and retreating beneath the curvature of the faded blue sky. Cypresses and crosses between the thick walls. The solitary Segral. The last part of Oleza: The tower of Our Father; the San Ginés hill.... A mountain came forward, its lower slopes stained the color of blood with red pepper. Mists and fields of cane. And a damp hill with a childlike hermitage remained there alone in the countryside. Up above, a bright star drop was trembling ....

NOTES

Introduction

1. Azorín wrote several articles in which he referred to the existence of a Generation of 1898 in Spain. In 1910 he wrote an article called "Dos generaciones;" In 1913 he wrote a series of articles to further develop the theme, entitled "La generación de 1898," in which he accepted this name. His last article, "Aquella generación" appeared in 1914.
2. Donald L. Shaw, *The Generation of 1898 in Spain* (London and Cambridge, MA: Ernest Benn, Ltd., 1975), 14.
3. Gabriel Miró, *Nuestro Padre San Daniel*, Manuel Ruiz-Funes, ed., intro. and notes (Madrid: Cátedra, 1988), 24. The section runs from pp. 24–33. The translation is mine.
4. Ruiz-Funes, 33. The translation is mine.
5. Ruiz-Funes, 33. The translation is mine.
6. Pio Baroja, *Obras completas.* Volume V (Madrid: Biblioteca Nueva, 1948), 1240. The translation is mine.
7. Baroja, 1241. The translation is mine.
8. Gabriel Miró, *El humo dormido*, Edmund L. King, ed., intro. and notes (New York: Dell Publishing Company, 1967), 16.
9. King, 24.
10. Ruiz-Funes, 11. The translation is mine.
11. King, 26.
12. King, 29.
13. Vicente Ramos, *Vida y obra de Gabriel Miró* (Madrid: El Grifón de la Plata, 1955), 63. Cited in Ruiz-Funes.
14. Ricardo Landeira, *An Annotated Bibliography of Gabriel Miró (1900–1978)* (Manhattan, KS: Society of Spanish and Spanish-American Studies, 1978), 27.
15. Ruiz-Funes, 15. The translation is mine.
16. José Ortega y Gasset, "Un libro: *El Obispo leproso: Novela por Gabriel Miró*," (*El Sol*, Madrid), Jan. 1927. It can also be found in Ortega's *Obras completas*, Vol. III, 3rd Ed. (Madrid: Revista de Occidente, 1955), 544–50.
17. Jorge Guillén, "Gabriel Miró" in *Lenguaje y poesía* (Madrid: Revista de Occidente, 1962).
18. Andrés Amorós, "Modernismo y post-modernismo," in *Literatura española en imágines* (Madrid: Ed. La Muralla, 1974).

19. Mariano Baquero Goyanes, *Qué es una novela?* (Buenos Aires: Ed. Columba, 1961), 7–18.

20. Ricardo Gullón, *La novelística* (Madrid: Ed Cátedra), 15–16. The translation is mine.

21. Richard E. Chandler and Kessel Schwartz, *A New History of Spanish Literature* (Baton Rouge, LA: Louisiana State University Press, 1961), 248.

22. G.G. Brown, *A Literary History of Spain : The Twentieth Century* (London: Ernest Benn Limited, New York: Barnes and Noble, 1972), 45–53.

23. Brown, 46

24. Salvador de Madariaga, *The Genius of Spain* (Freeport, N.Y.: Books for Libraries Press, 1968), 160.

25. Madariaga, 161–64.

26. Brown, 50.

27. King, 36–53.

28. Ruiz-Funes, 38–42.

29. Ruiz-Funes, 38. The translation is mine.

30. Arthur Machen, "Introduction" to Gabriel Miró, *Our Father San Daniel*, tr. Charlotte Remfrey-Kidd (London: Ernest Benn Limited, 1930), ix.

31. Ruiz-Funes, 42. The translation is mine.

32. C.A. Longhurst, *Nuestro Padre San Daniel and El Obispo Leproso* (London: Grant and Cutler, 1994).

33. Longhurst, 17.

34. Longhurst, 122.

35. Brown, 53.

36. Gabriel Miró, *El obispo leproso*, Manuel Ruiz-Funes, ed., intro. and notes (Madrid: Cátedra, 1989), 57–63.

37. G.G. Brown, "Gabriel (Francisco Victor) Miró Ferrer" in *Twentieth Century Literary Criticism*, Sharon K. Hall, ed. Vol V (Detroit, MI: Gale Publishing Company, 1981), 333.

38. Marcus Parr, ""Gabriel Miró: *The Years and the Leagues*," Ph.D. dissertation (Salt Lake City, UT: University of Utah, 1958).

39. Jorge Guillén, *Language and Poetry: Some Poets of Spain* (Cambridge, MA: Harvard University Press, 1961).

40. Guillén, 196.

41. Azorín, "Gabriel Miró (1879–1930) In Memoriam," in Azorín, *Obras completas*, Vol.VI (Madrid: Aguilar, 1962), 225. The translation is mine.

42. Azorín, 997. The translation is mine.

The Leper Bishop

The most helpful source of information for the notes for this novel were the footnotes prepared by Manuel Ruiz-Funes for the edition of the novel *El obispo leproso* published by Catedra (Madrid, 1989). The 477 notes prepared by him for this outstanding edition were an invaluable help for me in the preparation of the translation into English of this novel, and especially for the 259 notes of my work.

1. The convent of the Visitation of Our Lady in Orihela was founded by the Infante Don Carlos María Isidro de Borbón and his wife Doña Francisca de Asís de Braganza in 1826 for the Salesian sisters there. The Silesian order had been founded in 1610 as the Order of the Visitation of Mary. The patron saint of Orihuela was María de Monserrate. The appearance of the Virgin at this site gave rise to the common belief that the earth surrounding the site was blessed and potters came here to find the clay to use for their pottery. It was held that drinking from them would make barren women become fertile.

2. Miró changes and even invents many of the major sites in Orihuela for the city he calls Oleza. He was a student here at the Colegio de Santo Domingo, run by the Jesuits, from 1886, when he was seven years old, until 1891. Scholars have tried to determine the exact location of many of his place names. The "costera de San Ginés," or the "cuesta," may well be the "Cuesta de San Miguel, that rises up to the seminary there. The "arrabal de San Ginés" could be the "Arrabal de Roig" or "de Rabaloche."

3. The church of San Bartolomé is difficult to identify. It is clearly not the church of Santa Justa y Rufina or the church of Santa Ana in the city.

4. The bishop's palace in Orihuela, called "Palacio" in the novel, was built in 1733.

5. The flood mentioned in the novel is described in great detail in the earlier novel, *Our Father San Daniel*. Part IV, Chapter VIII.

6. The remark is attributed to Lucius Coelius Anticipator (1st century A.D.) He was a Roman historian who wrote 7 volumes on the history of the Second Punic War.

7. In the bishop's palace in Orihuela, there is a room containing portraits of past bishops of the see, a number of them by the painter Vicente López.

8. The new bishop was introduced in *Our Father San Daniel*, in Part II, Chapter VI, as Don Francisco de Paula Céspedes y Beneyto, the archpriest of Tarragona.

9. Saint Godfrey was a Benedictine monk of Mont-Saint Quentin, who served

as abbot of the monastery of St. Rogent-sous-Concy in Champagne. He was born in 1066, later became bishop of Amiens in 1104, and died in 1115.

10. The term "lord" alludes to Carlos VII, the Carlist pretender to the throne of Spain. Carlos de Borbón de Austria Este, duke of Madrid (1848–1909). He married Margarita de Borbón, daughter of the duke of Parma. He was the grandson of Don Carlos María Isidro (Carlos V) and the son of Juan Carlos de Borbón de Braganza (Juan III). His partisans started the third Carlist War in 1873, and it ended in 1876 when he fled into exile.

11. The pseudonym *Carolus Alba-Longa* is derived from the Latin. Alba-Longa, cited in Virgil's *Aeneid*, was the city of Ascanius, son of Aeneas (Book VIII). The choice of so inappropriate a name makes him appear even more ridiculous.

12. The Poor Clares of San Gregorio are Franciscan Urbanist sisters. The order was founded by Saint Clare of Assisi in 1212. The convent of San Juan Bautista de la Penitencia was founded in Orihuela in 1493. Miró changes the name of the convent to San Gregorio, perhaps because the inhabitants of the fertile plain considered the saint as their patron as a protection against flooding.

13. The Augustinian sisters resided in the convent built in 1591 at the site of the old hermitage of San Sebastián in the section of the city called San Agustín. It was beset by scandals and lawsuits over a period of years and caused bad feelings between the bishops and the sister of the order.

14. The *Verónicas* were Franciscan sisters. Although no such order existed in Orihuela, there was one in nearby Murcia.

15. Santiago el Mayor is a very lovely church in Orihuela, noted for its outer architecture and its interior. It has one gothic style portal and another of baroque style. Its central nave, the retable of the high altar and the sculpture of Salcillo have made it highly praiseworthy.

16. The Mothers of San Jerónimo are the female branch of the Congregation of San Jerónimo de Estridón.

17. The Association of Hijas de María is a pious order of women that considered the Virgin Mary as a model for spiritual life. The first congregation (Prima) was founded in Rome in 1560 at a Jesuit school. Popes Gregory XIII and Sextus V, in 1584 and 1586, gave it official recognition. In Orihuela, the Jesuit fathers at the Colegio de Santo Domingo established their chapter in the late 19th century.

18. There is no such group in Orihuela and is an invention of the author.

19. The Horas Santas is a devotion started in the late 19th century that continued to the middle of the 20th. It was an act of withdrawal and reflection before the Holy Eucharist displayed for the faithful.

20. Gandía is a town in the province of Valencia. When Elvira Galindo and her brother came to live in Oleza, she brought her old maidservant from Gandía with her.

21. "Jeaús" is the Colegio de Santo Domingo where the author spent five years of his childhood as a boarding student.

22. It was a custom at this time in Spain for children to be given water containing iron to improve their color.

23. The material dealing with "Cara-rajada (Scar-face)" can be found in *Our Father San Daniel* (Part III, Chapter V).

24. The chronicler of Oleza, Espuch y Lóriga appears at the beginning of the novel *Our Father San Daniel*. Here he is seen as the uncle of Don Amancio. Some critics feel the models for the chronicler may be the jurist Ernesto Gisbert, or the chronicler of Orihuela Rufino Gea, who wrote at the turn of the century.

25. In his novel *El libro de Siguenza*, in which he introduces the character who will represent him, Miró described the school, built between 1552 and 1626, the work of several architects. He goes into greater detail here and offers an accurate description of the school.

26. There is such a grotto in the school in Orihuela and it is modeled after the French original in Lourdes.

27. The verses are a *redondilla*, a poem of four octosyllabic verses, and they are found in a book about the school by Justo García Soriano (1918), in which he describes the cell and the words on the wall, and other writings there as well.

28. The comments by Espuch y Loriga are taken from a book by Rufino Gea Martínez about the history of Orihuela (1900).

29. Juan de Ochoa was in reality Don Fernando Loazes (1498–1568), who first studied in Orihuela and went on to hold a number of offices as an inquisitor, a bishop and archbishop. He was said to have suffered from leprosy and believed he was cured by waters provided by the Dominicans in Orihuela. This led him to order the construction of the school there.

30. The Cortes of Monzón in 1563 ordered the definitive separation of the Church of Orihuela from the one in Cartagena.

31. The University of Alcalá de Henares was one of the best known in Spain. It was begun through the efforts of Cardinal Cisneros in 1498. The first completed structure became the Colegio de San Ildefonso in 1508.

32. The University of Santo Tomás de Avila was opened in 1504 and became a university in 1550. It was associated with the Inquisitor General Tomás de Torquemada. Miró wrote an article about the convent and church there in 1922.

33.   Francisco Ximénez de Cisneros (1436—1517) was a noted Franciscan churchman and statesman, a confessor to Queen Isabel I, an archbishop and cardinal, who helped reform his order.

34.   Tomás de Torquemada (1420–98) was a Dominican churchman, who is most remembered as Inquisitor General of Castile and Aragon. His harsh measures and abuse of power brought the wrath of the pope down upon him.

35.   The sepulcher described here is that of Fernando de Loazes; it is in the presbytery of the church of Santo Domingo in Orihuela, which was destroyed during the Spanish Civil War.

36.   In the disentailment of church property during the 1850's, the school was given over to the control of the bishop.

37.   This humorous incident of the bishop and the playing card appears in Ernesto Gisbert's *Historia de Orihuela*, and refers to a bishop who occupied the office from 1670 to 1700. The bishop who presided over the installation of the Jesuits in Santo Domingo was don Pedro María Cuberto y López de Padilla, who imposed the condition that children native to the city could attend without paying.

38.   The description of the installation of the Jesuits is described in Juan Sansano's history of Orihuela (1954). The bishop called upon the Jesuits to establish the Colegio de San Estanislao in 1868, on the site of the old university. This was the year of the revolution against the queen and there were many delays. In 1872, when it was officially opened, there were additional obstacles because of the attitude of the newly established republic.

39.   The name given to the academic assembly hall, *De profundis*, is taken from the first line of Psalm 30, "Out of the depths. . . ."

40.   Juan Sansano, in his history of Orihuela, and Manuel Revuelta González, in an article about the school, give us the names of the Jesuit officials and teachers, the numbers and names of lay teachers, and other pertinent facts. One of the Brothers was a Brother Canudas, whom Miró calls Canalda. This Brother went into town to buy food for the school dressed as a peasant.

41.   Revuelta González offers the data with regard to the two types of students. When the school opened in 1872, there were three boarding students and one hundred day students. After the Restoration of Alfonso XII, boarding students increased in numbers, and by the 1880's, they dominated and by 1886, there were 149 boarding students and only twenty-two day students.

42.   The Rector Father was in charge of the operations of the school, the Prefect Father was charged with the education of the boys, and the Minister Father was more of an administrator. There was also a Spiritual Father responsible for the religious development of the students.

43.   This song is a corruption of a French song, "A mon beau chateau. . . !"

44. Personal friendships between the students were a cause of great concern among the Jesuits to the point of obsession. The rules went back to a guide of 1591, *Ratio studiorum societatis Jesu.*

45. Miguel Hilarión Eslava (1807–78) was a Spanish composer and musicologist and a professor of Harmony in the Conservatory in Madrid. He composed religious songs, operas and a famous "Miserere." He was also the author of pedagogical works on musical subjects.

46. This is the order of the Carmelites, founded in 1156 by the crusader Saint Berthold on Mount Carmel, then inhabited by some anchorites who lived in grottoes on the mountain. The order gained approval in the 13th century; they adhered to silence, poverty, abstinence and fasting. St. John of the Cross brought about modifications. A division distinguished between those with bare feet, and those wearing sandals (calzados and descalzos). Franciscans in Orihuela were called *franciscos.*

47. The holy day is celebrated on the 25th of March.

48. The bishop has considerable knowledge about his disease. He has studied the pertinent sections of the Old Testament, Chapter 13 of *Leviticus.* This section deals with diseases of the skin as they pertain to purity and expiation.

49. The relationship between the homeopath and Dr. Grifol is explained in Part III, Chapter II of *Our Father San Daniel.*

50. The three things mentioned here, "memoria," "entendimiento," and "voluntad" are the three powers of the soul found in the Spanish catechisms and are taken from the *De Trinitate* of Saint Augustine.

51. The story of the dean's nephew and Doña Corazón can be found in Chapter III, Part II of *Our Father San Daniel.*

52. *San Pánfilo* – Saint Pamphylus of Caesarea was a native of Beirut who settled in Caesarea in Palestine. He was a noted biblical scholar, was imprisoned and tortured during the rein of the emperor Galerius and was martyred along with 10 companions in 309 A.D.
    San Blas – Saint Blaise (Blasius) was an Armenian bishop martyred in 316 A.D. who became the patron of wool carders because he was tortured by a large comb.
    San Luciano – Saint Lucian of Antioch lived in the 3rd and 4th centuries. He studied Aristotle and was influenced by the heretic Peter of Samosata. He died a martyr.
    San Marcelo – Saint Marcellus was a native of Apimea in Syria. He founded a monastery for monks called "Akimetes" in Constantinople. He died c.485 A.D.
    San Platón – Saint Plato was a Greek monk of the 8th and 9th centuries A.D.,

who was the superior of the monastery of Symboleon on Mt. Olympus.

San Teodoro el Studita – Saint Theodore Studites (759–826) was a native of Constantinople and a monk of the monastery of Studios, serving as abbot in 799.

El patriarca Méthodo – Saint Methodius the Confessor was a Sicilian who founded the monastery on the isle of Cheos. He became the patriarch of Constantinople and died in 847.

José el Himnógrafo – He was Joseph the Hymnographer, also known as Joseph of the Studium, and lived in the 9th century A.D. He was a patriarch of Constantinople and the sacred vases there were under his care. He composed poems and hymns.

El monje Juan – This could be a number of people. They include three saints: Saint John Climacus, also known as John Scholasticus, a hermit of the 6th and 7th centuries A.D.; John Damascene, who lived 7th and 8th centuries A.D.; John Gualberto, an Italian of the 10th and 11th centuries A.D.

El monje Cosmas – He was known as Cosmas Indikoplepleustes and was a cosmographer of the 8th century A.D., who traveled to India and wrote a number of curious works on topography and geography.

San Doroteo de Gaza – Saint Dorotheus was a monk of the 7th century A.D. who wrote in Greek about monastic life and died c.640.

53. Saint Nicholas was a monk who lived in Crete in the 9th century A.D. at the monastery of Studium, serving as Archimandrite there.

54. Saint Nicon was a monk in Asia Minor in the 10th century A.D. who lived for years in a monastery and left to go out to preach, emphasizing the importance of penance.

55. Leontius of Byzantium lived in the 5th and 6th centuries A.D. and was a Byzantine monk and theologian living in Constantinople.
Nicephorus I was a patriarch of Constantinople in the 8th and 9th centuries A.D. He wrote theological works and a history of the Greek empire. He died in 828. Cyril of Scythopolis was a monk of the 6th century A.D. who wrote a biography of Saint Sabas.

56. La Platería and La Trapería were two of the principal commercial streets of old Murcia.

57. In *Our Father San Daniel*, a barber had cut Paulina's hair when she was ill with a fever.

58. The word *gafe* does have a special meaning, but here it is used as a French word that should be *gaffe* (a *faux pas* or mistake).

59. Francisco Salcillo (1707–83) was a Spanish sculptor who was born and

died in Murcia. He was the son of a noted Italian sculptor and wanted to be a monk, but changed his mind when his father died and he took over his workshop. His was a Baroque Italian style.

60.   This is a quotation from the Greek physician Hippocrates (460–377 B.C.). It is a fundamental principle of his medical theory and implies that a cure can be had by applying the laws of nature.

61.   The beneficiary in Murcia is mistaken because the sculpture does have an olive tree and not a palm tree.

62.   "Gethsemane" means "olive press," and is located near Jerusalem not far from the Mount of Olives.

63.   Lord Wellington (1769–1852) was also the Viscount of Talavera and Duke of Ciudad Rodrigo, and had come to Spain to fight against Napoleon, defeating the French at Salamanca.

64.   Added details about the holy days in Murcia can be found in a book by Pedro Díaz Casou.

65.   Origen (185?–254?) was an early Christian philosopher and writer. He lived in Caesarea and died after being tortured by the Romans. He believed that all knowledge comes from God and is best revealed in Christianity. He wrote over 60 books on religious themes. His library was kept by Saint Pamphylus.

66.   The Spanish novelist Ramón Pérez de Ayala (1880–1964), in his novel *AMDG* (1910) has offered a picture of education in a Jesuit school and its emphasis on militarism and authoritarianism. The use of "brigades" in the school is only one example.

67.   In 1882, the Jesuits prescribed a code of dress as a uniform for the schoolboys; it included a jacket, gold buttons, black trousers and a black hat embroidered with gold trimming.

68.   The reference is to Saint Francis de Sales (1567–1622), who in 1612 founded the Salesian order of la Visitación. He used the words she cites in his *Directory for Nuns*.

69.   Saint Mary Magdalene de Pazzi (1566–1604) was a Carmelite nun who, due to her poor health, attained a high level of mysticism and spirituality.

70.   Miró was very much taken by the story of the Samaritan women found in John, 11: 1–45, and he used it as the last chapter of his work about Jesus and his time in *Figures of the Passion of the Lord*. The conversation between the woman of Samaria and Jesus at the well in Sicar moved him to include it in his work.

71.   The author makes a small change in this novel from *Our Father San Manuel*.

When the Loriz family first arrived in Oleza (Part III, Chapter VII), the countess was the one with the title and not her husband. Now, eight years later, the presence of the countess's brother Máximo and her son make it clear that her husband holds the title. Otherwise, her brother would have inherited the title.

72.   Dr. Grifol had been attending the ailing bishop earlier in the novel. We now learn of his death since that time. Mosén Orduña had appeared in the earlier novel and he too has died. The legend of angels making the image can be found in Gisbert's book on the history of Orihuela.

73.   In Part IV, Chapter III of *Our Father San Daniel*, there were only three daughters mentioned.

74.   Critics have seen an excellent example of a humanist in Don Magín. He compares himself to Dante's hypocrites (Canto XXIII of the *Divine Comedy.*

75.   There had been a Spanish tie with Oran since the time of Cardinal Cisneros in the 16th century. Alicante had commercial relations with Morocco and Algeria for many years.

76.   The Farmer's Club represented the most conservative and traditional values in Oleza. They were the strongest supporters of the Carlist cause and most opposed to the policies of the government in Madrid.

77.   The scenes describing the enthusiastic welcoming of Carlist forces can be found in Part II, Chapter II of *Our Father San Daniel.*

78.   There was a "Casino Orcelitano" in Orihuela founded in 1864 and it occupied the former Pinaza Inn, where it stands today.

79.   The previous bishop had died of palsy, as described in Part II, Chapter II of *Our Father San Daniel.*

80.   The separation of the sexes at events sponsored by the church has a lengthy history and can be traced back to the 4th century A.D.

81.   *Life is a Dream* is one of the most famous Spanish plays of the Golden Age and was written by Pedro Calderón de la Barca (1600–1681). The other play was very likely *La tragedia de San Hermenegildo,* an anonymous work of the 17th century. Since women were not permitted to perform in such performances, many of the roles were changed to male roles.

82.   For the Daughters of Mary, see note 17. The *Luises* are the members of the Marian Congregation of San Luis Gonzaga. At the school in Orihuela there were two congregations established to help develop religious feelings in the boy, the one being the *luises* for boarding students and the other of San Juan Berchmans for the day students.

83.   The tertiary branches of the Orders were associations attached to a particular order. There were such orders of Saint Francis, Saint Dominic and Saint Augustine; all these were brought to Orihuela in the 17th century.

84.   Francisco Cascales (1564–1642) was a Murcian author of a *Tabla poética* dealing with literary aspects of the Renaissance. Miró cites a letter he wrote to his brother-in-law about silk worms.

85.   This is a reference to San Luis Gonzaga, a Jesuit novice who died in 1591 and who always appeared dressed in this fashion.

86.   Some of the activities ascribed to this bishop were actually those of an earlier bishop, Don José Torino who served from 1767 to 1790.

87.   These are the words spoken by Don Magín in Part I, Chapter IV of *Our Father San Daniel*.

88.   G.H. Armaner Hansen (1841–1912) was a Norwegian physician who discovered the bacillus causing leprosy in 1874 and whose name was given to the disease. Albert Ludwig Heisser (1855–1916) was a German physician and bacteriologist who also investigated the disease.

89.   This is a quotation from Ovid's *Metamorphoses*, Book II, verse 553, and deals with Mercury and Herse.

90.   This is a religious association that stands watch over the Holy Eucharist. It was first formed in Rome in 1809 and in Madrid in 1878.

91.   The Council of Trent (1545–63), in their efforts to counteract the impact of the Reformation, ordered the establishment of both Seminaries and schools as centers of study for those aspiring to the priesthood. The Jesuits were prominent in this effort. Universities had long maintained Faculties of Theology, but by the 19th century, they were disappearing. The Seminaries were now divided into Minor and Major. The former stressed Humanistic studies, while the latter stressed Philosophy, Canon Law and Theology.

92.   Seminary students, in theology, seeking "minor orders," were divided into ostiaries (gatekeepers), instructors of the Gospel, exorcisers and acolytes.

93.   These were apologetic lectures on religion. They were first conceived in France in the early 19th century by Frayssinous, and strengthened by Father Lacordaire. When they died out there, they were continued in Spain during Lent.

94.   There is no evidence of such a confraternity. The one devoted to the Seizure of Jesus was first organized in Orihuela in 1761.

95.   The Congregación del Pilar in Orihuela organized a procession and in 1854 they received authorization for the presence of Roman centurions, called "ármaos," to escort the float of the Seizure of Jesus.

96. She is speaking of Queen Isabel II who was to marry her cousin, the count of Montemolín in order to resolve the Carlist dilemma. Instead, she married another cousin, Francisco de Asís de Borbón. It proved to be an unhappy relationship from the start and the queen proceeded to take a number of lovers over the years. The scene described here refers to an illegitimate child conceived from her union with José María de Arana. The scandalous behaviour of the queen was a subject for historians and novelists. The heir to the throne, Alfonso XII, was born in 1857.

97. Manises is a town in the province of Valencia famous for its ceramic industry dating back to the medieval period.

98. The devotion to the Sacred Heart of Jesus was a part of Catholic worship since ancient times. It developed more in the 17th century due to the efforts of St. John Eudes and Saint Margaret Mary of Alacoque. Pius IX in 1856 established the holy day dedicated to the spread of the ideal in Europe.

99. The words "I shall reign" was part of a remark by Father Hoyos, "I shall reign in Spain and with greater veneration than in other places." The first rector of the school in Orihuela, Father Jacas, founded the association, The Apostolate of the Prayer, dedicated to the cult of the theology of the Sacred Heart of Jesus.

100. This is a reference to the woman mentioned in St. Mark, St. Luke and St. John.

101. A "santero" or "santera" was a person who went around from house to house asking for alms, leaving behind in any one house the image they carried. They were very poor and would visit the house of a person listed on the small portable chapel, and receive a small donation deposited there.

102. The Forty Hours is a religious devotion before the Eucharist originating from the forty hours Jesus lay in his sepulcher.

103. The quotation is taken from a letter Spinoza wrote to Hugo Boxel.

104. The Dominican sisters of Santa Lucía are a religious order of St. Dominic established in Toulouse when Santo Domingo de Guzmán converted a number of heretical women. The convent of the Dominican sisters in Orihuela was founded in 1602.

105. Saint John the Baptist was baptized in the Jordan River.

106. Santo Domingo de Guzmán (1170–1221) was the founder of the Order of the Preachers (Dominican Order). While traveling in southern France, he was disturbed by the spread of the Albigensian heresy and decided to found an order of preachers to counteract heresy. After the pope's approval, the order spread to Spain and Italy.

107.   Saint Jane Francis Fréymot de Chantal (1571–1641) joined with St. Francis de Sales after she was widowed, and helped found the Institute of the Visitation of the Blessed Virgin (Salesians).

108.   This Sunday before Ash Wednesday receives it name from the fact that it is fifty days before Easter Sunday.

109.   Saint Goar (VI-VIIth centuries) was a Gallic saint, who was an anchorite in Aquitaine. He was born about 585 and died in 649. He withdrew to a village in Germany and dedicated himself to prayer and penance. He was admonished by his bishop, cleared his name by a miracle and was named bishop by King Sigeberto III of Austrasia.

110.   Lent consisted of the 46 days from Ash Wednesday to Easter Sunday. The early church was given to much preparation and prayer to commemorate the time Jesus spent in the desert.

111.   The Feast of the Assumption of the Virgin Mary is on August 15.

112.   Saint Paul wrote these lines in the First Epistle of Saint Paul the Apostle to the Corinthians (Chapter 14: 30).

113.   The quotation is from Saint Teresa in *Las Constituciones*, Number 27. She was a Carmelite nun born in 1515 and one of the most important mystics of her time. She remained in the convent of the Incarnation in Avila all her life.

114.   The quotation is from Chapter IV of the *Directory for Nuns* by Saint Francis de Sales.

115.   The two stanzas are marked by unfinished endings of final words. The first may be from a collection by Braulio Vigón, *Juegos y rimas infantiles*. The second may be by the author himself.

116.   The two quotations by the mother superior are from the directory of Saint Francis de Sales.

117.   The reference is to *Genesis*, 25: 24–25.

118.   The "Little Sisters of the Poor" was the congregation founded by Jeanne Jugan (1792–1879) in Saint-Servan, France.

119.   The petitionary table was set up in public places – churches, streets – where persons of social and religious importance, took turns sitting, soliciting donations for charitable purposes.

120.   In this order, the superior was referred to as the "Good Mother," and the sisters were considered the 'Little Family."

121.   One of Monera's sisters, after her parents' deaths, served in the household of the canon-penitentiary. The other was a lay sister with the Clares.

122.   The deep silence on Wednesday and Thursday was due to the prohibition

against carriages on the streets and against the ringing of the church bells.

123. These were trees or poles set up in a public place during May where young men and women would dance and celebrate the coming of spring.

124. The author is accurately describing the liturgical events of Holy Week. From Passion Sunday to Palm Sunday, images and crucifixes were covered with purple veils. On Maundy Thursday and Good Friday, the altars were stripped of everything on them. The *Tenebrario*, the triangular candelabrum with fifteen candles was lit, and they were extinguished, one by one, after the chanting of all the psalms and offices recited.

125. The Order of Santa María de la Merced was founded by Saint Peter Nolasco to redeem captives in Arabic lands. It was established in Orihuela in 1377. The Carmelites came to the city in 1584, the Franciscans in 1449 and officially in 1464, and a reformed branch was begun by San Pedro de Alcanatara in the church of San Gregorio in 1600.

126. The office of Tenebrae was celebrated at that time on Thursday and Friday of Holy Week. It was a nocturnal service at first and then was changed to the evening. The service is named from the candelabrum used.

127. There was very little mixing of the sexes in social life in Oleza.

128. Between the Seminary and the cathedral lies the section of the city called la Peña. A brothel was supposedly here.

129. On Maundy Thursday, the rite of the "Washing of the Feet" was observed. The biblical source is in John, 13: 1–20.

130. Students in Jesuit schools were grouped according to age, regardless of their programs. These groups, or "brigades" shared study halls. dormitories and other facilities. This was done to avoid harmful influences from being passed on to younger boys.

131. The puritanical character of the rules for the young students was similar to that found in Victorian England and in France. Boys were compelled to remain at school for Christmas and Easter to avoid outside corruption. Special events and activities were planned for these periods.

132. The Prefect uses the words "Thanks to God" to permit a relaxation of discipline, especially silence. This strict, almost military discipline included crossing one's hands so as not to make use of them for frivolous or indecent purposes. Keeping one's hands in one's pockets was taboo.

133. Jesus was brought here to be judged. John, 18.

134. "Behold the Man" were the words with which Pontius Pilate presented Christ, crowned with thorns, to his accusers. John, 19:5. In Orihuela, the float of *Ecce homo* was first seen during Holy Week in 1777.

135. This is the goddess Juno.
136. Miró draws his inspiration from parades he witnessed during Holy Week in Orihuela and Murcia, and he combines elements from both, creating additional material from his imagination.
137. Shechem was a city in Samaria. After the Babylonian exile, Shechem was converted into a cultural center of the Samarians.
138. The words are part of a popular religious song heard all over Spain.
139. As far back as 1761, a platform of "Our Lady of Sorrows" was part of the procession. A Sisterhood honoring the Virgin was established in the Church of Santiago in Orihuela in 1852.
140. Miró once again combines scenes he witnessed in the two cities. In Orihuela, the platform was carried on a wagon. He does include many of the anachronisms common at such events, like cannons.
141. The scene is from Mark, 14:47. The float was organized by the Congregación del Pilar in 1761. Malko is not mentioned in the Scriptures and is part of a later Christian tradition.
142. This prayer was offered in the church at three in the afternoon on Good Friday. The preacher repeated and commented on the seven words spoken by Christ on the cross. Mark, 23: 46.
143. The *Miserere* is a song used in the Catholic liturgy composed of Psalm 50.
144. The Society of Jesus has two levels. After two years of the novitiate, some continue in order to become priests. Others become lay brothers: or coadjutor brothers, or assume lesser roles like gatekeepers, gardeners and administrators.
145. San Alonso Rodríguez (1533?–1617) was from Segovia, and, after losing his wife and sons, he was not permitted to become a Jesuit, he went to Valencia and became a brother coadjutor and served as a gatekeeper in Mallorca, writing ascetic works.
146. The informational booklet distributed to students' families discouraged excessive family visits, and enforced the rule by censoring mail and rarely permitting students to leave the school.
147. The image generally called "The Recumbent Christ" was carried during the "Procession of the Holy Burial" in Orihuela. It was destroyed during the Spanish Civil War and replaced.
148. Tradition required that professional men, lawyers, doctors and soldiers, carry the platform.
149. These are the last lines of the novel *Our Father San Daniel*.
150. Paulina is not attending a service. She is participating in a tradition in

Orihuela and Murcia called "The Solitude of Mary," in which groups of women take turns for one hour each praying to Mary on Good Friday for a period of several hours.

151. "Visita ad limina Apostolorum" means "a visit to the threshold of the apostles." It implies an obligatory trip to Rome for bishops every four years to talk of the state of their diocese.

152. Venus, whom the Greeks called Aphrodite, was the goddess of love and beauty. She was the mother of Cupid, son of Mars, and the dove was sacred to her. Her chariot was drawn by doves.

153. Miró takes this metaphor from a poem by the Spanish poet of the 11th century Gonzalo de Berceo and uses it quite ironically.

154. This is a feast day in honor of the Eucharist, celebrated on the Thursday after Trinity Sunday, the Sunday after Pentecost.

155. The festival of Corpus Christi was initiated by Juliana de Mont-Cornillon in 1193; it was approved by the church in 1246 and accepted by Pope Urban IV for everyone in 1264. Miró felt a special attachment for this day because he associated it nostalgically with his childhood.

156. The Church of the Holy Sepulcher stands on the hill of Calvary (Golgotha), where Christ was crucified and buried. The Roman emperor Hadrian forbade its worship for Christians, but in 135 A.D., the emperor Constantine put up a monument that became the church.

157. The Via Dolorosa (Way of Sorrow) is the route Christ followed carrying his cross to Calvary. On Good Friday, worshippers follow the route chanting prayers.

158. An apostolic vicar governs a territory in the name of the pope and is not beholden to a local bishop. The office was first established in the 19th century.

159. This is the Carlist pretender, Charles VII, living in exile.

160. The words are from the *Confessions* of Saint Augustine, 8, 5, 10.

161. Military religious orders were an outgrowth of the Crusades in the late 11th century. Urban II encouraged their growth. In Spain, there were the Orders of Calatrava, Alcántara and Santiago (1171).

162. One can compare Miró's irony and humor in this graduation scene to the bitter sarcasm of a similar description in the novel *AMDG* by Miró's contemporary Ramón Pérez de Ayala.

163. The word comes from the Provençal and French "mascoto," or "mascotte," which means a "talisman." The word is a diminutive of a Latin word for "witch," and is related to the word in English.

164. The technique of ending a chapter with a colon, in order to leave the reader in suspense and anticipation, is found in some chapters of Cervantes's *Don Quixote.*

165.   This is a prayer based on a song popular in Spain at the time, possibly composed by San Alonso María de Ligorio, founder of the Congregation of the Most Holy Redeemer, set up to evangelize the masses.

166.   Erhard Ratdolt or Ratdolf (1443–1528) was a German professor of astronomy who lived in Venice and published a book on Euclid there in 1482.

167.   The *Elements* is the major work of Euclid and deals with Geometry. It is divided into 13 books. There are no works of his entitled *Specularia* or *Perspectiva*. However, a book by Pedro Ondéniz published in 1585 on Euclid's *Optics* was entitled *La perspectiva y especularia*.

168.   This work by Euclid was on astronomy.

169.   José Zaragosa (1627–1678) was a Jesuit mathematician in Spain who lived in Valencia. Robert Simson (1687–1768) was a Scottish mathematician who published a widely read translation of the *Elements* in 1756. He also reconstructed a lost work of Euclid on prisms.

170.   Pedro Ambrosio Ondéniz was a 19th century Spanish geographer and mathematician.

171.   Omar Khayyam (1050?–1123?) was a noted Persian poet, astronomer and mathematician. He is best known for his long poem *The Rubáiyát*, translated into English in 1859 by Edward Fitzgerald.

172.   The Capuchin order was founded by Matteo Bassi, an Italian monk who sought to bring back the old Franciscan ideal of total poverty and evangelical life. It was formally accepted in 1528 by Pope Clement VI. The superior is called a "guardián." It came to Orihuela in 1614.

173.   Masonic lodges were condemned by Roman Catholic authorities since their inception. They are secret associations of men professing fraternity and use various devices to communicate with each other. The early Masons, as far back as the 14th century, had a lesser influence on the outside world, but later Masons, after the 19th century, were active and extended throughout the world. They adhered to vague deistic religious ideas and were dedicated to philanthropy. Numerous popes severely and publicly condemned them. For traditional Spaniards, they were almost a Satanic symbol of evil activity.

174.   Saint Sabas (439–532) was a monk who helped found religious colonies in the Holy Land for anchorites.

175.   The Jewish historian Flavius Josephus (37–100? A.D.), in his *Jewish Antiquities*, told of how Herod built towers in Jerusalem to shelter the doves.

176.   A disciple of Saint Sabas, Cyril of Scitopolis, created the legend of how the saint encountered a lion and removed a thorn from its paw.

177. A number of scholars have pointed out the autobiographical elements of this chapter.

178. This was a fortnightly Catholic publication. It was first published by Adolfo Clavarana y Garriga in 1883 and was dedicated to the working classes. It ceased publication in July of 1936. It had 65,000 subscribers. Its founder had been an ardent liberal but shifted his politics to become a Catholic conservative.

179. The quote is from the Sermon on the Mount (Luke, 6:23).

180. This quote is from Mark, 2:21.

181. The worship of the Eucharist, going back to the 15th century, is described here. The Exposition of the Holy Eucharist consisted of the singing of the hymn "Pange lingua," the Adoration, the Benediction and the singing of "Tantum ergo." The Reservation concluded the service.

182. He is referring to the *Iliad* (verses 146–160), in which the old Trojans speak of how Helen's beauty brought about their downfall.

183. The Infanta María Isabel de Borbón y Borbón first came to Orihuela in October 1862 with her parents Queen Isabel II and the consort Francisco Asís de Borbón.

184. The story of the woman who spread perfume on Christ's feet is found in Matthew, 26: 6–13, Mark, 14: 3–9 and John, 12: 1–8. Only Saint John refers to her as Mary, sister of Lazarus.

185. Dioscorides was a Greek doctor of the 1st century B.C., who loved botany and traveled widely. He wrote *Materia medica*. A Spanish translation of his work by Andrés Laguna appeared in 1555.

186. Don Magín's intimate knowledge in this area derives from his reading of ancient authors and what he found in the Scriptures.

187. Gaius Plinius Secundus lived in the 1st century B.C. and was a Roman soldier, politician and scholar. He wrote about nards in Books XII to XXVII of his *Naturae historiarium*. He died in the eruption of Mt. Vesuvius.

188. Mijnheer Lecour was a Dutch floriculturalist about whom Don Magín had read in the literature of his day.

189. The events discussed here took place in Coldingham, England in 874.

190. Eusebius of Caesarea was a Greek bishop and writer (265–340 A.D.) who bishop in Caesarea in 333 A.D. and was a favorite of emperor Constantine. He is considered a founder of ecclesiastical historiography and wrote a biography of the emperor.

191. Miró reveals a precise awareness of the hierarchy of angels. This was established in the 5th century and includes three levels, including cherubim, seraphim, archangels and angels.

192. Saint Margaret of Cortona (1249–1297) was a nun of the Third Order of Saint Francis who fled with her lover and bore his child, before entering a Franciscan convent as a penitent.

193. Saint Pelagia of Antioch was a beautiful woman given to vice who was converted, went to Jerusalem and lived an austere, ecstatic life in a mountain cave.

194. He was a solitary, born in Chidana in Mesopotamia in the year 300 A.D. He fled his wedding and sought isolation in a cave., where he stayed 30 years. He abandoned this life to become a priest and to convert others. He died in 365 A.D. He was the subject of a play by Roswitha von Gandersheim, another by the Spanish dramatist of the Golden Age, Mira de Amescua and a book by Anatole France.

195. The killing and the torture of animals and birds plays a major role in the novel, and the acts of Father Bellod and the Keeper of the Keys are seen as extremely sadistic.

196. The two rosaries, one at dawn and the other in the early evening, were devotions to the Virgin Mary and sung in procession.

197. These verses were written by Francisco de Velasco and were sung in religious penitential services that go back to the early 17th century.

198. These are tiny sacred books containing text from the Scriptures and were hung around a child's neck. They were like medals and amulets.

199. The final quotation is a rewording of lines in the *Apocalypse* of Saint John, 3:16. The quotation from Pope Leon XII is very likely from one of his encyclicals.

200. In the face of the onslaught of the most conservative forces in the city, led by the Jesuits at the school, the bishop felt that his reputation had been defamed and countered what he considered excessive and hypocritical piety by rejecting the honor given him.

201. See note #41.

202. It was a custom in these schools to put a board on a cleric's door listing where he could be found. The Jesuits introduced the large-headed pins for these boards.

203. This is a rewording of a statement Jesuits repeated about themselves stressing poverty and obedience.

204. The Society of Jesus had geographical divisions in Spain that varied from the provincial designations. The provincial in Aragon supervised the region of Valencia.

205. The quote is from *Guzmán de Alfarache*, a picaresque Spanish novel by Mateo Alemán (1547?–1614?).

206. The old gardener speaks in a dialect common to the rural peasants on the Murcian irrigated plain.

207. The style of language the author uses here recalls many of the lines in the *Coplas* of Jorge Manrique (1440–78).

208. The Roman Catholic Church often assigned older priests and those with failing eyesight to celebrate the Votive Mass for the Virgin.

209. The events of this paragraph actually occurred in the 15th century, not in 1625, They are described in detail in a history of Orihela by Rufino Gea.

210. The actions of the bishop referred to here occurred in Orihuela when Juan Elías de Terán served from 1738 to 1758. Some critics see him as the model for the bishop of this novel.

211. The background for this scene is from Part IV, Chapter III of *Our Father San Daniel*.

212. The sacrifice of Isaac is described in *Genesis*, 22: 11–13.

213. The parable of Jesus and the rich man is in Mark, 10: 17–30 and tells of the encounter with him and Lazarus.

214. This publication is discussed in *Our Father San Daniel*. It was issued every Sunday. Only two publications using the word "truth" existed in the region of Alicante at that time. One was a literary weekly and the other an independent liberal monarchist daily.

215. He uses examples of early Christians whose marriages were atypical. Saint Cecilia was a virgin who died a martyr with her husband in 292 A.D.. She was forced to marry Valerian, a pagan, whom she converted and convinced to respect her virginity.

216. Saint Galatian and Saint Epesteme were both Christian martyrs. Little is known of them other than that they were martyred at Emesa.

217. Saint Paulinus was a poet who became bishop of Nola during the 4th or 5th century. He married Therasia, was baptized at 47 and gave away all he owned to the poor. He withdrew from the world with his wife.

218. Saint Marcelus and Saint Nona lived in the 3rd century A.D. He was a centurion. He found his way to Leon, where he is worshipped to this day. He, his wife and 12 children were all martyrs.

219. Work began on the railroad line in 1882. The first locomotive ran on January 18, 1884. In May of that year there was an inauguration of the line. Cánovas de Castillo, the prime minister and other dignitaries attended, including bishop Guisasola.

220. *The Christian Year* is a recapitulation of the lives of the saints. Miró had copies in his library.

221. The *Messenger of the Sacred Heart* is the author's version of *El Mensajero del Corazón de Jesús*, published by the Jesuits after 1866 in Barcelona. It was a widely read monthly.

222. The work the author mentions is a combination of various existing books on the religious history of Orihuela.

223. This is an actual work by Mosén Pedro Bellot, a priest from Catral. It covers the 14th to the 16th centuries.

224. These were publications appearing regularly on the anniversary of the saint and distributed to the public.

225. Antoine Arnald (1612–1694) was called "Le gran Arnald" in France. He became an avid Jansenist and wrote attacks on the Jesuits, leading to his expulsion from the Sorbonne.

226. There was a book with this title published in 1764.

227. This work was published in Zaragoza in 1610.

228. The Abbé Tirón is the author of the *Historia y trajes de órdenes religiosos* published in two volumes in Barcelona in 1845.

229. This is the actual dedication of Tirón's book. Cardinal Lambruschini (1776–1854) was an archbishop of Genoa and secretary of state for Pope Gregory XVI.

230. Miró draws all his very accurate descriptions of the nuns and their habits from the pictures in Tirón's book.

231. This very likely Saint Basil the Great (330379 A.D.) who founded many monasteries and was widely revered. The Fuldan refers to a monastery in Fulda in Germany. The Knights Hospitalers originated during the first Crusade (1096–99), and are named after a hospital in Jerusalem. It was a religious, military order.

232. This work is *The Journey of Antenor Through Greece and Asia, with Notions about Egypt*, by Etienne-François de Lantiere.

233. The Protestant Huguenots in France had been fighting the Catholic regime since 1562, and would continue till 1598. In spite of several peace treaties, Admiral Coligny, a Huguenot, and many ordinary citizens were massacred by French mobs in Paris and the provinces on St, Barthomew's Day. Atrocities were committed on both sides over the years.

234. Elvira's prayer was widely known and used in Spain.

235. Saint Encratia (d. 304 A.D.) was martyred along with 18 others from Zaragoza. She is the subject of the poem by Prudentius.

236. Marcus Aurelius Prudentius Clemens (348–415 A.D.) was a Christian poet. He was born in Spain and was a professor of Rhetoric and a lawyer. He began

writing poetry at 50 and wrote allegorical and apologetic poems. These lines are from his *Perisiphanon*, in honor of Christian martyrs.

237. The Spanish brought furniture from their colony in the Philippines till the end of the 19th century. They were made of bamboo and often from the camphor tree.

238. The Angelus bell could be heard three times a day – early morning, midday and evening. It was a time for praise of the Virgin Mary and was a devotion in memory of the Annunciation.

239. In the Egyptian story, Rhodopis is a Greek slave girl who lives in Egypt and is teased by other servants because of her coloring. Her rosy-gold slipper is carried to the Pharaoh's court and he searches everywhere for the girl and finds her. Charles Perrault (1628–1703) was a French writer known for his *Mother Goose Tales*, that included the story of Cinderella.

240. The allusion is to the Carlist pretender Charles VII. Even though the last armed conflict had ended in February 1876 and Don Carlos had fled, his followers continued to support his cause.

241. Miró has given us a contrast between the three bishops, the first, active and communicative, Bishop Salom, ascetic and withdrawn, and the present bishop, studious, liberal and spiritual.

242. The words are from Matthew, 7:7. They are cited in *Our Father San Daniel* in Part II, Chapter VI. The first bishop of Oleza, used the words, spoken by Jesus, on his shield, "Pulsate et aprietur vobis."

243. Miguel Lozano Herrero (1842–79) was a Carlist officer who had deserted the government forces in 1873. His forces fought in Alicante and Murcia in September 1874 till he was captured and shot.

244. The "accursed one" refers to the legend of the "Wandering Jew." It is based on the story that Jesus, on the way to Calvary, was struck by a man, who was later condemned to wander without rest till the Day of Judgment. After the 12th century, the legend named three possible individuals: Joseph Cartafilus, a servant of Pilate, Buttadeo, known in Italy, or Malco, a character in dramatic mysteries. In the 17th century in Germany, he was presented as a "wandering Jew" and called Asuerus. Since then, the character has been portrayed in all genres by writers like Goethe. Eugène Sue's *Le juif errant* is perhaps the most important. Miró uses the character in his *El humo dormido*, in two chapters: "Don Jesús y el Judío errante" and "El alma del Judío errante y don Jesús."

245. This work is the first compilation of Castilian law prepared by Alfonso Díaz de Montalvo at the behest of Ferdinand and Isabel. It derives from the laws of Alfonso XI. The quotation is from Book I, law XXI.

246. The *Crónica de Oleza* is Miró's name for Rufino Gea's *Historia de los oriolanos* (1920). The passage is found on page 96, Paragraph 68 under "Varios Excomuniones."

247. The quotation is from Seneca's *Troades*, where Andromache says these words to Ulysses, "Utinam timerem (Would that I were afraid)," in Act III, Scene IV.

248. The railroad that is the chapter title is the line from Murcia to Orihuela to Alicante and its branch line from Albatera to Torrevieja on the coast. On its first trip in May 1882, one coach overturned and the official party had to continue by coach.

249. The *Antorcha* was a scientific and literary journal published weekly in Alicante from 1881–82.

250. Don Amancio sees himself as a later St. John the Baptist, who will help restore the Carlists to the throne.

251. This *Glorieta* was constructed in the 1880's on lands funded by the municipal government, while the gardens were a gift of the Duke of Tamames.

252. The historical basis for the "Crown of Aragon" dates back to the 12th and 13th centuries, and involved a union between the territory of Aragon and Catalonia.

253. He cites an old Spanish *refrán* (saying), referring to those who have lost their fear of being reprehended.

254. Some critics see the evidence of Epicurean influences in Don Magín's ideas in this stream of consciousness passage. The author has quoted the Odes of Pindar and other works and may reflect this here.

255. Thomas à Kempis (1380?–1471) was a medieval Christian religious writer, author of the *Imitation of Christ*. The quotation is from Part I, Chapter XIII, Section V.

256. The author takes three lines from his own work, *El humo dormido* in a chapter entitled "San Juan, San Pedro y San Pablo." He attributes it to a *villanesco* by Alfonso de Alcabdete.

257. He takes the term "morada" (mansion or dwelling) from Saint Teresa and her work *Las moradas o El castillo interior*. It is from the Second Morada.

258. These lines are from the "Coplas a la muerte del Maestro don Rodrigo, su padre" (1476) (Verses 13–18) by the Spanish poet Jorge Manrique (1440?–79).

259. The words *perro gordo* refer to a copper coin that had a lion on the reverse side and was worth ten *céntimos*. Popular usage in Madrid made the lion into a dog and it became feminine *perra*. The phonetic changes to the word are regional.